The Book Store on Lexington Avenue

by
Calvin E. Tyrrell

RoseDog 🐾 Books
PITTSBURGH, PENNSYLVANIA 15238

RoseDog Books
585 Alpha Drive
Suite 103
Pittsburgh, PA 15238
Visit our website at www.rosedogbookstore.com

ISBN: 978-1-4809-7547-7
eISBN: 978-1-4809-7570-5

PREFACE

THE NUTS AND BOLTS
OF
MURDER
ARE
A
GRAY
AREA
WHAT
MATTERS
MATTERS!

Calvin E. Tyrrell
1/12/2016

The Book Store
on Lexington Avenue

Part 1

CHAPTER - 1

On March 28, 1948, a panicked phone call from the downtown area of Philadelphia was received at the Philadelphia Fire Department at 10:33 P.M.

"Help! Help! Please hurry, Brooke's Book Store is on fire, the windows are exploding, glass and bricks are flying everywhere, for God's sake hurry before the whole block burns down, the building looks as if could collapse any minute."

In Philadelphia Pennsylvania, William Brooke, owner of Brookes Book Store, was about to lock up for the night. It was Monday and it had been a slow day. It was 7:56 P.M. just four minutes before closing time and he was anxious to go home and have supper with his wife of fifty three years. They had raised two children who had gone to a University where they graduated with honors in their respective fields and were pursuing their own careers at the time.

William had recently put his store up for sale advertising it in the usual Book Store Trade Papers. He had several prospective buyers peruse his book shelves for the previous two weeks but so far no one had made a solid offer.

Just as he was about to put the key in the door an average looking middle aged gentleman begged his indulgence to let him in so he could look at some the rare first edition books the owner had advertised for sale. The customer explained he was in town on business and was leaving by plane the first thing in the morning to return home. William relented and let him in so he could have a look around. He took the man to the area of the store where his most expensive rare first edition books were in a locked glass counter display cabinet.

The customer asked to see them all and said if he liked the books he may make a reasonable offer for the entire store as long as he was there. William, although very tired from the uneventful day, opened the case and took out several books so the customer could look them over. There were many more in the case and someone would have to box them up to carry them home if he or she were to buy all of them. William told the customer he was expected home soon for supper with his ailing wife who had been ill for several months. She told no one including William that she had stage four cancer and was terminal. The customer suggested he call his wife and tell her he still had several customers in the store and had to stay open until at least nine o'clock but promised he would lock up soon after the last customer was served. He was to tell her that if a particular customer liked what he saw that he may make a good offer on the whole store. William did just as the customer had suggested and called home apologizing to his wife doing exactly as the customer had asked. William was never seen alive again. At 10:33 that night a passer by called the Fire Department and told them that Brookes Book Store was on fire.

The next day the newspapers read in huge headlines, 'Prominent Book Store Owner William Brooke, owner of BROOKE'S BOOK STORE, found dead in the basement of his store after fire completely destroyed his building. The fire Marshall's preliminary finding is that William went downstairs to check on his large portable kerosene heater that he used to keep the damp basement dry for book storage and somehow tripped over it while trying to turn on an overhead light that appeared to have had a burned out bulb. It probably exploded with a muted sound and he was knocked unconscious when his head hit the concrete floor. This was an older unit, explained the Fire Marshall, that had no safety feature on it that would have turned the burner off immediately after being accidently turned over. An autopsy will be performed to determine the exact cause of death but it does appear to be accidental at this time.'

The heater he had been using was his old faithful heater of many years that had never given him any trouble with a thermostat on it so it would only run when the temperature dropped to a certain level which William had set on the unit. It kept the old basement at an acceptable level of dryness to prevent mold from growing on his book inventory. William, it was known to many people, had failing eyesight and even with strong glasses he had trouble reading any size print. He was well liked by everyone who knew him. His store had been in business over fifty years after he inherited it from his father who died of a heart attack leaving the store to his only son and heir William, so the store was all he ever knew.

Unbeknown to anyone, all of the valuable books of any significance had been removed, packed into boxes and put in the trunk of a late model four door sedan that had special suspension under it so it could carry heavy loads of books without appearing to be loaded down as seen from behind the car. It appeared level no matter what was in the trunk and was controlled with a switch under the dashboard.

Soon after showing the customer all the books of any value the customer had asked to see the basement storage. William was knocked unconscious with a blow to the back of his head by a large caliber weapon, a pistol. The customer tied some twine he found down there around the handle the large portable kerosene heater and just prior to his leaving the store's basement at the top of the stairs he pulled on the twine very hard knocking the burning heater over spilling fuel from a loosened filler cap that spilled fuel around the body of the unconscious owner. No one had been seen the mystery man entering or leaving the store that evening.

A couple of weeks went by and the Insurance Company determined that the fire was an accident and paid the widow for the loss of her husband, the business and the building. It did little good, she died a few weeks later from the cancer.

It was further assumed that the store's inventory was a total lost due to the intense fire in the old two story building. The remaining books were so badly burned and all of the cabinets and shelving were destroyed as well so no one had attempted to take an inventory of the books that had been in there to see if there had been a theft or perhaps a murder as well.

CHAPTER - 2

Several months went by and a man arrived in Poughkeepsie New York on June 9, 1948, a small town at the time near the Hudson River a few years after the Second World War was over. This was a quaint town with houses, shops and stores of every size and description many of which were badly run down. The man looked around and asked questions about the age of the buildings and what might be for sale. He didn't care about the condition of the building per say mostly the age of it, how big is was and did it have a basement that was unfinished maybe part concrete and the rest dirt. He was looking for a two or three story building with a basement, wood or brick construction that would fit his needs at the time. Sixty percent of the commercial type buildings were of red brick with wood frame construction on the inside or were all wood frame buildings with shingles or clapboard siding.

Finally he found exactly what he had been looking for. The sign said; For Sale by Owner with a phone number listed. He called the number and set a time to meet with the owner.

It had been a Woolen Factory during the big mills hey days like they had in a lot of cities and they manufactured clothing there. They were all suffering like a lot of other towns and cities when the big Mills closed down. There were deep depression areas and some property could be bought very reasonably in many cases. It was much bigger than what he needed but the price was right, dirt cheap. Outwardly it appeared to be in poor condition near the railroad tracks with freight trains and an occasional passenger trains passing through now and then on their regularly scheduled runs.

The stature of the man looking at the building appeared to be five feet six inches tall, weighing about one hundred and twenty five pounds. He looked old beyond his years from the outside. He seemed to be walking with some difficulty as though he had a bad hip or maybe one leg was shorter than the other and appeared bent over as though he suffered from a bad back. All in all he didn't look very healthy and people took him to be in his early sixties or thereabouts at the time. In reality he was in his mid thirties.

Several years ago he had Graduated from the University of Maryland though he told no one. He spoke very quietly when he talked to people and it sounded like he had a raspy voice like he was hoarse from smoking all the time. He wore the same worn out faded brown overcoat whether it was 30 degrees out or 90 degrees out. He wore brown shoes with holes in the soles and when he made a purchase he pulled out a small old fashioned black change purse from his pants pocket and opened the old metal clasp at the top and took out some old looking folded paper money from within. The money had been folded several times and looked as though it may fall apart giving the impression that he seldom spent any money.

Finally the owner showed up and they began talking about the age and condition of the building and its price. When he finally decided on buying the building the owner asked him how he would like to pay for it.

"Are you going to take out a mortgage at one of the local banks sir?"

"No, I'll pay cash for it if you'll come down on the price just a bit," answered the buyer.

The two of them talked and dickered a bit on the price of one hundred and sixty nine thousand dollars and finally settled on a price of one hundred and fifty thousands dollars after the buyer explained that the man would have all of his money in one day instead of having to wait up to several weeks or more for a bank to make a mortgage loan.

"Very good sir, would you be able to settle up on Friday this week or do you need time to clear some things out or prepare a deed or something?" asked the buyer.

"Oh no sir, we can close the deal anytime this Friday."

"Alright then how about 11:45 A.M."

"Sure, that will be fine sir; oh by the way what name should I put on the deed for you, you know like your name or a company name?"

"No names I'm afraid, I'm going to form a Corporation and I want the deed in the Corporation's name."

"And just what would the name be sir, for the deed you know?"

"Well you are a few steps ahead of me I haven't quite figured that out just yet, things are moving a bit too fast for me right now. Let's see," he began to mumble about initials, "hmm, I could use my own initials, no that won't work, um how about, no that won't work either, oh I just don't know, I will have to think about it some more." The buyer thoughtfully paused;

"My initials won't, it would sound like a silly name to anyone who didn't know me."

"Why, what are they?" asked the seller innocently.

"Its S.O.D. my name is Solomon Oscar Devine but I go by Sol."

"Oh I see what you mean," as he chuckled to himself.

"I know; we'll call it the R. O. B. Corporation," said the buyer.

"May I ask what it stands for sir, just out of curiosity understand, you haven't told me what the building is going to be used for?"

"Well not that it's any of your business but I intend to open a used book store in here. The initials stand for, Really Old Books." In the back of his mind he was thinking rare old books but he felt the seller was being too curious at this point. He would also sell newly published books and magazines.

"I see, now that does make sense, but isn't the building a little big for a used book store?"

"Maybe to the untrained eye but I also restore old manuscripts and other old books as well. I need the basement to store equipment and supplies and that's where my laboratory will be. The first floor will be the book store to sell rare books as well as newer books that no one wants anymore and then new books that I will buy from Publishing Houses. The second story will be storage and the third floor will be apartments for my employee's and myself."

"Still that's an awful lot of square footage, there's no way you'll be able to use all of it."

"No need for you to worry. I'll need a couple of other stores near me to house things like Office Supplies that I will need and other related stores, maybe a restaurant. I can turn the whole top floor into apartments as well. Employees need a place to stay while they search out suitable housing for themselves you know."

"Yes I see what you mean, that all makes sense. Well alright I guess we've covered everything until Friday morning, where would you like to meet?

"How about right here in the building, I'm sure we can find someplace to sign papers."

"Sure, I mean why not. What are you going to carry all the money in when you come on Friday; a hundred and fifty thousand dollars is an awful lot of money for a man of your stature to carry around isn't it?"

"I'll have it in a couple of suitcases; I don't trust banks or Attorneys."

The following Friday at precisely 11:45 A.M. the seller showed up at the front door with the keys to the building. The buyer was waiting for him with two old brown leather suit cases with two leather straps on each one with discolored brass buckles. The seller was ecstatic, cold hard cash, more than he'd ever seen in his lifetime. His father left him the building in a will and it was old and dilapidated then just as it was today and he could no longer afford to pay the taxes and insurance on the old vacant building. He was glad to be rid of it at any price and the buyer was happy as well.

"Just give me a minute and I'll have the door open and we'll go inside." He put the key in the front door and opened it. "There we are, come in and we'll find a place for us to sign the papers transferring ownership from me to you and I'll give you the new deed." "Sounds fine, just fine." The buyer picked up the suitcases and struggled to get them in the door as if they were very heavy. They looked around for somewhere to sign the papers the seller had in his hand, one was a contract for sale and purchase and the other was the new deed he had prepared through a local Attorney to be sure it was correct.. They finally found an old built in desk against an inside wall that probably belonged to a Time Keeper for the Mill. They signed the necessary papers and the seller handed the buyer the deed and the keys.

"I want to thank you my friend." He opened one suitcase so the seller could see the cash Inside all in small denominations from one hundred dollars bills to smaller ones. "By the way could you show me around a little bit more so I can see the lay out?"

"Sure I'd be only too happy to oblige."

They placed the suitcases near the front door and walked through the upper floors.

"How about the basement," asked the buyer, "it's very important for me you see. I will have my Laboratory down there and equipment to restore the oldest books."

"Sure follow me."

They walked across the main floor to the center of the room where there was a door to what looked like a closet but it was a door leading downstairs to the basement.

"I haven't been down here in years understand so it could be quite dusty and dirty."

"That's fine. By the way you never said; do you live here in town and what are you going to do with all that money?"

"I live here in a very small house; I'm a widower and have no children or family left."

"I see, well that's too bad, living alone I mean, no friends either?"

"Well I have a couple of friends I guess you could call them but they mean nothing to me, they hang around waiting for me to come into some money when I sell this place so they can free load off me."

"You mean like here today?"

"Yes, this is just the very thing they would like to see happen."

"Have you told anyone about our deal yet?"

"No, not a soul, they would be clinging onto me trying to get at my money."

"Oh I see," said the buyer, "I guess that's good for you anyway. Say that part way over there, is that part of the cellar?"

"Yes, of course but it's never been excavated before for some reason."

"That would be a great place to bury valuables wouldn't it?"

"I believe you're right, it's a great place to bury things you don't want anyone to see. If you don't mind could we go back upstairs, this place gives me the willies?" asked the seller.

"Sure we can go back upstairs. Wait just a minute, what's that way over there?"

"Over where, I don't see anything?" the seller said as he turned around to look.

The buyer was pointing over towards a pile of dirt that was in almost complete darkness. There was a thud and a groan and the buyer went back upstairs alone. He had slipped in there during the night and dug a large hole in the basement's dirt floor large enough to bury a body. The seller was never seen or heard from again.

The buyer began getting people together, mostly homeless people with some skills or trades that he needed and they went to work fixing up the old building that was structurally solid.

The first order of business was getting the building cleared out of all things he didn't want on the top floor where he would build three apartments, one for himself and two others for single employees that already worked for him in another location but tiny compared to this one. Here they would have room to expand and grow their business. Only his two friends had ever seen or knew who their employer was and what he looked like and just how young or old he really was and that was his Partner Fred Samuel of many, many years and Greta Snodgrass who was running their original store and she would manage this new store as well.

The two friends had started out in another friend's borrowed garage mixing chemicals and creating inks of different kinds then they bought a small used Book Store whose owner had become mysteriously ill. They bought it for pennies on the dollar, the owner disappeared the day after the sale and was never seen again.

CHAPTER- 3

Four weeks later on a Monday morning after the building was purchased a man showed up carrying a clip board with several papers on it wearing a hard hat. He was clean shaven and appeared to be thirty five to forty years old. He his name was embroidered on the coveralls he wore so he looked like a superintendent. It was not his real name however; the stolen coveralls were from another construction site in another town far away so no one would notice the name or identify it as bogus. No one noticed the man's work shoes either; they had a two and a half inch lift in them. The shoes were very expensive and were made in a way that if a man or woman were wearing long pants or slacks no one could tell the shoes were built up. The company designed the shoes to look perfectly natural disguising that fact that they had a lift in them.

The man walked around talking to some disheveled looking homeless type people who seemed to be happy just having something to do. There were men and women who wore worn and tattered clothing and looked like they hadn't had a bath in months There was a food wagon on wheels built on a small pickup truck chassis that came around three times a day and fed these people and never charged them any money. It was all prepaid and taken care of by the owner of the building they were working on although they never knowingly saw him.

The first things to go in were bathrooms and kitchens in the upper apartments and two restrooms downstairs where the Book Store would be. In the basement another restroom was being installed complete with a shower for the work area with all of its equipment, work benches and long tables with two sets of double stainless steel industrial sinks and another double size sink made of soap stone. They were all specially treated sinks. Hundreds and hundreds of two" by four" studs which had to be cut for partition walls and gypsum board, precursor to drywall, hung and the sanding of the gypsum boards after the joints were sealed with gypsum sealer created a lot of new dust and debris. That debris was piled up and removed by dump trucks.

Every time one of the Building Inspectors from the City Building Department came around they couldn't help but marvel at the expertise of the craftsmen's work being done by a bunch of what they called bums from around town. The electrical work was not only impeccable it was correct to code as was all the plumbing and construction work. No Inspector could find fault with any part of the work.

All of the windows in the building whose floor space was going to be used right away were replaced with new windows and new storm windows constructed to insulate against the cold and the heat loss from inside or outside. It appeared that no expense was too great for the strange man who had purchased the property that no one else had apparently seen either. There were truck loads of insulation going into the building on all floors, including the basement, Heating and Air Conditioning was also being installed on all floors. The boss explained to those who asked that the building had to be climatically controlled for the valuable books that would be stored there and their restoration business as well. Painting it seems was another stickler, it too was perfect, there was no bleed through like cheap paint would make and all lines were perfectly straight. Every corner was exact even in the most problem areas of painting like some small inside corners that were almost impossible to get a paint brush into. Everyone on the job site understood that this building would be a show place when complete and they took pride in their work and it showed plus the fact they were generously paid cash under the table each week.

CHAPTER- 4

One day a friend of the seller's could no longer contain his curiosity and walked up to the man he saw with the clipboard who appeared to be the superintendant running the job. "I say there mister, do you know the owner of this project?"

"Yes I do as a matter of fact?"

The friend thought for a minute trying to place the man's accent. "Say, you're not from around these parts are you, where you from, England?"

"No, actually I'm from Australia; I was hired to head up this project by the new owner."

"Oh I see. The reason I'm curious is that my friend who used to own this building hasn't been seen for the past several weeks, would you happen to know where he is?"

"I believe he told the owner he was going to the Caribbean for a few weeks and would return on the first of next month so he could pay his utilities and other bills."

"Oh, I see; then he should be back by next Tuesday which is the first of the month."

"Yes I believe that's right."

"You see, sometimes we room together when he and I are low on cash."

"I see; are you running a little short of money right now?"

"Well actually yes, I'm a little short near the end of every month, I get my disability check on the first of every month just like my friend does."

"I see, what was your profession?"

"I built custom cabinets for kitchens and bathrooms, I am a master cabinet maker," the man puffed out his chest showing pride of his profession.

"Well as it so happens I don't have a cabinet maker on the payroll just yet for the new store. Would you be interested in building cabinets, counters and book cases for the new store I'm putting in on the ground floor? It would require some night work so as to stay ahead and out of the way of the finish carpenters and painters. I'm afraid I have already contracted out all of the kitchens and bathrooms for the apartments upstairs but I haven't got around to the Store level yet. And one more thing, we're putting in a restroom in the basement and we will need cabinets down there under the big sinks and around the room floor to ceiling to hold vessels for liquids, chemicals and dry storage as well. I have drawings for all that. Can you read blueprints?"

"Why yes sir! Here's the thing though, I was injured on the job a few years ago and won a disability settlement so I can't hold a regular job you see and still get my check every month. I would have to have cash under the table or I'll be in trouble."

"That's no problem, most of the workers receive their money under the table and we pay top wages for quality work. A lot of them are in the same boat as you are. Now if I put you on the payroll your hours will be your own so you can come and go as you please but please bear in mind I know exactly to the dollar what custom work costs so it you try to pad your hours on the job I'll fire you in a minute, understood?"

"Yes sir, that's very clear."

"Alright before I say yes there is one more thing I must insist on. Your measurements must be exact according to the plans, any deviation will be harshly dealt with. Everything being installed must be built exactly to the smallest degree or some things just won't fit in spaces allotted. Do you understand what I'm saying.?"

"Of course I do, if the cabinets aren't done to specs then the counter tops won't fit and that will hold up the job and I can see that you're trying to maximize every space to conserve square footage."

"Well said; the owner insists on perfection for the money he is laying out. No mistakes, no matter how small will be tolerated and no drinking on the job whatsoever, you drink you're fired, is that clear?"

"Yes sir, does that mean I have a job?"

"It does, when can you start?"

"Tomorrow morning first thing if you want?"

"Alright tomorrow morning come dressed for work, old clothes, you don't have to shave or shower, you'll get plenty dirty working here. One thing that's very important to the owner is that we will provide you with your own two Shop Vacuums for the floor where you'll be working. When you use them be most careful to separate the dust and the dirt. Vacuum up the old dirt and empty that Vacuum into the appropriate barrel in the basement. Vacuum up the new dirt and sawdust you create and place it in the new dust barrel next to the old, they are clearly marked as are the vacuums. The scrap wood and debris goes in the pile around back. Once again I must insist on perfection, anything less will mean immediate dismissal, okay?"

"Yes sir, I understand perfectly. Then it's alright for me to work after dark?"

"Yes of course it is I thought I made that abundantly clear."

"I just wanted to clarify it so there is no mistake."

"One thing more I may be able to help you out with; if you would like to change your address to this building I am going to be adding several more apartments to the top floor and we can custom build one up there for you if you'd like to stay on in the employ of the boss?"

"What's the catch?"

"No catch, its just if you work out this could end up being a place for you to work and live as well. A couple of others have already signed on, it helps with the financing as well you know. The bank loves it when people sign up for apartments ahead of time with us. By the way I probably shouldn't tell you this but your friend who used to own this building has a lifetime apartment for as long as he lives rent free but he has to pay his own utilities. We're already working on his unit, its number five. Think it over and if you're interested you can have number eight at a reduced rate if you work out like you say you will."

"I don't have to think it over, I'll take it! I'll see you in the morning and I'll change my address at the post office to here effective tomorrow if it's alright with you, I see you already have twelve mailboxes in the hallway."

"That will be fine with me and I'm sure the boss won't mind."

The man left thinking this was his lucky day, what he didn't know was he wouldn't be alive on his next birthday but his checks would still be coming to his mailbox and cashed with his forged signature. He also didn't know his friend's Social Security Checks were coming to his mailbox as well and his checks were being forged by the owner and deposited even though he no longer existed. The mysterious owner was still not seen on the project and the building was always bustling with workers and the work was perfect.

The store's cabinets went in, the bookshelves were built to spec. and installed, even the counters with their glass tops were in for customers to pay their bills for the books when they made purchases. The second floor was built with several large rooms partitioned off and painted with sturdy shelves made to hold heavy boxes of books to be stored. Each room had a letter over the doorway denoting its area of storage where the boxes would be kept until they were needed. The basement was coming along with its cabinets installed and the concrete floors were tiled that had been bare concrete. The walls had been patched and painted an off white, the space was spic and span and sterile to the point of looking like an operating room.

The unfinished part of the basement remained dirty, unfinished and was closed off but a door was installed for access. The remodeling was nearing completion in just over eighteen months and the workers became fewer and fewer with less than twenty five percent of the building actually done, more would be done later as the need arose. To local residents it appeared as though the workers seemed to be moving south to escape the cold winter that would arrive shortly so no one really missed them.

They were mostly homeless people anyway; out of sight out of mind was the way residents of the area felt. The mailboxes were full every month with disability and Social Security checks and were signed over to the Corporation and deposited into its account as rent payments which supposedly included power and water and other bills that were incurred by the tenants. The Bank didn't care about money going into the business account because they knew the people living there were perfectly happy with the arrangement. They turned a blind eye and no one paid any attention to the lack of workers.

The Corporation was paying all of their utility bills and taxes on the building and to any on looker it appeared perfectly normal. There were always a few people coming and going and they all area where tenants would sometimes stop by and eat a meal once in a while when work was winding down on the building. The food truck was cancelled, people kept coming in and the faces were constantly changing yet no one paid any attention to it.

The Bank accepted deposits from several people all in one bank bag or sometimes two if there were a lot of deposits that had to be made all at once. Everyone was happy with the status quo and no one was going to question the strange operations of the new Book store in town.

CHAPTER - 5

A huge Grand Opening for the new store was planned for May 15, 1950. People were curious to see what kind of merchandise the store held. There were several counters with glass fronts and tops with locks on their doors for the more valuable rare books and valuable first editions. Each item had a three by five inch card in front of it with the books name and author on it along with the price which seemed high if you weren't a book collector. There were three divisions of rooms, one for the rare books, one for used books where you traded two books for one in exchange and the third room was the largest; it was all new books, magazines and inventories of book stores the owner had purchased from stores going out of business.

Coming in the front door you could go right or left to the new or used books rooms, if you were interested in old rare books there was a well lit corridor in the center that led people back to a private screening room where the rare books were but anyone could go back there and look around if they were curious because it was felt that they would tell their friends and their friends would tell their friends etc. and besides everything was under lock and key. It was felt by the owner that this would be a good business practice. Everyone who came in was in awe of the books and how well they were categorized and easy to find either by genre, by title or by the Author's name.

You were able to browse to your hearts content. In the new book section of the store there were several comfortable over stuffed chairs where you could lounge around and read as long as you wanted and there was a hot beverage bar where you could purchase hot chocolate, coffee or buy a soda from a vending machine. Under the counter was a large glass topped case where there were doughnuts, large cookies and pastries for sale fresh every day. There were large restrooms also available for the customers both near the food beverage counter and in the rear of the store. The employees on this floor had their own restroom in the back and a small break room where they could eat a lunch or supper when the store was open late which was two nights a week unless they had a special sale. The store was years and years ahead of its time.

Little by little other merchandise was added to compliment the Book Store such as book marks with quotes and sayings on them and racks and racks of gifts that could be purchased for holidays, weddings etc. Eventually a huge greeting card section was added as well.

No one but employees had access to the second floor which was only used for storage of books that were being shipped in from across the Country from other book buyers or sellers as well as from the owner when he made large purchases while out on the road. He shipped them back by freight or used a Moving Company to save the mailing fees which were much higher because of the weight of the boxes. On the top floor were the owners completed apartments and the employee's apartments which numbered eight of the twelve units. The book store owner only hired people who were single for a reason and no one cared or asked why. Part of the requirement for employment was that the person had to agree to remain single for at least two years, then if they got married or wanted to move in with a girlfriend or a boyfriend they were released from their apartment lease without prejudice and would get a favorable letter of recommendation for another apartment or assistance with buying a house.

If they separated from employment without prejudice they would be given a letter of recommendation for another job or at least that's what they perceived. It was all a tidy operation and people talked with pride about where they worked when on the outside of the store when shopping or running errands. The four remaining empty apartments kept getting mail and the mail disappeared daily just as if someone was living there. Their Bank accounts got their deposits and checks were signed as normal transactions. It was a little mysterious that no one living there ever saw anyone around and if you were to ask questions about them you would simply disappear never to be heard from again. Even the Postman didn't question anything when he had several envelopes for the same apartment with several different names on them and the same original twelve mail boxes still existed on the main floor for the Postman to leave all of the mail. The postman did go into the store each day to leave the store's mail with Greta, the Store manager who was an old friend of the owners. As far as the other boxes went he figured that some people had simply moved in together to share the rent. No one was any the wiser. Later the owners added another eight mail boxes with apartment numbers on them for non existing apartments which also began receiving mail.

The Master Mind of the operation was Solomon Oscar Devine, which was his given name.

CHAPTER - 6

The small stature bald headed man in the basement was Fred Samuel, Sol's partner and an expert on paper aging and the manufacture of paper that looked ancient as well as fine modern textured paper such as expensive linen writing paper. He was the same age as Sol except he was older by three months but no one knew for sure except his partner. Fred had a slight build, neither fat nor skinny and he seldom put on or lost weight. His meals were mostly prepared for him at a local restaurant and delivered to the store at precisely at the time he specified each day. One of the employees of the store would take his downstairs to him. He turned out excellent work fooling the experts of the day to where they couldn't swear the book they were looking at was a fake, a copy or an original first edition. They would all eventually agree that it was in fact an original and it would be sold as such at a very high price once documented by the experts.

The store made most of its big money this way and held its own just as it had been intended to be, just a Book Store on Lexington Avenue.

The basement changed little over the years, gradually six to eight feet of earth four to six inches deep was removed across the width of the building and new concrete was poured to enlarge the basement or so people thought. The man in the basement was a wizard, he used dust from the old dust barrels to give a little dusting to cover a book and around the edges of the cover and the pages giving the book the appearance of being stored away somewhere for a very long time with dust that when tested proved to be over one hundred years old. The man had to be careful what dust he put on the books, he wouldn't want the experts to look at one hundred years of dust on a book that was only twenty or thirty years old, that wouldn't do. He was meticulous in his work and was well compensated for it, he wanted for nothing. If he wanted time off to travel he took it and was encouraged to keep an eye out while he traveled for old book stores. He didn't mind mixing a little business with pleasure because he really enjoyed the old loved rare books, it was what he lived for.

There wasn't a lot of entertainment in town in those days so people quite often came in the store just to look around and most always found something to purchase anyway. The owners of the building did very little to the outside of the building other than painting the wood trim around the windows and doors and putting signs on the inside of the windows to keep weather from affecting them. The building retained for the most part the original look of an old factory and if it weren't for the new windows and signs on the building and a large marquis out front one could assume it was just another factory. The top floor however gave it away because of the curtains the residents put in whenever someone came or went as renters often do and curtains were changed out with new ones from time to time.

Then there was the other partner, who was he, where was he from, as far as anyone knew he'd never been seen except by the man in the basement who knew who he was and the older woman who managed their store and kept a couple of young people busy running other things. In fact the other owner or partner was very much alive and well and he often traveled throughout Europe and the United States looking for old and rare books and following sales of other Book Stores going out of business. When he was in residence it was known because the lights were constantly on. He ordered in almost all of his meals in and they were left outside his apartment door. There would be an envelope on the floor in the hall with the restaurant's name on it along with the correct money for the food and a tip for whoever brought it over to him.

The inside of his apartment was spacious, there were book shelves everywhere however and then there were tables and tables of unsolved murder mysteries and files from police departments around the world. He would visit one and tell them that he was a mystery writer and was looking for unsolved mysteries to study so he could write a new book, it almost always worked. He had accumulated literally hundreds of them over the years. He would pore over them night after night day after day until he knew the plot of the murder in question by heart and the mistakes he had seen during Police investigations or maybe they overlooked them due to the heavy case load they apparently all had. He would then plan the exact duplicate murder down to the last degree of probability then go out and find a victim somewhere a long way from where the crime had originally been committed; he of course would always have a solid alibi. If the murder had been in a big town such as New York he would commit the murder in a city in the mid-west. He left few clues at any scene, he always wore old fashioned rubbers over his shoes, cotton gloves over his hands and he also practiced leaving no hair at the scene that could be traced back to him by wearing protective hair bonnets, the kind workers have to wear when cooking or working with food or in hospitals. All of these things he would dispose of in garbage receptacles around town far away from one another and far from the crime scene so that they couldn't be tied to the actual crime.

He also studied the time the garbage receptacles would be picked up or emptied and would commit the murder the night before so that the bins would be emptied most likely by the time the Police got around to checking on them. He planned each crime meticulously. This went on for years and years and he never went to the same town or city twice to commit a crime and he made sure he was at least a hundred miles away from the scene of the last one before committing a new one. The Police had no idea he was a serial killer when in fact he was and of the worst kind.

He got a thrill out of killing a person, man or woman, white man or black, it made no difference as long as it was by the book, the last one he read of course. Some of the crimes had money involved with them, small amounts to millions of dollars in cash, cars and yachts. It seemed as though there was no limit as to what the murderer would do or the lengths he would go to so as not to get caught. And of course there were the women that committed the murders it just wasn't men who did them. For this the mystery man would dress up as a woman to do the killing deed so it would appear that it had been a woman right down to the shoeprints left that he made by wearing the old fashioned women's shoes and women's rubbers over them where he would sometimes leave tracks in the mud, snow, dirt or dust behind just to drive the authorities crazy.

Part 2

CHAPTER - 7

The second part of this man's story begins in Milwaukee Wisconsin in 1970 with a wealthy bank executive who had a cheating wife. She apparently wants the husband killed so she can collect millions of dollars in Insurance and inherit his estate. She would get the house they live in as well as their summer house, the horse farm where they raised championship horses and stored an antique collection of cars and their yacht moored in a marina. The mystery man watches and waits, he studies the movements of the husband and wife. He has never been here before to do business but as before with a lot of his crimes he may come back to town to buy books from local book sellers he has contacted and made a date to come by and see what they have usually weeks from the time of his crime when things have settled down.

He thinks this through and yes it's the same type of crime committed by a woman years ago and she got away with killing her husband and collecting on everything they owned. As he watches the wife cheating on her husband something inside him clicks and instead of killing the husband he feels empathy for the first time and decides to kill the wife instead. He has suddenly left the comfort zone of his well planned murders. The husband is unaware of his wife's infidelity and therefore blissfully unaware that she intends to kill him. The mystery man spent two weeks studying the movements to match the crime to another one he had read about but this one is derailing his thought processes.

His head begins to ache as he tries to get back on track with his plan but it won't work. Something has suddenly snapped inside and he has gone from planning to rage. The wife leaves one day for a rendezvous with her lover and he tracked her to where they met. He watches and waits for the perfect opportunity. He has never killed anyone before in broad daylight, he'd always used the cover of darkness. The two met in a secluded park not far from the woman's home. The mystery man slipped up on them quietly and when they were through with their love making and while the man was struggling to pull his trousers up the mystery man shoved a large stainless steel 357 magnum revolver against the woman's head through the open window on the right side of the car and fired one shot literally blowing her brains out all over the man who had just made love to her.

She died instantly holding her pink underpants in her hands, she didn't have time to put them back on. The man with her was so shocked by the gunshot and the scene of the dead body next to him that he wet his pants and passed out without ever seeing the man who had pulled the trigger. The side of the man's face was covered with her brain matter and blood spatter.

It's still an unsolved mystery because the husband had a perfect alibi. He was at work with dozens of employees to vouch for him within his building where his office was. The killer now had a new motive all of a sudden. He thought of himself now as an avenger, righting the world's wrongs. He continued to kill indiscriminately but every now and then he would avenge another person in his own mind being sure that the intended targeted spouse opposite had an air tight alibi which no one could dispute. Then he began to make a mistake now and then. He was still careful not to leave any physical evidence but his rule of no witnesses left behind may undo him if he wasn't more careful. He had been seen in the park near the car where the woman died.

The killer was described to the police as a heavy set man, six feet tall, with light colored hair, maybe a man in his twenties or thirties and he was wearing an old black full length wool overcoat. The description couldn't have been more wrong. No one noticed the gloves that he wore and the old fashioned rubbers over his shoes and it was a sunny day with only a slight chance of rain. He couldn't have looked more out of place but no one noticed the little things. He had gotten clean away with another murder.

The shock of hearing a gunshot in the park had sent some people running away from the noise while others ran towards it to see what had happened. After shedding his disguise tossing it in several refuse bins the man simply joined the crowd wearing a brown pin striped business suit, white shirt and fashionable tie and seemed curious like everyone else. He had a full head of black hair and was wearing a soft brown business hat to match his suit. He went totally unnoticed. He meandered around a little while as the police ran themselves ragged checking out eye witness accounts of the killer. Since he didn't come close to fitting the description and was not a witness he walked away looking at his watch as if he was going to be late getting back to work. He simply vanished among the throng of curious bystanders.

CHAPTER - 8

Back at the mystery man's Book Store in Poughkeepsie his employees were unpacking books and storing them according to the type of books they were then marking the boxes on the outside to identify them. They had received two separate shipments of books this week from different cites but from within the same State. They didn't question the types of books because frequently the Store's owner would buy up huge inventories of books from Library Book Sales and other Book Stores who were going out of business. Many times he was given several boxes of books just so people could reduce unsold or slow inventory movers which couldn't be returned to the Publishing Houses. He really didn't care about the books or what they contained, he was really looking for unsolved mysteries mainly about murders in book form or from police reports he had procured.

This part of his business didn't change He was also on the lookout for any information about rare books, who owned them and where they lived. First he would try to buy the books legitimately and if they couldn't agree on a price he would later return to kill the owner then steal the books and make it look like a simple robbery gone awry as if the owner had caught the burglar in the middle of the theft, had confronted him and lost his or her life in the end. So far the man had been getting away with everything never leaving the authorities a modus operandi or M/O for short.

The local authorities couldn't connect any of the crimes from across the United States to another. However once they did trace some marked money the mystery man had accidentally taken and crossed state lines with, then the

F.B.I was called in. Still they couldn't find anything that would tie any of the crimes together. Mainly the lack of clues stumped them all, Local, State and F.B.I. Agencies. As far as they were concerned none of the crimes were related to one another. It appeared to be a stale mate of enormous proportions and they were all clueless.

They even traced the money to the killer's Book Store and the employee's were able to prove that they took the money in payment for several books and had the receipts to prove it and they could not tell the authorities whether it was a man or a woman who had purchased the book due to the high volume of the business. Once again he eluded police investigations, the mystery man seemed invincible.

The F.B.I. then called in their best Investigator, a detective named Richard Jefferies, who came from a long line of law enforcement family of men and women. From his father, grandfather and great grandfather to his in laws, one of them down the line had been in law enforcement of one type or another going back three generations. He was the forth generation now and he had two boys and two girls and was a graduate of the F.B.I. Academy as well as the Military Police where he excelled in Investigations while in the Navy as a J.A.G. Officer. This appeared to be the only hope anyone had to track the money which was the only lead the Authorities had at the time. The Agency hoped that new blood with fresh new eyes may turn up something where they couldn't or at least they hadn't yet. His wife had died in a failed robbery attempt and shootout a few years ago so now he was single.

Meanwhile, in a small Ohio town the mystery man traced a lead he had received from an old friend where an older man was confined to a wheelchair was reported to have in his possession several rare books that museums and collectors would like to get their hands on but the old man wouldn't let go of any of them at any price so far. He lived in a two story older frame house in a modest part of town and the killer waited outside in his car across the street for complete darkness.

Once it was dark he sat back upright in his seat, checked all directions for anyone who may be out walking on such a beautiful night as this. He saw some children playing two doors away from his target house and he waited until a woman opened the front door and called them in to supper. Perfect he thought to himself. He opened his car door and closed it quietly so as not to attract any unwanted attention.

He was made up to look the part of a College Professor complete with a soft hat, suit, bow tie and was sporting a handlebar mustache with long side-burns, bushy eyebrows and his hair was all black. He wore an old tweed top coat and had on elevated shoes that made him look approximately five feet nine inches tall. He strolled up to the man's front door and knocked loudly three times. He had been told by his contact that this was a code to let someone in, that it was safe.

After several minutes the door opened slightly and he peered inside a little so as not to startle the man on the other side. He saw a man in a wheelchair with white hair and a well trimmed beard.

"Professor McLaughlin I presume?"

"Yes, that's me, who are you?"

"I'm Professor Stevens from Columbia University, I believe you know who I am."

"Yes I've heard the name but that is all." "Well professor, I am researching some work that is literary in nature and I was told by a friend that you may have a book on the subject I am working on."

"Yes, so what?"

"May I please come in sir, people are watching us and I don't like people staring at me, it makes me uncomfortable unless I am in the classroom teaching?"

"Yes of course, I feel the same way. I don't teach anymore you understand but some of my older students still come by to check on me now and then. It was very rude of me, please come do in. Now then what was the subject you were interested in?"

"Colonialism in America, The Beginning."

"Yes I know the books that cover that, there were several written on the subject but there is only one I put any faith in. Would you care for a cup of tea Professor?"

"Yes I would if it wouldn't be too much trouble."

"Here you are, take a seat over there and I'll put the kettle on and be right back."

He watched as the aged Professor wheeled himself into the kitchen, fill a tea kettle with water and put it on a gas stove, then he turned on the stove and lit a match to light the burner. How perfect is that, the old fool has an old fashioned gas stove with no pilot light he observed? He wheeled himself back in and went right over to a bookcase filled from floor to the ceiling and it ran around the room on three sides with hundreds of old and extremely rare books.

"This is quite a collection you have here professor." His eyes roved around the room like a shark sizing up its prey.

"Thank you. Now let's see, the volume you want is right there just out of my reach, can you get it for me, I'll point it out with my cane?" He reached into the side of his wheelchair and produced an old wooden cane. "There it is right up there" and he tapped a volume with his cane tip pointing it out to his visitor.

"Oh yes I see it, say these books are in great shape, ever thought about selling any?"

"No, I won't part with a single one! I have willed them to my University where I earned my degree in literature and taught!"

"I understand from my friend that you have a Doctorate as well as a Master's Degree in science, is that correct sir?" asked the visitor.

"Yes it is, you are very well informed sir and may I ask what your academia credentials are as well?"

"Yes of course, I attended school in Brookshire England to get my masters in Literature and then did undergraduate work at Princeton and Columbia where I got my Doctorate in Literature."

"Impressive, very impressive, I have heard of all those schools as well you see."

"Yes I thought you might have. Now then let's cut the bull, I want your entire collection of books and I will pay a fair price for them, now then what is your price sir?"

"I told you just like I told the others, none of my books are not for sale, they will go to the University of my choice after my death and not before. I hate to be rude Professor but I think you should leave. Apparently you have come here under false pretenses. You have not looked at one book, you have only perused the titles of some of them. Further more I don't believe a word of what you said about the schools you claim to have attended. So I am asking you politely sir, please leave my home, our conversation is concluded."

"I can't do that, I came here to buy your entire collection and I'll not leave here until we have agreed on a price that will make you happy."

"Are you threatening me sir?"

"Not at all sir, I just want to come to a fair understanding about your collection of books. I am also an avid collector and conservator of fine books." Oops he thought to himself, I should have left out the conservator part, he'll think I'm only interested in copying his books to resell. Of course that's the truth and I'm not leaving without the books I want. The old buzzard doesn't know who he's up against, he will be dead very soon if he doesn't decide pretty quick, I'll not waste any more time with him.

The man stood up towering over the smaller man in the wheelchair. He laid his hands on the arms of the chair and asked, "well what do you say, what's your price and make it quick I don't have all night?"

"I told you before the answer is no, I won't sell any of my books regardless of price, I don't need the money, I live quite comfortably on the income I receive from the University where I taught. Now please, for the last time, leave me be in peace!"

Ah, so he doesn't need the money the mystery man thought, perhaps there is something else he would like to have. "May I ask you one more question before I depart, since you don't need the money maybe there is something else you would like to have that you don't have now, could that be it?"

"No, there's nothing else! Everything I ever dreamed of is right here on my shelves!"

"You're sure now, there's nothing in this world you wouldn't like to have, you never know, I may already possess it?" asked the mystery man.

The man in the wheelchair thought for just a minute or so. He looked back up at the intruder in his life. "No there's nothing I can think of, now please won't you just leave me be and do it quietly."

"Yes of course, my apology to you sir, I am sorry for troubling this evening. I just got caught up in all the wonderful books you have." He reached out his right hand as if to shake the older man's hand and with his left hand he came down hard with the butt of a 9mm semi automatic pistol on the back of his head knocking him unconscious. The Professor slumped in his wheelchair. The man pushed his wheelchair over to the bottom of the stairs that led upstairs to his bedroom and sat him on the edge of the automatic chairlift that ran up and down the wall.

He had a wheelchair at the top of the stairs and one downstairs, both were alike in every way. He ran the chairlift upstairs almost to the top then rolled the unconscious man off the chair lift and let him tumble down the stairs. To any investigator it would look like he simply forgot to fasten the safety belt on the chair lift before starting it down the staircase and simply fell off breaking his neck in the process as he rolled down the stairs. To be sure he broke the man's neck and left him where he landed in a heap.

He went into the kitchen to see if the stove was still on and it was. Then he went to check the fireplace, it was gas fed as well. Perfect he thought to himself, just perfect. He turned the burner under the kettle down very low then went to the back door and checked outside.

He found that there was an alley which ran for a couple of blocks in back of the houses. He went around to the front, got into his car and waited until he saw no traffic or anyone else on the street and brought his car across the street and drove into the alley behind the Professor's house. He began loading up the books he wanted. He was very selective taking only the rarest and most valuable of the book collection. He had other boxes of books he had already bought and as he took four or five books out he would replace them with others he had in boxes in the trunk of his new sedan, a four door Lincoln. He had air bags installed under the car so he could raise or lower it as the weight in the back increased or decreased. No one would guess he carried several hundred pounds of precious books in his back seat or trunk.

When he had removed all the books he wanted he took a rag and a pair of pliers and went to the gas line in the fireplace and loosened a fitting just a tiny bit using the rag on the pliers to protect the brass fitting from any marks he may leave from the sharp jaws of the pliers so the gas would escape very slowly. He locked the front door from within and went out the back door turning the lock in the door knob locking it from the inside as he left. He wore cotton gloves similar to the ones coin investors wear while examining rare coins so as not to leave any smudges on the coins or fingerprints. He drove down the alley with his lights turned off then out onto the street and headed for the next city and a motel to spend the night.

The next morning there was a News Program on the TV describing the unfortunate death of a famous University Professor. It seemed as though he had a gas leak in the house and had put a kettle of water on to boil in the kitchen and when the leaking gas fumes got to the flame on the stove the house simply exploded. The walls blew out and the roof and the second floor collapsed onto the first floor destroying his famous collection of rare books which were consumed in the resulting fire. The whole thing was determined an accident. They deduced that he had fallen from his chairlift as when they had found it was at the bottom of the stairs with the controls in the down position and his body was found at the bottom of the stairs near the chair lift as well. The authorities figured that he had simply failed to put on the seat belt and fasten it on his chairlift and had fallen from it therefore breaking his neck. Some of his friends who knew him well said that he would sometimes skip putting on the seat belt on his chairlift because it took too much time and was inconvenient.

The man in the Motel changed his clothes and washed off his makeup, put on a regular pair of sneakers which matched his jogging suit and checked out of the Motel then headed for home in his car.

He smiled all the way back to Poughkeepsie after spending two more days on the road. His partner Fred he knew would be pleased when he saw this load. The trunk was full as was the back seat of boxed up books. Almost every available nook and cranny in his new car now contained books. In his mind on the way back he was trying to figure how much they would make on the resale of the books. Let's see he thought, the one book is worth upwards of ten thousand dollars by itself. If Fred and I make a copy and sell both as original first editions we'll double our money on the one book by itself.

By the time he got back to his own Book Store in Poughkeepsie New York he figured they would make around fifty thousand dollars or there about on this haul of extremely rare and first edition books.

CHAPTER - 9

Sol arrived back in Poughkeepsie two days later. He took his time on the way back and visited other Book Stores to see if any of them had anything new in their back inventories he could use. When he got back he said hello to everyone and told them his trip had been successful and he would be unloading his car soon then went straight down to the basement.

"Good day Fred, I had a very good trip and have some books for you to work your magic on today."

Fred Samuel was the miracle man alright, he could restore any book and make copies of it that fooled the experts of the day. Fred and Sol had been friends all the way through school.

They got their start one day when they borrowed a friend's garage to use and mix chemicals in. It was a detached garage so there was little danger of burning down the house in case of an accidental fire.

Then Sol's father died suddenly and left both property and money to his only heir Sol. Now they had the money they needed to work with. It turned out that Sol's dad was a skinflint, he always looked broke but had money to burn only no one knew it. Sol took it to heart and saw how his father had always dressed down to appear poor.

The boys got their first break one day when a man came into Fred's book store where he worked to sell some books. One of the books Fred saw right away was an old classic seldom seen in such fine condition as this. He held it apart from the other books he bought that day so the store's owner wouldn't see it then snuck it out to show Sol. They copied the book three times and sold each copy as an original first edition to some book collectors they had come to know over the years.

One day they counted up the cash they had stashed over time and it came more than $200,000 dollars in the days before World War Two. After the war they bought the old Mill in Poughkeepsie New York in1948 and began the re-modeling right away.

Fred knew there was a seedy and dangerous side to Sol in his work but he ignored it. The thrill of the hunt and finding rare books to restore and copy was all he lived for in those days. Neither man married and their work was all that they knew or cared about. Their combined bank accounts grew in leaps and bounds after the Second World war things really picked up. The economy was growing fast and people had more money to spend.

Finally one day they were contacted by someone from England who had heard about their rare book finds and he gave them a list of books he wanted to invest in for his own collection. They were about to go International from their meager beginnings of only a few years ago.

Neither one saw any action in World War II due to their physical disabilities. Sol was too short, an inch under height standards and Fred's bad back kept him from Military service as well.

During the depression and the war years they had a bonanza of buying up old books. People sold their heirloom collections for pennies on the dollar to put food on their tables. All the men had to do was to wait out the war and things would get back to normal. Only the very wealthy were not burdened by the war.

In their new Store they had a matronly looking lady managing it. She had the look of a real librarian though she wore a grey wig to make her look older than she was. Her name was Greta Snodgrass and she had been with the men since they opened their first small book store. She was petite in every way and was single. She stood five feet five, was slender and had no figure that anyone could make out. If you saw her you wouldn't give her a second look but she knew her books and where every book in the store was and if they didn't have what the customer wanted they would get it for them in a day or two.

She had three employees to start with but as things picked up she had to hire two more people, a young man and a young lady both studying and working their way through a University. Each had their own apartment upstairs as did all the employees who came and went over the years. When they decided to quit however upon graduating from school they simply disappeared. The men thought they knew too much and forged paper work to show that they had moved without notice. They had everything done right down to the change of addresses which they supplied to the Post Office to show they had moved and where. The men paid all of the utilities for the renters except for the telephone bills so there was little to do to show they had moved away. It was all very clean and crisp, almost too professional for young people to think about. Problem was everything checked out right down to the forwarding addresses of where they supposedly had moved to. Someone paid the first and last months rent at the new locations but no one ever moved in.

The men sometimes hired others to do their dirty deeds, mostly down and out drug abusers or alcoholics who were young enough to pass as a renter. They too disappeared after doing the dirty work for the men. They were supplied with whatever their drug of choice was or whatever their taste in alcohol was but it was tainted with a substance that would kill leaving little trace. They would simply appear to have overdosed on their drugs or died from alcoholic poisoning if the bodies were ever found. It was all clear cut for the men, no witnesses anywhere.

They sometimes let the municipalities take care of the burial details and could not be tied to the crime in any way.

Fred had a chance to look over the boxes of books that Sol had brought back. To his delight he found two extremely rare books that he had neither heard of or seen before. He had trouble making out the paper they were printed on and the ink that had been used then he settled on papyrus. It was definitely a rare form of paper and ink. He of course knew of these things but had never held it in his hands before. This would truly be a challenge to reproduce and do it right. He loved the challenge of course, he thrived on it.

He had also seen cuneiforms before but not in this style and not in book form. He studied the binding and found it to be of the right type and age predating anything known of in existence at this time. A few covers were made of hand tooled leather. This was the mother lode of all mother lodes, this alone could make them rich beyond their wildest dreams. The only thing they shied away from was notoriety.

They had to remain anonymous at all cost to continue their illegal enterprise. Fred and Sol knew their business and their craft and one could not survive without the other. That was the tie that bound them together. Fred had research to do, he had to find out more about what he held in his hands, who created it and where it came from. In the same box was a book of handwritten notes that Sol had thoughtfully found and included in this latest heist.

For two days Fred poured over the notes piecing together what they needed to save and what had to be disposed of. They couldn't keep anything that was in the Professor's handwriting that might tie them to his murder if anyone snooped around long enough. Fred finally dated the material and found that Hitler's henchmen, who unknown to many people, was interested in the occult and History of Germanic people and where they originated from and this was stolen from a Museum in Israel in the mid 1930s. He wondered how a Professor could have come by it either before or during the war. This material was still hot and had to be handled with great care. They could be in big trouble if they sold it to the wrong person.

Sol would masquerade as another person to do the actual transaction. This was not Fred's worry, his job was to copy the book which was an odd size. It measured twelve inches in width to twelve and one half inches in height on cover, which meant the pages were eleven and a half inches wide by eleven and one half inches in height. That's odd he thought as he reached for a slide rule. Ah, I've got it he thought to himself on the third day of research when he finally got all of the pieces to fit.

He copied off the Professor's work he needed then burned the original notes.

Soon a young man came downstairs to the men's laboratory to check on Fred. "Sir, would you care for some coffee this afternoon?"

"Yes Benjamin thank you. Would you please ask Sol to come downstairs, tell him I had a breakthrough in my research, its very important."

"It must be sir you haven't left the basement for three days now."

"Be off with you and don't be impertinent, go get Sol and hurry please!"

"Yes sir, right away." The young man took to the stairs two at a time in his rush. He knew that when one of them wanted the other it was right now without haste.

Benjamin was twenty years old and a sophomore at Boston University almost through his second year. Fred and Sol took a liking to him soon after Greta had hired him. He enjoyed Literature and marveled at some of the books the men had for sale in the store. To him they were ancient works of art. Benjamin was slight in build and tall at an even six feet, he weighed one hundred and forty five pounds had sandy colored hair with a tiny shock of white in front. His given name was Benjamin James Silas and his friends all called him BJ.

CHAPTER - 10

Upstairs Sol was working on the second floor storage area, Benjamin had a time finding him because he wasn't allowed in the area all alone just yet. He knocked loudly and impatiently on the door.

"Yes, what is it, who is it?" came Sol's impatient gruff voice.

"Sorry to disturb you sir but its Benjamin, Fred wants to see you down in the basement right away, he said he has had an important break through to discuss with you."

"Right, thank you Benjamin, I'll go down strait away then!"

"Would you also like some coffee brought down for you sir?"

"Yes, thank you, what a nice gesture Benjamin, most kind of you," his voice softened.

"Thank you sir!"

By the time Sol had unlocked the door the young man had already run downstairs to to the main floor to get their coffee.

Sol went ahead on down to the basement to where Fred was waiting for him with his arms folded and a smirk on his face. "You do realize that these books are hot don't you Sol?"

"Of course I do, I stole them!"

"That's not what I meant. The Professor also had in his possession stolen property, its from a Museum in Israel from the 1930s; We could be in really big trouble if we were found with these in our possession."

Unbeknown to them Benjamin had opened the door at just the right time and had heard that the books were stolen when and where from. He hadn't heard the rest of it, at least not yet; He quietly closed the door then reopened it again loudly enough so that they had heard the door open and someone was descending the stairs.

"Coffee gentlemen!" announced Benjamin.

"Why thank you BJ" said Sol, referring to his nickname all of a sudden.

"Coffee for the two of us Fred?"

"Yes Sol, I need some now that I have identified this book you brought me. I have spent the last three days going over the notes and the other books."

"Oh, I am sorry; thank you Benjamin, that will be all for now." Sol did not realized the young man was standing there staring at the books on the work bench. Bad move you fool he thought to himself. This young man is smart though, we might need him one day as our protégé.

Sol had heard the door close as well and asked, "well alright Fred, what else do you have?"

Fred went on to tell Sol what other important details he had found.

"Oh, so the old man wasn't such a fool after all Fred, no wonder he didn't want me snooping around especially when I saw these two books. He knew they were hot and figured once he was dead, the University would receive the books with open arms and say nothing about where they were from, right?"

"Right you are Sol! Now then, we are in kind of a pickle here ourselves. I'm not worried about selling the books two and three times over but we have to be sure they can never be traced back to us."

"No problem Fred, I'll take care of it. We'll use the drop box we used before at that post office look alike place, I forget the name but it's over on Elm Street. I've maintained the box for a purpose just like this. We'll use a young woman this time to send and pick up our mail and pay for the box in person and that way it can't be traced back to us, okay?"

"Yes Sol, you're the expert when it comes to subterfuge especially of this magnitude."

"Say Fred, I have another idea, neither of us is getting any younger, one day we will want to retire, how about we take young Benjamin into our confidence? I have an interesting idea that just came to me. You know the young man is smart and resourceful and is always short of money. I think if we confide in him a little at a time we'll be alright, I'm thinking of course that maybe we should offer him a full time job when he graduates and further more I think we should pay his tuition for the next two years therefore obligating him to us. We'll have him over a barrel, one he can't afford to walk away from. We can do it with your help of course, we'll draw up a contract which you can forge his signature to. We'll have him between the proverbial rock and a hard place I believe."

"You've got a point Sol, I'd love to pass on what I know to someone younger so they can get the hang of it before I die."

"Me too Fred, but let's start slowly however. I think maybe he has already heard more than he should have." Sol was right BJ was upstairs wondering what was going on in that basement. He knew they restored rare books but didn't know how they came by them. He knew deep inside that something wasn't quite right about the basement activities but he couldn't get down there to snoop around because Fred was always there it seemed. He decided that he would just have to wait until he could get down there and look around when they were both out of the building. His main problem was he had no key to the basement. He went on about his business unaware of the plotting going on in the basement at that very moment which would change his life forever, both professionally and financially.

CHAPTER - 11

Another week went by with Fred and Sol meeting secretly and planning how they would market their latest find. Every other day they would let BJ learn a little bit more about the process of creating old pages for books from newly engineered paper. BJ wasn't allowed to see the two rare books again, only others being restored.

One day Fred asked him outright; "BJ, how would you like to learn the process we use to recreate old paper. Sol and I have talked about you and how you seem to be very interested in our work. What we do is restore an old page or pages in a book and recreate the faded page and ink to make it appear original so even the experts can't tell an original from a copy. We do it for posterity's sake. Our work will live on beyond the ages, people will be able to enjoy the original works of the Literary Masters indefinitely. We may not go down in history for our work but someone will and no one has the formulas that we do."

"But isn't it illegal to do that and sell it as an original?"

"Not at all BJ. We tell the customer which pages have been restored or replaced so they know right up front that the book they are about to receive isn't one hundred percent original. We have been able to fool the experts into thinking that what we have done is part of the original book, our work is that good. It hurts no one if we tell them right up front that some of the book has been restored."

'Think of it this way. You buy an old junk car that doesn't run. You take it to a restorer expert and he restores the car to like new condition, sometimes better than new and the car will always be a restored original using original parts. In some cases they are able to get new old parts or what is called NOS parts from companies who have a large stock of obsolete parts."

"Yes I can see now why its important to make it look like the rest of the book with some pages beyond repair that need replacing but you don't completely restore the book like a car is done, you only make it look like the rest of the book in its present condition."

"By George I believe you have it now, good explanation, I couldn't have said it better. There are people out there who would kill to get their hands on our formulas so we must be tight lipped and our customers also know this, that's why we only deal with reputable people museums or collectors. We have at our disposal the knowledge to create new old paper from scratch just like they did in olden days when these books right here were written."

He pointed to a small stack of books he was working on. "We even import papyrus from abroad and make our own papyrus paper right here. In the old days some paper was made from rags as well as wood pulp. There is a lot of science that goes into what we do and we learned it all in school. That is when I made the best discoveries, of course and I told no one except Sol who was and still is my best friend,. Am I making sense son?"

"Yes, I think I have a better understanding now of what you do but what does Sol do?"

"Ah, you want to know how we come by all of these books don't you?"

"Yes you could say that, the second floor storage area is full of boxes of books, I've only been in there a couple of times to locate a box that Sol or Greta wanted."

"Well put your mind at ease, Sol buys all the books he can, good ones as well as the junk books. Those books we use to make new old paper with, we recycle the paper you see, nothing goes to waste around here. Sol travels the country attending large book sales held by anyone but especially the older used book stores going out of business. Some of them don't realize the gold beneath their feet. He has spent years talking with used book store owners asking them to let him know if they come across any old books that might be special. When he hears from one of them he goes on the road. He doesn't waste his trips either, he searches out any used book stores in the area while he is there visiting a particular store, that's why the second floor is so full of books waiting for one of us to go through.

We're hoping that you will accept our offer to train you in the way we restore books. Sol and I wont live forever, we want to retire one day and we would like you to take over the business then if you like. Don't give us an answer right now, its a career changing decision for you. Just the other day Sol mentioned that his old four door Lincoln was about wore out and he thinks maybe we should invest in a new three quarter ton van with a diesel engine to conserve fuel and wear and tear on the engine. We also discussed asking you if you might like to go on one of his forays to find rare books so you can see how we operate. I have no interest in traveling about. I have everything I've ever wanted right here at my finger tips."

He pointed to his table filled with jars of chemicals and stacks of paper which were all blank. "Each stack of these papers, he explained, "are ready for ink." That is another skill that has to be learned very slowly. Much of what was written in ancient times was in cuneiforms, some in Greek, Latin, English and Hebrew and so on. You will have to learn how to do the printing which I will show you. In another room around the corner here we have old type writers, old printing presses and old type setters, what do you think of all this?"

"I'm actually over whelmed Fred, the two of you have devoted your lives to restoring old manuscripts, books and parchments haven't you?"

"Yes BJ, it has been our life's work and we are extremely proud of our accomplishments as you shall be one day."

"Wow this is too much to take in for one day, when can we start Fred?"

"You started just over two weeks ago. Little by little we have been revealing to you what we do down here and how we do it. Now here is the big question, if you decide to come on board with us as an apprentice we're prepared to pay your next two years tuition and all other costs and when you get your Degree we hope it will have some Literature, Engineering and Science in it.

Don't answer me now; think on it, it is a very big decision for you to consider. One day you could be running this whole operation as a partner with us then we could retire. When we pass on the whole business will be yours as neither of us have any heirs to leave anything to."

"Now then go back upstairs and in a few days when you come to a decision you can tell one of us, Sol and I have no secrets between us."

"Thank you Fred, I don't know quite what to say, this is a tremendous opportunity for me. You'll pay me a living wage when I begin?"

"We'll do better than that, you can have a small percentage of the profits we make when we make a big sale, how does that sit with you?"

"You're right, I need to take some time and figure this out as to whether I want to make this my career instead of teaching." BJ grabbed Fred's right hand which surprised him and shook it vigorously. "I can't thank the two of you enough for the offer, I will give it the attention it deserves, thank you very much!" He continued to shake his hand until Fred made him let go.

Fred went back to his work and BJ ran upstairs two at a time full of excitement. Well so much for small talk, let's see what happens over the next few days Fred was thinking.

BJ couldn't contain his enthusiasm as he went about his day whistling, waiting on customers with new energy always trying to please them. Sol went out and traded in his four door Lincoln and bought a brand new Ford three quarter ton van just like he wanted. He had air bag suspension installed underneath instead of regular shocks, he thought he might get a better ride out of it. It was a non descript white stretch van with no markings on it whatsoever. He wanted to blend in, not stand out. He had the van beefed up with overload springs underneath to carry more weight than intended and had a false floor installed beneath the original five and a half inches deep so it wasn't perceptible to the naked eye. There he could hide any stolen masterpieces he happened to pick up illegally. If he were to be stopped by the police the van would appear clean with the stolen merchandise beneath the floor. He bought a heavy rubber mat made for pickup trucks and vans to protected the paint beneath it and installed it. Sol had come up with an ingenious design and told no one about it, not even Fred.

He drove the van every day learning its good points and its faults but he found no faults with it. It cornered well and had great pickup with its turbo charged V8 diesel engine. This was more like driving a race car rather than a big three quarter ton van with an ten foot loading area. He had a curtain installed behind the passenger seat so he could keep prying eyes from seeing what was in the back, there were no side widows only two tinted back windows in the doors. He could make the van to appear empty or full with the use of the air bags. With the sale of just one book he had stolen from the deceased Professor he could have bought several vans like this but Sol was tight with the money so he could buy all the books he wanted without worry and have money to back his enterprise at the store. He spared no expense when it came to the Store. He also planned to hide his disguises and elevated shoes beneath the floor and any other tools of the trade that he would need from time to time.

Over time he added more and more features to the van. He had installed a heavy gauge wire cage behind the seats that could be moved backward or forward on fixed tracks in case he had extra passengers and the cage would protect them in case he had to stop quickly. Heavy items would not impact the passengers that way.

CHAPTER - 12

Another week went by before BJ was ready to talk to either Sol or Fred. One day as he was bringing coffee down to Fred in the basement he finally spoke up; "Here's your coffee Fred, how are things going with you today?"

"Just fine BJ, have you thought about the offer we made you?"

He seemed a little hesitant but finally said, "yes I have Fred, I gave it very careful consideration. As you know teaching is my first love but being short of cash and my parents are no longer able to help me with tuition, books, rent and so forth, so I have decided to take you and Sol up on your offer. I think this will give me a better opportunity and I can certainly make more money here at the store than I can teaching and one day who knows, maybe I'll retire and teach anyway after I teach someone else the ropes about the Book Store's Operations."

"That's fine son, just fine, why don't you go up to the second floor storeroom and tell Sol, I'm sure he'll appreciate hearing from you as well. You're a fine young man and you've made the right decision. He has a new shipment of books that arrived recently from one of his contacts that went out of business, just knock loudly twice, you know the routine."

"Thank you Fred, enjoy your coffee." The young man went upstairs one at a time, he felt a foreboding of some kind and chills suddenly ran up and down his spine but he saw no reason for it as he ascended the stairs from the brightly lit laboratory.

Fred was thinking; I'm glad that's done. He'll need Chemistry classes now but I'll bring that up later. He went about his business, he was mixing a new ink formula to make the ink appear old and faded for an old Masterpiece that Sol had picked up a couple of weeks ago, the one that BJ saw but didn't connect with. The stage was now set and the show was about to start for them. They had their new recruit and possible fall guy. The next thing to be done was to get him to sign a contract so they could get his signature then forge it to a second contract. Later they would draft a confession and forge his signature to it like so many forgeries they had done in the past to protect themselves in the event the authorities eventually got wise to them. After all who would expect two little old men of doing anything criminal.

In a few more days Sol and Fred had a very simple contract for BJ to sign. It said that he had to keep his end of the bargain by graduating in the top twenty five percent of his class and he must get his Degree in Literature signing his life away effectively to them but it didn't say that in so many words. It was a simple bargain, do as we ask, we pay all your tuition, don't and you have to pay us back over a ten year period. That they did put in writing. On the surface it looked perfectly normal, all he had to do was to perform as he was asked to.

"BJ, could you come here for a minute," asked Sol, "Fred and I want to talk to you. They were in the store by the front counter, they had asked everyone else to give them five minutes alone with BJ.

"Here is the contract for you to sign between the three of us. Please read it over and if there is something you don't understand let us know," Sol asked.

BJ picked it up and read it over. "Wait a minute, it says here I can live here in my own apartment for the rest of my life rent free or until I get married, then I have a choice of staying here or getting my own place somewhere else. We didn't talk this far into the future but I like it, you are just too generous with me." "Nonsense, we like you is all there is to it and we would like you to take this place over one day if you want. It simplifies life for you, you can live and work in one building and you can come and go as you please."

"Are you sure you want to take the chance on me not screwing something up?"

"We're sure BJ, here's a pen or would you like to think it over some more?"

"No hand me the pen please, I'll sign it right now!" he said excitedly.

Sol handed him the pen and after he signed it they ran it through their

Pitney Bowes flat bed copy machine they had in the store. "Here's your copy BJ, we'll keep the original to put in our safe."

They had a large fire proof safe to keep their most valuable books and documents in on the main floor, it was disguised as a wall of book shelves that slid open from one corner like a huge door that revealed a safe. All the employees knew it was there but only three knew the combination and that was Sol, Fred and Greta.

Greta had been watching as BJ signed the contract and she winked at Sol as the boy signed his name and Sol winked back at her. The three of them shook hands all around and Greta came back over to where they were to welcome BJ into the store's firm as she called it. She knew what the men had planned for BJ and went along with it wholeheartedly. She wasn't privy to the things BJ was about to learn however, she was perfectly content running the store and the rental units above the store and she was an absolute whiz when it came to keeping business records.

CHAPTER - 13

A few weeks went by and BJ would have to start a new semester soon as a Junior. Sol approached him one Monday morning. "Good morning BJ, would you like to make a trip with me up to Buffalo? There's a store going out of business there and I have been contacted to see if there are any books we might be able to use. It would be a learning experience for you to see how we operate. The store has been in operation close to a hundred years and there may be a treasure trove of books people may have forgotten about. If we act quickly we can scoop the whole deal. I'll pay all of the expenses, food lodging and so forth, your job will be to observe my technique in dealing with people, are you game for this kind of a trip?"

"Yes of course, I'd love to go with you."

"Alright then tomorrow morning we leave, we should be back in four or five days if we hit pay dirt, less if it's a bum steer. Better bring a couple changes of clothes with you and throw in some of the oldest clothes you have for when we visit the store, we don't want to appear too affluent, the price would go up considerably if they knew we could afford to buy them out lock stock and barrel and never miss the money. That's where you come in to observe and just acknowledge anything I might say. I'll see you in the morning and we could get plenty dirty crawling around an older store, that's the reason for the oldest clothes."

"Got it Sol, I'll be ready."

The next morning BJ was ready, he carried an old suitcase and it was the first time he would see the new van. Sol kept it garaged under the warehouse portion of the old Mill in back where there were several small and larger garage spaces used in the old days for pick ups and deliveries by big trucks. Inside there was a huge loading dock with a ramp built in so the trucks more or less descended to the loading platform to unload their goods. Sol had the ramp where he kept the new van parked raised so that he could back up against the dock and he could raise or lower the van as needed to off load his merchandise. BJ had no idea about the van's intricacies other than it had a diesel engine and was a new vehicle. The two of them were finally ready and Sol drove pulling out onto the street and they headed for Buffalo. It was a very long drive and by the time they got there they were both tired so they found a Motel close in to town and stayed in adjoining rooms overnight.

In the morning Sol got BJ up very early, he wasn't even dressed and hadn't shaved yet. He knocked rather loudly on BJ's inner door.

"Come on BJ get a move on we need to get there before anyone else, the advertised sale won't be for another week but the owner has contacted a few people to come and look over his inventory before he advertises it for sale to the general public. He hopes one of us will buy him out so he won't have to stand around selling a few books at a time then end up having a whole lot of books left over that no one wants."

"But Sol, I need to shave and shower this morning."

"Nonsense, we want to look poor not well to do, remember what I said, I didn't' shave either and I'm in the oldest clothes I own."

BJ looked at him through his bleary eyes and realized he barely recognized the man standing there. He looked disheveled, unshaven standing there in an old overcoat and old shoes which were badly scuffed up and had seen better days.

"I'll be right with you sir, sorry I wasn't ready sooner, you forgot to tell me we were starting so early."

"Well come on get a move on, we'll eat at a place I know and get a good breakfast in us."

In a matter of minutes BJ was ready and followed Sol down the hall out onto the street where they had parked the van overnight. They got in and drove several minutes until Sol suddenly pulled over and said, "we're here."

It was a mom and pop style restaurant that had a sign outside that said: GOOD FOOD - CHEAP PRICES! They went in and had trouble finding a place to sit.

A waitress came over and didn't give them a second look as she took their drink orders and after she served them their beverages she took their food order. "Hey, just a minute there mister, I know you! Sol, its been a long, long time there honey."

"Yes it has Francis, this is a new employee, his name is Benjamin but we call him BJ."

"Well howdy there BJ, any friend of Sol's is a friend of ours as well."

"Why thank you ma'am, that's very kind of you."

"Wow and polite as well Sol, maybe some of that will rub off on you, hey?"

"Maybe Francis but I doubt it, I'm pretty well set in my ways as you already know."

"Still not married huh Sol, too bad you missed your chance with me, I got married a year ago to a real bum; he sits at home while I do all the work to keep us afloat."

"I'm sorry Francis, is there anything I can do to help?"

"You could knock him off I suppose," she said quietly, "I took out a big Insurance Policy on him but he has to die accidental like or they won't pay me much."

"Before I leave Francis write down your address for me, tell me what he looks like and I'll see what I can do."

She walked away and left BJ with his mouth agape. "You can't be serious Sol, murder I mean?" BJ was in shock at what he had heard.

"She's an old lover of mine BJ from my University days, I would do anything to help."

"But murder Sol? that's illegal as hell!"

"Hush yourself, you'll make a scene. Can we help it if he gets run over or something? Here comes breakfast, not another word now about what was said."

"Yes sir, mums the word."

They ate their bacon and eggs, home fries and toast. Francis came over to the table to give Sol the bill and handed him a piece of paper with her address on it and a recent small snap shot of her husband. "Your bill is all taken care of Sol, thanks for thinking about me and stopping in again, see you later I hope?"

"You can count on it Francis! Does the man drink a lot?"

"Yeah Sol, he drinks something terrible and beats me sometimes so bad I can't come to work because of a black eye or internal injuries."

"Just what does he like to drink best Francis?"

"He likes any kind of whiskey especially the cheap kind, he can buy more of it that way."

"I know what you mean Francis, well goodbye for now."

"Goodbye Sol"

" BJ,I am pleased that I met you. see you both later."

BJ caught a glimpse of her crying, it seemed to him that she still loved ole Sol here.

They got to the Book Store they were looking for right at nine o'clock. Sol gave BJ some last minute instructions but he couldn't get Francis off his mind. They went inside and the place was devoid of customers. There was an old man sitting behind a counter with snow white hair balding down the center of his head all the way back.

"Mr. Fletcher, we are here about your contacting me regarding the closing of your store and the need to sell your entire inventory."

"That's right sir, are you interested in any of my stock?"

"Yes possibly, maybe all of it depending on how many books you have and the quality."

"Well what you see out here then in the back I have a lot more in boxes, many of them older slow movers the publishers wouldn't take back."

"Mind if I show myself around sir?"

"No, take your time, I'm not going anywhere, I have cancer you see and less than a couple of months to live so I'm pretty weak."

Damn it Sol thought, the perfect set up and I have this kid to lug around with me.

"Come on BJ let's have a look around in back."

BJ followed Sol through some saloon type bat wing doors into a huge room filled with boxes and boxes of new and some older books. Sol started to sift through some of them while BJ did the same and he called out to Sol about what was in the box he was looking at. "Gees Sol, this looks like a lot of junk to me."

"Yeah me too BJ, keep looking though, we came a long way to give up so soon." They checked box after box but it wasn't the treasure trove Sol had hoped for. "Keep looking BJ,

I'm going out front to see the old man for a minute." Sol disappeared and BJ kept looking. In a minute or so Sol was back grinning from ear to ear.

"Basement BJ." Sol kept walking until he came to what looked like an old cupboard.

"Here it is BJ, the door to the cellar; the old man says he hasn't been down here in years." He found a light switch and turned it on. They descended the steep narrow stairs into the gloom of what looked like a nightmare. Cobwebs were everywhere, dust and dirt were abundant. Sol located some strings hanging from the ceiling which were attached to old fashioned white porcelain light fixtures and pulled on each one as he found them.

"My gosh Sol, the man was right, it doesn't look like anyone's been down here in years, look at all the boxes of books, these would never fit in the new van."

"Hush now BJ, I told you what to look for and this is where you earn your money, I have been doing this for years now so just keep looking." They looked into each and every box they came across. Suddenly Sol spoke up rather loudly, "got it BJ, this is what we're here for."

BJ walked over to where Sol stood amongst the dust and dirt, he was staring into a box of books. "What is it Sol, what did you find?"

"Just look at these books, they're as pristine as the day they were printed."

"Those are just old mystery books aren't they Sol?"

"To the naked eye maybe, but if you look closely some are unsolved mysteries and most are written by the most famous Mystery Writer of all time. Just look at a couple of others in this box, its a series of Sherlock Holmes and here are some first editions by Charles Dickens too."

"Does that make them special Sol?"

"To me yes, they still sell like hotcakes if you get the ones by great writers and this is it.

We'll take this box upstairs after we look around some more." They searched about another fifteen minutes or so when Sol spoke out again. "Over here BJ, the mother lode!"

BJ went over and stood next to Sol; "just look at this right here, he must have forgotten all about these over the years, the old rascal may have been hoarding them all this time."

"What are they Sol?"

"Classics my boy, just look at the authors names. Why some of these date back before Uncle Tom's Cabin and so on, here is one from 1756 from England. Here's an author signed First Edition First Issue of Frankenstein, my word this box is solid gold. They are in great condition, I've never seen so many classics in one place. We have to have this box as well."

They moved it around to where they could see it for when they went back upstairs they could carry them up with them. They continued looking and found eight more big boxes too heavy for Sol to lift by himself. When they were done they had fourteen boxes in all from the basement alone they wanted and hadn't looked in all the boxes yet.

"BJ, its time we went upstairs and got some fresh air, I'll talk to the old man while you check the bookshelves over up there, sing out if something looks interesting to you."

"Right behind you Sol, basements like this make me creepy anyway."

They went upstairs and Sol went to chat with the old man while BJ checked the book shelves out with renewed interest now that he knew what Sol liked and he too took a new interest in the hunt. BJ found over a dozen books for Sol to look over and then found some that read unsolved Mysteries so he grabbed some of them as well. He began to carry them over to the counter where the old man was talking with Sol setting down a few at a time.

"What do you think about these Sol, any interest in them?"

"I'm afraid not BJ," but he winked at him so BJ just kept bringing them over.

"Well BJ, he and I have come to an agreement, he said we had to take all the books or none for a price. I can live with the price but I don't know how we can possibly get all of these back to Poughkeepsie, there's not enough here to hire a freight or a moving company."

"What about renting one of those moving trucks that you rent one way, could we get them all in one big truck?"

Sol began to scratch his chin, "maybe, I'm sure we could get all of the ones I want for now in the two trucks I suppose. The old man says he has plenty of boxes in the back to pack all of these up, I just don't need all of these books that are here in the sales room, he won't take no for an answer though, its all or nothing like I said. Say I have an idea how to speed things along."

"What is it Sol, your idea that is?"

"Let me think on it a minute then I'll decide."

They were silent for several minutes, Sol leaned over to whisper something in the old man's ear now and then.

"Alright I thought it over and we'll take it all, I made him a new offer because he is forcing us take all of them and I'll need extra help and maybe a couple of trucks so I lowered my price and he said okay, he understands the challenge of removing all of the books. Can you drive a big rig BJ?"

"How big of a rig are you talking Sol?"

"Just tell me how big of a rig you can legally drive then I'll tell you what I think."

"My license is good for anything up to five tons, but I have driven bigger trucks."

CHAPTER - 14

"Five ton box truck will do BJ, I think we can find one that big to rent alright. We'll leave now and go find a truck, that's the next order of business. They left and went looking for a truck, moving truck, straight truck or a small semi tractor trailer.

After driving around for a while they found one at a Moving Company which had one for sale and it was just what they needed. It was an ugly three colored straight box truck with a faded blue top, a faded wide white stripe around the middle of the truck then coral on the bottom of it, the cab itself was blue and white. The truck's doors had the company's name painted out and the truck was rated for ten thousands pounds carrying capacity. Sol found that it was cheaper to buy this clunker of a truck than to rent one. It was recently inspected and deemed road worthy so Sol negotiated on the price and bought it for a song and had BJ follow him back to the store with it.

"BJ, stay here and start boxing up the books in the main store, I'm going to get us some help to pack and load all of this, its just too much for the two of us."

Sol left and headed for the seedy part of town where all the bums and alcoholics hung out. He found six men who were strong enough to carry heavy cartons of books and took them back to the store in the back of the van. He took them inside and set them to work helping BJ. Sol went to work carefully packing boxes while others carried boxes up from the basement out to the truck or van. Sol checked each box and marked some of them before allowing them to be loaded. In several hours they were done.

Sol paid off the men in cash and told them they would have to find their own way back to where he had picked them up. "BJ, can you find your way back to the main highway while I finish up my business with the owner here?"

"Yes of course but we have to check out of the motel yet and its way past lunchtime, don't you think we should wait until tomorrow to leave, we could get an early start if you like. t will be a long drive and I'd feel more secure if you followed me back to Poughkeepsie in case I breakdown and I don't have the money to fill this bad boy up, it's a diesel and it only has a quarter of a tank of fuel right now plus it has two tanks and the other one is slap empty."

"Yes of course you're right, I should have thought of that; I am sorry, we'll get both of the vehicles filled up and spend the night at the motel and leave early in the morning, that way it will give me a chance to say goodbye to Francis."

Something that Sol had done caught BJ's eye; he handed one man the picture and address of Francis's house and he gave the man an extra wad of bills but he said nothing and made out like he didn't see it. That's why he thought Sol was in a hurry to leave. Nothing more was said, they left the store together and went to a gas station which was close to the Motel where they were staying to fill both vehicles up with diesel fuel.

"BJ why don't you go ahead to the Motel, I need to go back and finish my business with the man at the Store, then I'll come get you and we'll have supper."

"So it's okay for me to shave and take a shower now Sol?"

"Yeah kid, do whatever you like from here on out, I'll be back soon."

BJ shaved, showered, changed his clothes and went next door to knock on Sol's door to see if he was ready. He was just about to knock when Sol came walking towards him down the long corridor.

"I'm back BJ, the old man was in a talkative mood so it was hard for me to leave. Give me a little time and I'll knock on your door when I'm ready."

The rest of the day was quiet, they rode around town looking at other stores but found nothing of interest and went back to the Motel after they had supper.

They got up early the next morning, washed up and shaved, checked out of the Motel and left the big truck where it was while they went to breakfast. Francis looked like hell, she looked as though she had been through a real battle of some kind, she didn't have any marks but she was short of breath and looked ill like her insides hurt something awful. She quietly took their orders and went about serving others while they ate their breakfast.

They were waiting to leave after paying their check when a uniformed police officer came in and asked for her.

" Are you Francis Salisbury ma'am?"

"Yes sir, what can I do for you? Oh shoot, can you wait just a minute while I take care of this man's bill?"

"Certainly ma'am."

"That's seven dollars and sixteen cents sir," talking to Sol.

"Thank you Ms. the food was excellent this morning," and Sol smiled at her.

They headed for the door but before they left they overheard the Policeman and Francis talking. "Ma'am, I don't like this kind of duty but your husband Burt was killed this morning when he accidently stepped off the curb and into the path of a City Bus, I'm afraid he is dead ma'am."

She looked down as if to weep into her apron and gave a wink to Sol as they were going out the door and get ready to cross the street. He returned the wink so no one saw them. They got in the van and headed back for the Motel.

"Funny huh?" said BJ.

"What do you mean?"

"Well one day the guy beats the snot out of his wife and the next day he gets run over by a big City Bus. I guess you could call that getting your just desert wouldn't you say?"

"I'd say you are right BJ, just imagine, that getting run over by a bus with witnesses all around." The witnesses he was eluding to just happened to be the men who had helped them load the truck and the van the day before but BJ couldn't have known it. When they were getting their vehicles ready to roll again Sol looked down at the front page in a newspaper box, it stated: 'Local Book Store Owner falls downstairs to his death yesterday after selling his business, horrible accident is all it was, according to the Coroner.'

They left out the meager amount of money he had deposited in his bank. It would take days if ever to find that out. The deposit slip they found in his pocket was smudged somewhat around the numbers of the amount but not the deposit Bank Account's numbers. The last people anyone remembered being at the store were several bums who had been loading boxes onto a large moving truck with no lettering or signs on it, they did say it was a big ugly truck. No one remembered the white van.

Fortunately for BJ he didn't see the newspaper, all he had were suppositions of what he perceived seeing in the Restaurant, even that he wasn't sure of. He was wondering if his eyes had deceived him.

The trip back was long, arduous and monotonous. The big truck ran pretty good but the steering was sloppy allowing the truck to wander all over the road on the Interstate and the brakes were about wore out. He felt as though someone hadn't done their job when the Inspection Sticker was put on the truck. The brakes constantly squealed metal on metal every time he had to brake for a vehicle but at least they worked. He felt that it would be a one way trip for this truck but what he didn't know was as soon as they got the truck unloaded Sol would call a wrecker friend of his to come and get the truck and take it to a crusher right away to be rid of it as soon as possible. He didn't want any evidence around and that truck would stick out like a sore thumb in January anywhere it was parked.

When they returned back to the Store they had been gone for four days. Sol went and found help like he had done before to help unload the big truck. He and BJ would unload the van themselves, that's where the most valuable books were. The chore took several hours with the homeless men having to stop every few minutes, they tired easily climbing two sets of stairs to the second floor and then back down again after carrying all the heavy boxes of books. Greta watched the procession of men coming and going, up and down the stairs, in and out, it looked like terribly laborious work to her which it was in actually.

"Well Sol it looks like you had a successful trip after all, how did our BJ do?"

"Just fine Greta, he knew when to be quiet and when to talk, he did great!"

It sounded to Greta like there had been a problem of some kind by the tone of Sol's voice. He didn't tell her much about the details of his business anyway, only Fred knew about this dark side of him and BJ was going to have to learn it as well.

As soon as they were done unloading the big truck Sol went into the store and made a phone call. In less than an hour a huge wrecker truck with signs on its doors that said, BIG AL'S RECOVERY SERVICE, showed up that was capable of hauling the big truck away. It would be crushed completely by five o'clock the driver told Sol and Sol handed him a fist full of cash. They shook hands and the big wrecker left with the other truck on its lift apparatus. The evidence linking them to Buffalo was gone for good, there would never be a record of its existence. Sol used a fictitious company to buy and register the truck with a temporary tag. Sol had thought of every minute detail while in Buffalo and Poughkeepsie. No one ever came around asking questions about anything or anyone who was missing, they were clean as a whistle once again.

CHAPTER - 15

In Washington DC at the Federal Building, Special Agent Richard Jefferies has become suspicious about some of the rare book collectors and Book Store owners who had suddenly died and in all cases the conclusion of written opinions were that they were accidents in all of the individual cases. To Jefferies none of it added up. There was no comparison of the deaths, nothing to tie them together yet he thought something was being overlooked somewhere.

The latest tragedy was about a wealthy retired University Professor who was known to have an extensive rare book collection and to him it just didn't measure up. The man was meticulous if nothing else and in his home nothing went unnoticed by him. Also he wondered what the Professor was doing on the second floor when he had a pot of water on the stove. He felt the Professor would have noticed gas leaking and would have shut down the offending gas line and turned off the stove before going upstairs but he hadn't. Too many unanswered questions for Jefferies.

The house had blown up in the wee hours of a Friday morning according to the newspaper article. All the items including the gas stove and its fittings and gas line from the kitchen were sent to the FBI Lab and the gas fireplace with the gas line and all its fittings were sent as well. Agent Jefferies had requested them and was going to get to the bottom of this supposed accident.

He went over the gas stove with a gas expert and they found nothing out of the ordinary.

The next day they turned their attention to the gas log fireplace. Nothing was out of line here either until Agent Jefferies took one more look at the fitting closest to the ceramic logs. He asked the technician to get some soapy water for a leak test.

"Herb lets charge the line with air from the farthest point with the valve in the off position like it is now and let's put some soapy water on the fittings, this one closest to the logs caught my eye."

"What did you see that I didn't?" asked Herb.

"I see a minute shiny brass thread that shouldn't be there unless it had been loosened."

"Let me have a look, none of us saw it before." Herb got down to where he could see it in a better light. "I don't see anything shiny anywhere Agent Jefferies."

"Use a magnifying glass then, I can see it plain as day."

Herb went and found a magnifying glass and took a second look. "Well I'll be darned Agent Jefferies, how the hell did you see that and we couldn't?" he asked.

"Trained eye I guess, lets charge the line and see if we have the smoking gun or not."

Herb signaled to one of his helpers in the Lab and he charged the line with air and held it at a small level so it acted like low pressure gas. Herb soaped the area of the fittings and they watched.

"Looks like we struck out Agent Jefferies."

"Give it time Herb, remember this is low pressure gas that runs these appliances, not high pressure."

They watched and waited. In a few minutes the first bubble appeared, then another.

"Suppose someone loosened this fitting which is obvious to us now, how long would it take for the gas to reach sufficient mass to be set off by the burner that we found still on when we examined the stove."

"A few hours to several hours depending on the size of the rooms in the house and as you know the gas would stay close to the floor until a sufficient amount of gas escaped and filled the room to where the stove would have ignited the fumes. Was it a very big house?"

"Yes it was and it had very high ceilings and massive rooms according to the people I talked to who had been in the house. They told me that the Professor had put in all new thermal pane windows two years ago and had the entire house insulated against the cold so it was real tight for an old Victorian house."

"How far would you guess it was from the living room to the kitchen then?"

"From what I was told it would be quite a ways, the fireplace was in the front wall of the house in the living room, to get to the kitchen one would have to cross half of that room, go through a large dining room and then into the kitchen and the gas stove was in the center of the kitchen on a center wall."

"So what are we talking in feet, twenty five to thirty feet or more?"

"I'd say thirty feet or more would be a good guesstimate."

"Well then there you have it, it would take several hours for the low pressure gas to reach the burner on the stove that was on if the burner had indeed been lit."

"The Fire Department concluded that the explosion originated at the kitchen stove"

"Well then we have it, its murder for sure," added Herb.

"Put that in your report to the Director and a copy to me of course, thank you Herb. There is one more thing I am curious about while we're here. The books the investigators found and the wall safe I'm told that was recovered, where are they right now?"

"The books or what's left of them are in room eight where our fire investigators are and the wall safe I believe is in room eleven where they are attempting to open it as you requested."

"Fine, I'll need the reports of the actual findings when they have them but right now I want to see the condition of the books, just out of curiosity understand. Thanks Herb see you later,"

Jefferies left the room and went to room eight where the burned books were being looked over. Jefferies walked in without knocking, he had full run of the Lab with his credentials and was well respected by his collogues. "Good morning gentlemen, I understand you're working on the burned books from the explosion we're investigating."

"Yes that's right, they are all laid out on these tables what's left of them, are you looking for something unusual Agent Jefferies?"

"Exactly Ben, anything that says these are extremely rare and valuable books which they are supposed to be."

"I thought you might be interested in this one then, have a look over here. We have identified this as an older Public Library Book sold a month or so ago and it has recent date stamps, rare books would not have Library stamps on them anywhere. Here have a look under the microscope, I just finished with it and was putting it in a report for you and the Director."

"How many have you found so far like this that are suspicious to you?"

"Using the microscope is the easiest way to see the burned pages that were not 100% consumed in the fire and so far we have seven for sure that are recent books in the last decade, not rare at all, perfectly common. If you look right here the name of the Library is still legible. I think I know what you are thinking now, someone came in and removed all the books he wanted and replaced them with other books that had been recently purchased or maybe even stolen from a Library Book Sale, that about it Agent Jefferies?"

"Since when are you a mind reader Ben? You hit the nail right on the head though, good work all of you."

`There were a total of six people in the burn lab working on the same things. "I think we have the smoking gun now, I just left Herb in the other lab and we found the gas leak in the house was definitely murder and arson, there is no doubt about it now. We have a serial killer of sorts out there preying on book collectors and book store owners. Lord only knows where he or she will strike next. Several of these things that are happening I'm sure are on a local level and the cases are being closed saying they were accidents. I'm going to ask the Director's permission to contact Law Enforcement Agencies in all the states and ask for their cases involving book store owners or rare book collectors. This whole mess makes me sick, why hasn't someone already caught this, it's as plain as day to me, don't people out there have eyes, are they all blind to the fact of murder?" Agent Jefferies had no idea that he had just uncovered the tip of a monstrous iceberg of crime moving throughout the United States.

CHAPTER - 16

Sol was blissfully unaware that anyone was onto his activities. As of yet they, the FBI, didn't know who they were looking for. Sol spent the next three weeks in solitude engrossed in novels he had recently come by from Buffalo. He was reading all of the unsolved mysteries he could and was looking for one that was unique. He had most of his meals sent in at appointed hours from the restaurant he liked just up the street called Louie's.

They fed just about all of the local people at one time or another during the day and they had an extensive menu and were open from 6:00 A.M. to 9:00 P.M. seven days a week. A boy runner would bring Sol's food over from the restaurant on a tray and leave it outside of Sol's door. He would pick up the previous tray with the dirty dishes on it and on the tray would be a slip of paper with instructions on it for his next meal with money and a tip and so it went day in and day out, it was all very convenient for Sol.

Finally one day Sol emerged from his room, as one would refer to it as his cocoon, he entered the store and saw Greta. "Good morning Greta, how are you today?" Sol was grinning with a mile wide smile from ear to ear.

"I'm fine Sol," she paused a little, "did you finally decide to join the human race again?"

"You might say that. He replied, "I have a little field trip in mind, I could be gone several days looking at book stores around the country. If I am fortunate I could be back in a week but I could be gone as long as two weeks depending on my discoveries."

"When do you plan to leave?"

"I'll know that after I check in with Fred downstairs."

"How can he stay down there for days on end and never see the sun?" asked Greta.

"I don't actually know how he does it. Even I sit by the window when I'm working or studying a situation I want to get involved in because I like to see the sun just as you do. Well I'll go check on Fred, do you need anything while I'm here?"

"No Sol, we're in good shape supply wise, we have been doing a good business shipping books that you and Fred have created in your magic shop downstairs."

"Magic Shop?, that's the first time I've heard Fred's dungeon called a magic shop, I like it, maybe I'll have a sign made to hang in the entrance to the basement, might be cute, see you later Greta."

Sol left and headed for the basement to see Fred. He strolled down the stairs and noticed how quiet it was, no radio music, no whistling or humming from Fred, no machinery running, it was almost too quiet. Then he saw Fred sitting on a high stool working intently on something. Sol knew not to startle Fred or he would get angry. He just made enough of a noise to let Fred know that someone was there in the basement Lab. He walked around to where Fred could see him from his peripheral vision and stopped without talking, he would let Fred speak first.

"What's wrong Sol, you're mighty quiet this morning?"

"Nothings wrong Fred, just wanted to check in with you, we haven't talked in a while. I wanted to see if there was anything you needed. I'm going to make a field trip to look at some book stores around the country tomorrow and may be gone a week or two depending on my luck."

" I can't think of anything special you can get me other than a bottle of indigo ink, a bottle of red and a bottle of dark blue and a bottle of midnight black as well. I also need some iron salts, some tannin, a thickener, some carbon ink, some iron gall ink, some pine tar, some solvents, dyes, pine tree resins, some pigments, some graphite and I have plenty of the other colors we use but these are the ones I use most in my base blends."

"Well that's quite a large order for someone who doesn't need anything Fred."

"I have a list here for everything Sol. I'm looking ahead. I'll be getting low by the time you get back and you know the colors we need as well as I do,. You could call it a stop gap measure if you want?"

"Whatever you say Fred, I'll bring it back with me from the supply house we use. I'll leave first thing in the morning in case you think of something else you can let me know between now and then."

"Alright Sol, see you later then, good hunting now!"

Sol turned and went back upstairs to the store.

"Greta, have you heard from BJ lately?"

"Yes he calls when he can skip a class to come in and work and he asks about you each time, you know, like, how is Sol doing, does he need me for anything special, things like that?"

"Oh I see, he's a good lad you know."

"Yes I know!"

"Well Greta I think I'll go to the restaurant and get a bite to eat for lunch, can I bring you anything back?"

"No Sol, I have an errand to run on my lunch hour and I'll eat somewhere while I'm out, but thank you for asking."

"No problem Greta, well see you."

"See you Sol."

Sol left and headed for Louie's Restaurant. He would leave a note on the last tray of food from Louie's asking them to stop delivering food until they heard from him again. An hour or so later he was back, Greta was at lunch and there was a young man and young lady there minding the store. Sol by-passed them and went straight up to his apartment.

He spent a good part of the afternoon packing what he needed for his trip. When he was done he had three suit cases full of clothes and four pairs of elevated shoes in another case. All but one of them would go under the floor in the new van and six pairs of different rubbers to slip over his shoes with different sole patterns on the bottom. He seldom left the same shoe print or style of shoe at any crime scene. He was ultra careful with every move he made so it would appear that different people were doing the crimes. He had a weight belt used for scuba diving he always kept in the van's hidden floor space, he used it when he wanted to look heavy with his fat suit on which was also in a suitcase.

Then he picked up a book he'd been reading the past few days and looked through it again to be sure he was familiar with the crime he was going to try to duplicate to the letter. He fell asleep in his chair somewhere around three thirty he assumed, it was almost five o'clock and suppertime for him. He got himself together, freshened up in the bathroom and headed out for Louie's again this time for supper.

CHAPTER - 17

The next morning Sol was up early, he packed the van with last minute items, locked it and walked across the street to Louie's for breakfast. He hadn't told a soul where he was headed, he would just disappear after breakfast.

Later he got into the van and headed south to the interstate before swinging west towards his ultimate destination. He took I-87 south to I-84 west and traveled west until he picked up I-76 then he continued on that until he hit the I-70 just outside of Pittsburg Pennsylvania and stayed on that until he got to Grand Junction Colorado, his destination. He had mailed away for brochures about Colorado and Grand Junction that fit the criteria for his plan in size and population numbers. He couldn't commit the same crime in the same place as it would be too obvious to anyone in Law Enforcement. Even a dummy would recognize the similarities, he needed a new location similar in size to pull off his next crime and Grand Junction had just what he wanted. He took four leisurely days to get here, still had been a long drive.

He rode around town a little, found a rental car lot and not too far away was a long term parking close to a small airport where he could leave the van as long as needed. He went to the long term parking lot and made a deal with the attendant there to leave the van for an undetermined length of stay and told the attendant he may be back picking up things he needed from time to time from the van. He explained he was traveling on business and his van was not very business like so he would rent a nice car to drive while he was in town and he would be staying at a local Motel. The attendant didn't question the strange looking man's motives; he gave him a placard to hang from his interior mirror that said 'LONG TERM PARKING PERMIT" and showed him where he could leave it.

The attendant looked at the man's Missouri driver's license and wrote down the license number from the license tag on the van which also said, Missouri. The attendant had no idea that both were stolen on the way to Colorado. Sol had done his homework and made unerring preparations to get this far unnoticed by anyone. He stole the license tag off a Funeral Home van and the license he picked up in a shopping mall when a man absentmindedly left his license out for a second or two to write a out check for some merchandise and Sol snatched the license without anyone noticing. The timing had been perfect to get away with it, a simple crime of opportunity. The man would later apply for a new license to replace the one he thought he had dropped or misplaced somewhere. It was almost too easy getting the things that Sol felt that he needed.

He called a taxi from the attendant's small building in the lot, the Taxi picked him up and took him to the car rental lot he had seen earlier. Sol paid the Taxi driver who didn't question the odd looking little man with cash. He went inside and rented a new four door Lincoln, which he had a passion for, it seemed the bigger heavier cars he liked the most and he also paid the man with cash.

After all the arrangements were made he drove the car out of the lot and went looking for a motel. When he found one moderately priced he pulled in and registered under the alias on the Driver's license which had his own picture on it now. The name on it was George C, Johnston, Columbia Missouri. He took everything up to his room then went looking for a restaurant to eat supper. He used the side entrances at the Motel when he came and went using his room key card. The last thing he wanted to do was to make an impression on someone who might remember the little man with the bald head. Starting tomorrow after getting his other luggage out of the van he would change into a disguise looking like a different person altogether.

The next morning he left the Motel wearing a new disguise, a taller heavier man with a soft business like hat with a wide brim and a brown pin striped business suit. He got into the car and began driving. He already had a city map that had been mailed to a drop box at the place he rented one just for this purpose under another assumed name. He had already circled the place he wanted to go and start his surveillance and took a lunch with him.

After three days he realized that the man and woman he was watching never varied their comings and goings from home by more than a minute or two here and there. He would strike tonight he decided, no sense wasting anymore time or money. He came back after dark. Now he appeared to be a fat man and wore the old fashioned black rubbers over his shoes and common brown cotton gloves on his hands. He watched and waited.

Finally his patience paid off, the woman left quietly in the middle of the night to go meet her lover. Sol waited and watched for a light to come on but there was none. He easily slipped into the house quiet as a mouse, climbed the stairs and found the man's bedroom. He quietly went in without waking him. He pulled a hypodermic needle from his pocket and injected some fluid under the man's armpit and he woke up from the stick of the needle. All he said was, "what?" and fell back asleep or so it seemed but he was dead from an apparent heart attack.

The newspapers the next day carried the story, 'Doctor George Salvatore died in his sleep last night of an apparent heart attack his grieving widow said. The rescue and hospital personnel came to the conclusion that it had been a definite heart attack; the Doctor had been suffering from a bad heart for over two years so there would be no autopsy due to a Doctor being in attendance with others declaring his death as natural causes.

Sol left the next morning with his things to go back to the van and put them back in before returning the car to the Rental Agency. There was no evidence of a break in at the Doctors House so Sol had been pleased with that. He did however have a nagging feeling about the killing. He thought to himself, did I kill the wrong person, perhaps I should have killed the wife and her lover? He was almost back with his vehicle when he abruptly turned around and went to another Motel because he had already checked out of the previous one.

He registered at the new Motel and went about his disguise work again. He watched the Doctor's house and when the woman left she left the lights on in a couple of rooms. He followed the woman with his car to see where she went. Soon they came to a house in another part of town. The Doctor's wife got out and went up to the door of the house and rang the door bell. A woman answered the door and looked right and left outside to make sure no one was watching and they hugged and kissed each other right there in the doorway.

Damn it, he thought to himself, a lesbian couple, I never thought of that. He watched and waited, it wasn't long before the lights went out in the front of the house and one came on at the back corner of the house. Must be the bedroom he thought. He got out of the car silently, crossed the street and went to the back of the house to find a way in.

He found the back door which had an old fashioned lock on the door above the door knob that was really easy to slip a credit card into and just open the door. He saw no sign of a dog or alarm system so he was in the house in seconds. He found himself in a hallway and at the end of it there was a light on and the door was ajar. He peeked in and saw the women cavorting on the bed and they were naked. He watched for a few minutes until they calmed down and both were on their knees hugging and kissing each other.

Sol almost got sick; this was a scene he had not expected. Both women were extremely attractive and well built, long slender legs, flat bellies, nice breasts and great hips. What a pity he thought. He unrolled something from his overcoat pocket, it was an rubber apron, the kind welders use to ward off hot sparks when welding pieces of metal together. He would have to subdue the women quickly to keep them from screaming out. Just the sight of him would be enough for anyone to cry out.

He waited until they were atop one another the other face to face and quiet. They were just kissing and then he seized his chance. He hit the one on top first with the butt of his 9mm pistol knocking her unconscious then smothered the other one with a pillow before she could cry out, it was all over in seconds. After the one on the bottom was dead he placed the pillow over the other one's face and smothered the unconscious woman. He left them like that, no blood, no mess, no bother. They were lying together as he left and there would be no mistake that they were lovers.

This was the second time he had broken his own code of stick to the script of the kill, no side tracks. He left the house as he had found it, but turned out the lights in the bedroom as he left. Sol was now gratified that he had done the right thing in his own twisted mind. He returned to his Motel and went to sleep.

CHAPTER - 18

The next morning Sol drove to the lot where the van was and put his luggage back inside. The attendant watched and took it all in, three suitcases, one large brown paper bag and a box with the top closed. Sol paid him no mind and took the car back to the Rental Agency and turned it in, He paid them the balance of his bill and caught a Taxi back to the Long Term Rental Lot.

While he was gone the attendant couldn't contain himself, he walked over to the van and looked into the back windows but the dark tint on them made it hard for him to see anything so he went around to the front and looked in but the curtain behind the seats was pulled closed and he couldn't see in there either. He shrugged his shoulders and walked back to his attendant's shack to wait for the next customer.

Sol happened to be the next one in the lot who had returned by Taxi. Sol paid the young attendant for the use of the lot and gave him a modest tip. The young man looked intently at Sol so Sol asked, "is everything alright young man?"

"Uh yes sir, I guess so, but somehow you don't look like the same man who drove in here a few days ago."

Sol felt the top of his head and he was wearing a hat, part of his other disguise. "Must be the new hat I bought while I was in town on business, my head kept getting cool so I bought one, you see I'm nearly bald," he whispered while smiling.

"Oh I see sir," and they both chuckled a little.

Sol walked over to the van but couldn't help notice the young man still staring at him for some reason. He shrugged his shoulders and got in, started it up and headed for home.

The front page of the morning newspapers read; 'Doctor's wife found dead with her deceased lesbian lover, deaths are under investigation and are suspicious.' The article went on to say that they both died of suffocation presumably with by a pillow and one woman had a nasty bump on her head and that happened before she died but no forced entry was found at the house, it appears to be a real mystery.

On the way home Sol found a roadside rest in the hills with a river running along the valley floor, it looked deserted so he threw the Missouri License plate and drivers license over the side of the hill and they floated on air before getting caught in some trees. That takes care of that he thought. One more errand he remembered, he had to pick up supplies for Fred before he got home. By the time he got back he would get back he would be gone eight days and had committed three murders and he had figure out where he went wrong for a second time.

After stopping at the Supply Store to buy the supplies Fred needed Sol decided to take a little side trip and drove up to Buffalo to see Francis. Something inside was nagging him, he really liked her after all these years. He knew he would spend three more days traveling there and back but he had to see her. By the time he would arrive back to his store he knew he will have been gone thirteen days instead of twelve but he told them he may be gone up to two weeks or more so he wasn't concerned about the extra side tour.

It seemed like no time at all and he was at the restaurant where Francis worked. He parked the van and went inside to have lunch. He didn't see her right away so he decided he would inquire about her. He sat down at a small table for two and waited. A young lady finally came over to take his order. "May I help you sir?"

"Yes I'd like a cup of coffee to start with, say is Francis here today?"

"No sir, she took today off, said she had some personal business to attend to regarding the passing of her husband. She'll be back here tomorrow though, I'm the owner's daughter, I fill in sometimes when someone is off."

"Well that is very nice of you, I would like a hamburger with all the fixings please?"

"Yes sir, would you like some french fries or chips with that?"

"No thank you, I'm trying to watch my weight, it's hard to do at my age you know."

"Yes sir, thank you sir, but you don't look old enough to have to worry about a thing."

"Why that's very kind of you young lady, thank you."

She left and Sol remembered he hadn't taken off his hair piece yet. He thought to himself, I must be more careful, that's three times I've slipped up in the past four months. His burger was there almost before he knew it. He went ahead and ate leisurely and read a newspaper that someone had left on the table next to him. He glanced from article to article not really reading anything just checking the head line above each column, he was busy trying to blend in. He was so engrossed in his paper that he didn't notice Francis come in until he heard her name mentioned at the cash register. She had come in to check to see if anyone had been asking for her or if she had any messages, that she would be tied up the rest of the day cleaning up her husband's affairs. He was close enough to hear most of the conversation when the young waitress mentioned that a man over there was asking about you this morning. She glanced his way but with the newspaper obscuring his face all she could see was the hair on his head. She didn't recognize Sol right away. She started to leave and as she passed his table he said in a low seductive voice, "hi there beautiful, busy tonight?"

She stopped dead in her tracks, she knew the voice and the tone, she reached across the table and pulled the newspaper down so she could see his face. "I knew it was you, you're the only one who ever used that line on me that worked, what are you doing here Sol?"

"Why that's a fine way to treat an old friend, I just got in from Colorado and made a detour up here to see you and see if maybe we could have dinner together tonight."

"Oh Sol, it's wonderful to see you again, I've missed you after all these years, you're the fish that got away you know. Ever since you opened that Book Store in Poughkeepsie you've been a stranger. Its good of you to check on me and we can have dinner tonight if you like."

"I'd like that, thank you. What time would you like me to pick you up?"

"Be at my place around seven o'clock, we'll eat in if it's alright with you."

"May I bring some wine, White Zinfandel if I remember right was your favorite."

"It still is and be sure it's chilled before you bring it and make it the large bottle, it could be a long late dinner with desert if you like."

"I'd like that."

"Where are you staying, do you have a Motel Room?"

"No, I just got into town and stopped here first for lunch to see if you were here."

"Don't bother getting a room; I have a perfectly good guestroom you can use for the night if you like."

"That's very generous of you." They both knew what it meant but it was said for the benefit for those who were watching and listening.

She said, "it's been a long time Sol, I've moved a few times, here's my new address and phone number." She took a small note pad from her purse and a pen and wrote down the information for him but she already knew he had it still or he wouldn't be here.

"We have a lot to catch up on since our University days, I'd like to hear how your family is doing and everything."

"Alright sounds good, I'll bring you up to date on everything including the new store, by the way its doing great these days." Everything they were saying was for the benefit of those watching and listening to every word intently. They all knew of Francis's poor choices in men but this one was different they were thinking. He sounded smart, he was handsome from what they could see of him, he was well dressed and polished in every way. For some reason he didn't look like the same man that was in a few weeks ago when her husband died after getting hit by a City Bus. None of them put two and two together.

They did notice that Francis simply was swooning over him, the light in her eyes was bright and seemed to reflect brighter than the sunlight. The owner, the cook from the kitchen and two waitresses were gathered behind the counter leaning on their elbows watching the scene unfold.

As Francis straightened up and tuned to leave she gave them an of handed wave and nodded like everything was alright and they went back to work quickly, their faces red because she had caught them watching them.

CHAPTER - 19

Sol spent the afternoon shopping. He bought two large bottles of white Zinfandel Wine at a Liquor Store from the salesperson there and asked him to
put them in the cooler and he would be back around seven thirty this evening
to pick them up so they would be cold. Then he bought a dozen red roses from
a Flower Shop close by and asked them when they closed and they said five
o'clock so he asked them to hold them for him and he would pick them up before five, he was afraid they would wilt inside the closed up van. Then he went
to a Jewelry Store and bought a broach to wear on a sweater or blouse with
diamonds set in twenty four carat gold. It had a big curved gold leaf in the
center and the diamonds were set inside of it so they sparkled in the light. It
was so pretty that Sol got weak in the knees when he saw it being wrapped for
him so he could give it to Francis as a token of their friendship.

Having more time to kill he went book shopping at every store he could
find from the malls to individual stores he had found in a phone book. He
went to a big chain book store last where they had chairs so a person could sit
and read. Here he was in his element, he picked out a mystery book and sat
down to read and kill time. He nearly lost track of time, before he knew it, it
was four thirty and he knew he must get to the Flower Shop before they closed.
It wasn't far and he could come back here to kill more time before picking up
the wine.

Then he headed to Francis's house. He grabbed the small gift, flowers,
wine and climbed the steps to a brownstone house where she lived. He rang
the bell and waited. In a minute or two Francis opened the door to let him in.

"Oh Sol, you shouldn't have, roses and wine, the wine would have been enough for me."

He had the broach in his pocket and he would give her that after they had supper.

"I hope you still like lasagna Sol, I made it with my own recipe. Have a seat on the couch over there and I'll put the roses in a vase and the wine in the fridge." She returned in a few minutes and sat down next to him.

"Well Francis, how are you getting along now with your husband gone and all?"

"Just fine Sol, I don't miss the beatings at all." She started laughing and got Sol to laughing as well. "He got a Social Security check every month that kept us in food and paid the rent but there wasn't enough left for the Utilities so I had to work and he became a couch bum, drunk every night when I got home from work."

While they were talking a timer went off in the kitchen and Francis excused herself and went into the kitchen to take up supper. The table was all set and she brought in a large baking dish containing lasagna and asked Sol to open the wine. She had a sideboard in the dining room where he found a cork screw to open the wine. He poured two glasses and they sat down to eat. They ate in quiet managing to get a word in edge wise once in a while. They gazed at each other dreamily across the small table that only sat four people but they didn't mind, it was fine for the two of them.

Sol helped her clear away the dishes and he refilled their wine glasses for a fourth time, they weren't very large glasses. They went back into the living room to sit and talk some more and let their dinner settle. She told him her husband had an Insurance Policy and with that and what little she had saved up she was able to buy herself a house.

They talked the better part of an hour about the old days and how they met in school and had gone their separate ways after graduation. They had been lovers in school the four years they were there. They saw one another only occasionally over the past thirty some odd years but the spark still there after all this time and her three failed marriages. Sol reignited the spark each time he saw her.

"Francis, I have something for you, a little memento of our friendship for all these years." He reached into his pocket and brought out the small package neatly wrapped in black paper with a small gold bow on the top.

"Oh Sol you shouldn't have, you don't have to buy me presents, I love you just the way you are." She opened it and tears began to form in her eyes, "that's the most beautiful broach I have ever seen in my life! Are those real diamonds?"

"Yes Francis they are real and twenty four carat gold. Its just a small token to show you how I still feel about you."

"Oh my goodness Sol, this must have cost you a fortune, you really shouldn't have spent so much money on me."

"You're worth every penny, my book store has made me a very wealthy man. I have been very fortunate to have found some of the rarest books known to man. Collectors and Museums around the world are dying to get to me so they can buy just one of the books. That broach cost less than ten percent of what I can make on a sale of just one book. We're known world wide for our restoration techniques that Fred and I have perfected over the years. Its good thing he and I took advance Chemistry courses while in school, it has made us both rich beyond our wildest dreams. You would be surprised what people are willing to pay for our restored manuscripts, books and parchments. We've discovered a way to protect and preserve them almost indefinitely. We have several patents pending right now among our older ones, we've even been contacted to see what we can do with the dead sea scrolls."

"I had no idea that you and Fred had been so successful with your techniques. The last time we talked the two of you were still working on formulas for preservatives and ink."

"Yes and at the new location we have our own huge lab where we make our own paper and parchments and you can't tell the new from the old, it works fantastically well as does all the inks, in fact I have lots of supplies and bottles of base ink to take back to Fred with me."

"And you came all this way just to see little ole me?"

"That's right sugar."

"My golly, you remembered that after all these years, you used to call me sugar back in school. Listen Sol, there is something," she never finished the sentence. Sol put his arms around her and kissed her.

"You were going to say something Francis?"

"It don't matter none, kiss me again."

They kissed for several minutes. Finally Francis stood up, straightened her skirt and said, "come with me Sol and I'll show you my new house." She led him directly to her bedroom. He looked at the bed, it was strewn with rose petals and there was a large scented candle burning on a small bedside table. She put her arms around his neck, drew him close and they kissed standing there, a long passionate moist kiss. She started to unbutton his shirt and he began to unbutton her blouse and in a few minutes they had undressed each other just like when they were lovers back in school. She threw back the covers on the bed and they lay down beside one another and began to make love like they had been doing it for years.

They made love a couple more times during the night into the morning hours before sun up. They finally got up around eight thirty in the morning.

Francis looked lazily at the clock.

"Oh Sol, I'm late for work."

"Do you have to work anymore Francis, why don't you come back to Poughkeepsie and live with me, I have plenty of room for you at my place."

"Thank you Sol but no, I couldn't. I love you dearly but you know you're married to your work, there's only time for us to have an interlude with each other once in a while. I know you have to travel a lot and now that you have apparently gone International you'll be away from home more than ever. Let me get up and get to work before I lose my job, its all I've ever wanted working there at the Restaurant and now that I can afford to buy it, I think I will!"

"Really Francis, I didn't know that it meant so much to you."

"It does Sol, the people who eat there have become my family and I promise you this, I'll never take another lover to bed or marry again as long as I live, you're the only man for me. I should have told you while we were still at the University but I couldn't come between you and Fred. There was a special bond between you two and I knew it and I also knew the two of you would make it big one day and I could never come between you. I love you too much to make a blunder like that."

Sol's eyes suddenly grew misty, "honestly Francis, I didn't know but you're right of course, I am married to my work, I've always known it. You need to know that although there have been a couple of other women in my life you and you alone have won my heart forever, no one else has ever come close."

"Yes my darling, please let me get up and get to work, I'll see you again, you know there will always be a warm bed here for you anytime and I'll be here for you."

"Oh my darling, please don't leave just yet."

"I have to Sol; please try to understand why its so important to me. You've made your mark on the world and now its my turn. I'll own the finest eatery in Buffalo, maybe I'll even franchise myself."

"Yes, who knows, if you ever need anything including financial backing don't hesitate to call me, I'll leave my address and phone number for you. I can let myself out. Oh, say, do you need a ride to work?"

"No silly, I do own a car you know, it's a little old but I'll buy a new one soon."

"Oh alight if you insist on going to work, I won't keep you."

"Thank you for understanding Sol, I love you so much it hurts."

CHAPTER - 20

In Washington DC the bulletin requesting information about book collectors and book store owner's deaths went out and results began to slowly trickle in. One a week, then two a week and before long they had nineteen Death Case Files to work on from around the country. It wasn't much but it was something to see if they could find a connection between cases. The man in charge, Special Agent Richard Jefferies, requested two more people be assigned to him to help sift through the files and look for anything at all suspicious that might be there and may have been overlooked by the original Investigative Agency in charge. Some files were several pages long others only a couple of pages but its what they didn't see that grabbed their interest. Very few eye witnesses or others were interviewed because the case was called accidental by the Attending Coroner or a Doctor at the Hospital where a patient was taken..

Jefferies knew better, he had already reviewed the Professor's case in the lab and found discrepancies very quickly. He instinctively knew there had to be more cases that had been over looked similar to this one which had been closed by three Agencies all agreeing that it was an accident when it was obvious to the trained eye that it was murder. Even the gas company didn't find the loose connection on the fireplace. Jefferies was beginning to wonder what kind of agencies he was up against that in his eyes didn't properly investigate what was obvious to him. He saw it almost immediately and wished everyone could be trained at the FBI in Washington and Quantico Virginia before becoming a Police Officer, Fireman or even a Coroner in some cases. He felt they were too quick to close the file and move on and not spend the time, money and effort to do a proper investigation.

He didn't know how right on he was at the time because that's exactly what had been done. If it looked like an accident, smelled like an accident, then it was an accident, whoopee case closed and the Agency moved on to more clear cut cases.

After a couple of weeks they were no closer except for the Professor's murder. This was an open and shut case of homicide beyond anyone's doubt by now. Agent Jefferies sent people out to interview every person they could find on the other cases while he concentrated on the Professor's death. It haunted him as to why he was killed other than someone stealing of a few of his books. Any professional killer would go in with a mask on and tie the person up but not kill him for no reason unless he could recognize the burglar's voice and mannerisms, maybe that was it. But still why kill an old man in a wheelchair who couldn't defend himself. These thoughts bothered Jefferies every day, the why of it all, nothing added up. He had to get to the bottom of who would want the rare books and why. Less than a handful of people even knew that he had a book collection of any value. He would start with them and see what turned up.

He turned the list of books from the professor's safe over to a researcher to check out every single entry on the list and see what the book was all about, its age and value. Then maybe he would have something to go on.

About two o'clock that afternoon he got a phone call from the Director himself asking him to come up to his office as soon as he could which meant of course, drop everything and get upstairs right now. So he did but he also took his time. He was already tired from reading and re-reading files and getting nowhere.

He knocked on the Directors private door and heard the Director say, "come on in Dick."

"You called me sir, it must be important for you to call me in on the carpet."

"You're not on the carpet yet Dick, have you found anything new about this Professor fellow who died in the explosion and house fire?"

"Yes sir, it was definitely not an accident, it was murder and arson!"

"Good job son, I knew if anyone could figure it out you could and you know by now that he and I were old friends. Now that you are here I'd like you to meet someone." He picked up his phone, called his secretary and said; "Sarah, you can send her in now."

A strikingly beautiful woman walked into the office and took Jefferies by surprise.

"Dick I want you to meet Jane Marlowe, Jane, Dick Jefferies, his name is Richard but he lets me get away with calling him Dick, you'd best call him Jefferies if you want to get along. "

Dick, she is assigned to you effective as of now. She has a long resume which I will not bore you with. She has a degree in criminology and was the top of her class five years ago at the Academy. She is now a seasoned veteran and has had some special assignments where I needed her expertise. I want her to give you a hand on this book fellow whoever he or she is. I should warn you not to get funny with her, she has several black belts in the Marshall Arts."

"But Director, I don't need anymore help right now, you just assigned two more men to me and right now there are four of them are out working on the cases that I gave them."

"This is not your choice; it 's an order, you will put her to work with you and not your other people, she has certain qualifications I feel will help in your investigation, do I make myself clear? She's your new partner!"

"Yes sir, quite clear, she'll be my right hand from now on! I got it!"

"Good, now get out of here you two and quit wasting my time, I'm a busy man you know!"

"Yes sir, foursome at four o'clock sir?"

"Yes damn it and you know the top brass will be there, I'll beat the President one of these days; he can't keep winning all the time."

"Check the score keeper sir."

"Oh go on you two, get out of here!"

They walked out the back door and headed for the private elevator.

"Is the Director always that gruff and short with you Richard?"

"No ma'am, that was actually quite cordial for him today, sometimes he chews nails for lunch and spits them at us when he's really mad; no it's just his way."

"Where is my, uh err, our office?"

"Ground floor basement, they call it the dungeon."

"Gees, no windows huh."

"That's right dark and dingy, just pretend you're a mushroom while you're working down there, it helps."

"Mushroom? I'm afraid I don't understand, I thought we were all Agents of the FBI."

"Think what you will but we're all mushrooms just the same, they keep us in the dark and feed us crap all day."

"Oh I see, a little levity for the office huh?"

"Think what you will but it sure is dark and gloomy down there."

She knew he was pulling her leg, she also knew he was not comfortable having a woman assigned to him as his new partner. She would have to earn her stripes in the jungle of men in the basement. The private elevator stopped and they stepped out into a huge open area with cubicles scattered everywhere, typewriters were going and computer screens were all moving, the place was as bright as day in there. Their Department was not street level in the front but it was in the back and that the front made it appear as the basement. There was also an underground garage for their special vehicles.

"Some jungle Richard."

"Do me a favor please, everyone down here refers to one another by their last names only. There are too many Linda's, Carols, Charlie's, Bobs and such that people get confused."

"Point well taken Agent Jefferies."

"Very good Agent Marlowe."

"I was serious about our Offices, don't we actually have an office or do we sit out here in the public area with the rest of the help."

"You call this the public area, this is where all the work gets done, this is known as the brain trust, each one of these individuals is a qualified agent and none of them have an office, our work is mostly out in the field which is just where you and I will be going as soon as you familiarize yourself with the case I'm working on right now."

He was hot under the collar and she knew it but this place was a mad house, how could anyone get anything done around here she thought. She followed him until they came to a door marked private, he opened the door and walked inside with her on his heels.

"Here we are Agent Marlowe, you'll sit at that desk opposite mine, I'll get the files and then we'll get your feet wet with the problems of this case because as soon as you're ready we're heading for the field."

Wow, this is more like it she thought, private office and all. I'm beginning to like this. It was a spacious Office that was more covert than she realized and it kept him close to the activity in the lab and close to the garage for easy access to his car in case of an emergency. The two desks faced one another and were pushed against each other tightly so that they would be able to see each other when working. She did not realize the importance of her new partner right away and why he was actually number two at the Department.

She sat down and barely got comfortable when he was back and dumped a huge file stuffed to the gills with papers and said, "come with me to the lab, I'll brief you while we walk."

She dutifully followed him like a puppy following its mother.

"Remember in the lab, last names only, it's a lot easier, believe me."

They entered through a door that said keep out qualified technicians only.

"The sign on the door said keep out, how come you ignored it Agent Jefferies?"

"Because I put it there to keep new Agents like you from bumbling and stumbling about through the lab destroying valuable evidence. Haven't you been in here before Agent Marlowe?"

"No, this is only the second time I've been in this building at all, I worked out of the Chicago and New York Offices before the Director called me and told me to get down here that you needed my expertise."

"I'm terribly sorry, I thought you'd been through the most thorough training we have which begins and ends with this famous Lab, this place is known throughout the world for the work we do here."

"Like I said I am sorry," she replied, "I've been in the other offices, just not in this one, this is all new to me."

"Alright, I'm sorry," Dick apologized, "we're kind of getting off on the wrong foot here. I'm irritated at the Director for going over my head and asking you to come down here from wherever without consulting me and preparing me a little first. I'm on the most difficult case the FBI has ever had. We have only now just proved that one of possibly hundreds of cases that were closed because they were supposedly an accident when they were in fact a murder case and I'm mad as hell at my fellow Law Enforcement Officials for not catching them. This case is as plain as the nose on your face. I'll walk you through the areas of the lab and see if you come to the same conclusions I have, fair enough?"

"That's fine with me, don't get your under ware in a tangle or whatever it is they say, don't take your shortcomings out on me, I didn't ask to come down here and baby sit a Neanderthal you know."

Dick let that remark slide, he knew he was being a jerk and that she had nothing whatsoever to do with her being assigned to him.

"Here is our first station to look at, the background on this is that a retired Professor was sitting in his house when it blew up and burned to the ground. There was nothing left but a pile of rubble for the most part. The fire department said it was a gas explosion and a broken neck that killed the man. The walls of the house blew out and the roof and the second floor collapsed onto the ground floor and here is what's left. A top of a gas range and a gas fireplace log heater with its pipe and fittings. Look them over and tell me if anything jumps out at you."

"How much time do I have before the quiz?"

"Take all the time you need, even my own lab tech's didn't see it at first, I had to point it out to them."

She looked at the stove for a minute, then she pulled a white pair of cotton gloves from her jacket pocket and went over the stove and its fittings. "Well first I see that the stove was on, was this the source of ignition Agent Jefferies?"

"That's what they tell me."

"Ah I see but this isn't the cause, any first year forensic student could see that."

Two Lab Technicians cowered when she said that.

"Okay so now we have a fireplace ceramic log heater, average I'd say" added Agent Marlowe, " and would and you look at that, there's your smoking gun Agent Jefferies, a loose gas fitting. Any first year student could have seen the shiny brass and the old discolored brass."

"Very good Agent Marlowe!"

"You people hear that!" hollered Agent Jefferies," any first year student could see that, you people get a move on and get me the rest of the answers and I mean right now!"

Every person in the lab was moving all at once, they had just been put down by an outsider and Agent Jefferies was not happy with the results they were getting for him given the tongue lashing he just gave them.

"Now then Agent Marlowe one of the really difficult tasks at hand, all of these books burned almost beyond recognition but my people here have actually identified some of the books after some brow beating. These were supposed to be very old and in some cases extremely rare books, some extremely valuable to any collector or museum but they identified many of them to be just average books anyone could buy at a book sale from a library or book store unloading slow movers to get new material in. This is where we are at right now." His voice had softened some while in another room as he knew now that she knew her job and would be an asset.

She began looking at some of the blowup photographs of the damaged pages and inside of the book covers. "Yes I see what you mean and I concur. Someone removed all the books of any value before this man was killed and his house set afire by the range being on in the kitchen and the log fireplace leaking gas. It would have probably given him several hours to get away from the house before it exploded."

"One hundred and ten percent correct Ms. Marlowe, I'm sorry, Agent Marlowe."

"Now then, where would you suggest we go from here Agent Jefferies?"

"No where just yet!"

"Have they identified all the possible pages and book covers?"

"Not yet and there is one thing I did leave out and I am sorry, it was not intentional. We found an inventory list of all of the man's books and its being gone over as we speak, let's see if we can find Agent Cartwright."

She followed Jefferies around the lab until they came to a small cubicle with a man sitting there listening intently on the telephone.

"You don't say, Israel huh, 1930s, uh huh, yes, I've got it. Thank you very much for your help, what was that, did we find the book, no sir I'm afraid we didn't but we'll let you know the first thing if and when we do," he hung up the phone.

"Hi Agent Jefferies. You were right sir, some of the books were so hot they would burn your fingers. A few of the books were stolen from a museum in Israel in the 1930s. I just got off the phone with the Museum there. What a find, if it weren't for your suspicions none of us would have noticed a thing, nice catch there Agent Jefferies, I'll let the Director know that we have it now. He was asking about it, the latest report you know. The Professor was an old friend of his,. he had him as a Professor at the University when he was there."

"Small world Agent Marlowe?"

"It certainly is Agent Jefferies, school out?"

"Yes ma'am, schools out, now you know as much as we do. The Professor was murdered by someone who knew about his valuable collection. They obviously sold the information for cash to the murderer directly or indirectly. Now we go to work, field trip tomorrow we're going to visit a little town call Jewett in eastern Ohio. Feel free to wander around, I'm waiting on a few reports to be finished so we can take them with us, I'm going to chew somebody's ass out but good for fouling this up. Terrible police and fire department work. They should have caught this!"

"Want to bet me some money that the excuse will be the same as always, lack of funds, lack of proper training for personnel."

"No, I never bet on a sure thing, I take it you've heard the excuses before. I'll be in our office if you need me. The I D you have will get you access anywhere in this building same as me, that makes three of us with the clearance you have, you and me and the Director but don't let it go to your head, employees seeing that I D Badge will make them quiver once they see you, its very intimidating too anyone, the Director must think very highly of you."

"Just as highly as he does you, but don't let it worry you, I wouldn't have your job, I'm too set in my ways, I like what I do better, get the bad guys and put them in cuffs."

"I do the same thing but first we have to identify the bad guys then go after them."

"You've been inside too long Agent Jefferies."

"Thanks, I owe you one."

Both of them were trying hard to get in the last word, people were watching and listening to see who would get the last word in and making bets for Jefferies to win and he did eventually with a few more jabs at one another. It was all in good fun now, they were still getting to know one another.

CHAPTER - 21

The next morning at eight am. Agent Jefferies asked Agent Marlowe; "are you ready to hit the bricks."

"That's an awful old cliché left over from the 1920s and 30s when they still had brick streets!"

"I'll have you know that several towns and cities around the U.S. still have brick streets even today, Pennsylvania for one, who knows we might find brick streets in Ohio where we're headed. Come on let's go to the Car Pool and see which pile of junk they will let us have for our road trip." The two gathered up the files and their luggage and headed to the end of the hall to the door marked garage. They walked out and an attendant approached them.

"Hi Agent Jefferies, headed for the field again I see. This must be Agent Marlowe, word about her is circulating and all the bachelors are going to be coming at you fast lady."

"If they know what's good for them they'll stay clear, I saw her first and believe me when I say don't cross her path and don't let her cross your path either. This she cat is armed to the teeth quite literally. The Director himself warned me about her black belts in the Marshall Arts of which she has many. So treat the lady like a lady Agent should be treated, with respect and no cat calls, am I clear on that Donny?"

"Yes Dick, quite clear, we were just wondering what you are working on now that has the Director so up in arms about?"

"An old school chum, a Professor, he was murdered a while back and everybody called it an accident but us here at the Bureau and he's mad as hell about it. He wants heads to roll so be careful how you address him for a while, he's a mite touchy. What kind of a junk pile do you have for us today Donny?"

"The one being pulled up here right now, just took delivery on this baby last week, it's got twenty five miles on it and all the toys and whistles you'll ever need."

"Holy cow! That's a brand new Ford Galaxie 500 four door, how come I rate it?"

"The Director told me personally to give you this car, your old gray pile of junk as you call it has been stripped and sent to the junk yard for crushing. Man you're hard on automobiles aren't you? By the way she has a 429 police interceptor engine under the hood."

"I get the job done, that's all that counts today. Thanks Donny, 429 huh, say how are the wife and kids?"

"Great Dick, just great, thanks for asking."

They got in the car and Donny lifted the barricade from across the entrance which is done electrically and made out of steel and would destroy the windshield and grill of any car that tried to speed through without stopping and they were on their way to Ohio.

"Now I am confused," said Agent Marlowe, " the two of you just called each other by your first names and nicknames, how come?" asked Marlowe.

"Old friends is how. Donny used to be my partner. We got into a really bad shootout one day and he lost a leg in the shooting. You wouldn't know it but he has an artificial leg and the Director liked him so much he kept him on at a small reduction in pay so his wife and kids could get along and he would still feel like part of the Department. With that kind of an injury you're not allowed to do any leg work like we're going to do and he didn't want a desk job, this one suits him fine and he knows he'll always have a desk waiting for him when he's ready, he's very bright and we miss his expertise in the field."

"What happened, were you injured?"

"I was hit three times and knocked unconscious when I was grazed in the head with the fourth shot, I didn't see Donny go down, he saved my life and killed three of them himself. I killed two before I went down, one of our other Agents was killed as well."

"Is that the shootout I saw on TV a year or so ago."

"Yes that's the one."

"You know both of you were lucky you weren't also killed, I understand you were out numbered and outgunned."

"That's right, when the shooting was over there were six dead perpetrators and one Agent, we held our own against superior fire power. We no longer have that problem as you'll see in the trunk, shotguns and rifles, two of each kind and there are three kinds back there with smoke grenades and other things."

"Is that what Donny was talking about, toys, whistles and things?"

"Yup, he checks out every vehicle to be sure it's properly armed and everything works. He doesn't get his hands dirty except for some gun oil and things like that sometimes."

"I've got a lot to learn don't I Agent Jefferies?"

"Yes ma'am, I'm afraid so, you've only seen the tip of the iceberg as they say. By the way how is your proficiency with firearms?"

"If you're questioning my abilities to fire weapons I rated expert with every weapon the FBI has, does that settle your troubled little mind?"

He turned the car without answering her towards a sign that read Interstate 495 north and followed it until the were on Interstate 95 then Interstate 83 headed in the general direction of Ohio. "In case you're wondering I've made the trip to Ohio before, I'm originally from Columbus myself. And to answer your remark about weapons, yes it did concern me but not any longer, I just wanted to be sure we could back each other up if it came to a shootout with a perpetrator or any other idiots."

"I can assure you I'm not gun shy."

"Me either, let's get the show on the road, shall we?"

CHAPTER - 22

Sol arrived in Poughkeepsie at the Book Store late in the afternoon the same day he left Francis in Buffalo. He had a lot of time to think on the way back. He had to get back on track, he had made three mistakes of not sticking to his script of unsolved murders. He was getting sloppy and he knew it. He got in so late in the day that he went across the street to eat supper without going into the store. The special of the day was pot roast so that's what he had to eat, it was just like home cooking and that's what kept him coming back. He was just finishing up when Greta came in and saw him.

"Why Sol, we didn't know you were back, Fred had another break through with his ink process and he's waiting for the base ink you told him you were going to pick up for him."

"I'm sorry, I didn't have a very good trip but I did bring back his ink, it's in the van in the garage. I'm all done eating, I'll pay my tab and go back to the store and surprise him with it in a few minutes."

"He'll like that, he thought for sure you'd be back two or three days ago. I have his dinner order with me, as soon as I'm done eating I'll bring his dinner over to him."

"Thanks Greta, you're a jewel among us thieves." They both laughed at the pun.

It wasn't long before Sol came through the basement door from the garage carrying two of the four large bottles of ink, he could only manage that many due to opening and closing of doors and they were a gallon of ink each and then there was the climbing up and down the stair steps from the basement garage where the van was then up a few steps to the lab.

"Fred, you around here somewhere?" Sol hollered out.

"Yeah Sol, over here behind the big printing machine. I just ran out of ink, got to mix up some more, did you bring my ink supplies?"

"Yes Fred, right here."

"Say there's only two of the one's I need the most here, where's the others, I need all my supplies to make the different mixes."

"They're in the van, don't worry I didn't forget. I'll set these down and go back for the rest, I'll be right back."

Sol was back before Fred had a chance to miss him, he was busy getting ready to make his new mixture that he had recently come up with. "Here you are Fred, just what the Doctor ordered."

"Thank God you got it, I had a breakthrough with the new process we talked about and it works great, we should be able to patent it and sell our own brands of ink after this. We already have two patents for the other inks and when we get this one I'm betting we could sell them all on the International Markets."

"You could be right Fred; it could put us on easy street especially if one of the big companies wants to buy us out to market it themselves. We're not doing so bad as we are, we've accumulated more money than we could ever spend in two or three lifetimes."

"I know that Sol, but think of the publicity, the fame it would bring us, I could finally be free of this basement environment."

"I didn't know it bothered you so much, is the musty air getting to your sinuses again?"

"Yes Sol, some days it gets pretty bad down here, if I didn't know better I'd say there was a graveyard down here with all of the odors I smell in the summer time."

Whew thought Sol, I didn't know there was any odor from the decomposing bodies down here. "Must be your imagination Fred, oh, before I forget I ran into Greta across the street while eating supper, she'll be along with your dinner in a little bit. You know Fred, we could move the lab up to the main floor now in the far end of the building, I'm sure the machinery could be insulated and quieted down enough so that it didn't bother the tenants we already have in the building. Why not think about it, we can afford to do it now."

"Alright Sol, I'll think about it, this is becoming more like a cave to me these past few months."

Fred was unaware that Sol had been burying both men and women down there over the years as he was finished with their services. He did know however about the other killings Sol had been doing in different parts of the country as well as book store owners to keep the store supplied with new almost free Inventory.

"Alright Fred, I've got to unload the van and get my gear put away upstairs, I had no luck finding any books this trip. See you tomorrow, I'm going to turn in early, I've been on the road the whole day."

"Okay Sol, see you tomorrow then and thanks for the supplies."

Sol went about removing his luggage from the van and carrying it all up three flights of stairs. Damn he thought to himself, why didn't we put in some of elevators when we renovated the building? Wait a just darned minute, we can still do it, it would be a lot easier on all our backs when it comes to lugging all of the boxes of books up two flights of stairs. I'll get with Fred and Greta in the morning and discuss it. Sol got his things put away he had brought upstairs but couldn't shake the picture of Francis in his mind and how lovely she still looked after all of these years. He picked up a book of unsolved murders and read himself to sleep.

The next morning after breakfast Sol got Greta and Fred together to ask them about his plan and get their take on it. "Listen you two, I value you both and your ideas. I have a solution to some of our headaches or rather backaches. Now that we're well established in the community why don't we start thinking about making our lives a little easier? I was thinking last night when I was carrying my heavy luggage from the garage in the basement to the top floor that there had to be an easier way. Suppose we look into putting in a couple of elevators in the building, one from the basement to all floors for us, one for our tenants and ourselves to our apartments and a freight elevator from the basement to the first and second floors only, what do you say to that?"

"I'd say," said Greta, "why didn't one of us think about this before?"

"That's a great idea, those boxes of books you bring back get awful heavy lugging them up and back down the stairs. The only problem I see is that our tenants don't need to be stopping on our second floor storage area, can you put in one that by passes that floor?" Fred asked.

"Why not, I'm thinking about an elevator for us from the basement to all floors and a tenant only elevator for the rest. We could arrange them side by side and put a private use only sign on ours and put some kind of a key lock on it so only we can use it with our own special key, what do you say, shall we look into it?"

"I'd say lets go ahead," Fred answered, "get a few companies to submit a bid and we'll look them over. Of course we'll have to supply some specs for them to go by, you know how big we want the cars, how much weight should they carry and things like that and they can help us by giving us some suggestions as well."

"What do you say Greta, you're as much a part of this as we are?" Sol asked.

"I say why are we standing around gabbing, lets put our own ideas on paper first then contact some companies to come here and look over the building and give us some help with ideas on how best to use them and maybe we could disguise our private elevators so the doors seem to disappear."

"So I take it you are both in agreement with me, its time to expand. There's no reason we shouldn't look further down the road, we could turn the entire third floor into apartments starting next spring and put an additional pair of elevators down that way to serve the tenants and we can use the same ideas for the other end of the building. We have the money, let's invest it in ourselves. Write down everything you can think of that you want in an elevator but no elevator music, I draw the line there!"

The three of them had a good laugh. Sol went back upstairs to his apartment to read. He would take time out later to write things down for his idea sheet but right now he needed to reinvigorate himself with his murder mysteries.

Three more days went by before they were ready to sit down again, Sol took all of their ideas and had Fred organize them in order and print them out for the three of them to sit down and go over, throw out the bad and keep the good. Two more days went by and they met again to go over the idea sheets. They pored over them the whole afternoon talking about the size of the cars, the width of the doors and some other things they didn't feel were needed. They threw out the cheap items and real expensive ones and came up with a middle of the stream outline for utility of purpose.

"Alright, I hate to ask you again Fred but would you consolidate all of our ideas then I'll contact three or four elevator companies to come look the job over and see what it is going to cost us?"

The next day paper in hand Sol began making calls to different companies to come out and give them some bids.

The next week on Friday the first of the companies showed up to take a look around and gave Sol some more ideas on where to place the elevators to take advantage of the space that was required to install them.

Then the following Monday another company showed up and did the same thing.

On Wednesday another company came by and did the same as the others. They made suggestions they hadn't thought of.

The fourth company declined saying the job was just too small for them, they only did high rise office buildings and three or four floors was just to small of a job

Two more weeks went by when one of the company's submitted a bid, two days later along came a second one and the third company respectfully declined in that they were spread too thin right now for the next two years to squeeze in this job, it was a nice apology.

"Well Fred, Greta, we only have two bids to go over, are the two of you able to sit down with me and see what we have soon?"

Greta apologized and said; "I have a shipment coming in this morning and another in the afternoon, tomorrow would be much better for me"

"Fred how about you, tomorrow alright with you to go over these and select one?"

"Yes Sol that would be best for me as well."

"Alright then tomorrow morning, nine o'clock here in the store?"

"Fine with me," Greta replied.

"Me too," answered Fred.

"Okay then until tomorrow, if anyone needs me I'll be in my apartment, you both have the number." The meeting broke up with everyone going back to work.

The next morning they met in the store and carefully went over the two bids and settled on an Elevator Company to do the job, a total of four would be installed right away when the contractor was ready to go. They had plans to build an additional two more in the middle of the building when it was time to build more stores and apartments.

Sol said, "listen Fred, before we all take off I read an add this morning in the newspaper about a company which scrubs air in buildings that have offensive odors. They literally clean the bad stuff out of the air and return fresh air into the building. Would you like me to see about it for the whole building, the second floor gets a musty smell to it like there's mold growing on the books and that could ruin many books, we could clean all the air in the building."

"I think that its a good idea to look into for all of us," answered Fred.

"What do you think Greta?"

"Same as Fred Sol, it could improve the different odors we all smell from the books."

"Alright I'll get right on it," answered Sol.

CHAPTER - 23

Agents Jefferies and Marlowe finally arrived in Jewett Ohio. "Well we're here, I'm not sure about a place to stay, why not look around a bit before we decide and see if we can find something the will fit our per diem money so we don't go out of pocket. I hate it when I have to spend my own money,"

"Me too Agent Jefferies, lets have a look around first." They rode around for almost an hour in the surrounding area. Most of the Motels were the mom and pop kind, family owned small roadside Motels, they couldn't seem to find a National Chain close by.

"There's one Agent Jefferies that should do us, The Jewett Family Inn, shall we have a look?"

"Why not, it looks neat and clean, I'd like to see a room before we decide though."

"I agree." They pulled into a covered entrance for automobiles and went inside. They went to the front desk but no one was there. Behind the desk was a room with a couch and a couple of chairs and there was a TV on. Dick saw a bell on the counter so he tapped it a couple of times and an elderly gentleman came out from the room behind the counter.

"Good afternoon folks, need a room do we?"

"Yes, two non-smoking single rooms please," asked Jefferies.

"Have a little spat did we?"

Agent Jefferies got miffed, pulled out his badge and showed it to the man. "We're on official business that is none of your affair, we'd appreciate it if you have two single rooms. Agent Marlowe and I have had a long ride and we're tired, Is there a place close by where we can also get something to eat?"

"Yes sir of course, whatever you want, never had any FBI men here before, oh excuse me, Agent Marlowe was it?"

"Yes and please answer his question," she showed her badge as well to shut him up and close his dirty little mind. She could tell he thought they were lovers or something. "We're not here to play games, we're here on business just as the man said."

"Well you don't have to get huffy with me you know, I pay my taxes like anyone else."

"How about we look at a room before we decide?" asked Jefferies.

They followed the elderly manager owner outside and down a long row of rooms. He finally stopped and opened a door and let them go inside and look around. I have two of these identical rooms available right now but that's all, if you take the two rooms I'll be full up and put out the no vacancy sign for the night."

"Where is the other room?"

"The second door down from this one, this is room 17 and the other is room 21."

"What do you think Agent Marlowe, shall we take these or move on?"

"I think these will be alright but I do have an important question I'd like an answer to."

"How far is the nearest Restaurant where we can get three meals a day sir?"

"Just a short walk down the street there's a family style Restaurant that's open twenty four seven; you don't need to drive there unless it's raining."

"Well then its fine with me Agent Jefferies, so whatever you want we'll do."

"I guess that means we'll take the two rooms then."

"Fine, lets go back to the Office so we can do the paperwork and I'll give you your keys. Just out of curiosity, are you investigating the Professor's death or something bigger?"

"We're not allowed to discuss business like that sir, sorry we can't tell you the answer."

"Well I figure it has to be the Professor's death, everyone in town is discussing it, we all knew him, he was a fine man and wouldn't do something dumb like leave a kettle on the stove and fall from in his chair lift. If he were making tea he would have done so and turned off the fire under the kettle. The man was meticulous in everything he did. It was also rumored he had a very important collection of books that must have been very valuable because he had doors that closed the whole area off and when they were closed it looked just like part of the room. No one would ever know he had book cases behind there unless he was showing the books to someone he knew. He was a very private man, didn't drink, smoke or fool around with wild women. He did have a steady girlfriend though who would sometimes spend the weekend with him. She cooked and cleaned for him and they were the talk of the town whenever she was there. People can't understand why she never moved in with him on a more permanent basis, they made a perfect couple. Well here we are would you please fill out these two cards for me, name, address, you know the usual things."

Neither of them spoke to one another until they got their respective keys, they were the old fashioned type, very large made of real brass with a large plastic key tag attached with the Motel's name and address on it so it could be returned to him if they were lost somewhere by simply by dropping them in a mailbox.

They went to eat supper and soon they were back. Once outside close to their rooms Agent Marlowe spoke up. "We could leave right now if you like; the Manager filled in all of the blanks we were missing."

"Not quite, we need to talk to this mystery woman about the Professor, first we find her and talk to some of his neighbors to co-berate the man's story he gave us, basic Detective work Agent Marlowe."

"Yes I know, I was just thinking of all the shoe leather we'll wear out doing it. Well good night Agent Jefferies, what time do you want to get up?"

"How about seven thirty, then we can shower, I can shave then we can eat and be ready to go to work hopefully by nine o'clock, sound good to you?"

"Yes, that's fine, you want me to call the front desk or would you rather call him?"

"I'll call him; I can cut him short real fast if he starts to talk again like he did at the front desk. I'll leave a wake up call for us. Good night Agent Marlowe."

"Good night Agent Jefferies."

In the morning the two of them met outside their rooms and walked down the street to the same Restaurant where they had supper. The manager was right, this was not a fast food joint everything was made from scratch right down to the homemade biscuits. By the time they ordered their food the place suddenly filled up with people on their way to work or headed someplace else. They finished their meal and went back to the Motel. They got what they needed to take with them and headed to where the Professors house used to be to talk to neighbors and see what more they could learn. By eleven o'clock they had interviewed six different people both next door to the house and across the street. They finally got a description of the female that would be there on almost every weekend but not a name. All they knew was that her car had an Ohio license plate and they got a partial number for it but not all of it. Agent Jefferies contacted the Department of Motor Vehicles and left his number at the Motel. It was two thirty and they had just finished talking with another couple who knew the Professor.

"What do you say Agent Marlowe, shall we go check and see if we have any messages at the Motel and then grab some coffee and relax for a few minutes?"

"Sounds good to me, we sure don't have much to go on just yet. No one remembers the Professor having a visitor the night the house blew up so right now we don't know anything more than we did last night."

"Yeah you're right, this is the boring part of our job."

They headed back to their Motel. They had no idea the confusion and unrest they had stirred up in the small community. They did tell everyone they talked to where they could be reached and left them their number.

When they got back they unlocked their doors, "no light flashing in my room Agent Jefferies, how about yours?"

"Yup, the red light's blinking on my telephone."

She locked her door and followed him into his room. The maids had already cleaned their rooms and made the beds. Agent Jefferies got his message from the D.M.V. and turned to face Agent Marlowe. "We have two possibilities from the D.M.V., both live in Columbus. I'd stake my life on the older of the two, one is in her sixties the other is a young female attending the University of Ohio. I have the name and address, we'll stay here tonight and head for Columbus early in the morning and check out this lady and keep our rooms here. We can pick up Interstate 70 and that will take us right there, I think with luck we can do it in one day there and back. How does that sound Agent Marlowe?"

"Sounds like a plan to me."

"How about some coffee and we can strategize what we're going to do tomorrow and talk about what we did or didn't learn today?"

"Sounds good to me as well."

CHAPTER - 24

The next day Dick and Jane arrived in Columbus to talk with a Ms. Elizabeth Rice. It took them time to find her house but at least she was home when they found it. They talked at length with her and heard much the same things that everyone else had mentioned.

"I'm sorry I couldn't have been more help to you folks, have a nice drive back now."

"Thank you Ms. Rice, you have a nice day also and thank you for the tea," Jane said.

"You're quite welcome my dear, goodbye now."

They were almost to their car when Ms. Rice called out. "Excuse me Ms. Marlowe, could I see you a moment?"

She shrugged her shoulders at Agent Jefferies.

"I'll wait with the car," he said.

Jane walked back over to the house. "Yes Ms. Rice what is it?"

"Well dear, I just remembered the poor Professor didn't have an enemy in the world but there was a man he said he didn't trust, I'd forgotten all about him until just this very minute.

He seemed awfully interested in his collection of books and was there with a friend one day and like I said, there was something about him he didn't trust, it was as if he was afraid of him telling someone about his collection of rare and valuable books."

"Very interesting Ms. Rice, do you remember his name or where he lived?"

"Yes, the Professor had me write his name and address down just in case someone broke in to steal his collection while he was out. Give me a minute to find it and I'll give it to you."

She went back inside and was back in a couple of minutes. "This may be nothing at all but the way you and your friend were asking questions I got the impression that the Professor was murdered although you didn't come right out and say it, otherwise why would the FBI be snooping around, know what I mean?"

"Yes Ms. Rice, I know exactly what you mean. We'll check it out. Thank you for the information."

"Goodbye Miss and you take care around that man, he looks kind of funny to me."

"Yes ma'am, I'll surely be careful." She left as Ms. Rice closed her door and Jane returned to their car smiling just a little.

"Well, find out anything interesting Agent Marlowe?"

"As a matter of fact yes. She gave me the name and address of a man she said the Professor was afraid of. He was there with a friend one day and the man paid a little too much attention to the Professors collection of books, she said he didn't trust the little man, that he might tell someone about his collection."

"Where to now Agent Marlowe?"

"Back to where we came from I'm afraid."

"Why did you say that?"

"Well the man we'll be looking for lives back there in Jewett."

"Oh I see, we'd better get a move on then hadn't we?" He pulled the car away from the curb and headed back towards Jewett. "If we don't hit any heavy traffic we can have supper back there by the Motel."

"Would you mind if I spoke my mind for once Agent Jefferies?"

"Probably, but go ahead anyway."

"I'm getting tired of Agent this or that while we're out on the road, can't we call each other by our first names when we're alone, like me Jane, you Richard or Dick, I prefer Dick myself. We can introduce ourselves to strangers as Agent this or that but I would prefer first names between us from now on."

"Boy you do speak your mind alright! Okay, it's alright with me when we're alone but around strangers we'll stick to being professional if it's all the same to you."

"Works for me!"

"Done, now let's get back to work."

Late that afternoon they arrived back in town just before dark, they went from the car to the Restaurant to get supper.

"May I see the note Ms. Rice gave you Jane?"

"Yes of course Dick, here it is."

"Umm, don't remember the name or where he lives, let's wait until tomorrow to look him up. Right now I'm hungry and don't feel like messing around in the dark in an unfamiliar town hunting for an address."

They finished their supper and went back to their Motel.

"Say Jane, would you be interested in having a drink with me if we can find a lounge in town somewhere."

"Yes, I'd like that, I'm ready to unwind a little, lets ask though back at the Restaurant about a lounge, I don't went to give our friend at the Motel a reason to talk behind our backs."

"Good idea"

They found a very small Lounge not too far from the Motel and had a night cap or two or three and went back to the Motel and went to bed, separate rooms of course.

CHAPTER - 25

The next morning it was back to work. They decided to ask at the Restaurant where they had been eating where this man lived that they wanted to talk to. One of the waitresses recognized the name and said he ate there occasionally but that he didn't work or have a job, he lived off his Social Security Disability checks. It seemed as though Johnny Jamison might pan out. They followed the directions the waitress had given them and went to the house. They were greeted with a road block and there were policemen everywhere, there was a Coroner's van backed up to the front door and they were loading a body inside.

"Uh oh, looks like we're a little late, let's have a talk with the police and see if this stiff is our man," Dick suggested.

They parked the car and walked up the street towards the house like they owned the place. A Police Captain stopped them.

"You folks can't come up here, this is a crime scene, you'll have to leave."

They both reached into their pockets and produced their badges identifying them as the FBI Special Agents. "We're not leaving Captain," said Jefferies, "we're looking for a man by the name of Johnny Jamison, he needs to answer some questions for us!"

"Not possible, they're picking his body up right now; he's been dead a couple weeks from the looks of the decomposition."

"Did you see any obvious foul play that you would care to share with us Captain?"

"Sure, from what the Coroner could tell, he thinks he was shot with a 9 mm semi automatic pistol to the temple on the right side. He died instantly, probably never saw who killed him either. He was sitting in a chair smoking a cigarette reading the newspaper. We found the burned out cigarette in his fingers and the newspaper in his lap. He probably didn't even know his attacker was in the house."

"Here's my card Captain, I'd really appreciate it if you'd send me the ballistics check on the bullet when you have it analyzed."

"This have anything to do with the Professor's death a few weeks ago?"

"It's possible they are connected but we'll know more when we have your report."

"But the Professor's death was accidental."

"Sorry to burst you're bubble but he was murdered, any first year student of Criminology would have caught it but all of you professionals here in town missed it."

"Just a minute there mister I don't like your inference that we're a bunch of amateurs around here."

"Listen buster if the shoe fits wear it and stay out of our way! Understood?" Dick was fuming at the sudden lack of professionalism by the Captain.

"Yeah I understand that you're not in Washington now, I'd be careful driving home you might get a ticket."

"Did you get that on the tape Agent Marlowe, harassing and threatening a Federal Officer in the line of duty during a criminal investigation is a crime against the Federal Government. I could run you in right now Captain, would you care to retract that statement right now?"

"Go to hell! You'll never see the analysis you wanted either."

"Oh I think you'll send it to me right away, if not I'll hold you personally responsible for your actions and we'll take action against you and the entire department, do I make myself clear?"

"Get the hell out of my town, you hear me you Federal bastard."

"Well, we'd better go before he blows a gasket Agent Marlowe, he just blew his retirement and his job all at the same time." They causally walked back to their car as if nothing had happened. They got in and before Dick could start the engine the Captain was next to Jefferies door tapping on his window. Dick lowered his window some and held his index finger to his lips glaring at the Captain. "Which way to the station house, you follow us or we'll follow you and do it now, I'm fed up!"

"Perhaps I was a bit hasty," said the Captain.

"Listen you dingle berry we have it all on tape, every word, every remark and I will use it against you as soon as we talk to your Chief, now get out of my way, you lead we'll follow."

"Come now, can't we work this out, listen, where are you two going to eat tonight?"

"We're staying at the Jewett Family Inn and we have been eating at the delightful little Restaurant right next door," answered Jefferies.

"Well how about this, I get off from work around six o'clock, I'll go home and change, pick up my wife and we can all go out to dinner. I'll buy and see if we can't bury the hatchet, we've been under a lot of stress around here with three unrelated deaths in the past five weeks."

"How do you know they are unrelated?"

"There's nothing to tie them together whatsoever, my boss is furious because we haven't got a clue who did what to whom and there is no apparent connection."

"How come you didn't connect these two together, the Professor and this man?"

"We didn't have a reason too, the Coroner and the fire Department both said the Professor's death was an accident, we had no reason to suspect otherwise until you just told me. We only have twenty men on our entire Department, how many do you have in Washington?"

"Good point, thing is though no one looked at the evidence, not the Coroner or the Fire Department, least of all the Fire Department should have seen it. It was as clear as the nose on my face, even Ms. Marlowe here saw it and she's only been on the case 48 hours."

"Our Fire Department is 100% Volunteer and I'm afraid they are not professionals. Please let me try to make it up to you two, we had no idea the Feds. were interested in our town. We don't have the resources and expertise you people have. We haven't had a murder here in over forty years and that was when a man killed his wife in a drunken rage over his burned supper. We just don't have crime is this little town of ours therefore we weren't looking for anything."

"This Professor of yours was an international criminal living in your midst and you didn't know that either?"

"No sir Mr. Jefferies I swear it, no one suspected the sweet little man in the wheelchair to be anything but what he led us to believe and that was that he was a retired University Professor living on his retirement income and Social Security. I didn't know he was wanted by anyone until you just told me. Give me a break here, you'll see I'm not a bad sort once you get to know me. I'll pick you both up around seven if that's alright with you two, what's your room number?"

"You've done it again, assuming we're lovers staying in the same room, I'm in room 17, she's in room 21. We've only known one another for three days and we've been on the road talking with witnesses the whole time except for going separately to our own rooms."

"Oh gees I am sorry, his face flushed tomato red suddenly, "slip of the tongue, I meant nothing by it, seven o'clock alright with the two of you?"

"Alright, you pay for the wine also," Dick said.

"Yes of course, I'd really like to talk with you both man to man woman to man as the case apparently is."

"Agent Marlowe, should we give this hayseed another chance; he's blown three chances already?"

"Only if I get to pick out the wine," answered Jane.

"You heard the lady, before the night is out you're going to be glad she didn't get mad at you as I did, right now you're looking at number two and three in the hierarchy of the FBI, only our boss is higher up than she and I."

"You're joking aren't you?"

"No joke Captain, she was brought in by the Director to work with me on this now International case and we just learned that three days ago ourselves when we fist met and here we are. One thing you probably should know, our titles are Special Agents Jefferies and Marlowe, we're the only ones with that Title at this time. If you'd care to complain you may call the Director of the FBI and check us out but if you think I have a temper just wait until our boss gets a load of you. He could have your entire Department's badges and you could all be out of work."

"Wow, I had no idea, now I know I have a lot to make up for. I'll see you both around seven; this is quite exciting, wait until I tell the Chief."

"You'll tell no one we are even here, no one is to know we're investigating these murders. You may tell your Chief tomorrow that you ran into a couple of Federal Officers laying over for the night in your quaint little town and further more I'm from Columbus myself, I'm no stranger around here, do we understand each other?"

"Yes of course, but what shall I tell my wife?"

"Tell her the truth as I tell you, make her swear to keep quiet or we'll be back here and turn this place inside out. Just tell her that we're a couple of Federal Officers passing through and you thought it would be courteous to take us out to a dinner is all. We've already told you more than we would ordinarily but you explained the situation and trust me we've heard it all before."

"Okay then, until this evening, I'll call my wife and brief her as soon as I can."

"Alright Captain, we'll see you later."

They drove away both of them laughing to themselves. "You were a bit hard on the Captain back there, did you really intend to go the Station House with him?" asked Jane.

"No but he doesn't know that, it got us a free dinner and we'll have someone else to talk to tonight."

"You were right to come down on him for the sloppy work between Departments and someone should have caught the same thing we did, it was almost too obvious."

"Yes but we remember we're trained to look for what is not obvious even when it isn't to someone else. Our own Lab Techs. missed it, only you and I saw it right away, that's why we make the big bucks, right?"

They laughed about that as well, they were not that well paid and had to watch every penny they spent to show the Director and get reimbursed when they got back from any trip on the Government's dime.

They had an excellent dinner and the wine was exquisite, a Chardonnay that Miss. Marlowe picked out. The Captain and his wife turned out to be a wonderful couple and full of fun. Before they left that night each of them exchanged business cards and left on a high note. They truly liked each other after all and the Captain kept his composure while inside he was thankful for their chance meeting. Dick and Jane knew that from this day forward their Departments would be more careful at any scene and would look for things that weren't obvious. The shakeup they caused with the Captain may do some good after all. At the very least they had a new ally they could depend on during their Investigation.

CHAPTER - 26

Back at the Book Store, Sol once again locked himself away in his apartment and was having his meals delivered to his door. No one wondered about his reading so much. They thought he just got so engrossed in his books that he didn't want to be interrupted and to a point they were right. What no one realized was that during this time he was plotting his next perfect murder down to the minutest detail. He couldn't forget his few past mistakes, he would have to be more careful from now on. So far his leaving no witness behind was working right down to the Professor's home. No one could place him at the scene. Even when he used homeless people to assist him, one by one they disappeared or were found dead from alcohol poisoning or dead from an overdose from their drug of choice. Not one of the deaths had been investigated as a crime of murder. His latest adventure as he called them would take him across the country to Utah where there was very little crime if any due to the Mormon Church beliefs and the beliefs of other church going people as well. For him to pull off the perfect murder would require his utmost attention to detail. He would quietly slip in and out town instead of sticking around within a hundred miles or so of the crime scene when his victims were found. He enjoyed watching the authorities on the news become frustrated from the apparent lack of clues.

However he hadn't figured on the FBI getting involved because some of his stolen money had crossed State lines that was from Federally Insured Bank Accounts and that had brought the FBI into the back to him he was thinking The stolen books didn't stay in his procession very long; he wanted a quick turn around of the books out of his and Fred's hands with no traceable evidence left behind. They were extremely careful not to leave a paper trail behind that would show they had ever had a stolen book in their hands.

In two weeks he was ready to go to Utah and do his carefully laid out copy-cat crime. He picked Bryce Canyon National Park. There had only been two deaths there in all the years it had been in operation and both cases had been closed. He was going to copy a crime from Yellowstone National Park where the body was found a year later and the killer was never found. He decided to fly into the Salt Lake City then rent a car there and drive to the National Park. His murder would be random and to him insignificant. He didn't care who it was, only that he commit the perfect crime. Someone would come up missing and he would leave a few clues like a blood trail leading off into the brush to tantalize the authorities but it would be a misdirection to cover where the actual body lay.

Soon he was ready to leave. He got one of the young people Greta had working in the store to give him a ride to the Airport in New York, he would have to change planes twice to get to where he was going but he was confident he could pull it off. The young man questioned why he needed the two big suitcases and a large carry on bag when he would only be gone for one or two weeks. Sol passed it off that he was carrying reading material for research to help Fred and that this was a working vacation. He told him that if he were successful he would be sending a shipment of books back to the store. The young man bought the plausible excuse. He dropped Sol at the airport and left.

Sol caught his plane, made his connections on time and got to Salt Lake City late that afternoon where he checked into a Motel. The next morning he rented a station wagon. He put the gear in that he would need and went south to a little town called Richfield where there was another Motel as well as a big Campground. He checked into that Motel using another name and credit card using a different disguise.

The next day he went to the Park to scout it out and find a location close to a hiking trail which he could use for his copycat murder. It had to be the right place with the right surroundings where he could duplicate the exact type of murder. The story he read in the book was one where the body had been found the following year by some hikers but the scavengers had dismembered the skeleton and scattered bones every which way. Once the skull had been found the woman was identified through dental records.

After a full days search he found the site that best fit the description. He went back to the Motel and spent the night once again, it was Friday and the weekend would bring tourists and hikers alike out to enjoy the fresh air and scenery.

Saturday morning he was up early and eager to get going because he knew that the Park should be filled with people. Today he put on a pair of regular hiking boots he'd bought weeks earlier and had shipped to him from a catalog. He also carried a pair of his old black rubbers in a backpack to put over his boots at the site he planned for the murder. He found his spot and waited out of sight. He watched as tight groups of hikers went by but there were no stragglers. He sat there the whole day eating cereal bars a few candy bars and drinking soda from a small cooler big enough to hold six cans of soda but the opportunity to kill someone never came.

He went back to the Motel and had a good night's sleep. This was not going to be the quick turnaround he hoped it would be. Instead of a couple days it could be several days or longer.

The next morning he repeated the process. He waited at the same spot until almost noon when he saw two couples coming up the trail where he was waiting. One of the young women seemed to have a pebble or something in her boot that was irritating her foot. She told the others to go on ahead and stay on the trail and she would catch up after she took off her boot and got it out.

She sat on a huge rock right in front of where Sol was hiding. He waited, his breathing coming in short uneven breaths as he waited in anticipation for just the right moment. There were no other hikers that he could see in either direction so he watched patiently for her to finish tying her boot back up. Just as she was ready to get up from the boulder where she had rested to remove her boot Sol reached around her, put one gloved hand over her mouth and pulled her backwards over the rock and quickly broke her neck with his powerful arms. She never made a whimper, she didn't have a chance too, it was a complete surprise and was over in seconds. The only shoe prints she left were where she had sat down to remove one of her hiking boots and re-lace it and tie it. It would seem to people looking for her that she had simply disappeared into thin air.

Sol now had to work fast, he cut her throat near a vein and caught some of the blood in a small empty squeeze type mustard container with a nozzle on it to leave his blood trail. He pulled her over to a ravine that could not be seen from the hiking trail after he had her blood and he shoved the body over the sheer drop to the jagged rocks a couple hundred feet below. Standing on the rim no one could possibly see the body down there. He left no trace whatsoever. He took his container of blood and a white sweater she had tied around her neck by the sleeves and went across the trail and up towards the way the hikers had been going until he met a hiker coming down the trail so he ducked into some trees and hid in the brush.

It was the woman's husband who had come back to look for her. He passed him by and in a few minutes he realized that he must have passed her somewhere on the trail that was well marked. He retraced his steps and caught up with the other couple. He thought she may have gone off into the woods for a nature break and hadn't come out yet so they waited where they were for her to reappear and catch up.

Sol, finding the trail clear again, came out of hiding and stayed on the opposite side of the trail from where he had murdered the woman and started to leave his blood trail uphill into the woods far from where she had been. He left blood droplets that any dog or searcher could find. The forest floor was perfect, nothing but lots of leaves off the trees and little wisps of grass here and there. He left no foot prints, only the blood droplets. He walked uphill until he was out of blood, there he dropped the sweater. He retraced his path careful not to leave any footprints anywhere until he got back to the site where he had killed the woman. He took the empty plastic container of blood and with everything he had he tossed it as far away from the body as he could over the edge. He knew suspicious scavengers would carry it around chewing on it for a while as well.

He packed up his black rubbers and walked backwards back out onto the trail and then headed down the trial back to the parking lot where he had left the car. As he walked he heard people far behind him yelling loudly; "Susan, Susan, where are you?"

I've done it he thought, it will be spring before anyone finds any part of her and he was right. Searchers that night and the next day found the blood trail and followed it until they found her sweater but the trail ended there.

Sol went back to his Motel, spent the night then checked out the next morning and headed back to Salt Lake City to return the car and spend one more night in the same Motel as before under the other name he had used when he checked in.

In total he'd used three pairs of shoes, his hiking boots, three wigs of different colors and styles. He wore two pair of pants, two shirts, two different hats, one a base ball cap and one was a safari hat that was soft enough to fold and hide in his backpack. Anyone that connected one of his disguises to the crime would be chasing a ghost that didn't exist.

Three days after the crime he was back in Poughkeepsie waiting for someone to pick him up at the airport. The same young man who had taken him there also picked him up.

"Hello Mr. Devine, how was your trip?"

"It didn't go too well, I ended up hiking my tail off going from store to store and all of the leads I had were bad but I did meet some real nice people."

"I'm sorry to hear that. Fred has been wondering when you would be back, he said he has something important to talk to you about but didn't say what it was. Sit back and relax and I'll have you back at the store in no time."

"Thank you son, I'm very tired actually."

When they got back to the store it was late in the day and the young man was nice enough to help Sol carry his heavy suitcases up to his apartment.

CHAPTER - 27

Back in Washington Agents Jefferies and Marlowe began to compare notes. "Agent Marlowe, in your opinion, where do you think we stand with the investigation regarding the professor's demise?"

"Right back where we started I'm afraid. We have a man who was well liked, didn't have an enemy anywhere, yet he's murdered over some rare stolen books he owned. It just doesn't make any sense. What are we missing?. I think we need to closely scrutinize every lead we come across. All the leads we had have hit a dead end with the killing of the only man who may have profited from the Professor's collection."

"You're absolutely right Agent Marlowe, let's see if anyone else has had any luck with book store owner deaths." One by one they checked with the other four agents who were also on the case and they had hit a dead end as well.

"Agent Jefferies how about we start a chart and call it suppositions," asked Agent Marlowe. "We put all of the deaths on a chart along with known stolen books and see what it looks like, maybe then we can find a common thread somewhere."

"That's a good idea, let's give it a whirl and see what comes up."

They took a big four foot by eight foot white dry erase board that wasn't currently in use and started their chart. By the end of the day they had completed most of it and all of the data wasn't in yet. Soon they trickled in every few days. New unexplained cases long forgotten by the Authorities who had investigated them. The board was soon filled up and they needed another.

"How far back do some of these cases go Agent Marlowe, maybe that's another factor we need to add in?"

"Alright Agent Jefferies, we'll give that a try also." They plugged in all the dates and the data grew and grew.

Six months later it was spring and they were still no closer to closing one case from another. Even the Director came downstairs one day to check their plot on the boards and was surprised by what he saw. Later the next day he called Agents Marlow and Jefferies to his Office on the top floor.

"Are we in trouble?" asked Jane on the way to the Directors Office.

"I hope not but I have to admit my frustration with not being able to solve one case, what we have here are only suppositions. The data mostly says the deaths were accidental, a lot of it I can't find fault with."

Soon they were in the Director's Office.

"Have a seat you two, let's talk about these book store killings. Have you been able to ascertain whether any of the other deaths were murder?"

"No sir, not one of them, every person died differently. A fall down the stairs to a heart attack to death from cancer to an explosion and fire, they all add up to accidents or death by natural causes and no witnesses."

"Don't the two of you find it strange that there's to not one witness to any of the deaths?"

"Of course we do Director, but there is no evidence that says otherwise," said Jefferies.

"Well I don't mean to mess with what you've found but here's my take on it. I believe we're looking for a very clever killer who is an avid book collector," said the Director. "He or she is not your typical serial killer, this one murders by wholesale if you get my drift."

"Yes sir we thought about that. We have charted every death suspicious or not over the past twenty years and we're still getting closed cases from across the Country. Not once have we gotten an open file on any of these cases. I think we just got lucky on the Professor's case, the killer missed one important detail, bright brass threads on a gas fitting," Jefferies said.

"Yes, yes I know all about that, but mark my word, someone is killing people out there and getting away with it and the reason there are no witnesses is that they are all killed as well."

"That's reaching awfully far isn't it sir?"

"Right Agent Jefferies but keep digging. If you found the Professor's killing was murder and not an accident then why not some of the others. The ones you have are all past Book Store owners or collectors aren't they?"

"I see your point sir."

"Agent Marlowe, do you have anything you'd like to add?"

"No Agent Jefferies, but the Director got me thinking. He could be dead right and we need to look at deaths two or three days before and two or three days after each of the book store deaths, maybe we can tie this altogether; that may be the thread I was talking about earlier."

"Alright you two, from now on you have Carte Blanch to get this mess cleaned up, you're now six strong, get to work and find me some answers before the Press gets wind of what we're sitting on here, now get going and good hunting."

The two of them left the Director's Office with more questions than answers. On the elevator Agent Marlowe asked, "Agent Jefferies, what we need is a king size map of the United States about eight feet high and thirty to forty feet long, how about it Agent Jefferies?"

"Can do Agent Marlowe," he replied smiling from ear to ear because he'd been thinking the same thing. A geographic study of the whole Country regarding book store owners, their deaths and time lines."

Now came the hard part, finding a wall in the basement where they could put such a map. They both began formatting on pieces of paper what they wanted to see on the map. They decided to leave about four feet at the left and right ends of the map for listing demographics providing they could find the wall space. Even if they only ended up with twenty feet of wall the plan would be the same.

The search began for wall space, cubicles may have to be moved and areas of other cubicles reorganized to provide wall space then they would have to find an artist that could do the job. Planning and moving some disgruntled employees around went on for two weeks once they had identified the space they would use. They put one Agent in charge of looking for an artist to do the job and get at least two or three to come in and look over what they wanted done. Of course they would not be told what the map was for and they could easily explain that the Director wanted a mural wall map showing all of the FBI locations on it. They even looked into putting a map made of wall paper or vinyl.

Three of the walls in the basement were windowless; the only windows were bullet proof glass doors at the end of the huge room that opened out into the underground garage. There were four other narrow high windows also made of bullet proof glass that ran almost floor to ceiling and they are about eighteen inches wide two on each side of the doors spaced evenly. Things were moving along swiftly but the new team was looking for results not artistry and comfort for the FBI Lab, techs., agents and employees. The wall paper and vinyl maps they found were way too small for what they needed so they ruled them out. They all knew the importance of each others jobs and complained little once things were set up and waiting for an artist to be hired.

Three different artists showed up all in one day evenly spaced apart so they wouldn't run into one another. They settled on a woman artist who said she could start immediately, the others had projects that wouldn't be done for several weeks yet and couldn't start until then.

The next day drop cloths went down, saw horses came in, ladders and some scaffolding were brought in as well. It seems that the artist chosen was only five feet four inches tall and needed the ladders and scaffolding to get her closer to the ten foot high ceiling. She went to work and the six Agents went back to work, fortunately they didn't have to disrupt their own limited work space. Things were finally coming together for them organizational wise. They really needed the map to visualize the areas of the country affected. It would also help pinpoint a central location where most criminals didn't strike close to their home base, usually. They didn't have a clue as to what they were really up against.

Another month went by with the artist bringing in helpers to paint in the States as she lined out the boundaries. All of them would be different colors so that no two colors touched each others boundaries, much like the jig saw puzzles for children to help them learn the states. It was coming together nicely, everyone in the basement took sneak peeks at the map wondering what was going on. Right now all they knew was that the Director ordered it and it would be done, the reason would come out later, they all had their own case loads to work on.

CHAPTER - 28

At the Book Store things were booming, Fred and Sol's patents for ink were bringing in special orders from around the world which kept them so busy they had to add extra employees in the production and packaging areas. They cleared out and remolded a section of the second floor to accommodate modern machinery to aid them in the processes they were not so familiar with. They were more into research and development rather than in the marketing, production and shipping. These they needed assistance with so they brought in professionals to help and let them run that part of the company. No one suspected their new employer was actually the serial killer who was loose in the country.

Nothing so far had connected him to the Book Store on Lexington Avenue.

Things were going so well for the Store and its subsidiaries now that Fred and Sol could retire if they wanted too and let the new corporation run itself. All this free time for Fred and Sol gave them the time they wanted to pursue their individual interests. Fred's was restoring and copying rare books so well that the experts couldn't tell the difference so he stayed in the basement perfecting and honing his craft to that end.

Sol continued reading True Unsolved Crime Mysteries and dreamed of his next perfect crime. He was averaging one or two murders a year of book store owners or book collectors.

Then to carry out his dream of committing the next perfect crime he continued his murder fetish a couple more times a year. He didn't want to over do that plan. Sometimes he would spend months studying and planning his next perfect crime. The book store killings he felt were just part of doing business. He was so clever that no one suspected him and the disguises he used kept the authorities confused as to who the buyer of each book store really was. Any leads they had all led to dead ends as to who was buying the stores and who was stealing the books and many times all the cash the owner had. Sol and Fred seldom kept a rare book long enough for it to be traced back to them. They used mailing services and forwarding mailing services from around the country to mail the valuable books to wealthy purchasers. There was no paper trail back to their Store.

Both Fred and Sol kept separate books of the transactions in case one of them died they would have a duplicate. Sol had gone one step further. During the construction of his apartment he had a fake wall installed in his walk in closet in his bedroom where he kept all of his daily wear. At the end of the closet concealed within a stack of shelves was a small button similar to an old door bell that opened the fake wall and led into three other rooms plus two more bedrooms and bathrooms. The wall was split into two sections so it slid both left and right inside the walls much like a pocket door would do only on a larger scale with nylon rollers that rolled silently when operated. In the other rooms was where he kept all of his extra elevated shoes and boots, his disguises, wigs of different shapes style and colors and lots of clothes to fit his fat suit or his elevated persona. All his books, magazines and files regarding unsolved murders were in there as well.

The only things in his own apartment were several suits of clothes that wore on an every day basis along with shirts and underwear and socks, everything else pertaining to his secret life was contained in the other rooms and he had book shelves in there with history books and geography books with maps of the world and others but no murder mystery books. He had a security system in his rooms so when someone would come to his door he could hear the knock on his door from anywhere in the rooms on both sides of the fake wall. He also installed a simple small buzzer in the floor under a floor mat at his front door so if someone approached his door he was warned immediately. Even if someone moved the floor mat they wouldn't see the buzzer button, it was concealed beneath a floorboard that operated the buzzer when someone put pressure on the board by simply stepping on it. The buzzer was situated where it could not be heard by the person approaching his front door. In case he didn't hear the buzzer he had some small red lights installed around the rooms of both units to where he couldn't miss them to warn him that someone was at his door.

He could slip in and out of either side of his unique set up of rooms without being heard from outside the door. All the walls in both units were sound proofed so no one could hear him when he was at home and he couldn't hear them either. Even Fred didn't know about this extravagant set up. Sol had telephones in both units as well as TV sets so he could be at home in either space. In his main apartment he had a kitchen and two full bathrooms along with two bedrooms in case he had a guest like his girlfriend Francis who may stay overnight or a male friend who needed a separate bed to sleep in.

The separate unit held his private life and so far he had shown it to no one. The man who had done the lion's share of the work had disappeared and with him went the secret of it all. Sol was a man of his word when he said leave no witnesses. He was extremely thorough, so thorough that he had few friends left other than Fred and Greta and his girlfriend Francis who idolized him.

CHAPTER - 29

In the Book Store Greta sorted all the mail for the Store, Sol's and Fred's as well but they seldom received any personal mail mostly it was addressed to the Book Store. There came a letter one day for the Store and Greta opened it then realized almost immediately that it was for Sol. It was sent in care of who-ever the buyer was for old and rare books. It was advertising the sale of a Book Store in a suburb of Boston Massachusetts called Brookline which Sol was not familiar with although he knew where Boston was. Greta summoned Sol by sending a young man upstairs with the letter to give to him and if he had ques-tions he could check in with Greta.

The young man knocked on Sol's door and Sol opened it almost immedi-ately upon his hearing the buzzer when the button was depressed beneath the floor mat at his door.

"A letter sir, from the store."

"Why thank you young man." Sol took the letter out of the envelope and read it over quickly. He got more and more interested as he read. Simply stated it said, 'the heirs of Stanley Rogers announce the untimely death of their father and uncle and the subsequent sale of his Book Collection and all of the books in his retail Book Store. You can preview the sale and or make an enclosed bid to purchase it all by previewing it on November 14th 1972 on the premises of his house or the store. We will accept sealed bids on either the store and its inventory or the owner's residence where his private collection is and the house and all that is in it will be sold. Everything must go, it is hoped that another entity will purchase the store and all of its contents and reopen in a new location because the lease on the current space expires on December 1st 1972 and is not renewable.' Perfect thought Sol, he'd take it all in one fell swoop if it had enough rare books to warrant a high bid. He read a note at the bottom. The lowest acceptable bid is $900,000.00 and only takes care of the bills due from the store and over due mortgage payments on the house. Please visit the Store at your convenience as it remains open and take a tour of the house anytime, a relative will be on hand to show any interested parties around. It gave the address but no phone numbers and no contact person.

Well, Sol thought to himself, someone is being a little mysterious about all of this because of the lack of contact information. Sol immediately began to make arrangements to go to Boston. He called around and found a Motel close to both Brookline and Boston. He made arrangements by phone and when he was asked for credit card information he said that he didn't have one, he always paid cash for everything he bought and gave them the name of his Bank and their phone number. The Motel called the Bank and was told to give that man anything he wants, he pays cash for everything and has the funds in the Bank to back any amount of money requested up to a high seven figures cash on hand. The Bank never divulges the full amount but it was well over three million dollars in the Bank in Sol's name. Fred has his own money in his own account at the same Bank in New York City.

Sol drove to Brookline Massachusetts and went to the Book Store first to view what was there. It was a first class operation with a complete stock of all kinds of books. Sol knew he didn't need the entire stock but some of what he saw intrigued him and it wasn't in the store but in the basement storage of the store. He figured the owner of the store must have been an elderly man due to the shipment dates on some boxes that had never been opened. It looked as though he had received them and had them put in the basement until later and simply forgot about them.

He asked for and was given the old bill of laden on the boxes and wondered just what was in them that the man had been so secretive about because he never opened them and the Bill of laden only said rare books for the store and its name.

Next he went to the house and took the tour of it along with the collection of some really old books and valuable ones to boot on the main floor in a spacious library. Mentally Sol took it all in. It was a young lady who showed him around and he asked if there was a basement. The young lady said yes and showed Sol where the door was but said she had never been down there and she had no intention of going down there because she was told it was haunted and full of spider webs. Sol went downstairs to the basement and it stank of mildew and mold. He milled around looking at several old rotting cartons that once contained books that had been sent to the house address. He rummaged around several minutes until something caught his eye. There was a semi circle of disturbed dirt and dust near a brick wall so he investigated and found a simple button like a modern door bell so he pushed it. To his amazement the wall swung open and there was a lighted room beyond the brick wall and it had a dehumidifier running and it wasn't dirty, dusty or smelly inside. The temperature was kept at an even 78 degrees with its own air conditioning system and heat. There he found hundreds of rare books on ornate book shelves that he drooled over to get his hands on. A veritable gold mine he thought to himself, this man had to be a book enthusiast or hoarder or maybe both. He had to buy this house even if he didn't buy the store. He went back upstairs and found the young lady.

"Miss, are you a relative of the deceased owner?"

"Yes, he was my grandfather."

"Well Miss, I wouldn't let anyone go down those stairs again, this house is infested with Termites and ought to be torn down, it's damaged beyond repair. I collect fine books and would like to buy all of the books in here but the house is in terrible condition, completely unsafe to live in. Do you have an attorney who represents all of the heirs or should I talk to you?"

"We have an Attorney in Boston who represents the family, you can discuss any terms or conditions you wish with him and you may give him any sealed contract or offer to purchase."

"Very well," he thought this over for minute, "may I have his information, I'd like to see him straight away."

"Yes sir here it is, this is his card, he left several on this table for just such an occasion."

"Well thank you Miss, I have enjoyed talking with you and you're probably right, the basement may be haunted. I did hear some strange sounds down there myself and there is nothing down there of any interest whatsoever. The foundation is in a shambles as well, I don't quite know what's holding the house up right now, good day to you Miss."

Sol left and went back to his Motel. The young woman was crushed, she had hoped to get some money after the sale but now it suddenly looked hopeless.

From there he made inquiry as to when he could see the Attorney whose name he had been given. He was told he could have fifteen minutes tomorrow morning or a half an hour the next afternoon at two thirty. He took the two thirty appointment, he had much to say and needed time to say it regarding the sale of everything he had seen.

The next day he was in Boston at two thirty to meet with the Attorney. He walked into the office and told the secretary at the desk who he was. "I am Mr. Stevens from New York here to see Mr. Wilson on an important matter."

"Yes of course Mr. Stevens, Mr. Wilson is with a client just now but he may be done in a minute, he's very punctual when it comes to his appointments."

In a couple of minutes an old lady came out in tears followed by a younger woman who was obviously upset about something and she was physically supporting the older woman as if she may have been a caregiver of sorts.

"Mr. Wilson, this is Mr. Stevens here about the Book Store and the Estate you are handling."

"Come in Mr. Stevens, can I get you some refreshment of some kind?"

"No thank you Mr. Wilson, I'd like to get down to brass tacks if we can. I'm interested in purchasing everything in the estate and I do mean everything."

"Yes of course Mr. Stevens, do you wish to make a bid for it all?"

"No! I told you I am here to buy it, not bid on it. I do not have time for your foolish games young man. Tell me the bottom price and I'll tell you if I am interested."

"Well, the highest bid I have seen so far is for $1,200,000 dollars for both properties."

"You are a cad and a liar sir, I have seen the house and it is a pile of junk, you and the family have misrepresented it and I'll see you disbarred for this if you're not careful."

"What are you talking about, the house is in perfectly good condition, there's nothing whatsoever wrong with it."

"Did you ever go in the basement?"

"No! Why would I?"

"Aha, I thought so, you're lying all of you. The place is infested with termites, the book collection is of no value to a collector such as myself and the book store is full of common everyday books and some of them are obsolete books that even a library wouldn't take if they were offered. Either you are all idiots or crooks, maybe both. I am prepared to offer you however $850,000 for the whole lot, including the junk house which I shall have immediately torn down."

"That's not possible, the estate owes $900,000 in debts."

"That is also a lie, show me the bills and mortgages or whatever and do it now, do not waste my time and I will not waste yours. I was told there was no mortgage on the house. What is your fee in all of this, $135,000 would be the normal fee for this kind of transaction."

"I'll not listen to your insinuations, just who do you think you are anyway?"

"Have your secretary make two phone calls, one to my office and one to my Bank, you'll know soon enough that I'm not fooling around. I have enough Attorneys on my staff to hold you up in court for the next twenty years for liable and fraud. Here are the numbers, have her make the calls and put it through to you one at a time." Sol's face was red with implied rage. He threw two business cards down on the Attorney's desk, one for his Corporation and one number for his bank. The secretary put through the first call to Sol's company and Fred came on the line; Sol had already told him what to say.

"Mr. Wilson here, just what is going on?"

The Attorney's face began to get red then it got redder and the veins on his head swelled and seemed as if they'd burst any second.

"Well I never, I," and the phone went dead as Fred had said his piece and hung up on him. "Well I never, I simply never;" he was saying into the dead phone connection. In a few minutes the secretary put through the next call.

"Mr. Wilson here, I'd like to know the credit worthiness of a Professor Stevens please? Give him what, are you sure? How much is he worth, are you sure about all this?" He slammed the phone down onto its cradle again, he'd been talking with Fred again who disguised his voice.

"It seems sir that you are someone terribly important and I didn't realize what I was up against, what will it take to make all of this go away?"

"You're signature deeding the house and all its contents to me as well as all of the contents down to lost change found on the floor of the defunct store and you'd best be thankful I'm in a charitable mood today, any other day I'd have reached across your desk and jerked you to your feet and beat the hell out of you!"

"Yeah tough guy? You can go to hell after I sign the paperwork for you, this is robbery and fraud when you come right down to it. You can pick up the papers tomorrow morning."

"I think not, cancel your appointments for the day, you will do the paperwork right now or take a dive out your window!"

"You wouldn't dare lay a hand on me!"

Sol reached across the desk and jerked the man to his feet and pulled him across his desk and the Attorney was so tall he had to look down at Sol. "Head first, feet first, it don't matter none to me?"

"Okay, okay, put me down will you, gees you're a hot head." He was shaking all over when the smaller but stronger man let him down slowly until his feet touched the floor. He called his secretary in and told her to get the paperwork ready and gave her the price and name to put on it which was a shell company of Sol's and sat back down in his chair. He was still visibly shaken when she finally finished her work and brought it all in for their signatures.

"You did the right thing Attorney Wilson and the smart thing because from what I have on you I could put you in jail for the rest of your life."

The Attorney just shook his head in disbelief and wondered just how much this stranger with the thick red hair and heavy set muscled build knew about him. He judged the smaller man to be about five foot ten inches tall as he was an even six feet two himself without shoes on so he was closer to six feet three with the designer Italian boots on he was wearing. He couldn't believe the strength of the man before him and didn't want to see him upset again. Sol handed the man his personal check for the entire Estate with one of his shell company's names on it so it couldn't be traced back to him and in return the Attorney handed him the new Deed.

"Well there you are Mr. Stevens and don't bother me again. You can see yourself out!"

"Thank you Mr. Wilson, I wish we had met under different circumstances, we might have become friends."

"I doubt it, I don't much care for filthy scum like you!"

"The feeling is mutual then, I'm sure!"

Sol turned to leave walking slowly towards the secretary's office on his way out.

"Jenny come in here please," asked Mr. Wilson, "I'm going to have to work late tonight, you can go on home if you like."

"How much later were you talking about Mr. Wilson?"

"Oh, probably not past eight o'clock if I can get caught up by then."

"Well then I'd like to stay, maybe you can buy me dinner after we're through."

"Yes well, that could be arranged I think."

Sol let himself out but heard the entire conversation about the plan. He went to eat by himself then went to his hotel room. He changed his clothes and his wig and went back to the Attorney's Office to pay them one last visit.

CHAPTER - 30

The next morning the Newspapers read, 'Attorney Stuart Wilson and his mistress of several years, his secretary, jump to their death fifteen stories from his office window despondent over lost gambling debts. His wife says she didn't suspect a thing.' The newspaper didn't divulge where the information came from, they didn't have to. 'The Attorney was in debt over his eye balls.'

The next day Sol had a moving company at the book store load everything up that wasn't nailed down.

Later there was another moving van sent to the house and he was there to meet that one as well. He directed them to pack up everything that the family members hadn't already removed and as soon as they were done he took two men down to the basement to remove the rest of the books from there as well. He left nothing at all in the house. The movers packed everything left in the house.

The following week on Friday a Company showed up to demolish the house, they had been told to tear it down and haul it to the nearest landfill, every stick, brick and piece of glass and to fill the basement with dirt and grade the lot.

After returning to Poughkeepsie Sol had some time to reflect on his recent haul of booksand old furniture he thought may contain some antiques.

As he was reading through some of the materials he himself brought back he came across a diary written in the owners own hand that read; 'Today I realized the dream of a lifetime when I opened my first Book Store in Brookline Massachusetts, dated this day the 15th of May 1898' He couldn't put the diary down, he had never seen one kept by a man. Later he read: 'My health is so bad that the pain is driving me crazy, I fear I have only one or two days to live, I have asked my son Stanley to take over the business, I hope he continues my work and my collecting of rare books, I have instructed him never to sell my collections of famous Authors whose collections I was able to obtain. It was dated August 19ᵗʰ 1929' He continued to read while it all sunk in and began to realize the value of what had been upstairs that he may have missed as well as the secret room in the basement which he had cleaned out himself letting the packers box up all the books.. He read further in some newspaper clippings and found that the house he had torn down was being considered as a Historical Land Mark and he sighed now that he had it destroyed. He thought to himself, I could have made millions on that old house if I had just left it alone. Sol thought to himself, my impulse will be my downfall that's four mistakes now.

Three months later the young lady who had waited on Sol and had shown him around the house received a deed for the vacant lot with a note of thanks from Sol signed by his alias he used to buy the estate. He said in a brief note; 'here is the Deed to your vacant lot, have it rezoned and sell it for whatever you can get for it and enjoy the fruits of your grandfather's love.' She could barely visualize the small man that had been there to see her and didn't remember his name. She sat there with a gladdened heart thanking the man silently whom she could barely remember.

CHAPTER - 31

Finally the map of the Untied States mural was finished in the basement of the FBI Building. Dick and Jane were standing back marveling at the art work. "Well Agent Marlowe, where do you suggest we start with this?"

"I haven't got a clue but why don't we take it by case by case and start with the one on top of the pile, that's the only suggestion I have, it is a bit overwhelming isn't it?"

"Yes it is, just think of all the people who have lost their lives and we haven't seen the tip of the iceberg yet."

They started with the file on top of the pile they had. Each Agent working a case would add theirs to the map as soon as Agents Marlowe and Jefferies finished theirs. It took ten days to get all of the cases up on the wall and marked. The entire wall was drywall so it was easy to put colored push pins in it and run bright colored thread from a pin to a legend on either side of the map. On the eleventh work day morning all the Agents gathered to compare notes and count the number of states that had Book Store Closings and a death related to it. On the Legend portion they placed the date that each had occurred with City and State and they were comparing notes as to the length of time between deaths and the store closings. They found no similarities or a pattern but something interesting did show up and that was the number of dead which was staggering but there was no proof of intent to murder except for the lone Professor's house and his was a private collection not a book store.

Standing near the wall Agent Jefferies had summoned all the Agents to meet with him. "Agent Marlowe, fellow Agents," said Jefferies, "I have a feeling we're missing something here. I'm suspicious by nature and I think we better re-visit each death that occurred and get the following information. Number one, the number of deaths the day before the store closings, number two, the number the day of the closings which is what we have and number three two to three days after the store closing. I think if we dig far enough we'll find that common thread. Something just isn't right about his whole set up now that we can see it all on the wall. Anyone else feel that way? I mean the hair on my neck is standing up, something has given me the chills all of a sudden. It's almost as if there is a spirit in here egging us on to keep looking and I don't for one don't believe in ghosts."

"Me neither," said a couple of the other Agents.

Then Agent Marlowe weighed in with her two cents. "I have to agree with Agent Jefferies, something is giving me the willies right now and I'm very uncomfortable as well. I don't believe in ghosts either but something just doesn't feel right in here."

They all went back to work contacting each agency who had sent them the cases and asked for the additional information of deaths related or not to the closing of each book store.

They themselves would determine whether or not the deaths were related through good old fashioned shoe leather and leg work. Three more weeks went by and then slowly but surely reports began to come in from around the nation. One report was recent from a town near Boston called Brookline.

"Agent Marlowe, feel like a road trip up to Boston soon?"

"Sure why not, I'm not at all busy this week Agent Jefferies," she said tongue in cheek.

The next morning they were on their way to Boston or rather nearby Brookline. They found a Motel close by and it happened to be the same one where Sol had stayed but they didn't know it. They looked up the granddaughter of the owner of the book store because she lived right there in Brookline and she said she knew all about the sale of her grandfather's book store. She welcomed the two Agents into her home and asked them what she could do to help.

"Well Miss this is Special Agent Marlowe and I'm Special Agent Jefferies and we'd like to ask you some questions. We're investigating all Book Store Sales around the country because some of them quite frankly have been rather strange transactions."

"Oh? Well I'm afraid you've wasted your time here, my grandfather died of cancer quite naturally and my father is too ill to run the store so the rest of us decided to sell the store and advertised it through the trade magazines all over the country. We had several people come and look then walk away for some reason and the man who bought it made an offer that our Attorney said was to good to pass up so he took it, paid off the bills and sent the rest of the money to the family members per my grandfather's instructions in his Will. We're all very happy with the outcome."

"Yes, from what I understand the police here in Brookline are a little concerned about the deaths of your Attorney and his Secretary the same day you closed the deal."

"Yes, we all thought it was strange as well but the papers said that he was deep in gambling debts from betting on the baseball and football games here in the Boston area and that's not at all unusual. A lot of people bet on the games, many employers allow baseball and football pools in their Company's for their people to take part in. We received our checks in the mail a couple of days later all dated the day of the sale."

"Yes, we're aware of all that. But don't you find it strange that a good Attorney with no problems would take his life and that of his secretary as well?"

"But the newspapers said he was deep in debt and had an affair with his secretary."

"Not true, we've already checked his records and he was clean, he loved his wife and children and his secretary was also devoted to her own husband and family. Someone wanted them dead because they witnessed something they shouldn't have. It may or may not be related to the sale of your book store and your grandfather's collection of books he had in his house,.Is the house available for us to go and look over?"

"No I'm afraid not, the man who bought everything had the house torn down because it was unsafe due to termites and just a couple of weeks ago he sent me the deed to the land where the house used to sit."

"He sent you the deed to a vacant lot?" Agent Jefferies asked, his eyebrows went up with a questioning look and his forehead wrinkled.

"Yes, that's correct."

"Well doggone it Miss, didn't you find that rather strange?" Jefferies asked.

"Yes of course I did, but I thought he was extremely rich from what our Attorney had said to us the same day so I didn't think anything of it, the note said, enjoy the fruit of your grandfather's work and love."

"Do you still have the letter?," asked agent Marlowe?

"Well no ma'am, I threw it away and put the property up for sale with a local Realtor."

"Do you remember what the man looked like who bought the property Miss?"

"No sir, well yes, maybe a little, he was an older man with red curly hair, heavy set but not fat, maybe around six feet tall maybe a little shorter, like five feet ten maybe. He could have been shorter or taller, I just don't remember that well, I only saw him for a few minutes and there were other people milling about asking questions all at the same time but I'm sure about the red hair and that he is the one who bought it all. He made sure everything that wasn't nailed down was loaded into moving trucks and hauled away."

"Moving trucks you say?" asked Jane.

"Yes that's right ma'am, he used a local Moving Company to move everything from here to wherever his Book Store was."

"Do you remember the city or town where he was from or the name of his store or anything or maybe the letter he sent with the deed, where it was from?"

"No, it was a very busy day and things were moving way too fast. Two days later everything was packed up and gone. The following Friday another company showed up and demolished the house and hauled it to a landfill somewhere. I am sorry, is it important?"

"Yes, well it could be, we think so, don't we Agent Jefferies?"

"Yes, any information would be of a help to us, any detail you may remember, here are our cards, please call us if you remember anything more."

"Wait, I do remember the Moving Company, the truck's sign said, Hobson's Moving Co. Local or Long Distance, its right here in Brookline."

"Thank you, they are bound to have records of some sort about the move, thank you Miss for your time and please call us if you remember any little detail, good bye now."

"Good bye to you both."

"Yes thank you, bye now" added Jane.

They went out and got in their car. "Well what do you think Jane?"

"Why would he send her the deed to a vacant lot, why not sell it himself. Another thing, what did the Attorney and his secretary see that got them killed and not this young woman?"

"Maybe the killer has a soft spot for young women?"

"Oh I don't know, lets go to Hobson's Moving and Storage Company, good thing she remembered them at least."

CHAPTER - 32

They drove straight to the Hobson's Moving Company to check out where the trucks delivered their loads to. They walked into the office of the Moving Company and encountered a middle aged secretary there.

"Good afternoon ma'am, we're with the FBI and would like to ask you some questions if we may?" asked Jefferies.

A man from an office behind the secretary came out who had overheard them. "What the hell does the FBI want with us?"

"Who are you sir?"

"I'm Thomas Hobson, I own this place and I don't like cops snooping around, you ain't got no business with me so get out of here!"

The two Agents looked at the big burly man with no neck, he was solid muscle from the looks of him, probably got that way from moving furniture all his life. He was bald as a cannon ball and looked as though he weighed about two hundred and sixty pounds and appeared to be in his mid fifties, it was hard to tell but one thing did show, he was no gentleman.

"Alright then sir, if you would care to come with us back to Washington and explain why you are withholding information from Federal Investigators we'd be glad to accommodate you," Jefferies offered.

"The hell you say, just who do you think you are coming in here and threatening me?"

"That wasn't a threat sir, we'll take you in if you like, we really don't care because one way or the other you'll answer our questions and I'll have the IRS step in here and let them have a look around while we're tied up in Washington with you."

"Alright, you got five minutes, state your case then get the hell out, I'm a busy man.!"

"I'm only going to warn you once sir, if you swear just one more time before these two ladies I'll bury you so deep in legal paperwork that you'll never see the light of day again, you got that?"

"Yeah I got it you son of a," his voice trailed off.

Agent Marlowe was waggling a finger at him and saying, "ah, ah, ah, naughty, naughty."

The man shut up and began to listen. Agent Jefferies laid the whole scenario out for him, the days and dates of his moving trucks. "Now then, we would like to know where the trucks delivered the goods and if possible we'd like to talk with the drivers."

"Well so would I. They left here with no word on their destination. They were to call me before they left town but never did and I haven't seen the men or my trucks since. For all I know they drove off the edge of the earth and disappeared!"

"I see, you were working a cash deal under the table so to speak."

"So what, we do it all the time for people who can afford it, that isn't anything new!" "Have you been paid for their services yet?"

"No,! They were to bring the money back here with them and all their expense receipts but they never returned I tell you!" The owner was obviously getting more and more agitated.

"Uh huh, you believe him Agent Marlowe?"

"No I believe he lies through his teeth."

"Watch it lady, no broad is going to push me around, I'll throw your ass right out into the street and your boss man right behind you."

"Oops," said Agent Jefferies, "I don't believe you should have said that."

Before the man could raise a hand to fight, he made a threatening move towards Agent Marlowe and she threw him off from her hip right outside into the dirt in a summersault before he could utter another word. The stunned man lay on his back there staring up at the sky.

"What the hell happened, did I trip over something?" he asked?

"You just met the tame side of Agent Marlowe," said Jefferies. "I wouldn't make her mad if I were you, she was just making a point. Now that we have your undivided attention, care to give us a description of your trucks and the men driving them?"

"Uh, I guess so, can I get up now?" The man got up dusting himself off and came back inside the office still trying to catch his breath.

"Elizabeth can you get them the information they want on the four men and give them copies of their photos if you have them and photos of the two trucks we're missing?"

"You know I've never been thrown by a broad before, what did you use on me, I never saw you lift a finger you moved so fast."

"The lady here is modest but I'm not, she has several black belts in the Marshall Arts as well as Military and FBI training so I would use some restraint if I were you and show the lady the respect she deserves."

Jane couldn't resist a snide remark to the owner as well, "if you think I'm mean, I'm a pussy cat compared to Agent Jefferies, he's the real bad ass. He lets me handle the light weight dummies and he handles the really dangerous types, not wimps like you"

Soon the secretary had everything copied they would need and she was grinning from ear to ear. "Thanks," she whispered to Agent Marlowe and gave her the information.

"You know Agent Marlowe, you really should learn to control your temper."

"Yes I know, but I had all I was going to take from that ingrate, he's lucky I didn't kill him because I was certainly thinking about it. You know Dick those men are dead and the trucks are gone as well don't you?"

"I'm afraid I have to agree with you on that one, too bad, they were probably promised the world and got a bullet to the brain, want to bet?"

"No bet, I'm pretty sure that's what happened, otherwise we would have witnesses. Whoever this is, he or she don't play nice."

"By the way Jane did you happen to notice that the man at the moving company seemed unperturbed at the missing men, all he asked about was his money and the two trucks."

"Yeah I noticed, he didn't care a thing about the missing men or their families."

"I wonder if the Insurance Company has any records that would help?" Dick asked.

"Don't know but it might be worth checking out," added Jane."

CHAPTER - 33

In Poughkeepsie Sol and Fred were going over the rare books that Sol had brought back from Brookline. "Sol you have gone and out done yourself this time, just look at these books, they are in fantastic shape for their age, how did you ever find them in such great condition."

"Believe it or not this bunch were in the old man's basement in a secret room that was protected from the heat, cold and humidity with the best equipment ever made. I almost didn't find them at all, even the heirs were unaware of it. The basement was old, dirty, dusty, smelly, damp, you name it, it was unspeakable! I happened to look down at the dirt strewn concrete floor and noticed there was a mark in the dust that looked like a quarter of a circle, you know, the kind that opening a door would make but there was a brick wall there and no door. I got lucky and found a button that operated an electric door, part of the wall swung out like a bank vault door silent as could be and inside the walls were covered in book shelves, a lamp an easy chair, a big couch and two or three floor lamps for reading and it was beautifully decorated inside but no windows and there was a small TV set in there as well. I bought the whole place and as soon as I had everything cleared out I had the house torn down and hauled away to a landfill. I told the man in charge that the house was full of termites and had to be torn down or burned down to destroy the insects. I didn't want anyone to see the room or they would realize something of value had been in there. If an heir had known about the room they wouldn't have sold the place so cheap."

"I lucked out on the store as well, there were boxes and boxes of unopened rare books in the basement that apparently no one knew about and I kept those separate for you to work on. That's why I was able to salvage so many books. The people either didn't know or care about what they had. All they knew was their grandfather had died and their father was too ill to run the Store any longer and they didn't want it so they sold it as is where is. We just got lucky, even the dumb Attorney didn't have enough sense to go looking and inventory what the family was sitting on. If he had they could have asked millions for the two places and got it. I don't feel a bit guilty of taking advantage of them. It's their own fault for being dumb and naive. I did do one nice thing though, the young lady who helped me out deserved something so I mailed her the deed to the vacant lot and told her to have it rezoned, sell it and enjoy the money she received."

"You didn't!"

"Don't worry, I used one of our shell companies to make the transaction look genuine, we can't be traced by it. I did however have to take care of two loose ends that pissed me off, I made it look like a double lover's suicide until I got clear of town, they probably know by now that it was murder but the man shouldn't have made me so angry."

"What did you do to them?"

"I went back to the Attorney's Office just before eight o'clock that night, hit them both in the back of the head with my 9mm pistol, opened one of the large windows, pulled them over to it and positioned them close together so when I pushed them out they would fall fifteen stories to the street below and land close together like lovers would have done. Why do you ask me about this one Fred, you don't usually care how I come by the books as long as I deliver?"

"I don't know, its just that someone really loved these old books and I was curious what you had to do to get them to let go of them and now I know. You didn't have to kill someone to get the books this time."

"Anyway Fred there's nothing behind us to tie us to any of the stores. Everything I've done was made to look like an accident or suicide like the last two."

"What happened to those nice men and the trucks that brought all this back?"

"I paid them off and got rid of them, who knows where they have gone. I made it worth their while to keep quiet and run off with the money I paid them. I have no idea what they did to get rid of the trucks. I told them to be sure and take them at least a hundred miles away from here before they disposed of them. They probably set them afire and walked away to a new life for all I know." He had lied through his teeth, he knew exactly what had been done with them.

Sol and Fred spent the next three weeks cataloging the books and making copies of each one before selling any of them abroad or in the U.S. The books they had were an easy sale, they had just enough dust on them to make it believable they were originals. Before a sale they would advertise them to the prospective buyer that they would be sold as is dust and all. They claimed that they had never been cleaned and were sold as they had been found or purchased from the previous owner. The dust made the buyer feel even more secure especially if they decided to have the dust analyzed for age. They were meticulous in their work of restoration when needed or when copying for profit. The business was after all about the bottom line, profit. If anyone took the time to think about the name of the Corporation they may have gotten a clue as to their purpose. It seemed easy for Sol to pick the name because it was what he and Fred were all about, Rare Old Books. Hence the initials for the store, 'ROB B Store' Kind of catchy but true. Buyers were being robbed because fifty percent of the rare books were copies, not originals. Later Fred and Sol got together and changed the Corporation to read R.O.B.S. Inc. for Rare Old Books Store, Inc. The big sign on the building stayed the same and simply read R.O.B. Store. It was just the way Sol wanted it in the end and the beginning.

CHAPTER - 34

It wasn't long before new reports began to drift in after the second request by the FBI for additional information of deaths the day before and the few days after any book store sales.

"How many States have we heard from now Agent Marlowe?," asked Jefferies.

"Last count I made was fourteen but there may be more who are searching their records more thoroughly going back several years" answered Marlowe.

"I've been so caught up in the study of these cases that I forgot how many years we asked the Departments to go back, do you remember Agent Marlowe?"

"Now you have got me, I'm not sure. Like you I've been studying case files one after another looking for anything that could point to murder. I'm not real sure but twenty years sticks in my mind. Let me ask Theresa Wilcox, she's the one who drafted the nation wide inquiry for us, I'll be back in a few minutes." She left their office and went looking for their Secretary. She was back in around ten minutes.

"It was twenty years Agent Jefferies, is there a problem with the time lines?"

"I'm not sure but just suppose these people have been at it for more than twenty years and are close to retiring."

"I never thought of it that way before."

"Me neither; it just dawned on me that we could be looking at a very long crime spree. I hate to go back and request more from the Departments, it could put a strain on some smaller Police Agencies. Many of them don't have the manpower to do a search like we're asking, everyone is slow about getting computers due to the high cost of them in the initial outlay. It could take them years to catch up."

"I agree but look at what we already have, why not go with that?"

"Yeah you're right, I'm reaching again. Let's take a look at something more recent. Let's see if we can find something in common with the buyers of the book stores," asked Dick.

"What are you looking for?"

"Something regarding height, weight, name, color of eyes and hair, age, things like that. I want to see if the same man shows up to buy each store or not."

"Suppose it isn't a man we're looking for? Isn't it possible that a man and a woman could be working together or two men and two women?" asked Jane.

"That's why I'm looking for a common denominator silly."

"Oh I got you now, I wasn't looking for that right up front, I was only interested in common names. It is entirely possible that the same people are pulling off these crimes using an alias now and then for instance."

"Uh huh, you just made our job worse didn't you Agent Marlowe?"

"I guess so. Say what about a day off Agent Jefferies, we haven't had one in the three weeks, the other Agents are starting to grumble as well."

"Yeah? Well, maybe we ought to talk to them."

"What's this 'we' business, you're the one driving the bus and everyone else so hard."

"Sorry, I'll talk to them and let them know that the Director is the one who wants answers, its not just me you know, besides murder never takes a day off."

"Oh yeah, and by the way I don't like your quotes either, they are too cliché."

"My, my Agent Marlowe, you do need a day off, we are a mite touchy aren't we?"

"You know what Agent Jefferies if you were a real gentleman you would notice the stress level is rising and you ought to ask the lady out to lunch."

"Point taken Agent Marlowe, where would you like to eat today for lunch, I'll buy."

"Some place quiet and not too crowded, I need time to think just like you do, it will do you good to get out of here as well for a little while."

"Okay, we have a choice of chicken, beef, oriental, you name, it we'll eat it."

"I think someplace that serves beef, people are a lot quieter for some reason when they are eating a good steak, they spend most of their time chewing instead of talking."

"I never heard it put more eloquent Agent Marlowe, beef it is, how about a nice inexpensive Steakhouse?"

"Where are you going to find one that's open for lunch?"

"I thought we'd go by a store, pick out a couple of steaks and go to my place and I'll cook them outside on my grill. We could have baked potato or anything else you like."

"I'd like to go to a Restaurant where people wait on us and we can talk civil like. We go to your place and we won't have time to talk, you'll be grilling outside and I'd be baking inside, too much work, I want to get away from work for a while."

"Okay peace treaty, you pick the restaurant and I'll buy."

"Now that's better. Lets find someplace away from downtown so we don't have to listen to Senators and Representatives voice their petty views and arguing all through lunch."

"I got it Agent Marlowe, I know a quiet little steak restaurant that's open for lunch just over the border in Virginia. They open at eleven A.M. for lunch and by the time we get there we'll miss the big lunch crowd, they have both booths and tables where we can eat in comfort and peace."

"Fine, but won't that take all afternoon to go there eat and come back?"

"I certainly hope so, I really need a break and didn't know how bad until you brought it to my attention."

"I have one rule while we're there, no talking shop, I've had it up to my ears today, I feel like I've run headlong into a stonewall,"

"Okay Agent Marlowe, lets get something to eat, someplace quiet just like you asked."

The two of them cleared up what had to be done right away then went out to the garage to get their car.

CHAPTER - 35

Jefferies and Marlowe got in their car and headed south on Interstate 95 for Virginia. In a little while they were across the Virginia State Border and Dick spotted the exit he wanted. He got off the Interstate and changed from one highway to another almost like he was trying to lose a tail on himself or so it seemed to Jane. "You do know where you're going don't you Dick?"

"Yes Jane, we'll be there in less than five minutes."

"Okay, just curious, my stomach is growling."

"Oh is that what it was, I thought I had transmission trouble."

"Very funny and don't get any old fashioned ideas like running out of gas or having a flat tire, the Director wouldn't believe you anyway if we're late getting back."

"Yes mother hen." Minutes later he declared, "well here we are," and he pulled the car into a dirt lot in front of a ram-shackled looking Restaurant.

"Lord have mercy what is this place, it looks like it's closed up or worse, ready to fall down, we're not going in there are we?" She looked at what appeared to be boarded up windows.

"Not to worry, its just a facade, once inside you'll change your mind, this is one of the Restaurants favored by Jimmy Hoffa and other high rollers of the day, its truly elegant inside. Only the brightest people know about this place so you won't find any politicians in here but you will find some computer geeks once in a while, otherwise it's full of business men, the movers and shakers of Industry getting away from it all as you'll soon see my pet."

"I am not your pet Dick, please remember that!" Jane was irritated at the ugly sight of the restaurant.

"Sorry about that, slip of the tongue is all." They walked in through a door that looked like it was about to fall off its hinges but it opened with a quiet grace. They walked though a a small alcove and found themselves in a slightly darkened room with hats and coats hung on racks until it looked like there was no room for more. A man in a tuxedo approached.

"Ah, Agent Jefferies and a lady friend, how have you been sir?"

"Just find Sam, how about yourself?"

"Just fine sir, thank you."

"How are the wife and kids?"

"Just fine sir, but my wife oh, um," he whispered to Dick, "she's pregnant again."

"Oh no, not again, how many does this make seven or is it number eight?"

"Where have you been sir, this is number nine and she wants more, she say she won't be happy until she has a baker's dozen."

"I'm almost afraid to ask Dick, but what's his last name?" Jane whispered.

"Why its Baker, Sam Baker, didn't I tell you, he owns this place and can afford as many kids as he wants, this is a gold mine of sorts, best beef in the country right here."

"Oh I am sorry," said Jane to Sam, "I thought you were the maitre d who worked here or the hat check person or, oh I don't know."

"Help me out here Dick?"

"You were doing fine before hat check person so why not try our host or Sam?"

"I like that even better Dick."

She held out her hand and Sam took her hand in his and said, "it is a pleasure to meet you I'm sure," and he kissed the back of her hand.

"By the way Sam she is no lady, this is Special Agent Jane Marlowe and her credentials may be higher than mine."

"But Agent Jefferies, everyone knows you're number two at the FBI."

"That may be but she is number three now. May we have a quiet out of the way table for two Sam?"

"Sure thing, I know exactly what you need."

"You understand Miss Marlowe, no one discusses business in here, it is forbidden other than that anything goes, within reason of course." He was blushing as he led them through what seemed to her as a maze of rooms that sat anywhere from four people to twenty four or more at a large table. They came to what appeared to be several small alcoves with tables for two. It was a very intimate setting Jane was thinking. As they sat down a waiter suddenly appeared and set two glasses of water down with a small bowl of lemon slices then disappeared. Another waiter appeared with menus and a wine list.

"Dick if I didn't know better, I'd think you were trying to get into my pants. This is an extremely personal and romantic setting."

"Listen Jane, you said somewhere quiet and reserved and this is it! You heard the man, no business spoken in here, what more could you possibly want?"

"I'm afraid to ask because a violin might magically appear from out of nowhere."

She had barely finished talking when a strikingly beautiful shapely female violinist walked quietly up to their table and asked in a quiet and seductive voice, "anything special you would like to hear today Dick?"

"No Susan, play your little heart out for the lady if you don't mind, she wants to be sure she isn't hallucinating."

"Whatever you say lover!" She began to play a haunting love tune that would melt any woman's heart, it was Autumn Leaves which was his favorite song.

"Oh Dick, how did you know?"

"How did I know what Jane?"

"I was born in November, its one of my favorite tunes when leaves are changing color."

"Oh my, how careless of me."

"You set this whole thing up ahead of time didn't you?" Jane was getting irritated again."

"Whoa there, hold on now, she always plays that song for me because she knows it's my favorite tune, I swear that's all there is to it!"

"Uh huh and I've got a bridge in Brooklyn that I'd like to sell you big boy!"

"Why don't you quit belly aching and find something to eat!"

"You tell me, what s the best steak of the house?"

"Well if you're asking me it's the rib eye, it falls apart and the flavor is exquisite."

"Then I'll have the rib eye and a baked sweet potato and corn."

"You can relax, we have a five course meal coming, how do you like your steak cooked."

"Medium rare will be fine, just so long as its not still moving when it gets here."

They were served soup, salad, then breadsticks with a garlic sauce and when the meal arrived she hadn't heard him order it, it was perfect, the steak was done to perfection and they had strawberry cheesecake for desert.

"Dick, I have to ask, how did they know what I wanted, I didn't hear you order the meal."

Dick snapped his fingers and a waiter suddenly appeared beside him. "He was listening Jane, they know my routine by heart, I get the same wine, the same meal and this time it was times two, you had the same thing I always order. The only difference was I like my steak medium and yours is medium rare, you had corn and I had green beans. There's no science to it at all, a waiter is always close by in case a customer wants something."

"Oh I see, you come here often with your girlfriends do you?"

"No Jane, there was a woman once but she was killed in a botched robbery and this is the first time I've been back here since she died; she was my wife!" he said sadly and now irritated.

"Oh I am sorry Dick, I had no idea. I have behaved badly without thinking, how can I make it up to you?"

"You can make it up to me by not getting me to talk shop, you want to get us thrown out of here, Sam means it when he says no shop talk."

"I knew it, you did have an ulterior motive bringing me here, you it did just so you could get into my underpants, the same thing you would have done at your place I'll bet!!"

"You're impossible Jane, I did everything I could to get you out to a nice quiet meal and you turn it into a dirty love match of some kind, do you want to walk back to DC because I can make that happen too!"

"Oh you men, always a one track mind, you're just like all the rest, unzip your pants to pee and your brains fall out. Take me back to the Office please, I'm ready to get back to work."

While she had been ranting Sam overheard what was said and came over to their table. "Miss you are mistaken and you have wronged this man. You must have a problem with the opposite sex because Dick did not set this up, we have not seen one another since his wife died then his partner was nearly killed. He was crushed and it brought the world down around his shoulders. This man is a good man, an honorable man and if you continue you rant and rave I will have to ask you to leave. Dick can stay because his honor is intact but I can see that someone has dishonored you somewhere in your past and you are taking it out on Dick and that's not fair. Mend your ways Miss and I mean right this minute or I will show you to the door!"

"You wouldn't dare!"

"Careful Agent Marlowe, you don't know who you're dealing with here, this man has more black belts than you'll ever see."

"She caught the Agent Marlowe thing and decided against an all out public brawl, perhaps she was wrong so she relented. "I can see I'm out manned, two to one isn't fair. I'll behave myself and you're right Sam, I have had difficulties with men in the past, but this man has been trying to get into my pants since the first day I met him."

"How so Miss, please explain?"

"The first day we met he eyed me up and down in the Directors Office. Then he tries to get me alone in the elevator every day,. He has invited me out to lunches and dinners and I've not gone because I feared he was just trying to get to me. There, I've said it, that's how I feel."

"Honestly Sam it's all in her head, none of that happened like she said. She asked me to take her to a quiet out of the way place away from the city and all the politicians and I did and this is how she repays me. I should have taken her to a fast food burger joint where she wouldn't have felt trapped. I apologize for ever bringing her here, I hope you can forgive me."

"You are welcome here anytime Dick. However this vixen cannot come back here again, she's trouble for you Dick, watch your back. She won't help you in a situation like your other partner did some time ago. He gave his life to save yours, I'm surprised this one is such a bitch. She has no honor at all. By the way, I feel so badly for you, the meals are on me!"

"Sam you don't have to," and Dick's voice died on thin air. Sam had his hand up as if to say, you have said enough. Sam pulled the chair out for Jane as she stood up.

"Honestly it's just like you men, always sticking together to gang up on a lady."

"Funny thing Dick I hear a voice but it does not come from a lady, she'll never know what a kind and gentle person you really are. She has a dirty little mind and A mouth to match. I feel sorry for you. The next time you come, come alone please and we'll eat together and talk of the old days when gentlemen were gentlemen and ladies were ladies."

"Thank you Sam you are too kind and I am sorry for her out burst, it will not happen again I promise you." They walked out to the car in total quiet, got in and drove back to DC in silence. Jane was boiling inside, mad as any woman could ever be, she was going to the Director and request a transfer anywhere away from him. Dick pulled the car into the space with his name on it without waiting for Donny to park it for them.

Donny walked up to greet them. "Hello Dick, Agent Marlowe, how did lunch go?" "Like crap!" Jane said and she stormed off to go upstairs to the Director's Office to complain.

CHAPTER - 36

At the Book Store things couldn't have been going better than they were this month. Sol advertised a book in a mail out to a select few that they had on their interested mailing list and got responses back almost immediately. This latest haul of books was a gold mine. Sol shipped an original first edition to a man in California and a copy of the same book he sold as an original first edition to a man in France. Both Books sold for thousand of dollars apiece. Sol always waited for the checks to clear the bank before he shipped the books to the buyers. Doing business this way he figured that the two buyers would never meet one another and claim to have the one and only known original book still existing out there.

They were shipping up to four rare books a week sometimes. On the low end of the spectrum Sol charged upwards of one thousand dollars or more for a book. Homer's original collection would bring a much higher price. He set two bidders against one another and when the bidding ceased to go any higher he wrote them both and told them they had the winning bid and shipped the original to one and the copy to the other. They both thought they had the only rare first edition existing by the author. He did the same thing with the manuscript originals and parchments. The parchments were sometimes original renderings of maps such as the Lewis and Clark expeditions which they claimed to have uncovered in an estate sale of one of their family members who had them stashed away in a trunk in an attic. The copies were so good that no one including the experts could tell the difference and the museums wondered if what they had were fakes when one of these surfaced.

They were so good at their forgeries that they reproduced fake letters of Presidents all the way back to George Washington and sold them for thousands of dollars collectively when things were slow in the book sale department.

Meanwhile their Book Store gained fame as having the widest selection of books so that people came from far and wide just to wander through the store isle by isle of old and rare books by the masters themselves. Of course they didn't know when they bought an original copy or a first edition; they all thought they were buying a very rare book mainly from the price on the book itself displayed with a three by five card in front of it with a brief description of the quality of the book in a locked glass display case that held several extremely rare books. Greta had to put on two more extra people just to work in the book store and she kept a couple of them busy going up and downstairs to bring more books down from the storage area to restock the shelves.

They never cleaned any of the rare books, they wanted them to appear worn and dusty to match their claim that the book had been bought through an estate sale. It was a very effective sales tool for them. Books were flying off the shelves with people buying them up figuring they had something both valuable and collectable. In fact they had many newer books that were collecting dust in the same fashion. Unbeknown to the employees the men had installed a separate air system that kept the room air conditioned and heated to a temperature where the books would not deteriorate and then once a week they would introduce an infinite amount of dust into the air on the whole second floor to cover the stored books in tiny dust particles from what they had cleaned up during the restoration and construction of the factory warehouse in which they were located. Even Greta was unaware of this process. She believed they bought the books at Estate Sales just like they claimed they had. In truth almost every used book had been stolen in one way or another, the scheme was working perfectly for them.

Time went by quickly for the two men, the elevators were installed in their end of the building and two more in the middle of the building which was being renovated a little at a time as new tenants were always moving in it seemed. A National Office Supply Chain opened their first Retail Store there.

The reputation of the Store itself had grown so much that people from around the Nation were contacting them from time to time to come and look at collections of their relatives and appraise them or purchase what the families didn't want. Some people smelled the musty odor of the books and didn't like it and didn't know what to do to clean the books safely hence a call to the Book Store on Lexington Avenue usually brought Sol out pretty quickly. He would fly into a city close by, rent a non descript run of the mill rental car and go and see the family that had contacted Greta about looking over the books they had on hand and didn't really want or knew what to do with them.

When the phone would ring Greta had a script next close to her there and acted as the men's secretary. She had a list of aliases Sol would go by and he explained to her that if everyone knew his real name he wouldn't have anytime to himself. She had five names for different parts of the United States. When she got a call from California she used that name for the area west then Midwest and so on. She would write Sol a note with that name at the top of the message so when he called that person back he called using that name from the script. When he showed up he wore a different disguise for each area of the U.S. No one outside of the store or Poughkeepsie knew that his name was Sol or what he really looked like for sure. He always had the look of mystery about him when he made personal calls on people that had called into the store for help with a collection of books. He may have two or three calls from within the same State so he scheduled his time so he could visit each one within a day or two of one another. It was however cutting into his time of reading and planning another perfect murder somewhere, only he knew where he would strike next but he would strike at least twice a year to feed his fetish with the perfect crime of murder.

CHAPTER - 37

Jane Marlowe stormed out of the garage and headed directly to the Director's Office on the top floor of the FBI Building. She barged into his Secretary's Office and said; "I demand to see the Director right now!!!"

"Do you have an appointment Miss Marlowe?" asked the secretary.

"Of course not, I need to see him right now, I'm not here to make an appointment!"

"Well I am sorry, without an appointment you can't see him. He isn't here right now anyway. He's at the White House going over something with the President and his group of Military Advisors, something big is up over there."

"I don't believe you, you lying bitch!" She brushed past the secretary as if she weren't there. She threw open the door and rushed into the Director's Office. It was empty, there wasn't a soul around. "Alright where is he?" Jane demanded once again.

"I told you Miss Marlowe, he is at the White House, I have no need to lie to you and besides I would never do that. If you don't leave here quietly I will be forced to report this incident to the Director, he doesn't take kindly to people barging into his office like you just did. You'd better get your head on straight before you see him, I have seen him fire people for less than what you have done, talk about insubordination, well I never!" The Secretary's face was as red as an over ripe tomato. She stood with her hands on her hips waiting for Jane's next move.

"Gees, you're just like all of the rest, opinionated, untrustworthy, rude and you go right along with the rest of the chauvinist pigs, you're in the wallow with them aren't you!!!"

"That's it Miss Marlowe, get out of here now or I'll have you thrown out on your ear by Security!"

"You and what Army stupid?" Jane said with hands on hips with a smart-alecky attitude.

"That's it Miss Marlowe I've had enough. All of what you have said is on tape and believe me when I say that the Director won't take kindly to this." She pressed a button and before Jane could open her mouth again four U.S. Marines in full battle dress appeared in the room along with a Marine in full Officer's dress.

"You heard Lieutenant?"

"Yes ma'am, we heard, front door or back?"

"Back door if you please and confiscate her I D, the Director will decide what to do with her, oh and make sure she isn't armed, that could be another infraction the Director doesn't take kindly to, no armed agents in his office."

"Yes Ma'am, consider it done. Miss, whatever your name is, you can walk with us or go out in handcuffs and shackles."

"You wouldn't dare!"

"Sergeant, handcuffs please."

"Wait just a minute, do you have any idea who I am?" Jane was really mad by now.

"Doesn't make any difference, if you were Agent Jefferies or someone else, we would do the same to him for his attitude. Fortunately he knows about this squad and is respectful when he's in the Director's Office."

`"Listen the five of you couldn't take me down if I didn't want you to!"

The Lieutenant was the only one in dress uniform, he snapped his white gloved fingers and six more men filled the room armed to the teeth.

"You were saying ma'am!"

"I was saying I'd be happy to follow you, lead the way asshole!"

"So long bitch," Jane added to the Director's Secretary as she left the office.

Agent Jefferies was still in the garage talking with Donny as the Squad of Marines came out with Jane Marlowe in tow.

"Good afternoon Lieutenant, problem upstairs?"

"Yes sir Agent Jefferies, this little lady is a spitfire and she is leaving the building for a while.

This weapon young lady, is this your own property or does it belong to the FBI?"

"It's mine you silly little twerp! "

"Your I.D. ma'am, may I have it please?"

She took it from around her neck and threw it on the ground in front of the Lieutenant.

"Ma'am, would you kindly pick it up and hand it to me, if not it will also go on your report as more insubordination?"

"Go to hell you bunch of jerks." She turned on her heels, put her 9mm pistol back in her purse and stormed out of the garage towards the street.

"Wow, what brought that outburst on Dick?"

"I have no idea Donny, one minute we were having lunch and the next minute she flew off the handle."

"Wow she sure looks pissed," added Donny.

"Lieutenant, what happened that you had to force her to leave?"

"Well Agent Jefferies, Donny, she burst into the Director's Office with no appointment and harassed his Secretary so she called us in to show her out. She's not allowed back in without proper I D and I have it now and will hold it until the Director tells me different. I'm afraid she is in a heap of trouble. This could easily get her fired and quick, the Director doesn't like insubordination from anyone. His Secretary has it all on tape as well as on video. Good day gentlemen."

"Good day Lieutenant."

The squad marched in unison back into the building and upstairs to their posts.

"Boy Dick, you sure have a way with partners don't you?"

"Must be my beguiling charms I guess, see you later partner."

"Later partner." They still called each other partner, they felt a kinship like no others could unless they had been in a life and death situation such as they had been in.

Dick went back to work as if nothing had happened. Only one person asked the where a bout's of Agent Jane Marlowe. He told him that she had decided to take a couple of days off due to the stress they all had been under.

Two days later Dick got a phone call asking him to come to the Director's Office post haste. He took the private express elevator from his Department upstairs to the Directors Office.

His Secretary showed him right in.

"You wanted to see me sir"

"Yes Agent Jefferies we, meaning you and I, have a little problem." Whenever the Director called him Agent Jefferies he knew it was something serious. "I want to hear your side of this thing with Agent Marlowe."

"Yes sir, but there really isn't very much to say. She had been riding me about going to lunch somewhere quiet away from work. I have been pushing people a little hard lately so I took her to Twin Willows over in Virginia and we had a nice lunch until suddenly she claimed that I'd set the whole lunch thing up just so I could get into her underpants so I brought her back here and you probably know more than I do now."

"Twin Willows you say?"

"Yes sir, as you know my family has two tables reserved there to use whenever we please. One that seats two people and one that seats four or more if we so desire."

"Yes I am well aware of that and extremely jealous that you haven't invited me there yet, it's so exclusive it means nothing to the owner if I showed up, he'd just show me out again. So you say she just went off on a tangent telling you that you just wanted to have sex with her and that's what the planned lunch was all about and that you set it up ahead of time?"

"Yes sir that's pretty much what she accused me of, but honestly sir, it was a spur of the moment thing."

"I am so sorry Dick, it seems that I owe you an apology. I thought she was over this. I should have warned you that she has claimed sexual harassment at every office she was at but she is a damn fine Agent and I don't want to lose her. You tell me she's gone and I'll fire here right here and now, I'll leave up to you. If she stays I'll hit her so hard it will take her months to come around and by hitting her hard I'm talking of course by the book. She made an absolute ass out of herself over nothing and she treated my Secretary like dirt."

"To tell you the truth sir she is a fine Agent but her attitude about men has to change, can you dig deeply enough to find out why she's acting like this?"

"Already done son, here's her jacket." He pushed a thick file over towards Dick to where he could reach it on top of his huge desk.

He began to read and didn't like what he saw. She had been raped a few times by a family member, an older man, when she was thirteen then raped again in high school by a couple of football jocks. It said in the jacket that she had a hard time adjusting to any man who was superior to her in rank. She had taken an anger management class that the FBI had made her go to but only nights for four weeks. She quit saying that the instructor was trying to get her to have sex with him. It also stated that she had never had a steady boyfriend, every date she had in the past resulted in just one date, she seldom saw a man more than once.

"If I am reading this right sir, she's never once had a sexual partner. She's thirty five years old, doesn't she ever wonder what it might be like to be in love with a man?"

"That I can't answer. But I will say this, if she doesn't receive the right professional help she's as good as done with this Department, no one would ever hire her again anywhere."

"Well sir you know how good an Agent she can be, are you willing to go the extra mile and order her to see someone, a professional I mean."

"Do you have someone in mind?"

"Yes sir, I just now thought about it while reading her jacket, forget the male instructors or professionals, I'm thinking of Doctor Joyce Brothers. You would of course have to use your clout to make her go but she respects you at least."

"Yes, well let me think that over, I have a friend of a friend if you get my drift that could make this happen and keep it out of her jacket but I'll need your help in the long run. Are you willing to step up to the plate next to me?"

"Yes sir of course I am, but right now she hates me."

"Are you familiar with blackmail Dick?"

"Of course sir."

"Well I'm about to blackmail you. If this works out and she gets through this crap she's been carrying around all these years you owe me and Sylvia dinner at Twin Willows."

"My offer to you is always open sir, your time just never coincides with mine is all."

"It will son, I could lose my job right here and now for what I'm about to do."

"No sir! She isn't worth going that far, no one is! Just fire her in a way so she can get a job somewhere else!"

"Not possible, this is her fourth time with insubordination over made up sexual harassment charges and it has to stop here and now!! There'll never be another chance for this gal. I will make some calls before I call her back in here and drop the hammer on her. I will give her in short an ultimatum she can't get out of."

"Sounds like you're going to be rough on her sir."

"That's exactly what I intend to do. Can you do without her for four to six weeks, I have no idea on how long this may take, Dr. Brothers as you know is one busy lady but I'll do my best to put the pressure where it will do the most good." The Director stood up signaling that the visit was over. The two of them shook hands and he walked Dick over to the door and opened it for him signaling all was well between them. Dick said goodbye and he walked him out to the Director's secretary's desk.

"I'm not real sure what Agent Marlowe said or did the other day ma'am but it wasn't her, I just leaned some very disturbing news about her past and I hope we can all forgive her."

"I don't know Agent Jefferies, a little respect and decency goes a long way around here and she has none of it! It will take a powerful apology from her to me and half the staff in this building before anyone will forgive her, apparently the word has gotten out about her attitude."

"Well she's going to be on administrative leave for a while and hopefully when and if she comes back, she'll be a changed person."

"If she isn't she will get the same treatment as before with the Marines escorting her out of this building, I won't have it! Understood Dick?"

"Yes ma'am, perfectly ma'am!"

Dick thought to himself, that kind person just called me by my nickname, I'll be darned. She must pity me for putting up with Agent Marlowe these past few months.

He was exactly on target because that's exactly how she felt. Behind the scenes things began to roll while the Director called in some favors, he sent all of Jane Marlowe's records to Dr. Brothers with the tapes from his office to show how upset she could get. The appointment was made and set in concrete, it was time to call her in for an interview and give her in short her ultimatums.

CHAPTER - 38

One day while Sol was alone in his apartment a young man from the store came to his door and knocked rather loudly.

"Yes who is it?" Sol called out gruffly.

"Its Norman sir, from the store, Ms. Greta sir, she wants you to come downstairs as soon as you can, she has an important message for you."

"Well alright boy, tell her I'll be there directly!"

"Yes sir, thank you sir." The boy left and ran down the stairs, he didn't want to use the elevator, he'd been told that it was just for business and tenants who lived upstairs.

After several minutes passed Sol strolled into the store, "you wanted to see me Greta?"

"Yes Sol, I've got a phone message you might want to look at."

"Alright, let me see it."

She handed him the message and he read what she had written. "Uh huh, did you just receive this?"

"Yes Sol, I thought it might be a good lead and not some crack pot trying to make a buck on us."

"Looks genuine, I'll check it out, thanks Greta."

"Anytime Sol." Deep in her heart she wished Sol would take to her in a personal way and marry her, but she knew Sol was not the marrying kind and he only thought about Francis.

Sol went back upstairs to return the phone call after a while; he didn't want too sound anxious about it just in case it was some poor bum who needed money to buy wine or whiskey. He read it over again a few times to let it sink in. It read, 'wealthy widow comes into millions, has hundreds of books in her late husbands library she doesn't' know what to do with. Please come and take a look. Name, Richard Longtree.' Huh, that's a funny name, sounds like it might be Native American Indian or something he was thinking. He dialed the number after an hour and a half. A voice answered on the other end and told him that they didn't know each other but a friend had given his Store name and phone Number. Sol listened intently but said very little.

"Listen," he finally replied, "I don't know you, send me a newspaper clipping before I decide to come all the way to California, if its on the up and up I'll call you back, don't call here again, we're just too busy this time of year, goodbye!" Sol hung up and didn't give it another thought. Three days later an envelope arrived for the store; Greta opened it and saw the note in it apparently addressed to Sol. With it was a newspaper clipping about the wealthy heiress? She immediately gave it to Norman to run upstairs with and to give to Sol. The young man knocked on Sol's door and he heard the floor buzzer as well.

"Yes what is it?"

"It's Norman sir, I have a Message from Ms. Greta in the store sir."

Sol opened the door and the frightened young man handed Sol the envelope that was resealed with cellophane tape. He opened it up and recognized the name again and decided maybe it was worth a trip to California after all. The young man stood there shaking in his shoes waiting for Sol to tell him to go or there might be a message for Greta for him to take back downstairs. Sol scared some of the people half to death with his apparent gruff short temper.

"What are you waiting for boy, get the hell back to work and hurry up about it, you going to stand around here all day?"

"Yes sir, no sir, thank you sir, right away sir." Norman took off at a run for the stairs at the end of the hall never looking back. Sol studied the clipping several times before he really decided to take the long trip to California. He'd been there twice already on bum steers and had committed one murder there in the past in a small town called Red Bluff located in the Sacramento Valley in northern California.

The next morning Sol went to the store after he had breakfast brought to up his apartment. "Greta, guess I'll head to California; I made a call to the airlines and found a straight through flight if I can get to the airport in New York

City by noon today. Got anyone who can take me to the airport who knows where it is?"

"Wait just a minute and I'll see."

She disappeared and soon came back. She had the same young man with her. "This is Norman Sol, he says he knows the way to the airport."

"Yes I've met Norman a few times, what do you say Norman, are you up for a trip to the big city?"

"Yes sir! What will we be driving?"

"You'll be driving the new van in the garage. I've already loaded my suit cases in, all you have to do is get me to the airport within then next three hours, can you do that?"

"Well sir it depends on what kind of an engine you have in the van, is it a six or a V-8"

"It's a big ole hulking turbocharged V-8 diesel racing engine son and it will blow anything off the road as you will soon find out."

"Yes sir! very good sir, do I have your permission to go Ms. Greta?"

"Yes of course you have, this man owns everything around here, he's the real boss."

Norman followed Sol to the freight elevator that took them to the basement. Sol pointed out the van was and tossed him the keys in the air. "Here you go son, catch, let's go!"

Norman caught them in the air, got in the van, turned the key and watched the instrument panel come to life and heard the guttural growl of the powerful diesel engine.

"Every drive a big turbocharged diesel my boy?"

"Sure, I've driven diesels before but not one with a turbocharger."

"Just wait until we're on the interstate, you can punch it then and get the feel of it, just don't get us any tickets, alright?"

Soon they were hurtling east towards the City of New York. The young man had never felt so much power even with a big V-8 gasoline engine. He saw the lighter side of Sol, the kinder side.

"Wow this sure is some rig sir, may I ask what I should call you sir besides sir?"

"You may call me Mr. Devine if you'd rather, that is my given name."

"Thank you Mr. Devine, I like that a lot more."

They made the airport with thirty minutes to spare.

"Help me with my luggage won't you, I'll get a sky cap to help me into the airport and get my bags to the plane. I'll call you when I'm ready to come back and you can pick me up with this please. Hang on to those keys; you just might be my chauffer for a while."

Young Norman puffed out his chest; he was driving a real live millionaire around as it was for now and he knew that from what Greta had said from time to time. Soon Norman was on his way back to the store behind the wheel of the fastest automobile, truck or van he'd ever driven, he couldn't believe the power and pickup the huge van had, he was literally flying back to Poughkeepsie.

Before long Sol was also flying but in the opposite direction to California. While on the plane Sol began to think about BJ and how long before he'd be out of school for the summer. He missed the boy, he really missed him.

CHAPTER - 39

Several weeks went by and the FBI was no closer to solving this case than before. Agent Jefferies had been working alone day and night piecing things together, tying up loose ends and looking for anything in common. No one had seen Agent Marlowe for the better part of a month or more, no one had time to pay attention about her missing, they were all focused on the wall map and number of pins that increased almost daily right along side of the others.

One day Dick's phone rang and it was the Director, he asked him to come up to his office right away. Dick went upstairs not knowing what to expect, it had been weeks since he'd seen the Director so he had no idea what might be up. He walked in, greeted the Director's Secretary and she picked up the phone and called to say that Dick had arrived. Several minutes passed when she finally told him to go on in. He was astonished to see Agent Marlowe was sitting in front of the Director's desk, her head hanging down seemingly staring at the floor.

"You called me sir?"

"Yes Dick sit down please, we have some fence mending to do. As you can see Agent Marlowe, scratch that, Miss Marlowe is currently here wondering if she still has a job or not and I told her that it was up to you. I told her about our talk and how I recommended that she be fired for the fiasco she caused with my secretary which you knew nothing about."

"I understand sir, but I feel that its up to Miss Marlowe whether or not she is reinstated as an Agent, does she understand that as well sir?"

"Yes, in a way she does. As I told you I would give her one last chance and that was to talk with and work with Dr. Joyce Brothers and that was my part in all of this. I have the report here from Dr. Brothers and it is a lengthy one. You don't want to know what's in it but it is a scathing report. It will be up to you and me if I reinstate her because I ultimately have the last say and I'm telling you up front that if you decide to take her back on as an Agent she will have a six months probation, one slip up and she's gone for good, end of story. Miss Marlowe, are you getting all of this?" asked the Director.

"Yes sir, I have to behave myself and not run off at the mouth anymore." She continued looking at the floor, she didn't want to or feel the need to make eye contact with the Director.

"There's more Miss Marlowe, we already discussed it so get busy and I mean right now!"

Dick could tell that the Director was irate because his face was red and the veins on it were standing out turning blue in color.

"Go on Miss Marlowe get on with it, Dr. Brothers told you what needed to be done and in front of witnesses!"

"Yes sir, but I've never once apologized to any man so you can't expect me to jump up and down with joy to do it!"

"Get on with it; you owe this man everything including your career, now we've stuck our necks way out for you and you had better appreciate it, now get on with it!!!"

"Agent Jefferies," she cleared her throat, "I made a fool of myself and I ask your forgiveness. The Director filled me in on why you are the way you are and I had no idea you were wealthy beyond compare and did this job because you wanted to make a difference in the world. I had no right whatsoever to act the way I did but there are things in my past I don't ever want to think about again. I am not going to beg you for my job; I only ask that you let me try to make up for all the dumb things I did and said. That's it, end of story. I will not grovel at your feet or anyone else's, so take it anyway you want! I am a person with some really bad baggage and Dr. Brothers has told me to get over it, that it was alienating me from everyone that I came in contact with. So take it or leave it, that's the way it is!"

"Director, did she just try to say she was sorry because I really didn't hear that part?"

"I don't know Dick, I didn't get a word of it, it looked as though she was talking to her feet and not to you or me and I just don't understand what it is she wants."

"Miss Marlowe, when you address someone look them in the eye and not talk to your feet, remember what Dr. Brothers told you about sincerity?"

"What do you want from me?" she growled at them both without looking up.

"You offered to give her job back but it sounds like to me she doesn't really want it Director," Dick said.

"You see that's what's wrong with the two of you, you're both just male chauvinist pigs, that's all there is to it," Jane spouted off loudly finally looking up then glancing at them both.

"Director I think you'd better call Dr Brothers back, its obvious she isn't ready to go back to work, she needs more time."

"I agree Dick, we've made a terrible mistake."

"Oh come on you two what do you want from me?" asked Miss Marlowe.

"A simple I'm sorry would do if you can manage it instead of going into one of your tirades again," said the Director.

"Ooh you men are all alike, you're never satisfied."

"Dick?"

"You're call Director, I'm done with it, she'll never change!"

"Alright, I'll give it one more shot and call her back." He rang for his Secretary to come in and soon she was there.

"Yes sir, what is it?"

"Would you please call Dr. Brothers back and let her know that Miss Marlowe needs more time."

"Yes sir, right away." She went back out front to make the call.

"You two weren't just kidding were you, you're actually going to send me back to that crazy woman." Jane's head was suddenly on a swivel looking at them both.

"That's right, you need more time, two more weeks should do it and this is no joke, we'll give you that much more time, no improvement, no job here or anywhere else ever."

"Alright, I know when I'm licked, where do I sign up for the loony bin."

The Director pushed a button to summon the marines again. They came in right away.

"You weren't fooling were you, the both of you, you just don't like me, either of you."

"That's it, I've heard enough, take her downstairs and out the back please, same routine as the last Lieutenant."

"Yes sir, come along Miss, peacefully this time I hope."

She hung her head and began to cry real tears, they were streaming down her face.

"Please Director, I'll do anything but I can't stand another minute with Dr Brothers."

"Take her downstairs please Lieutenant!" asked the Director sternly.

"Yes sir, right away."

"Oh and when you get to the ground floor, please give this back to her," the Director said quietly. He handed him Jane's I D card with the chain on it she wore around her neck.

"Now get her out of my office, I've heard enough for one day!" the Director added.

She was crying uncontrollably now as she went down the elevator with the Marines at her side. When they got to the ground floor the Lieutenant handed her the I D card and chain.

"Here you are Miss Marlowe. I don't know why the Director said to give this back to you but here it is, not my call, I just follow orders! Good day ma'am."

Jane stood there not knowing what to do. Finally Dick came out of the other elevator.

"What are you doing Jane?"

She looked up at him through her tears and said, "dear God, I don't deserve this but I'll try to make it up to you and the rest as best I can."

"What are you talking about Jane?"

"This you silly brute, my I D card, he gave it back to me so I guess you're stuck with me for a while."

"Yeah, looks that way, go to the ladies room and make yourself presentable you have a lot of catching up to do Agent Marlowe."

CHAPTER - 40

Sol's plane landed in Los Angeles California that afternoon just before five o'-clock. He got off the plane and went to retrieve his bags and then to another level to the rental car companies locations and once again picked out the most non descript car he could that would not call attention to it or to him. He put his bags in the car and headed for the Hotel he had already made reservations for. Finding it he got settled in and phoned his contact to inform him he was in town and that he'd like to meet him over breakfast in the morning to discus the heiress and how much he really knew about the situation. He wanted to know what she looked like and what she drove if she drove her own car at all etc. How many rare books did she have was what he was most interested in.

The next morning they met in the restaurant of the hotel and Sol had told the man to ask for Mr. Steven Shultz's table and he would be shown to where he was sitting. The man was there right on time and was dressed very well to do. This was no bum about town so he would have to handle him with care.

"Good morning Mr. Shultz, my name is Richard Longtree, we spoke by telephone a few days ago."

"Yes that s right, won't you have a seat Richard, have you had breakfast yet?"

"No, I thought perhaps we could eat together and get to know one another a little more."

"That's a grand idea, we can start by your telling me everything you know about this lady and her collection of books."

Richard went on to tell Sol everything he knew about her right down to her values and things that pleased her.

"My goodness you seem to know a lot about this woman, may I ask how come you seem to know her so well?"

"Certainly, she is my first cousin on my father's side and we're reasonably good friends. I will take you to meet her then I will discreetly leave and let the two of you get acquainted for a while then you can ask about the books. I have seen some of the collection but many of the books are still boxed up from where her late husband recently acquired them. Its an extensive collection and she doesn't know whether to sell them or donate them to a museum. I suggested she should talk to you first that you were an avid collector and fine conservator of the best of rare books and that you would know how best to dispose of them and trust me, she doesn't need the money from the sale and there are hundreds of them."

They both had Eggs Benedict, sausage links, wheat toast, coffee and orange juice.

"Well that was a great meal Richard, is Longtree your real name?"

"No it isn't, it's one of the alias's I use."

"Well how about that, my name isn't Steven Shultz for obvious reasons. If people knew my real name I'd have to drive them away with a club or something."

"Yes I gathered that when I called your store's number, the lady who answered was very vague when I asked questions about you," answered Richard. "Isn't this interesting, both of us are afraid to give our real names out in public, they can be an awful bore sometimes you know. Before we conclude our business you will know my true identity and by the way don't even think about paying me off with money. I'm so filthy rich you see that I don't need the money, but ah, it's the adventure and excitement in my life now that I now crave."

"Well wouldn't you know it, so do I, it seems as though we have the same interests at heart. Well what do you say I pay the bill and we take a ride in your car or mine so you can point out to me where she lives so I can get an idea of what to wear when I see her for the first time. Tell me does she like the sophisticated type or the more down to earth manly type. I'd like to make a good first impression you see, by the way I'm driving a rental car."

"Well then if you don't mind we'll take mine, I'm here with my Chauffeur and my car. I'm afraid it does draw a lot of attention but the windows are tinted real dark so they can't tell who is in the car. May I suggest you allow me to drop you off for the first meeting and pick you up then you can decide if you need to rent a more fancy car. She undoubtedly will want to have you to dinner because that is how she usually transacts all of her business and she will want to use her limousine as well if she decides to go out to dine with you. You will still need a nicer car to drive up in and someone will take your keys from you and park your car while you are there. She will get a report on what you are driving even if she doesn't see your car so she will know how well heeled you really are. You don't need to rent a stretch limo, a Rolls Royce rental would be best or maybe a Bentley. I can hook you up with a reputable automobile Rental Agency that won't steal you blind for a few days worth of driving around in one of their cars."

"I can assure you Richard that if I need a car I can buy the best there is several times over without batting an eye but I am a frugal man and I put everything I can back into my business. Sometimes I have to pay millions of dollars for a really large collection and I pay in cold hard cash or in gold or silver if that is what the party wants, it is of no consequence to me."

"I feel better already because my cousin will worm it out of you anyway but don't be afraid of her, she means well she just doesn't want to get screwed in the process of a sale. She doesn't like it when someone takes advantage of her. Trust me, she is a very smart woman. If you're ready to go, then I am as well?" Richard reached into his pocket and pressed a small button on what looked like a miniature garage door opener as small as a book of matches. They walked out in front of the Hotel and a long maroon colored stretch limo pulled up to where they were standing. A man got out and came around and opened the door to let the men into the very back seat. Richard picked up a two way phone form the center of the seat in front on him and spoke into it quietly. "George, take us past my cousin Lorelei's place if you please." The car pulled away from the curb and they were on their way.

"Tell me Richard, is there anything more personal that you can tell me, like the kind of flowers she likes, the kind of perfume, candy or anything else you can think of."

"All in good time my friend, we will spend the day together and I'll fill in all the blanks."

They drove all around Los Angles and the surrounding country side so that Sol could get the basic lay of the land and find landmarks that he could recognize to find his own way to his cousin's place. They had a delightful time together feeling each other out and finding many similarities about themselves. They got on so well that before they knew it, it was suppertime so they ate together once again. Now remember you will follow my car tomorrow to my cousin's place and I will introduce the two of you and then you're on your own, here is my private number that will find me wherever I may be if you have a problem."

"Thank you but I still don't understand what you expect from me in return for the favor."

"We'll have time to discuss that before you depart back to New York State, it is a trivial thing, no monetary value whatsoever. Well here we are back at your Hotel, now remember to call this number I gave you and a Bentley will be parked out in front waiting for you with a driver, cash is the name of the game, everything under the table."

"Yeah, that's my kind of game alright."

They parted at the Hotel and Sol went upstairs to his room to get some rest, he was tired from riding all over town and being shown this place and that and he was just plain bored all at the same time. He had to come up with a new plan. He hadn't counted on having a personal associate of any kind along the way. But there it was and he was apparently stuck with Richard, at least for the time being.

CHAPTER - 41

Jane was having a hard time adjusting to her new life of not bitching about men all the time. Dr Brothers told her it would take time to heal the wounds of incest and rape but that she needed to put it all behind her and find a good man to lean on. The question was who would be that man? The logical answer was Dick Jefferies but dating among Agents was forbidden by the Director so maybe she could talk to him more like brother and sister. All she knew for now was that it was fence mending time. This was on her mind all the time now due to the close contact of them working together on a daily basis. She was going to need one or two days a week off to give time so as to recoup her battered mind, that's what the Doctor had ordered. She had so many things going on in her head that she was finding it difficult to focus on the business at hand, connecting the Book Store Sales to murder and proving it beyond any doubt. They had already proved that the Professor's death was murder, now they had to find others and put it all into perspective. Six people were now working in two person teams poring over files every day now concentrating on finding the smoking gun. They did have one thing going in their favor, some of the deaths had autopsies done that were definitive, heart attack or stroke followed by a shutdown of all internal organs resulting in the death. The autopsies that they were mostly concerned with were, Cause of Death undetermined, those got an immediate red flag.

All in all after a total of six months they had seventeen cases to look at for a second time. No two were in the same state and were scattered all over the United States. Agents Jefferies and Marlowe would do almost all of the field work because Jefferies had a sense about him that smelled trouble when others didn't see it or sense it. Just like in the Professor's case it was Jefferies who smelled a rat and found it.

They drove to Decatur Illinois to investigate a Book Store called The Book Salon LTD. It was a non descript type building so the store was hard to find in a huge strip mall where every store appeared to be a cookie cutter in style shape and color, one had to read the names on the windows, a small sign over each covered doorway and the street number in small numbers above each front door. They finally arrived and checked it out by getting the Mall's Manager to let them in so they could look around and get a feel for what used to be there. All of the shelving along the three walls had been removed, all the book display areas with isles between them had been removed and the store was stripped clean so they asked questions of the Mall Manager.

"Miss, could you tell us please who removed the interior of this store, usually all of the shelving stays in the Store until a new tenant is found, isn't that right?"

"Yes Mr. Jefferies but I happened to be here on site while the books were being loaded into a moving truck and the man in charge told them to take everything right down to the curtains and curtain rods that were in the windows. The man who bought the contents left nothing behind which said to me he either already has a store and needed more shelving or he is going to open one somewhere and needs the shelving for that."

"Uh huh, so the man stripped the whole place?"

"Yes sir, that's right."

"Tell me is there a break room, storage room, receiving room or anything like that here?"

"Yes, please follow me, its cleverly concealed behind this back wall where the mirror is. There are three small rooms back there and a restroom that is unisex with disabled access."

"May we have a look back there?"

"Of course, I haven't been back there since the sale." They walked the length of the slightly narrow store to the mirrored back wall. "The checkout counter used to be right here," and she pointed to the floor where they could see that an L shaped counter used to sit there due to the lines of dirt and dust. She walked up to the eight foot wide set of mirrors and pressed against the outside of one of the mirrors. "This mirror has a magnetic strip along here," which she pointed out. "By pressing lightly at this point you release the magnetic catch a lot like a magnetic kitchen cabinet door and it pulls out towards you and then you can get into the back of the store. The owner designed it like this to stop people from coming in to the use the restroom or snooping around where they shouldn't be. Oh my, would you look at this, no one has been back here, everything is the same as the last time I saw it. I guess Frank, the owner, forgot to tell the buyer about the rooms back here." There were several boxes of new books that had been received but never put out on the shelves.

"Can you tell when these shipments arrived here, was it before or after the owner died?," asked Agent Jefferies.

She checked three or four boxes that were clearly marked to whom and from where and the date of shipping was on there but not the date received.

"No I'm sorry there's no telling unless we can find the bill of lading."

"They went into another room and found a small desk in there along with two chairs.

"Do you want me to look in there Mr. Jefferies?"

"No, let Miss Marlowe and I have a look, we know what we're looking for and its more than a bill of lading, we need the owner's phone records, notes or phone messages as well." They each took one side of the desk and they wore white cotton gloves and were careful not to smudge any possible prints. They each found several things that the buyer would have never left behind. There were several phone messages in the top right hand drawer that Dick found. On the other side in the top left drawer was an appointment book that read like a diary of sorts.

"Bingo Dick, appointment book up to the last date he was alive. Too bad we don't have a bigger car we could take the whole desk back to Washington and go through it"

"Miss, I hate to ask you but would you possibly have a couple of empty boxes somewhere that we could put the contents of the desk into?"

"No but I have an excellent idea, right here in the Mall there is an Office Supply Store, why not go in and buy some manuscript boxes which are letter size and not very deep, you could put the contents of each drawer into each box and mark them however you wish."

"That's a great idea, Agent Marlowe, would you go with this nice lady and get some of those boxes? We'll need, one, two, three, four, five boxes total. Hopefully they come in sets of six. Oh and don't forget the receipt so we can get reimbursed."

"Uh, Agent Jefferies, do you have any spare cash on you, all I have is plastic with me, no sense in putting it on plastic when they don't cost very much?"

"Sure, here's a twenty, that should cover it, won't it Miss?"

"Oh yes they don't cost very much," answered the manager.

"One more thing Agent Jefferies, how about a black marker to mark the boxes with, I don't have one with me, how about you?"

"No Agent Marlowe I didn't bring one of them either, go ahead and pick up whatever you need, there should be enough cash for that. Uh, wait a minute." He reached back into his pocket and grabbed another twenty dollar bill and handed it to her. "Let's not take any chances, here's another twenty, maybe you should get a roll of shipping tape and some address size labels, we'll have to carry this all back to the Office."

"Right, we'll be back soon." She knew he wanted to be alone there without the manager looking over his shoulder. The two women strolled out and headed back down the long row of stores. The Office Supply Store was the biggest store in there taking up the entire south end of the L shaped Mall.

"That's funny Miss we drove right past there and didn't even see this store," Jane said.

"Yes ma'am, you have to look at the huge Marquis Sign in front and then look for the store you want."

"Ah, that's different." They walked into the store and Jane did her best to stall the manager as long as she could without being too obvious but the lady knew her way around the store and they were in and out in a few minutes with everything Jane could think of. She bought clear shipping tape to seal the boxes and labels to put their initials on them for identification back in Washington for when they got back to work.

When they got back to the store they were both shocked at what greeted them. Agent Jefferies had his suit jacket off and was laying on the floor beneath the desk on his back.

"What in the world Agent Jefferies?"

"Sorry, but you know how things get lost in a desk sometimes. They fall down behind other things, I had to have a look."

"Did you find anything Agent Jefferies?" asked Agent Marlowe.

"Nope, clean as a whistle down here, I've never seen a desk this neat before."

What he was actually telling Miss Marlowe was that he had indeed found something and she needed to get the manager out front for a minute while he removed whatever it was that he had found. Agent Marlowe asked the manager to come back out front for a minute so she could talk to her.

"Ma'am, could you tell me anything personal about the habits of the man who used to lease this space, like was he a drinker, womanizer or anything like that?"

"No Miss Marlowe, he was a married man and devoted to his family, he went to church every Sunday with his wife. I do know however the reason he sold the Store's contents. I probably shouldn't tell you this but in his Ad that he placed in his trade papers as he called them, he put, 'selling out to the walls due to illness.' He was in perfect health but his wife has breast cancer and is dying, there's nothing that can be done for her. The cancer has spread throughout almost every organ in her body. He was getting strapped financially and had borrowed every dime he could to pay for her treatment and medical bills."

Immediately a red flag went up inside Jane's head. He wasn't ill like they thought, it was his wife, he wasn't dying she was. They kept talking and the more they talked the more suspicious Jane became. There was no autopsy done on the man because he accidentally fell down a flight of stairs and broke his neck in public. Several people saw him falling but didn't see anyone near him that may have tripped him other than a little old frail looking man who was holding onto the railing himself so he wouldn't fall. The police said it was an open and shut case. They never got the old man's name, just a couple of people were talked too and no one saw anything suspicious at the time.

In a few minutes Dick called out, "Agent Marlowe, could you give me a hand please?"

The two women went back into the office where he was and he was sitting on the small desk chair, his white shirt was filthy from squirming around on the floor.

"I'm ready to box things up so we can take them back to the Office with us, that is if its alright with the Manager."

"I'll watch while the two of you do your thing, I doubt that there's anything of value in the desk that his family would want so go ahead, I'll stay out of your way and let you work."

The two of them went to work cleaning out each drawer and putting the contents in the corresponding boxes as they marked them as to which drawer they came from. A little over a half an hour went by when they finished cleaning out the desk.

"Agent Marlowe if you would stand by here for a minute or so, I'll go outside and see if I can park our car closer to the building so that we can load up the trunk with these boxes?"

He disappeared for a few minutes and soon he was back. "Agent Marlowe if you'll stay with the car I'll bring the boxes out."

She went outside followed by the still curious manager who wanted to watch. Jane opened the trunk and the manager was stunned when she saw all the guns in the trunk.

"My word, do the two of you need all those guns and know how to use them?"

"Yes ma'am, every Agent in the FBI has to know how to use certain weapons, both Agent Jefferies and I are experts when it comes to weapons of any kind."

Pretty soon Dick was coming out with a stack of four boxes.

"Where's the last box Agent Jefferies?"

"Still inside I've got to go back and get it and my suit jacket, I'll be back shortly."

"Are your jobs that dangerous that you need all of those guns Miss Marlowe?"

"Yes, a few years ago there was a huge shoot out, Dick was shot four times, another Agent was killed, Dick's partner had his leg shot off and six bad guys were killed in the process."

"I think I remember that shootout, it said that the Agents were outnumbered and outgunned at the time."

"Yes that's the one, every since then the FBI has increased the fire power available to certain Agents, we happen to be two of them. Also Dick lost his wife a few years ago, she took a bullet to the heart in botched robbery attempt in a grocery store. It took him a long time to get over the guilt of why her and not him. He and I share a tie when it comes to accuracy on the gun range. The Director had a talk with us several months back and sent us out together as a team and well, here we are."

"I had no idea your jobs were so dangerous Miss Marlowe."

"Well we do have a lot of down time, we aren't always in the field like we are today, when we get back we have to sift through every piece of paper and see what we can determine about the man's death who sold the store. By the way I understand that his store manger also lost her life the day after he died."

"Yes she was killed crossing the street by a big white van with out of state plates."

"You don't say, they never found the van did they?"

"No, they said someone got the license plate number but the plates were stolen from a Funeral Home van that was all black."

"My you do have a memory for detail don't you?"

"You have to, when managing a Mall of this size."

"Yes I see what you mean." She looked around to take in the entire size of the Mall. "This far end to the north, is that also part of the Mall?"

"Yes the Grocery Store is one of our anchor stores, the Office Supply is another one of our anchors, that's what pulls the customers into the Mall, we do quite well actually."

Finally Dick came out with his suit jacket over his arm and the last box. He put it in the trunk and closed the trunk lid because he didn't want the manager looking in there anymore.

"Well Agent Marlowe, we'd better be going."

"Miss, can we come back later today or tomorrow if we need to?"

"Yes of course, you know where my office is, just stop by and I'll let you take the key, if you remove anything just let me know so I can see it in case a family member asks questions, then I can tell them that the FBI has it but will give it back as soon as they can, is that alright?"

"No I'm afraid not, if we find what we expect this could end of in a Court of Law and there could be a trial, so it could be years before we can release any of the things we take but they will get it back one day, I promise."

"Well that's good enough for me because I didn't see one thing that the children could possibly want but in case an Attorney for the family asks I'll be able to tell him something."

"Agent Marlowe lets give her our cards so we can be contacted in case there is a question about the property we've confiscated."

"I think that's a good idea, here you are ma'am, here's our cards."

"Thank you both, I've never met real FBI people before, you have been most gracious, thank you both."

"Yes ma'am, we thank you for your help as well. Goodbye for now, we're staying in town for a while, we may be back in touch with you."

The two agents headed back to their Hotel where they could compare notes without fear of someone looking over their shoulders and asking lots of questions.

CHAPTER - 42

In LA Sol got up the next morning, went downstairs and had breakfast alone. He had a simple breakfast of eggs over easy, bacon, fried potatoes, wheat toast, coffee and tomato juice. It gave him time to think some more about his meeting with the heiress at 10:30 this morning. He decided on a pair elevated shoes for the day, his brown wig cut short and natural looking and blue colored eye contact lenses to change the color of his eyes from brown to blue, a deep, deep, blue. His shoes would make him appear to be five ten inches tall and his makeup would take his now sixty three years of age and make him look a youthful forty five to fifty years old. Maybe I should add a little grey to the sides of the wig to make it more distinguished looking he was thinking. He couldn't over do the makeup, she was a well traveled woman herself and obviously used makeup so she would see right through his facade. He finished reading the LA Times, set it down, picked up his check and headed for the cashier to pay for his meal.

"How was everything today sir?"

"Just fine, thank you." He was short and curt but not rude, he wanted to give the appearance of a man here on a business trip who was preoccupied and carried it off very well. After all he was actually here on business but what kind even he wasn't sure of after meeting his contact yesterday.

He went upstairs to his room to change and get ready to leave. He dressed in his best suit for the height and weight he would portray and put on his wig after touching up the sides of it just a bit, put in his contact lenses and was ready to leave. He was a half an hour early because he wanted to stop and get a bouquet of roses to give the lady of the house where he was headed. The first impression had to be right. He went to the concierge desk and asked to use the phone and he was cheerfully allowed to do so.

"May I get your car for you sir?"

"No thank you, my chauffer is waiting outside for me, I'll just give him a ring to let him know I'm ready to leave.

He had no idea who was bringing him the car only that it might be a Bentley. He made the call and walked towards the front door. A beautiful white classic Bentley came along side the curb. A young woman got out dressed similar to a male chauffeur and opened the back door for him. He looked to his left and saw his friend's limo pulled to the curb a few car lengths away. He gratefully got into the back seat, his friend had seen to everything. On the seat were a dozen long stemmed red roses they had talked about. Between he and the front seat was bullet proof glass and two phones, One was marked driver and one marked outside line. Before he hardly got situated the outside phone line rang. He picked it up and wasn't surprised when his friend's voice came on the line.

"Good morning Steven, did you sleep well last night?"

"Yes as a matter of fact I did."

"How do you like the touch of the female chauffeur I picked out for you?"

"I thought the deal was that I would drive myself around."

"Nonsense live a little, you have got to impress my cousin. The automobile you're sitting in belonged to a famous movie star and is now in the stables of my friend's classic automobile rental business. You don't have to pay for a thing, I've taken care of it all. I want you to look the part we both know you are playing so we can cut the crap and get down to business. I want to see my cousin happy and for her to get rid of those ridiculous books she has all over the house. You know that I have an ulterior motive and once you have made the deal to buy the books you and I will sit down and get some other things done. I may not even let you pay for the car and so forth if things go the way I plan, we should be all done within a week."

"It doesn't take me that long to make a book deal, I'm usually all done in a matter of hours. I either pick up the books myself or I send a moving company truck to pick them up if it is too big of a load for me to carry. I have sometimes purchased only one or two books from people because they were all I wanted. What makes this deal so different?"

"It's the actual size of the collection as you will see, you'll need one or two trucks when you see what she has. The difficulty comes from her distrust of men in general, me included. We don't see eye to eye on anything as you'll soon see. Just go along with any of her whims, you'll know when it's time to strike the book deal and there may be no deal at all if she likes you, she may just give you the entire collection for little to nothing, it all depends on your charms etcetera."

"It's the etcetera that worries me?"

"You'll have to be patient with us both, just let things happen, you won't be disappointed I promise. You have my direct number and I live just a few houses away up the hill from her place so I'll never be far away. Now I've given your driver specific information about where she is going and what she is supposed to do. You can dismiss her anytime you like and tell her when to be back and she will do it. She's a Professional Driver who grew up here in LA and knows every street. She will take you directly to the house so I won't have to follow. All you have to do is ring the door bell and give her the same name you gave me and she will invite you in. I have already briefed her that you're an International representative of Books and their Historical Restoration and Preservation, I believe that is correct isn't it?"

"Right on the money to be exact. My partner and I have several patents for our restoration techniques and are in high demand for our services from around the world."

"That's what has me all excited you know, I told you we'd be great friends. Go on with you now, just pick up the other phone and tell your driver you're ready to leave, she will get you there at exactly 10:30 not a minute before or after. By the way her name is Sissy."

"Thank you Richard, I'm ready to get on with this whole charade."

"Yippy!" came the happy childlike reply over the phone from his friend behind him.

Sol hung it up wondering what he had gotten himself into, this sounds like a bunch of hooey and foolishness he thought to himself. The man he was dealing with didn't sound all that serious to me when it comes to running the Business of a Book Store. He picked up the other phone and said quietly; "I'm ready when you are my dear."

She raised her black gloved right hand in a kind of off handed salute to let him know that she had heard him, she didn't respond and he wondered about that. The car pulled away ever so smoothly and quietly from the curb and they were on their way.

Inside the Hotel the concierge had taken it all in. He was thinking to himself, I wonder who he is to have a car like that waiting for him day and night with a woman at the wheel, that he'd never seen before. Most of the Chauffeurs he had seen were black men dressed to the nines. This woman was well built, long flowing blond hair over her shoulders like a Hollywood starlet, a discreet short skirt and dressed all in black. What a great looker she was is all he could think about and what a very lucky man he was.

Sol was finally on his way to meet the woman he had come to see and had no idea what to expect. All of the arrangements had been made by his new friend and he didn't even know the other lady's name he was about to meet. At exactly 10:29 she drove up in front a beautiful white mansion with huge pillars out front, he thought for a minute he was at the White House in Washington. The car stopped and a footman came out to see to the car and was waved off by his driver. She opened the door for Sol mounted the steps to the porch and he rang the door bell at the exact appointed time. A butler answered the door. The stuffed shirt ram rod straight kind who sounded very British. "Yes sir, you rang?"

"Yes, Mr. Schultz to see the lady of the house, I believe I am expected."

The butler looked him over slightly trying not to be overly suspicious of the stranger.

CHAPTER - 43

Agents Jefferies and Marlowe arrived back at their Motel to look over what they had taken from the closed Book Store. They went into Dick's room taking the diary with them.

"Dick, I have to ask, what did you find beneath the man's desk?"

"I don't really know. There was an envelope taped to the bottom of the desk and its in my suit jacket inside pocket. I didn't have time to look at the contents, I only had time to remove the the tape from it and put it away while the two of you were out of the room for a few minutes. Look over his diary or appointment book and I'll go outside and get my jacket out of the car."

She opened the small book and began to look at the way it was written. There were all kinds of entries, when he went to the bank, who had appointments with him the time and the date and shipment received dates for some reason. Apparently he didn't ship any books as there were no entries for those. She was about to skip ahead to the end of the entries when Dick came in with the envelope.

He sat down next to Jane at the small desk in the room where there were two comfortable chairs and then a little way from there was a round table and four chairs but they chose the desk because the light was better there. Dick opened the envelope. "Well Jane let's see what the man was hiding." He pulled out two sheets of letter size paper and began to study them.

"Can you see this Jane, look at it and what it says, 'I don't trust the man who purchased my store, he paid for everything in cash he had brought with him in a suitcase. It was the exact amount we had agreed on two days earlier and he encouraged me to take it to the bank and deposit it right away, he said he would mind the store for a few minutes. When I returned things looked normal. I have taped this envelope to the underside of my desk in case something unforeseen happens to me. I have not let him back here into these rooms and I won't until I know all is secure then I'll show him what's back here to see if there is anything else he may want as he is welcome to it all. For some reason I just don't feel just right. When I picked up my checkbook from under the front counter I noticed that two or three checks seemed to be missing. I could have made a mistake but I don't think so. It stops there before he finished it. Let's find out when he died and when the store was cleaned out. There's a chance we may have something here finally. You know it may sound like I'm on fishing expedition but I'm wondering. Do you have the mall manager's phone number handy, I'd like to ask her about the day he died and the day the place was cleaned out."

"No problem, I'll call her right now, I have her business number right here." Jane made the call and began to write things down on a piece of Motel Room Stationary. "Uh huh, thank you, you have been a big help."

"Well Dick you were right about fishing, I think you just caught a big one. She remembers the buyer being there on a Friday and the owner going to the Bank all excited like. He died Saturday night at a shopping mall when he was using the stairs, it was an old building that had a couple of elevators but they weren't all that reliable and that's why he used the stairs. She said the man that bought the place was here all day Monday and most of the day Tuesday supervising the packing of the books in boxes and the loading of the moving truck, it was a big tractor trailer set up she said. After he had removed everything he gave her back the keys, said thank you and left."

"We need the man's checking account number so we can see what transactions had been made the day after his death if any. I wonder if there's a chance he took the checkbook home with him for safe keeping or something. It certainly wasn't in his desk which I find very strange, if he was murdered he could also have left his checkbook under the counter like the note said. Would you mind terribly calling the manager back and seeing if we can go by his house and see if the checkbook is there or not I really need the account number to save time.?" Asked Dick.

"Sure, no problem, I'll call her right back."

"Oh and ask her if there is a chance if there is a next of kin of his in the area just in case we hit a pot hole?"

"Anything else Dick?"

"No that's all I can think of unless you have something you'd like to add."

"If I think of something I'll ask her while I'm on the phone."

She dialed the manager back and asked her the questions and was writing something down on paper again. "Dick, you're not going to like this, she said we could go by the house and see the wife but that she is in the care of Hospice since her husband died. She has given up on living, stopped eating and everything. She said we should probably hurry and that there were no next of kin on either side she was aware of, but there may be some children somewhere, his Attorney handled it all."

"Right, we had better ask about a Will and see if we can get our hands on a copy as well. I guess we'd better get going then, did you get directions to her house?"

"Right here Dick and I agree that we'd better go right now, everything else can wait."

The two of them left in a hurry, got into the car and headed for her house using the directions Jane had. This was a visit neither of them relished in making.

In another half an hour they pulled into a driveway of a well maintained modest house. The shrubs were well trimmed and in good condition and the lawn had recently been mowed and there was only one car in the driveway and they thought that it probably belonged to the Hospice worker. They went up onto a spacious front porch of the quaint house and rang the door bell. A nice looking middle aged lady answered the door. "Yes, can I help you?"

Jane handled the introductions as delicate as she could without telling her about the reason for their visit. "Would it be possible to talk to the lady of the house just for a minute or so, we're just tying up some loose ends on an ongoing investigation that does not involve her or her husband."

"Well you can try to talk to her but you'd better ask them by yourself, she is devastated that her husband is gone and very despondent and may not want to talk to you."

"Would you kindly show me the way please ma'am?"

"Sure right this way, we have a hospital bed in the dining room set up for her where she can see her flower garden from the windows there."

Jane followed the Hospice worker and Dick stayed near the door and waited. When the worker returned to where he was he decided to ask her some questions that she may know the answers to.

"Please ma'am, you may be able to help us a little as well. We're looking into the activities of the man who bought their Book Store, did you ever happen to see him?"

"No, we have a different girl here now and then so we can all have a day off. This lady has been under the Hospice care for two weeks now, she hasn't long to live. Her husband sold the store to pay off her medical bills."

"Oh that is too bad, they might have been able to help out otherwise."

They talked about things in general until Jane came back almost in tears, her eyes were very red. "We'd better go now Dick, I have all the information we need."

"What about the checkbook or account number?"

"Oh, I almost forgot, she said its in the top right hand drawer of his desk in his den. She said we could take it, where she is going she won't need it." She began to sob lightly, "she is such a wonderful woman, it is so sad."

"Where's the den Jane?"

"Oh its back this way, she told me to go ahead and take whatever I needed, she was so sweet and only fifty five years old."

They went past the dining room and Jane steered Dick to the den's door which was open. They went in and saw the desk right away.

"Here it is Jane." Dick pulled the checkbook out and read the last entry, six hundred and thirty thousand dollars deposited and that brought the balance up to just over $631,542.00 with what the checkbook said was a transfer from savings to checking. There were no checks written or deposits made past the date he died. Dick went though the checkbook thoroughly and found three checks missing from different pages in the huge business type checkbook with three checks to a page. He also saw the note in the front where either he or his wife could sign checks.

"Well Jane its all there just as I feared, I'm betting that the checkbook balance is near zero or soon will be. Something has been gnawing at my insides and that's it. After the sale he kills the owner, steals a few checks then empties the balance in the checkbook by writing checks back to himself or maybe a shell company, either one could be happening as we speak. Let's head to their Bank right now, maybe we can stop this guy from stealing the balance of the money."

They arrived at the bank and found the Manager who was only too willing to help due to the circumstances as he knew both the depositor's. "Well there you are, the account has been closed. There's the date, Tuesday two weeks ago it was closed in his own handwriting."

"Impossible, the man had been dead for more than a week when that was signed."

"I can't help it, that's his signature, there's no doubt in my mind."

"May I have copies of his hand writing to take back with us for analysis in our own lab?"

"Sure, no problem, the account is dead for all intent and purposes. How far back do you want me to go in his records?"

"Six months of activity should be enough, oh and I'd like a sample of his wife's handwriting as well if you can find it. We already saw her; she isn't very well right now."

"Yes I know, the bank was to handle the estate after they both were gone according to their Attorney and what they put in the Will."

"Yes and that's our next stop; we want a copy of the Will."

"You know he doesn't have to give you one if he doesn't want to."

"He'll be glad to give us one or face an investigation by the FBI and the IRS."

"I'd say anyone would cooperate with that hanging over their heads. No one would want that, even me and I'm squeaky clean when it comes to numbers and money, I have to be or the Fed. would close the Bank."

"You're right about that, mind if we have a seat while you find the information for us?"

"No, go right ahead sit anywhere you like, it may take a few minutes but I'll tell the girls to put a rush on it." Twenty minutes went by and they had all they needed. The banker had the girls put the paperwork in a large empty box that had once held copy paper.

"Good day to you sir and thank you," said Dick.

"I don't know what you're really looking for but good luck and goodbye."

They put the box in the trunk and headed for the Attorneys Office they had directions to already. They got the copy of the Will with little problem once they explained the facts to him about a possible Federal Investigation. Jane read it on the way back to the Motel. "Wow, these must have been nice church going people, they left the house to the church and all cash to the Library here in town. Dick, I just thought of something, there's quite a lot of brand new books and furniture and other items the Library might be able to use, do you think we ought to direct the Mall Manager to give all of it to the Library, we have all we need and she'll need to rent the space out again."

"I like that idea Jane, I wonder if the Attorney got paid up front to execute the Will for the couple?"

"Good question Dick but not our problem, we've got a mole hill slowly becoming a mountain right here in our own hands."

"Give the lady at the Mall another call if you don't mind Jane and let her know she should call the Attorney and request disposition of the things in the store that are still there."

"Okay I can do that, she and I have become rather friendly today."

They were quiet on the ride back to the Motel. They had made up their minds to head back to Washington and go over the rest of the things they had including the diary or address book. They wanted the name of the buyer of the Book Store and any other information they might be able to find making a trail to his door. They really wanted him badly for the heartlessness of what he had just done to these fine people, one who was already dead and one who soon would be plus the firsthand witness information they had regarding the buyer of the store from the Mall's Manager.

CHAPTER - 44

"Follow me please," the Butler at the Wynn Mansion gestured with his right hand and closed the door once Sol was inside. The butler was dressed formally complete with black tails, a white shirt and black bow tie and sported white gloves. He was a white man with an obvious British accent. They walked a short ways down a hall and he stopped outside of a door that was ajar. "This is the receiving room sir, sit anywhere you would like, Madam will join you shortly." The Butler would formally introduce the two of them as soon as she came downstairs. Sol didn't have to wait long. He had barley sat down on a love seat when the Butler appeared in the doorway and Sol stood up.

"Ms. Lorelei Wynn, Mr. Shultz, Mr. Shultz, Ms. Lorelei Wynn."

She walked into the room with all of the grace of a ballet dancer, very light on her feet. Sol noticed right away that she was an extremely beautiful woman, her eyes flashed with a light similar to the refraction diamonds. Her eyes were a deep blue, very alluring, almost haunting. He was spellbound, she held out her white gloved hand for him to acknowledge or to kiss her hand, her gloves went all the way up to the elbow. He got weak in the knees as he reached out, took her hand in his then lightly kissed the back of her gloved right hand.

"Very pleased to make your acquaintance Ms. Wynn!"

She replied in uninterested dry tone, "charmed, I'm sure."

The butler filled the doorway with his ramrod straight physic as he awaited orders from his employer.

"That will be all Henry; we may wish to have some tea or wine in a little while after I find out what this gentleman wants."

"Why Ms. Wynn, didn't your cousin tell you, I traveled all the way from New York just to see the collection of books your late husband left?"

"Yes of course he did, but you would not be the first man to try and get into this house on a false pretence and my cousin as you call him is a cunning no good uncouth man. He has money to burn and burns all he can. I see that you were brought here in a classic Bentley, obviously appropriated by my cousin as well. He is always trying to cause me trouble; he wants my estate you see, the house and all forty acres. He's extremely jealous of the stable of riding horses I have. I breed and train horses for the elite of California and I get a very good price for them. They are all championship horses from the best stock money can buy. Now then sir, shall we get down to the real purpose of why you are here?"

"Yes of course, but I am not used to having to repeat myself." Sol was irritated at the delay in what he perceived as negotiations for bunch of books he hadn't seen yet.

"Henry! Bring me the file on this man."

The butler reappeared with a sheaf of papers and handed them off to his employer.

"I have all your references right here Mr. Shultz."

She read through them briefly before speaking again. "It seems Mr. Shultz that you and your partner have been very successful in your book selling enterprises. I see here that you have marketed classics to wealthy people all over the world and that you currently hold several patents for your restoration techniques. You seem to be highly motivated but the question still stands, why do you want to see my late husband's collection of books?"

"Why I thought you knew why, I am a collector of fine Literature as well. I own my own Book Store that sells retail to people from all over the country who want the best reading material they can find and I provide it for them. So I must continue to seek out new supplies of books and I was intrigued by the newspaper report regarding your collection. I will not sit here and be interrogated; I came to look at your books and that is all. I may or may not be interested in them and if I am not interested I'll be on a plane out of here this afternoon. If they interest me then we shall get down to negotiations about the price and I can be very generous. So, there you have it, my reason for being here is strictly business!"

"Ah, yes, I see, you are strictly here on business. Do you not find me attractive Mr. Shultz?"

"I find you extremely attractive ma'am, but I do not mix business with pleasures of the flesh."

"Oh, I see, then you would not be interested in having lunch with me today?"

"I didn't say anything about meals, just that I don't mix the affairs of a fine lady such as yourself with business."

"I am having a problem deciphering your meaning of business and pleasure, on one hand you say no while on the other hand you say you might like to have lunch with me, you see I am a little confused."

"Yes I can see how that would confuse you. You see for me the morning is almost gone and it is apparent that we will not be talking business until after lunch, that's the way I read you."

"Very intuitive Mr. Schultz and I doubt very much that it is your real name, I understand the need for an alias now and then in business to keep the wolf from the door so to speak."

"Then we understand one another. How should I address you, in the way of a first name or nickname or Ms. Wynn?"

"My friends all call me Li if that is sufficient for you."

"That's fine with me, Li it is then."

"And you Mr. Schultz or whatever your name is, how shall I address you?"

"Well I'm traveling as you know under an assumed name, for now you can call me either Steven or Steve, whichever suits you. I often use the name in my travels to keep people away that might otherwise recognize my real name and then they would be asking questions, looking for advice and bothering me about things which I have no time for, if you know what I mean."

"Yes, I completely understand what you are saying but before you leave will you reveal your true identity?"

"That all depends on whether or not we do business. We do business and I will tell you my real name before I leave town."

"Very well then I guess we have an understanding of sorts, you will see the collection when I am ready to show it to you and not before and I must tell you that it is huge in size and it is in my way, I'd like to be rid of it as soon as I can."

"Ah," Sol thought a minute, "are we talking a moving truck or tractor trailer size truck?"

"Tractor trailer I think is what will be needed, some of it is in the basement already in boxes, and other's are in still his library. The basement is outfitted with heat and air conditioning to protect his precious books. I believe you could call my ex-husband a hoarder of books, most of which he tried to explain were rare classics, whatever that means. Reading to me is a great waste of time to me don't you see."

"Now that is interesting. A few months ago in Massachusetts I ran into a similar situation with a man who had passed away and I dealt with the grand-daughter, together we found a satisfactory solution where none of his family cared anything about his rare book collection at home or his Book Store all of which I purchased entirely."

"Well enough talk for now, I am a little hungry, I'll order lunch for us and we can take tea and lunch as well out on the porch next to the pool, will that be alright with you?"

"That will be fine Li, I'd like that and fresh air is good for the soul."

They adjourned to the pool area where the huge screened in porch had sliding glass panels that disappeared in wall pockets when not in use. They had soup, salad and a sandwich out in the fresh air where they could look at her lovely gardens and the blue sky reflecting from the surface of the pool which at times was blinding when the sun hit it just right. They discussed all their likes and dislikes over the long lunch getting to know one another a little more. At the very end of the lunch she claimed to be tired and wanted to lie down for a nap.

"You'll have to excuse me Steven, I need to lie down for a while, we'll do dinner here tonight if that is alright with you, say 7:30?"

"That will be fine me Li, till tonight then." He kissed her still gloved hand and the butler was near by and showed him out to his car which was being brought around from somewhere in the back he presumed to pick him up. The female driver got out and opened the door for him and they were off. The phone in the back seat buzzed as they neared the end of the driveway. He picked it up. "Yes, what is it?"

"Where to now sir?," came the squeaky voice over the phone.

"Back to my Hotel I guess, I won't need you again until around 6:30 this evening."

CHAPTER - 45

Back in Washington Agents Jeffries and Marlowe were poring over what they'd brought back from Decatur Illinois. Jane was going over the man's appointment book looking for any clues up to the date of the last entry. All she found was a phone call from a man that was from out of State but it didn't name the State or phone number. It simply said, will arrive at 3:45 P.M. your time, will rent car to drive from the airport to your location. In parentheses it said, (Horace Corbett), all in the store owner's handwriting. Could this Corbett be our smoking gun Agent Marlowe was thinking? She read further on but could find nothing more to go on. The FBI had a huge Computer now and everyone had been plugging in information over the past couple of years including their new team of Agents.

"Find anything yet Agent Marlowe?"

"Yes Agent Jefferies I have a name but no address or phone number but I'm sure the call came from out of State. Do you suppose we could get the man's phone records for the last two months and see if we can match a phone number with a name?"

"Sure, do you want to do it or should I put someone else on it seeing as how we are so busy with this case?"

"I'd appreciate it if someone else could handle the more mundane things at this point. We're finally getting somewhere and I'd hate to lose my concentration over some phone calls."

"Consider it done; I've been able to get us our own private secretary to take over some of those details by bugging the Director."

"For goodness sake don't irritate the man and get him mad at me again!" said Marlowe."

"No chance, you're in solid now, just cool it until your probation is over."

"I hear that and thank you. Did you uncover anything more about the man's death?"

"Nothing I can hang my hat on, just suspicions. I'm sure someone was in a hurry. I did find out he had a really bad back so he didn't carry all those heavy boxes of books up and down the stairs."

"So now we're sure that he was murdered?"

"No, not for sure factually. He had to have had someone working part time for him that came in on a regular basis. I'm afraid all of the employee records were in the counter up in front so we don't have a name to put to anyone, we could contact the man's wife but I don't know if she is still alive or not, I'd hate to have to bother her again. He could have easily have had someone bringing things upstairs for him to work on like a box of books once in a while and the employee could have helped him stock the shelves and put slow movers or sellers back in the basement when he was through with them. I think that's why things were over looked by the killer because he was in a rush to get in and out as fast as he could."

"Yeah, sounds plausible to me as well."

"Keep digging Agent Marlowe, we're close, I can feel it!" They used the rest of the day going through what little they could find but they felt that something was still eluding them.

A few more days went by with no lose ends getting tied together. Then a package came in the overnight mail from the phone company in Decatur Addressed to Agent Marlowe.

"Bingo Agent Jefferies, we have the phone bills we've been waiting for."

"Lets go to our office with them Agent Marlowe, I need to sit down and take something for a headache."

"I've got some aspirin in my purse or do you need something heavy duty?"

"Something heavy duty I'm afraid."

"Did you take time to eat anything today Agent Jefferies?"

"As a matter of fact I don't think so."

"Well no wonder you've got a headache, you need to eat some food for a change, pouring only coffee down your gullet won't help your stomach any either."

"Yes mother hen I know. Come sit down next to me and we can go over them together."

Jane opened the envelope and they started with the last calls. The last one was to his wife at home. The one before that was to a pharmacy probably for her medication or his. A day before that was a call from and unpublished phone number in New York State somewhere. There was an asterisk to the left of the number. They read down, they would need higher authorization to trace the phone number.

"Agent Marlowe, want to flip a coin to see who gets to tell the Director we need help from on high?"

"No! you'd better do it, he's liable to yell at me for the way my hair is fixed."

"Are we chicken today?" Jefferies asked sarcastically but with humor.

"No, just common sense, you're a man he's a man, you know, birds of a feather flock?"

"Now that will do!" he cut her short, "you're going to take it up to him right now or Apologize all over again."

"Got it; will do Sergeant."

"And can the sarcasm."

"You're taking all of the fun out of living you know!" she answered a little frustrated.

"Out now, get on with it!"

"Yes Master." She ran out of there because he'd come off his chair like a bull entering a ring and was chasing her. It was all in good fun but it got things done. In twenty five minutes she was back.

"The Director said he would handle it personally and get back to us as soon as he got an answer. How many drawers left in those boxes Agent Jefferies?"

"Three more to sift through the two bottom file drawers and one single drawer that has very little in it."

"I'll take the little one, you can start on one of the others then I'll take the last one and catch up with you."

"Don't forget to check the back and front of every piece of paper, he may have left us a clue of some kind I hope."

"Roger Dodger that sir, will-co and out."

"And what was that supposed to mean Agent Marlowe?"

"Pilot lingo from World War II Agent Jefferies, we're both flying this desk you know."

"Oh brother what next?" They were just finishing the last drawer together when the phone rang on Dick's desk. They both tried to catch it but Dick let her grab it first.

"You don't say sir, you don't say, that's all? Yes sir I understand, yes sir we will."

"Alright spill it, what did he say?"

"He said that the number is one of the Post Office Rental places where you rent a box with a street address with phone forwarding and your phone call is routed to anywhere in the world and billed to that address."

"So where is it located?"

"Downtown New York City where there are hundreds of them just like that, everyone uses the number as an office phone it seems along with mail boxes. The phone calls go through a router of some kind to the individuals real business phones. I was told that it cuts out of lot of junk or soliciting calls."

"So we're talking a dead end then?"

"Maybe, maybe not, I just don't know."

"I'm not familiar with those things are you?"

"No, my family still uses the old technology, you have a phone, a phone book and an address and they are the same thing in the same place."

"I'm afraid we have hit a brick wall on that lead then."

"What next Agent Jefferies?"

"Back to square one and lots of shoe leather, we do it the hard way."

"Oh my aching back" added Jane.

"Mine too!"

"Hey what about this Horace Corbett, can this computer thing help us out there?"

"We can try it but I'm betting it's an alias for the phony Post Office Street Address and phone number."

"But can't we at least try it and see what happens?"

"Sure, we'll give it a shot, I'll give the name to our new secretary to run through the system, maybe he'll turn out to be someone after all." Jefferies looked up their new secretary and handed her the name and asked her to run it through the new Computer System.

An hour later the Secretary came back with the same slip of paper with the man's name on it. "Sorry Agent Jefferies but the information on this particular name and initials turn out to be a dead man buried in a Cemetery somewhere in Pennsylvania. He died six years ago at the age of 93."

"Wait a minute Agent Marlowe; I'm willing to bet someone has been getting names off tombstones and is using them as aliases."

"You could be right Agent Jefferies!"

CHAPTER - 46

Sol called Sissy, his female driver with the squeaky voice, at precisely 6:45 P.M. to pick him up in front of his Hotel. He walked out front just as she pulled up to the curb. Sissy came around and dutifully opened the door for Sol and he climbed into the gleaming Bentley. The plush red leather seats were welcoming as he sat down and she closed the door. She no sooner had gotten back in herself when Sol was on the car phone.

"Yes sir?"

"Do you know what a gentleman who is calling on a real lady ought to take to her as a small gift?"

"Yes sir, judging from what I was told by our friend the lady can afford anything in the world so I would guess a really nice box of expensive chocolates would be what the lady deserves."

"Would you happen to know where I could buy such a gift?"

"Of course sir, that is part of our service, knowing all the best places to buy special gifts. There is a shop on our way, we can stop there and you can pick out whatever you like."

"Very well, sounds like the right thing to do, would you mind stopping there for me?"

"Yes sir, no problem, consider it done." She pulled the big car away from the curb and Sol could hardly believe they were moving it was that smooth. This was not your standard Bentley; it had been lengthened six feet to allow distance between the driver's cabin and the back seats. There were two large bench seats facing each other and two seats along both sides for extra passengers and a center bar and table where almost everyone could reach it for refreshments. It had a built in refrigerator with a small ice maker. The bar was kept stocked with wine, champagne, expensive imported and domestic beer, whiskey, scotch, gin, rum and vodka.

Along side that rack was a shelf holding several different kinds of mixers including sodas. There were glasses available and a small sink to leave the dirty glasses in and a small built in refuse basket that was hidden in the unit but marked with a refuse sign. There were several built in drink holders that accepted different sizes of glasses, cans or bottles around the interior for the rider's convenience. Sol relaxed as she drove the next couple of miles when suddenly she pulled to the curb in front of a store that had Specialty Gifts written on the large front window. Sol's phone in the back purred, it was his driver.

"We're here sir, just a moment and I'll come around and open the door for you."

He hung up the phone without saying anything. When she opened his door he asked;

"Miss, would you mind picking out a box of chocolates for me, I don't have a clue of what to buy, I don't eat candy as a rule?"

"No sir, I don't mind a bit."

"Can I give you some money Miss?"

"No need sir, we're equipped for these things such as candy and flowers, it gets charged to the car and you pay for it along with the rental."

"My goodness that sounds easy."

"Yes sir, we carry a credit card that is keyed to the automobile we are driving and we make many purchases this way such as gas, car washes and things like that." She closed the door and went inside without a purse or a wallet. He watched as she carefully chose a box of chocolates and reached into a pocket in her uniform and produced a credit card. She paid for the candy, had it wrapped with a bow put on it and came back out. She opened his door and handed him the neatly wrapped box of candy.

"Thank you Miss, this means a lot to me."

"You are most welcome sir, we're only too glad to be of service." She closed the door and they were off again to the Wynn residence. At exactly 7:29 she pulled up in front of the mansion to an extremely smooth stop. She got out and opened his door as she glanced at her watch. "Exactly 7:30 as you requested sir, right on her time schedule."

He got out, thanked her and went to the door with the box of candy beneath his arm. He rang the door bell and the butler must have been watching out the window in anticipation of his arrival because he instantly opened the door and greeted him. "Good evening Mr. Shultz, Ms. Lorelei will be down any moment, won't you please follow me?"

Sol didn't say a word but handed the butler his hat as they walked one behind the other.

Sol knew that he was way out classed but tried not to show it. They went to the same sitting room as before. As he looked around it reminded him of a Doctor's waiting room in a way. He had paid little attention to it before, he'd been too nervous to look around then. It was arranged in a semicircle with chairs and two love seats around the perimeter. There was one large overstuffed high back chair with the back towards the outside wall with high windows where Lorelei could sit and see everyone that was there without turning her body to look around. It was an effective set up he marveled at. This lady has it together he thought to himself. While he was pondering this she entered the room gliding with such grace that he didn't hear her footfalls as she walked. She was wearing a full length evening gown like a person would wear when going out to the theater or to a fancy candle lit dinner. It was black from top to bottom and she wore a large pearl necklace around her neck and a gold bracelet on her left arm. She also was wearing a purple Orchid Corsage pined to her gown which had a deep plunging neckline which revealed her more than ample cleavage between her larger than average sized breasts. She was ravishingly more beautiful than when he had seen her earlier.

"Good evening Steven, I am so glad you have arrived."

"Good evening Li, thank you for inviting me back."

"Would you like to join me in the drawing room?"

"Yes of course, after you." He followed her a few rooms further down the huge hall.

"Here we are;" She glided through a doorway into a room that had the appearance more like a family room rather than a formal receiving room with a full bar and bartender on duty. Sol looked around and guessed that it would hold around twenty to twenty five people comfortably.

"Do you like this room Steven?"

"Yes Li, its a lovely room, so big and roomy." Damn it he thought to himself, how childish to say something dumb like that. She was looking at the package under his arm and he finally realized that she was staring at it.

"For me?" she finally said startling him out of a trance like state.

It jarred Sol's awareness. "This, oh yes this, this is for you." He handed her the smartlywrapped package of chocolates.

"Why thank you Steven, you didn't have to really, it is my pleasure to have you here this evening." She tore the paper off the beautifully wrapped package. "Why Steven, you have done your homework, these are my favorite brand of chocolates.

"Really?" He acted very surprised. "Only the best my dear for my new friend."

"Well said Steven. Why don't we sit over here for a few minutes, dinner will be served at eight o'clock sharp." She led Sol by the hand over to a large fabric covered over stuffed love seat. They sat down and giggled at one another like a little of couple of school kids. "Would you like something to drink Steven?"

"Yes I'd like that, scotch and soda if you please, on the rocks."

She nodded at the bartender and he brought them both the same thing.

"Do you also like Scotch and soda Li?"

"Yes, its my favorite before and after diner drink. Of course right after dinner I like to have a cordial then the Scotch and soda."

"Oh and what kind of cordial do you enjoy most?"

She leaned over and whispered to him; "I like a good a crème de menthe but my late husband always ordered me things that I detested, I think he did it on purpose like dram buoy"

While they were talking Lorelei glanced at the diamond studded watch on her wrist and said quietly, "its time to eat Steven."

The two of them stood up and went into a small formal dining room that only sat a total of eight people.

"I like this room Steven because it is a more intimate than the big one my late husband always decided to eat in with just the two of us. We're having filet minion if that's alright with you. I have the butcher cut me two large ones each time he gets a new shipment of beef in. He caters only to the higher end clientele you see, he has no store, he calls my cook, she orders whatever I want and he delivers it to the house. Personally I think he likes my cook because he's here quite often."

"I see, that is a unique service."

"Now then Steven, tell me more about your book business, it sounds quite fascinating although books are a bit of a bore to me. I don't even read the newspaper let alone a book."

"Well there isn't very much to tell that you don't already know. I met my partner at the same University and we saw that we liked the same subjects and we learned so much in chemistry class that we decided to start a business once we were out of school in a friend's garage and then it just blossomed, the business that is. We have several patents and more pending. We have been able to reproduce ancient text on all kinds of paper such as papyrus, parchment and the latest is a rag concoction that makes marvelous expensive linen writing paper.

We've produced our own brands of ink and have patents on those as well. We are highly regarded in the preservation industry for our restorations of old and rare books. I can produce an exact copy of ancient text on the same delicate paper with the same faded ink and the experts can't tell the new from the old. I'm not bragging, we really are that good. When this country broke away from England during the Revolutionary War we have been able to match the ink that faded to brown of the day on all important documents such as The Declaration of Independence and other important historical documents as well. You realize don't you that they didn't have black ink in those days, mostly it was a blue that faded to brown over time. We're also in high demand from Museums around the world to preserve and protect their ancient texts and other works that are deteriorating quickly before their very eyes. It all turns to dust when handled if one is not extremely careful. They are willing to pay hundreds or thousands of dollars for our services which cause me to travel to far and wide destinations to see what their problems are before I can suggest a formula to save their works and of course they must be shipped to us and then shipped back to them. It's a highly secure business dealing with such artifacts when they arrive. They come to us in an unmarked armored car sometimes complete with guards but once in our hands we have our own security on hand, then they can leave We call the same ones who brought the items to us to come back and pick them up when we are finished. Our whole operation is conducted on three floors of an old Woolen Mill plus a secure concrete basement where our Laboratory is and everything is done in top secret conditions so in essence you could say we have a four story building with apartments for employees on the top floor with ample storage.

Stores that we rent out space to such as Office Supply Stores and other companies related to our business and soon we'll have a full service restaurant so we don't have to send out for meals anymore or walk or drive several blocks to get three meals a day."

Lorelei was sitting there spellbound by now. "You see Steven, books aren't boring when you talk about them, you have a sincere love for your work. I still find them terribly stodgy but you bring them to life and make it sound interesting and exciting."

"Why thank you Li! One thing we recently did was to install elevators throughout the building, three sets for people and freight elevators to serve all the floors. It's better than the old way of carrying heavy boxes of books up several flights of stairs from the basement like we used to do. You see under the back of the building we have loading docks where any size of tractor trailer or small vans like our own can back up to a loading dock and off load or load their merchandise. One day we hope to have the whole Mill remodeled and completely filled with stores and apartments for the employees who want to live close to where they work."

"You certainly have a unique vision Steven."

"Why thank you Li!"

"I think we'd best slow down on the talking and get on with eating our dinner before it gets cold and cook has to heat it up again, she wouldn't like that very much, she is very proud of her cooking don't you see."

"Yes and it certainly is good and I apologize if I went a little overboard about my business, I don't usually talk shop with anyone, you are the first person I have confided in about my company in this way."

"Well then I am certainly flattered Steven."

They spent the next twenty minutes eating and just smiling at one another. Sol was thinking to himself however, I must be more careful with whom I talk business with; I don't want to divulge too many secrets to anyone. Finally they were done with desert and their cordials.

"What would you like to do next Steven?"

"I'm not sure I'm usually in bed by this time of night or I am reading one of my books."

"And what kind of book might that be Steven."

He almost blurted out unsolved murder mysteries but caught himself just in time. "Why right now I'm reading the history of this nation, the Colonizing of America."

"Oh my but that sounds awfully boring. Say Steven, I have a great idea, because its so late why don't you spend the night in one of my guest bedrooms and we can take up your work again in the morning and maybe then we can go through some of my late husband's books?"

"That sound just fine Li, but I have my car waiting outside."

"I can send word for her to depart and return tomorrow morning around say 10:30 if that is alright with you?"

"Why yes Li, that's okay with me if you don't mind."

"Consider it done Steven." She clapped her hands ever so lightly and the butler suddenly appeared. She whispered to him and he was gone. "There, all taken care of. Come, I will show you to your room, there are plenty of pajamas of all sizes and colors as well as robes and you can check out your room while we're upstairs, I'd like to get out of this dress and into something more comfortable then perhaps we can have coffee in the sitting room upstairs near the bedrooms. Oh and there are bathrooms attached to each bedroom with shaving things for the men and other personal items for the ladies who sometimes spend the night here."

"Why thank you Li you are a very gracious hostess."

CHAPTER - 47

He followed her upstairs, she pointed out a room and turned the light on for him then she stepped directly across the hall to her room to change. It seemed like no time at all that she was knocking lightly on his door.

"Steven, are you decent yet?"

"Yes almost, I won't be but another moment." In his haste to get a pair of pajamas on he had forgotten about his elevated shoes which he had taken off. He wasn't sure what kind of impression he would make now that he was much shorter than she was at dinner. Well, it's too late now, guess I'll find out soon he thought.. He opened the door and she was standing there almost eyeball to eyeball with him. She must have had some lifts in her shoes as well he thought; he couldn't see her feet beneath her dress earlier so maybe it was it was her high heels. They were almost exactly the same height, in fact he felt about an inch taller than she appeared to be.

"Well now then Steven, isn't this nice, we can both see our short comings now." They both laughed at their appearance of being so much shorter than before.

"You know, I had an idea that you were not the person you were trying to be."

"Oh but I am on the inside, nothing has changed there," answered Sol.

"Come with me, the sitting room is just down here a door or two." They walked a short distance then she opened a door and they walked in with her leading the way. There were two love seats and six chairs in the sitting room with several small tables containing the latest in reading materials on them. Newspapers, magazines and the latest best seller books.

She said, "let's sit here, coffee is on the way up."

She was pointing to a love seat. They sat down and within minutes the coffee arrived and Lorelei dismissed the young female maid saying, "you may go now, you won't be needed anymore this evening." The young lady made a small bow and left without a word. "Well now isn't this a perfect ending for a beautiful evening Steven?"

"Yes Li, it's almost too perfect, just right."

"How do you take your coffee Steven, sweet with cream like your women friends?"

"No Li, just black please."

She made a little pout with her lips and Sol just smiled back at her without saying anything more. They sat there in almost absolute silence watching one another while sipping the piping hot coffee. In a few more minutes they were done. Lorelei yawned a little and stretched her arms up and out in front of her a little and as she did the front of her robe fell open to reveal her breasts a little more than had been revealed with her dress. She paid little attention to it. "Oh my Steven, I am so sorry, that was very rude of me to yawn like that in front of you."

"Think nothing of it, I was thinking about the same thing myself."

She slowly brought her arms down and fiddled with the cord around her middle that held her robe closed. She uncrossed her legs and let the robe open a little more. She was wearing a black see through negligee but he couldn't tell just how short it was but he guessed that it came down to just above her knees or thereabouts. She began to yawn again with her arms way outstretched going up out in front of her then she raised them over her head to reveal more of her nightgown as she stretched.

"Oh my, I am so sorry, I guess I am a little bit sleepier than I realized."

"That's alright Li, I'm a little tired myself, maybe we should both turn in."

They stood up and she let her robe open completely. He could see all of her now every detail, it was as if she wasn't wearing anything beneath her robe. There was no mystery and this could only mean one thing, her bed or his. As they stood up she took his hand and put it to her right breast.

"Are you ready for bed right now Steven or perhaps you would like some desert?"

"I'd like both if it's alright with you Li!"

They strolled across the hall holding hands to her bedroom and as she got close to the bed she dropped the robe from off her shoulders and let it slide to the floor. Sol followed her lead and took off his robe and dropped it to the floor as well. He took her in his arms and they kissed a long passionate moist hot kiss. They were trembling with anticipation by now.

"You don't have to be gentle with me Steven, but not too rough either." She sighed longingly as he lifted her up in his strong arms and set her down on the bed then she watched as he took removed his pajamas slowly. She looked at his love making equipment and smiled.

"Now lover?"

"Yes, now lover."

She stood up and they embraced and kissed with a long passionate kiss. When they broke off the kiss he reached down to the bottom hem of her nightgown, grasped it in his hands and pulled it up over her head and they kissed again.

CHAPTER - 48

The FBI Agents finally had something concrete to go on but there were thousands of Cemeteries throughout the United States and no one knew which cemetery their bad guy may be using so they were right back to where they had started.

"Well Agent Marlowe, what we have here is a real Mystery."

"I agree Agent Jefferies, a real Unsolved Mystery."

"Wait just a darned minute, what you just said. All these collateral deaths around the time of the Book Store murders, we were missing something and I think you just found it."

"What, what did I say to set off your smoking memory banks?"

"What you just said, Unsolved Mysteries, that has to have something to do with this."

"Oh no, your trolley has jumped the tracks this time Dick"

"No Agent Marlowe, think about it, if you wanted to cover your tracks what better way than to misdirect the investigations into a possible murder." She caught the Agent Marlowe thing. He only called her that when something big was up.

"But honestly Agent Jefferies some of these deaths are miles away from one another."

"I can't help it, I feel deep inside that we are being sent all over the place so we don't' look in the right place. Let's have another look at our wall map and see if we can see something that jumps off the wall at us," said Jefferies.

"Okay, we'll take another look." They went back to the wall map and started to look it over from one end to the other.

"I don't see anything we have overlooked other than there are several states that haven't reported anything recently."

"It has to be here right in front of us. Tell you what, let's put our new secretary on putting all of the deaths on paper in alphabetical order by State and see if it does anything to stimulate our minds which right now are going no where but to sleep with all the pins and needles."

"We are not using any needles here Dick."

"Slip of the tongue Agent Marlowe, pay no attention to it. I'm really sticking to the unsolved murder mysteries though."

"Why don't you take some petty cash and go to a book store and buy some material for us to look through then?"

"Right, why didn't you think about that before Agent Marlowe,? come on let's go."

"Whoa there Lone Ranger, I'm not Tonto and I for one don't jump to conclusions."

"Oh come on, getting out will put some color in your cheeks."

She gave in and followed Dick around as he made excuses and picked up some petty cash and they were off. They went to the nearest big Chain Book Store and found all kinds of books and magazines on the subject of unsolved murders. They both grabbed an armful and headed for the checkout counter.

Back at the FBI building they went straight to their office.

"Alright Agent Marlowe, lets get busy and do some reading."

"Whoa there cowboy, what's this 'we' business again?"

"Well we are partners and we're supposed to help each other, right?"

"To a point, but I'm a forensics specialist, not a lackey."

"But we're supposed to work together, help each other, right?"

"Maybe we should get a ruling from the Director about goofing off reading crime novels and novelettes."

"Ah but remember what the Director said, spare no expense, I want this thing solved and now! This is a part of our investigation as I see it!"

"But that's not the way I see it Agent Jefferies!" Jane said sternly.

"Oh come on this could be fun, who knows what other crimes we might uncover and solve while we're reading some of these. One of them may ring a bell in regards to the other cases."

"Now that did get my attention, the possibility that we could solve some other unsolved crimes which we already have questions about."

"You know there is a possibility that we have a copycat killer on our hands who's doing the same thing we're about to do."

"You know you brought that up once before, do you still feel that way about a copycat killer?"

"I don't know but I'm tired of grasping at straws and coming up with the short straw, whatever is going on is right in front of us, we just have to figure it out."

"Yeah well I guess you're right, I might as well lend a hand, your office or mine?"

Dick was grinning from ear to ear about her pun regarding the office being his or hers.

"Your office this time Agent Marlowe."

They shared the same office so they teased one another about whose office it really was. They carried all of the materials they had bought into their office and went to work. They spent the rest of the day poring over story after story and into the next day with the same routine. On the third day of scrutinizing article after article Dick finally hollered out loudly! BINGO!"

"What do you have Dick?"

"Here's a story about a young lady who was lost in a park in Utah, she wasn't found until the next spring by some hikers. She died from a broken neck ostensibly when she fell off a ledge of some kind. They think she had gone into the bushes to relieve herself from an urge of nature and maybe lost her balance and didn't realize she was so close to the edge of a precipice. All they had were skeletal remains, scavengers had scattered her bones all over the place and they never found all of her. It goes on to say that the previous summer when she disappeared they had followed a blood trail off into the woods and they found an article of clothing that one her friends recognized but her body was found hundreds of feet away in a huge chasm, it doesn't add up to anything but murder. I found an almost identical article of a death some twenty years ago in another State Park almost identical to this one in detail. Talk about copycat this has to be our guy. We've got to check this out, both cases are almost identical. I still think our murderer is the guy who's buying up book stores across the Country but I don't know what to make of these other murders or how can we tie them together? Let's head for Utah, we've got to go over this one and check it out."

"I think you're reaching for straws that don't exist on this one Dick, how can you possibly tie this one to any of the others?"

"I don't know Jane but like I said, I think this guy is an avid reader of mysteries and gets his jollies recreating unsolved murders by killing book store owners in a way he read in about in a magazine or a book and that he does the other murders because he likes the rush when he doesn't have any book stores to buy and kill the owners and any witnesses that may have seen him or her and I also think that the key is, no witnesses!!!"

"But Dick, the few people we have interviewed all describe a different man, red hair, black hair, no hair, curly hair, fat man, thin man, tall man, short man and an average man. None of them match any of the other descriptions we have."

"Yeah and that part bothers me. We could be dealing with at least two men who work together and another thing all of these other murders I don't believe are coincidences I think they are all done by the same man."

"Like I said Dick, I think you're really reaching here but you've been right on the money with everything else so I'm going to go along with you on this one as well. Something definitely smells about this scenario and its just wild enough to be true. Let's get booked on a flight to Utah."

"Now you're talking Agent Marlowe, let's get a move on and really earn our pay."

CHAPTER - 49

Back in LA. Sol woke up an instant before Lorelei did. He stretched and yawned as she woke up and did the same.

"Wow that was some night honey."

"I'll say," answered Sol.

"It doesn't have to be over just yet you know, let me shower and brush my teeth and we can go again if you like."

"Sounds good to me, I'll go shave and shower as well and meet you back here in a few minutes."

Sol got up totally naked in front of her and she did the same, both had slept naked in one another's arms all night long. Sol went about brushing his teeth and shaving while trying to compare his Francis with Lorelei but he couldn't draw a comparison. Lorelei was talented, resourceful, experienced in bed with men and it showed. He had known few women in his life because he was too set in his ways and didn't want to get married; he decided that if he were to get married that Francis would win the battle of the sexes for him. He could never trust this woman he was sleeping with right now. He finished his shower, dried off then went back to Lorelei's room where she was drying her hair with a blow dryer. He went into her room and sat on the bed where she could see him in the mirror while she continued to dry her hair.

"Be with you in a minute Steven." She finally finished came back in and sat down beside him. "Ready lover?"

"Yes lover, I'm more than ready this time." They lay down in each other's arms and kissed and made love for close to an hour.

After a brief nap they finally got dressed and went downstairs for some breakfast. They ate greedily like they hadn't eaten in days. They went out by the pool to enjoy their last cup of coffee and said little, they were watching one another. "Tell me Steven what is your real name?"

"Are you sure you want to know?"

"Yes I'm sure, I know it isn't Steven, so what is it?"

"Actually it is Solomon, my middle name is Oscar and my last name is Devine and everyone calls me Sol and many more do call me Steven." He had blurted it out before he knew what had happened, he'd let the cat out of the bag quite unintentionally. Another mistake he shouldn't have made.

"You're kidding, really?" she said a little shocked.

"Oh yes and it is my true name. You can check my University credentials if you like, they are under my real name."

"Well you're the first honest man I've met in a while and I think I'm falling in love with you because of your extreme honesty in the bedroom, it brings out the best in you. As soon as we're done with our coffee I'll show you my late husband's book collection, it isn't far from where we are right now."

"Thank you, that's very kind of Li, I'd almost forgotten why I came here."

In a few minutes they were done and she got up first. "Follow me Sol, we'll go this way."

He dutifully followed her like a puppy follows its mother as if he'd follow her to the ends of the earth. She slid open a couple of ornate hand carved solid wood doors that looked like mahogany through their patina. They walked into a spacious Library furnished with brown leather chairs with reading lamps next to each one. The ceiling was dotted with concealed flush lighting called can lights. The walls were painted a beige color soft on the eyes, there was a large stone fireplace on the inside wall and there were a few wall sconces around the room that looked like an after thought by the builder he presumed.

"This is a beautiful room Li, much better than my own Library back home in New York." He almost gave his location away. What's going on he thought to himself, am I also falling for Lorelei? Suddenly he was confused, she called him Sol instead of Steven, but she soon brought him out of his trance and back to reality.

"Take a look at these classics Sol, are they worth anything on the market these days?"

"Well let me have a look and I'll let you know." He had no more reason to lie to her now, she suddenly knew almost everything about him. "Yes, well, a couple of these might be, let me look at a few more before I say what I think." He continued to peruse the titles of most of the books. Every now and then he would take one out and look at it by leafing through the pages a little. "Well your husband must have had more money than brains, some of these are very poor copies of First Editions someone has tried to duplicate and copies of other rare books, I could re-do them and make them appear as originals at a pretty high expense but it could be done."

"Are you saying you can take a fake and make it look like an original that would fool even the experts?"

"That's exactly what I'm saying."

"You are a strange and complex man aren't you Sol?"

"Maybe to your way of thinking but I don't work alone, I have other employees to do the hard work for me. I simply travel the world looking for manuscripts and books and of course rare first editions to make money from then bring them back to make copies of then we sell them on the open book market Internationally. We do quite well actually. Did you say you have other books as well?"

"Yes but they are in the basement and I don't go down there much. If I need something I send Henry down to get it, there are several boxes of books down there he tells me."

"May I see them next, I'm interested in almost all of what is here, you said you want all of the books gone from the premises?"

"Yes that s right, I will choose what to replace them with from my own tastes. In case you didn't notice most of the books deal with murder mysteries and the macabre which I don't care for. Follow me Sol and I'll show you where the basement door is, do you want me to call my butler to go down there with you?"

"If you don't mind, that would save me the trouble of wandering all around your basement looking for boxes the rest of the morning."

Lorelei made a movement which he didn't catch but all of a sudden the butler was standing next to them. He figured he must have been watching from somewhere close by.

"Take Mr. Shultz downstairs Henry and show him the boxes of books that were my late husband's and if he wants them maybe you can help him bring them upstairs if you don't mind."

The butler said nothing, he bowed slightly, opened the door and said; "please follow me sir." They descended the stairs to a brightly lit basement that held everything under the sun. The butler walked to their right directly to several rows of boxes some up to thirty feet long that contained books that were stacked four boxes high. He simply pointed to them and said, "there you are sir." Then the butler stepped back and stood still awaiting further instructions.

"Is there another way into the basement down here?" Sol asked.

"Yes sir, over this way there's a set of double doors which swing in and allow trucks to back up here and either unload or load up things we no longer need."

"Wouldn't it be easier if I were to send a truck down here to pick these up from there rather than cart these all upstairs then out the front door? This is a tremendous amount of boxes for anyone to have to carry upstairs."

"Oh yes sir much easier. May I suggest something else, we have a rather strong dumb waiter to every floor and to several rooms like the kitchen and dining room. We could box up the books in the Masters Library and send them down here on the dumb waiter, it's plenty strong enough to do the job, then everything could be loaded up from here."

"Thank you for your help, I believe I've seen enough, I'll try and make a deal for the entire collection and have someone to come round to pick them up. You can supervise, you won't have to get your hands dirty moving any of this, it isn't your worry." Sol looked at the butler who had a sad faraway look about him. "I say there my man, are you feeling alright?"

"Yes sir, I am sorry sir, it's just, well it's just, oh I don't know, it just doesn't seem right her getting rid of all the Master's books like this."

"Did you ever read any of them?"

"Oh yes sir, the Master let me read anything I wanted and told me not to tell his wife. I do have some favorites," his face brightened up as he smiled broadly.

"Very good. Here is what you must do then and with my authority. When I make the deal to buy the collection you may take whatever books you want to your quarters and hide them if you must but keep them for yourself, understood?"

"Oh yes sir, thank you sir, I understand perfectly." He was a changed man. Henry was grinning from ear to ear. Sol would now be well taken care of, he would see to that.

They went back upstairs to where Lorelei was waiting. "Well did you find what you were looking for Mr. Shultz?"

"Well yes and no, I'm afraid your husband did not have an eye for the great works of the Masters of Literature. Most of what is down there are similar to these, just poor copies but there may be a few that could be valuable."

He reached into his jacket pocket and took out a small pad of paper and a pen. He did some scribbling or what looked like doodling then looked at Lorelei once again. "I'll give you ten thousand dollars cash for what you have in here and in the basement."

"Is that the best you can do Mr. Shultz?" she asked pouting just a little.

"Yes, I'm afraid it's the best that I can offer."

"May I see your pen and paper for a minute?"

"Yes of course." He handed them to her. She flipped to an unused page and wrote a big zero with a line drawn through it diagonally. "This is what I want for the entire collection, take it or leave it. It is of no concern to me whatever if you take it or not," she said in a kind of haughty attitude.

Sol realized now that this was a show for the butler who had to be close by watching.

"Well I don't know Ms. Lorelei, that's pretty steep even for me. But, well, alright if that's what it will take, we have a deal. I'll need to go into town and get a moving crew to come out here and box up everything and ship it back to my store though, it might take a few days."

"That will be fine. Say listen here's a thought, my man Henry could do that for you, he knows all the ins and outs of moving things around."

"Well alright if you insist."

"I do," and she made another almost imperceptible movement and the butler was back at her side again.

"Yes ma'am, you wanted me?"

"Yes I do, this man has purchased the entire collection of books both here in the library and in the basement, I'd like you to arrange for a Moving Company to come here and box everything up and take it to this man's store which I think is somewhere in New York City, the Moving Company will want to know where they are headed."

"Yes ma'am, right away ma'am." He gave a slight wink to Sol, he didn't miss it but he hoped Lorelei did.

"Well then it's almost time for lunch, what do you say Sol, stay for lunch?"

"Yes Li, I'd like that." The two of them went back out by the patio near the pool, had lunch and made more small talk.

"Sol, I'd love to come by your store one day and have you give me a tour of your establishment, it sounds extremely interesting. I've never seen let alone heard of your kind of restoration techniques or the making of paper from used paper and rags as you say."

"We'll have to set up a special tour for you but I'll have to talk with my partner first, he is the brains when it comes to the science. I come up with ideas or problems and he solves them and makes them work, that's what makes us a great team. I'm more of an Engineer who designs then builds the equipment and he has the scientific mind for the techniques we use. Listen, I really hate to eat and run but I could be back later for cocktails if the invitation was made."

"What time would you consider too late for cocktails?"

"Oh I'd say after ten o'clock is too late for cocktails, its time for a night cap then."

"Oh I like the sounds of a night cap much better so should we say around 9:30 then and we can do both?"

"Sounds absolutely delicious, it will give me time to call the store and let them know I have procured another load of books and that they should be there within a week or ten days depending on how many stops the moving truck has to make by the time it gets to my place. Even though I own the Store they like me to check in just in case they have another lead like this one for me to check out while I'm on the road."

"I certainly hope you don't have more stops like this one. I'd hate to be upstaged by another woman."

"No worry there, ninety nine percent of my business deals are with little old men in wheelchairs or professors who don't know their butt from a hole in the ground when it comes to the classics."

"Have you really had that kind of experience before?"

"Yes, earlier this year and once last year both situations came up."

"You know something I seem to remember a rather famous Professor who was at home when his house literally exploded killing him and burning all of his books to a crisp, it was all over the TV. Were you there to see him?"

"As a matter of fact I did go to see him but he had died the day before I got there and I didn't know about it until I saw it in the newspaper while I was having breakfast at my Motel so I just up and left and went back home. That's what we call a dry run, nothing but empty pockets is all that's left after all of the expenses of getting there and back, big waste of my time and money I'm afraid."

"Have you had many experiences like that in the past?"

"No, fortunately about ninety five percent of the time I end up buying anything from a few books to a whole Store full that is going out of business like the one before I got here. It took two trucks to clear the place out, I bought everything right down to the curtains and all the furnishings including desks, counters, shelving etc."

"That must have cost you a bundle then."

"Actually it wasn't all that bad. The man was ill with cancer, he was getting old and feeble, he just wanted someone to get his store at a price that he set and trust me, it was a fair price for the whole shooting match. After paying off his medical bills he passed away anyway and he lived in a modest home that was paid for, he didn't even own a car. He could walk anywhere he wanted to in town and get everything he ever needed. Between what he had left what I paid him he left his home and all he owned to his wife."

"Did he have children still living?"

"Yes of course, they keep in touch with me now and then and give me leads when one of them reads something of interest to me in one of his Trade Papers."

"Oh I see, then you made other friends in your travels."

"I don't know that you could call them friends, I'll never see them again but they have my card and they call the store and talks with my partner who has a very sympathetic ear from time to time. I'm seldom there for very long when I'm in town. Like I said before I travel the world in search of the finest books money can by and preserve them for posterity."

"That sounds very noble, but you have to admit that you make money from most of your Ventures, don't you?"

"Most of the time but I do have a few visits a year when I don't buy a darn thing. It goes along with the work that I do." Sol had lied through his teeth once again about the man with the store he had killed. He was now flying by the seat of his pants.

She casually looked at her watch, "if you don't get a move on soon you won't make it back here for cocktails or a night cap."

"Oh my goodness Li, you're right, if you'll excuse me I'd better be going, I'll see you around 9:30, okay?"

"That sounds great Sol, give us a kiss before you go."

"What about your butler, won't he see us?"

"He may but so what, if he knows what's good for him he'll look the other way."

They kissed and as if by magic Sol's car drove up with his female driver just as he stepped outside.

CHAPTER - 50

Agents Jefferies and Marlowe arrived in Salt Lake City around 5:00 P.M. the following Monday afternoon after clearing up several loose ends around the Office. The first thing they did was to rent a full size four door passenger car to travel around in and carry what little gear they brought with them to aid in their investigation while in the Park where the missing woman's remains were found. The second thing they had to do was to go to the Motel where they had reservations then have supper. They had all of the information with them that the Utah Authorities had sent them so all they needed was someone from the Utah State Police to go with them and a Park Ranger to point out the places of interest. They had made appointments with them both ahead of time to save time and time is what they had to use effectively before the killer may possibly strike again.

They next day at 9:00 A.M. a State Police Officer met them at their Motel and they were ready to leave. The first question that came up was whether to use his car or their rental? They opted for his car, a black unmarked model four door Ford. They had time to talk with the Officer whose name was Roger McKenzie, Captain in charge of the case there in Utah, so he was familiar with the case. It was a long ride so they stopped for coffee at a roadside café.

"Tell me Agents Marlowe and Jefferies, what makes you think this was murder and not an accident. The coroner said it was an accident, she broke her neck when she fell."

"Well Captain McKenzie, we wondered why there was a blood trail going the opposite direction from where her remains were found. How did your people feel about that?" asked Jefferies.

"Well our investigators thought that she may have had a slight injury and wandered away from the trail uphill. She may have been a little confused and went looking for help. She lost her sweater and retraced her steps back to where she had been and just walked off the edge of the precipice falling into the canyon to her death because she was probably somewhat disoriented."

"Okay plausible, but do you believe that scenario?" replied Jefferies.

"I don't know what to think now that the two of you are here. I'm sure you suspect some kind of foul play but everyone has been accounted for and interviewed and you have all the information with you I take it."

"Agent Marlowe why don't you give him your take on this then I'll tell him what I think?" asked Jefferies.

"Okay!"

"Captain, we believe she was murdered in cold blood but we differ somewhat on how it was done. I think that it was a crime of opportunity, someone saw her, decided to rape her, he pulled her into some bushes and a fight ensued and she may have fought off her attacker but was slightly injured in the process and wandered off in the wrong direction trying to get back to where she had been and fell off into the canyon by herself. Your turn Agent Jefferies."

"Okay, I think that it was also cold blooded murder and that the murderer staked out a likely place to commit the crime and she happened to come along and was alone. He saw the opportunity and struck. I believe he knocked her out cold. Before he threw her over the edge into the canyon I think he cut her neck near an artery with a knife and collected the blood in some kind of vessel before she died and her heart stopped. Then the killer left a blood trail up through the woods and left her sweater there to make it look like she had been confused and just wandered off then getting lost. I think it was misdirection by the killer to get your people searching the park in the wrong direction for her so you wouldn't find the actual crime scene."

"That seems pretty far fetched, what made you think of that may I ask?" said McKenzie.

"Well don't laugh but we think collectively that we have a copycat murderer on the loose and he reads both real crime stories or novels of unsolved murders then he goes out and tries to duplicate the same thing to see if he can get away with it. Currently we have several unsolved homicides from around the country and they resemble unsolved crime stories from not only books but the tabloids, you know the kind of things you find in your Supermarkets."

"So you think he is reading about murders then goes out and commits them, is that about it?"

"Yes, that's it in a nutshell and we have already solved some closed cases and have reopened them that were supposed to be accidents but were definitely murder and this one matches a death in another State Park right down to the smallest detail."

"That's a pretty incredible statement, but if you are right we have a huge amount of ground to cover across the United States then don't we?"

"That's exactly what the two of us think along with the Director of the FBI who put us on the trail of these murders or so called accidents. There is no such thing as the perfect crime, the killer always forgets one small detail. That's what we're looking for, that one detail he forgot to cover his trail with."

"Very interesting! I'll do my best to keep an open mind on this, it could prove to be an interesting crime scene if it's true. Well shall we go, we still have a long ride ahead of us, my time is your time though, my Boss like your Boss wants some answers and he didn't believe the scenario from the coroner for what its worth."

The three law officers paid for their coffees and hit the road once again for the Park. They got there just before noon and asked for a Park Ranger by name who was supposed to lead them to the place where they found the remains, or rather the canyon rim above where the skeletal bones were found. The Captain went into the Main Office and soon returned with a Park Ranger walking along side of him. "The Ranger asked if we could follow him, he said he would take us to the spot but that he was needed back at the Office, he said an emergency has come up regarding a bear and he was needed back here a.s.a.p."

The Ranger got into a green pickup truck with the Park's name on the door and waved out his left side window for them to follow him and they were off. Twenty minutes later of following winding narrow roads they came to a spot on a fairly steep incline where he stopped. He motioned them to park off to the right side as far as they could to let other cars and bicycles through. "Well folks here you are," he walked over to the rim and pointed down to where most of the scattered bones were found.

"Sorry I can't stay but I've got to get right back," said the Park Ranger.

"Just a minute please, one question," the Captain asked, "where approximately was the blood trail the police and your people found?"

"Why that's about over here" and he walked forward several feet then pointed uphill into the woods. "I'd be careful about wandering around, we have a report of a bear stalking people in this area."

"Point well taken, thank you Ranger."

"You're very welcome but be careful, you people shouldn't be out here in street clothes and shoes, you really should be wearing hiking clothes and boots."

"Thank you, bye now."

The Ranger nodded his head and got into his truck; with some difficulty he turned his truck around on the narrow path and headed back down the trail to his Headquarters.

"Well folks, where would you like to start?"

"I'm not sure Captain but I'm going to walk along the rim over here and see if I can find a good place to hide like a murderer would use," said Jefferies.

"Agent Marlowe, have a look around but I doubt we'll find any evidence because its been almost a year now and they have had snow and rain up here so anything we might be looking for may have already been washed away."

"Alright Dick, I'm going to walk uphill just for the heck of it and see if I can figure out where the killer may have walked and see if I can find the area where he left the blood trail."

The Captain simply walked along the edge of the road looking for anything that may help support one of their theories. He knew they were here for a reason, they weren't just killing time.

About a half an hour went by and they had found nothing. Then while Dick was walking back though some brush he saw a large boulder and hollered out to Agent Marlowe. "Jane, I think we have it, come over here!"

It took her a few minutes before she arrived with the Captain close behind.

"This big boulder Jane, sit down or lean against it like you had to tie a shoe, I want to try something." Dick reached over the rock from behind and easily grabbed her by her head and pulled her backwards over the big boulder.

"Well Jane, Roger, I think this is the place, its perfectively concealed from the road. The killer could have easily hid behind the bushes here, then crept forward a couple of steps, grabbed the woman by surprise from behind clamping his hand over her mouth so she couldn't scream. He could have easily choked her unconscious or knocked her out then he cut her neck, drained some blood into some kind of bottle, put the bottle down then rolled her body off the rim right here just a few feet away into the canyon. Take a look over here and see what you two think."

The Captain followed Jane to have a look.

"Now from here, if this is where it happened, he could have easily walked up the hill across the road and left a blood trail and her sweater to lead investigators away from here!"

"You know Dick, I think you've got the murder site, it all fits right up to the blood trail to misdirect the cops and everyone else that was searching for the woman," answered Jane.

"Well Captain what are your thoughts on this now?" Dick asked.

"I'm afraid I have to agree with you Agent Jefferies or is it Dick, I heard Agent Marlowe refer to you as Dick?"

"You can call me Dick out here, we're far enough away from town so that we both use our first names in a situation like this."

"Good that makes it much easier and friendlier. I think you proved your theory to where even a jury would believe you; it all fits perfectly. You know if you don't mind I'd like you send me a copy of that article on the killing in the other State's Park."

"Sure thing Roger, that's what this is all about, sharing of information."

"Jane would you mind retrieving the camera from our bags we brought along? I'd like to get several pictures so we can show to the Director when we get back, this is most interesting.

Captain, I'm sorry, Roger, I'd like to try one more thing. We don't have any idea how tall the killer is, would you mind getting behind the bushes then come up from behind and try to grab me like I did Jane, you're a couple inches shorter than I am."

"Sure I'd be more than happy to help." They did the same thing Dick had done to Jane, he had no effort grabbing Dick from behind covering his mouth with his right hand.

"Alright, now we know that it was a man or woman with strength at around five feet six inches tall or taller who grabbed the girl and pulled her over the rock. Jane would you stand in front of the rock one more time and Roger would you get behind the bushes in a crouch like you're hiding? I want to take photos of what I just did to Jane but using you because you are a little shorter than I am so I can prove to the Boss that this is the way I believe she was killed."

They went through the actions and Dick snapped off a roll of film in their 35mm camera. "There got it all, this is great, what luck we found this area so quickly, thanks of course to you Roger and the Park Ranger. Now not a word to the Ranger about our suspicions, he has enough to worry about other than the FBI and the State Police poking around his Park. Roger, I don't know about you but I could do with some lunch, how about you Jane?"

"Yeah, sounds good Dick, lets hit the road."

Dick was absolutely giddy, like a school kid who was skipping school for the first time.

CHAPTER - 51

Sol went out front and got into the Bentley. He picked up the phone to talk to his female driver Sissy. "Miss, how did you know I was ready to leave?"

"A man called my private number and said you were about to leave and would I please drive up to the house and well, here I am."

"Alright, thank you for the prompt service. I guess you can head for my Hotel now."

"Alright sir but your friend wants you to call him as soon as we're clear of the driveway, the number is already keyed into your phone, all you have to do is pick it up and press redial."

"Thank you Miss."

"Sol pressed redial as soon as they were clear of the long sweeping driveway where he couldn't be seen from the Mansion. Richard soon answered. "Richard, this is Sol, you wanted to talk to me?"

"Yes I do, how is the book deal going?"

"Just fine, we agreed on a price."

"May I ask how much it was?"

"Yes of course, so far it has cost me two sexual escapades with your beautiful cousin and I'm due back later tonight for a third round of all night sex."

"Yippy!!!," hollered Richard, "wonderful just wonderful, this is much better news than I expected, I would like to meet with you and discuss some private issues so would dinner be alright with you tonight, I'll buy?"

"Yes of course, I'll need to go take a shower at the Hotel and change clothes and get something to change into in the morning but after that I'm free until around 9:00, I have to be at her place by 9:30 for cocktails and a night cap."

"Superb, you have my number, call me before you leave your room to come downstairs and I'll pick you up, I'll give your driver a couple of hours off and tell her where to pick you up and she can take you back to Lorelei's place and she can go home from there and then pick you up later in the morning, if it's alright with you."

"That sounds fine, I'll give you a call then when I'm ready."

Later on after Sol had had his shower and changed his clothes he got some things together to take back to Lorelei's and he gave Richard a call. "Richard, its Sol, I'm about ready to head downstairs and I have a small overnight bag that I'm bringing along to take to your cousin's place."

"Fine I'm in the area I'll pick you up out front in about ten minutes."

"Very good then, see you in a few minutes." Sol picked up his small overnight bag, left the room and locked it on his way out. He couldn't get past the concierge though without being seen and he had a wise crack that he couldn't contain and had a sly smirk on his face all in good humor.

"I see you got lucky, very lucky sir, she must be a real looker."

"Not that it's any of your business but the old codger I'm here to do business with can't stay up past eight o'clock so he invited me to spend the night with he and his family."

"Yes sir, of course sir" but he was smiling the I know the truth smile as Sol walked past.

Almost as soon as Sol stepped outside Richard's limo was making a U turn to come back around and pick him up, he had been going the opposite direction. Sol waited for the driver to come around and open the door of the stretch limo and got in. "Well Richard here we are again, right where we started a few days ago."

"Tell me Sol, was the collection as good as I was led to believe?"

"Well yes and no, there were some very poor copies that her husband had bought but there were also a few copies that were genuine. I may break even after I pay all my expenses for my trip out here."

"Oh I am sorry. I tell you what, I'll help you cover those expenses. I'll take care of your Hotel and the rental car, okay?"

"Yes of course, they will cost me a pretty penny as you know."

"Yes well, things cost more out here than on the east coast."

"Tell me, what is it you wanted to talk about anyway?"

"How about we talk over dinner, I know a place where we can talk and eat in complete privacy and no one dares eves drop on conversations?"

"Okay the buck is on you I believe this evening."

"Yes, well I never heard it put quite that way but I get the idea." He picked up the car phone and spoke quietly to his driver. In a few minutes they pulled around to the back of a non descript building with a back door that read Private, Members Only. They got out and Sol followed Richard to the door.

Richard knocked twice and a little door slid open about eye level for recognition and the door soon opened for them. A tall man dressed in a black tuxedo greeted them; "good evening Richard, so good of you to drop by."

They were quietly taken to a table for two that was big enough to seat four to six. There were comfortable high back over stuffed chairs tastefully done in a soft mauve tapestry type material. It was obvious to Sol that this was a place for the movers and shakers of Industry probably built for and catered to the movie moguls in the earlier days of movies. Now it catered to the wealthy business people, there was room for a secretary at some tables where they would have room to write, negotiate and seal deals right at their own tables while eating and drinking the night away. Almost as soon as they sat down a waiter showed up with glasses of chilled water and a wine list. They also had a bar to serve the most odd of tastes when it came to drinks, the bar was for table service only, it was not a bar where you could sit and drink. Everything and everyone was on a first name basis right down to and including the waiters or waitresses.

"Richard, this is a lovely get away for meals and deals."

"Yes Sol, I come here often alone, I've run the gambit of women in this town; I need a new stock of ladies to charm and take home. Sol, what I want to talk to you about may come as a bit of a shock to you so I hope you will indulge me and let me finish what I am going to say before asking any questions. Let me know when you think you are ready to listen. We will not be bothered as long as we are talking. Its one of the perks here, they don't interrupt conversations or listen in on them. Remember please no questions until I am through. Shall we order drinks or wine first; we can also place our meal order at the same time? They will leave us a small black box on the table that will buzz gently that will let us know that our meals are ready to come out and when we're ready to eat we push the red button and the meal will be brought out right away. We can also use the box to hail a waiter or waitress; they will bring it when we order drinks or wine. So if you are ready for a glass of the bubbly or something else let me know and we'll order whatever you like, the night is on me and before the night is out you will see just how generous I can be."

"Well, this sounds like a lot to digest right away; I'll leave it up to you to run the show, I'll behave myself and be quiet."

"That's the spirit Sol." Richard hailed a waiter the old fashioned way by raising his hand and waving towards their table. The waiter was there toot sweet.

"Yes Richard, are you ready for refreshments?"

"Yes George, I'll have the usual Scotch on the rocks, Sol?"

"I'd like a scotch and soda tonight I believe."

"Your name please sir?"

"Call me Sol, everyone does."

"Yes sir very good sir, I'll be back shortly."

"We'll wait for his return, you might want to take a few sips once I get started."

"One thing before we get started," Sol asked, "where are the menus, I don't see any?"

"No need too, they have their own butcher in the kitchen and you can order any kind of meal you can imagine from duck to filet minion to venison, you name it they have it including fresh lobster flown in from Maine."

While they were still chatting about food the waiter returned with their drinks.

"Here you are Richard, Sol, please try them to be sure they are alright, I can make any adjustments as Richard can attest to."

They both took a sip and gestured by nodding that they were alright.. "I think George we'll wait a few minutes to order our meal, we have some business to transact."

"I understand perfectly Richard, buzz me when you are ready." George left as silently as he had arrived.

"Well then Sol, have a big sip then I'll get started. I assure you it won't cost you a dime and will be of benefit to us both."

Sol took a long slow swig afraid of what he might hear in the next few minutes and he wanted to brace himself just in case.

"Alright, if you're ready here we go. Sol as you know I have everything a man of my means could desire except two things, excitement in my life and a stable of horses. This is where you come in. My entire life has been a terrible bore, money can't buy everything."

Sol nodded his head in agreement, he knew exactly what Richard meant.

CHAPTER - 52

Richard began to talk with Sol hanging on to every word.

"Before I contacted you I had you checked out thoroughly by my own Private Investigators so I know quite a bit about you, that's why I wanted to meet you in person. I know almost everything there is to know about you from where you were born to where you went to school. I know about Francis and how you helped her out of a difficult situation, about your partner Fred and his discoveries along with yours etc. That's the background I have on you and it will go no further than myself and I have already destroyed any documentation I had. I have no interest in your past but I do have an interest in your future which brings us here tonight. In the short of it I want my cousin's place and she doesn't wish to sell it to me. I want you to arrange an accident to befall her, perhaps a horse riding accident where she breaks her fool neck. Then I want her Will doctored so that I inherit everything she has, she won't need it in Hell which is where she is going. She killed her late husband you know and got away with it. I understand that with your forgery techniques and your expertise with accidental deaths you can make all of this happen. Now I am also a little greedy in that I want to come to your store and I'd like to meet your partner Fred and see how your operation works. This is the excitement I crave, seeing the inner workings of your operation. I want to see just how you do what you do on that end of your business and in return I will keep you informed of all my contacts who own vast private collections of art, books, manuscripts and other things and you can get your hands on by whatever means you wish, it is of no consequence to me and I won't give you a bum steer. No wasted trips or shooting in the dark. Our continued association will be a benefit to us all and I will also benefit by the thrill of seeing things done and reading about them in the newspapers. Now then, what do you say to all that?"

Sol reached up and scratched his chin thoughtfully. "I realize now that you are a very dangerous man to let live, but you will only live as I see fit, understand that! You already know of my activities and now you want to become a part of them not as a partner, just a person of interest. As you already know I can make it all happen in a whisper either way I want. Killing your cousin won't give me any pleasure but it would be justice for your dead friend. Do you mind if I kind of digest all of this while we eat? You have made me a very interesting proposition and I can surely see the benefit for all of us. As you said it may shock me and it has a little in that I thought I had covered my tracks very thoroughly but I see that people still talk if approached in the right way. Let's go ahead and order and you can tell me more about your cousin's schedule when it comes to riding horses and where exactly she goes on her rides. I'll need times and places so I can check things out for myself. No one will know when it happens and that way it appears to be more of an accident. Now the really hard part, can you get your hands on a copy of her Will and can you get it to me soon?"

"Yes on everything, I already have a copy of the Will my Investigators procured for me, they have no scruples you know, they do it only for the money."

"Yes, well very good; I'll need a few days to set things up and the name of a person you can trust to do the dirty work on your cousin. A broken neck from falling off a horse is easy enough to do. I'll need someone to do the work, breaking her neck I mean, so we are not anywhere close by when it happens, alright with you? Oh and this man you find make sure he isn't someone you like because as you must already know I don't leave witnesses behind anywhere. I have used many homeless people because they are hard to trace for the authorities, they work for cash and move around so much that no one misses them for months on end."

"What did you do with them?"

"They got a proper Christian type burial when there was no one there to send them off to the nether world. You do realize the chance you are taking just talking with me don't you, I don't like loose ends."

"I've considered everything and that's why I contacted you for the job, I know you can pull it off. When would you like me to drop off the Will?"

"Tonight or tomorrow, I'll have to go back to the store to do what you asked and it will cost you, a plane trip both ways for me to carry the document back and forth, I won't trust the mail with something this important and dangerous."

"I can help you there, I will fly out to your location and you can give me the tour I asked for and I can bring the Will back with me."

"I see you have already planned everything. Does it bother you any that I'm sleeping with your cousin?"

"No not at all, she's slept with half the men in this town already, it means nothing to me how many times you sleep with her, if she's good in bed then enjoy it as long as you want, all I want is the Will and her dead, okay?"

"Yes Richard its perfectly clear. You know this could be a very interesting proposition you have made me. I'm beginning to like it more and more, maybe I'll even do the job myself; I already have a plan in mind for her. We can make this work to both of our benefits but what about your Private Investigators, surely you know I'll have to get rid of them, they already know too much and their files will have to be dealt with, a fire in their office should do it with them inside. Does that concern you in any way?"

"No, they mean nothing to me! I paid them a huge amount of money and they earned it but as good as you are you could clean out their bank accounts and do whatever you want with the money. I hope you can see the logic in what I have done? You know, I just had a thought, as good as you are you could point the blame to some poor sucker who got divorced because of them and point the finger at him."

"Now you're thinking just like me Richard, I knew I'd like you the minute we met."

"So I take it we have a deal?"

"Yes of course we do, I like it. As you may already know I do a lot of reading about unsolved mysteries and then I go out and recreate the killings to see if I can get away with it."

"Yes I know Sol, that's what gets me so excited, just knowing you is an honor because I have seen where you have righted some wrongs in Justice already and my cousin is one of those who has wronged someone. Beware of her as well Sol, she sleeps with a gun under her pillow."

"I know, I've already found it and have removed the ammunition, its a 9mm pistol similar to the one I use, I have it on me right now in a shoulder holster."

"Oh my goodness this is getting more exciting all the time." Richard was smiling and clapping his hands like a child would quietly. "I've never been this close to a firearm before!"

"When we get into the car if you'd like to hold it I'll let you. I've only killed with it a few times." Sol was stretching the truth here a little bit, he had used a snub nosed chrome 357 caliber pistol but it had made so much noise that he hid it in his apartment and got the 9mm that he now carried and he had a silencer for it just in case he wanted to be quiet but he didn't want Richard to know everything right away.

"Oh how exciting, I wish I could have been there to see it."

"By the way, you should know that I have many disguises so the next time you see me you may not recognize me at all. I can make myself tall, fat, skinny, old, bald, red hair, blond hair, black hair or brown hair all in different styles of haircuts."

"This gets better all the time, I can't wait to see your Book Store and your operation and how you do things. We'd better order now before it gets any later otherwise my cousin may not wait up for you, we must keep her happy for a little while longer."

"I agree with you, push the buzzer so we can eat."

After they were done with supper Richard kept his word and got Sol to where the Bentley was parked waiting for them and he got to Lorelei's place precisely at 9:30.

CHAPTER - 53

Once back in Washington Agent Jefferies was in a hurry to get their film developed in house so he could show the Director what they had learned while they were in Utah but it wouldn't get them any closer to the killer. It was back to square one as far as Jefferies and Marlowe were concerned. They had proved another accident was murder but what would be next? Where and when would he strike? Then there was the why of it all, those were the really big questions.

"Well Agent Marlowe as soon as the film is developed we'll go see the Director, okay?"

"Yes Agent Jefferies whatever you say."

"Is something troubling you Agent Marlowe?"

"Yes as a matter of fact there is." Jane was standing with her hands on her hips. "You seem to find the problem almost too quickly, like you've been there before as in de ja vu."

"Well maybe if you read as much as I have you would have figured this out as well."

"No, I think that it's all in the interpretation of what you read, what you see, your scenario makes the most sense as the two of us saw when you re-enacted the scene for us, that is the Captain and I anyway."

"Can't you find a better theory of your own other than my scenario, its makes me look bad, like I'm grandstanding or something."

"Yes well alright, I see your point but I've tried other scenarios and they just don't work as well as yours Agent Jefferies."

"Okay, I give in, where do you suggest we take this investigation now, I want to hear your thoughts on this guy we're looking for."

"Well it's like you said before," said Jane, "I believe just as you do that this guy is a book nut, an aficionado of literature maybe, there has to be a reason why he buys so many books. What does he do with them, does he sell some and keep some or what? I feel he must have his own retail outlet for them but where is his operation is the question. We don't have a single common thread to go on, every witness saw someone different at each book sale, so which one is our bad guy?"

"That's what we would all like to know. We've been over this all before; we're missing a key link somewhere. There must be thousands of legitimate Book Stores across the Untied States, so which one will he hit next."

"Well we can rule out one of them," said Dick, "we already sent an investigator to that great big Book Store in Poughkeepsie New York and we're sure that one isn't it, it's run by a couple of older men in their sixties and they were both short in stature and their manager was interviewed and we came up empty because they were squeaky clean. They run a legitimate business restoring old manuscripts and the two of them are worth more money than you can shake a stick at. They hold several patents which have already made them millionaires several times over and have several more patents pending. They have no need or reason to pilfer Book Stores and kill the owners or kill any other people that may be a witness just for the hell of it."

"Okay then, lets take another look at the map, I'd like to make a trip to that store anyway and have a look around sometime. I've heard they are big in the International Markets with their preservation techniques with collectors and Museums all clamoring for their help. I don't see how they would have time to go out and do the things that we are looking into and besides how harmless can two old men be, their credentials checked out and both of them are near geniuses!"

"Good question Agent Marlowe I'm with you, we're at another dead end and its time to regroup the troops and take another look at the map."

"Wait a minute Agent Jefferies, I just thought of something. When we sent out flyers looking for information regarding deaths some twenty years back, did we bother to ask anyone to send us immediately any information on the recent death of a Book Store Owner surrounding the sale of a store as in the near future?"

"I think you have just struck a nerve Agent Marlowe, where is that new secretary, lets put her on it right now and see what we have. I've already forgotten what the flyer looked like that went out to all Law Enforcement Agencies across the U.S. it was so long ago."

"Okay, I'm on it, be back shortly." She disappeared and was gone for a good half hour.

"Sorry I was gone so long but I had to read and re-read the notice several times and it depends on who is reading it as to how they may interpret it. It doesn't actually say that we need to be notified immediately about any new deaths but it does allude to it, like I said it depends on who's reading it."

"Alright then lets get the thing re-done and sent back out like it hasn't been sent out before, I want a whole new look to it and it needs to be specific this time. I could have sworn we did it right the first time."

"But Agent Jefferies, it depends on who's typing it up. They are directed to make things clear and to punctuate and sometimes interpret what's being said and rewrite if necessary."

"Please be quiet Agent Marlowe, you're giving me a headache. I still want to see a copy of what was sent out and we need to see a proof before another one goes out and this time I insist on it!"

"Yes sir Mr. Jefferies, right away Mr. Jefferies!" She gave him an off handed salute and was being funny but she knew that someone must have dropped the ball on this even after they had approved the copy to be sent out. Someone had forgotten to add future Store Owners Deaths in the copy to keep them appraised of the situation. A fresh trail is better to follow then one that is a year old or more like the one in Utah that was over a year ago. The closet thing they had was the Professor's death and the other one in Buffalo where the man had a sick wife and he apparently had fallen down some Mall's stairs and was killed. They needed fresher cases to work on, somewhere someone would slip up and they'd be there to pick up the bad guy this time at they were hoping.

A couple days went by and while the six Agents were all meeting in Jefferies and Marlowe's Office. Dick's telephone rang and he picked it up. His face got red immediately as he said; "sir, yes sir, right away sir!" he hung the phone up. "Shit!" he hollered at no one in particular. "Come on Agent Marlowe we have an audience request from the man upstairs."

"Are you telling me that God just called you on your phone?"

"No and that's not funny, the Director wants to see us right away. We must be in some kind of trouble because he never calls us direct, he always has his secretary call us when he wants to see us, that was the man himself. Come on get a move on, when he says right now he means right now."

They walked into the Director's outer Office and his Secretary waved them right in.

"You wanted to see us Director?"

"Yes that's why I called you! Where are you on this latest investigation that took you all the way to Utah?" he asked as if he were under some duress.

"Well sir, I believe that it was murder, it was no accident!"

"Do you concur with him Agent Marlowe?"

"Yes sir, I agree with Agent Jefferies assessment one hundred percent now."

"Do you mean to say you didn't agree with him at first?"

"Yes sir, uh no sir, we both had different scenarios as did the Captain of the State Police that went with us but once we looked at all the details Agent Jefferies had the right one. We both had to agree with his theory."

"Beyond any doubt Agent Marlowe?"

"Yes sir, beyond any doubt, even a jury would be able to see that it was murder."

"The reason I asked these questions is that someone screwed up and gave me the photos you took in Utah."

"Care to explain why Agent Marlowe is bent over backwards on a boulder by a State Policeman Dick?"

Uh oh, he thought, he called me by my name as he broke out in a sweat. "Yes sir, may I see the pictures first so I can put them in order of the way we took them?"

The Director reluctantly gave the pictures to Dick as he reached across his desk for them. He enjoyed grilling the two of them, it was one of the few pleasures he got as he drummed his fingers impatiently on his desk.

"You know Dick the reason I put the two of you together on this case is that I wanted the two of you to play off one another's theories, I knew you wouldn't agree on anything one hundred percent but you do on this one and that does surprise me."

Dick went through the motions of explaining each photo and the Director sat back in his chair and smiled when Dick was done. "Good job you two, that's what I pay you for, results! Now I am going to ask a simple hard and direct question and no waffling, got it?"

"Yes sir no waffling, we got it," they both answered.

"Now then, I know you have put out bulletins to all the Police Agencies across the United States and that's good work. I also understand that a new bulletin is going out today, correct?"

"Yes sir, that's correct, we revised the original so there could be no vague gray areas or misunderstandings, it is more direct and to the point."

"Very good Dick, now then here's the big question, did either of you think to subscribe to any of the Trade Magazines where Book Store Sales may be advertised to other Book Dealers so they could come by and view what was for sale and maybe make an offer on the merchandise because our killer evidently does. That's probably why he is there and gone before we are aware of it. I want the two of you to go undercover a.s.a.p. as buyers of Books Stores or at least as interested parties. I will see that you get the credentials that you need that will fool anyone and the credit on paper in the form of a Letter Of Credit from our local Bank we do business with."

Dick and Jane looked at one another with a questioning look. "No sir we didn't think of that, we've been too busy setting up our wall map and getting all the information put on it that we've gathered."

"I thought as much, I didn't bring you in here to grill you but it's the only fun I have anymore. I know Agents can sometimes take their eye off the ball for a minute or two and I have to assume that the two of you would have realized this Trade Paper thing sooner or later. Alright, take your photos and show them to the rest of your task force you have set up and get busy, I want some answers and soon!" He pounded his fist once on his desk for emphasis.

"Yes sir, thank you for understanding sir." The two of them left sweating their nervous tails off.

"How come we didn't think of that before Dick?"

"Beats me Jane, how could we both have missed the obvious?"

"That's why the Director gets paid the big bucks I guess."

"How come one of us is always saying that when we have been on the carpet?"

"Oh hell, I don't know, let's get back to work and find out how we can get a subscription to Book Store Trade Papers."

"I have an idea Dick, there is a big Chain Book Store just up the street a few blocks, we could stop in there and make some inquiries on our way to lunch or on the way back."

"How about we eat first then stop by the store, if we're lucky maybe we can talk the manager out of some copies of what we're looking for. I've never seen a Trade Paper before if that's what they are even called."

CHAPTER - 54

After lunch they stopped by the Book Store Jane had mentioned and asked to see the Manager. Lucky for them he'd just returned from lunch. They showed their badges and told him why they were there and asked about Trade Papers they might have to subscribe to.

"I'll tell you what Agents Jefferies and Marlowe, there are several but only two that I would suggest and if you'll give me a minute to look them up I'll make you copies of the latest ones we have and you can take them with you. I would suggest that you call the Editor of each one, tell them who you are and what you want and I'm sure they will cooperate with you. People in our business are all humming with conversations of who is going to die next."

"How come no one has come to us for help?" asked Jefferies.

"Why in the world would the FBI be interested in a Book Store Owner's murder or accidental death, isn't that usually left up to the local authorities?"

"Yes, but money has disappeared from Federally Insured Banks and have crossed State lines and now it does concern us."

"Well that's something none of us were aware of. Please give me a couple of minutes and I'll have the information ready for you." He disappeared from his office and left the two of them sitting there while he went to make copies. They had not even said anything to one another when he was back. "One of my cahiers is looking them up and will make a copy for you and she'll bring them in to us when she's done. Should I mention to any of my employees or friends that you're investigating the deaths of book store owners now?"

"Absolutely not, no one is to know that we were even here, we don't want word to get out, we need to catch whoever is doing this and soon before anyone else dies."

"I understand, when my gal asks me who this was for I'll simply tell her that you're thinking of opening a Book Store somewhere away from here so it won't worry them about competing with another store, we have enough competition as it is right now. There are literally hundreds, maybe even thousands of local mom and pop type owned stores across the country and it seems like those are the ones getting picked on all the time for some reason. I haven't heard a thing about big Chain Stores like ours being sold let alone someone being killed."

"We agree and you would not believe how far we have traveled in our investigations and what we have uncovered and of course we can't discuss any of the details with anyone."

"Of course and I wouldn't pry either, but that doesn't mean I'm not curious about what you've found out."

"Of course not, there's nothing wrong with being curious."

Just as they finished talking a knock came at his door. "Come in Shirley it's alright."

A petite twenty something girl sauntered in catching Agent Jefferies eye. He let out a soft whistle under his breath that only Jane caught. She handed the Manager some papers that he went through and stapled some together so that they wouldn't get mixed up and in doing so he circled in red ink the editor that they needed to speak with by phone to start a subscription. He handed the papers to Jefferies. "Well there you are you two, have a nice day and stop by anytime, we have a great selection of mystery books you know."

"Yes, thank you, we are aware of all that but we're in the business of solving them not reading about the botched jobs of others."

The three of them laughed lightly as he walked with them all the way to the front door.

"Whew Jane, isn't this the same Store we went to earlier?"

Yes it is and I thought sure someone would recognize us but they didn't apparently or they would have said hello or at the very least given us a little wave."

Once back at their Headquarters Agent Marlowe took on the job of making the calls and requested they be put on the mailing list right away and gave them a Post Office Box number they used as a drop for all of the Agents. Each one of them used an alias of one kind or another and the girl that picked up the mail every day had a list of the aliases with the Agents real name beside it so she could get them to the right person every time. Agent's Jefferies and Marlowe had picked names well before this case of any undercover work. They had picked John Wesley Smith and Shelly Anne Cooper. Those were the names she gave to the Trade Papers so they would both be able to get them at the same time. In effect they each got their own copy of the Trade Paper they wanted just in case one of them was away from the Office the other one could stay up to date.

"Agent Jefferies, we should be getting something in the mail within the next two weeks, I called in between issues and I requested a back issue for us both just for the heck of it to show our interest. I know we both have the latest but I'm trying to set up a scenario for us for when we go undercover."

"Very good Agent Marlowe, then we can make copies for the rest of our team. How are you fixed for undercover ware Agent Marlowe?"

"Are you inquiring about my under ware or my street clothes?"

"You're street clothes of course, please don't misread what I say, I'm not going to hit on you, we're professionals after all!"

"Yes, of course I knew that, please disregard the last remark."

"Done and over with, so how are you fixed for clothes for undercover work?"

"Alright I think; I have a business suit that makes me look like a Studious Literate person that bleeds professionalism all over. How about you Agent Jefferies?"

"I'm good, I have some white shirts with worn out at the sleeve cuffs that remind you of a busy Attorney and a couple of suits to match that persona plus a couple of blazers that go with anything, depends on my mood or what I'm trying to project."

"So what you are trying to say is that you're all set."

"Yeah, all I have to do is to repack my luggage."

"Me too, time to repack mine as well. This might be fun playing real people and not cops and robbers for a while."

"I was thinking the same thing, how about that, birds of a feather——."

"Don't say that, I hate clichés Agent Jefferies!"

CHAPTER - 55

Sol took Richard's proposal to heart, he felt as though he had made a new friend for life. Although Richard could be dangerous to Sol, he and Fred knew they were getting to an age where they needed to think about retiring one day and that was the reason for hiring BJ the way they did and he could always kill Richard at a time of his own choosing if he became an implied risk. BJ was their future, he could keep the Company going even after their deaths.

Together Sol and Lorelei with the butler's help worked out a plan to have a Moving Company come in and pack up all of the books and ship them back to his Store in New York.

Moving day was soon here and Sol was there to oversee the packing of the books. Some were more valuable than others and Sol didn't tell anyone about the different values other than he had stacks of books in a pile that went into a box he had marked Special Handling. Greta and Fred would know what it meant if Sol were not on hand the day the Moving Truck arrived with the shipment. Sol continued to see Lorelei and sleep with her for the better part of a week while the arrangements were being made to box everything up and ship the books. Both of them knew Sol would be leaving soon to go back to New York State.

"Sol, how soon do you have to leave?"

"I won't leave for a couple of days yet Li, I can't just run off in the middle of the night and leave you, I have grown very fond of you and couldn't do that. Still, I do have a business to run back home. Maybe you could come out and see me, we could do up the City of New York, Broadway, Restaurants with all the trimmings. We could have a great time for a couple of weeks, at least we would have some time together. I think you'll be surprised at the success my partner and I have achieved after all these years, we have really have made our mark on the world."

"Sounds wonderful Sol, I'd like that, there's nothing here to hold me but I do have a life I have built here along with my horses and I don't want to leave here on a permanent basis. You know we could visit one another you a few times a year and have a long distance relationship."

"That sounds fine Li., I'd better go now and see how the packing is going, they should be done and loaded up soon. The day I leave will be one of the saddest days of my life, you truly are a remarkable woman. If you'll excuse me I'll go check on the packing of the boxes and see if they are about ready to load up yet, I have a specific way I want them loaded so as not to put too much pressure or weight on top of each box which could crush some of the oldest books, it could ruin the bindings you know and some book jackets as well."

"Yes Sol I know, you're married to your work and I know it and I appreciate you're being so forthright with me."

Sol got up from the love seat they'd been sharing and went to find the men who were doing the packing to be sure his instructions were being carried out to the letter. First he checked the truck, it was a big air ride suspension tractor trailer, a double axle in the rear and a sleeper cab that he had hired them to haul only this shipment for him back to Poughkeepsie. There would be nothing on this truck but his books. By the time it was loaded his boxes would nearly cover the entire floor which was forty four feet long inside with an additional six feet of space up in front of the trailer over the fifth wheel coupler that attached the trailer to the cab pulling it which he would not use. This space right now was filled with moving pads; a thick blanket quilted like material which came in different sizes and colors for the loads they protected. Sol looked over the trailer inside then came back into the house and checked on the boxing up of the books. Some of the boxes could not be completely filled due to odd thickness of some books and he had them put packing materials of different kinds in the ends of the boxes so that the books would not shift around and cause unneeded wear and tear against the hard covers or the thin paper dust covers.

The man in charge came over to see Sol. "Sir, are you the owner of these books?"

"Yes that's right, I purchased them from the Estate and the woman I bought them from is in the sitting room just down the hall, I believe you have seen her around here today."

"Yes sir I have and she is a looker, I mean to say she's a beautiful woman alright. I need to ask, would you care to insure this shipment, it must be quite valuable with all the care you have my men taking?"

"Yes some of them are priceless my friend and I would like you to insure them for one million five hundred thousand dollars please, your company can handle that much Insurance can't they?"

"Yes sir, of course sir, would you like me to add it in to the overall price, this is going to be a bit expensive you know."

"Yes I know, the shipment is going to my Store in New York State, I will give you sealed directions on how to get there and who to talk to when you arrive. I hope to be there myself by the time you arrive."

"Yes sir, my boss has instructed me to personally drive the truck and take another driver with me. On the side you want us to drive straight through to New York State, is that right sir?"

"Yes that's correct, you do have a sleeper cab as I requested on this truck don't you?"

"Yes sir, it sleeps up to two people at a time if necessary, we can do the job but like I said it will cost a little extra."

"Listen to what I'm going to say next, it is very important. If you men do a good job and get there within my five day limit and by the way it shouldn't take you more than four days, I will pay each one of you an extra one hundred dollars cash in hand after you unload this truck. I appreciate good and honest help. For every day you shave off the five day limit I will give each of you an extra fifty dollar bill, fair enough? One thing though if you so much as damage one book I won't pay you a bonus of any kind. You'll treat and handle this load as if were an expensive set of the finest fragile antique china."

"Fair enough sir, we'll handle the boxes with kid gloves." The gloves he referred to are gloves from made from young goats called kid skin.

"Good and don't forget to tell your packers to be careful, it could cost you bonus money before you get it all loaded."

"Yes sir, I'll take care of that right now."

"One more thing, tell your packers that if they do a real good job of packing there is a twenty dollar bill extra for each one of them."

"I'll let them know, they are under appreciated you know, packing is eighty percent of the job of getting the goods to their destination safely anyway."

"Yes I know that, I do this several times a year, that is buying up large collections of books and shipping them back to my store. You will be amazed when you back this truck up to the loading dock in back of my warehouse. I'll show you men around a little so you can see how we handle valuable books, some of these may go as far away as Europe or somewhere else like the Middle East."

"I had no idea you were an International Book Broker."

"Well now you know, so govern yourselves accordingly."

"Yes sir," was the enthusiastic answer and the man took off at a fast walk to spread the word to the six men who were busy packing books. They had arrived in a separate van. He and the van driver left to go back to the shop and pick up the additional driver. The man in charge didn't inquire as to why it was so important to get the shipment there with such haste but he didn't care, they were going to be well paid by the company and return loads to pick up in New York City anyway so they would get paid both directions for the long haul.

Sol went back to be with Lorelei and talk some more with her.

"How is it coming along Sol?"

"They are doing a fine job, really careful packers. I just talked with the driver who will be bringing them back to New York State for me. I offered him a bonus if they didn't damage any of the books in transit and he seemed excited about it."

"Isn't this going to cost you a lot of money Sol?"

"Yes, it's going to be very expensive but its the way I want it done. To me all books are like fine china, ruin one and I could lose anything from a few dollars to thousands of dollars on a single book."

"I had no idea that books were that valuable Sol."

"Not many of them are, but I take the utmost care with all of my books. For instance, a book with a torn or missing dust jacket on it, would you buy it if there was one next to it on the same shelf for the same price, you'd choose the book with the better dust jacket wouldn't you?"

"Of course, anyone would."

"Exactly, so you see the need for great care to be taken in their packing then don't you?"

"I do now Sol; you've really opened my eyes when it comes to books now, thank you so much for getting me to appreciate them more now than I ever did before. I'm beginning to see why you enjoy reading so much. There really is more to a book than just its cover. I always thought reading was such a bore. Could you suggest some literature that I may enjoy reading?"

"Sure, but you can answer that question yourself. Here I'll give you an example. You like horse breeding, raising horses and building the right stables don't you?"

"Yes of course, its all I live for."

"How did you learn about breeding and raising horses?"

"Why I bought some books and read up on the subject so that I could become an expert. Then I hired the right qualified people to do the actual mundane day to day work."

"Uh huh, and when you needed to build the stables you have, what did you do?"

"Why I bought books on stables and how they are used, how they were built and why and it made me an expert."

"Where are those books now?"

"Why they're in a bookcase in my bedroom."

"Okay now let's suppose you wanted to know more about Morgan horses or Arabian horses, what would you do?"

"I would go to a Book Store like before and buy the books on the subject and learn all I could about it."

"Alright now, I forgot what your question was, do you remember?"

"Why of course I remember, I was telling you what a bore I thought books were and why I should bother reading any of them. Oh my;" her faced flushed a bright red. "Sol, you really embarrassed me, how foolish I was to question you. I answered my own question didn't I?"

"Yes and don't feel embarrassed, a lot of people think the same way as you do but turn to books now and then for all kinds of reasons."

"What other books do you read Sol, I know you read a lot and you have learned a lot from books like in your restoration practices?"

He thought quickly and said the first thing that came to mind. "Why I like the history of the world and the individual cultures, the politics of things like the building of Rome."

"Wow that is terribly ambitious isn't it?"

"Maybe for some people but I have on hand all the books I'll ever be able to read. My apartment above our store is full of book cases and books that I use for reference. I'm constantly reading something and sometimes a completely different subject if it interests me enough at the time, I go ahead and read up on it as well. I guess you could say that my store is my own personal Library."

"Just how many square feet is your Store Sol?"

"Oh my gosh, I'm not really sure. We started out with four thousand square feet and have enlarged the store several times over the last twenty five years or so. I'd have to guess but I think its right around forty to sixty thousand square feet, perhaps more." Sol was being conservative, he didn't want her to think he was bragging but it was more than five times the size he had told her and took up a total of two stories without the lab.

"That's a huge Store, how do you staff it.?"

"I have a woman who's been with me since the beginning, she is nearly seventy now and an old maid, her world is her library as she calls the store. She knows where very book is and hires young college men and women to help her especially in the summer. We even ship books out of the store; we have a huge shipping room in the back of the store that handles all that. We have a second floor above the store with identical space that we use as storage as new shipments arrive. She runs that as well and we're putting a new young man in charge of all of that as soon as he graduates from the University next year. He has been with us for more than two years and is learning the business from the ground up. When I retire my partner Fred and I will leave him the business because Fred and I don't have any family to leave anything to. He will become a multimillionaire overnight when we sign it over to him. He has already made a few buying trips with me to Book Stores who were going out of business and he's a quick learner."

"It sounds as it you have your life very well planned out for the future. Have you and your friend been able to make any secure investments over the years?"

"Believe it or not, we have only invested in ourselves, we hold several patents that earn us a million dollars a year apiece. We will always have those and upon our deaths we will leave them also to our young man who will take over for us. You would not believe how much money we make just from our ink inventions and patents, its mind boggling. Then we have all of our paper products patents and machinery patents and it's the same thing, they're worth millions. The parchment paper alone we invented makes us rich year after year, it's in high demand by many industries who want to preserve their documents on our paper for posterity and then there are the book publishers that publish many books a year including the Bible and they like our parchment paper for their introductions in front of their books. Am I starting to ramble Li?"

"Yes you are Sol but it sounds absolutely wonderful this dynasty you have built for yourselves, you should see the sparkle in your eyes and the pride on your face when you talk about books."

CHAPTER - 56

Just as Lorelei finished the sentence about Sol's Store a man came to the doorway and asked for the owner of the books.

"That's me now," said Sol, "what do you want?"

"We are through packing sir, sorry it took us so long but we were told to pack with special care and we did. We have everything loaded on the truck, would you like to take a look around and be sure we didn't miss anything?"

"Yes of course, thank you."

"I'm sorry Li, but I'd better check around, would you like to come with us and make sure we have everything?"

"Yes thank you Sol, I'd like that."

The two of them followed the middle aged moving man and checked out the Library which was completely empty then they all went to the basement to have a look around.

"Sol, did I tell you about the other room down here, I don't remember if I asked Henry to show it to you or not?"

"No, I don't think so, he only showed me this big area of books already in boxes that were right over here. I'm afraid I don't remember another room down here."

"My late husband set up a reading room for himself down here, he called it his man get away room, I call it the man cave." They walked to the opposite end of the basement where it was very dark, she found a light switch and turned it on. "There it is, over there Sol."

"Over where, I don't see anything but an old mirror leaning against the wall?"

"Yes, that's it, that's the door, take hold of the mirror and pull, it should open easily."

Sol grabbed the mirror by one side but it was stuck fast so he took hold of the opposite side and a door pulled open. It was dark inside but it was an apparent room.

"There's a light switch on the left just inside the door I think Sol, take a look."

Sol felt all over the wall, both up and down and sideways until finally he found it on the opposite wall. "Got it Li," and he turned it on. It lit up a room about fourteen feet by thirty six feet and the walls were plastered with book cases full of books floor to ceiling.

"I am sorry if I forgot about this room Sol, can they pack this up and get it out of here."

The man in charge of packing was standing there with them in absolute awe of the immense size of the room and all of its books. "We can do it folks, I have plenty more packing material and boxes, I will go get the men and get them to work on this if it's alright with you.?"

"Yes of course, go ahead" said Sol. He was amazed at the amount of books in this room. He started to go through some one at a time.

"Sol you had better hurry he will be back here any minute."

"Yes of course Li, I'm just a little shocked at all this fine Literature."

"Literature? isn't this the same as what was upstairs?"

"No, almost every one of these books is gilded with gold indicating their quality and they may be more valuable than all of the rest put together. You must let me pay you for these Li."

"No Sol, a deal is a deal, I said you could have all of the books which included these."

"But Li, any one of these may be a priceless heirloom; it will take me days to go through each one of them. Look here, there are some with very old hand tooled leather covers as well."

"Just pack them up and get them out of here, I want nothing whatsoever to do with any of the books my husband left behind, they must all go!" Her voice then softened some. "Please Sol, take them all I beg of you." Suddenly Lorelei seemed terribly distraught to Sol, she was trembling all over and he knew she hated the basement anyway.

"Yes, alright when you put it that way, I'll take them but these are the cream of the crop, they are absolutely beautiful. I've never seen such wonderful pieces of Literature in all my life."

She reached over to him and kissed him on his cheek; then they are yours my darling, you have earned them."

"I don't know what to say; no one has ever treated me as well as you have Li, no one." He turned in towards her and their lips met in an equally passionate kiss. They broke it off when they heard several footsteps coming down the stairs to the basement.

It was the packers and the driver ready to go to work on the forgotten books. "Well we're back folks and ready to box these up, anything special for them sir?"

"Yes, these get extra special treatment especially when you're packing them, some of them may be quite fragile so if you don't mind put extremely fragile on the outside of each box and treat them as if they were the finest fragile china plates you have ever seen."

"Must be pretty valuable huh?"

"Priceless my friend, priceless, you have no idea on how valuable these are. Please instruct your men to handle these with extreme care, you would not want to see me upset, that I can guarantee. These my good man are the best of the best when it comes to the classics." "Yes sir, we will surely be careful then."

He turned to his packers who were behind him and said, "you heard the man, be careful and treat these as if they were expensive antique china."

"I don't want to hear about past mistakes either, just don't make any with my books!" Sol added for effect.

"Yes sir, we got the message."

"Sol, you're not needed down here are you, I think you'll just make these men nervous and they might make a mistake if they get rattled, what do you say we get some lunch?"

"Yes of course Li, but these books, they are the best I have ever seen all in one place, how can I ever repay you?" I feel simply awful taking these without paying for them in some way, these obviously are the finest books I have ever seen."

"No need, they were my husband's not mine, if they were mine I might ask a pretty price for them but they have little value to me."

They had their lunch and at 5:30 the moving truck was ready to leave. Sol gave all of the men the tip he'd promised and they were a happy bunch. He also handed the driver his instructions in a sealed envelope. Sol stayed for supper and spent the night once again indulging in sex. It was almost too good to be true. They both knew that in the morning Sol would be on the plane back to his store and he had to call them that the truck was on its way. Unbeknown to her he still had some loose ends too attend to in LA before he would leave.

CHAPTER - 57

Three weeks had gone by and the change in the bulletin Jefferies and Marlowe had made began to pan out as new cases began to trickle in. Almost every one of them were marked closed with the reason for death as accidental due to an overdose of their drug or alcohol of choice. Agent Jefferies was beside himself, didn't anyone bother to question the deaths instead of conveniently calling them accidental. Jefferies was once again questioning the other agency's investigative work and wished he could line them up then fire them all and start over with better trained people like his own agents. They were trained to look beyond the obvious, look for a reason of murder or homicide rather than just closing the cases to clear their desks. Each one of his hand picked men began to pick apart cases and little by little things began to change, they had serious questions for the field investigators who had been on the cases in other States.

"Agent Marlowe, have you seen any forensics at all reported in these cases we are getting?"

"Few to none actually Agent Jefferies."

"Just as I thought, almost every one of these are apparently open and shut cases. I can't remember when I've seen sloppier Police work in all my life. I can shoot holes in nearly every one of these new cases which are showing up. Just look at the hit and run cases, it appears to me that they never went looking for the car or truck that hit someone, They just didn't disappear off the face of the earth, someone had to steal a car or a truck or rent one to do all of these but I find nothing in the notes where they actually went looking for the vehicle or the driver. In a lot of the cases I have here when there was a hit and run a homeless person ends up dead the next day from alcohol poisoning or something. It's all too neat and too convenient for the cops on the beat out there to overlook things with their tremendous work load. Do you get what I'm saying? There is a tremendous amount of cases over the years that are similar in a lot of ways."

"Yeah I know," answered Agent Marlowe, "I'm seeing the same things now that you mention it. It's like who cares about a deceased homeless person the next day or the day after a high profile person is killed."

"Do you think maybe we have found the common thread at last Agent Marlowe?"

"I would have to agree with you on that assessment. What would you like to do, reopen some of these cases that really stink or stick out from the rest?"

"You know Agent Marlowe if we're on the right track maybe we need to look at missing persons reports from families looking for a homeless person or alcoholics, that's one avenue we haven't yet explored."

"Yes, you're right about that but I sure hate to send out another bulletin looking for lost homeless people or alcoholics who move around a lot due to bad weather in one region where they move south to another region such as Florida to escape the cold and snow. I don't know about you but I sure don't want to go back to the director asking for permission to send out another bulletin, it already looks like we don't know our own jobs."

"Yeah you're right, but this has just come up, I swear it. There was nothing said about any of this in any of the other cases."

"You do realize Dick that when some of these people die no one bothers to go looking for them, not even their own kind, they simply absorb the dead person's belongings and get on with their life, even they don't want to draw attention to themselves. I tell you what, if you want to go to the boss with this, I'll back you one hundred percent because you have been right almost every time and I think you have something here with this question. You know we could word it so it looks like a new investigation where family members are coming forward asking where their loved ones are to find out if they are still alive or dead."

"By golly I think you have it Jane, let's give it a shot with that in mind."

The two of them got all their ducks in a row and called the Director's Office for an appointment. This was way too important they felt not to involve the Director himself.

"Alright Agent Marlowe we have a fifteen minute window tomorrow afternoon to see the boss, lets make our case before then so we don't waste his time going through reports to figure this out along with us, it has to be overwhelming and convincing."

"I agree Dick; let's get as much together as we can to show him our concern."

"Thank you Agent Marlowe, your support of my theory means a lot to me. After all, these people were brothers, sisters and in some cases mothers and fathers of someone out there."

The next day they made their case and the Director went along with their idea of a new separate bulletin regarding missing homeless people and alcoholics as well. They would carefully craft the new bulletin to look like it was a separate request from the cases they were working on. In essence it would say,

[SPECIAL BULLETON FOM THE F.B.I. ATTENTION: Special; Agent Jefferies, Washington, D.C THE FEDERAL BUILDING].

[Many people have contacted this agency regarding missing loved ones who are either homeless or alcoholics, in some cases both. They cannot find their relatives and we need your help through this bulletin in finding some of these lost souls.

If you have a number of unidentified people either missing or dead we would appreciate your assistance in this matter.]

This was the very first draft and they would go over it several more times to get it just right before sending out the plea. Early the next morning it went out over the airways much like an old telex but the age of computers was here and today it would be considered similar to an email or a fax, agency to agency.

It worked, the agencies reporting said the same thing, they had been contacted about missing loved ones but no one was seriously looking for them due to their moving around all the time. Now the pressure was on with the FBI being involved. Agencies began to work a lot harder but it would take weeks before lists would begin to show up back at FBI Headquarters. Agents Jefferies and Marlowe had struck a chord that other Agencies had hoped would simply go away. They didn't have the resources to try and find unidentified corpse's families.

Another week went by with few results and they were still waiting for their trade papers to arrive. Finally one arrived advertising an upcoming sale in

Oklahoma near Tulsa, they would be ready and get there ahead of everyone else they hoped. It was advertised as a [Going Out of Business Sale, Everything Must Go.] However no reason was given for the sudden sale but they would go anyway and the date given was a week away so they had time to get moving and get their new act together.

They spent the next week trying on different clothes then playing off one another with one being the good guy the other an agnostic. Jane decided to be the odd one while Dick decided he would do better as the smarter one, knowledgeable about books and book stores. She would be the one holding the purse strings and reluctant to buy anything let alone a whole store full of books. They worked out several scenarios to try out on one another and finally were confident enough that they could pull of their imposter roles.

CHAPTER - 58

The following morning in LA. Sol arose and knew he had to get moving with his latest plans. Although he enjoyed his time in bed with Lorelei he knew it was time to get back to work. To Sol this had been a very nice interlude between trips but now he had things to do before going back to his own store. He shaved and showered just ahead of Lorelei, they both got dressed and went downstairs for breakfast. They were extremely quiet because they knew it was getting close to the time to say goodbye and it may be some time before they saw one another again. After breakfast Lorelei asked Sol to come outside to her favorite spot near the pool to have another cup of coffee alone.

"Sol I hate saying goodbyes, they seem so final when all is said and done."

"Yes I know, sometimes it seems that way but remember we'll see each other soon. If you don't come out to the east coast then I'll come back here to see you. One way or another we'll see each other 'real' soon."

"I certainly hope so; it has been a long time since a man satisfied me in bed the way you have. Besides the sex I enjoy your company and now I have a new respect for books and the passion you have for books is truly remarkable, I'll never look at a book the same way again."

"Thank you Li, what a nice thing to say. I've always taken my passion for books for granted, I never looked at them the way you do and I have learned something new as well."

They moved their chairs closer together and kissed a long moist kiss. "Well my dear, I really must be going, my car is probably waiting for me as we speak and I still have to check out of my Hotel and get to the airport to catch a 1:00 flight to New York."

"Yes I know my love, I just can't seem to let go even though I know we'll be together again soon, but that doesn't make it any easier!"

"Let me grab my overnight bag from upstairs and you can walk me to the door where we can say goodbye, okay?"

"Sure, go ahead and get your things, I know you must leave soon my sweet."

Sol went upstairs and picked up his gear as it were and came back down to the huge foyer near the front door to where Lorelei was waiting for him.

"Well Li, I guess this is it?"

"I guess so, be safe my love and we'll see one another very soon."

"You too my sweet, take care of yourself and please be careful when you are riding horseback, horses scare me so and to me they are awfully unpredictable."

"Oh no, my horses all are safe and gentle and well trained or I wouldn't have them here, you must let me show you how to ride sometime."

"No, I think not, I'll stick to keeping my feet on the ground, flying is the only thing I do to get my feet off the ground."

"Yes of course you do, but maybe I can change your mind about horses one day."

"Perhaps, but I'll not ride one of those beasts. Like I said they scare me! they are so big and we're so small, what's to stop them from running away with one of us on their backs or bucking us off?"

"Nothing, but my horses are so well trained that nothing bothers them."

"All right my sweet give us a kiss goodbye so I can make my connections."

They embraced one another and kissed a long hot moist passionate kiss. Even the Butler who was nearby was blushing. They finally said a last goodbye and as Sol stepped out onto the front porch his Bentley was driving up with Sissy at the wheel.

"Well good bye Lorelei, I'll never forget our time together."

"Neither will I Sol; goodbye my dear."

Sol got into the back seat as soon as his door was opened. He waved from the car window as they pulled away then on down the driveway. As soon as they were out of sight Sol asked his driver how to get in touch with Richard who had handled the rental for Sol. She said to give her a minute and she would put his number on his phone so all he had to do was to hit redial and he will answer. He put down one phone and got ready to pick up the other when his driver gave him the high sign from the front seat. Soon he saw her wave and he picked up the other phone and hit redial, Richard answered on the third ring.

"Richard here,oh good morning Sol, how goes it?"

"Everything is great but I do have one very large concern. This morning I felt Lorelei out about riding horseback and she informed me that her horses were really well trained and nothing would spook them. So maybe her being thrown by one of them isn't such a good idea after all."

"Don't worry we'll go to plan B and we'll have our man meet her out in the pasture where its secluded. I'll have him break her neck as planned and I'll have him loosen or cut the cinch strap on the horse so it will look like a simple riding accident when the saddle fell down around the horse's middle section or have the saddle appear to have fallen completely off with a broken cinch strap causing her to fall off striking her head on a rock thus breaking her neck as well as getting a knock on the head. It will look like an unfortunate accident and we'll put the blame on the stable boy who saddled her horse that day. There will be no problem and I do have a plan C if need be, another sacrificial lamb, another one of the stable boys."

"Okay, sounds like you have it all worked out, are you sure you can implicate one of them in the accident if need be?"

"Sure, I can fix it so he looks like a jilted lover with some of Lorelei's under ware to be found in his things where they sleep. Don't worry I'll handle that, I need your expertise to make it fool proof. I'll give you the name and description of the man who actually does the killing before your plane leaves today. How do you plan to get him? Are you flying back the same day or tomorrow or something?"

"None of the above, I'm not leaving, Sol is, they will see me get on the plane then I'll get off as a different person saying I got on the wrong plane and disappear in the terminal, then I'll go to another Hotel or Motel and check in under another name then I'll take care of our business and catch the next plane out as that man and still be back in time to meet the moving van when it arrives at my store."

"Wow, sounds like an ambitious plan, I like it. Everyone is away clean, you and I both get what we want."

"Exactly, when I get to the airport I'll turn Sissy loose and send her back to wherever it is she has to go. I'll get a Cab from the Airport and go to another Hotel like I said. I'll see you in Poughkeepsie one day soon and we'll drink a toast to this caper."

"I'll be looking forward to it Sol, I can't thank you enough."

"The book collection is more than enough, I plan to make close to a million at least on the sale of her individual books, of course I'll duplicate the best ones and sell them twice."

"You're a devilish man Sol, that's why I like you so much I guess; I wish we'd met twenty years ago."

"Me too Richard, me too."

"Goodbye and good luck Sol, see you soon."

"Goodbye Richard, looking forward to your visit to New York State."

The two of them hung up, each had received or almost everything they wanted and so far all it had cost Sol was two plane tickets, half down with the moving company and the better part of a week in bed with a beautiful woman."

CHAPTER - 59

Two days later the LA Newspapers all had the same headline.

[Wealthy Heiress Lorelei Wynn dies in horrible horseback riding accident on her ranch. Detectives found that the cinch strap which held her saddle on had been cut part way through with a sharp knife. Stable boy suspected after detectives found part of her undergarments along with a sharp knife instable boy's locker upstairs in the stables where he slept in a small apartment. Butler confirms he has seen the two of them together. The heiress was also under suspicion that she poisoned her late husband. Rumors are that all of her property has been left to her only cousin; she has no surviving relatives who are known at this time.]

The next day the newspapers carried more interesting front page news:

[Bull's Eye Private Detective Agency burned to the ground with the Owner, his assistant and his secretary all inside. Police suspect a disgruntled divorced man set the fire after killing the three of them with a gun then he set the fire to finish them off.]

The following day there was a small inconspicuous article near the death notices that read,

[Today a homeless man's body was discovered inside a newspaper recycling bin when it was dumped and readied for recycling. Coroners report said he died of alcohol poisoning, he was thought to have gotten in under some newspapers to escape and unusual cold night to stay warm and simply passed away due to exposure from the elements. His death was found to be accidental therefore there will be no further investigation.]

Sol in the meantime had arrived back at his store and was making ready to welcome the Moving Truck when it arrived. On the fourth day since they left California they arrived at the store and inquired where to unload from a young man in the store. He rode around to the back of the building with them after telling Sol they were there and showed them to the loading dock they were to back up to. The man who Sol had talked with was the one to back the truck in. He got out of the truck and climbed a short set of steps to the loading dock and wasn't surprised when Sol was there to greet him.

"Well gentlemen, you made good time," said Sol.

Both the drivers were on the dock by then. Sol shook their hands individually and then showed them to the elevator they would use to take the books up to the second floor where they would be stored and sorted later. The specially marked boxes were to be taken immediately to the laboratory where Fred was, he would show them where to put the special boxes. He would make two separate stacks of only two boxes high so as not to damage the books by their own sheer weight. The driver that remembered Sol spoke to him once again.

"Mr. Shultz, you certainly have a wonderful building here, I had no idea that this place was so big, three stories huh?"

"Yes, but counting the basement there are four, the top floor are all apartments for our employees who need one, we don't rent them to anyone else, only those who are actually working in the building itself. The first floor is full of shops and other stores as well. When we started out we were the only store here and we've enlarged it twice since then. Wait until you see our factory where we manufacture our own ink and paper products, it's quite a sight. We restore old books as well as old manuscripts to original condition if that is what the owner wishes, we also do a lot of preservation work for museums. Well you and your fellow driver have earned yourselves quite a bonus and remember you're not to tell anyone about our side agreement."

"No sir, we won't tell a soul, the man with me really didn't want to make such a long trip until I told him of your generosity."

"Well you men have done a remarkable job, I hope you will allow me to by you lunch before you depart. We can eat before your unloading is done because no one wants to work on an empty stomach. My deal with you only required you to get to the loading dock in five days or less, you can take your time unloading, you are on your boss's clock for now."

"Yes sir, thank you sir and may I add its been a pleasure working for you, I had no idea the value of such books, I have a new respect for them now, I feel as though I've just delivered a big load of history to the world."

"And you are correct it that assumption because some of these will be going overseas to wealthy collectors of fine literature, they have you to thank for getting them this far safely. After this it will be my responsibility to get them to their final destination and in pristine condition."

They went to eat after a few minutes and spent the rest of the day leisurely unloading the truck. Norman and another young man from the Store helped during the unloading process and when the drivers were done technically they had a free day to do with as they wished. The contract to deliver the books said only that they would be delivered by five days, any longer and the Moving Company would have to pay Sol a penalty.

"I will need your names; I'll give you receipts for your meals to turn in to your boss so he can repay you both."

"But we drove straight through, we ate fast food on the go to get here and only stopped to get fuel and use restrooms."

"You and I know that but your boss won't know it. I'll take care of everything, that's part of our agreement you didn't know about. You men should make a tidy little profit when you get back and don't forget to complain about the food and filthy conditions of where you ate having to pay a high price for the food."

"I got it; I'll have to do it because he don't know how to get a long with my boss like I do. I know how to work it depending on the receipts you make out for us. He gave me some cash for that which I still have because we still have a load to pick up in two more days in the City of New York, I have to be there to do that. That's one reason the boss told us to bring the bigger trailer because of what we need to bring back with us, we will have the trailer full to the top with the amount of furniture and things we're picking up from a total of five stops."

"I'll take care of everything," said Sol, "you have no idea the things we can create around here."

While the men were repacking their truck with all the moving pads and things they had to fold up Sol went to check on Fred to see how he was coming with the phony receipts for the drivers. When he got downstairs

Fred was all done and he handed the small pile of receipts to Sol so he could look them over.

"They look great Fred, these men have earned a little extra for what they have done for us. By the way have you had a chance to look over any of the boxes yet?"

"No Sol, this receipt business has kept me pretty busy what with meal tickets and receipts and all but it wasn't too bad just a lot of them, you know, three meals a day apiece covering five days. I'm glad you gave me what receipts they had, that made it easier to figure of the different State Sales Tax percentages."

"No problem, we'll talk some more after they leave, they have a free day and night in New York City now so they can live it up with the bonus money I gave them. I've got to go now and give them their new receipts, keep the others for reference for another job and I'll tell them goodbye for you."

"Thank you Sol, they were nice young men weren't they?"

That night Richard called Sol at his apartment and told him about the newspaper articles regarding Lorelei and the homeless man plus the devastating deaths of three people in a Private Detective's Agency's Office who perished. There were no witnesses, the building was completely destroyed by fire. Reports say that there were two men and a woman found in the debris after the fire was out. Police are looking into a tip about a disgruntled husband who got a divorce because of their Detective work who had gone broke.

"Sol, I don't know anyone who can be in two places at once and get away with it."

"But I wasn't there, I've been here the whole time."

He could hear Richard laughing hysterically over the phone. "Boy I can't wait to meet you on your own turf."

"I don't live the high life here Richard, I'm just another average business man who makes several trips a year around the States or somewhere else in the World. You can come this way anytime you feel like it, we can go into New York and catch some of the big Stage Plays if you want. I know a person who can get us tickets anytime I want and back stage passes if you like."

"Back Stage Passes, are you kidding?"

"Certainly not, anytime anywhere and anyone you would like to meet."

"What's the best paper for me to read about the plays, what and where they are playing?"

"Try the New York Times I guess or there is a magazine called Playbill I believe or something like that, you should be able to pick them up anywhere in LA and check them out."

"Okay Sol, I have to go, I'll be in touch and let you know a few days ahead of time before I decide to fly out there to be sure you're in town and not off somewhere gallivanting." "Okay I got it as you like to say, give me a ring ahead of time, you know my routine."

"Right you are Sol, bye for now."

"Bye Richard, good talking with you."

CHAPTER - 60

Agents Jefferies and Marlowe had their act down to where the other Agents who they were trying out their undercover act on almost believed them. At first it sounded corny but then the Agents began to help them with suggestions rather than their out and out uncontrollable laughter. After three weeks of practicing in front of mirrors at home alone they had their acts down so well that they could switch roles with little problem, they almost knew what the other one was thinking. They finally had it down to where it would fool almost anyone. Their request for odd deaths of the homeless was so good that someone sent them the entire pages from a LA newspaper that carried the death notices for both Lorelei Wynn and the homeless man found in the newspaper recycling bin and a feature article about a fire at a Detective Agency where three people were found dead.

"Hey Agent Marlowe, did you see this one yet?"

"Which one Agent Jefferies?"

"This one from a few days ago in LA. An heiress died after being thrown from her horse and a homeless man found dead in a newspaper recycling bin, how strange is that?"

"Sounds perfectly normal to me, people die after being thrown from a horse at least once a week somewhere in the world."

"Maybe so, but the Police say this was murder. They say that a jilted young man who worked for the lady in her stables cut the saddle cinch strap, whatever that is, nearly in half and that she fell from the horse when the saddle loosened and broke her neck. Broke her neck, ring a bell does it? That's three broken necks this year or is it four, I've lost count."

"I hear you and I know that suspicious mind of yours is always looking for trouble."

"That may be to the unknowing person but this one is definitely murder and there is the homeless man found dead as well. I wonder, maybe I ought to call the LA Cops and see if there was a book collection intertwined here in some way? There is another article here on the same page about a Detective agency that burned to the ground with three people inside but it says here a divorced man is suspected of setting the fire due to the agency work that caused his divorce which then caused him to go broke as well. That one doesn't seem to concern us but I am suspicious about the other two articles.

"You're reaching again Dick, how in heavens name can you possibly tie it all together."

"I don't know but it fits with what we're looking at."

"How do you figure, let me see the article before you go off half cocked?"

Jane read the articles through and through again and again. "It's an open and shut case, didn't you read the part abut the knife and her under ware being found in the boy's locker and the Butler said he'd seen them together before."

"Sure, but its also possible the Butler only thought he saw what he thinks he saw."

"Huh, come again?"

"Well think about it. I'm sure the house and stables are quite a ways apart and I'm also sure that someone saddled the lady's horse for her and I am sure she checked it out before riding like any good rider would have."

"So what's your point?"

"Couldn't someone else have saddled her horse and cut the cinch belt strap or whatever you call that thing that is supposed to hold the saddle on for you."

"Are you saying the Butler could be confused?"

"No, not at all, what I am suggesting is that almost anyone could have saddled that horse and not be seen from the house. I'm sure the butler has seen the two together many times but I don't believe he meant it in a romantic way. If they wanted to make love wouldn't they go into the barn out of sight of everyone in the house and everywhere else?"

"Well you and I would have of course but you're talking about a wealthy heiress who probably doesn't give a flip, let me read it through again?" She read the whole article again twice. "Dick, did you happen to notice she was under suspicion poisoning her late husband?"

"No, must have missed that part, but so what, he's dead now she's dead."

"I've got it!" said Jane.

"What Jane, did you think of something?," Dick asked excitedly.

"Yes, I know who did it!"

"Who did what to who woman, make some sense!"

"Well it's as plain as the nose on your face Dick, the Butler did it of course, he killed them both."

Dick held his head in his hands. "Oh no, I'm working with a crazy woman!"

"Alright Dick, I'll bite but I know I'm going to be sorry. What about the homeless man, who killed him?"

"Accident just like the Police said, pure and simple."

"Are you saying his death was still an accident when even the newspapers agree with the cops, it was a cold night and he died from alcohol poisoning?."

"I don't buy all of it Jane but something just isn't right here. I want to go to LA and talk to the Butler and whoever else works there on the estate."

"Alright Dick you haven't been wrong yet, something is eating at you but what about our Book Store guy?"

"He's involved in this somehow I know it, I just know it. I just want to check this out. Let's make the arrangements, we can check in by phone back here, we shouldn't be gone more than a couple of days or so."

"Okay, but you can clear it with the Director this time, not me, you're on your own with this one, I can't see one flaw with the story that's in the newspaper."

"What about the cops, they make mistakes like some of the other cases we received. I want the strap brought back here for our people to go over along with the knife."

"Okay, okay, you deal with the Director and I'll take care of the plane reservations and Hotel rooms."

Dick got his things together mainly the newspaper clippings and headed upstairs in hopes he could see the Director right away between appointments. He had to wait almost an hour but finally got the wave in from the secretary. He told the Director what he suspected and wanted permission to make this quick trip and bring the evidence back with him; he would need the boss's authority to do that. He got that and more, he got chewed out for wasting time standing around talking when he should have been on his way to the airport. He thanked the Director and headed back downstairs to where Agent Marlowe should have been waiting. He didn't see her right away. Then he thought, dummy, check your office, she was going to make reservations.

"Where have you been Dick, we need to catch a ride to the airport right now or wait a couple of days for another flight."

"Donny can take us, it will be quicker if he just lets us off at the outside boarding thing for the airline. Someone can cover for him besides he likes to use the lights and sirens still in our marked cars, he can't get it out of his blood."

"Damn it Dick, you think of everything."

"Yeah but I can also forget a lot, I only have an overnight bag here, how about you?"

"Same thing, only an over night bag."

"We'll work it out when we get there, let's go." They were surprised when they saw Donny waiting there for them with a car in the garage parking lot.

"Hi guys, the Director called me and said you might need a ride to the airport, I have a marked car all ready to go."

"How did he know we needed a ride right now Jane?"

"Damn if I know Dick, must have read your mind, certainly not mine, I was against this as you know."

"Yeah, yeah, just get in."

"Let's get moving Donny."

"Do you mind telling me where to?"

"Certainly!" said Dick

"Jane where are we going?"

"Oh, I'm sorry guys, Dulles Donny and step on it, we can make it if we hurry, it was the only airport with a straight through flight going out today to LA with vacant seats."

There were three airports to chose from in and around Washington. Donny hit the lights and siren, he was back in a car again and it felt good. Dulles was a thirty to forty five minute ride or so in a cab in normal traffic and they didn't have time to mess around so the marked FBI car came in handy after all.

CHAPTER - 61

At 3:30 that afternoon LA time they landed at LAX and immediately rented a full size sedan. They headed for a Hotel that Jane had found with two adjoining rooms but she didn't tell Dick that just yet. She didn't want him to get his male hopes up. Dick followed her instructions and they got checked in then immediately left for the local Sheriff's Department who was handling the heiress's case. Once there they were met with suspicion themselves, the Sheriff's Department Deputies wanted to know why the FBI was there and really didn't want to cooperate because they had already closed the case. After a lot of haggling and some threats the Deputies relented and gave up the evidence they had found at the stables. Every single officer was convinced the young stable boy did it because of what they had found in his locker.

Number one Agent Jefferies and Marlowe found that the lockers had no locks on them, anyone could come and go any time without being seen. The Department they were at was a Sheriff's Sub Station used to service rural LA County. Dick was livid about the lack of respect they had received and the run around they got when they arrived. Dick started to berate the Deputies who were gathered there.

"Don't you people ever read the bulletins we send out? If you had you would know we are looking for a serial killer. All of you probably trampled all over the crime scene where the body was found and at the stables, am I right?"

"Yes I'm afraid so Agent Jefferies, we had no idea the FBI would be interested in this particular case. It's clearly an open and shut case, the young man did it and we have no doubt about that."

One man, a uniformed Deputy Sheriff, apparently was speaking for most of them who were gathered there.

"Oh really, why is that?"

"Like I just told you, we found the knife that cut the leather on the saddle in his locker."

"Look, obviously you are the biggest bunch of amateurs I have ever seen. Did you even bother to check for fingerprints on the knife before you handled it?"

"No sir no need to, it was his knife."

"Did he say it was?"

"No! He said he had lost his only knife and that it was a small folding pocket knife that he lost a few days before the killing."

"Did any of you check out his story?"

"No, like we said, he did it clear as day, the knife was in his locker."

"Bull crap, no jury will ever convict him on this flimsy evidence. I'm taking it all back to DC with us and run it through our crime lab and I'm betting that this isn't even the knife that cut the leather you're talking about. Did you bother to see if the leather was torn or was it cut all the way through, because if it is a clean cut it was done after the lady was killed, am I getting through to any of you now? Let me see that piece of leather?" Dick was really livid by now.

A man produced the short piece of leather strap approximately six inches long. Dick took the piece of leather in his hands and asked where the rest of it was.

"Well sir, we cut that piece off the saddle and brought it here, we couldn't very well bring in the whole saddle now could we?"

"And why the hell not, don't you people realize you've tampered with evidence, which end is the cut end from the knife you have, they both look the same to me?"

"Well now I'm not rightly sure which end is which now that you ask."

"I'm going to give you all a direct order and you will carry it out right this very minute or I'll arrest every damn one of you for tampering with Federal Authority's evidence in the course of our duties and investigation, do I make my self clear?" The veins on Dick's neck and face were standing out by now and his face was getting redder with each answer he got from the men who were there.

Another Deputy piped up obviously fed up with Dick's tirade. "Yeah we hear you big mouth, you're in California now I'd be careful where you cross the street and where you drive, you just might get a ticket or get hit in a cross walk, who cares?"

"Agent Marlowe, did you get that outburst on tape?"

"Yes I did Agent Jefferies, every word!"

"Now I want that man's name, he'll be the first one fired or goes to jail if you don't get you asses in gear and bring that saddle back here and in one piece or so help me Go;"

Agent Marlowe grabbed his arm as he was reaching for his concealed weapon. "If I were one of you I would do what this man asks or be arrested, we are not here to play games or bust balls, we're here because a murder has been committed and you obviously have the wrong person in jail you damned idiots!"

"Cool off Agent Jefferies!" Jane added as she held his arm more loosely now.

"I want that man's name and badge number, hell I want his badge right now, you no longer work here Jack, every man in here heard you threaten two FBI Agents and we won't stand for it. You have stonewalled us every since we walked in the door. If it were up to me I'd lock every single one of you up in your own jail right now, where the hell is your chief located?"

"Well sir he, the Sheriff that is, has an office in City Hall up town, this is only a Sub Station" offered another Deputy.

"Uh huh, a bunch of wana be cowboys or is it cops you wana be?"

"No sir, I mean yes sir, oh hell I'll run out to the estate and get the damn saddle if no one else will," said a third man who wasn't talking back just yet. The young man left by the front door while the rest of the Deputies just kind of milled around not knowing when Jefferies would blow up next but he had made a point and some of the men had red faces. One man standing near the back of the group of officers tried to leave through the back door without being seen. Agent Marlowe saw the man sidling sideways towards a door in the back of the huge front office.

"Don't even think about it Mack, get back here and face the music, once we get through going over this with your boss in all likelihood you'll all be let go. We Law Enforcement Officers are supposed to cooperate with each other but you people to a man have gathered against us and confronted us in a most unprofessional way. I mean how small can you people get warning us to be careful crossing the street even in a cross walk we may be run down or driving anywhere in your jurisdiction that we may get a ticket over nothing. Talk about Police harassment, this is the worst I have ever seen and I've been around gentlemen."

One of the Deputies in the back of the group said under his breath, "just who the hell does this dumb broad think she is?"

"Alright buster I heard that, step out here for a minute and we'll conduct a class," Jane added.

The uniformed Deputy stepped out from the back of the group; he was a tall mean looking man, very muscular in stature, his muscles looked as though they'd break through his shirt seams if he took a deep breath .

"Another man in the group said, "be careful now Johnny, don't hurt the lady, she has dishes to do when she's through here." A subtle laugh went through the group of nine men.

"Uh Agent Marlowe," said Jefferies, "I don't think this is necessary, why not let me talk to them before you start breaking bones, Workman's Comp may not cover a man's broken arm or leg horsing around the office."

"No fooling around Agent Jefferies, we're going to conduct a class in self defense."

"Alright you men you heard the lady, schools in session. I think I should tell you she came in first in every one of her self defenses classes at the Academy. She also holds several records just behind me and is also an expert in firearms of every kind you can imagine, so gentlemen, I guess school is in session!"

The big man approached Agent Marlowe with ease, he was a heavy set man but he looked like it was all muscle, still he moved with grace and moved like a cat as he approached Agent Marlowe looking for an opening to strike quickly.

"Come on big man with the big mouth, take me out with your bare hands if you please, I wouldn't suggest using a knife, you could end up with a broken arm or worse."

He began to circle Jane to the left then to the right, he looked like a lion sizing up its kill before attacking, then he made a lightning quick move and with hardly any effort she threw his big body to the floor with a thud that shook everything in the room and the dust flew. He lay there on the floor with the wind knocked out of him.

"What, what happened, did I trip over something?" he asked as he got his breath back.

"No you big lug but you're lucky to be alive, I could have easily killed you, and you're too big and too slow to be a cop, anyone else care to try my patience?"

"Uh no ma'am," came the reply from around the room.

"Alright now, have we made our point, we won't tolerate any more insubordination?"

"Yes ma'am, no problem, we'll tell you whatever it is you want to know."

"Alright, consider yourselves lucky because Agent Jefferies has killed men with his bare hands who challenged him with weapons, understood? In fact you may have seen the shootout on TV a year or so ago about a shooing where several men were killed along with an FBI Agent. One of those Agents was Agent Jefferies partner and he nearly gave his life to save his, I'm his new partner and he or I would do the same for one another. We're professional Law Enforcement Officers and Federal Agents; do you understand what Federal means you bozos?"

"Yes ma'am, if we didn't we do now."

"Right, it trumps Local and State Police agencies all the way to the top and believe me when I tell you that you wouldn't ever want to see our boss mad, he even scares us that's why he is where he is and we're still Agents. Now then gentlemen, do we have your full attention?"

"Yes ma'am, sorry we came off like we did but we're proud of our office, we feel like we do a real good job and service to our community," answered one man.

"We're not faulting your work in general but you do understand that in this case you have no case and you have deliberately destroyed valuable evidence that could free the man you have in custody and maybe also convict the man we're after. Hell we don't even have an accurate description of him. One of you may have already met him and didn't bother to check his credentials which we believe are false identification items and if you had bothered to check him out you would have caught him and the murdered heiress and another unfortunate man may still be still alive. You had him right here in your midst and not one of you bothered to read our bulletins. I hope it makes you all feel real good because a lot more people are going to die due to your own ineptness. I want one of you to locate the last three bulletins we sent out, I want them posted on your bulletin board and I want to see it done right now!"

"Yes ma'am." Every one of them took off in every direction looking for any sign of the bulletins in question. None of them wanted to raise the ire of Special Agents Jefferies and Marlowe again now that they knew they meant business. Not one of them went to the bulletin board behind the massive counter to check it out.

"Ahem gentlemen," said Jefferies, "you might check your bulletin board."

One man went over and leafed through every page stuck with push pins to the board.

"Nope, nothing here Agent Jefferies."

"Well they have to be somewhere, we sent out an all points bulletin three different times on this guy and we want him bad, he's already killed more than twenty people that we know of and there could be many more that were overlooked just like your case right here. I suggest that you get with the prosecutor and tell him what's happened and see if he won't release that young man. he in no way had anything to do with the heiress's death. I'm really surprised no one here saw through the planting of evidence, it was really amateurish of every man in here. Even a rookie cop would have known the difference. You looked the wrong way and let the bad guy make his escape. Do you see the problem with what you all have collectively done to that young man you have in jail? I want one man to leave here right now and go and find your Captain or Lieutenant or whoever is supposed to be in charge here. I want to know why one of them wasn't here watching the station house, I don't even see a Sergeant among you here."

"Yes sir, I mean no sir, it's his day off."

"Alright let's work down the chain of command, is there a corporal in here at least?"

"No sir, I don't know where he is, he could be in the restroom for all we know."

"My God, this is worse than I expected" offered Jefferies.

"Agent Marlowe, is there anything you'd like to ask of these men?"

"No, I can't fault them anymore, it appears that we start at the top and work down, these men apparently didn't know anything other than what they were told, I suggest we lighten up on them and chew out the top dogs but good when they get here."

"I agree with you, we'll let the chips fall where they may. I want the man who was in charge of this investigation, he's the one who's responsible. I'm going to call the boss; he'll want a piece of them when I tell him what has happened here, where is your nearest phone mister?"

"Right over here behind the counter, you can get an outside line easy," said a Deputy.

Agent Jefferies sat down and in a few minutes he was talking with his boss. He explained the nest or angry hornets they had run into and what was going on as they spoke. He asked him if it would be alright for him to call back as soon as the Captain and or the Lieutenant got back so he could talk to them. He was on the phone a good twenty minutes and didn't pull any punches.

"Alright, that's done, from now on we wait Agent Marlowe; we wait for the head of this department to show up. Did anyone find the bulletins we sent you?"

"No sir we're still looking!" said another Deputy.

"I'm betting that one of the men we are waiting for knows exactly where they are."

Everyone found a seat while they were waiting for the return of their boss when they couldn't find the bulletins.

CHAPTER - 62

An hour and a half went by; it was nearly lunchtime when the two officers in command walked in.

Agents Jefferies and Marlowe introduced themselves and told them why they were there and demanded answers to their questions. There were a bunch of elusive answers and it was evident that the two men didn't want to answer them directly or cooperate either.

"Gentlemen, I have someone who would like to talk to you both, can we use an office where the two of you can get on the phone?," asked Jefferies.

"Yeah we got a place but you're wasting your time, we did our job and the case is officially closed," said the Captain.

"I figured as much after talking with your men Captain." As they were getting ready to move to a private office the young Deputy came in the front door lugging the saddle.

"What the hell do you think you're doing you idiot, get that piece of crap out of here, throw it in a dumpster or whatever but get rid of it," bellowed the Captain.

"Don't move Deputy, put the saddle down and find a seat we're going to have a chat with your boss," said Jefferies.

"You can't countermand a direct order by me just who the hell do you think you are?"

Agent Jefferies was boiling under his collar as he walked behind the two men with Agent Marlowe right behind him. They went into a small office with a single desk that had two telephones. Dick picked up a phone and dialed an outside line. In a few minutes he had their boss on the line, the Director of the FBI. "Director, we have the Captain and the Lieutenant here finally and they would like to explain all the insubordination and the actions of their own due to the wrongful arrest of a fine young man who's as innocent as he can be. They still want to prosecute him. I advised them to take it up with the prosecutor of this case and tell him everything that's transpired, I believe the young man will be released before the end of the day, here's the Captain and the Lieutenant, they both can hear you sir. Oh and by the way we have the saddle now, we'll be sending back the evidence we need so the lab can go over it." He handed the telephone to the Captain and the Lieutenant picked up the other phone. Agent Jefferies and Marlowe stood by the door and watched their reactions as they introduced themselves and said a few words then began to listen intently. The conversation lasted several minutes. As the time ticked off the men's faces got redder and redder, they both broke out in a sweat. In another five minutes they both said goodbye after saying yes sir several times. The Captain handed the phone to Agent Jefferies, "your boss wants a word with you."

He took the phone and listened. "Yes sir, we can handle it, yes sir, consider it done."

"Captain, I'll have your badge, you're under arrest for failure to do your duty and will be given a hearing to determine your fate, you do understand don't you?"

"Yes Agent Jefferies, I left my post with no one in charge and I'll show you where those bulletins are, I tossed them away just this morning. I guess that's part of the dereliction of duty your boss mentioned," replied the Captain.

"We had no idea anyone would commit such a crime here," added the Lieutenant.

"Problem is Captain, how many more people have to die because of your incompetence."

"Yes sir, I understand now, your boss was very explicit, he told me every-thing and also said we were to cooperate fully or you'd lock up everyone in the station house."

"You do believe now that we mean business now don't you?"

"Yes but what about my Lieutenant, what will become of him now?"

"That's up to a board of inquiry but I think the responsibility is yours and yours alone, understood?"

"Yeah I got it and you're right, I was bull headed and wanted to look good in my own boss's eyes. I rushed my men to conclusions, please don't fault them, they were only following orders."

"Well I'll say this for you; you're taking this like a man should;" and he slapped the cuffs around the Captain's wrists.

"Lieutenant you're in charge now until this can be investigated further. You may or may not be implicated in this but together you are going to cost someone else their lives, you'll both have to live with that, now go ahead and process the Captain as you would any other prisoner."

"Yes sir, I understand, but like the rest I followed orders, we're at fault collectively."

"I understand, but the inquiry will decide what is to be done, suffice to say all of your jobs are in jeopardy and I'm sure none of you will work together again and that there will be some re-training for several of your men."

"Yes sir, I guess we deserve it."

"Well there is one man out there who will not suffer your own demise; I will give him a letter exonerating him from any discipline. He was the only one who had the balls to stand up and do what we requested. He recognized the fact that something was dreadfully wrong here."

"Yes sir, may I go now and explain to them what has happened and set up their patrols for the day?"

"You're telling me that no one is on the street and hasn't been all morning are you?"

"Yes sir that's exactly what I'm saying," said the Lieutenant. "The Captain asked me to go with him for a few minutes before I could get the schedule finished and I guess time got away from us."

"Well I can't fault you for following orders very well, get them out on the street and now, it will be better for them if they are out of here when heads start to roll. I have to call your boss the Sheriff Lieutenant, he will want to see you as well."

"Yes sir, thank you sir and for what's its worth I am sorry, I had no intention of being gone for more than a few minutes."

He went back out front to talk with his men while Agent Jefferies called their boss, the Sheriff, and told him there had been some trouble and that he was needed there right away.

CHAPTER - 63

The Agents spent the rest of the day briefing the Sheriff after the three of them went to lunch to get away from the office for a while. Heads would certainly roll for many reasons, not just because the Feds had shown up and had disrupted their routine but because of what had been done out at the stables and the arrest of the young man who was a stable boy. Once the Sheriff had all the details he swore there would be an overhaul and Agent Jefferies asked leniency for one man and gave his hand written letter to the Sheriff. They took the saddle with them, had it encased in a plastic covering it much like you encapsulate a boat for winter storage and sent it back by Air Freight to FBI Headquarters in Washington.

After everything was finished they borrowed a Sheriff's marked car and a driver and went to the Estate of Lorelei Wynn to talk with the servants, not just the butler. One by one they came up with differing stories of a man who came and stayed overnight and bought all the books in the house. No two descriptions appeared to be close. The last man they talked with was the butler Henry who seemed to be constantly near Lorelei and looked after her every need. He became their suspect for a while until they shot holes in his story and decided he was a compulsive liar, con man or both. Either way he didn't fit the profile of their killer and it seemed to them that he had no knowledge of what had really happened to his boss, the heiress.

"Well Agent Marlowe, now we know there was a sale of books intertwined here after all with our killer but no one saw any money change hands. Could it be he was seeing this woman romantically and she gave him the books just to be rid of them. Apparently from what everyone says she hated books unless it had something to do with horses and she loved some men but was choosy. What troubles me is no two people seem to have seen the same man twice. One day he's short, another day he is taller, one day he appears bald wearing a soft wide brimmed hat, one brown hair, one black hair, I wonder he's masquerading as several people to throw us off track."

"I don't know Dick; its possible but why, why hide your identity when in the presence of the same woman? It doesn't make sense to me, couldn't she have been seeing different men each day and one of them bought the collection of books like the butler said?"

"I suppose it's possible but he would have to be here on the day that the truck they told us about came to pick them up. I'm sure he would had been here to supervise the packing of the boxes and loading, especially if they were as valuable as they tell us they were."

After interviewing every one of the staff in the house they took a walk down to the stables and found two men there who acted like they were absolutely lost. Since Ms. Wynn's death they were unsure whether or not they were going to have a job in the future. They told the Agents that the Will had not been read yet and they were not sure who the new owner might be or even if the new owner liked horses. They showed them the horse she had been riding that day and their lockers where they kept their belongings. They also said what a nice a boss Ms. Wynn had been to work for. They showed the Agent's their small apartments above the Stables where single people were allowed to live rent free. They did pay their own utilities and phone bills. It gave them a chance to see how easy it would be for someone to come and go without being heard or seen anytime of day.

"Alright we're beating a dead horse here, lets go see if we can find the Moving Company that picked up the books and where they were delivered," Dick asked Jane.

They had the name of the Company from one of the servants who had seen it in the driveway on a truck backed up to the side of the house. They asked their driver to take them to the Moving Company.

A half an hour later they were there. They checked with the owner and he showed them the bill of laden and it went to an address in New York City. He told them his men had trouble finding it and just made it under the five day deadline of delivering the load. Unfortunately the men were out with other trucks doing pick ups and making deliveries all over the States.

"Well we have an address although its probably bogus," commented Agent Jefferies, "that may be why they had a hard time finding the location, they probably called a number and we're told to stay put until someone came to show them the way to the delivery address."

"Is that what you really think Dick?"

"No I think we've been had and mislead over all creation is what I really think!"

"I agree with you, whoever this guy is he bribes people with enough cash to the point that they won't help us, either that or they are scared he may come back and kill them." "I think you're right on both counts, this man must be some larger than life character."

"What do you say, shall we go back to our own little hell hole and start from scratch?"

"Yes, I'm with you on that but I also want to write down all of the descriptions of this guy and see if we can't come up with the same one once in a while, maybe trip him up when he's in disguise."

"You really feel the way I do now don't you Dick? This is a man of many disguises!"

"Yes I totally agree with you now after talking with that staff at the Estate of Ms. Wynn's. I'm afraid your instincts were right on the money all the time."

They took the ride back to the Sheriff's Office, picked up their rental car and went back to the Hotel to book a flight back to Washington and call Donny to tell him when they wanted to be picked up. They got a flight out the first thing in the morning, there had been a two person cancellation so they got a flight out almost right away.

CHAPTER - 64

Two weeks went by and the Book Store was humming along smoothly. Sol and Fred had both been through several of the specially marked boxes from LA and found some very rare books but only a handful were real, many were poor copies just as Sol had said. Fred threw out the poorest copies, they were worthless to them, they could make millions their way and they knew it. The books that were thrown out were recycled through their own paper mill. It was small but they turned out magical quality paper beyond compare. They were getting orders for different shades of colored paper and on each box contained the words, 'ROB Fine Linen Stationary.' They had several blends of white and beige. Their most popular colors were soft pink for the ladies, blue for the men in different hues. They could also custom make any color the client wanted. They got orders from middle east countries for reds and purples and a canary color for the Canary Islands from bright yellow to a soft yellow and they could imprint a canary into the paper to make it more attractive. They could also put in the clients own choice of water marks for security reasons. Larger companies could not compete with small orders like they could. It was just too costly for a big company to make small runs of paper; they existed on huge runs at cheap prices. Once again Sol and Fred could easily retire and sell out to any company of their choice but they enjoyed the challenges themselves, it kept their adrenalin flowing.

One evening after supper Sol was in his room reading. He checked his phone answering machine and found that Richard had called and left a call back number he didn't recognize. He called him back at 8:00 P.M. eastern standard time.

"Hi Richard, Sol here, everything okay with you?"

"Yes Sol, couldn't be better, the Will was read yesterday and no one could find fault with it, nice job the two of you did. I'm looking forward to meeting your partner. Are you going to be in next Monday, I've got a few days respite I've arranged to take and I'd like to come out there and meet with you and see your operation?"

"Certainly, come on out, fly into New York City and catch a shuttle aircraft out here to Poughkeepsie or I can pick you up in the City."

"Would you mind meeting me in New York, that's one place I've never been to other than quick business trips, I'd love to see the City lit up at night."

"Sure I can do that, one thing though, believe it or not I drive a stretch van, a three quarter ton to be exact. Its perfect for any of my work close by you know within a thousand miles or so. You'll like it once you see it. Only seats two though, I need the room to haul books around to and from sales you know. I do have an extra seat I can throw in if need be, you know in case you want to see some of the lovelies of New York or I can rent a car there and drive us around but I'd love for you to see the van we have, you won't believe your eyes, its like a James Bond Movie Vehicle."

"I'll leave it up to you Sol, I like the latter best though."

"Okay, I'll drive in to the airport, pick you up and we'll rent a car from a contact I know and maybe he'll even give us a driver so you'll feel at home, how does that sound?"

"Wonderful just wonderful, I'll call Sunday night with my arrival time and see you in New York then."

"It's a date, see you then." The two of them hung up. Sol immediately had a sinking feeling in his gut about seeing Richard, he was the one loose end he had to be rid of one day but not until they had some fun and Richard saw his operation. He made a call to New York and talked with his friend and asked him about a limo and a driver for the next week starting on Monday. He told him it would be cash as usual and that they needed room in the car in case they picked up some ladies from the theater district, actresses and singers, not ladies of the night. He agreed and Sol asked for a white Lincoln or Cadillac, it didn't matter but it had to have red leather inside because that was what Richard was used to and now Sol had come to enjoy it as well.

Sol hung up and went into his reading rooms where he actually lived, the front part was only for show. His quarters were actually quite comfortable although a bit sparse in decorator touches on the walls and furniture. He wanted utility not glamour. He leafed through several books and magazines looking for anything to do with airplanes, if he were going to kill Richard like he knew he should he wanted it to be on a grand scale and untraceable. He had in mind to plant an explosive device in Richard's suitcase but needed information as to what to use and how to do it. He wanted the plane to blow up near its destination not anywhere near New York. He couldn't find anything and began to have second thoughts, there would be plenty of time to kill him; Richard was a true globe trotter when it came to travel."

Sunday night he got the call from Richard with his flight number and destination time. They decided as before that Sol would pick him up in his van then they would go pick the car Sol had rented while they were in the City. Sol decided to go ahead with having a driver drive them around town because the driver would have more knowledge about New York City than he would especially when it came to the theater district.

Sol arrived in the City about thirty minutes ahead of Richard's plane landing, he found a place to park and met Richard, got his bags to the pick up area and Sol went after the van to come back and pick him up at the baggage claim doors.

"Richard this is the van I was telling you about, it's just an average looking vehicle until you look under the hood at the turbo charged diesel V8 engine, the biggest fastest engine I could fit in here under the hood. It's a little sluggish on a fast take off from a traffic light but if you baby it just a little you can catch up real quick with traffic and once on the highway this will out run many police cars because you can drive this at top speed and out run the cops while they are blowing up their engines because they are not built to run at high speeds for an extended period like this engine is. You can drive it full out with out worry of overheating it or damaging it. No one can keep up with me. This big brute flies down the road and the suspension I added makes it stick to the road like glue. This is built like a high speed race car underneath right down to over sized brakes and special tires for traction on all types of highways."

He pulled up to a traffic light. "Here Richard, I'll give you a little demonstration." He waited for the light to change. When it turned green he hit the accelerator pedal about medium foot pressure instead of stomping on it.

"You see how I pulled away, kind of easy like, if I had hit the gas pedal with great force I could overload the fuel injection system and blown out a huge cloud of black smoke and wouldn't have gone any faster. This way I'll catch up within a few feet and watch what happens next." He steadily pushed the pedal to the floor and shot past the traffic and was soon pulling ahead leaving them in the dust of the City streets. The speed he hit and the force of pulling away from the traffic pushed Richard into the back of his seat giving him an exhilarating experience similar to fast roller coasters.

"Wow Sol, that was great where did you find this vehicle?"

"I didn't find it; I bought a brand new stock three quarter ton van with a diesel engine and took it to someone I know who builds racing engines for cars and trucks. They pulled the engine out and put in one of their truck racing diesel engines. I'm sure at one time or another you've seen on TV the big trucks racing like semi tractor trailer trucks without the trailers going around a track to see who can go the fastest and there are other races for pickup trucks of all sizes as well."

"Yes, I saw it once but didn't pay any attention to it."

"Well you just experienced it now for yourself."

"Oh I get it now, I see what you mean, holy smoke this thing really does go like hell."

"That's the point of the van, it looks just like any other one on the highway but try and catch me and they can't unless they have a helicopter. In traffic they can't really see me because I blend in with the traffic so well. There are literally millions of plain white vans across the U.S. Oh and one more thing, reading my license plate is a waste of time. I have fixed a system on the back where I can change plates manually in here by remote while I'm driving and I have four plates I can rotate one behind the other so even it they do catch up with me the plate can be different from the one called in and they just let me go on about my business without stopping me. Also I have four different out of state plates to really throw them off. Now if you really want a laugh the plates are all linked to a funeral home, cops don't want to stop someone hauling a dead body around waiting to be embalmed or cremated."

"Wow, sounds like you have thought of everything."

"Everything but an airplane or a helicopter chasing me but I'm working on that with some graphics for the roof that look like air vents or huge numbers for tracking that can be opened or closed from inside again by remote control. We're trying to work out a graphic that can change like a hologram. I believe its possible to create something like that."

"Gees, this is great, I can hardly believe that a big hunk of machinery can handle like this one does, it seems light and agile all at the same time."

"Oh there is one more thing I added that will blow your mind. I have air ride suspension underneath, I can raise or lower the van to make it look full of cargo or make it ride it high like its empty when its actually full of merchandise."

"Now I have seen the impossible, who but you would think up these things, air ride suspension you say on a work van, wow!"

CHAPTER - 65

After a half an hour later of riding around and talking Sol pulled into an apparent blind alley that was wide enough to accommodate two vehicles side by side so they could pass one another in a pinch if need be. He pulled a hard left and stopped in front of a solid brick wall. He reached up to his visor and pressed something that looked like a garage door opener but smaller and flatter and blew the van's horn twice. The brick wall lifted up and went inside of the building. It was just a garage door made to look like a brick wall.

"What's this place Sol, why are we stopping here?" Richard suddenly appeared nervous and apprehensive all at the same time. He didn't like the feel of being in dead end alley.

"This is the rental place where we pick up our ride while we are in town, my friend wants to borrow my van and we need a car so he's using my van and he's giving us a limo with a driver. It's an even swap for as long as we want. I'll pay cash to his driver and he is also going to copy all of my spec's which I have for him, he wants to build a similar type vehicle."

"Dare I ask why all of this is happening?"

"No, its better you that you don't know my friend."

"Okay Sol, you lead and I'll follow, this is the most excitement I've had in years."

They got out of the van and Richard saw a dozen or more Limos, almost all alike. Some of them were of different manufactures but almost every one of them was white and some were longer than others.

A man came up to Sol and shook his hand and asked; "Is this the van I heard about my friend?"

"Yes John this is the one and only, there is none other like it. Do whatever you like but please put it back together the way you found it. I suggest you take lots of pictures and that you put it up on a lift and check out the under-carriage, it is also very important."

"Alright no problem, I didn't believe I was going too actually see it up close like this. You're ride is right over here and Reginald will drive you any-where you want but call him Reggie, he hates his first name."

"He's been briefed that he will be hauling two sightseers around has he?"

"Yes and he knows all the right places to go including the theater district and restaurants. Is this the man you told me about from California?"

"Yes this is Richard, Richard this is John."

"First names only in our business, hey Sol?"

"Yes Richard, its best for everyone."

"One more thing Sol, you know I'll be using your van for a couple of jobs, right?"

"Yes, it as we agreed John."

"Please show me your license plate remote control you told me about. I am intrigued that you have it registered to a Funeral home for a pick up vehicle to transport stiffs," John asked.

"Sure, it saves lots of excuses if you get stopped by a cop, you tell them you have a fresh body back there and it needs to get to the Funeral Home to be embalmed soon and chances are they will let you go with a warning to slow down some or watch for stop signs and so forth. I haven't been stopped yet because no one has been able to catch me." He showed John all of the features that he could use from inside the van then he and Richard got into the stretch limo with Reggie at the wheel and they drove off.

"Well Richard, it's almost time for dinner, are you hungry yet?"

"Not really I'm a few hours behind time, back in California it's only cock-tail time. I suppose I could eat a sandwich then maybe we could see a show and then eat dinner."

"Alright, consider it done."

Sol picked up a phone that went direct to the chauffeur and Reggie an-swered right away.

"Yes sir, how can I be of service to you?"

"Hi Reggie, my friend and I would like a sandwich then we would like to take in a show, can you find us a sandwich shop, a nice one understand but a place that has sandwiches?"

"No problem sir, there's one just around the corner from where we are. Do you gentlemen have any particular show in mind? If you do, while you're eating, I'll call ahead and get tickets and as I understand it you want back stage passes as well, correct?"

"Yes that's right, are you coming along with us to the show?"

"No probably not, I've already seen most of them with John."

"Well Richard, any idea of what you would like to see?"

"Yes, I'm dying to see Fiddler on the Roof."

"No problem." He spoke to Reggie again and told him what they wanted to see.

"Consider it done sir, your tickets will be waiting at the ticket counter as you go in."

"What name will they be in?"

"Any name you wish sir, John is picking up the tab; you can use his name or any other name you wish."

"Can I use my own name to put them under," asked Richard.?

"Sure, I'll tell him."

Sol spoke into the phone again and told Reggie to put the tickets under the name of Richard Suitor, Richard's real name.

"Very good sir I'll have it done before you know it. I'll give you my card with the car phone number on it and you can call me when you're ready to leave the lunch counter and when you're ready to leave the theater after you've met all the lovely ladies behind closed doors."

"How did he know we wanted backstage passes Sol?"

"Because I told John ahead of time what we wanted to do and where we wanted to go. He said he'd need my van for a total of three nights and three days starting today so we can pick it up anytime after that."

They ate their sandwiches and to Richards surprise the place was called The Lunch Counter but it was open twenty four seven due to all of the theater traffic and they catered to anyone's tastes. They went to see the show then went backstage to meet the people who had been in the show. Richard took his time talking to each person as if he had known them all his life congratulating each one of them. He had the poise and knowledge to pull it off. By the time they were ready to leave two beautiful women had their room number and hotel where they were staying so they called Reggie to come and pick them up along with two female guests who would be going to dinner with them and later back to their Hotel for the night. They spent the next two nights doing the same thing, different Theaters, different shows, different restaurants and different ladies each night in their separate rooms. When their time was up to return the car and pick up Sol's van they had Reggie take them and their luggage back to the garage and they switched vehicles again and John was beside himself with joy.

"Sol you old son of a gun, that's the best set up get away vehicle I have ever seen, it worked like clock work. I got my jobs done with no scratches whatsoever on the van. We made copies of everything we could regarding your set up, even the President of the United States doesn't have anything like this. Its great, what a beautiful job your friend did installing the engine and setting everything up. Would it be alright for me to get in touch with him and more or less duplicate the same set up on a vehicle or two for us to use here in the City?"

"Sure, here is his card and phone number, you can mention my name and he has my real name same as you do, oh and Richard here knows as well."

"Is this man alright Sol?"

"Yes, I did him a favor and he did me one, we're almost even, he is returning to Poughkeepsie to see my operation before he returns to California."

Sol and Richard left the garage and headed for Poughkeepsie.

"Sol, forgive me for asking but how do you get license plates to match funeral homes?"

"I really don't know the details, I give a friend an order for a plate that should match a Funeral Home and he does the rest. I guess he has a friend who actually makes the duplicate plates somewhere in the Prison System to match the Funeral Home's plates. I suppose he has a friend in the Licensing Plate Office or Registrar's Office from whom he gets the details. The thing is that they have to match the vehicle description as well. All I know for sure is that he can come up with a plate within a few days of my request and Fred and I duplicate the Registration form."

"Hmm," was all Richard could say.

CHAPTER - 66

Agents Jefferies and Marlowe arrived back in Washington the same day the saddle arrived by air freight. They met in the Lab to discuss what they were looking for with the lab techs. Agent Marlowe was the forensics expert so Jefferies let her handle the saddle question and she began with talking to the techs.

"The important thing for us is to figure out is how the strap called the cinch was cut. Was it cut before or after the lady was killed. What I'm trying to get across is did the cut fail and tear the strap in two or was it simply cut most of the way through then torn in two by hand. We need to prove that a young man has been falsely accused who is in jail right now, check the knife and cut mark to see if this was the actual knife that cut the leather. Do you understand what I am trying to say?" .

"We think so Agent Marlowe but which cut is the one we're supposed to be looking at, it's been cut twice almost clear through?" asked one tech.

"That's a good question, does anyone know anything about horses and saddles in here?"

"No ma'am, we're all city boys and girls but we could check around the building and see if there is anyone who does know their way around horses."

"Good, well get going then, we need the answers like yesterday, a young man's life is at stake here. Call myself or Agent Jefferies when you know anything, okay?"

"Yes ma'am we're on it."

She left to go find Agent Jefferies. She found him in their office going over some of the information they had brought back with them. "What are you doing now Dick?"

"I'm going over all the descriptions of the men who were at the house before during and after she sold the books to someone and it's that someone we're looking for I believe. Every time he is at a sale someone dies and I want to know why and most of all who is he. There is no mention of any women coming to the estate to look at books so we know we are looking for a man. I don't have one thread of evidence to tie anyone to this crime but at least we know that two murders were committed and we need to tie them together somehow, I know they were made by our man, I know it, I just know it!" He was sitting on the back side of his desk pounding his fist on the top of it. "Damn it Jane, why can't we figure this out, what are we missing?"

"Well I think just like you said earlier before we went to California, we are looking for a very cleaver man who can alter his disguise to look like anyone but himself."

"I know that but which one of these is the real man? Not one of these descriptions says whether or not there was anything in common like his height or weight for instance, every description is different. Not one of these shows up twice in a five day period. One of these men is the man we want. Let me go back to the day the Moving Truck was getting ready to leave, let's see which man was there that day. Yes here it is, a man about five feet ten inches tall, around one hundred and eighty five pounds, dark hair a little long like he needed a haircut. No it just isn't right, none of these match up with any other descriptions we have from other crime scenes. Would you like to take a crack at it Jane?"

"Sure, why don't you take a break, maybe something will ring a bell? In the meantime I'll see if anything jumps out at me."

Jefferies got up and went to the lab to watch them work their magic.

"Agent Jefferies, good to see you," said the same lab tech who had talked with Jane, "take a look at this under the microscope. Both ends of this piece of leather you brought in along with the saddle, we know now which side was cut by the cops, see right here how uneven it is, its cut by someone who was in a big hurry. Now this other one was cut nearly all the way through to a point where a man with any strength at all could easily break the other part of this with his bare hands, there's only a tiny piece holding it together. See it right there!"

"Yes I see it, good work, that's what we we're looking for, the killer did this out in the pasture after he killed the heiress then he broke it with the strength of his arms to make it look like the stable boy did it but it's impossible for him to have done it I think."

Another tech offered a better explanation. "Sir, she couldn't have gotten up on the horse if it had been cut at the stables, it would have instantly snapped under the lady's weight as she tried to swing her leg up and over the saddle."

The first tech then added, "oh and the knife sir, it didn't make either of the cut marks."

"I didn't think it did, it was done to throw the cops off the track just long enough for the killer to get out of town and those clowns in LA all fell for it. Alright, write it up and I'll sign it then please call LA and ask for the Sheriff's main Office but don't talk to anyone but him, got it?"

"Yes sir, we have it."

"Good job all of you, you just confirmed my suspicions that the stable boy was a fall guy for the killer. Thank you all of you, and you too whoever you are, you seem to be the expert when it comes to horses, saddles and leather."

"Yes sir, thank you sir, names Broderick sir."

"Well done Broderick, I'll let the director know who solved this mess."

"Thank you sir, may I go back to the mailroom now sir?"

"Mailroom?" Jefferies said with a surprised look on his face, "aren't you one of our lab techs or Agents?"

"No sir, mailroom clerk, I sort mail for the whole building sir."

"Well just the same you may have just saved a young man's life with your expertise."

"Thank you sir, I'm glad I was able to be of help in some small way."

Dick went right back to their office to tell Jane the news that his theory had been right.

"Dick you came back too quick, I haven't had time to analyze all of these descriptions."

"Say Jane, I just had another idea, I don't know why we didn't think of this before, lets get a big dry erase board like we had before and put every single description that we've gathered on the board, some of them have got to match somehow."

"That's a great idea why didn't we do that before?"

"Hell I don't know, usually we have only one suspect but here we have several, I believe they are all the same man though. There may be something else we have over looked, what about orthopedic built up shoes like people have when one leg is shorter than the other or when a person wants to appear taller than another?"

"That's another good point, want to put one of our other people on it checking out Specialty Shoe Manufacturers?"

"Yes and right away, we'll trip this guy up somehow and if we are right we could have a name and address in a couple of days."

"I'll put one of the older Agents on it with a lot of experience, be back shortly Dick."

Several days went by with manufacturers sending in information on the types and styles of orthopedic shoes they provided for those who needed special shoes but none of them offered pairs of shoes just for a lift to make people look taller. Just as Dick had suspected they did make a special shoe for people who had one leg shorter that the other and those kinds of shoes were not sold in pairs. They were right back to square one.

"Alright Agent Marlowe, I have one more idea up my sleeve."

"What is it Dick; I'm about wore out from chasing ghosts around the country."

"Well think about this, I saw a documentary about movies and how they are made. For short actors opposite tall actors, especially with women in general being shorter, they sometimes build platforms for the shorter ladies to stand on when they had lines to say with a six foot or taller actor. It used to be done all the time. It made the actors appear as though they were all approximately the same height as one another. Suppose we contact a couple of movie studios, maybe they could shed some light on our problem. I think its worth a shot, someone somewhere must make shoes for height challenged people to lift their height up as little as and inch to maybe a little more. That has to be it, but its only speculation again."

"I think you are really reaching again Dick, are men and women really that self conscious about their height these days?"

"I don't know but I think we have to explore every possibility until we catch a break."

"Okay, do you want me to put someone else on this task, we're about to wear a couple of our people out using the phone, they need to get back to the actual leg work and studying the facts instead of chasing the ghosts you keep coming up with. I'm not faulting you, we're all doing the best we can under the circumstances."

"Yeah I know Jane and I know the pressure our people are under, you and I feel it as well but at least we have field work to do, the rest of the Agents are stuck inside fighting dragons with pencil and paper, not very effective I'm afraid."

CHAPTER - 67

Several more days went by then a lead came in by way of one of the Trade Paper bulletins they had requested.

"Hey Dick, did you see this in your mailbox this morning?"

"What is it Jane I haven't checked mine in a couple of days?"

"There's a Book Store closing its doors and everything is for sale right down to the bare walls, fixtures, book shelving, books, magazines, everything must be sold because a new tenant is moving in and the Book Store is in serious financial trouble due to a huge rent increase by the owner of the mall. It says here that a new anchor tenant is moving in to create one large space of fifty thousand square feet for what they need. What do you say, time for a field trip?"

"Well tell me where it is and how old the actual store is, you know how long as it been in business in the community, the older the better, the guy we want likes really old books, he could care less about newer ones it seems."

"Well let me read some more and maybe I can tell you, I just read the highlights of it. I've got it, its a really old town in Connecticut called Waterbury, it's a pretty affluent area I believe. I had a cousin who used to live there until she retired and moved to Florida, but If I remember right it's a really nice town or it may be a city by now for all I know. Also this store has been in only two locations all of its years, the present owner took it over from his parents and it's been in existence since 1923 in the same family."

"Well now this could be interesting, chances are they may have some old books in a private collection at home like some book store owners do, they like to collect the best of the best when it comes to Literature in general, maybe we'd better check it out. We can take our car, its unmarked and we can make it to Connecticut in one day easy. I'll let the Director know what we have in mind. One more thing, do you have your traveling clothes with you here that we bought specifically for this kind of event?"

"Yes, I have everything in my locker including a suitcase; I can travel in what I'm wearing."

"Oh, one more thing, when is the big sale, we'll need to be there to look things over just like our killer, I'm sure he checks things out prior to the sale so he can buy the whole shooting match if he wants before the general sale opens to the public?"

"It's this Saturday and today is Wednesday so we'd better get on the road right now, its only 9:30 A.M. we'll miss the major traffic if we get on I-95 and head north."

"Right you are, maybe we can get a good look at this guy if he shows up."

They spent the next fifteen minutes grabbing their gear and telling people where they were headed. At 10:00 they were pulling out of the FBI underground garage and I-95 was just a few blocks away and ran right through Washington so they didn't bother with the bypass, they knew they would save some time going straight up 95 this time of day.

Several hours later they approached Waterbury, it was a bigger more sprawling city than Jane recalled but she hadn't been there since she was twelve years old when she with her family visited her older cousin. She remembered the huge house with its six bedrooms and several bathrooms, the kitchen was accessible from both the living room and the dining room and there was a big back porch off from there that led out to a spacious humongous backyard. In the front was a huge high porch held up with four great big white wood columns that made the front look a little bit like a cotton plantation mansion in south with its formal entry. She remembered getting lost more than once in the big two story house that sported a big attic and spacious basement. The walls were made of what is called field stone. It was so rocky in some New England States that every rock was used in some way when they were plowed up in the fields. They built stone walls and basements and sometimes laid up walls of stone for farm houses. It's not unusual to find houses built completely of stone throughout New England.

As soon as they arrived in the City limits they began looking for a Motel that wouldn't be too far from restaurants and shopping and not to expensive but would still have to fit what they were portraying to be, wealthy and eccentric couple who liked books. They both had glasses that were just plain glass but it made them look the part when they went in to register at the Motel they finally chose. They really looked like a couple of geeks and carried almost empty briefcases. All that was in them was a pad of paper each and a few pens and pencils that they would later use as props when they visited the Book Store.

CHAPTER - 68

Sol and Richard arrived in Poughkeepsie around 3:00 pm that afternoon. Sol drove around the back of the huge warehouse and store complex and parked in the special garage he had under the building now with his own garage door that looked like part of the brick warehouse.

"Sol, did you copy this garage door from your friend's in New York?"

"Yes, we copy each other's ideas quite a lot lately, he's been here and has seen what I am going to show you and agreed with me that I need better security. You won't notice of course but there are cameras watching us everywhere and if anything is out of the ordinary an alarm will sound very loudly, enough that it will hurt your ear drums. They got their luggage out of the van and Sol led the way over to the elevator that he used to go from floor to floor without being seen from outsiders who may be around the building or in the store.

"I have to tell you Sol, I'd give anything to have a vehicle like yours that I could use around LA what with all the gangs and things, no one is safe anymore especially someone like me who bespeaks money. I'd like to find some anonymity somehow like what you have done." "That's no problem, have your people get in touch with my people, my secrets are yours Richard because I like you, we think alike in several ways. For instance this elevator is accessible only to me, it has to be opened by the right key then I can go anywhere in the building I please without being seen or heard by anyone, its also my escape route in case of emergency. Just wait until you lay eyes on my apartment, it's to die for."

Before Richard knew it they were on the third floor just outside the door to Sol's apartment. When Sol closed the door to the elevator it disappeared and became part of the wall.

"Holy cow, it disappeared, the door to the elevator I mean."

"Just another illusion I had built in Richard."

He unlocked his apartment door and let Richard go in first. "This is a little small Sol, is this where you live?"

"Yes it is actually, to the outsider at least, but we're friends so I'll show you the rest." He walked towards a bookcase and pushed a concealed button that was so well hidden Richard couldn't pick it out.

"The button you're looking for doesn't exist; it's made to look like a knot in the natural wood of the bookcase, look closely right here." He showed him the place and said, "okay now push the knot very lightly."

Richard pushed on it and the wall that had been open closed. He pushed it again and it opened again.

"This is where I really live Richard, there's two bedrooms, two bathrooms, a eat in kitchen and dining area, my private library and reading room I recently completed for myself."

"This is more like it, it's you all over, my goodness look at all of the books, this place is a man's place, no frilly stuff for you huh Sol?"

"That's right Richard, although I do have one occasional female visitor here she is the only one who has seen what I've done here and she is more or less my steady girl. We would have been married long before this but I have this travel bug in me. And along with my not being home much and my love for the printed words leaves very little room for a woman so we see each other when we can. We do love each other but neither one of us wants to get married and she has been married two or three times to spite me. She's single again now since her last husband was run over by a City Bus and died."

"Oh nice touch Sol, a City Bus you say?"

"That's right, he was drunk and stepped off the curb into the path of the bus, there were several witnesses."

"Let me guess, they were homeless people or alcoholics out for a walk."

"Something like that but the fact remains he was proven drunk, it was ruled an accident."

"Still I say it was a nice touch, did he beat her a lot?"

"Yeah, every time he got drunk he left her visibly bruised and battered."

"Then he got what he asked for I'd say."

"I agree with you there, come let's put our things away and we'll go downstairs so you can meet everyone."

They unpacked and went downstairs to the store by way of another elevator.

"This is our store Richard, this is where many of your cousin's books are right now, some we had to throw out and some we have sold to overseas buyers and we ship a few out nearly every day." He took him on a tour of the whole store pointing out the many security cameras that were so well disguised that Sol had trouble pointing some of them out.

"Wow I've never seen so many books in one place before, this place is huge."

"Yes Richard, we have such a great reputation that people come from around the world just to walk through our store and it seems like every person who comes in leaves by buying something. Check out our break area for those who want to spend the better part of the day with us, plenty of varieties of drinks, pastries, cookies, snacks and things."

"It seems as though you've thought of almost everything, I can't tell if you forgot a single thing; are those tables and chairs for customers as well?"

"Yes and there are several areas where people can sit and read under their own reading lamp to see if the book they have in their hands is the one they want. Come with me and I'll show you the second floor, it will blow your mind."

Richard followed Sol to another out of the way elevator that he explained was for employees only and only went between the first and second floors. They stepped off the elevator and into humongous rooms that looked like they went on forever.

"What's this place Sol?"

"This is our storage area where we bring in recently purchased books, we store them here until we have to replace depleted stock downstairs. Come on, I'll walk you around." He took Richard through several of the rooms and explained what each room held and how they were cataloged so anyone could come upstairs and get a book that someone had requested that was out of stock on the shelves downstairs.

"This is absolutely amazing Sol, you must have thousands of books up here alone."

"Wrong, we passed one million books on hand in storage already without your cousin's. Come with me, I'll show you the fate for some of her books."

They went to a freight elevator on the same floor and went to the basement.

"Come along Richard, don't be afraid there's nothing down here that will harm you. Sol took him over to where Fred was seated on a high stool working intently on a book to be copied.

"Fred, I want you to meet Richard, this is the gentleman that hooked us up with the last load of books, do you have any of her books handy that you're working on by chance?"

"As a matter of fact I do, are you sure this guy is alright Sol?"

"Yes Fred he's okay, you can shake his hand."

Fred reached out and pumped Richards hand vigorously.

"Pleased to meet you Fred, so this is where the real action happens huh?"

"Yes, this is our work area, laboratory and factory down here, I take it Sol that you're going to give him the grand tour?"

"Yes Fred."

"Follow me Richard, we can talk while we walk then we'll go back and check on Fred, he's very protective of our work you understand."

"Yes, from what you've told me I'd have armed guards all over the place."

"We have excellent security and if an alarm goes off we simply call the local police."

They walked along a little further into another large room.

"Alright Richard, this our paper making factory where we use one of several patents to create old time paper from the past. We use this when we make copies of the most valuable books we get in from time to time. We won't go any further; the fumes of the factory will make you ill. We have treat the air before we release it back outside or we'd hear about the odors from the residents around here. Right over there where it so dark is where we manufacture several kinds of ink, brown, blue, black, red and several other blends that we use in our copying process. You can't tell it from the ancient inks, not one expert has been able to tell the difference between our ink and the ancients, some we manufacture the same way as the ancients would have, its foolproof."

"Are they some of your patents that you mentioned?"

"Yes, almost every one of them is our own blend."

"Wow, like you said it would be an experience."

"I will allow you to stay and watch Fred at work if you like so you two can get acquainted a little, he can show you which elevator to take to come back up to the store or go directly to our floor to the apartments."

"I'd like that but I don't know anything about ink or paper."

"You just watch Fred work his magic, it will amaze you and he's working on one of your cousin's books making an identical copy so we can sell one original here in the States and the other we'll sell abroad and both will think they have a First Edition, only Fred can tell them apart." They walked back through a maze of rooms again back to the Lab where Fred was.

"Alright Fred, Sol said you were working on one of my cousin's books can you tell me what you're doing in layman terms?" asked Richard.

"Sure, I've already duplicated the exact paper the book is made of, now all I have to do is duplicate the exact faded look of the ink then copy the pages by choosing the print style the publisher used and run the pages one at a time though our own duplicator machine."

"That looks just like a regular copy machine to me."

"Don't let the looks fool you, this is one that Sol designed himself, it can duplicate each print style or font and run any ink we decide to use in it. It prints the old way using real letters and ink and there's no other machine like this in the world."

"Did you two patent this as well?"

"No, we don't want anyone to know that we have the capability of doing what we do, it works so well that the experts can't tell a copied page from an original so we call it a duplicating machine because it really does duplicate an original from an original. Here watch as I place the book face down on the glass, this custom built top comes off and can be replaced with another different size so that the dark from the light coming in from around the edges doesn't show up on the copied page or duplicate page and the pages are cut to size before the duplicating process."

"Wow this is one huge operation you have but on a smaller scale than the big companies like the ones who make paper from scratch. What do they use, isn't it some kind of wood pulp or something?"

"Yes they use wood pulp but we're using lots of old paper, newspapers and any kind of used paper even colored construction paper like they use in the schools. We have a driver who visits schools and hospitals and places like that where they use a lot of paper. We pick it up for free and guarantee its destruction so no one will ever see it. We shred it in our huge paper shredder then process it down into a liquid slurry and remake the paper using the formulary we want to reproduce and copy old looking paper and we use old rags to make very fine linen paper. We don't use any cardboard in our paper, we only want real paper none of that brown stuff, it contaminates what we are trying to accomplish. We're able to sell our fine linen paper overseas as well as in the United States and as with everything we use a dummy or shell company with several Post Office boxes that no one can connect back here to us, there is no way to trace any illicit sales back to us because of the shell companies. We use different people to pick up the mail and forward it to us through another mail service like some military families use and others like retirees who travel a lot. They use a central mail service that distributes their mail by forwarding it to wherever they are in the world. This works great for us as well. We are so well known just by our Book Store that we could go International and sell franchises all over the world and get even richer but we already have more money now than we could ever spend. We enjoy the challenge of discovering something new and maybe we will let the world in on it one day. Right now though we enjoy the challenges that lay ahead of us, we actually hunger for something new to discover.

We have one or two more kinds of paper to reproduce like the Dead Sea scrolls paper; we haven't done that one yet mainly because we don't have a sample of the paper they are made from. If we are allowed to reproduce the paper we could completely reproduce the whole document for posterity's sake. Actually we could make several copies and put them in museums around the world for everyone to enjoy instead of just one in one location. Of course we would have to label ours; Copied from the Original, just imagine letting others see your work around the world, what a great accomplishment that would be. Now if you would like to watch me for a minute while I duplicate these pages from one of your cousins books that's really rare and when I'm done with a page hold it up next to the original page and see if you can tell the difference? Like Sol and I told you we only make one copy, one stays here in the States with an anonymous collector and the other will be sold overseas to another collector who will also remain anonymous. None of them want anyone to know that they have a rare first edition. Some of them are so valuable that others would break into their homes or business to try and steal one of them and resell them on the black market. They lay out huge amounts of money sometimes for these rare books. That's how we can experiment at our leisure to discover new ways of doing things. Sol is currently thinking about contacting some of the large companies like Pitney Bowes and IBM to sell them our plans for our duplicator machine. Sol used several brands of copy and printing machines to make the one we're using but he made engineering plans for each and every piece as he built it. There isn't another machine that can do what this one does. Just imagine it in the wrong hands, someone could flood the market with copies of rare first edition books and it would drive the prices we are getting down to almost nothing, you could buy a copy of an original classic for $12.95 in any book store and that's not fair to collectors. Today's copy machines do a good job but they don't have the paper, ink or print heads that we do so we at least have the corner on the paper and ink products. You know that duplicating machines have been around for years and years but have been replaced by copy machines recently that essentially do the same thing quicker and cheaper."

"Yeah I know about that but I'm not familiar with duplicator machines. I've never even seen one, when I need copies I go to the post office and make them myself for a dime. This whole operation is mind boggling; all of this is being done in the basement of an old factory beneath a real Book Store. Its unbelievable what you two have accomplished. I was telling Sol that I may be of great assistance to you in that I travel a lot internationally and have contacts that I can use to secure more rare book collections. In case Sol didn't tell you I asked him if I could possibly be of some service to you, it won't cost either of you a dime. I'm looking for the thrill of doing something that could be considered a little outside of the law but not serious enough to get me arrested or either of you, as you say nothing can be traced back to back to you."

"Yes Sol and I talked it over but I withheld my okay until I got a chance to meet you and now I concur with Sol, you could be of help to us and save us both time and money. Several times Sol has spent a number of weeks chasing down worthless book stores or collectors. Just like your cousin's collection here. Quite a lot of it was junk but we did find some good really good books we can make money on. Others turned out to be just everyday run of the mill books you can buy anywhere. This is how we have grown our business by providing books that are really hard to find and of course we sell others at a marked down price to get people into the store and once they are in here they almost always leave with one or two books or refreshments.

CHAPTER - 69

Still in the Lab beneath the Store Fred still has some questions of Richard.

Richard. has Sol shown you our private viewing area where we bring in high profile collectors to show them some of our rarest books?" asked Fred

"No he hasn't shown me that yet."

"He is probably letting you and I get acquainted before showing you everything we have. Once I tell him that you're okay with me he'll finish the tour by showing you everything I'm sure. You're a fine man Richard, I knew it the minute we shook hands. You have a firm and honest grip. When I looked you in the eyes you didn't flinch. A liar won't have a firm grip and he won't look you in the eye. He'll look down and away from you averting them at all costs and his hand grip, well imagine a fresh dead fish, limp, wet and a little warm, you wouldn't want to shake hands with that person again now would you?"

"No I sure wouldn't, thanks for the tip, I didn't know that, look them in the eyes and if they look up, down and away you don't want them for a friend or a business associate either."

"That's right, works every time, that way you'll know whether a person is sincere or not and whether or not they can be trusted. It may keep you out of trouble in the future especially if you're dealing with big money people, watch their eyes and feel their hand shake, if you don't like what you see and feel get away from them as fast as you can gracefully so as not to arouse suspicion, you could avoid a trap or worse, death. You know what they say, the eyes are the window to the soul, remember it and use it."

"I will Fred, I don't know how I can ever thank you or Sol; I hope we'll always be friends."

"I believe we will Richard, I can see why Sol let you come here, we can use your expertise and you can get a thrill working with us knowing how hard we have worked to build this company. This has been our dream since we met at the University and saw that we were both taking almost the same exact courses for the same reasons and well, here we are some twenty five years later after starting out in a borrowed garage of a friend."

"Well I think you've done a magnificent job. I never had the urge to work as hard as you two, everything I have was handed down to me through generations of business dealings and I have more money than I could ever spend and here I am with the two of you whom I now consider my only true friends because you don't need the money same as me. The other people who hang around with me do it so they can get some of my money because they know I always pick up the tab for whatever it is we're doing. I don't even have a girlfriend anymore, once a woman finds out I'm worth millions the love and courtship stop and they get that hunger for diamonds or gold in their eyes and don't give a damn about me anymore."

"Have you met any ladies with Sol?"

"Yes I have and they were all nice but they knew between he and I one of us must be rich because of the car we were in or hotel we were staying at."

"Now you know the reason Sol drives the van, a real woman doesn't give him a second thought when she sees the van, either she likes him like he is or not, take it or leave it. Those are the real women and they are real people, either they like you for what they see or they don't."

"Do you have a girlfriend Fred or are you married?"

"I do have a girlfriend who thinks I'm a business man, she hasn't been here before but she likes me for what I am and I like it that way. Now Sol, he does have a real girlfriend who was here once long ago and he wants to bring her here for a weekend so she can see the store, she knows that he is into books and their resale but that I believe is about it. He's known her since our University days."

"I believe he told me about her, the one up in Buffalo or somewhere."

"Yes that's the one, I myself haven't seen her in several years but he says she still looks good and he would marry her but for his traveling all the time that it wouldn't be fair to her. I know he loves her and she loves him and they get together every now and then when the urge strikes one of them. She has his phone number for his apartment."

"Yes he showed me his place, very smart indeed. Well Fred if it's alright with you I'd like to go find Sol and see what we are doing about meals."

"You'll like it where he is going to take you, do you have any causal clothes with you?"

"No, all I brought were several suits because that's all I wear."

"Well Sol will get you fixed up in a more causal way so that no one will take notice of you but those who might give a damn."

"You know that's exactly what Sol said, I've got to go somewhere and get some street clothes as you call them."

"He can take you downtown before you eat and get you all fixed up, you need to dress down here in Poughkeepsie, you shouldn't dress like you're in California, that will only draw attention to you and that's the last thing you want if you want to be a real person and have real friends. One more question, do you play golf?"

"Certainly not, that's not me, I'm nothing like that!"

"Neither of us do either but it doesn't hurt to wear a pull over sweater or shirt like some golfers do, it throws people off and that's good because they won't be sure what's under the clothes, they don't see the real man, at least not yet."

"Gees Fred thank you, this is a whole new experience for me circulating among real people instead of phony millionaires who don't give a damn about anyone but that's California for you, at least where I live. Maybe now is the time for me to change my image and go back to LA looking like a normal person, I'm sure many people won't even notice me."

"The people who count in your life will take notice and those are the ones you want as true friends. You'll seldom see Sol in an expensive suit and tie, he likes his suits to look like it's the only one he owns, works wonders in a crowd, real people will come and talk to him and leave the jet setters alone with their groupies or cadre of fake friends."

"Wow Fred I can't thank you enough for the tips, I really must go and find Sol now."

"Sure go right ahead, just go up to the store and ask Greta where Sol is, she usually knows his whereabouts in the building."

"Alright, bye now, see you later my friend."

"Goodbye Richard, we'll eat supper together later this evening, alright?"

"Yes I'd like that." Richard disappeared into the elevator that would take him to the first floor of the store. He was really impressed with the well thought out scheme of things and his two new friends.

CHAPTER - 70

In Waterbury Connecticut Dick and Jane got settled into their rooms and decided to take a ride around town and go by the Book Store that was for sale which they would look at the first thing in the morning. He let her drive so she could re-acquaint herself with the town which she remembered from her childhood. They had a nice ride checking out local restaurants and other stores and drove by the Book Store at the same time.

"Well Dick did you see any special restaurant where you would like to eat tonight?"

"Yes actually I did, do you feel like a steak tonight?"

"Yeah I could go for a small rib eye."

"You would, that's just about the best steak there is for taste and tenderness, sounds good to me as well. We passed a nice looking Restaurant back there a couple of blocks, see if you can turn around or go around the block here and try to come out where we just were and we'll find it on the way back."

She turned right at a traffic light and went around the block but there was a one way street the wrong way and they had to take a street further down back the way they had come. When they came back out to main street Jefferies saw it across the street. "There it is, across the street where it says Papa Jim's Fine Food."

"You're kidding, a family restaurant full of squabbling kids who don't want to eat their vegetables and stuff."

"Yeah maybe, but let's give it a try and if we don't like the looks of it you get to make the next choice."

"Alright we'll try it your way, who knows it might not be too bad." She parked the car and they strolled back down the street a ways to the restaurant and went in the front door. It was bedlam inside, someone was having a birthday party for kids on one side and the other side was full of retired senior's a lot older than they were so the opted out of that idea and got back in the car and started driving again.

"Whew!', said Dick, "that was pretty bad back there, hope you have better luck."

They drove for several blocks then suddenly she saw something that caught her eye. "Back there Dick, the perfect place, it looks quaint and all."

"What did the sign say?"

"I don't know, I saw neon lights and thought we ought to check it out." She turned around and pulled up slowly across the street from a quaint looking place just the way she had described it. Dick was staring past her trying to read a sign in the front window, it said; 'STEAK YOUR WAY', we only take out the moo under it.

"What sort of a place is that, we only take out the moo. Do cows go moo when you cook them?" asked Dick.

"No silly, all cows moo when they are contented or want something. Come on lets take a look, it might be a nice place."

They got out and went across the street. Dick causally opened the door and they went into a dimply lit alcove setting with a podium sitting in the middle of the room that said, 'please wait to be seated.'

Dick said, "uh oh we've seen this scene before. Maybe we better find someplace else."

Just then a gentleman came up in dressed in black slacks, white shirt and a black bow tie wearing a short apron in front of him with straws sticking out of one of the pockets. "May I be of service folks?"

"Well maybe," said Dick, "do you have Happy Hour?"

"No sir, this is a family style restaurant and we don't do happy hour however if you like we have a full bar over that way were you can eat and drink. You can get cocktails, wine or beer if you like. In the other direction is for families with small children who don't want them to associate alcohol with eating."

"Thank you, we'll take the bar side if you please."

"Just the two of you tonight?"

"Yes, just us."

"Very well, please come this way." He took them over to a huge room with a piano bar where a man was playing soft dinner music and it was less than half full. Dick didn't say a word, he pulled a chair out from a table that held four people easily and then sat down opposite of her. The waiter laid a menu in front of them and said he would return shortly with water for them. He came back with two tall glasses of water, gave them a straw and left again. A few minutes later a young man who looked like he was college age came over and introduced himself. "Good evening folks, my name is Ben and I'll be your server tonight. Can I start you off with a cocktail or wine perhaps?"

"Yes I think so, what would you like Jane?"

"I feel like a blooming bloody mary."

"Yes ma'am and you sir?"

"Scotch on the rocks please."

"Very good sir, are you ready to order or shall I get your drinks first?"

"Drinks first, we haven't had time to peruse the menu just yet."

"Very good sir, I'll be back shortly."

They picked up their menus both smiling as they began to read the choices of meats. There was every kind of meat on there except lamb and fish. They both had already decided they wanted steak, the question was which cut. There were some cuts neither of them had heard of before. They both found the rib eye that they had talked about earlier and decided on that with baked potatoes and sour cream with green beans for Dick and corn for Jane. They both ordered their steak medium this time for tenderness.

When the steaks arrived they were cooked to perfection, they felt like they were in heaven, the meal was that good. So far the night had been perfect when all of a sudden the piano player started to play 'autumn leaves.'

Dick shrugged his shoulders and said, "hey don't look at me, I didn't pick this place."

They both chuckled quietly to themselves at the pun, Jane knew it was a coincidence.

After they consumed as much food to satisfy themselves they left and rode around some in their car more looking for a movie theater but not finding any they went back to their Motel to spend the rest of the evening.

As they walked into the lobby they heard music coming from a back room somewhere. They looked at each other and the desk clerk saw them and responded, "piano bars open until midnight, nice place to unwind if you like."

They nodded their heads and headed in the direction of the music. They stayed there until nearly closing time. It was a very relaxing evening they both needed, neither one drank too much. They had to be up early to preview the book store and get the lay of the land so to speak. They went upstairs to their rooms and stopped just outside of Jane's room as if Dick had taken her home and walked her to her door.

"This has been a lovely evening Dick but I'm afraid that I'm out of coffee or I'd invite you in for a cup so good night for now, see you in the morning." She kissed him lightly on his cheek, unlocked her door and went in. He felt his face get red but didn't understand why, maybe it was too much scotch he thought as he opened his door and went on to bed.

The next morning they were up and ready about the same time. They had on their street clothes they had brought with them and looked the part of two geeks. Dick even had on a soft hat with a wide brim and the front of the brim was folded slightly up like he couldn't see unless it was. It was part of the plan. She looked more like a studious school girl throwback from the sixties. They used their real first names but that was all, they never gave their real last name to anyone even when they asked for it.

"Well Dick where would you like to eat breakfast"

"What's wrong with right here Jane?"

"Its fine with me Dick, I just want some eggs and toast."

"Alright lets go in and see what they have on their menu."

They went in and were seated right away. They both got eggs but Dick wanted some home fried sliced potatoes, bacon and sausage and wheat toast, orange juice and coffee. He was really hungry.

By five minutes of nine they were out of the restaurant and in the car with Jane driving again heading for the book store so they could check it out. They arrived at the store, parked the car and went in to look around. A middle aged man came up to them and asked; "excuse me, but are you here about the sale Saturday?"

"Yes we are, we came in to check and see what kind of inventory you have," answered Dick

"Well, we have all the latest titles by all the best authors, I represent the bank that holds the paper on the business you see, I'm here to protect our interests."

"Are you telling us you loan money to people to buy books, sell them and then borrow some more to buy more books and sell them etc.," asked Jane.

"In a manner of speaking yes ma'am, that's about how it works but you see the owner needed more money to spruce up the store, he painted and did all new shelving and so on and well, here it is. As you can see he is being forced to move out for no good reason except someone wants this space and he can no longer afford the rent and he has no place to move the store to either. The whole mess has made him extremely ill, I'm afraid, he may not live to spend what little money he may realize from the sale."

"Is this all he has, no collection of rare books, no rare first editions, only current titles?" Dick asked.

"Yes I'm afraid this is it, its all he has in the world."

"Oh my goodness, I'm afraid we made a mistake driving all this way for nothing. Come along my dear there's absolutely nothing for us here I'm afraid, we'll have to look elsewhere," said Jane.

"Just what are you looking for my friends?"

"Why Literature my good man, fine books of Literature, we thought this man had a collection of old and possibly rare books, we would have bought the whole shooting match if he had what we were looking for like even new first editions."

"I am sorry, I don't know a soul who collects those kinds of books, I'd tell you if I knew. Sorry you had to drive such a long way just to see run of the mill books anybody could buy anywhere."

"Thank you sir, well come along dear, we'll head for home and wait for another sale to come along," Jane said.

They left dejected that there was nothing there, they figured the man was going to lose his shirt, who would buy all the books here when they could get them anywhere and closer to home as well probably for a lot less money. They got into the car, went for an early lunch checked out of their Motel and headed back for Washington.

"Well that sure was a bummer Dick, just when I thought we had a chance. Our guy won't show up for this one, what did we miss, the ad said selling out to the walls didn't it?"

"Yeah, that's what it said but it said nothing about new or old, I wonder how he knows the difference."

"Maybe he telephones ahead and asks the owner or someone else or maybe he has a guy who gives him tips as to who has the old books."

"No that's not it. No, now wait just a minute Jane, I think I know, the word old just struck me like a bolt of lightning!

Of course, that's it! That's what tips him off, the age or how long the store has been in business. The older the store is the better chance the owner may have of having an old collection of rare books at his store or at home like the Professor did. Damn it why didn't I see that before, old is the key, that's where we'll find him next. When we read the next ad for sale we'll see how long the store has been in business like if it says since 1965 we'll dismiss that one but if it says in continuous business since 1903 or something, that's the one we'll jump on next, that has to be it, that has to be the key which we've been missing. Oh I am so mad at myself I could spit nails."

"Fingernails Dick?"

"No roofing nails, the big ones, how could we have missed that one little word,' old, a rookie cop would have thought of that one."

"Maybe Dick but we've had a lot of stumbling blocks thrown at us not to mention the misdirection's, we might as well say it; we've been had, again."

"Yes I guess you're right, oh hell, take us home Jane, I'm fed up."

Jane put the pedal to the metal as they say and they were soon hurtling back towards Washington after checking out of their Motel. On the way back Dick had a dream about he and Jane the night before when she had invited him in for a night cap and they had made love until the wee hours of the morning. When he woke up they were almost back in Washington.

Jane glanced over at him. "Nice nap Dick?"

"Oh my word, you have no idea Jane, whew!" he said as he brushed his hand across his forehead.

She looked over at him and there were beads of sweat across his forehead as she drove into the underground parking garage where Donny saw them and came over to greet them.

"How did it go, catch the bad guy this time?"

"I'm afraid it was a dry run Donny, maybe next time, boy I sure am beat."

"He had a tough day at the Office I think Donny," and she winked at him.

CHAPTER - 71

Richard went upstairs looking for Greta to ask her where Sol might be. He approached her and she pointed towards a door that led to a room marked Mysteries. He walked up and down a couple of isles until he found Sol who was simply perusing some newly arrived books from publishers.

"Hi Richard," he said in a low voice as if in a Library, "how did it go with Fred?"

"Oh Sol, I am in heaven, I have met two really great friends, how could I be so blest? Fred mentioned that maybe I should find some street duds rather than wearing my pricey suits."

"I agree, whenever you are ready we'll go downtown and get some street clothes for you that you can wear anywhere in the U.S. and not look out of place. You shouldn't stand out in the wrong way which will cause people to stare at you making them wonder what planet you just came from."

"Thanks, I didn't know I looked so out of place. We can go whenever you like, oh and Fred gave me some really good insights into people and how they react, he gave me some warning signs to look out for and so forth."

"Well you and I will continue to work on that. You'll find that there are two prices for people, one only the rich can afford and price two for the normal people which is what I plan to transform you into. Maybe I'll take you up to Buffalo to meet my girl. I'm sure she could scare up a friend for you if you like. Now these are real women understand, not your typical floozies like we met in the City who know you have money and are just along for the ride so they can get some expensive gifts. Those are fake painted ladies is all they are.

You need to meet a real woman if only for the experience of conversation. You won't believe how pleasant it can be just talking with someone over a glass of wine during dinner. Its the most invigorating and relaxing thing you can do and if she likes you well enough, well who knows she may even take you home for the night."

"Wow, that sounds almost too good to be true."

"Tell you what, I'll call Francis and tell her an old friend is in town and I'd like to bring you up there to meet her and have dinner with us and I'll drop a little hint that maybe if she has a friend she could bring her along. One thing to remember is to be yourself, don't hint at the word money; say you own a medium size book store somewhere in California and that you're moderately successful according to California life styles. You're a business man same as me but we need to tone you down some and maybe change your haircut just a little."

"What's wrong with my haircut?"

"Well Richard its evident that you visit a hair stylist quite often probably as much as twice a week, maybe more. You need to go to a regular barber so you don't stand out so much, any woman will notice it."

"Oh I see what you mean, its part of me trying to look like a regular guy then."

"Yes that's it Richard, a regular guy like me. I can put on the airs with the best of them when I have to and fit in with a certain crowd. You know I'm as bald as a billiard ball?"

"No I didn't know that."

"Well I am. I have several wigs I take with me so I can fit in anywhere, your cousin wanted the real me bald head and all. She didn't like the made up person where I looked just any other average man, she wanted someone different and that's what she got, something she could never forget. Even where she ended up she'll have a smile on her face which nothing can wipe away. Enough talk for now I have no regrets. Let's see about dinner and on the way we'll shop a little bit and get you set up with some real street clothes."

"What about Fred; he mentioned he would like to eat with us as well?"

"I left word for him where to meet us, there's a little restaurant where we get the best steaks you ever had, nice home cooking kind of place like the old days of the late 1800s and early 1900s before everything started commercializing and the mom & pop places were all replaced with diners and restaurant chains. He'll meet us there at 7:00, this way you'll get to see a little of Poughkeepsie the way used to be years ago."

"Well okay then all I need to do is to go to my room and get some money, I feel naked without my wallet."

"You won't need it. You took real good care of me in LA and now it's my turn to return the favor, besides I made a handsome profit on a couple of your cousin's books already. Say I never asked you, why was she in such a hurry to get rid of all those books in the first place?"

"You may not believe it but she told me one night after she had a little too much to drink that she read in a couple of his books how to kill a person to where no one could prove it was murder. Anyway she got him quite drunk and he just died. Of course it was after he passed out that she gave him a shot of something under his arm pit where it wouldn't be noticed and he just stopped breathing. She left him where he was in his chair in his library. She went upstairs to bed and let the servants find him the next morning apparently passed out dead drunk but he was stone cold dead. She had unwittingly left several notes in the margins and dog eared a few of his books and she couldn't remember which ones they were or where she had placed them back in his bookshelves so she decided to get rid of every last book in the house to be sure she was rid of the evidence. That's the story she gave me and I swore I wouldn't tell anyone. So there you are, someone somewhere one day will find her notes but won't be able to trace them back to her and now it won't make any difference anyway."

Soon they were driving into the downtown area to get Richard some new street duds as Sol had called them. After some shopping Richard finally had some new normal looking street clothes. They met Fred for supper where they all had steak, although they each had a different cut, Sol opted for a rib eye, Fred opted for a T bone and Richard went for the filet mignon with bacon wrap. They all had a different vegetable but also had baked potatoes loaded with toppings. They had a lot of fun reminiscing about their old days as children, each one had a unique story about their parents and how they were disciplined and where they went to school and stories about their girlfriends.

"Fred, I'm going to call Francis tonight and see if she's busy tomorrow night or the night after and take Richard up to Buffalo to meet her and maybe she can find him a date with a real woman, would you like to come along and make it a threesome of couples?"

"I think I'll pass this time, you two go on ahead, I want to finish the work on his cousin's books so we can get them sold and mailed out of the store. You do know that I have a steady girlfriend now don't you Sol?"

"Well I guessed as much," said Sol, "but I didn't know for sure, I haven't met her yet, is she attractive?"

"Oh my yes, her name is Kelly Braden. She lives and works in New York City where she has her own apartment and all she knows about me is that I own a Book Store with a partner here in Poughkeepsie. She works in the fashion design industry for women, she plans to retire when I do She says then we can travel all the whole world over and never have to worry about money. She has no idea that you and I are worth millions. I told her that we make a decent living and that I do have a little nest egg."

"Well Richard with your new street clothes we'll get you dressed down to a decent looking income but not over the top. Francis knows we have the larger store but she doesn't really know how successful we have been. She knows I make a decent living by the presents I buy for her but I don't go overboard or she would get suspicious about where that kind of money came from, she'd probably accuse me of robbing a bank."

They all had a good laugh over that. Soon they were all talked out and Sol stood up to go pay the bill. Fred left a healthy tip as he always did. Most people in town respected the two recluse type men as they called them and gave them great service whenever they needed something such as food, clothing or other goods. Many of the town's people were also very good customers who came in regularly to see what new books had arrived in the latest shipments. They got two regular shipments a month plus the books that Sol bought while out on the road. They had recently set up a mail order business like a book a month club to see how it went over and it took off because of the many titles they offered their customers to choose from and they almost put other book sellers by mail out of business. Their catalogues were three times as big as their competitors and their prices were much lower due to the way Sol was able to purchase stock from other stores going out of business. Their regular suppliers noticed the amount of books they carried and gave them a much lower price per book due to the huge volume of orders per month. They hired more help to package, sort and mail out books just for that part of their business. They opened a new location on the second floor of the old factory just for their mail order business and had their own shipping and receiving location as well. They called the new Business simply; "Entertainment, Books By Mail" or EBBM for short. Their sign out front and logo looked something like this:

EBBM
ENTERTAINMENT!
BOOKS BY MAIL

They thought it was kind of catchy and did it ever catch on. Book clubs were formed by the dozen around the country to read all the new novels that were coming out. They kept the Publishers very happy and in doing so it kept all their costs down as well.

Sol and Richard went upstairs to Sol's apartment and Sol called Francis on his phone.

"Francis my dear how are you?" "Yes I'm fine as well, listen I have a male friend of mine who is visiting me from out of town and I'd like to bring him up to meet you and I wonder maybe if you could find a nice wholesome girl like yourself to maybe double date with us.

No he's never been married, like me his work keeps him on the road quite a bit. Oh I met him in LA, we had a mutual friend there and we just bumped into one another then a few weeks went by and he came out here from the west coast to see our Book Store in operation. How old is he, well I'm not quite sure, he's a bit younger than this old fossil, let me ask him; he says he's fifty six, is that a problem? No, alright, very well then, why don't you ring me back. We would like to come up tomorrow if we can to see you. Well okay, bye for now," he hung up. "She's going to check around and find a suitable girl for you, Francis is a waitress at a local restaurant up there and is very well liked. You'll like her as well, she is as down to earth as one can be. How about a night cap Richard, she'll call back in a little while?"

"No thanks Sol. Listen, I don't know about this blind date thing, I had one once and it was a disaster, I vowed never to have one again."

"I promise you a good time Richard, what you do after will be up to you. If you and your date hit it off maybe she will invite you over for coffee and whatever if you get my meaning?"

"Yes I've been around, I've apparently been around too much is part of the problem."

"Just be a good listener and let your date decide what she wants. The very worst will be that we will have a great dinner and go to bed early then come back home the next day."

While they were talking the phone rang. Sol picked it up and listened intently. "Yes, well aright, then we'll see you later tomorrow afternoon."

"Well there you are Richard, we're all set, she has a friend from the local bank where she has her account who would love to meet you, she said she's a dynamite looker, much better than herself and my Francis is real super attractive and her body is to die for. So if she is anything like my Francis you are in for a delight tomorrow night. She says the lady is divorced and isn't sure if she'll ever marry again, she's a natural blond, blue eyes and has a great figure."

"This is sounding better all the time. When do you plan on leaving in the morning?"

"How about around nine o'clock right after breakfast, we can eat across the street where most of us do every day or we have it sent over to us."

"Sounds good to me, if its all the same to you I'd like to eat out in the morning."

CHAPTER - 72

The next morning true to his word Sol and Richard were on the road to Buffalo soon after breakfast. They rolled into Buffalo later that afternoon and Sol decided to call Francis at home from a phone booth, before going to the restaurant where she worked the last time he saw her. Finding that she was home and had the day off and tomorrow as well Sol drove straight to her house so she could meet Richard and they could talk a little before going out to dinner and a movie. Sol had given the ladies a choice of where they would like to eat, then go to a movie or one of the all night nightclubs for dancing and they both decided that the movie would be the best ice breaker for Richard and Cecile so they could get to know one another.

Francis took to Richard right off. "I can see why you like Richard so much Sol, he is a lot like you in many ways, you both have your work that takes you all over the country and I can see that he is well traveled as well. Cecile is coming over here and we're going to go out to eat in her car if its alright with the you two. She has a big four door sedan, one I could never afford before but now with the loss of my husband I can afford one almost as nice as hers."

"What happened to your husband if you don't mind my asking?" asked Richard? Sol had given him a brief description of what had happened, Richard just wanted to start a dialog.

"The man was dangerous when he drank which was nearly every day to excess and when I got home from work I'd be dog tired and he would be pissed off that his supper wasn't ready the minute I walked in the door so he beat the hell out of me about every other night and then one day he got really mad and very drunk. He decided to come down to the restaurant where I work and stepped off the sidewalk to catch a bus but it wasn't the right bus and the Bus ran him over killing him. The Police came and told me at work, fortunately I had a decent insurance policy on him so I only work four days a week now and I got my place fixed up, replaced all of the broken mirrors and doors, patched all the holes in the walls where he punched them and if it hadn't been for my old flame Sol here I'd probably ended up killing myself to be rid of the misery I brought on myself by marrying that jerk instead of Sol. Sol has always been my man but he can't stay put for long and I still love him just because I can and will the rest of my life. We have a strange relationship but we're always there for one another, I've learned my lesson now and will never marry again. This man right here is all I'll ever need. He's offered to set me up in my own apartment in his building but I have all my friends here and could never leave them just like he can't go off and leave Fred, his best friend. So we have an understanding between us. We'll love one another long distance and make it work for us and we have and we do.

"So Richard what's your story?" asked Francis.

"I think that can wait until your friend Cecile gets here. I'm really nervous about meeting her, this is only the second blind date I've ever been on you know."

"Well you can relax, Sol met Cecile a few years ago when he went to the bank with me one day, do remember her now Sol?"

"No, can't say that I do."

"Well she is the one who waited on me at the counter, you know where all the tellers are, anyway you thought she was cute back then. Now she's a Wall Street Pro in the Investment Industry spending other people's money and loving it and she's good at it. She invested a small amount for me some time ago and it's doing quite well. She buys and sells for me and never even asks if she should. I told her to do whatever she thought was right."

Just then the front door bell rang. Francis went to the door and it was Cecile. She was in a dark blue skirt with a white blouse and a type of a large navy blue bow tie that hung down about three inches below a plunging neck line to show off her cleavage. She wore a pearl necklace around her neck and looked just like any other lady who was moderately successful. She wore a pair of black high heels about half as high as normal, the kind that looked comfortable on her.

"Well good afternoon everyone, Francis, Sol, and I believe and this other fine looking gentleman must be Richard. Delighted to meet you Richard you must tell me all about yourself." She gently thrust out her hand for him to either shake or kiss and he went for the kiss on the back of her hand.

"Delighted, I'm sure," he added. He stood there staring, absolutely memorized in awe of the most beautiful woman he could ever remember seeing standing right there before him.

"Is there something wrong Richard; are my eyes crossed again or something?" Cecile asked.

"Oh no Cecile everything is simply lovely, I was just telling them how nervous I was about a blind date, I've only had one and it was a disaster!"

"Oh me too when I was younger. I went on one and promised that I'd never to go on another but then when Francis called and told me a little about you and Sol both coming up well I just couldn't resist. I hope I don't bore you with money talk but that's all I know from my banking days to now when I'm working on Wall Street with the big boys of finance,. Do you have any Investments Richard?"

"Well yes, I have a little nest egg set aside but like you I spend other people's money in a way. I travel throughout the world on business buying up other businesses for clients you see."

"Oh my, how very interesting, we do have a lot in common. Well what do you say, are we ready to go? I'm glad I dressed the way I did, I'm ready for anything tonight!"

"Well yes more or less, we were just having some coffee would you like a cup also?," Francis asked.

"Yes if it's already made. Would you mind if I stole Richard and went into the living room where we can talk a little and find out more about one another?" As soon as she got her coffee she and Richard disappeared into the living room. Pretty soon Sol and Francis could hear both of them laughing and giggling like a couple of school kids.

"Well Sol, sounds like a match made in heaven from here, I kind of hate to break it up." She cleaned up the coffee pot and the cups from the kitchen, Richards and Cecile's could wait until later.

"Ready to go you two?" asked Francis as she entered the living room.

"Gosh is it time to go already, Richard and I were on a roll about Money Market Accounts, I've never met a man who could keep up with me in a money conversation."

The four of them piled into Cecile's four door sedan, a new Mercury Marquis Brougham and headed out for a Restaurant that the ladies had already picked out in the affluent part of the City of Buffalo.

They had a marvelous dinner then went to a club for a couple of drinks and some slow dancing rather than a movie, things were going that well.

"Richard you dance divinely, so smooth, it's a pleasure dancing with you."

"Thank you Cecile, the pleasure is all mine, I assure you."

"How about you come home with me for a night cap and we let the two love birds off at Francis's house?"

"That's fine with me, I have no plans for tomorrow but I know Sol wants to get back to the store the day after tomorrow, something about a big shipment going out overseas. I don't understand his book business but it certainly is fascinating and he's done very well for himself. He told me all about his expansion and how he was bringing in new businesses all the time to enhance his own. He even created his own mail order book business within their building."

"I'd rather talk about your business, it's much more fascinating than smelly ole books. Tell me Richard, do you travel out of the country much?"

"Why yes I do, I travel all over Europe, the Middle East, South America; you name it I've probably been there at one time or another."

"See that's much more exciting than books, now you said something about buying and selling businesses for clients, how do you go about that?"

"Usually I get an inside tip that a company is short of money and running into problems due primarily to growth. I check their balance sheet and if I like it I buy it or pass it on to someone else I know who can handle the deal. It can be very exciting for the right person."

"Oh yes I find it terribly exciting, go on tell me more, I find it very interesting. A friend of mine used to work for a large corporation which was swallowed up by another corporation, they fired all the top brass and brought in their own and that business today is one of the largest in the world."

"Oh, do you remember the name of it?"

"Yes I do, but I'll whisper it to you, someone might overhear me and recognize it."

She whispered the initials of the company into Richards's ear. "You ever hear of that company Richard?"

His face immediately turned a bright red, "I'm afraid I have, I'm the one who bought it and I'm embarrassed to say it's making millions for me every year."

"Oh so you're the rascal who bought it and turned it inside out upside down and let it run away with itself."

"Yes I'm afraid I'm the one responsible."

"I hear the company has since frozen everyone else out of the product line, it seems as though you almost have a monopoly in world trade for that line of products."

"Really, I didn't know it was that successful. I have nothing to do with the company any longer. I put the right people in place and let them run with it. If one business should fail I write it off as a loss against taxes, it works very well for me that way."

"Like I said I find you absolutely fascinating and you're the only man I've ever met that can keep up with my brain and be tactful about it, even modest and you're much too modest Richard, I think that's why I like you so much. You are a down to earth man but when it counts in the business world you are to be feared as well as respected for your tenacity. I can't wait to get you alone and just talk, lets hurry those two up a bit. You yawn, I'll yawn and I'll tell them I'm taking you home with me for a night cap and spend the night as well and we'll drop them off then go to my place if you don't think I'm being too forward?"

"Heavens no, I find you extremely attractive and knowledgeable and that's hard to find in a woman these days. I like you as well, in fact I'm a bit over-whelmed by all of this. Usually I date a girl only once because when they learn I have a few bucks all they want are expensive present's, cars and their rent paid for by me so I don't see them again. I don't want a kept woman I want a woman who can keep up with me with intelligence and so far you are the first woman I have ever met who has it all in one package. This could turn out to be a wonderful friendship after all, at least I hope it does."

"Good, then that's settled lets get those two off the dance floor and head for home. I can't tell you what a wonderful night this has been. I wish it could last forever but we all have jobs so we have to make the best of what time we do have together, make sense to you Richard?"

"Oh yes, it all makes perfect sense."

Finally Sol and Francis saw Richard and Cecile trying to signal them back to their table.

"Aren't the two of you going to dance some more?" asked Sol.

"No we have other plans if it is alright with you two. Cecile and I find that we have a lot in common and she has invited me to spend the night so we can get to know one another a little better away from all the hubbub of the club scene."

Francis looked at Cecile who was absolutely beaming. "Is that what you want Cecile?"

"Oh my yes, Richard is the most wonderful and charming man I have ever met. We have so much in common that its scary, it's as if we're soul mates who have just met. I want to take him home with me after we drop you two off, then I can bring him back tomorrow. say around lunchtime if that's alright, I know Sol has too get back to work soon and so do we?"

"Sol, would you like to spend the night with me?" asked Francis.

"Of course I would, you know how I love your coffee with all the trimmings."

"Well okay I guess that's settled, we're glad the two of you hit it off so well."

They left the club, Cecile dropped Sol and Francis off at her place then she took Richard home with her.

CHAPTER - 73

Soon they were at Cecile's house. "Well here we are Richard, this is my home away from home so to speak."

"This is a lovely home, late 1800s I'd say from the architecture."

"Yes I bought it when I still lived here then this job opened up for me in the City so I bought an apartment there as well. I split my time between the two places but I love being here. I catch a commuter plane here in Buffalo that takes me into the City and I catch a cab to work or to my apartment. I keep the car here, there's little parking in the City as I'm sure you found out when Sol picked you up at the Airport and showed you around town. Well come on in and I'll show you around." They went into the spacious house and she showed Richard the entire house. "I'm glad you brought your things with you so you could spend the night," said Cecile.

"That was Sol's idea, he said if things work out we may be staying with Francis. I'm glad things worked out the way they did."

"So am I." They walked back into the dining room. "Richard, would you care for some coffee, perhaps a glass of wine or something stronger?"

"No thank you, actually my bladder is full, may I use your facilities?"

"You mean the bathroom of course."

"Yes, of course."

"Why Richard the man a bout town is actually blushing."

"Yes well, I never asked a lady if I could use her bathroom before either."

"Of course it's right this way," and she was smiling.

He followed her past the dining room into the kitchen.

"It's right in here, handy huh, for the lady who likes to cook anyway."

It was in one end of the kitchen only a half bath but that was all that was needed anyway, there were a total of four bathrooms in the house and five bedrooms with a master suite that was to die for. Richard was soon out of the bathroom and Cecile asked him to bring his things upstairs. They went straight to the master bedroom that had its own huge bathroom with a shower that would easily fit four people in and a soaking tub to the right of the shower that was high at both ends so two could take a bath together or just soak.

"Oh now this is nice, I wish I had this in my own place back in LA."

"Well maybe I could help you with that, how big is your place in LA?" asked Cecile.

"Well actually its way to big for one person, I'm seldom there, I do have a staff of two that keeps the inside running smoothly and then I have a gardener who takes care of the lawn and shrubbery year round. I don't even know why I keep it. I got it real cheap so maybe that's it."

"Uh huh, Richard if you don't mind my being so bold, life is short and I need to slip into something more comfortable and get out of these high heels, you can change in the bathroom or in here if you'd like."

"I'll take the bathroom, you have to get your things out to put on and my things are right here together in one bag. I'll knock on the door before I come out to make sure you're decent."

"Aright, sounds good."

He went into the bathroom and changed into a long pair of lounging type pajamas but didn't put on his robe, he saw no use in doing that. They were both adults and would soon be in bed anyway. In a few minutes he was ready, he brushed his teeth and took a little extra time knowing she would take longer to get ready and that she would have to brush her teeth as well. Finally he knocked lightly on the door.

"Give me another minute Richard, then come in." He waited like any gentleman would and before long she said; "alright Richard!"

He felt funny about the way she put it, he thought she would have said, you can come out now, but guessed she had her reason. He came out and she was standing near the foot of the bed in a long dark blue robe that hid her completely from her neck to her toes.

"I've got to brush my teeth Richard, won't be but a minute." She went into the bathroom and closed the door. He heard the water running then soon heard it stop. Soon she stepped out from the bathroom smiling. She walked over close to where he stood and untied the belt that held her rode closed. She shrugged from her shoulders and let it fall to the floor.

`Richard was standing a couple of feet from her and couldn't help himself, he gasped out loud. "Oh my word, you are more beautiful than I could ever have imagined!" He found himself starring in disbelief. She was standing with her legs spread apart just a little, she had on a black negligee that only came to just below her hips, he could see through most of it, Her nipples were hidden by little flowered things woven into the material that hid them just a little. She wore a tiny pair of bikini type under pants, also black that he could plainly see through.

"Well Richard, say something; do you like what you see?"

"Everything I see I like," he blurted out, "actually, I'm pleasantly surprised I might add."

"Fine, then how about a hug?"

"Yes of course; how uncivilized of me!"

"No Richard, I expected no less than what I just saw, you know a real lady when you see one, it surely does show."

He stepped up to her and hugged her, then they kissed a long passionate kiss. They spent the night making love to each other like they made love all the time, hungry like teenagers in heat, searching out every part of one another's bodies a little at a time.

In the morning Cecile got up, showered and went downstairs to start breakfast for them. Richard woke up as she left the room in her night gown and he shaved and got a shower as well and put his pajamas back on and went downstairs. He walked up behind her and hugged her from behind. "Not now Richard our food will get cold."

They both laughed and had a solid breakfast of sausage and eggs, sliced friend potatoes and wheat toast. He helped her clear the table and they just put everything in the sink. They went back upstairs and made love once more.

On their way back to Poughkeepsie Sol had to ask; "well Richard, how was your night?"

"One word Sol, unbelievable, just unbelievable."

"She was pretty good between the sheets then.?"

"Between the sheets on top of the sheets on the floor on top of the covers, you name it we did it! she is such a wonderful woman that we want to see each other again. She wants to come out to LA and spend a week with me, then she wants me to come to New York and spend a week with her. I'm in heaven and I think we're in love, no retract that, we know we're in love! She's a fantastic woman, how can I ever thank you and Francis?"

"No need to Richard, we're both glad it worked out between you two."

"I have to tell you Sol, she is the first woman I ever slept with that was perfect for me, one that I would want to see again. And I can see why you like Francis she's a great gal as well and pretty as a picture."

"I'm glad you like her, I think you and I and the girls may have a future together after all, maybe a European cruise or a Mediterranean cruise or something?"

"Sounds like fun, maybe we could talk the two of them into something along that line."

Before they knew it they were pulling into Poughkeepsie once again.

Richard thanked Sol and asked him if he minded if he left the next day to go back to LA.

To Sol, Richard looked dumb struck and he could only imagine how it must have been for him. He was happy for all of them, each and everyone including Fred.

CHAPTER - 74

Three more weeks went by before Agents Jefferies and Marlowe got another lead and this one looked pretty good as they were in their office going over their latest flyer. "Agent Jefferies have you seen this latest bulletin, it's for a quick sale of a book store, it says everything must go, selling out to the floor and walls. Illness forces sale of Old Time Book Store, son of previous owner has cancer and must sell to pay medical bills."

"Say that sounds familiar doesn't it?"

"Do you think you have seen the ad somewhere before?"

"Yes I do, unless two owners have had the same problem for some reason, lets check it out anyway, it may be nothing." They got together and compared notes asking each other questions to see if anything rang a bell but nothing did. "Where's the location of the sale?" asked Dick.

"It says it's Albuquerque, New Mexico, how could there be an Old Book Store out there, I thought the oldest ones were in the northeast?"

"Read on a little more and maybe you'll find your answer."

"Oh I see it now, it says the Store been in operation since the days of dime novels in the same family for more than a hundred years. How is that possible, New Mexico hasn't been a State that long has it?."

"Sure it's possible, back in the old days when the Pony Express and Stage Coaches carried the mail and passengers and New Mexico was a territory of Mexico, it was the newspapers and dime novels that kept the people of the territories informed. They even printed Wanted Posters for criminals and sent them across the plains to other territories and States. That was before the telegraph maybe, I'm not sure when the telegraph was being used back then but we could find out I suppose if we had to. I do know the telegraph was in use during the Civil War because that's how everyone kept in touch when there was trouble in Dodge so to speak back in the 1860's, that's just over a hundred years ago."

"I don't think we need all the History, lets make a couple of calls and check out the story. The ad I remember said that owner had pancreatic cancer let's see what this man has?"

"Suppose it's a woman?"

"Then we'll know its not the same one won't we?"

They both picked up the phone and called someone different. Since they had only one phone and had to share it early on, Dick had become frustrated and had another phone line and phone installed for them. It wasn't long before they had their answer, the man had stage four prostrate cancer that had spread throughout his body and involved so many organs that it was too late to help the man with surgery or chemo therapy. Dick was told that the man's wife had to sell to pay all of the bills which were mounting up. They owed quite a lot in back rent and shipping bills from Publishers and back pay to two employees in the store. They were desperate. For them going bankrupt was not the answer, he needed medication and Hospice had just come in to help the man and his wife out at home. The two clerks were keeping things running until the sale was concluded then they would get their back pay and vacation time paid for as part of the sale.

"I don't know Jane, this doesn't sound like our guy would be interested in this one." He went on to tell her what he had heard.

She didn't have any better news.

"The age of the store has to be the common thread we have been looking for Jane, I'll tell the boss we may have a live one this time, its way too good for our guy to miss out on."

Dick took off and so did Jane. It was early in the day so she got on the phone to the Airlines and found a couple of seats on a plane going to New Mexico but the seats weren't together but she didn't care, she wanted them on that flight as bad as he did. The flight was at 1:00 so they had a little time to kill and would let Donny take them to the airport. Luck was with them, they had four days before the final sale besides today. She didn't bother with a

Motel, it was off season she was told for where they were going so there would be plenty of rooms available.

By 10:30 they had all their gear together and headed out to get the car and Donny. Late that afternoon they landed in New Mexico due to the time change and they had to make some adjustment for the time difference. For them it was supper time but the clock didn't say so. They picked up a rental car at the airport and drove into town and began looking for a motel. They found a national chain Hotel that advertised competitive rates with the bigger Hotels and Motels so they picked that one and went in and registered. He registered as John Wesley Smith and she registered as Shelly Anne Cooper. They had separate rooms which were adjoining but Dick hadn't paid any attention to, at least not yet. Jane picked up on it right away, this was the second trip where they had adjoining rooms and this one for some reason made her a little uncomfortable. They put their luggage away but didn't get into character, that would come tomorrow. They had supper and watched TV in the lounge there at the Motel. They stayed there a good part of the evening watching TV and discussing their plans for tomorrow.

"Suppose Dick that our guy just happens to stay at our Motel, what do you want to do?"

"Nothing Jane, we'll stay in character until we go to our rooms, that's all we can do at this point besides we don't even know who we are looking for right now."

"Yeah you're right, I'm putting the horse behind the cart again or wagon before the horse, I know its something like that. I've got a weird feeling we're up against some kind of chameleon."

"I feel the same way Jane, this guy is too good not to have been caught by now. In fact no one but us even suspect that he is the person who is committing these murders, as far as he is concerned he has gotten clean away with all of them. But with this trip I think we have a good chance of finding out who he is before he can commit another murder. The family of the man who has the cancer sounds like a nice family, too nice to have them killed over nothing."

Finally they grew tired and headed upstairs for bed. "Call me in the morning Dick after you shave and shower or whatever and we'll do breakfast."

"Okay, I'll do that." They went to bed for the night.

The next morning they were up early and eager to get started with their ruse of being literate Book Store buyers. They were in complete character once again and they looked believable this time, much more so than their first dry run a few weeks ago. They went to breakfast in character and no one paid them any mind although they did stand out just a little. They looked like a pair of geek's right down to their fake glasses that looked very real but were only clear glass with lines in them to look like bifocals. They ordered two different types of breakfasts opting for the odd rather then the norm again as practice just in case their man happened to be there. They finished their meal, paid their bill, left the restaurant and went to their car. They already knew where they were going so they walked as if they had a purpose, like their minds were made up for some kind of activity. The people who had been eating around them were kind enough to hold their tongues until they left then they talked behind their backs laughing and mimicking their mannerisms.

"Did you get a load of those two jerks?" one woman asked her husband.

Another man said to his wife, "wow how weird was that, what the hell did they order for breakfast, I didn't see any eggs, bacon, sausage or anything, it looked like one of them was eating some kind of grass, maybe bean sprouts or something worse!" The talk was rampant around the dining room. There was even some giggling among the waitresses and waiters as they pointed fingers at one another and made faces. But the Agents were gone by now and were out of the parking lot headed down the street unaware of the fun of them being made behind their backs. But this is what it was all about, fooling people to the point of the ridiculous leaving a lasting impression on anyone who saw them or came in contact with them so they didn't appear obvious as FBI Agents on a case which would be easy to pick out in a crowd.

Soon they were within the same block as the store they wanted to look over. They had rehearsed everything they were going to say and would play off one another's emotions appearing not to agree on anything.

They were lucky to find a place to park on the street close to the Store within walking distance. They got out of the car and they had a pad of paper and a mechanical pencil apiece but they were different makes and models. They walked into the store as if they already owned it. They strolled up and down each isle making doodling notes on their pads nodding their heads and saying things like, uh huh, or oh my goodness and things designed to confuse anyone that may be watching their act. Finally a female approached Dick. She was dressed in a professional business suit made for women.

"May I help you with something sir?"

"Not unless you own the place, we're thinking about purchasing it and moving everything to a new location."

"Well if you are interested in buying up the inventory perhaps you should talk to the Bank Representative who is here on site today."

"Oh, and who might that be miss?" Dick asked.

"Well actually that's me; I am the Bank's Representative here on site," she straightened her shoulders, crossed her arms and looked as if she were the boss.

"Oh? Well alright, I'm not used to dealing with a woman in charge of such a large transaction as this may be, what is the Bank's absolute bottom line here?"

"Sorry but I can't discuss that with you or anyone else. If you would like to submit an offer then you may do so but I have been asked not to try and lead a prospective buyer into making a ridiculous offer if you get my drift?" She said it in a sarcastic tone so badly that Dick wanted to break out laughing. He held his emotions in check and tried really hard not to smile.

"Well Miss, whoever you are; apparently you don't want to sell this place very bad. Usually in our trade papers they list an approximate value or an appraised value or bills and mortgages owed so that prospective buyers know whether or not they want to make an offer, you are very silly you know, who is your boss, maybe he is the one I should be talking to?" he said it with his own haughty attitude now.

Her face got red as if she were about to explode, she knew he was right but she also didn't know he had no idea what he was talking about. "Well sir, I am the Executive Vice President of the Bank that holds the note on this whole operation and I have every right to throw you out right of here now, I do not care for your attitude!"

"Well you go right ahead and try."

"Oh sis, would you mind coming over here and setting this broad straight?" he called out to Jane.

Jane came walking over slowly, she had overheard the outburst just as everyone else had.

"This woman is being impossible, she won't answer the simplest of questions and she is downright indignant and rude, see if you can get anything out of her?" And he made a questioning mannerism with his arms aloft almost in a feminine like gesture.

"Yes, well alright John, I'll do my best."

"Miss, come over here with me where we can talk in private, my cousin is a little high strung, he doesn't relate well towards women. He is terribly bright you know, he holds a Masters Degree in Literature and a Masters in world history. So you see he is no dummy, we have enough power and money to throw your ass out into the street right now, do I make myself clear?"

"Oh!" She stomped her foot hard on the old tongue and groove flooring raising a small amount of dust; "I've never been talked to in that tone of voice, just who the hell do you think you are?"

"Oh, did I fail to mention that we may own your pitiful little bank very soon, in case you haven't heard it's called a hostile stock takeover, we buy and sell businesses for profit."

"Of course I've heard of that, I'm no dummy either, I have an associate's degree in banking and finance, so what do you have?" She asked it in such a smart-alecky attitude that she irritated Jane now.

"I have a Masters Degree in Investment Banking and Finance, now what's your next stupid question?"

"Why I, I, oh hell I don't know, I need to go over to the Bank and get someone else over here to deal with you two, you're both acting like complete idiots!"

"A word of caution Miss, I wouldn't mention the possible take over just yet, we haven't decided who is going to stay or go. I think you'll be alright because you stood up for yourself and your bank so you'll probably be kept on with our approval that is and I'll talk to John and try to make him understand that you were only doing your job. Will that be alright? As you can see you are way out of your league here."

"Yes, well thank you for understanding my position, I didn't ask for this assignment you know. I feel terrible about the owner's situation but the bank has to look after its assets and interests after all."

"Yes well you're probably right, you'd best run along, don't worry about sending anyone else over, we're in complete control here anyway, not your precious little Bank, understood?"

"Yes, thank you for understanding my own position."

"Alright then run along and keep this between us until the story breaks, alright?"

"Yes ma'am, may I have your name please?"

"Shelly Anne Cooper, why do you ask?"

"Call it curiosity, I'm going to check you out on our new computer system and see what comes up." Jane had a second thought and invited the woman outside to talk alone.

Once on the sidewalk and out of earshot of anyone else Jane started in on her again. "Good luck checking us out because we don't use our real names, if we did everyone in town would want to get to know us, we are famous Philanthropists and we're listed by Corporation on Wall Street and won't I tell you that name either. If you'd care to run a background check on us you are welcome to do so but I doubt you'll learn anything more than I've already told you.

"I see, maybe I'll run you through our system anyway and see what comes up."

"Like I said before, we're not here to play games, this is business to us. If we want the store we'll get it with or without your knowledge, you won't know who the actual buyer is when its purchased. It will be one our associates who is with us and I'll not tell you who it is but remember the obvious is not the truth, watch for the odd just like us. We are not geeks at all, but do posses the degrees I told you about, the key to making a large purchase is getting to know who the seller really is and its not you, we already know that. So go ahead back to your job, either inside here or at the bank, you make the choice. Understand that we're real people and we'll deal harshly with anyone who stands in our way, do you understand what I'm saying?"

"Yes I think so, I'll keep a low profile from here on out but I'd really like to stay in the store if you can keep that man away from me."

"I can make that happen as long as you keep your mouth shut, but remember I hold your future in my hand."

"I understand, really I do, can we go back inside, you really make me nervous."

The two of them went back into the store and Jane went to huddle with Dick. "Hey Dick, I almost blew our cover or rather we did, but I got her attention and she is a little scared. I told her we have two Master's degrees in different things. She's scared of you now and that's good. She won't bother us anymore and in case of danger she'll stay of the way which is the way we want anyway. We can come and go now with ease, just act aloof like you can't stand her guts and it will be fine. Sneer at her once in awhile if you catch her watching you, it will scare the underpants right off of her, that is if she's wearing any under ware."

"Damn, I wish I could have seen you work, I just wanted to agitate her a little to get her attention, we don't want her in our way if we have a shootout with our man or something worse, I don't want anyone to get hurt unless its our man."

They spent the better part of the day looking around and occasionally they would pick up a book and shake their heads in disbelief and they kept it up almost all day. Finally they threw in the towel. "We might as well go back to the Motel, I have another idea I want to run by you."

"Okay Jane, I'm ready to go now anyhow."

Back at the Motel they were able to get out of character and unwind. "Dick while we were there I had time to think and tried to put myself in the bad guy's shoes. Suppose he's the type that waits until its late in the sale, like when its getting close to the deadline. Suddenly he shows up and makes the deal saving the owner any embarrassment. Maybe he has someone go in ahead of him to scope out the situation."

"Oh yeah Jane, now who is reaching but you do have a point. In fact you may have mashed the nail it right on the head, what is it they say, you whacked the nail or something."

"Oh Dick sometimes you can be so juvenile, its hit the nail on the head not whacked, whacked is when someone gets shot and killed."

"Yeah I knew that but the word hit just didn't surface in time. So we have a little down time, how about splitting our forces and we each take a shift in the store while the other watches from outside for someone strange looking or out of the ordinary."

"Wait a minute Dick, that word ordinary you just said, we're looking in the wrong direction, we need to be looking for the everyday type of Joe, not the oddity."

"By gosh you may be right Jane; we'll try it your way this time. Lets see now, this is Thursday and the final sale is Saturday at five o'clock here at the store. They will accept offers right up until then. I'll bet the killer will show up on Friday, take a look around, get the lay of the land then come back on

Saturday afternoon and be the last one to make an offer and trump all of the others if there are any."

"I think we've figured it out this time Dick, we're wasting our time until Friday afternoon, we can watch the store from somewhere outside."

"Hey here's an idea; did you happen to see the coffee shop across the street from the store?"

"Yes I did, what are you thinking, do you want to sit in there and sip coffee all afternoon until we see something suspicious and then one of us go over and check it out?"

"You've got it, that's exactly what we should do!"

"So until tomorrow we have some time to kill. Shall we aggravate the restaurant employees again?" Jane asked smiling.

CHAPTER - 75

Back in Poughkeepsie Sol noticed that BJ had a few days off from school and had come in to see if he could work until the following Monday, his classes didn't start back up until the following Wednesday.

"Hi BJ, how is school going these days?"

"Just great Mr. Devine."

"Please BJ, you can call me Sol while we're here. Listen I have an idea, there is a large Book Store for sale in Albuquerque in New Mexico. would you like to go with me and see if we can buy the place, I'll go as your grandfather and you can pose as my grandson?"

"Well of course sir, I mean yes Sol, I'm anxious to learn all I can from you and Fred, but as usual I'm a little short of cash."

"Don't worry about a thing; I'll take care of all the expenses. I've already made my reservations but let me see if I can get you on the same flight as me and the Hotel is no problem I always get a double room."

Sol disappeared and left BJ standing inside near the cash register counter with Greta.

In about an hour Sol was back and asked BJ if he would d like to have lunch with him. The two of them went across the street to the restaurant and made their final plans to go to New Mexico. Sol would give him more details once in the air and more when they got to their Motel.

They arrived in New Mexico late Thursday afternoon, checked into their Motel and already had a rental car that Sol had made arrangements for ahead of time. "Well here we are BJ, Albuquerque, nice looking town isn't it?"

"Yes sir; I've never even been out of New England before, this is very special."

Sol began to go over the disguise he would wear and BJ was to be himself. The story BJ would give people was that he had lost his parents in a automobile accident a few months ago and had no one left but his grandfather Sol. The ruse was that Sol would buy contents of the store and have it shipped back to a storage center in Connecticut while they searched for a suitable location for BJ's new store.

"Why Connecticut Sol?"

"Well we don't want anyone to know where we're from, its part of the ruse I always use. If anyone should ask you recently graduated from the University of Connecticut, okay?"

"Yes sir, I can handle that."

"If they probe further you got the same degree that you are working on right now, that way it will only be a small lie. You know enough about the book business to carry it off now."

"Yes sir, sorry, Sol, I can handle that."

"Now just so you will know, I'm not going as myself. I'll use a different name and I'll be using a cane and walk like a hunch back old man. I'll do my best not to look up at anyone but I'll do the deal using you as a go between. We'll act as if I'm a little hard of hearing as well, got it?"

"Yes I've got it, you'll almost be just like my great grandpa who is ninety one years old and looks a little like what you just described. He walks with some difficulty and is hard of hearing as well."

"Very good, then we'll relax for a while and tomorrow we'll have a look at the store, case it or scope it out as some would say."

The next morning was Friday, Sol was in no hurry to get going and somehow seemed a little anxious. They shared the double room.

"BJ, you awake yet?"

"Yes Sol, what time is it?"

"Its 8:30, don't you think we ought to get up?"

"Yes sir I guess so but I'm still tired from our plane trip I guess."

"It's the change in time son that's all, its still dark at home I suppose or maybe the sun is about to come up, I'm not sure. Anyway I'm going to get a shower and shave then we'll go downstairs to eat. Do you need to shave and shower this morning as well?"

"Yes sir, damn it I meant Sol, I really should so I can look my best I suppose."

"Well then, after me you're first, okay?"

"Very funny sir; shoot I've done it again, okay Sol."

An hour later they were on their way downstairs to eat in the Motel's Restaurant. Sol ordered his usual bacon and eggs, eggs over easy, sliced fried potatoes, wheat toast, juice and coffee. BJ ordered sausage links, eggs sunny side up, sliced fried potatoes, white toast, juice and a glass of milk. They ate their breakfast in leisure talking only about books and their varied interests in them. Sol paid the bill, left a tip, then they went back up to the room for Sol to get into his disguise. He made himself up, put on a white wig so that the hair fell below the soft brown wide brimmed hat he would wear then he asked BJ his opinion. "Well BJ how do I look, can I pass for your grandfather do you think?"

"Yes sir you're the right height and weight and have the look alright of a man in his eighties I suppose."

"Close enough, with the cane and this pad I'm going to put under my coat it will be the right look I believe. I want to look like a tottering old man." He took down an old dark brown overcoat and opened it up so BJ could see inside. "BJ, have a look at this; see inside here, there are three sets of really big pockets sewn into the coat?"

"Yes Sol."

"Well this is where I insert a pad to make me look a hunched back person to varying degrees. I'll use the highest one today and the pad I have is hard just like my boney back would be so if someone were to come up to me and pat me on my back it will feel exactly like my back but the underside is soft so it won't hurt me but I'll still feel it. It should fool anyone who gets close enough to check us out. So if you're ready I'll put the finishing touches on and we'll go but we'll leave by the back door and go to the car from that direction. When I'm in disguise I don't want anyone else to see me around the Motel, it could raise questions I don't want to answer."

They got into their four door sedan rental car and Sol let BJ drive while they went to look for the store. One of the waitresses was kind enough to give them directions. In a half an hour of driving around and looking around they found it and BJ pulled to the curb about a block away as Sol had directed.

"Alright BJ, here is your big chance. You go in the store and take a look around, hopefully someone will come around to help you out. Engage them in some idle conversation about the store. Gather every bit of information you can and then explain that your elderly grandfather is actually the one who will buy the store for you with cash from your trust fund if you like it. Tell them about your family being killed in an automobile accident while you were away at school and now that you've graduated your grandfather has graciously agreed buy you the book store of your dreams when we found one. Play it up big, act upset when you talk about your dead parents but don't cry, some people can spot fake crying right off. So no tears unless they are genuine. Remember to tell them that I'm not well but if we are interested we'll make our decision before the deadline tomorrow, okay?"

"Yes Sol, I got it."

"Alright then off with you and good luck, I'll stay with the car."

BJ got out and puffed out his chest, this was it his big chance to show Sol he could carry off the ruse and get away with it. He confidently walked into the store but no one bothered him, he simply looked like any college kid looking for school books. After a half an hour of checking everything out that he could he decided to ask someone for help. He went to the front counter and there was a gorgeous young college age girl behind the cash register.

"Excuse me Miss, is there someone here I could talk to about buying the store?"

"Why yes there is, just a moment please." She went into the back behind the counter through some tapestry that was hanging over the doorway and then she was back again followed by another woman. "This is Ms. Jackson; she represents the bank that holds the note on the Store, she can answer all your questions."

"What would you like to know young man?"

"Well I'm here about buying the store complete with all the works, shelving counters and everything."

"Oh I see, and just what do you think you'll do for money young man?"

Her tone was very sarcastic; BJ didn't like it one bit. "For your information I will use part of my trust fund to buy the store, my elderly grandfather is outside in the car and will make good on the purchase."

"Oh I see, so you aren't buying the store after all, your grandfather who is outside in the car is, right?"

"When you put it like that, I guess it is. I came in here to check the place out for him so you wouldn't waste his time."

"How much is your trust fund worth in today's dollars?"

"Just a tad over two million give or take a dollar or two. I recently graduated from the University of Connecticut with a Masters Degree in Literature and another Masters in business. I may look young but I can assure you I started college at age 16 and then the University at 18 and here I am."

"Just how old are you young man?"

"I'm twenty one would you care to see my driver's license from Connecticut or something? Another thing ma'am, I don't care for your attitude towards me, I'd be very careful how you address me from this moment on, very careful," he waggled his index finger at her for effect.

"Are you threatening me young man?"

"If the shoe fits lady then wear it, if I have to go out there and haul my grandfather in here I can assure you he will tear this place apart starting with you."

"Oh that would be rich, just who the hell do you think I am, remember I have to approve the sale or there won't be any."

"Let me ask you a question ma'am, how long have you worked at your bank?"

"I'll not answer that after you have already insulted me."

"Okay, have it your way." He walked out as if in a huff and went back to the car.

"You're on grandpa; I did all I could and really riled up a female Bank Representative while I was at it."

"Tell me BJ, is she a bitch or not?"

"First class bitch I'd say, she's probably never been married and is hungry for a real man to take her to bed and soon."

"That bad huh?"

"Yes Sol, she's that bad and more, she's full of herself if you know what I mean."

"I know just what you mean, her little bit of power has gone to her head, well I can fix that, let me have a crack at her."

BJ stepped back and made believe he was helping Sol out of the car. The woman was watching this unfold from the store's front window. They slowly made their way to the store.

Once inside Sol asked BJ in a very gravely voice, "which one son?"

"This lady right here grandpa, she says her name is Miss. Jackson."

"Am I to understand that you got a little smart-alecky with my grandson here Miss. Jackson?" He wasn't looking up at her but at the floor near her feet.

"You could say that sir, he was very smart-alecky to me you see. He gave me a really tall tale about you buying him the store and it wasn't at all believable to me."

"Uh huh, believe me he was right, if I decide to buy this place it will be for cash and it's the boy's own money and the money is in the car."

"Oh yeah, well you're the second jerk to pull that one on me this week so get in line buster."

"I don't understand Ms. Jackson, what do you mean the second one?"

"Well yesterday, a couple from somewhere, New York I think they said, pulled the same type of routine on me. So what, you have some money, first it has to clear the bank and I mean every bill, I'll not take a chance on one of you giving me counterfeit bills or a bad check!"

"Oh I see, well would you care to look over our money just in case so you can satisfy your own curiosity? By the way did you check out the other people's money or credit?"

"Well no, not actually, but I did run their names through our banking computer system and their story more or less checked out."

"Well then I submit to you that you and I should go over to your bank and unload the money I have brought with me so you can look it over and assure yourself that we are on the up and up and I tell you here and now that the others are probably imposters. Do I look like a crook to you Ms. Jackson?"

"No of course not!"

"Alright describe the others to me if you can."

"Well they were funny looking both of them, a man and a woman in their thirties I'd say, both of them wore thick glasses which looked like bifocals I think and they carried a pad of paper and pencils and they told me not to try and check them out that they just bought our bank in a hostile stock takeover which is very possible you know."

"Yes I know all that, I have done some of that myself, go on anything else?"

"No not that I can think of other than they told me they would put in a good word for me with the new owners of the bank who they claimed to be."

"Doesn't that sound a little fishy to you?"

"Well no, there has been a lot of stock activity with our bank. Like I said I checked their credentials through Washington and they were on the up and up, I just didn't like them."

"Yes I see, so how did you check them out exactly?"

"By Computer, we have the latest thing in computers, it takes up a big room that we had to add onto our building to house it and give the room heat and air conditioning because they are susceptible to hot and cold both you know, you probably have one yourself."

"Of course my company does, come let us go to your bank. I'll have my grandson drive over there and you can check with my banker while someone counts the cash and checks it out."

"That will be fine sir; I appreciate your candor and your manners as well."

Sol went outside and got into the car next to BJ who was at the wheel.

"I think we're in some trouble here BJ, it will take me some time to figure this out but in the meantime I'm going to humor the bitch and you were right she is one, we're going to let them go through our money. It's all clean no worry there and I'm going to let her call my banker who is actually Fred. He has a special phone marked bank and he will answer it in the phony bank's name and verify that our account in the millions of dollars and that ought to shut the ole biddy up."

They drove across the street a ways to her Bank and parked in front. Sol got out and asked if they had an armed guard and she said they did and he said well then get him out here to carry the money satchels in.

"Yes sir, right away sir." She went back inside and came out with an elderly gentleman who couldn't lift either one of the satchels as Sol called them, he was elderly himself and extremely thin and looked like he was on his last legs, he trembled all over like just standing up was an effort for him.

"Son, would you bring those inside for me?"

"Yes grandpa, whatever you say." BJ took the two old leather bags out and closed the trunk lid, picked them up and headed inside to the bank. Things went like clockwork.

"Well sir your story checked out, your Banker asked how you were and I told him you were just fine and a real gentleman. The money checked out as well, they counted out one and a half million, is that about right?"

"Yes that's correct; I didn't want the boy to blow his entire trust fund on one project all at once you see. He has more where that came from and it's his now to do with as he pleases. He is over twenty one now, I'm just along to advise the boy don't you see."

"Yes well it seems as though you are very wealthy in your own right according to your Banker."

"Oh I don't know about that. I am the boys only surviving relative though, what I have will one day be his, I just want to get him set up in a business to occupy his time until he takes over my conglomerate of businesses."

"Well it has a pleasure to meet you; I hope to see you tomorrow by the closing of the sale so you can buy the store and not those other two idiots who were here yesterday."

"Well, we'll have to see Miss. Jackson, this day has been very strenuous for me and I am sorry but you should have listened to the boy, he spoke the truth and now you know. Good day Miss. Jackson."

BJ loaded the bags back into the trunk and said to Sol; "Where to now grandpa?"

"I think this is a bust, I have a bad feeling about this. I think we'll head for home first thing in the morning." They drove back towards their Motel.

CHAPTER 76

Dick and Jane were doing the same thing, relaxing before setting up their little stake out for Saturday. "Suppose Dick our killer doesn't show up, then what?"

"We'll wait for the next sale and the next sale and the next until we catch him."

"I hate to think how many people may die at his hands until then."

"You know Jane we could still be wrong, maybe he doesn't kill all of his victims, maybe he lets some of them live out their days like this man with prostate cancer."

"Maybe, but I think he kills them to get his money back by raiding their bank accounts before the family can cash even one check to pay for the burial, how could any man be so cruel as to take money away from those who deserve it?"

"Well I personally believe that the man has no conscience, he kills in cold blood just as he pleases not unlike some of the stories we read about in the crime magazines and unsolved mystery books."

"I know all that, we've been over it and over it but it doesn't lead us anywhere except right back to square one and that is who is this man?"

"Yeah, that's the number one question back at headquarters, who is this guy? That's just what all of us want to know and don't feel sorry for him when we find him, if he shoots at us shoot to kill, is that clear?"

"Yes Dick, clear as a bell. I've got all that, we watch each others back and protect one another, trust me I got it! It's just that something isn't right with this whole series of killings. I want to know who this man is. I want him alive to answer all the haunting questions of every man and woman he has ever harmed and that's the why of it all; why did someone have to die in his eyes and for what purpose if they were about to die soon anyway?"

"Like I said, I think he wants his money back that he paid for their store, with them out of the way its simple to take the money back, all he needs is an account number and the bank where they have their accounts. We've traced every check he's written to a Post Office Box of a company that doesn't even exist, so he must be an excellent forger as well."

"Yes, I know all that, it keeps creeping back into my dreams so I feel like I'm haunted!"

"Alright how about a nap then supper and we'll call it an early night as well unless you'd like to go to a movie or something?"

"We'll talk about a nap right now, I'm really tired and my brain is on over-load with a headache."

"Mine too; you're room or mine?"

"What do you mean?"

"Well we both have two beds, you could take a nap on one and I could take a nap on the other one."

"Oh go to your room Dick, I just want to lie down for a while!"

Dick took the hint and walked through the connecting doors to his room and lay down where they took a long nap, separate from Jane.

Dick finally woke up and it was a quarter of seven. He went to knock on her inner door and found that she had locked it but he heard her shower running so he waited for her to knock on his door. After a short time the shower stopped next door, Dick waited patiently on his bed. Then he had an idea, maybe I should freshen up myself and take her out for a nice dinner and conversation. That's it, we need time to talk about other things other than this murder case. Dick had just finished up in his bathroom when he heard a soft knock on his inner door.

"Dick, you up yet?" whispered Jane.

He spoke in a normal tone of voice, "yes I'm up, I just have to put on a shirt and I'll be ready to go out for dinner or supper, whichever we decide I'll be dressed for either. Give me a couple minutes and I'll knock on your door out in the hall."

"Okay, I'm all ready."

Dick slipped into his suit coat, adjusted his tie and went out into the hall. He knocked on Jane's door and she opened it, checked out what Dick was wearing and must have agreed with his appearance, she closed her door, locked it and they headed downstairs.

"Well Jane what would you like to do tonight, a candle lit supper in a fine Restaurant or eat here in the cardboard food Motel?"

"Cardboard food, what's up with that?"

"Well I think all Motels who have their own restaurants serve plain ole food without any flavor, all the salt and pepper and hot sauce won't help the food, it's still plain."

"Oh I see, so that's what the food tastes like here, cardboard huh?"

"Kind of, I'm used to more highly refined food and atmosphere if you get my meaning."

"I think I do, you want more flavor in the way of ambience and atmosphere with your food."

"Yes, that's pretty much it I guess, I never thought about fine food in that way."

"Okay so what do you suggest?"

"Well let's see if there is a concierge here and we'll ask his opinion of where to find great food with some atmosphere."

Soon they arrived in the lobby and Dick went to the registration desk and asked about a concierge. The man shook his head no so Dick asked him about taking a lady out to eat, would you suggest some place for them to go for a quiet meal. He wrote something down for Dick and he looked over in the direction of Jane who had on high heels and looked fabulous and he nodded to Dick and told him this was the place to go to get it all and he winked at Dick. He didn't catch the wink but Jane saw it and shrugged it off because she saw Dick reading the note that the manager had given him, he hadn't been watching the manager's mannerisms.

"The manager says that this place has real good food and it has atmosphere, he did say the theme was southwestern and kind of frowned at our dress but he said for us to give it a try, he said that there's plenty of room to become lost away from the dance floor in a more intimate setting as he called it, I guess he thinks you and I are an item or something."

"I'd say or something would be correct, we're not exactly dressed for a southwestern theme restaurant are we?"

"No I'm afraid we'll stand out like all the rest of the tourists who go there dressed the same as us."

"Oh and that s supposed too make me feel better?"

"No, just stating a fact, he said all the tourists go there for the food and fun."

"Well let's go, it's something to do and we just might have some fun as well."

"Then we agree, he said the food is out of this world. They drove for almost an hour in the dark before they found the place. It was on the main highway and was appropriately called the OLD COACH INN. Local lore claimed that the restaurant was a favorite stop for Stage Coaches where folks could eat while the horses were being changed out and many famous outlaws were said to have stopped there as well. Dick parked the car and with some trepidation they walked into the local hot spot for some dinner and dancing.

They walked in and were greeted by a young lady dressed as a cowgirl complete with cowboy hat, a red and white checkered shirt and a short white skirt that was much like western style square dancers wear and white cowgirl boots. They took a minute to look around and up over their heads hung an antique Stage Coach suspended from the ceiling by heavy cables. There were all kinds of western memorabilia on shelves just out of reach of the customers but where they could see them. It was a truly awesome sight to behold.

"Would you folks care to sit in the cowboy cowgirl area near the dance floor or on the far side where the tenderfoots sit?" asked the waitress.

"Well take the tenderfoot's side if you please," answered Dick.

"Certainly, please follow me" and she wound around tables full of people dressed in western clothes and some were in regular street clothes with sneakers and the farther back they went the more dimly lit it became. She sat them at a table that at first looked like a wagon wheel but then they noticed that it was only a painted wagon wheel on a flat surface but it was so well done it looked like 3-D. She left them with two huge menus and soon came back with glasses of water for them in red glasses that resembled the red lights that you would have seen on old time cabooses following a train. The ambience was unforgettable. They searched the room with their eyes trying to take everything in.

"This place is full of history Dick, just look at all the things they have in here, it almost feels like a train or stagecoach is about to arrive and you expect to hear horses coming in any minute, its all very realistic."

"Then I take it you like it. I'm told back in DC that this kind of theme restaurant is catching on, there's even talk about a Roy Rogers fast food chain."

"I didn't know that, but this place is extremely interesting, I've never seen anything like this." They began to look over the menu. "Dick did you see the burger menu, buffalo burgers your way, wild boar barbecue hot and tasty, what is this, a wild game food restaurant or what? I want good old fashioned American burgers, roast beef, steak, things like that."

"I agree with you, I'll ask the waitress when she comes back." In a few minutes she returned to take their orders. "Excuse me Miss, what are these buffalo burgers, is it hamburger or is it really buffalo?" asked Dick.

"Why this is a theme restaurant sir, we serve only the best mid western beef, not buffalo, we only call them buffalo burgers to go along with the theme of the restaurant you see."

"Yes of course, thank you."

"Are the two of you ready to order yet or do you need a little more time?"

"Jane, do you know what you want?"

"Yes I want the best steak you have cooked medium please, with baked potato and what are the vegetables today?"

"Well you can have a choice of green beans, peas, carrots or white corn or corn nib-lets, some people call it baby corn but its very good and sweet."

"I'll have the corn then, it sounds delicious."

"And you sir?"

"I'll have the same steak cooked the same way but I'd like the carrots please and baked potato with sour cream and what's the bread this evening?"

"Well we have choices of corn bread, white rolls, Texas garlic toast and sourdough bread and butter."

"I'd like the Texas garlic toast please."

"And you ma'am, would you like some bread?"

"Yes, I'll have the cornbread please."

"Thank you, may I ask where you all are from?"

"Washington DC." They answered collectively.

"Wow, you are a ways from home aren't you?"

"Yes we are but we love this town already, everyone is very friendly save one bitch."

"Jane watch your tongue!"

"It's alright sir, a bitch around here is a female dog and there is nothing wrong when talking about your dog, we're all country people round here, it don't mean a thing."

"Well you have to admit Dick, she was a dog of sorts."

They both started to laugh as the waitress walked away. A little while later they got their steaks and they turned out to be huge bone in rib eye steaks that filled the whole plate, they were a good inch and a half thick after cooking, they were the biggest steaks either of them had ever seen.

"Wow, would you look at that cow on our plates, those are huge Jane."

"You're not kidding, I hope you brought your appetite for this and look at the size of those baked potatoes, I've seen shoe boxes smaller than those."

"Oh I don't know about this; I was expecting a small six once piece of meat not two pounds of cow, holy smokes what a meal and look at the size of my Texas toast, they must have come from Texas all the way here, they are huge, two pieces, holy smokes!"

They both dove into their meal but didn't finish half of it, there was just too much to savor and eat as well.

"Dick I am stuffed, I've never eaten anything as tasty as this, its by far the most wonderful meal I've ever had and by far the largest quantity of food I've ever seen."

"I feel the same way Jane, it was wonderful wasn't it. Remind me to thank the manager when we go back to the Motel, the meal was extraordinary." They were just about to push back their chairs from the table a little when they heard a voice over an intercom announce; "well folks and all you tenderfoots out there this is what you have been waiting for, the floor show is about to commence with the Albuquerque Square Dance Ensemble, give them a big howdy as loud as you can." The place broke out in bedlam. They decided to sit still and watch, they had a small view between the backs of chairs out to the dance floor. They danced several different kinds of square dances then another group of dancers came out, they were the Albuquerque Cloggers' who danced several dances to the delight of all the customers. Then they slowed things down and opened up dancing for everyone in the crowd.

Soon the waitress came over and asked if they were done and could she clear the table for them. They said yes but the music was very loud so they just nodded their heads. When she was done she asked if they'd like to stay a while and maybe dance. They said they would and she told them about a bar and she would take their drink orders if they liked. Dick ordered scotch on the rocks and Jane got a scotch and soda, it was more lady like she felt and she could toss down as many as Dick could if she wanted to. After having a few drinks Jane asked Dick if he would like to dance. He said yes and stood up and they danced. He wanted to hold her close but not too close, he didn't want her to feel any discomfort from being held too darned close remembering her bad experiences with men in the past. By the third slow dance he was holding her real close like lovers would hold each other on the dance floor. They were oblivious to those around them, it was a mix of tourists dressed in different attire. Everything from boots to sneakers, street clothes to suits and ties, high heels so they were not alone and didn't look or feel at all out of place. By the fifth slow dance during the night they were dancing cheek to cheek, she could smell Dick's cologne and he drank in her perfume and it was subtle, just right and not at all strong. They stayed through midnight and finally they told the waitress they were ready to leave and she brought Dick the bill. He raised his eyebrows as he checked the figures like he didn't agree with them.

"Is something wrong Dick, was it that expensive?"

"On the contrary, it isn't expensive at all, it's only sixty eight dollars and thirty two cents, that's extremely reasonable for a night out like this. In DC a night out like this would cost a couple of hundred dollars and then some with tips."

"Wow that is reasonable and we had a great time to boot."

Dick paid the bill and he left a hefty twenty dollar tip for their waitress, he knew she had worked her buns off for them and everyone else she had waited on. They got into their rental car and headed back to their Motel.

They went upstairs and like a gentleman Dick walked Jane to her door. He took her key and unlocked the door for her. "I had a wonderful time tonight Jane; I hope you had one as well."

"Yes I did Dick and thank you for not pressuring me and being patient with me."

"You're quite welcome Jane, good night now." He started to turn towards his door when she stopped him by gently touching his elbow.

"Just a minute Dick," she reached up with one hand and took his chin in it and turned his head slightly and kissed him lightly on his left cheek. "Thank you for understanding and not pushing me; I'll never forget this night as long as I live, goodnight Dick."

"Goodnight Jane." He went to his door, unlocked it and went in. Wonder what she meant, thank you for not pressuring me or pushing me, what was that all about? The kiss on the cheek was a nice touch as well, appreciated but not expected he was thinking.

CHAPTER - 77

On the way back to their Motel Sol had a thought. "BJ, I just had an idea, the flyer we have about the sale, didn't it say the owner had a rather large collection of books at his home as well as the inventory at the store?"

"I think so, but maybe we ought to read it again though."

"Do you have it with you son?"

"No, not on me, but if I remember right there's one in the trunk in one of my small bags."

"You mean like an overnight bag?"

"Yeah, I threw one in before we left and I don't think I took it out at the Motel yet, it may still be in the trunk."

"Please pull over and check please, I have an idea that we may save this trip yet."

BJ pulled to the side of the road in a grassy flat area and stopped, went to the trunk and came back with the overnight bag. In it he found the copy of the flyer that Sol had given him so he would have his own. "Here we are Sol, I was right. I also have some stuff in here in case I need something."

"Oh, and what do you have just out of curiosity?"

"Well there are a couple of different kinds of screw drivers, an ice pick, a roll of duct tape, a roll of black electrical tape, a folding knife, a small first aid kit, some ¼" nylon rope and a pair of soft cotton brown gloves. "

"That's a rather odd assortment of things isn't it?"

"Well you told me to be prepared for any eventuality when we left for somewhere so this is my own little bag of tricks I'd guess you'd call it."

"Umm, that's not a bad idea but you don't want to get caught with those kinds of things, where did you buy them?"

"I didn't buy them, I had a homeless man purchase those things for me at a Hardware Store near school and I paid him with cash for his trouble. I figured a while ago if I was going to work with you I'd better start to think like you so no one ever saw me buy a thing and the poor man died two weeks later from alcohol poisoning and cancer of the liver from too much drinking. All I did was to contribute to his drinking by giving him enough money to buy the good stuff or whatever his alcohol of choice was and he probably drank it all down straight from the bottle but I bet he died with a smile on his face. He reeked of cheap whisky when I met him."

"Alright then good job, always get someone else to do your dirty work when you can."

"It says here at the very bottom in small print Sol that the seller has a collection of rare and old books at his home that have been in his family since the store opened. It gives the man's name but no address, we'll have to find a phone booth and see if we can find it in there." BJ turned around because they were almost back to the Motel and headed back the way they had come until he saw a phone booth. He pulled over to the curb and got out to check. "No phone book in there Sol, someone has ripped it off I guess, we'll have to look for another one." They drove until he found another phone booth. "There's a phone book in here Sol."

"Good, put your gloves on so you don't leave any prints and here's the flyer and a pen. If he is in there write down his address and see if there is a map of the city in the phone book, if there is rip it out so we can use it to find the man's house."

BJ did as he was told, the man's name and address were in the book and there was a map of the city in it so he got them both and returned to the car making sure that no one had seen him. "What are you thinking Sol?"

"Well I figure if we didn't remember his private collection then maybe the people ahead of us didn't either. I've got a feeling it's the cops and maybe they have finally figured out what I've been up to for the past twenty five years. They already showed their hand which shows they don't know a thing about buying a business because they went about it all wrong. I wonder just how long they have been onto me? Oh well no mater, they will never catch you and I, we are way too smart for them and I am going to teach them a lesson tonight. Lets go find the house then we'll grab something to eat early then we'll go and see them just before they have their supper. If they have any suspicions or the cops have talked to them we'll disarm their fears with our ruse. We'll do the same thing that we did at the store but this time I'll do the talking and tell them I'm buying the books to put in your new store on display under glass with lock and key. If that doesn't work I'll think of something else, at least we'll get them to show us where the books are in the house then we'll take care of business." They looked over the map and found the street they wanted and headed in that direction. Sol was very quiet; BJ could see that he was devising a plan of some sort because every once in a while his lips would curl into a smile and his fingers were moving like he was building something. They finally found the house on a secluded street with huge trees lining both sides of the street a long ways out of town town. BJ slowed but didn't stop and Sol was checking the houses nearest to the one they wanted.

"Perfect BJ, just perfect, lets go back to the Motel, I need my own little magic bag then we'll eat an supper early and pay them a visit. If they have what I hope they do we'll find a truck rental place before they close and get us a you drive it one way truck and load up the books then we'll have some real fun. I want to change clothes back to myself as well."

They swung back by the Motel and Sol used the back entrance to go to their room they shared and got Sol's little magic bag as he called it and came back down to meet BJ. They went to eat and had a chance to talk some more and Sol let him in on part of the plan, he didn't give him any details because he didn't know about the books and whether or not he would want them.

As soon as they were done with supper Sol thought it would be a good idea to check out a few Truck Rental places and Hardware Stores for the things that they would need later.

At 6:00P.M. they went straight to the house to meet the owner of the store. They were met at the door by a kindly elderly woman who let them in. Sol introduced himself and BJ using their real names without any disguises. There was no reason to hide their names, these people would soon be dead. The man they came to see was in a hospital bed in the dining room where he could look out to the street and watch cars and people who were walking go by.

"Sir, I am Sol Devine and this is my grandson BJ, we are interested in seeing your collection of Literature. We've already been to the store and liked what we saw and will probably buy it tomorrow before the deadline if we can. I can out bid any of the written bids and the lady from the Bank said she would accept the highest bid."

"Then you have met Miss Jackson I take it, she's a bit of a spinster woman with a bit of an attitude but she knows her banking and is an astute business person as well."

"Yes we found her to be very knowledgeable about your store. May we perhaps see your collection, if we like it I will pay you in cash for it tonight so I'll be free to take on the business of buying your store tomorrow afternoon."

"She told you how to find me then?"

"Yes, she was very cooperative once she checked out my credentials and BJs and she also talked with my Banker, I'd say she is very thorough in her work."

"Yes that's her alright, always watching out for the bad guys if you know what I mean."

"Lucy, would you come here a moment dear? Lucy is my wife and caregiver when Hospice isn't here and they have gone for the day you see."

"Lucy dear would you show these men to my library, they may be interested in buying my entire collection."

"Yes of course honey, right this way gentlemen." They followed her past a couple of rooms and came to a large library with double sliding solid wood doors almost black with age and patina, they looked like they were mahogany. "Here you are gentlemen, whenever you want to talk with my husband you know where he is, just go back down the hall the way we came, I'll leave you both to peruse the books."

She left and Sol almost gasped out loud. "Would you look at these BJ, dime novels from the 1800s, I've never even seen one and here are dozens in almost perfect condition." He kept looking and went over nearly every book that was there and every now and then he pulled one book out to look at it and said, "yup, first edition, this is great, just look at all these books, some with gilded pages, what a find, this is the mother lode for sure. Alright BJ this is it, we'll take the whole lot. I'll give him whatever he wants for it all, lets go talk to the man." They went back to the dining room that had the table removed but the chairs were left for people to sit when they were visiting the couple.

"Sir, you undoubtedly have the finest collection of rare books and first edition books I have ever seen. Do you have a price in mind?, please remember that I am a collector as well and have some of your books but your collection added to mine would make mine greater than most of the collections found in the world's finest museums, any doubles you have of mine, I will give to my grandson to put in his new store in glass locked display cases for people to see."

"Yes, I think that twenty-five thousand dollars ought to be a fair price for just over thirty two hundred very rare books, don't you?"

"Very reasonable sir. Will cash be alright, I have it with me and your Ms. Jackson has already checked it out to be sure there is no funny money in there?"

"Yes of course, cash is always nice, no banks, no income tax and things. I would keep the books but alas I have no one to pass them down to who would want them, they wouldn't appreciate them like you and I would anyway."

"Oh yes sir, you are right about that! Would it be alright with you if we left for a while, we need to rent a truck anyway, get some supper and I wouldn't trust a shipper or mover of freight with these. I'll have BJ drive the truck back to my place in New York State. When we buy your inventory at the store I'll have a local moving company come in and pack everything and ship it to my store in New York."

"I thought you said you were a collector sir?"

"Oh but I am, but you should see our store though, I bought an old three story Woolen Mill and warehouse. The top floor is where I live and I have my own huge Library there. That is where I keep my own collection and we rent out several apartments for people who work for me and the other stores in the building. I turned the ground floor into stores of every kind imaginable that compliment my own huge retail store and the second floor is used for storage only for incoming shipments not unlike yours and others. We also have a huge shipping and receiving department where we ship books all over the world retail. However I will not break up my own collection unless I have doubles and I won't break yours up either. I don't mean to brag but my partner and I have made millions using our restoration techniques, we have patents for machinery we have built for producing our different inks, different kinds of paper and you should see the fine linen paper we manufacture. We have museums from around the world sending us books to restore for posterity as well."

"Oh my that is wonderful, I am so glad to have met you, Sol wasn't it?"

"Yes sir, just Sol will do. Well then if I may take your leave you're probably getting ready to eat and we should go and find a truck and some packing boxes then we'll come back and conclude our transaction, if that is alright with you sir?"

"Yes that's fine, you go on ahead, I'm really very tired right now."

"Very good sir, we'll be back before you know it, give us about an hour and a half and we should be back, that will give you and your lovely wife time to eat as well."

Sol and BJ, who was standing nearby, left the room, thanked the man's wife and told her they would be back soon.

They left and went to the first truck rental place that was closest to town and furthest from the man's house. Sol had a plan but was not telling BJ what it was just yet. He apparently was still formulating it as they went. They got all the packing boxes and filler for the boxes from the one rental place along with a thirty foot long one and a half ton box truck. Soon BJ was ready to leave and Sol would follow him in the car. Sol told BJ to stop at several large hardware and home improvement stores he had seen and gave him money to buy six propane tanks like you would use on a home barbecue grill. Then they headed back to the house. The man and his wife had finished supper and she had cleared away the dishes from a stout card table next to the man's hospital bed and she was doing the dishes as they returned. She met them at the door.

"Good evening gentlemen, I see you are back, how very nice of you, please come in."

"Thank you ma'am, would it be alright if my grandson backed our truck up to the front door so we can start to box up and load your husband's books?"

"Actually it would be closer if you backed into the driveway all the way to the back side door; its a shorter distance to carry heavy boxes of books. Confidentially I am glad that you are taking them, I wouldn't know what to do with them and if I were to try and sell them I'm sure someone would take advantage of a little old lady and steal me blind," she whispered quietly.

"Yes ma'am they probably would. We're here to pay top dollar for them though, you and your husband should have no more financial worries whatsoever from now on."

"Bless you sir and thank you."

BJ backed the truck in as the wife had asked them to do and began to bring in the boxes that were all broken down flat and had to be put together to make a box which only took seconds to do for each one and they used shipping tape to secure the bottoms that the truck rental company also supplied for them. The man's wife volunteered to help by packing and putting boxes together as they went. Sol had a magic marker and was marking certain boxes as they filled them. The propane tanks stayed on the truck in the right front corner out of sight as it was getting dark. They were almost finished loading when the wife mentioned the money. "Oh my yes," said Sol, "let me get it out from the trunk in my car, I'll be right back. He returned carrying two bags, his magic bag and the other was one of his money bags. He plopped the money bag down on the floor, which was just an old suitcase with worn leather straps and faded brass buckles and counted out all the money in front of them both putting them both at ease. He laid the full amount of cash they had agreed on at the foot of the man's bed, he had to move his legs over to accommodate room for the money. The couple were hugging and gushing all over. Sol stepped back a ways, turned his back while he screwed on a silencer to the 9mm semi automatic pistol he carried. He walked up behind the woman while she was hugging her husband and shot her in the back of the head at point blank range and she slumped to the floor.

Her husband said; "what's wrong dear too much excitement?"

Sol shot him in his head killing him instantly. Sol scooped up the money, put it back in the bag and returned it to the car. He came back like nothing was wrong and helped BJ put the last few boxes in the truck. As the truck filled up BJ moved the propane gas tanks back a little at a time until they were at the very rear of the truck.

"What do you want the gas tanks for Sol and how come so many stops at different stores to buy them?"

"We are going to send these nice folks off with a big bang and I didn't want you to draw to much attention to yourself by buying all the tanks at one store, people would question why you needed so many tanks all at once. Bring them in and put one in every big room you find and one in the room where they are taking a nap."

"Sleeping at a time like this?" a surprised BJ asked.

"Yes and they won't wake up anytime soon, you'll see."

BJ put one in the dining room and quickly saw that they were dead, both had been shot in the head but he had heard no shots. Then it hit him, Sol had to be using a silencer but he had seen no gun so where was it? BJ went about his business following Sol's every lead.

"Alright BJ time to learn your craft. What I have in my hand is called C4 explosive."

"Huh? Looks like plain gray putty to me."

"Right but when it goes off you don't want to be around. We're going to take a little bit of this and roll it around with your finger's until it looks like the thickness of a lead pencil, and then we wrap this small piece around the neck of the gas tank right where the valve connects to the tank then another piece around the tank where this seam is around the middle and we'll connect them together with another piece. When we set the explosives off the valve will effectively be cut off from the tank body, then the tank will cut itself in two and will explode and if we do it right each tank will blow at the same time. We'll run this wire which is called det. cord, short for detonation cord, from each tank to where the center of the explosion will take place. We'll put our timer right there. Go ahead and place a string of explosive around the neck of each tank then I'll show you how to attach the det. cord." They went about their ghostly chore and in another hour they were all done. "Alright now we are going to attach the cord to each tank and run a length to the center of the hall where I put the small kitchen timer I found. It will give us an hour to get a long way away from the blast which should be heard for miles and will completely destroy the house and everything in it. The only thing left will be the ashes and the only way they can figure this one out is to bring in the FBI but they won't come here so they will have to send everything to Washington to the FBI Lab for analysis. Before we are done we will have completely covered our tracks and will have left nothing much behind for them to look at. Is everything done now, are these all the cords?"

"Yes Sol that's all of it."

Sol noticed that BJ showed no emotion, he was ready for the excitement of blowing the house sky high. Sol showed BJ how to open all the gas controls on the kitchen stove wide open along with each small gas tank opened to leak extra gas into the house as well to make the explosion even bigger. Sol also made sure that all the windows and doors were closed tight as well. Sol set the timer that was connected to a 9 volt battery he had BJ buy when he bought the gas tanks. BJ went to the truck and Sol went to the car and they left the neighborhood with no one being the wiser. They got close to their Motel and Sol signaled BJ to pull over behind him which he did.

"What's up Sol, I thought you wanted to get a long way away from here."

"I do but we have more work to do. Park the truck in the back of the Motel away from any bright lights and I'll pick you up there, we're going to pick up another rental truck."

"Another truck, are you kidding?"

"No, I'm very serious, we can't take a chance on someone who may have seen the truck back there at the house, we're going to ditch this one out of town somewhere and set it ablaze after we have transferred everything into the other truck. I'll steal a couple of license plates from other vehicles that won't be missed for a while then we'll do the switch and if the house blows before we're done she blows. Every cop and fireman for miles around will head there because of the size of the explosion giving us time to hit the road in a different truck other than what any neighbors may have seen. We'll abandon the car somewhere and point it in the opposite direction of our travel."

"I see, I know what you are doing now, you've set this up very nicely if I do say so myself, you're one smart man Sol, very ingenious."

"Alright, lets get the truck parked back there behind the Motel and I'll get the bags out then get us checked out. You come through the center of the Motel from behind and meet me inside the lobby and we'll be off and pick up the second truck."

Everything they did went off without a hitch, they found a canyon way out of town and dumped the first truck there then set it on fire with gasoline they had bought in two five gallon cans they had also purchased at different places. They made sure that it was on the opposite side of town that they would be traveling, no one would notice them going the opposite direction. They switched the loads using two homeless men Sol had found. Suddenly the house blew up and all they saw was a glow in the night sky and a barely audible rumble from the explosion.

The next morning was Saturday, the papers read: 'Prominent couple dies in house explosion, the owner of the book store and his wife died in the fire. The next door neighbor's houses on both sides of them also burned to the ground killing everyone in those houses. One house was a friendly neighborhood couple, on the other side was a family of five, they and their pets never had a chance to escape due to the high explosive nature and the resulting fire. The Fire Marshall is investigating but says that it looks like a terrible accident at this time.'

Sol and BJ saw the story on TV and were surprised at the early reports. They were in a Motel fifty miles away resting up from their arduous journey of Friday night where they packed the first truck with books then repacked them on another truck then they drove all night without sleep. They lay over for a few hours on Saturday before resuming their journey. BJ was impressed with Sol's ability to think under pressure and plan the way he did. It was his misdirection's that BJ valued most. Sol explained to BJ that between the two fires it would keep both the Police and Fire Departments busy all night long and probably through the next day as well investigating the fires, looking for clues as well as recovering the bodies of the deceased.

CHAPTER - 78

Dick and Jane awoke Saturday morning to headline news on television about the couple who owned the Book Store. They died in an explosion and resulting fire that destroyed two other homes in their neighborhood as well as their own. Dick had been in the bathroom getting ready to shave and take a shower when he heard the news on his TV but he couldn't believe his ears. It can't be he thought. He ran to the doors which connected the two rooms and just as he was about to knock on her door Jane knocked on his door from the other side first.

"Dick, Dick, are you up yet, let me in, there's something on TV you've got to see."

He unlocked his door and she ran into his room all excited. "Did you see what was just on TV?"

"No but I heard it, I was in the bathroom getting ready to shave when I heard the news."

All of a sudden Jane started to giggle. "I'm sorry if I caught you at a bad time Dick." She was laughing and giggling all at the same time. He had been in a hurry and forgot he only had his pajama bottoms on and saving cream all over his face.

He looked at Jane and he began to chuckle himself. "I wouldn't talk there sweetheart," he tried vainly to mimic Humphrey Bogart, "have you looked in the mirror lately?"

She was in a short black nightgown with a plunging neckline and she had cold cream all over her face and didn't look much different from Dick with the shaving cream on his face. They both began to laugh uncontrollably.

"Hell of a way for couple of professional FBI Agents to start the day isn't it Jane?"

"Yes Dick I have to admit we do look a bit silly but don't you think we should get dressed and check out the reports?"

"I need to finish shaving and grab a shower, knock on my door when you're ready, I should be close to ready by then."

They went their separate ways, Dick shaved and showered and Jane finished putting on her makeup and she was ready a few minutes before Dick. She knocked impatiently on his door.

"Give me a second Jane;" but it was too late she was already in the room.

He was busy fastening his trousers, zipping up his fly and getting ready to put his belt in the trousers loops when he realized Jane was standing there watching him.

"Love your polka dot boxer shorts there Agent Jefferies."

He turned to see her with a red face. "That's not fair Jane I wasn't ready yet!"

"Sorry Dick but I'm in a big a hurry same as you. What do you say we grab a quick breakfast here and then find directions to the houses and go find them?"

"Sounds good Jane, I'm almost ready now." He put his pistol in his shoulder holster.

"Do you have your weapon Jane?"

"Yes it's in my purse please, let's go."

They went downstairs to the restaurant to eat some breakfast. All of the waitresses and other help were buzzing about the explosion and resulting fires. As soon as they were done eating they chose one person whom they'd overheard talking with others and felt she may know the neighborhood. They called her over to their table to talk to her.

"Miss, could you tell us how to get to the houses that caught fire last night?"

"Yes of course, I live at the far end of the same street and heard the explosion and felt it as well. It shook every house on the whole block and then some including mine, we thought an airplane had crashed, you could see flames in the sky for miles some people told me today."

"You heard only one explosion, is that right?"

"Yes sir, one great big huge explosion like a ferocious thump, nothing after that!"

"Did you see anyone or hear of anyone injured Miss?"

"No ma'am but I knew everyone in the block, we were all friends growing up and I went to school with some of them. Are you people the police or something, there has been a lot of talk about your movements around here, you seem to be asking a lot of questions for tourists?"

"Yes Miss you could say we are the Police but actually we're Federal Officers doing an investigation, more than that I cannot tell you."

"Yes sir, didn't mean to pry but seeing the two of you together, well most of us knew you weren't exactly girlfriend or boyfriend if you get my meaning?"

"Thank you for not prying further, could you write down the directions for us, once we're there we'll ask questions of the authorities and they will tell us what we need to know."

"Certainly, do you have a paper and pencil," the waitress asked

"Of course just a minute." Dick reached into this inside jacket pocket and pulled out a small spiral pad of paper that flipped over from the top to back. The girl gasped when she saw the pistol in his shoulder holster. "Sorry Miss but we're required to carry firearms."

"Does the lady carry one also?"

"As a matter of fact, I carry two, both out of sight but I can pull them quick enough if I have to defend myself or both of us."

"Oh I see, I am sorry but guns frighten me."

"That's quite understandable Miss, please don't tell a soul who we are, we are on a case, that's enough for you to know, anything you might say could endanger someone else if they, the perpetrators, find out we're in town."

"Well alright if you say so but my co- workers are going to grill me when I get back to the kitchen."

"Just tell them we're journalists who happen to be passing through and we thought we would take a look at the fire scene as long as we are here anyway."

"Okay, I think they'll believe that story."

"Thank you Miss." They got up from the table Dick left a tip and they went to the cashier to pay for their meals. They went straight to their car and headed out of town to the suburbs following the directions the waitress had given them.

Within forty five minutes they were pulling onto the street where the fire had been and a City Cop stopped them abruptly with his car blocking the street.

"Sorry folks, this is a far as you go."

"Jane time to fess up, I guess he's got us on this one."

"Don't get smart young feller, a lot of people were killed here last night and we don't take kindly to strangers butting in, so state your business and be on your way."

Dick reached into his other jacket pocket slowly and handed his I D to the Officer, Jane retrieved hers from her purse and handed it to Dick and he handed hers to the Officer.

"What the hell? What's the FBI doing butting in here?" he asked obviously upset.

"Sorry, we can't say, we are on a case and if I'm not mistaken one of the people killed last night was the Book Store Owner from town."

"How did you know that?"

"Lucky guess, lets just say I'm naturally suspicious plus it was all over the news this morning. Now if you will kindly hand our I Ds back to us we will go check out the crime scene for ourselves."

"There isn't a crime scene buster, the Fire Marshall says the explosion and fire was an accident, there's no need for you to go snooping around up there."

"Alright I asked nicely, where's your boss, get him out here right now or face charges of impeding a crime investigation by Federal Officers, got it? Sorry if I stepped on your precious little toes but we have work to do and we mean to do it."

"Not if I hold you here you won't."

"Get your boss out here right now or I will put you under arrest myself, cuff you and lock you up in your own squad car. I'm not going to play petty games about territory around here; people are dying because you won't help, it could all be on your head," Dick's face suddenly turned red, he didn't like having to answer questions from the local constabulary.

"Just a darned minute there bub, calm down, I'll call this in and see what I'm supposed to do. I don't have the authority to let you in here. My orders are that no one is to have access to those houses but the police and fire department and I aim to follow my orders so don't get huffy with me buster! I'm an old hard headed cop due to retire soon and I don't need no young whip-persnappers telling me what to do!" He left and went to his marked squad car. He was gone several minutes and they could see him on his radio probably talking with someone at headquarters. He finally came back and his face was a little red like he was either mad, embarrassed or both. "Hey you, FBI man, my boss wants a word with you, in my car if you please, the lady can stay there." Dick went with him back to his car and got in the passenger's side door.

"Here, depress that button."

"I know how to work a radio Mack," he snatched the mike from the officer's hand." Dick spoke into the mike identifying himself and listened. He nodded his head a couple of times and then gave the man he was talking to a phone number and they waited. In several minutes the man came back on the radio. He told the officer to stand aside, let them in that they were only trying to help and that he'd better cooperate or lose his pension. That got his attention real quick.

"Sorry mister, I was only doing my job you know."

"No I don't know, where the hell do you get off telling me off, if you were a young man I'd have you fired. Since when does a City Cop tell us off when we are only trying to help?"

"Sorry mister but like I said I was only following orders. Here's your I Ds, I'll move my car and let you through."

Dick walked back to his car in disbelief. He got into their car and drove past the officer who had a bewildered look on his face. He could only imagine what the Director had told the Chief or his boss. They drove over some Keep Out yellow fire warning tape and pulled in behind a fire truck. A fireman approached as he stopped the car. "Hey mister, you can't park there didn't the police tell you, you can't come up here?"

"Yes as a matter of fact he did but he changed his mind." Dick reached into his pocket and pulled out his I D again. "Federal Agents and we are on a case. This was murder, this was no accident!" He brushed past the fireman who was in disbelief himself by now; he didn't want any strangers snooping around his fire scene. Dick was back in a couple of minutes.

"Where's the Fire Marshall or his Investigator?"

"They have gone for the day, this was an accident pure and simple they said."

"Sorry, but this is a crime scene, murder was committed here, how many bodies have you recovered so far?"

"Well none in the house to the far left, four in the middle house all adults and five in the house right here, two adults and three children."

"Let me ask you a question, have you ever seen an oxygen tank explode?"

"No sir can't say that I have."

"That's what they said it was on the news; let me tell you something, it might blow out a couple of windows maybe but not level three houses! How about the propane tank we heard about on the news, where is the debris from that?"

"Well all of what we found is right over here, this way folks."

They followed the fireman to what had been the middle house. "This is the driveway and this is all the metal we have recovered from the house."

"Uh huh, call your Fire Marshall back here and tell him to bring evidence bags with him, lots of them, I want every single piece of metal bagged and tagged and sent to FBI Headquarters Lab in Washington and I want it done today, not tomorrow or the next day but today and tell him this is a murder scene and get on it now!"

"Jane do you see what I see?"

"I think so, it looks like more than one propane tank blew up here, if I had to guess I'd say several blew up at the same time, say four to six or more maybe?"

"Exactly what I saw, how could a Fire Marshall mistake a thing like that?"

"I'll guess we'll find out when he gets back here."

"Yeah, in the meantime let's see what else they missed, I don't smell any gasoline so I'm guessing that the propane blew the building up, probably blew out the walls and the rest fell down and caught fire and some of the debris must been blown onto the other houses setting them afire as well. Look at the burn patterns any rookie could see this was arson and murder. This was no accident!" While they were talking they saw Miss Jackson from the bank approaching.

"Oh no it's the broad from the bank again. Jane please handle her I'm still mad at her."

"Sure thing Dick."

"Miss Jackson, how nice to see you again."

"Huh, do I know you?"

"No probably not, we were told you would be coming up here so we expected you and you're the only Miss Jackson around so it fits as they say."

"That's funny your voice seems familiar but then I talk to a lot of people every day. The coroner called and asked if I could I D two of the bodies for him, then he could deduce who the other couple was that way. I guess I beat him back here but he should be along pretty soon. Too bad about my friends, they were such a nice couple, such a terrible accident."

"Well we'll determine that I'm sure Miss Jackson."

"Say just who are you and what business do you have here?"

"FBI ma'am and that's all you need to know, kindly step aside and watch out for nails and glass, its all over the place."

"Yes well thank you Ms, Ms.?"

"Its Special Agent Marlowe Miss Jackson and Special Agent Jefferies is over there. We are securing this scene as a murder investigation."

"Murder; but everyone says it was an accident."

"May I ask you something Miss Jackson; did anyone come to look at the book store yesterday who looked a little out of place to you?"

"Well there was a man and woman who came in and were extremely rude to me."

"Yes we already know about them, they were not involved in this, we already checked them out, they were eccentric but not dangerous. Was there anyone else there with money?"

"Well yes actually there was a really nice old man and his grandson, he said he would buy the store for his grandson but they suddenly changed their minds and left when I mentioned the other couple who were interested it buying it as well."

"You only had two serious buyers the whole time?"

"Yes only two that had the money to make the purchase. Part of my job was to be sure that the sale brought enough money in to pay off the Bank's notes and that the buyers were qualified to make the purchase."

"How about the owner who lived here, did he have any other books perhaps, like old or rare books of any value?"

"Why yes as a matter of fact he had a rather extensive collection of very rare books that only a handful of us knew about."

"How about the other two men did they know about the collection?"

"Well probably, there was information about it in the Ad at the bottom of the page of the trade paper flyer for anyone who may have been interested in a rare old book collection."

"Hey Dick, bingo! over here!"

"What is it Jane, trouble?"

"On the contrary she says there was a rather large book collection here in this house and that it stated it in the ad in the flyer we saw."

"Give me a minute Jane, I'll get the flyer and be right back."

"I'm sorry Miss, may I see your credentials please?"

"Certainly, here you are."

"Uh huh Special Agent Marlowe and you said his name was?"

"Special Agent Richard Jefferies but we call each other by our first names it makes it easier when we're talking business like this."

Dick soon returned with the flyer. "Miss Jackson would you show me where the wording is please?"

"Certainly, may I see your credentials please?"

"What is it today, all these people who are being suspicious for some reason, here you are Miss!" He handed her his I D as well.

"First the cops then the fire department and now a complete stranger who says she's from the bank, how come we have to show our I Ds and they don't, answer me that?"

Jane shrugged her shoulders as Miss Jackson returned her I D to her and then Dick's I D back to him. "You know it's strange but it seems like we've met somewhere before."

"I doubt it Miss Jackson unless we arrested you in the past or have interviewed you in a Federal Prison, this is the first time we've been to New Mexico. Now tell us Miss Jackson as best you can, what did this other man look like never mind the boy, what did the man look like?"

She began to describe him and they wrote it all down. "You know there was one thing, the man said it several times about the boy and how smart he was and how he had recently graduated from the University of Connecticut at the age of twenty one and before that he had attended a college at sixteen, graduated from there at age seventeen but didn't say what College it was just the University was all he mentioned and he did say his major was Literature and a secondary in Business I believe. The man said he owned a conglomerate of Businesses that the boy would inherit because both of his parents had died in an automobile accident a few years ago and he took the boy in, that's about all I can remember."

"You have no idea how much help you have been Miss Jackson, thank you very much."

"Well you're welcome I'm sure, I'm glad I was of some help."

Just as they finishing talking the Coroner showed up. He asked her who they were and she told him there were Federal Investigators and let it go at that. The Coroner walked Miss Jackson over to where four bodies had been laid out, they were in the Coroners body bags. He uncovered one of the bodies. She shook her head no. He uncovered the face of the next one and she said yes that's the book store owner and the next one was his wife and she identified her. During the fire they had both ended up face down so only their backsides were badly burned.

"Thank you Miss Jackson, now I know who is who for sure. The other two lived next door over there and he pointed to a pile of debris that used to be a home. Now I can notify the next of kin but I'm not sure about this couple, the one's you said owned the book store; do they have any next of kin you know of?"

"None that I'm aware of Doctor but I can check their bank records, something may turn up there, if it does I'll call you."

"Thank you Miss Jackson, sorry to have had to drag you out here but you knew them as well as anyone I guess. I'll have my van here in a little while, we've had another accident with a truck and two bodies are in it that we are still trying to recover, good day now."

"Excuse me Doctor, can you tell me anything about the truck, like how big it is or who was in it?" asked Jefferies.

"Well I'll tell you what we do know, there were two adults in the truck burned beyond recognition, I don't even know if I'll be able to tell how old they were or anything else."

"The truck Doctor, what kind was it, a pick up, tractor trailer or what?"

"From what we could tell it was a rental box truck I'd say a ton and a half or two and a half ton maybe, not any bigger than that though."

"But it was big enough to haul away several boxes of books, say eighty or more boxes?"

"Yes it could easily have carried that much but the truck was empty I tell you."

"Thank you Doctor you may go now."

The Coroner left shaking his head at all the strange questions.

Dick and Jane were doing the same, wondering what it all meant.

CHAPTER - 79

At the fire scene Dick and Jane were still discussing their perpetrator. "This guy is real crafty Jane, talk about misdirecting the authorities, this guy is good. Let's do some leg work and check the local Truck Rental Agencies around here and see if we think it's the same pair, my guess is that it will be the same ones with different disguises."

"Wait a minute Dick one of us has to stay here to talk to the Fire Marshall, why don't you stay, I'll check truck rental agencies, they shouldn't be to hard to find, then I'll come back to get you."

"Sounds like a good idea Jane, here are the keys go ahead, I'll hang around here." Dick was wondering what the killer had up his sleeve next, where is he I wonder, did he go east or west, north or south. He wandered around a little more while waiting for the Fire Marshall to return. He had some tough questions to ask him.

To his surprise an hour and a half later a young female Lieutenant approached him in a fire fighters dress uniform with a clip board.

"Are you the Federal Agent in charge around here now sir?"

"Yes that's right, Special Agent Richard Jefferies."

"How do you do sir, I'm Lieutenant Agnes Hull, acting Fire Marshall for the day."

"For the day, for the day? Where's the head man he's the one I want to chew out."

"I'm afraid you'll have to wait, he knew all of these people. He suffered a heart attck when he returned to the station and was rushed to the hospital, I'm afraid he may not make it."

"That bad huh?"

"Yes sir, this wasn't his first one, it was one of many I heard about today but he wouldn't retire like he should have, he said too many people depended on him for answers."

"Well he sure screwed this up, do you have any special training for this job Miss?"

"No sir, I'm still in training as a fireman."

"Oh I see, I thought by the uniform you may have already been a fireman."

"Oh I have been on the department but in budget and finance and I earned these silver bars on my shoulders the hard way through schooling and training for a firefighter."

"Yes Miss, but that's not what troubles me, you have a total of nine people dead here at the murder scene and someone need's to tell us what happened and that's your job. Did you bring the things with you that I requested?"

"Yes sir they're in my vehicle parked behind the fire truck right there."

"Then I suggest you go get them, I will assist you in bagging and tagging everything that I give you, I don't suppose you brought any help with you did you?"

"No, should I have?"

"Yes! I suggest you get on the horn and get at least four or five more people over here to help, you're not in clothes that you should be digging around in piles of broken glass and nails with and neither is my partner or I."

"Who else is with you, I don't see anyone?"

"Special Agent Marlowe will be back anytime now, she's doing some background checks right now."

"Your partner is a woman then?"

"Yes, is there something wrong with that, she graduated top of her class at the Academy and is currently number three on the old totem pole of the FBI."

"Oh and I suppose you're going to tell me your number two as well, is that it?"

"You got it sister! Now get to work or do I need to call your boss as well?"

"Go ahead and call him I'm sure he'd love to talk to the cops." She left him standing there and went to her vehicle to get the envelopes Dick had asked for.

Dick began to stew, he decided to wait and see how many men or women she could get to help her out. She came back alone with about a half dozen number ten white envelopes.

"Is that all you have, where is the help I asked for and the larger manila envelopes?"

"I'm it, we're a little short handed today, we got a wrecked truck a few miles from here and that 's tied up most of our other people."

"Uh huh, what about the men who are here?"

"What about them?"

"Go get them to help and do it now before it gets dark damn it, we've got nine bodies here, we want to know how they died and you are going to help us figure this out right now!"

"Well maybe you ought to talk to my boss really, I can't ask these men to do anymore than they have, they have been here all night as it is."

"Oh alright, take me to your radio."

"Very good, follow me and watch your tongue or I'll walk away from here and leave you on your own."

"Look lady I've had a hard day, nine people are dead and two more in that truck you already know about and the killer slipped past us somehow. Doesn't that upset you just a little?"

"Why no, why should it, the bodies have all been removed from here by now."

"Hold on just a minute, what do you call those bodies lined up there right behind you?"

"Huh, where?"

"Right behind you on the ground in those body bags."

She turned to look and her face went from white to green to purple then gray as she passed out over backwards right into Dick's arms.

Just then Jane came walking up. "What's this Dick, the lady swoon over backwards?"

"No Jane she fainted when she saw the body bags, this is our Fire Marshall for the day."

"Please tell me you're kidding

"I'm afraid not, she said the Fire Marshall had a heart attack after he left here and is in the Hospital, he isn't doing very well."

"Oh dear what next?"

"We get her to come around and talk to her boss on the radio, hopefully the Fire Chief."

"They sat her down in a sitting position with her head in Jane's lap and facing away from the bodies. In a few minutes she began to moan and come slowly around.

"Are you back with us Lieutenant?"

"I guess so, who's this?"

"I'm Special Agent Jane Marlowe, FBI."

"Oh more trouble," she closed her eyes as if she had a headache or something.

"There's going to be a pile of trouble if we don't get to the bottom of these murders," Dick told her.

"Wait a just a darned minute, no one said anything about any murders!"

"Sorry to burst your bubble but these people didn't commit suicide you know," Dick said.

"But we were told that it was an accident."

"Someone somewhere dropped the ball lady, its murder and we need your help and we need it right now."

"But murder, oh my God, murder?"

"That's right sweetheart, now go call your boss, we want to talk to him right now."

"Yes sir, yes ma'am, um whatever, you'll have to help me up my legs feel like rubber."

"Right you are, let's go."

The two of them, one on each side of her, helped her to her feet and walked her back to her vehicle where she called in and asked to talk with the Chief. She talked with him for a minute or two then handed the mike to Dick.

"Chief, this is FBI Special Agent Richard Jefferies, we need some assistance out here with a murder investigation and we need manpower and need it right now before it gets dark."

"What are you talking about, no ones been murdered anywhere."

"We beg to differ with you Chief, we're the pros out here and nine people have been murdered and no one has done a damned thing about it not even the cops, are you all ignorant or stupid around here or what?"

"Say just who do you think you are talking to, I'm the boss around here."

"Listen to me carefully now before I have your badge and the Police Chief's badge. Call the Chief of Police and he will verify that we're not fooling around here. If I don't hear some sirens coming down the road in the next five minutes I'll have you all in jail and you're precious little badges as well, do I make myself clear?"

"Go to hell!" and he cut Dick off.

"Oh great Dick you have some rapport with the locals around here, now what?"

"We wait Jane, no sirens in a few minutes we'll go into town and we'll lock up the whole damned town if they don't jump to." Five minutes went by then six, then seven then there was a faint sound of a single siren in the distance. I do believe the Calvary is on the way Jane."

"I believe you're right Dick. While I have your attention both truck places that rented trucks out last night said that a young man told them they were headed for California."

"California? So that means they headed back east somewhere."

As they waited two fire trucks pulled up beside the other truck that was still there. The men of that truck refused to help until the others showed up and told them what was going on and that they had to assist the FBI Investigators. All told there were ten men on the two trucks and four other men who had been standing around waiting for orders from someone higher up in their department for a total of fourteen men to help now. They broke them up into two teams of five between Jefferies and Marlowe with the others were sent to help the young Lieutenant. Methodically they went though the wreckage of the middle house looking for metal fragments of any kind and identifying them as best they could. Pieces of plumbing were discarded into a single pile to be gone over later. They were trying to find every piece of propane tanks they could identify as such. They never did find any pieces to an oxygen tank as reported by the Fire Marshall and Dick was quick to point it out to the young Lieutenant. He told her that people often jump to conclusions not based on facts and science. She learned more in those few hours than she could ever learn in a classroom; she was fascinated as she watched Dick and Jane go through bits of wreckage and she didn't know what it was they were looking at but she soon learned what to look for and dug in herself. Someone sent somebody to get sandwiches so that the work could continue otherwise they didn't stop to eat or drink unless they had too. By the end of the day an enormous amount of metal had been found as well as parts of the gas stove from the kitchen in the middle house. By dark they had bagged and cataloged and marked where each piece had been found and photographs had been taken to assist the FBI in piecing everything together back in Washington. Dick gathered everyone together when they were done.

"Listen up people, its getting dark; I have given the Lieutenant instructions on how to ship everything back to the FBI in Washington including the top of the gas stove with all its burners which were in the switched on position which allowed more gas to build up in the house. As you can see there is or was no pilot light and the extra gas escaping into the house helped make the explosion even bigger than the propane tanks did alone. I want to thank all of you for helping out this very bright young lady, she has done a remarkable job. Now tomorrow morning we need to come back here and split up like we did today and sort through the other two houses for more fragments just like we did here today. I don't anticipate finding much more because it is evident to anyone that the house in the middle blew up and the other two caught on fire from the debris and the heat from the fire in the middle house. Now if someone can tell me where we can get some supper we'll all get a bite to eat. I'm buying, every meal and every bit of refreshment, that means beer for those who don't know."

A rousing cheer went up from the crowd and the young Lieutenant was blushing and suddenly sobbing.

Dick went over to comfort her. "Here now, what is this, tears my dear?"

"Oh it's just that I was so mean and nasty to you and then you give a speech telling everyone how great I was and I'm nothing but a damn clerk."

"Not anymore, when my letter of acknowledgment and recommendation hits your boss's desk you may be the new Fire Marshall here which I can almost guarantee, alright?"

"Yes of course, how can I ever thank you?" She reached up and kissed Dick on his cheek in front of everyone.

"Well are you people hungry for steak, burgers, fried chicken, or what, make up your minds and let's go."

They all piled into cars and trucks and Dick and Jane brought up the rear of the procession. "Did I do the right thing this time Jane?"

"Yes my hero you did just fine, there is still room for improvement though."

They laughed the rest of the way until everyone turned off at a steak eatery called, 'The Steak Place.'

The lone policeman was still there when they left to keep out any looters and he was wondering about his own position on the Police Force and when and if someone was going to relieve him anytime soon so he could go eat.

The next day brought more of the same even though it was Sunday by noon they were all done. Dick and Jane personally thanked everyone and they left and headed back to their Motel.

The Coroner removed the burned bodies of the men found in the truck but they were never identified which Dick had figured on.

CHAPTER - 80

Sol and BJ took two more days to drive back to Poughkeepsie with their load of rare books which was a treasure trove to Sol. They had a lot of time to talk on the way back and BJ had some tough questions for Sol. "Tell me Sol, why did you kill that couple back there?"

"Number one they were elderly, number two the man was obviously dying and on his last legs and number three you could see that his wife was still very much in love with him and I have seen couples like this that when one spouse dies the other is sure to follow shortly due to depression so I thought it would be kinder to send them on their journey together and fourth I have to teach the authorities a lesson now and then."

"Okay, I understand your thinking now; I just wanted to hear your own reasons. My first thoughts were that you didn't want to leave any witnesses behind."

"Actually that would be reason number five. And don't forget the money, I seldom pay the asking price for anything if you know what I mean. Let's see now, I guess you could say I purchase books at the lowest possible price. Don't forget I had plane fares, Motel bills and three meals a day for the two of us, various in sundry other hardware items like the propane tanks, two five gallon cans of gasoline then there are the rentals for the two trucks, fuel for them and more food bills and Motel bills on the way home. When all is said and done I may have lost money if I had paid for the books with the rest of the ex-penses. The upside is once Fred and I have gone through the books there may be some we can duplicate and sell both versions of like we have done with others. Even if someone were to find out that there were two original copies sold as one they would probably never discover the fake copy in our lifetimes so you see it can be a win, win situation for all of us plus we may make some money after all. As you already know we're not perfect. I have purchased books in the past that were worthless copies so we shredded them and made new paper from the old pages. We redid hard covers for other books of the same size giving credence to our own copies of First Editions. Understand I'm not complaining, I'm just explaining our work."

"I get it Sol, I just wanted a little better understanding of the way you think, I believe the three of us make a great team."

"Better make that four as of last week. We have a new book prospector working with us without pay, he is helping us for the thrill of the experience is all. He will alert us about anyone who has collections of old or rare books and tell us what they have. He won't be along for the ride like you and I just took. We're paying you for your work with us and we intend to set you up for the rest of your life. You will have to be careful who you date and how just much you tell your girlfriend. If and when you do get married she will have to be on board with you all the way with no secrets. She could destroy you and the whole operation if she went to the authorities."

"I understand Sol. I have been looking for just such a girlfriend who is interested in the science of books and their restoration techniques. What I really need is a girlfriend who is taking the same classes as I am but all of them so far have been real geeks, skinny, ugly, they wear thick glasses, they carry large stacks of books and spend most of their off time reading books of every kind imaginable instead of sticking to their course studies, not very attractive at all. Why one day I saw one of them reading a magazine on how to pick up guys you like and want to date. That kind of girl I'd run away from, I want a girl with the same basic tastes as mine when it comes to life and the studying of our courses."

"Yeah I know what you mean and that's one of the reasons I never married but at least I have my Francis. Did you know Fred has a steady lady of his own now?"

"No, that's great, he needs someone to keep company with other than all the chemicals and machinery. He told me one day if you listen just right, the machinery will talk to you, they will tell you when they need attention."

"Yes I know and I feel the same way. It's easy to catch a machine before it breaks down if you listen to it. When one breaks down if you've done your job right the repairs can be minimal but if you ignore the sounds they make you might have to replace the whole machine instead of just one part. Some of the equipment we built is one of a kind, there is no way to replace the machine if it breaks down. We have always designed and built our own machinery. We sent our designs to tool makers and factories to have them built to our specifications and nearly every part of each machine is custom built for us, there are no spare parts. If something breaks we simply send the design for that particular part back to the factory that made it for us and they make another one and send it back to us. With this new computer thing there is so much talk about I suppose one day we'll have to buy one as well but we just might build a better faster machine and market it ourselves. We have the capability to do almost anything we want except go to the moon and that's already been done."

"I believe you Sol, you don't have to sell me on your ideas, I'm along for the whole ride now. You and Fred have made an investment in me I can never repay, your faith in me shall be rewarded."

"It already has BJ. You proved it back there when you didn't flinch after seeing the deceased couple. We should be home soon, it will be good to get back to the store."

"I agree. By the way what are you going to do with this truck when we're done?"

"You young man will take it to the salvage yard I tell you too and it will be completely crushed never to be seen again."

"What about the Insurance policy you had to put up to rent the two trucks?"

"They were insurance cards and policies for proof of Insurance Fred and I made in the basement with aliases."

"Oh I see, so the owners of the trucks will have to eat the loss then?"

"On the contrary, they have insurance against stolen or damaged trucks, they won't be out a dime and will be able to buy new trucks with the money they get from their Insurance Companies. Everybody wins but the Insurance Company."

"Wow, it seems like you and Fred have covered all the bases after all."

"Let's hope so son."

The next day they arrived in Poughkeepsie and unloaded the truck, Sol made a phone call to a friend and told BJ where to take the truck and Sol followed in the van and picked him at the Salvage Yard. All BJ saw was Sol shake hands with a man and pass him a small envelope he assumed contained cash, they left and went back to the store. BJ had to leave before the end of the day to go back to school; he had classes starting Wednesday morning.

The next day Fred and Sol had a chance to look over the specially marked boxes that contained the rarest of the books. "Sol this is a great find, these titles should bring in thousands and with the copies we'll double that. Tell me, how did our BJ do?"

"He did excellent. After I killed the couple and he saw them he asked me nothing until on the ride home and I told him why I killed them and why I killed anyone else who got a good look at us. When their house exploded it took out the house on the right and the left killing anyone else who may have seen us. I used two rental trucks, one we crashed and burned and the other truck just went to the crusher."

"Great job by both of you."

"Would you like to pick out the most valuable book you see and start the duplicating process?" asked Sol.

"Certainly let's try this one. Wow, this is a first edition sent to the Author, it's even autographed by him, what do you know about that and he's been dead over a hundred years."

"Yes I recognize the author's name, what a wonderful find; I wonder how this man came by it."

"Who knows, maybe a friend of a friend who knew the Author passed it on down?"

The men began making copies of first one book and then another, they had a list of wants from prospective buyers around the world who had gotten word of them simply by word of mouth between collectors. Collectors often traded copies with one another when they had duplicates of a certain book. By trading among themselves they kept others from finding out what rare books they had in each of their respective collections.

CHAPTER - 81

Dick and Jane were finally back in Washington in their Office. "Boy it sure is good to be back home Jane."

"I agree Dick, working around those dead bodies made me a little queasy."

"How come, you've seen body bags before?"

"Yes I know but this was different somehow, they were killed in milliseconds of one another, probably never knew what hit them,"

"We can only hope that's the way it happened, better instantaneously than burning to death slowly in your home. I can't imagine a more horrible death. I jump up and down and holler like hell when I burn my finger a little on the stove."

"I know what you mean. Did anyone tell you about the family of five and whether or not they were found together like eating supper or something or were they in separate rooms?"

"No Jane we'll have to wait for the final report from our friend the local Fire Marshall and hope she remembers to add it in her notes and hopefully we'll hear something soon and the packages we filled and marked ought to be arriving anytime as well."

Another day went by and nothing, then the third day a large parcel arrived by air freight.

"Would you look at this, we beat the evidence back here by three days, what's up with that I wonder?"

"I don't know Jane, maybe they didn't send it out right away or maybe they had to have someone package it for them. Let's take it to the lab, maybe our friend the Lieutenant put something in there we missed." They used a two wheel dolly to take the box to the lab a few doors away. Everyone had been waiting for its arrival. They eagerly unwrapped the parcel and handed out envelopes to everyone. Also in the box was the top of the gas stove with all the control valves turned to the high position including the oven.

"Alright people, what we're looking for is any metal that could be from small propane tanks like those used on home barbeques. We think we have several so you'll have to work to try and piece the tanks together as best you can. One more thing, watch for pieces of an oxygen tank although I don't believe you'll find any. I never heard of anyone needing oxygen who had prostate cancer."

"I believe you're right Dick," added Jane.

"Further more we need to check back with the Doctors who cared for them and ascertain whether either of them were smokers or not. Call it a suspicious nature but it is possible someone may have paid off the Fire Marshall who is in the hospital with a heart attack right now, he may be able to tell us something about who was there and who paid him off; Jane?"

"I got the ball Dick; I'll be in the Office on the phone if you need me,"

Every Lab Tech. went to work as Dick walked around the room pointing out pieces. He had made copies of where each bag of debris was found and he gave the Lab Tech. with the corresponding bag number the copy that went with the one they had so they could see where each piece came from in the debris field that had been three homes. Hours went by with Dick hovering around the tables with piles of what looked like junk to the naked eye but to the trained eye white pieces of gas tanks began to materialize. Dick knew it may take weeks or a month or more to piece all this together and he also knew that a few pieces could have been lost in the bodies when shrapnel became embedded in them from the blast.

Dick soon headed back to his office to talk with Jane where she was making phone calls to Doctors in New Mexico. "Damn it, Dick how did you know about the oxygen tank?"

"There wasn't one was there Jane?"

"No Dick, neither of the victims in the house were smokers and the same thing with the two on the left of their house who happened to be in the wrong place at the wrong time, they weren't smokers either."

"I suspected as much. Now one more unanswered question. See if you can get hold of our new friend back there the girl, shoot I forgot her name, the young Lieutenant with the Fire Department we talked to. See if she can get a hold of the Fire Marshall's Bank account for us. I want to see if he made a large deposit before the explosion. I'm guessing mind you but knowing the pattern of our man I'm willing to bet that he deposited around $5,000 plus or minus a few bucks the day before or maybe the day of the explosion if my suspicions are correct."

Dick disappeared again for more than an hour. Soon she found him and called him aside from the Lab Techs with a long face. "Dick I hate to be the bearer of bad news but the Fire Marshall passed away yesterday. I got the Lieutenant to talk to his wife though and she said the wife found two deposit slips for their Bank's savings account in the shirt pocket of his uniform. They were two days apart each for $2,500, how did you know the amount?"

"I used the SWAG theory of math."

"Oh no not again, I know I'm going to be sorry for asking you this; just what the hell is the swag theory of math?"

"It's the sophisticated wild ass guess theory, works every time. Are they going to do an autopsy on the Fire Marshall, if not why not, press for one legally for the FBI if they aren't."

"What are you looking for now?" she asked now with an anxious voice.

"I'm betting the man was healthy and that maybe he was poisoned with a slow acting poison in something he was given to eat or drink. Have them check for chemicals of any kind that would produce something mimicking a heart attack on an otherwise healthy person. I'm only guessing, but this guy has us jumping through hoops and I'm thinking that's exactly what he wants us to be doing."

"Alright Dick, but remember what the Lieutenant said about her boss's heart, she said he had a bad heart. Oh and by the way her name is Agnes Hull."

"Yes I know Jane, just ask please."

"I know where you're going now, I'm on it!" Jane took off in a run for their office and the phone she was beginning to hate but now she understood Dick's way of thinking and was just as excited for him as much as she was for herself. Now she began to think like him. Finally they were a team with the same goal in mind. It was getting near the end of their shift and neither of them had bothered to stop for lunch. She finally came back looking for Dick with another long face.

"What's wrong Jane, don't tell me they cremated the body?"

"Almost Dick, you better call the in big brass right now, they are about to cremate his body but there's a time difference and they're going to do it at 6:00 P.M. their time. Better advise the boss, maybe he can stop it. They only have to hold the body for three days, times up today."

"Thank you Jane, can you watch things here for a few minutes, I'll see if I can get hold of the boss right now."

Dick took off at a run for their office and the phone. It was his turn to get down and dirty. He called upstairs and the boss's secretary said he was about to leave, he told her to stop him anyway she could, he was on his way up to see him and it was an emergency. He found the Director waiting for him in his secretary's office. He was drumming his fingers on her desk impatiently. "This had better be important Dick I'm late now for a meeting with the Cabinet up the street."

"Yes sir, it's a matter of life and death in a way. They are about to cremate a witness to murder and I need that body here to do an autopsy. I know the man was murdered as sure as I'm standing here talking to you. Something smells really bad and it's not the man's body, please sir pull whatever strings you have to, but put a stop to that cremation and order the body sent here please"

"It's that important to your case that you'd jeopardize your job over a body of someone you don't even know?"

"Yes sir, the man is or rather was the Fire Marshall back in Albuquerque and I believe he knew the man who committed these murders or at least had met him. I have to know if he was murdered or not. So far we have eleven bodies we can connect to the killer, this man could be number twelve, I don't have the authority to stop this but you do."

"Alright Dick but this is going to cost you big time, you'll be taking me to dinner at your club soon and I want to eat there so I'll do this for you. My Secretary will make my excuses to the Cabinet; they'll just have to start late grilling me over my budget some more."

"Thank you sir, can you have your secretary ring me when a decision has been reached?"

"Sure thing, run along. I also heard that you got your evidence parcel today and I know you are anxious to put the puzzle together."

Dick gave him an off handed salute with his right hand and took off for the elevator again. The Director sighed and walked back into his office while his Secretary was already on her phone to the Funeral Home number that Dick had scrawled on a scrap of paper. She knew this was the Director's priority; she would wait for the call to go through before calling the Chairman of the Cabinet. Fifteen minutes later Dick's phone rang.

"Dick, the Director would like to talk to you," said his secretary.

"Yes sir, I'm here!"

"Dick, we cut that close, the body was already for the cremation fire chamber when I came down on them. I didn't go through channels because I knew we didn't have time. Anyway I got it stopped. I scared the snot out of the Funeral Director when I talked to him. I asked him who gave him the authority to cremate a body that belonged to the FBI. Next you owe my Secretary more than a lunch and you better get back up here and sit down with her and dictate an official looking document and send it overnight mail to that Funeral Home claiming the body in the name of the FBI and don't forget to mark it carbon copy so it will scare the hell out of Funeral Home Director again. He thinks he misplaced the document you are going to be sending."

Dick made a quick trip back to the lab to tell Jane what was going on and then took off at a run for the Director's Office again.

At 7:00 P.M. Dick told everyone to go home, they could pick up again in the morning and he had called a pizza delivery company and had pizzas delivered to the front door and one of the night watchmen brought them down and Dick asked him to join them as well. It was party time in the Lab; it had been a very good day.

The next morning Dick and Jane were there early but said nothing when one or two of the Lab Techs were a little late, the last one came in at five minutes past nine. Yesterday they knew had been a long day especially when they all worked eleven hours almost straight. There were a lot of people yawning during the day but they all did their work by chugging down lots of coffee. Little by little things were coming together. First the better part of one gas tank and then another, he had told them to look for propane tank serial numbers and date of manufacture and any other information they could find. Next he put one of his other Agents on contacting any place in Albuquerque that sold propane tanks to see if anyone bought more than one tank the day before and the day of the explosion. He was trying to find out if a person bought one or two or maybe several from the same store. Eight of the stores had sold several the same day but didn't remember anyone buying more than one at a time. Now Dick had the answer. Whoever bought them went to several stores so as not to raise suspicion for themselves by buying more than one at a time. Dick was at his desk with his feet up. He was deep in thought when Jane came in.

Jane came in to their office and saw Dick's face. "You're awful quiet Dick, do you feel alright?"

"Yes, I'm just trying to put myself in the criminal's shoes and I keep getting the same answers. One of them had to be out buying propane tanks while the other one was doing what, it's the what that has me perplexed at the moment."

"Listen Dick, is there a chance our killer is getting to the age where he can't do the job anymore and the young man from Connecticut is his protégé and is working full time now

"Its possible but he could have also been in disguise as an old man to throw us off."

"Maybe he suspects we are onto him now so he is being more selective of his marks."

"I think Miss Jackson told them we had been there after she made me so mad that I could have spit nails. I've never met such a bitch in all my life."

"She was very nice to us the other day once we got her confidence but I have to admit she pissed me off pretty good there at the crime scene. I could have easily throttled the woman. Her problem is that she is an old maid with zero prospects for a man in her life and she has just enough power for it go to her head and she's very controlling as well"

"Why Jane, are you harboring a grudge or resentment against a fellow woman?"

"She's no lady and I doubt she could be called a woman, she's a first class a bitch as far as I'm concerned, she just pissed me off is all."

"Well so did the firemen and that cop even when they knew who we were they didn't exactly greet us with open arms."

"You're right Dick, maybe we should let it lay and give them a chance to reply to us."

"That's not going to happen, ten to one each one of them threw away our cards right after we handed them to them."

"Uh huh, you're right again. Let's start at the top and place the blame where it belongs, with the people in charge and don't forget you owe the young good looking Lieutenant an official commendation letter from us about her by way of her boss."

"Good point Jane, do we have a secretary who could draft a few letters for us to mail or do we need to get another one from the secretarial pool upstairs?"

"Honestly I don't know, our secretary has help for herself now and she is still backed up. I almost never mail letters from here, we always let the Director's Secretary handle all that."

"I know but I don't dare bring this up to her, she'll have to tell the boss and then he's going to want to know why we're bothering with people we'll never see again."

"Okay, I'll have a look around amongst our people and see what I can do," and Jane disappeared.

CHAPTER - 82

Another day went by and Dick went back to wandering around the giant lab with huge stainless steel lab tables against other lab tables taking up almost all of the space. A man from outside who looked the part of a truck driver approached one of the Lab Techs. Dick saw him across the table from where he was and the man asked a Lab Tech; "hey buddy, anyone here order a body from New Mexico, I have one outside in the parking lot on my truck?"

Dick raced over to where the man was standing. "Yes, yes, where did you say it was?" Dick asked excitedly.

"Outside on my truck in your parking lot, some guy out there almost took my head off until I told him that I had a body addressed to Special Agent Jefferies of the FBI, then he let me park my truck and showed me to the door and here I am. Now then, where can I dump the body, it scares me to death."

"Why, he can't hurt you, he's dead."

"Oh come on mister, just sign this sheet for me so I can unload this thing and get out of here, I don't like dead bodies."

"Haven't you been around bodies before?"

"No sir and I'm telling my boss not to give me another one, some of our guys quit because they had to pick up a body in a crate or a coffin from airplane and they didn't like it either. Why can't a Funeral Home handle things like this?"

"Alright, alright, show me where your truck is and I'll have someone come out there and get it so you won't have to watch, are you okay with that?"

"Yes sir, just sign my paperwork so I can get going, you cops make me nervous as well."

"We're not cops, we don't go around in cars with sirens blaring all over town, I'm Special Agent Jefferies and I do have Federal arrest powers but usually it's the bad guys we're chasing who get arrested, not John Doe citizen."

"Yes sir I got it; please just sign these papers for me?" he pleaded again and again.

"Sure, let me have them!"

Dick looked over his shoulder and hollered back inside. "The body is here guys, can you give us a hand to bring it in please?"

Two men in white lab coats came out with a hospital type gurney built from stainless steel with no bed pad on it to get the body and the driver seeing that nearly passed out.

"Oh gees, are you going to put the body on that?"

"Yes of course unless you'd rather carry the body in yourself."

"Oh no, please mister I got a weak stomach, I'm about to throw up as it is."

"Alright, turn around and don't watch and we'll have it off your truck in a jiffy."

They took the generic coffin off the truck which looked some what like a wood shipping crate and placed it on their hospital gurney and wheeled it back inside to the lab while the driver woefully looked out at the parking lot towards the street he came in on wishing right now that he was at home watching TV with his family. He didn't actually have to load or unload the truck himself, just the thought of carrying around a body in his box type enclosed truck was enough to make him sick to his stomach, at least he didn't hurl like he thought he would. Dick walked over to the Driver, handed him his signed paperwork and told him it was all over and he could leave whenever he was ready.

Donny came over to see what was happening and stood next to Dick. "What happened Dick? This guy was green around the gills when he asked directions to our lab so I escorted him in after I showed him where he could leave his truck temporarily."

"He just delivered a body from New Mexico that we want to do an autopsy on and he doesn't like dead bodies. I explained to him that the guy was dead, he wasn't going to bother anyone. He is terrified of the dead is all! If you'll excuse me Donny I got to get back inside with my patient, I don't want him to have to wait all day for his autopsy."

"Okay Dick, I'll see you later."

Dick went back inside to find out where his body was. He found him in the special autopsy room already with their on staff Doctor waiting to talk to Dick before he started on the Fire Marshall's body.

"Hi Doctor Richfield, ready for my patient?"

"Did you kill this guy or did Marlowe?"

"Neither one Doc, the County Coroner in New Mexico said he died from a heart attack and I for one don't believe it. I want you to concentrate on the heart itself and see if he had a healthy heart or not then check for any strange toxins that may be in his blood stream or heart. I know there is a drug out there I've read about that if ingested it can cause death and mimic a heart attack. I think this guy was murdered but I need absolute proof to show the Director. I'll be in my office or in with the lab boys if you need me."

"Thank you Dick at least I have a starting point, I may have an answer soon unless there is a toxin like you think that I don't recognize and have to do some research."

"Thanks Doc, I really appreciate it, it's more important to our case than you can imagine. We can already tie our guy to eleven deaths and if I'm right this guy is number twelve and there could be more somewhere we are not yet aware of." Dick left the Doc and his assistant to do their grisly work of slicing and dicing as the Detectives around the building called it. Dick nervously paced around the room full of lab Techs working furiously on piecing together what seemed to be an impossible task, rearrange bits and pieces of white metal that used to be propane gas tanks and try to figure out just how many were used and how they were detonated. One by one the Techs. came up with different serial numbers and date of manufacture. After going around the tables several times Dick asked; "how many of you have different serial numbers and date of manufactures right now?"

Five hands went up. "How about you Tim?"

"I'm not sure Agent Jefferies I don't have a complete serial number or date of manufacture yet. Do any of you have a few partial numbers that don't match what you have, if so may I see them, they could be the missing pieces I need." No one spoke as they all went through the jumble of pieces then one by one they began to come up with a fragment here and there and gave them to him. Tim went to work and finally told Dick; "I have a complete serial number and date of manufacture now as well Agent Jefferies."

"Okay, good work all of you, so we have a total of six cylinders of propane that exploded simultaneously. Next thing I need is how they were detonated, you may only have bits and pieces of valves from the tops of the tanks but our guy somehow managed to blow them all at the same time, look for a detonation device, detonators and their wiring."

"That's going to take a long time Dick, we may not have everything we need at hand. It all depends on how well the people you used picked the site clean of metal fragments."

"I know its going to be tough but you guys are the best in the world at what you do, good hunting."

"Thanks Agent Jefferies!" was the resounding answer.

He went to find Jane and see how she was doing with her research. He found her in their office. "Hi Jane, anything new with you?"

"No Dick, not a single person can accurately describe anyone who purchased the propane tanks. Do you have a count yet?"

"Yes, we have a total of six tanks."

"So that's what did the damage, they all went off at once, probably enough power there if the house was closed up to blow the roof off and the walls out. The fire would have started immediately and the house was consumed by fire along with the neighbors.

"Don't forget Jane the gas stove in the kitchen had all of its burners and the oven in the on position with the door probably open and no pilot light and all of that escaping gas also figures into the equation of the explosion of gas buildup in the house."

"I'm been giving that some more thought too Dick. Suppose both families on each side of the man's house saw the truck and our guys loading it. After the truck was loaded our guy probably shot and killed the owners of the books. Then they went about setting out the propane tanks in different rooms and tied them together with detonating cord and used some kind of a timer to set them off when they were well away from the scene and the couple next door couldn't contain their curiosity and went over to see if they had sold their book collection and maybe the store. They find the couple dead; see the gas tanks and wiring and before they can run outside the place blows up killing them as well."

"That's exactly the scenario I've been mulling over; I can't see any flaws in it Jane.

That's what I'm putting in my report, you can agree or not and make your own report. The Director will want to see what we have as soon as we have it. There is one thing however, there may have been more than six tanks and we only have six or it could be only six, we may never know. I have in mind to run a test and explode six tanks all together at the same time and see if the explosive power is enough to flatten a two story house if put in the right arrangement. From the looks of the houses on the street they all seemed to have been built around the late forties or so, maybe earlier but I doubt it. Let's see what we can find out about that timeline, it might take less explosive power to blow up an older home than a newer one. We won't know until we test the theory. Would you mind contacting our new Lieutenant friend back in Albuquerque to see if she can get us that information?"

"You just want the approximate year that the houses were built on that street, right?"

"Yes that's it and thank her for me if you would."

CHAPTER - 83

Another week went by and Sol's phone rang while he was in his apartment reading. He glanced at his clock and it said 7:45 P.M. Who could be calling me at this time of night he thought. He picked up the telephone by his chair and answered. He said hello and was surprised when he heard Richard's voice on the other end. He wanted to thank Sol once again for the date he had fixed him up with and told him that Cecile had come to LA and that he was coming to see Sol soon. Sol noticed that he was a little giddy while they were talking so Sol asked him if he'd been drinking and he said no that he got his HIGH from life itself. He said he'd never felt more alive since meeting Sol and then the Cecile.

Sol figured it out after a minute or two and realized that Richard was in love for the first time in his life. He went on and on about Cecile. He asked Sol about his schedule and when would be a good time to come by to see him. Sol told him that he had just come across a large collection of rare and wonderful books and that he and Fred were getting close to being done with the copying process and that they were in such great shape that none of them needed restoring. Sol thought for a few minutes then told Richard; "listen Richard, its Wednesday night, if you come by either Tuesday or Wednesday of next week we should be done with this load of books to where I can take a few days off. I can't run off and leave poor Fred all alone with work piling up even if he does like it that way. He hasn't taken a day off in months, but that's just the way he is. When he has a date with his girl he simply tells me he's going to be gone a few days and that's that. He can let certain work pile up except the work I bring in by the truck load, it has to be gone through right away and mailed out of here just in case some cops get nosy and start poking around.

Oh one more thing we made a change in the basement you'll be proud of. Remember the loading dock elevators, both of them only go to the first floor unless you have the key I was talking about then you can go to the second floor. My elevator and Fred's that goes to the apartment floor is the same way, you have to have the right key to get to our floor from the loading area of basement or his lab. My parking garage door for the van is there but not there. It has been very cleverly redesigned by the security company we hired to do the work. It looks like a solid continuous brick wall now instead of a hole in the brick where you could see the seams that looked like a door. Now its seams are staggered so it looks more like the natural brick of the building. They all did a masterful job on the work we had done."

"So you'll be here next Wednesday?

Very good, call me and I'll pick you up in New York like I did last time."

The rest of that week went by and soon it was time to meet Richards's plane. Sol drove into New York and picked him up at the same place where they had met before. Richard was still acting giddy about something and it wasn't because of women. It was 3:10 P.M. when Richard got in the van. "Well Richard where to first, out on the town or back to the store?"

"Back to the store Sol, we need to talk!" he said in a serious solemn tone that was not like him at all.

"Sounds serious Richard, are you in some kind of trouble?"

"No and my girl isn't pregnant either, just go on and drive!" he said again with a firm but careful tone in his voice. Then he started giggling all over again and it was about to drive Sol nuts. One minute he was quiet and stoic like and the next he was fidgeting about then smiling to himself then giggling some more.

"What is it Richard, you're giggling like a little kid who's hiding a secret and is about to burst if he doesn't tell someone?"

"Well if you must know I got a line on some books for you and I was thinking maybe we could take the girls along, this is a deal that has to be on the up and up and you won't be a bit disappointed when I tell you what and where."

"Now Richard you know I don't do any deals quite like that, there has to be money involved somewhere and good money to boot or I won't budge."

"Oh there's good money in it for you, I'll pay my own way and my girl's as well so you'll just have you and Francis to worry about if you like."

"Okay I can hardly wait, this sounds like a very serious deal for us in some way."

"It is and I'll tell you what little I do know and let you figure out the details and arrangements to transfer money between countries. Let me put it this way; it's full of international intrigue. I told the head of a certain country that you could move their Country's most valuable effects, namely books of such value that a new World War could start over this if word got out as to who had certain books and papers in their possession. Remember the Dead Sea Scrolls Sol?"

"Yes of course, we've been contacted about using some of our preservation techniques on them but a decision hasn't been made yet as to when."

"You do know they are priceless, right?"

"Right, so what?"

"Think of this proposition then as the scrolls being worth a penny American and the book I'm talking you about being worth hundreds of millions of dollars, in other words a thousand times more priceless than the Dead Sea Scrolls."

"What did you do Richard, find the lost books of the Bible for goodness sake?"

"Oh my gosh, you guessed it," and he began to laugh hysterically. "Can you believe it, having the original lost works of the Bible that no one knows are really in existence in your own hands and being able to copy it for your own use; you could become a billionaire overnight. The best part of the deal is my man is willing to pay you whatever price you ask to pick these up and bring them back to America for safe keeping until the conflict in his country is resolved and my insiders are telling me he may be assonated within thirty days from this Friday. Seeing as though he is the only person in the world to know of the document's existence, if he dies they become yours because there will be no trace of them once you remove them from his country."

"Just how big is this box we'll be transporting."

"I have no idea, we won't know until we see them."

"Oh I don't know about this, it sounds way too big for us to carry off and what about the girls, they could be endangered if things got rough and the paper they are written on is probably very fragile due to its age and will need special handling as well."

"Not to worry, we'll let the girls go shopping and we'll go look at the papers or books or whatever they are. You do know that the Bible itself has been translated from several supposedly books and so forth."

"Yes, of course I know all that."

"Well there are some discrepancies in the books of the Bible in that they had to fill in a lot of blanks, but these works were all done by one man who was with Jesus and done in his own hand so to speak. This set of works are the missing pieces of the Bible and they are complete. The Bible was done after Jesus died and by memory of events, but this is all of it together. The works had become split up between rulers over the years but this bunch has never seen the light of day. These are not only the missing pieces of the puzzle but all of it has been in one place from the get go. Whoever has these holds the world by the throat as far as the Bible goes.

Everyone will want it and will pay anything to get their hands on it. Thing is, who will own it and control it? Your turn Sol."

"I don't know what to say. Of course it's widely known that all of the books of the Bible are not there, there are many gaps between the written words of the individual books and many more versions have been written over the years for different faiths and each faith believes theirs is the right version. People and the experts have been agreeing and disagreeing about it over the centuries and the debate will continue as to what the correct language of the Bible was or is. I'll have to think this over, how much time do you have before you have to return to LA?"

"I have all the time in the world, I'm at your disposal, my horses and other animals and all my holdings are under excellent care and do not require my attention for months. I have told everyone that I may be gone for as long as a month or more."

"Okay then if it's alright with you we can go back to the Store and check this thing out on a world map and you can point out to me where things are in relationship to Sea Ports, Airports and the exact location of the books which we think are simply manuscripts bound together probably by tightly woven hemp and I would think and the hemp is probably very fragile as well as the paper the manuscripts are on so whoever is moving the package or box containing the works will have to handle them or it with extreme care. I'm thinking as we ride that maybe we could mark the box or whatever we pack it in, 'Extremely Fragile - Antique China!' I think that whoever is doing the handling would be more careful if they were marked that way."

"Are you saying you'll take the job then?"

"Not yet! I need to think this through very carefully and it will take meticulous planning for every imaginable event such as high jacking the load maybe. Tell me Richard how much do you actually know about the location of the works."

"Well in my luggage I have a detailed map of where they are right now. They are in a cave guarded by a dozen men. All anyone knows is that there is a body in the cave of a past Ruler they don't want disturbed until the right people can be brought in to remove the body and that's where you come in. You could pose as a world renowned Archeologist and you are there to observe and direct the safe removal of the body and it will supposedly then be taken to the Museum in Egypt for analysis and preservation. I am told everything is wrapped in really old linen similar to the way a body would have been wrapped in those days. You're an expert in preservation so you should be able to fool the simple minded guards with names of chemicals and things you might use. They won't have a clue what you'll be talking about anyway; all they know is that someone is coming to remove the body."

"This sounds more interesting when you put it that way, at least we'll have the protection of the guards."

"Oh and the army will be on hand, out of sight of course, but there nonetheless in case another country gets wind of the body and wants to lay claim to it. You know how jealous these Middle East Countries are, they battle over the slightest thing when it comes to territory, boundaries or anything else."

A couple of hours later they were back in Poughkeepsie. They stopped along the way for diesel fuel and got a snack. Poor Richard couldn't keep still; if he wasn't talking he was squirming and fidgeting in his seat. They parked the van beneath the store and Sol showed Richard his latest idea of the disappearing doors in the loading area. It looked as though there was no access to the building from the back of it. Richard was totally amazed at the difference to the look of it there were no visible seems on the brick wall of the building but they were there if you knew where to look. They took Richard's bags upstairs.

"Richard shall we go out for a late supper or would you like me to have it sent up here, we can do either one?"

"If it's all the same to you Sol I could make do with a hamburger or something due to the time change between here and LA.."

"Well let me make a call and see what the special of the day is?"

"Sol picked up the phone and called the restaurant across the street, they were used to the late dinner calls from above the store. After he called he said to Richard," the special of the day is beef stew, how about we get a couple of bowls of that?"

"That's sounds even better than a hamburger Sol, I'm good with that."

Sol ordered two piping hot bowls of stew in real bowls, no cardboard or plastic bowls, rolls and butter. In about twenty minutes Sol heard a knock at the door. He waited a minute or so then opened the door. The food was on a stainless steel tray and the delivery person had picked up the envelope of money Sol had left outside the door for him that included the tip. They told Sol how much the bill would be before he hung up so he was already ready for the delivery of the meals when they arrived.

Unbeknown to Sol the employees in the restaurant had to take turns to deliver the meals because there had been some in fighting over who would go because the tip that was very generous, that way Sol always got exactly what he wanted when he wanted it They ate their supper and chatted about their girls and whether or not to take them on what could be a perilous journey and they weren't even sure how long they would be gone and whether or not the girls could take enough time off to go with them.

"Richard, I don't know about you but I'd rather let the rest of this go until tomorrow morning, I have a headache now just thinking about the possibilities and the chances we could be taking, this could turn out to be extremely dangerous as you probably already know."

"Sure Sol, it will keep until morning I'm very tired as well; I have to adjust my inner clock to get on Eastern Standard Time again, how about we both turn in."

"Fine by me Richard"

CHAPTER - 84

Dick and Jane were still hard at work with the propane tanks. Dick wanted the lab techs. to come up with exact serial numbers so he could trace the six tanks back to the stores that sold them so he could talk to the person who made the actual sale. He wanted to put the store on the spot about whoever it was bought the tank and who sold it so he could get some sort of description of the young man now working with their Perp., short for Perpetrator. He hoped to rattle someone enough to jar their memory for a better description than they gave the first time. He knew he was reaching again but he had to do something he felt and if it meant going back to New Mexico to scare the crap out of someone and get something more tangible than they had right now they would do it. Dick studied all the material the lab techs provided him with and he still couldn't figure out what blew the tanks up, it had to be something extremely powerful.

One of the lab techs came into their office with part of a valve from one of the propane tanks. "Agent Jefferies, do you have a moment?"

"Sure what is it?"

"Well sir, I have a piece of a valve from one of the tanks and I've only seen this type of a cut using what is called a shape charge. I spent time in the Army Engineers and we used stuff called C4 to blow things up. It's used in demolition, you can shape a charge out of the putty like substance to form it around almost anything and when it goes off it leaves a reasonable clean cut through the metal its attached to. So I'm thinking that your guy used a hand molded shape charge around the neck of the tanks just below the valve and if he did that to all six of those tanks full of propane you'd get quite an explosion. It works by literally cutting through the threaded brass below the valve cutting it clean off and the resulting explosion of the valve being blown off resulted in blowing up all the tanks at the same time and I also believe that they put another piece of C4 around the middle of the tank as well and that's why we have so many small pieces. Had it been blown by just cutting the valve off the cylinder they would have opened up like peeling part of a banana and the tank would have remained basically intact. We haven't found a timing device yet but we are piecing something together that could be your timer. So for what its worth I'm going with the theory that your perp. has access to C4 somewhere, its not something you can buy on the street like common nuts and bolts."

"Thanks you for your insight, I believe you have the answer. Have your guys check every valve they can find and see if it's the same as yours, if it is than that's it, they used C4 explosive with a timer and hooked the tanks together then wired all of it to a timer and a battery."

The rest of the day went by quietly until the same lab tech. came bursting into Dicks office all excited this time. "Agent Jefferies, they used a common kitchen timer and a 9 volt battery for an electrical charge to set them all off at the same time, its absolutely ingenious."

"You're sure about this, there's no doubt?"

"Yes sir absolutely sure, they could have used a timer from the victims own house as well as the 9 volt battery. All they would have to buy was the C4 and a small amount of electrical wire and any kind of electrical tape to secure each connection and of course the propane tanks."

"Eureka, then we've got it, I can take this to the Director then?"

"Yes sir, we'll all stand behind it."

"Thank you my good man." Dick ushered him out so he could find Jane and tell her the news that had just been brought to him confirming everything they had a theory on, he was ecstatic. He went looking for Jane but couldn't find her anywhere. Finally he went outside where he saw Donny. "Hey Donny have you seen Agent Marlowe?"

Donny pointed over towards the back of the parking garage where the sun was shining through that part of the open garage. He found Jane standing in the sun light looking out at empty space. "Jane, Jane, are you alright?" Dick asked excitedly.

"Yes, of course I am, I came out here to clear my head with some fresh air, were you looking for me?"

"Of course I was, we had a tremendous breakthrough! We have a total of six propane tanks set off by C4 explosive using a 9 volt battery and a kitchen timer of all things."

"Yes well I've heard about that before in a bulletin we got over a year ago, someplace was blown up using the same thing, they called it a terrorist plot."

"How did I miss that I wonder?"

"Its called being preoccupied, wasn't that about the time you and Donny both got shot?"

"Yeah, could have been."

"Well then there you have it, your mind was somewhere else, it was by the bed of your friend and partner."

"I suppose you're right," Dick felt a little deflated, Jane didn't seem excited at all.

Several more days went by with no new leads or better descriptions. Dick and Jane were at a dead end once again. They went back over everything they had done on all their cases. "Jane we haven't found that common thread other than he likes rare books, there's still the how and the why of it all, what does he get out of this? I feel like its right in front of us but we have yet to find it. Maybe we need to take another look at the past cases and see if we can tie our guy to those deaths that have been coming in and we have had some strange ones and I'm beginning to think that it's the strange situations that set him off, maybe it's just not just the books but the thrill of the hunt and the kill like hunters say."

"Could it be that maybe this guy is like an avenger setting some wrongs right Dick?"

"You know I never looked at it that way but let's take that slant and see where it goes."

They continued going over cases they had and they hadn't had time to really look at them that closely they had been focused on the Book Store theory alone. They finally came across a few that looked like it might fit the same guy they were hunting. Some of the deaths were from a 9mm semi automatic pistol and it had been used several times in murder cases. They had the bullet fragments animalized and they all came from the same pistol.

"Jane, the case we just finished in New Mexico, did we determine how the couple was killed, was it before the explosion or did the explosion kill them?"

"What are you thinking?"

"I'm thinking our perp. has made a mistake by using the same weapon over and over."

"Ah ha; maybe that's one common thread," Jane said.

"Jane!"

"I'm on it already; I'll call Albuquerque and see what happened to the bodies of theBook Store Owners?" She got on the phone to their new friend who was now the Fire Marshall, she had graduated fire school and had finished her training and now she was Captain in charge of three other men as Fire Marshals and she had her own office and department now.

In a few minutes she was off the phone. "Dick, bad news in a way, they were badly burned but not cremated and were buried, do you want the bodies exhumed?"

"No, first I want to know who signed the certificate of death then I want to know if he or she examined the bodies or not or just signed off to get the file off their desk, then I'll let you know. Heads may roll back there some more, I've never seen such sloppy police and fire investigative work."

"I agree, I'll get right on it." Twenty minutes later Jane was back. "Better talk to the Boss again Dick, the bodies it seems were deemed almost unrecognizable due to the fire and it was assumed they died from the explosion and fire, no autopsy was done on either one of them."

"Damn it, what's wrong with people?"

"Problem is Dick they aren't you and don't look for trouble when it isn't obvious, you can't blame everyone, you're the best there is or you wouldn't be here today, same as me."

"Yeah well alright, I'll call the Boss; better yet I'll set up a meeting, want to come with me for moral support?"

"Sure Dick, I'd be pleased to meet with you and the Boss again now that we're getting somewhere."

Dick picked up his phone now that he was back in his office and called the Director's secretary to make the appointment. It was Tuesday and the Department was very busy as usual and the Secretary couldn't get them in to see the Director until Thursday afternoon at 2:30 P.M. He made the appointment.

He was just about to leave their office when his phone rang. It was the Doctor who had been doing the autopsy on the Fire Marshall from New Mexico. He wanted to see Dick right away. Dick almost ran people down getting to the autopsy lab at the far end of the hall that connected the departments together. He ran into the Autopsy room almost out of breath. "Yes Doctor, you said you had something for me?"

"As a matter of fact I do and I'm releasing the body back to New Mexico for cremation and have notified the family of the deceased. Now then, the reason I took so long was because you asked me to look for something specific. I don't know how you knew this man was a hearty individual but he was. He had a perfectly good heart, it was a toxic substance that killed him."

"Wait a minute we were told by the authorities that he had a bad heart."

"Maybe it was an excuse for some really bad indigestion, he had a Hiatal Hernia but his heart didn't fail, he was murdered just as you thought. Now the thing that killed him is something that is unique to the United States. In fact there isn't any here at all. It comes from the Middle East from a lab there that manufactures weapons of mass destruction for anyone who has the cash to pay for it. Apparently your guy has lots of cash because this is one expensive little white pill similar in size to a baby aspirin and it dissolves in any liquid and is tasteless, odorless and colorless. I've never seen such a scary thing. Can you imagine a man killing his wife with a single pill that leaves no residue whatsoever? No Doctor would have ever caught it if you hadn't acted so fast because it dissipates in as little as seventy two hours to a week. You were right in between time constraints and if we hadn't done the autopsy when we did no one would have ever known. The effect of this thing acts just like a heart attack. In fact it attacks the heart muscle and it takes its time to kill but usually death occurs within forty eight to seventy two hours and there is no way to stop it once ingested, damn fine catch there young man, what I'd like to know is how you knew."

"Fits our guy's M/O Doctor and I didn't know. I was grasping at straws and took a huge risk. If I had been wrong I could be gone as early as tomorrow morning for overstepping my bounds but fortunately I was right and the boss doesn't end up with egg on his face or me looking like a fool. It was an educated guess is all it was. Thanks again Doc, are you going to send the family an autopsy report so they know he was murdered and didn't have a heart attack?"

"Yes son, I'm going to do just that, they have a right to know and I'm sure the Insurance Company who insured him would like to know as well. You sure are clearing up some weird cases around here lately."

"Yeah Doc and the thing is they are all committed by the same man."

"Sounds like you're up against a genius son."

"That may be but one day he'll make a mistake and I'll be there to slap the cuffs on him when he does."

"I'm betting on you as well, good job son."

"Thanks again Doc!" Dick left and went back to his office all smiles now because he had been right after all.

Thursday morning came and went with no further progress in the case. Dick and Jane went out to get a good lunch and go over what they would tell the Director when they saw him at 2:30 pm.

When it was almost time they got on the elevator and headed upstairs to the Director's Office. They waited another fifteen minutes until it was their turn. Finally the secretary waved them into the Director's office.

"Come in your two, what can I do for you today, I understand that you both wanted to see me so I guess that means the two of you finally made a team out of one another."

"Yes sir, thank you sir, did you get our latest reports?"

"I think so, the last one I got was the autopsy done on the fireman from New Mexico, the Doctor had some fine things to say about you Dick, he was really impressed. Now then what has your under ware in a wad today son?"

"Well sir plain and simple we would like you to order the exhumations of the Book Store owner and his wife in New Mexico. I believe that they were murdered prior to the explosion and fire but no autopsy was performed on them due to the severely burned condition of the bodies. The coroner out there said it was evident that the explosion and fire killed them, no one could have lived through anything like that."

"So why the autopsy and exhumations then?"

Dick glanced sideways to Jane. "Sir we believe the killer has used the same pistol in several of his crimes. Our ballistics have shown that many of the bodies were shot with the same 9 mm semi automatic pistol and we believe the couple in New Mexico were shot as well. They would not have stood by while someone set out six propane tanks and wired them to explode and set a timer for an hour to give the perp. time to get out of town so to speak."

"Uh huh, makes perfect sense to me Jane and you're both right; there should have been an autopsy done on them. Don't fault others for what they have done, they don't have the resources we do."

"Problem is sir if they don't properly investigate they won't get to the truth either."

"I have to agree with that but I know the restraints of budgets only too well. You two don't realize it but we're so far over budget on this one case, well you get my meaning I'm sure. Thing is I have to keep reminding the Cabinet that this isn't just one crime we're solving, its dozens and who knows how many more, it could be in the hundreds if this guy keeps on killing indiscriminately. You'll get your exhumations and now I'd like to suggest something to you both. I want you to go to New Mexico and be on hand when the local Coroner does his thing so you can tell him yourselves, tactfully of course, what it is you are looking for and I sure hope you're both right on this one. I have to justify each and every expense of this investigation as you know. Now get out of here so I can get some work done and make your plane reservations right away because I'm putting a rush on this pair of autopsies."

"Yes sir, thank you sir." The two of them were flying high, maybe this would be the straw that broke the camel's back, had the killer finally met his match in wits? As soon as they were back in their office Jane got on the phone and made reservations for the earliest flight out to Albuquerque and reservations at the same motel they stayed in before. Their flight was for 11:15 tomorrow morning and their seats weren't together but at least they were on the same flight.

"Packing light for tomorrow Dick?"

"Yes, two or three day's worth of clothes should do it because the Director put a rush on the pair of Autopsies so it shouldn't take too long. I'm guessing but if I were the killer I would have shot both of them in the head at point blank range so the bullets should still be in their heads. Lets hope they weren't in and out wounds which could prove really embarrassing."

The next morning before noon they were in the air and on their way. A little over four hours more of flying time and they were landing back in Albuquerque. They got off the plane, picked up a white Ford four door sedan rental and headed for their Motel. They had no sooner got settled in then Dick was on the phone to the County Coroners Office. He went next door to tell Jane the news. "Tomorrow morning at nine o'clock the bodies will be dug up, we ought to be at the cemetery to show our support and show them we're on the job as well."

"I agree, I wonder what the Director said to get them moving so fast."

"Who knows, what would you like to do for supper tonight?"

"I'd like to go back to the same place we went to when we were here last, the food was great as well as the entertainment."

"Consider it done."

The next morning precisely at nine o'clock they were at the Cemetery to watch the exhumation of the two bodies. The Coroner was there as well, mad as hell, but at least he was there. They went over and introduced themselves and all they got out of him was an, "uh huh." They watched as two black unmarked vans were loaded one each with the caskets. They followed the vans with their car, the Coroner was in the lead van. It was nearly lunchtime for everyone when the bodies were unloaded and put in the Coroners lab for their autopsies and the Coroner sent everyone to lunch and said he'd do the autopsies right after they came back.

Dick and Jane took the hint and went the opposite direction of the others to eat.

They were all back by two thirty and the Coroner asked Dick if there was something specific he was looking for before he started cutting.

"Actually there is something Doctor, we suspect the couple were shot to death prior to the explosion and fire. I would guess that they were both shot in the head at relatively close range."

"Thank you, then maybe we won't be here all day after all. Is this all just a guess or do you have a solid basis for your argument."

"We're hunting a pervert Doctor, I'm speaking low so your colleagues won't hear me.

He's killed dozens of people across the Untied States and your own Fire Marshall was murdered by him as well. It was not a heart attack and it was us that discovered it, not you or your people who should have. Now get to work or I'll tear this place apart and hire new people to take your stupid jobs because its evident that none of you know what you are doing and if you so much as snicker I'll wipe that grin off your face for good. Do I make myself clear, we're not here to bust balls but are on a fact finding mission and we wouldn't go through all of this unless this was important, understood?"

"Yeah I got it sonny boy, you're going to be seriously embarrassed when we find nothing but I'll do as you ask because you're Boss already told me the same thing yesterday and he said he was a saint compared to the two of you so I'd best cooperate with you so I will. Now keep out of my light!"

Almost an hour went by when he heard the Doctor; "Well I'll be a monkeys uncle there's a slug in the old man's head, large caliber at that."

Dick stepped up next to the Doctor quietly. "Well Doc, are we vindicated or not?"

"Yes young man, I stand corrected it was a gun shot to the forehead of the man at his hair line, now lets see what his wife can tell us." He went to work on her next. He studied her while she was on her back then shook his head no and turned the body over so she lay face down.

About forty five minutes went by and he said it again. "Well I'll be a monkey's uncle right where you said they might be, good thinking there young man. Sorry I missed it but with almost every ounce of flesh burned away there wasn't much sense looking for a gun shot wound, I mean where would you start?"

"Look for the obvious Doctor then look beyond and you'll find your answers. I'll take what you said as an apology, we all make mistakes but you made three in a row here when you include your Fire Marshall. Next time don't be in a hurry to rush to conclusions!"

"I guess I'd better try harder, huh son?"

"That's the spirit Doc., would you please put each of the slugs in a bag and mark them as to which body they came from as well as where they were found in the head with entrance wound and so on?"

"Yes of course I'll do that for you and for what its worth I am sorry I jumped to conclusions when you two were here before but we just couldn't believe someone committed murder here in our town."

"Duly noted Doctor. You realize now that twelve people died don't you? I'll also wager that the two men found in the burned out truck were shot as well but from what I was told there wasn't enough left to do an autopsy on them, if there were any bullets in them they could have easily been consumed by the fire. We'll be leaving in the morning back to Washington with the evidence, you have your pictures and when we're done I'll mail everything back to you.

"Thank you Special Agent Jefferies."

"Special Agent Marlowe, it was nice to see you again as well."

They went back to their Motel, called the airlines for the trip back to DC. This time they were able to get seats next to one another for the long ride home.

They went to their favorite steak house once again to eat super and in the morning they had breakfast at the Motel. After they ate they went back to their rooms to get their luggage ready and they had to check out by eleven o'clock A.M. Their flight was at 1:10 P.M. so they ate lunch early to avoid the food on the plane if there was any. Dick had called Donny to meet them at the airport back in Washington as usual.

The following morning Dick and Jane gave the two bullets to their forensics team and they checked the ballistics and the bullets were a match to many others which had been taken from bodies around the U.S.; Dick had done it again. There was little for them to do now but wait and go through old files and check and recheck everything. One by one Dick came up with different items that intrigued him, more bullets were sent for from murders and the ballistics began to match what they had. There was one case however that stumped Dick, a killing in a park of a woman whose infidelity inflamed someone so bad that she was killed with a 357 magnum revolver and no other bullets from any other crimes matched the 357's bullet. He began to wonder if this was not related to the other cases but something stuck in his craw about it. It was the one case they called the avenger in disguise. He wondered about the little man back in New Mexico, he wondered if it was him and the power of the gun maybe scared him and was much too loud and powerful for him to handle. Maybe that's when he changed to his 9mm semi automatic pistol and he also wondered if he used a silencer at the last couple's home so that neither of them heard gunshots. He decided that he was on the right track due to the possible disguises and different people the witnesses thought they saw. Could it be their man could alter his height and weight enough to fool a lot of people who were afraid to come forward that he may come back and kill them? There had to be a reason for so few witnesses. While he contemplated it all something popped back into his memory. Then he had it, leave no witness to testify against him. He had thought about it before but this last tragedy of twelve people dying cemented it into his brain just that way. That had to be the reason for so many deaths at one crime scene like the last one. Then he came across the Book Store in Buffalo again. There were no bullets found in any of the bodies and two people died surrounded by witnesses but no one saw the killer. He read along further and found the report of a man who walked out in front of a bus, a drunk and wife abuser, was this work of his avenger and killer he was thinking? He had to find a link somewhere but where was it? His people had been to Buffalo and interviewed several witnesses and came back empty handed, no one saw or heard anything unusual. They concluded that the two incidents were just accidents. Still the hair on the back of his neck stood up every time he read about this thing in Buffalo. He didn't doubt his own Agents but wondered if they had asked the right questions of the right people. He fell asleep on the stack of files. No one bothered to wake him everyone knew he had been putting in more hours than anyone else with the exception of Agent Marlowe and she was usually at his elbow as well. She was not around when he drifted off to sleep.

CHAPTER -85

The next morning Sol and Richard got up, shaved and showered then went across the street for breakfast before diving back into the unknown as Sol was now calling the next adventure. Back at Sol's apartment he had lots of questions. "So Richard, can you tell me where this cave is and how we're going to get to it?"

"Ah Sol, there's the problem, it's in the mountains where Afghanistan, Pakistan and Tibet all converge. As you know two of those countries have been squabbling over their boundaries for years, Tibet says very little and lets the other two fight it out. The cave is so well camouflaged in the mountains that it can't be seen from the ground or from the air and Infrared Imaging doesn't help due to the difficult terrain. Now with those difficulties out of the way the books could be brought down the mountains for us in several ways, my contact awaits your thoughts on the matter."

"Well it sounds like he's already solved part of the problem in as far as his men know they are guarding an ancient body. Why not do this, let's say there is a body in there and the men go into the cave to remove it. It is extremely fragile and they have to be very careful how they handle it, any jostling of it could destroy the bones turning them into dust. You said the books were well wrapped or packed in something, right?"

"Yeah he said that but I don't know how they are disguised."

"Well here is my suggestion. Carry the makings of two coffins made from plain wood much like the Military would use over there to bury a dead soldier. Put half of the books in one coffin the men can put together on the mountain inside the cave and put the other half in the second coffin that they can put together the same as the first. The reason for the two coffins is that I don't want any undue pressure put on the tops of the fragile paper the works are on, they could be ruined before we even move them. If he needs a cover story for the dead men who are there he could say that when one body was removed another one was found beneath it hence the need for a second coffin. Now here's the worst of it. Once the coffins have been brought down to wherever we are to pick them up, the men who were in the cave who may have seen anything resembling the books will have to be quickly dispatched unceremoniously. The story could be put out that they fell to their deaths in a missed step in the mountains and when one fell he pulled the other one down with him because they were tied together like mountain climbers do, end of witnesses. Do you follow me? That shouldn't be a problem in the part of the world, they don't seem to care much for human life like we do here in the west."

"Brilliant Sol, that's what he wanted to hear. He said the guards were hand picked, so no families, no married men."

"Well there you are, he answered some of his own questions. Now when bringing down the coffins it will be important for them not to put anyone's national flag on them like we do or the Israelis do and other countries as well to mark the passing of a soldier. The story he could use is that these two men were known deserters and once the bodies were recovered they were buried without any ceremony once that was realized. He can word it anyway he wants too. I am told that they are all very good at subterfuge. Now to keep us out of it the two coffins should be re-crated for air freight and marked 'FRAGILE ANTIQUITIES,' 'HANDLE WITH UTMOST CARE!.' Now one more very important note, those words should be in several languages due to wherever the plane has to make stops. Now to get us there and back in one piece I had another thought. Are we going to be able to pick these coffins up in a safe haven type of an airport where no questions will be asked?"

"As far as I know we will be in no danger, the big question my man had was how to package the books and you have solved that one already, the rest I will relay to him."

"Okay now here's another thought, suppose we charter a plane big enough to carry say eight to ten people with a hold in the airplane that's pressurized to protect the books and used that for our so called escape. We'd have to find an airplane and plane driver or pilot who can keep quiet. The only thing the pilot has to know is that he's picking up two coffins packed as air freight and that he's flying family members to and from the pick up point. He could be told the bodies were on an expedition that ran into trouble and two of the men died of exposure or that they fell to their deaths in the mountains. Right now what I'm telling you is all speculation, things that we could do to get out of there safe and avoid Custom's check points. Once back here in the U.S. a good pilot could get us past all check points, customs etc. and land right back here in Poughkeepsie. We would of course have to pay off the airport manager and we'd have to make it well worth his while because if caught he could lose his Airport Operators License. I just had another thought about their pilot if he were caught. With our expertise we could provide the pilot with false papers and alter his identity and if he's caught the fake papers will be the one to lose the license and he'll walk Scot Free. He will have zero liability unless we're caught dodging customs but I'm told that there are pilots out there who love the thrill, the excitement and the money involved and they'll do anything for a buck. That's the kind of man we need and again as with the others, no family and no wife in the remote chance we have to off him."

"What do you mean off him Sol?"

"Kill him Richard, a bullet to the brain and the body dumped somewhere so it can't be traced back to us."

"Oh I got it now, silence him once and for all."

"By golly Richard I like your choice of words."

"Thank you Sol."

"Now, one more thing, from the sound of this I don't believe that it would be a good idea to bring the girls along. They would know we are riding around with a couple of dead bodies. It's not the kind of thing I would do to Francis so I have an alternative. Here's how we could work it. You and I are taking a business trip to the Mideast about some rare books and when we return we can take the ladies on a cruise, Alaska, Hawaii, the Caribbean, Europe, any-where they like and let them pick where they want to go."

"Great idea Sol, I like it, what fun that would be especially since we're going off without them this time."

"One more thing Richard, also check with your contact about the fact that we may have to kill a couple of his men and be sure he's alright with that and see what contacts he may have in the airline business and ways to get around customs because that is not my forte."

"Alright Sol, would you like me to contact him today with preliminary suggestions?"

"I guess it wouldn't hurt to show our interest in helping him and one more thing, see if he will pick up the tab since we're taking all the chances, that will tell us if he's sincere or not?"

"Should I call him right now then?"

"I guess it won't hurt, we haven't exactly said yes yet. Tell you what I'll go down to the store and when you are done you can come down and join me there." Sol left and took the elevator down to the store's level and got off. He said good morning to Greta and went to the area of the store that had mysteries in it. He began to thumb through them not really caring or looking for anything in particular when he thought to himself, World History, that's where I should be looking. He changed his line of thinking and went to the History and Geography section of the Store which was huge and complete with many different kinds and sizes of World Atlas's, wall maps and several World Globes in different sizes. He found the section that said middle East Countries and started to look through them for points of reference. He found quite a lot on Afghanistan, Pakistan and Tibet. He took all three humongous volumes up to the front counter and set them down so Greta could see them.

"I'm borrowing these for a few days Greta, I'll bring them back down when I'm through." She made a note of each one just in case a customer came in looking for one of those volumes then she could call Sol and ask him to bring that volume back downstairs for the customer. This was not unusual for Sol he often borrowed books to read and then brought them back downstairs and gave them to Greta to be put away. He was just about to go back upstairs when Richard strolled into the store.

"Glad I caught up with you Sol, my man had some questions but I think I handled them alright, he said he'd call back later today and for us to hang out near the phone."

"Alright Richard, I got some material to give myself a little background on where we may be going. Remember I didn't say yes yet, it depends on your contact now and how bad he needs our expertise."

The two of them went back to the elevator and went back up to Sol's apartment. Sol was dying to look at the parts of the region where the cave was located. Then he would check and see where the airports were closest to the site. He knew the two countries were nervous about their boundaries and air space and they would have to be careful not to alert one of them while they were making their move. This meant lots of camouflaged vehicles and men. They worked through lunch and had it sent over. Three o'clock came and went then at three forty five the phone rang. Sol wasn't expecting any calls so he let Richard answer it.

Richard picked up the phone and acknowledged that it was him and that it was a secure line then he listened, nodding his head now and then as if the person on the other end could hear him. "Alright let me get this right," said Richard, "one million five hundred thousand dollars American to help pay our way and another one million five hundred thousand apiece when we get the package back here safe and sound. We have to guarantee its safety while it is in our hands, yes no problem there." He listened some more nodding his head again and said he'd let him know later this evening Eastern Standard Time. "Sol, he said he could arrange for first class transportation on an unmarked aircraft that flies in and out of clandestine airports and we can switch planes at one of them and he said if we needed more cash he would wire it immediately, apparently time is now of the essence, we have to let him know later tonight from here. He's really anxious about his tenable situation, he needs to leave the Country soon and he wants the package as he calls it gone before he leaves, what do you say?"

"I say we call him back later tonight, we don't want to seem too anxious about this but it does sound tempting, whoever controls and owns the books can control the religions of the world as well as world trade and their country's incomes, wouldn't you say?"

"I'd say that's a fair assessment."

"You know Richard I'm dying to see what the books look like, I just hope that his whole thing isn't a hoax for some wise guy to control the world like some Dictator. I'm basing my word on your faith in this man that he is on the up and up, we don't want to start another World War now do we?"

"No, that's for sure. Are you trying to read up on the region where we may be going?"

"Something like that Richard, oh did he say when the money would be transferred into my account?"

"Yes, he said the minute you give him the go ahead and your account number it will be done instantaneously, that's the beauty of wire transfers."

"Yes but there is one difficulty, I can't contact my bank until after nine o'-clock in the morning to see if the money got there, I'm not budging until I see he has made the transfer and its in my account, that's only good business but you already know that."

"Yes Sol and I've done business with him before on the sly and he was always very generous with me."

"Alright then I'll read while we wait. Would you like to look through one of these?"

"Yes I would, may I have the one on Tibet, that place has always intrigued me and that's one place I've never been. I've been to the other two countries several times on business with my friend. Usually I launder cash for him through my business accounts then send it back to him for products I never received, its all a very clean business."

"Why Richard you are a sly scoundrel after all, I knew there was something else I liked about you."

Richard and Sol had supper, a glass of wine and at seven forty five that evening Sol decided it was time to make contact and say that they would do the job for sure. Richard made the call and after several anxious moments his contact came on the line. Richard mostly listened then motioned for a deposit slip of Sol's, once he had it in hand he read off the account number and said that he'd be in touch after nine thirty am. Eastern Standard Time to confirm that the money had arrived in the account and that they would make their plans to fly to wherever his contact asked them to. Sol heard him say; "Okay, I'll call you with our flight itinerary tomorrow as soon as we have it." Richard hung up the phone.

"Well Sol its all set. He suggested that we not arrive in street clothes, you know suits and ties, it may create suspicion of the wrong kind. I knew you would have an idea on that so we can go shopping tomorrow for some clothes to fit the situation."

Sol didn't answer he was thinking. "Wait, you said no street clothes and remember you mentioned me as an archeologist who was traveling to pick up the bodies, I have an idea now and you'll be dressed as my assistant."

CHAPTER - 86

Dick and Jane were going through some new files that had come in since their last request. Dick found something strange in two of them. Outside a window at two different houses where people had died it appeared as though someone had been standing in a flower bed in the dirt for a rather long period of time. There seemed to be shoe prints under the window that were the same size shoe but a different print had been made as if it were another shoe, one that Dick had never seen a print of so it seemed very strange to him. He sent it through the new Computer system the FBI had recently installed and it came back with no known matches. He showed the shoe prints to Jane. "Ever seen a print made like this Jane, look at the imprints of each shoe, they are similar but not the same at two different murder scenes. Our vast Computer can't find a match anywhere, its vaguely familiar but I can't quite put my finger on it."

"No Dick I don't remember anything like those, it could be that they are from two different people couldn't it?"

"Maybe, I'll pass them around the lab and see if anyone has any ideas on it." He took the photos and started one pair of prints from one end of the room and the other set from the other end of the room. He asked everyone to take a good look at them and see if they rang bell with anyone. There was a lot of shaking of heads like they were saying no until the last set of prints were handed back to him.

One man suddenly spoke up; "wait a minute Agent Jefferies, I know what they are.

They are from rubbers, the old fashioned kind people used to put over their shoes on a rainy day to protect their shoes from the elements. My maw made me wear them back in Texas when I was going to High School and had to walk there and back every day in bad weather. I didn't know they still made them and mine were black if I recall."

"Maybe they don't", answered Dick, "these could be very old rubbers indeed, just like our killer I'll bet. I'll wager he has more than one pair just like his disguises, he has several of those too is my guess, nice going there Jimmy"

"Thank you Agent Jefferies."

"Dick are you talking about those smelly old things like my father used to wear over his shoes in the snow?"

"That's it Jane, the very same ones."

"I wonder how many pairs the killer owns and how do you know they belong to him?"

"Variation Jane, that's what the killer is all about, misdirection like magicians use, they get you looking the wrong way and poof, they're gone."

"You know Dick you never cease to amaze me, where did you get the gift you have?"

"Dad or mom, I don't know. What I do know is how we're going to catch this guy now. We've been following the direction he wanted us to follow, now we'll go the opposite way whatever it is. Just like the last case, everything pointed to California when he was headed for New England somewhere but where is the question. We need to find his base of operations."

"I know what you mean Dick, but where do we start?"

"I don't know but one thing we do know is that some of the worst criminals hide in plain sight right under the authority's nose's and go unnoticed for years."

"Yeah, I heard about escaped prisoners who have done that as well. I recently heard about a man who escaped from prison live amongst us all in plain sight and even held a great job, got married, had a family then someone saw a poster in a Post Office and recognized something about the man and turned him in. It turned out that he was the man and he went back to prison to serve the rest of his term and they tacked on a few years because he had escaped but now he's getting out early due to good behavior since being in jail and what he had done since his escape but doesn't excuse his escape. The Judge took into account that he had been trouble free and led an exemplary life on the outside so he's getting an early release from jail for being a good boy. Talk about rewarding a criminal, he got rewarded for being just that but in my book it doesn't excuse the fact that a criminal is a criminal until his release from prison and only after he or she has served their full sentence. It just galls me that some criminals get out early and go right back to committing crimes until they are caught again."

"I agree with you Jane but the Courts and the Attorneys are the ones who make those decisions, not us."

"I know but sometimes it's like shoveling sand against the tide, it doesn't get you anywhere."

"Maybe you ought to take a break, you're getting worked up and losing your focus."

"No, I'm alright, I just had a moment of frustration about our guy, it seems like we take one step forward and two steps back, this guy is always one step ahead of us."

"Tell you what Jane why don't you help our friend across the table there research the old fashioned rubbers our man used over his shoes. See if you can develop a lead from that, maybe we can find out who the manufacturer of the rubbers is and what part of the country they sell the most of that style of rubbers in and see it they still make them."

"You're right Dick that's one thing I'm good at, tracking down old rubbers, thanks a lot for the vote of confidence." She was smiling so Dick never gave it a second thought. He figured she knew that she needed a reality check and she got it from her partner. They both needed to refocus now and then due to the many twists and turns their perp. was giving them.

An hour went by and Dick decided to call a meeting of all the lab techs and Agents who were working the case with them. He gave them a good pep talk about what he and Jane had just been through in New Mexico. They needed even the smallest detail brought to light, just like the man who wore the rubbers. This man had been intentionally using different size shoes and posing from a heavy short man to a taller thin man to a fat man. He told them they were dealing with a master of disguise and that's why they were having so much trouble with witnesses remembering a description because the man had several ways to throw them off. He went on to tell them that the man was obviously wearing wigs and sometimes appeared to be nearly bald to bald; short or tall it was the same man right down to the different style and size shoe prints they found. He told them about the misdirection with vehicles that he rented and what he told the people he rented them from. When he told them they were going west, they were really going east and vise versa north to south. "Damn it people I just had a thought, has anyone bothered to check back with the Rental places to see when they got their Trucks back and what the mileage was when they got them back. Somebody get on that right away please."

Jane immediately got her two cents worth in. "Can I help with that Dick; I'm really good at researching those kinds of things?"

"Sure Jane go to it but get help from someone else as well. I don't know why we didn't think about this before. Jane start with New Mexico and work backwards please."

"We're on it and she looked at the other Agents for a volunteer, seeing one she crooked her finger in a come here move and they went into the office and got on the two phones in there with separate lines and got to work.

It was the next day before results started to come in. One by one the Truck Rental Companies reported and told almost the same story. The truck that was rented the day of or the day before the murders was never seen again and was turned it into the Insurance Company for reimbursement for a stolen truck and had notified the local authorities. "Dick you're not going to like this, the trucks have just plain disappeared along with some of the drivers of the moving companies like we learned about in Boston.."

"One more thing Jane, check with the Rental Companies Insurance Carrier and see what they have done if anything to try and recover their stolen vehicles."

"Okay Dick but I still think the trucks are gone, they'll never to be seen again."

Dick picked up a piece of scrap paper off the floor, wadded it up absentmindedly and tossed it in the wastebasket. He looked at the wastebasket and called Jane back to where he was.

"Jane take a look at this and tell me what you see. I'm going to wad up piece of paper and throw it away." He tossed another piece of paper away. "Now what happens to the trash in the wastebasket?"

"They put it in our big paper shredder as we do with all our documents."

"Then what?"

"They go into a machine that bundles the paper in one big bundle and its sold to a wastepaper company who then picks it up."

"Right, now suppose I want to get rid of a car or a truck, what would I do?"

"I guess you'd take it to a junkyard or salvage yard to be crushed and sold as scrap."

"You just nailed it Jane, Scrap Yards!"

"Huh, I don't understand?"

"Think about it for a minute, you have a car that no longer runs you take it to a Salvage Yard and what do they do with it?"

"Oh I see now, either they shred the vehicle or crush it flat or crush it into a cube and sell it for scrap. I see what you're getting at, you think all of the trucks have been to a crusher and not one of those places that just flattens them but really crushes them into a small block of metal like I've seen on TV. That would be a good way to get rid of a body or prints on a vehicle, the same would hold true if the vehicle was shredded."

"If you've seen it don't you think the criminals have seen it?"

"You're right Dick but where do we start looking?"

"We don't but now we have the answer, there is no way to find a needle in the haystack in this case because a lot of the scrap is put on ships then sent over seas to be melted down into new metal in any number of countries, it's an ingenious plan with a fast turnover."

"I see, no wonder all the subterfuge, we could spend years spinning our wheels chasing trucks that no longer exist."

"Now you have it, we have the complete picture now. Somehow we have to follow one of the trucks from the beginning to the end of the truck."

"We could bug a few trucks and follow them in a helicopter."

"No good Jane, which State which City, where is this guy going to turn up next?"

"I see what you mean but I still think it could be done if we knew where the next big Book Store Sale is going to be. Even if we have two sales at the same time which I admit is highly unlikely, we could send one of our Agents to truck rental places in the town or City where the Sale is going to be held and if someone looks off center he could walk around the truck pretending to check it out and put a bug underneath while he's at it."

"Thanks fine but just like in New Mexico there were several truck companies there and they rented two trucks from two companies to throw us off."

"Right, but we have enough Agents now to cover all that and we only have to concentrate on the truck that leaves the area. Remember the first truck they intentionally let run off the road and then they burned it and while everyone was concentrating on that truck they left the area in the other one going the opposite direction."

"I'll work on it but in the meantime check with the Insurance companies, they have their own investigators who go looking for missing trucks, let's be sure that we're right on this part."

"You're right Dick I'll get back to them but it will take time, they aren't the quickest people to respond you know."

"Don't I know it, have a little accident and you're forever getting it straightened out. Do what you can, the more we learn the closer we're going to be to taking this guy out."

CHAPTER - 87

The next morning Sol and Richard went out for breakfast. Sol was still not sure about this trip proposed to him by Richard because he was getting information second or third hand but he liked Richard therefore trusted him explicitly. They had a hearty breakfast and returned to Sol's apartment.

Sol picked up the phone, and called his Bank, it was 9:25 A.M., he told the Bank who he was and that he wanted to see if there had been a recent deposit made by wire in the last 24 hours and if it was over six figures. He waited, they asked for his account number and he waited again then the woman he'd been talking with came back on the line and asked him to hold for the Bank's Manager. He finally came on the line and confirmed that indeed a seven figure amount deposit had been made just hours before the bank opened from an off shore bank he declined to name due to political turmoil in the region. He went on to tell Sol that if he had any more business dealings pending he should get them completed soon because the situation looked terribly unstable and customers were moving money in and out of accounts all over the immediate area.

"Well Richard the money is there just as your man said it would be but the Bank Manager also stressed that if I had any unfinished business in the region I should conclude it as as quickly as possible. Now here is what I suggest we should do next. Call your contact and tell him to get the package moving downhill, he'll know what you mean. Then ask him where we should fly into from here, what Country with a big Airport with another one nearby where his men and a pilot can pick us up. He will have to do the planning from there back to the USA by air. Once here I can arrange passage but that part of the world is his expertise. Tell him we can be ready to leave today if we have too but also let him know that we now know the shortness of time is dire. Tell him that from start to finish we should be done in three days that's loading the boxes on the plane and leaving the Country back to the USA. It will take me a day to arrange to get back to New York State. Oh and one thing more, does he know where we are right now?"

"I don't know Sol; all I told him was that I was with my friend."

"Alright then go ahead and call him so we can get things moving. We need directions to the airport where we're supposed to land, that's going to be his call."

"Okay Sol but stay close in case I forget something this time please?"

"I'm not going anywhere Richard, I'm staying real close."

Richard sat on Sol's couch picked up the phone and dialed a number then waited, pad of paper and pencil in hand. In an hour the arrangements were all made.

"Sol, my contact said please hurry, things are happening he can't control much longer, by the time we get to the airport I wrote down, we will met there and taken to the packages then his pilot is ours and the airplane too. He said fly it to the USA and park it somewhere if we have too and he will make it worth our while."

"We can't be baby sitting some airplane and where in hell would I hide one?"

"He stressed that it would be part of the deal or no deal, he'd go to the Russians, he said they have no scruples. He did mention he may have someone available to fly the plane back to his Country and that he's working on it but to be prepared for any eventually. He also stressed that we'd be well compensated for the valuable cargo and language won't be a problem."

"Okay, we have a deal then I guess. Did he happen to say anything else we should know about?"

"He did suggest that maybe we should each carry a gun of some kind. Me, I don't like guns, never did as you know."

"I'll carry a couple just in case; I have one that's big enough to scare the pants off of anyone." He still had the shiny stainless steel 357 magnum stashed in his apartment.

"Can you tell me our destination now Richard?"

"Last stop where we'll be picked up is Karachi, Pakistan."

"Why that's half way round the World isn't it?"

"Probably, but he told me to go there and to wait in the terminal for someone to approach me who would speak perfect English. He will introduce himself to us then we'll leave for the next destination with him. Our itinerary to return to the States is being worked out, private airports where they don't ask questions and its cash only as we go and he will take care of it all."

"Alright, I'd better get on the phone and get us in the air as soon as I can, we can always buy clothes on the run so to speak at lay over's. Oh, how about cash for us, should we take $100,000 with us split between us for contingencies?"

"Might not be a bad idea but I'd feel better with $100,000 apiece, $50,000 won't go far if we run into any situations where we may have to make payoffs to officials along the way."

"I agree with you, I've got that much right here, no need to run to the bank, you won't believe the safe I had installed, so we'll take $100,000.00 each. First let me call the airlines and see if we can arrange this outing of ours, let's not even talk to the girls until we return."

"Good idea Sol."

Sol picked up the phone and went to work. An hour and a half later he was done. "Would you believe no one goes there anymore, we have to change Airline's three times just to get to Pakistan. First flight today is at 3:00 this afternoon. I'd better alert BJ, shoot I can't do that he's already gone back at school, I'll ask Greta for one of her employees or we'll have to take a cab."

"What about an airport shuttle from here to New York."

"There are the Commuter Planes but they're usually filled to capacity, I tried it once, been driving to New York ever since." Sol called Greta and she said Norman could take them into the airport in New York.

They made their flight with ease and were in the air before they knew it carrying only enough clothes and under ware for a few days. They had made a quick trip downtown and purchased tan shirts, slacks and soft hats like professional men might wear on the job. Sol was filled with wonder about what he had gotten himself into.

After changing planes for the last time they still had a long ride to Karachi Pakistan. Once on the ground there they got their suitcases and waited in the terminal where Richard's contact had told them they would be met.

Jet lag caught up with them now. An hour went by, then another and they found themselves napping. Richard awoke as someone was tapping the bottom of his foot with a cane or something. He sat up and looked into the brown eyes of a tall English looking gentleman.

"I say there my good man, might you be Richard from LA?" That was the code for them.

"Sol, wake up we're ready to go."

Sol looked up at the gentleman with the wood cane with what appeared to be a metal housing over the end of it. Cane gun, he saw it immediately. The man was dressed all in black including a black bowler hat. "If you gentleman are ready, our automobile awaits?"

"Yes sir lead the way." They followed him out to a Rolls Royce Limousine that was waiting at the curb. Hmm Sol was thinking first class all the way I guess. They followed the strange man's directions and were soon seated in luxury. The car pulled away effortlessly and took a highway to somewhere but being in a strange country Sol knew better than to ask questions. Three hours later they arrived at a desolate looking place that turned out to be an airport, an old one with dirt and grass landing strips.

"Your plane is the blue and white one over there with two engines, you are to leave immediately, the Pilot's getting ready to warm up the engines." The plane looked as if it were brand new but had no markings on it whatsoever. The rear door was open and Richard and Sol tossed in their bags and climbed the four steps into the cabin. It was both spacious and beautiful. It could easily sit twenty people, it was obviously an executive's airplane or so they thought. They never saw the pilot just a man in street clothes that showed them where to sit and didn't offer his name a handshake or anything else. It seemed to the men that the whole situation was getting very mysterious.

The Captain soon came over the intercom and said, "welcome aboard gentlemen I will be flying you to your destination where you will change planes for your return to the USA. We will make two stops for fuel before we get there, the weather looks grand for the day so sit back and relax. Yusuf will get you anything you desire, he speaks some English but not as well as I so please be patient with him and if you want something he doesn't understand hit the button over head that says intercom, I'll answer and translate for you. When we stop I suggest you eat if you're hungry, it will be almost dark when we get to where we're going and if there's trouble there I have alternative Airports so don't fret we'll get you there in one piece."

Sol looked at Richard, he was all smiles, he was loving it, flying into the unknown, it was what he craved, what he lived for. Sol rested his head and tried to relax.

Their first stop didn't have a restaurant but had sandwiches, Sol and Richard opted out of the sandwiches and waited for a restaurant. They would eat when the Pilot did they figured that way they couldn't go wrong. They knew he had sandwiches in the cockpit and only went to the bathroom when they stopped. In the cabin there were two sets of seats that turned around and there was a drawing table that folded down when not in use. The seats were extra wide and very comfortable, one on each side of the aisle reclined almost completely flat so a person could sleep if they wanted to and in the extreme rear there was a small bathroom like on a larger passenger airplane. The entire inside of the plane was done in beige leather.

At the very next stop both Richard and Sol followed the pilot and his man off the plane and went looking for food. The pilot and his man however weren't looking for food, they were busy talking and arguing about fuel for the plane. There was a sandwich shop inside the small terminal and they grabbed what they could to eat. They stayed away from anything made of hamburger. Sol ended up with a ham and cheese sandwich with mustard on the roll and Richard got a roast beef sandwich piled high with chunks of meat. They both bought a soda and headed back for the plane. They had been on the road or in the air as it were for well over twenty four hours and were tired of sitting.

Finally they landed at their destination and it was nearly dark. As soon as the plane rolled to a stop twenty armed men with automatic weapons quickly surrounded the plane.

CHAPTER - 88

Sol and Richard followed their man off the plane as he retrieved their luggage for them. He pointed out and away from the airplane and said; "You go, that way!"

A uniformed guard approached them with a machine pistol, he gestured for them to follow him which they obediently did. No one spoke as they walked quickly in the failing light of day, all they could see was dirt or desert in every direction. They walked which must have seemed like a quarter of a mile until they came to another airplane, this one was huge with four prop jet engines. Their bags were carried by others aboard the aircraft. This was a passenger plane not a cargo plane as they had expected. They could see the plane was white with the belly painted in light blue but couldn't make out any other colors on it. They were motioned to stand in place by some solders, so they waited and waited.

In the distance they could see headlights of vehicles approaching at high speed. It was a caravan of four vehicles; two Russian Jeep type vehicles and two Russian big trucks like those that carry troops. A soldier spoke in broken English; "your package has arrived and will be loaded for you and you can be on your way." They could only watch as the vehicles peeled off from one another, one big truck stopped near the plane then backed up to the loading ramp for passengers. Four men took each of the boxes, about half the size of an inexpensive coffin that people are buried in, in middle east countries, and loaded them on board being extremely careful to handle them with great care. Sol was about to say something about the speeding trucks and a man recognized the anxiety on Sol's face and told him; "air ride suspension, the best money can by."

Sol thought, now how did he know what I was going to say, he must have seen the anguish on my face?

Another soldier walked up and said; "You go now, quickly," he pointed his rifle up the stairs to the plane. Richard and Sol looked at one another and went up the steps as directed just as one engine came to life. Once inside the aircraft they found that they seemed to be all alone again. The seatbelt sign came on over the cabin door to the cockpit so they fastened their seat belts. Before the plane started to taxi two female flight attendants came out of the cabin where the pilot and co pilot were. They were dressed in kaki uniforms similar to what Middle East Country's Military was using but with no insignias or other identifications. The men couldn't tell what nationality they were but both had worried looks on their faces as shooting broke out behind the airplane which had begun taxiing to the runway. As the plane turned they could see headlights of other vehicles speeding their way. One of the girls said, "keep your heads down we have been found out, we're only going with you to your first stop for fuel, there we will leave and others will take our place. The gunfire is from the opposition forces who want communism but we are a free country and don't want it, there is going to be a Civil War and I am afraid you have been caught up in it. If your pilot is good enough we will be out of here soon. If not we will die right here for what we have done." Sol and Richard stared at each other wondering what they had gotten themselves into.

Before they knew it they were airborne and flying away from danger, at least that was what they hoped.

A couple of hours went by and they felt the plane descending. One of the girls spoke up again; "we're flying lower to avoid radar right now it will not be long before we touch down and get new fuel. Would either of you like a drink, we're a little nervous about the boxes back there because we were told there are bodies in them and that they were zealots of some kind and that you're escorting them home to wherever they came from for burial."

"Yes that's correct, they're quite dead and can't bother anyone," Sol answered.

"Sol, what do you say, how about a scotch or something?," asked Richard.

"A scotch sounds great to me, how about it ladies do you have scotch on board?"

"Oh yes sir, several brands."

"Well hold a bottle up and if we recognize the label we'll have that over the rocks. They both held up two different bottles each,

"Ah there it is Sol; I'd recognize that label anywhere."

"We'll have two of the one in your left hand my dear."

The girl on the right smiled at them and put the one bottle away while the other girl put her two bottles away. She made two stiff drinks but they watched her carefully and she stood aside so they could watch her pour so they wouldn't think she was trying to poison them. She brought the two drinks back to the men. Several rows of seats behind them had been removed to make room for the two boxes that held the fake corpses. They had been stowed in a way which suspended them somewhat in air so if the plane made a sudden move up or down, left or right or had to bank sharply for some reason the crates would remain level and the contents would be protected from damage. It was an expert job by whoever the loadmaster was. So far so good they thought. About twenty minutes after they finished their drinks they felt the plane descend again, this time more rapidly than before.

"We're about to land gentlemen, please tighten your seat belts, the runway here is very short for such a big airplane and our pilot will be standing hard on the brakes as soon as we touch down, do not to worry though, we have flown in and out of here before." True to her word the plane had barely touched down when the pilot reversed the props on the engines then stood on the brakes. The plane shook violently for several seconds until it rolled to a stop then turned around and taxied back the way they had just come from on the ground to get fuel. The girls said goodbye and waited for the ramp to be rolled out to the plane by four men they could barley see

Then another woman climbed the stairs and the men could feel something being loaded onto the plane from outside. The petite young woman saw the wonder on their faces and said, "its alright gentlemen, it's only food and water being loaded and the bathrooms are being emptied for the long flight ahead of us and we are taking on extra fuel."

She was dressed in a light blue jumpsuit that covered all of her female features but the men noticed immediately how attractive she was. She had natural dark blond hair, brown eyes and appeared to be in her mid thirties and unmarried. At least she wasn't wearing any jewelry of any kind other than a complicated type of watch that the men couldn't make out at first. It was a type worn by paratroopers in the sixties that told not only the time but an altimeter to tell them how high in the air they were as they plummeted towards the ground.

"Is this our last stop before the States Miss?"

"Well yes but I'm not supposed to know any details but I happen to know this aircraft and they are adding fuel in the extra tanks where the cargo usually goes."

"What a fantastic idea, you could have an almost unlimited range," added Sol.

"Yes and this aircraft, although it isn't brand new, has the ability to go into smaller private airports where the really big jets can't go and her turbo prop engines are whisper quiet so unless you pour on the power to her she's quieter than most prop driven planes due to the extensive work done on improving her engines. These are not the factory installed engines but the latest thing in engine power quietness and safety. Any airport that can handle executive jets this one can land and take off from. This is so new they call it a STOL Aircraft, short take off and landing, every country in the world will soon want this technology for larger aircraft."

"Miss, can you tell us where we just took off from, I mean what Country?"

"Yes sir but you and I are not supposed to know in case we fall into enemy hands. Your first leg home on this trip originated in Afghanistan, then you landed in Pakistan where we just left from and the airstrip that you originally were at is in hostile hands right now in Afghanistan, now if that isn't confusing enough we are going to land very soon in Ankara Turkey where we will take on more fuel then we'll head for the states flying once again below radar. Its the land based radar we worry about and if we encounter any country's warship they may think we are a hostile aircraft and try to shoot us down but the captain has all the countries of the world I-D signals aboard and the captain will simply radio that we have lost an engine on their frequency and are attempting to restart it and are flying low just in case we have to ditch because we are low on fuel. As we cross date lines and veer away from certain countries the captain will tune to the country that we are flying close to so there can be no mishaps we hope. Anyway that is what's going on right now so strap yourselves in tightly because this is a small airport and the Officials have all been paid off so we can refuel to capacity then we'll head for the USA and please no more questions. I have told you much more than you need to know. The reason is if we are captured with the drugs they have today like truth serum, you would tell the enemy everything they wanted to know except things you didn't know. Please rest assured that your cargo is very safe aboard this aircraft.

Just so you know who I am, I used to be with the CIA before going independent and selling my services to the highest bidder that isn't hostile to our own country and I'm doing it with the knowledge of the White House but technically I don't exist if I am caught. My mission does not tell me who you are or what you are up to, only that you are U.S. Citizens and therefore entitled to my protection and cooperation as long as you don't break any Federal Laws."

"Whew Richard, what did you get us into, I've seen Russian vehicles and what I thought to be Israeli Vehicles, obviously Afghan marked vehicles and lord only knows how many others we have seen. Miss, I have to ask, are you armed?"

"Of course I am, you don't think I'd fly around these hostile countries bare naked without weapons do you?"

"Just had to ask, we're also armed if it makes you feel any better."

"It doesn't, I don't like it when civilians carry weapons and don't know how to use them effectively."

"I can assure you Miss, we're both experts with a gun of any kind, you're not dealing with a couple of rookies you know. We're used to being in control on our own turf, being out of our comfort zone makes us uneasy because we don't know who the enemy is. We were hired as you must know by a foreign country to spirit a couple of bodies away from their country due to an imminent take over of power. They are of great value to the Christian Faith, more than that I cannot tell you."

"Well for one thing I don't believe you, those are not bodies back there any expert could see through your subterfuge. They are secured in a way to cushion them from any dramatic change in the attitude of this aircraft like evasive maneuvers we may have to make."

"Ah perhaps, but it was only meant to fool the solders who were doing the loading and as for the ones who did the packaging of the material they are dead by now by order of the man who hired us. I have no idea of the value of what is in the crates and I could care less, they're going to a secure area only we know about, that's our part of the job."

"Are you guys new to the CIA or some other agency?"

"You could say its top secret, even the President doesn't know about it, at least not yet."

"I thought as much, neither of you are dressed for the part you are playing so I guessed you were trying to throw everyone off your trail."

"Pretty close but not quite right, but not a bad guess my dear." Just as he finished the sentence they felt the plane descending very quickly.

"Time to Land gentlemen, please hold on!" They all tightened their seat belts and held on tight. The plane hit with a thud and as before the pilot reversed the props and stood on the brakes almost at the same time, shortly afterward they rolled to a stop.

"Damn whoever is flying this thing knows their stuff alright, that was a great landing, very smooth." The landing almost jarred the men's teeth loose and they thought for sure that the plane would disintegrate before it stopped. They both gave a sigh of relief when it did.

"Say Miss," Sol asked, "you seem to know an awful lot about aircraft, are you also a pilot?"

"But of course, you'll discover the reason why when we get to our final destination." Sit tight now we'll be taking two more people on board very soon."

"May I ask why Miss?"

"Yes, we have several more hours of flying ahead of us. I will soon join the captain up front and we'll share flying duties so we can have bathroom breaks and we're taking on two professional flight attendants who are friendly military personal."

"How utterly convenient," answered Sol.

"Well yes you might say that, we're going to be taking a circuitous route away from and around hostile air space and soon we will have disappeared from everyone's radar that we don't want to see us. We'll soon be assumed lost in the mountains which we have already crossed. You can trust your captain because we know what we are doing, we have flown together many times before in and out of hostile areas where we were being shot at. The skin on this plane has been replaced here and there many times over. The fuselage has experimental Kevlar between the skin and us so not to worry even if we are stuck by bullets they can't penetrate the Kevlar."

"Well that does make me feel better, how about you Richard?"

He nodded at him but Sol could tell that this was way over his head and he hoped that his heart would hold out until they got back to Poughkeepsie and safe haven back at the Book Store.

"Gentlemen a word of warning when we're in the air, I would keep your seat belts fastened securely in case we have to take evasive maneuvers in case a ship below us decides that we are not friendly and fires a missile at us. We have defensive measures on board but sometimes it is best to out maneuver something rather than to tip your hand at your protection."

"Yes ma'am, warning duly noted, we were not expecting all this attention."

"Well whatever it is you are carrying, someone else wants it back really bad."

"That we don't know, we've dealt with only one man, even I don't know his identity."

Soon the refueling and everything else was completed and at the very last minute two young ladies climbed the stairs and stepped into the cabin where they were seated. They were wearing desert tan jumpsuits like the military wore but less all of the markings to identify the branch of service they were in. Their hair was cropped short and tied in the back with a small rubber band and they could almost be twins except for the difference in the color of their hair. One had soft light brown hair and the other one had fire engine red hair, it was natural as well.

"Gentlemen, please do not ask these ladies any questions other then when you want something to drink or eat. They will be serving the two of us up front, the two flight engineers and themselves as well so service should be fast and smooth and before I forget if you have to use the restroom either in the back or the front please sit down and put on the seat belt that is attached to the toilet there just in case we have to maneuver the aircraft rather quickly to avoid a missile or another aircraft. They have their instructions and they are also armed so please behave yourselves." She went into the cockpit and disappeared. Sol and Richard eyed the two young ladies and the ladies sized them up as well. Neither of them spoke, just smiled at the men and moved up forward and turned two seats around that were on a swivel apparatus that they hadn't noticed earlier.

CHAPTER - 89

What Sol and Richard couldn't see in the dark was the plane they were on was a military version of the C130 cargo aircraft the Air Force and Army were using at this time. The company that owned the plane bought it then stripped it completely and outfitted it to look like a stubby kind of Airliner that had been cut short and made to look fat. It had the fiberglass nose of an airliner and the back portion which covered the ramp that could be lowered in flight was only a fiberglass shell that could be jettisoned at anytime in flight or on the ground. It was enough to fool most people in that it was just a funny looking kind of Airliner and they gave little thought about its use. Fooling people just long enough to land, refuel and take off again was all they needed. Officially this airplane didn't exist anywhere. Inside the aircraft had the men completely fooled, it was fashioned just like any other Airliner of the day with a beautiful decor with comfortable extra wide seating with plenty of leg room for passengers. The bulkhead in front of the aircraft could have been one of many Airline Companies, it was generic. What was different was the performance of the plane. It was a go anywhere anytime anyplace kind of an aircraft. They left Turkey behind and were soon out over the Mediterranean Sea but at a very low altitude. They were headed home and that's all the men thought about. The plane performed flawlessly for hundreds of miles.

Suddenly the plane made an abrupt turn and decent then another turn and they looked out the window to see a missile flying by only a few feet away from the airplane, or so it seemed. The plane stood on its side to the left and then again to the right as another missile flew past them on the other side of the aircraft that looked like the a telephone pole painted white.

"Who the hell is shooting at us," asked Sol?

There was no answer. Soon a voice they recognized as the lady who had flown in the back with them spoke over the intercom. Sorry about that folks but that fishing trawler beneath us didn't believe our signals, we think its Russian but we can't be sure, she flies no flag and has no markings on the ship. Anyhow we are out of range for now, she may have another warship nearby however so be prepared for more defensive measures. If you would like something to eat go ahead, we're hungry up here as well. The girls will take care of you two first then it will be our turn. You'll have to ask them what they have to eat for a menu, we don't hand them out on this economy type of a flight." They could hear her giggling to the captain who they had yet to see or meet. The two young ladies approached Richard and Sol and spoke in almost perfect English but it was obvious to the men that they were multi lingual. They asked first if they wanted breakfast, lunch or dinner then went through what was available on the menu for whatever meal they chose. Richard ordered the roast beef dinner complete with potatoes and carrots, rolls and butter and it sounded so good Sol said he would have the same but he preferred green beans as a vegetable. The men had no idea it was breakfast time and not dinner time due to the datelines they crisscrossed with time changes.

The pilots both ordered breakfast. As soon as the girls had served everyone they sat down up in front with their tray tables and giggled quietly as they ate their eggs, bacon, hash brown potatoes, toast and jelly. The two men passed it off as a private joke but they had missed two meals over all and had made do with sandwiches which weren't all that palatable but the food on the plane they found to be delicious. Before they knew it the two flight attendants were coming back to pick up their plates and asked them if they'd like something more to drink. They ordered a scotch and water on ice which they were served again with giggles because of the time of day it was to them. They paid them no mind as the plane droned on and on. It wasn't long before they laid their seats back and fell fast asleep, they had been on the go for just over 60 hours now but didn't realize it.

After several more hours of flying the flight attendant who had been back there with them for a while came back and asked them where they would like to land. Sol said as close to Poughkeepsie New York as possible and a man would meet them when they landed but he had to know where and what time to tell them to come pick them up. "

"Yes of course we can do that but we'll be coming in over Canada at a very low altitude but we'll need a favor from you?"

"Okay shoot, what is it you need?"

"A couple thousand gallons of military grade fuel for turbo prop engines, can one of you arrange for a truck to be high jacked, we certainly can't go through channels now can we?"

"Have you a phone I can use that is secure and I do mean secure?"

"Of course there's a phone right in front of you to use."

"Yes I know, but is it secure is what I'm asking?"

"Yes of course, otherwise I wouldn't tell you to use it," the stewardess said sternly. Sol picked up the phone and made a few calls. Then Sol asked the big question as to where and how soon do you need it?

She looked at her watch then reset it; "let's see eastern standard time right now is 1:30 pm, can you tell them that we'll need it at approximately 3:10 pm?"

"Damn, that's short notice, I didn't know we were that close to home."

"We're not but in an hour and a half we could make up a lot of time with a short cut along the mountain ranges using the terrain following radar."

"What kind of radar?"

"Terrain following radar, it allows us to follow the variations in the ground, you know like over hills and through valleys without bumping into a mountain, a thing like that could ruin your day, it's the latest thing in experimental radar on Military airplanes."

"I'll see what I can do;" and Sol made another call. "My guy says he might be able to make it around 3:30 but not much sooner."

"Okay I'll tell the captain to slow down some, give this number to your man and tell him to call when he knows the exact time, we can speed up or slow down and meet the exact time, the less time we are on the ground the better."

"Alright, consider it done," said Sol.

"Now when you find out the exact time call me and I'll come back here so you can tell me then we'll try to match it. Tell him we'll be at the abandoned Poughkeepsie Airport that's on our map. Now then, do your people know where the airport in question is?"

"Yes, it's the old airport, a new one has been built but I haven't flown out of there yet."

"You better make sure because once we have our fuel on board the aircraft I'll be taking this baby off myself and flying her back to Jordan."

"Jordan, why Jordan?"

"Because they own this aircraft."

"Oh I see, that's okay I was just wondering how you were going to get back is all."

"We have airports where we can stop and refuel on the trip home; our job was to get you this far and dump you on your doorstep and that's all!"

"Oh? Okay, I think I follow you now." Sol wasn't sure now if she had been telling the truth at all about who she was or who she worked for. Why would she be flying one of Jordan's own aircraft if she worked for the U.S. Government. It was beginning to confuse him now.

"It's also vitally important that you don't stay at the airport too long yourselves; the authorities will have helicopters in the air looking for the fuel truck once its reported missing, that's why we can't linger on the ground, we have to be in and out as quickly as possible."

"Very good, I understand now, I've never dealt with anything that had to move as fast as an airplane. Trucks, busses and trains are more up my alley, those I can time down to the smallest degree of probability and everything works out okay, I mean look at me I'm sixty five years old and have been making my living on the edge all these years."

"Yes and you're none the worse for wear, you look too good to be that old."

"Well thank you kindly my dear."

She went back up the isle to the cockpit. Sol called the store and gave the news to Greta to have his van brought round to the old abandoned airport by 3:15, he didn't want to wait until the last minute, better the van was waiting for them than for them to have to wait for it. Then he had a last minute thought, he called Greta back and told her to have whoever was picking them up to throw in the bench seat for the van, there would be Sol and Richard and whoever drove the van who would have to ride back in it so they would need the extra seat. It was finally done. It was out of his hands now and in the hands of others. They only had to wait for the plane to touch down. Sol had time to contemplate, just how many pilots are on this aircraft he was wondering.

At exactly 3:29 the plane touched down, the pilot reversed the props then stood on the brakes and it felt like they skidded to a stop. It was an all grass runway and the grass was dry and hadn't been cut lately, they would be lucky if the grass didn't catch fire during the unloading of the packages and the transfer of gas from the fuel truck in the process. The pilot shut down the engines and let the dust settle some and was wondering where the fuel truck was when they saw a tractor trailer hurtling down the street. It crashed through double the gates of the eight foot high chain link fence and headed straight for the airplane. It had a red and white cab and a shiny aluminum trailer. The driver pulled up, jumped out and hollered up to the pilot; "someone call for a special fuel mixture for a turbo prop?"

The pilot pointed to the fill point on the left wing and the driver got up on the wing, put the nozzle of the hose in and started pumping. He hollered up from the ground; "she won't take no five thousand gallons Captain"

The pilot hollered back and pointed below the wing to another point and said, "auxiliary tanks, under the fuselage," he nodded and kept on pumping.

When both the wing tanks were full he opened the cap on the other tank where the pilot had pointed to and began emptying his truck of fuel.

"Got you a total of three thousand five hundred gallons okay,?" the truck driver hollered.

The pilot nodded and now Sol and Richard were off the plane and wondering where the van was when it came from around the other side of the plane and pulled up near them. A young man jumped out and Sol recognized that it was Justin, another young man from the store.

"Justin, you made good time, everything ready that I asked for?"

"Yes sir, the extra seat is in and we're ready to load up."

"Who is we, I only asked for one person."

"Well Greta thought you might need some help with the packages so I brought Mike with me, a friend of mine, I hope you don't mind, this is all very exciting you know."

"Yes I know, alright use the ladder that's being put down for you hop up onto the airplane, there are two large crates, bring them down the ladder as quickly and carefully as you can please, the contents are extremely fragile."

After he climbed up into the plane and hefted one of the crates he called out to Sol, "my goodness, they aren't all that heavy Mr. Devine."

"Yes I know, the wood in the crates are probably heavier than what is in them. Load them in the back in the van, we must hurry this plane is about to leave and we've got to get away from the prop's exhaust. They got the second crate loaded and here came the truck driver trotting over to them.

"I'll need a ride Sol, the truck stays here but I'm not staying with it."

Sol grinned and pointed to the van, "climb in Arthur you've earned a ride back with me."

CHAPTER - 90

Soon the van was loaded and everyone was in a seat. There was Sol, Richard, Justin, Mike and Arthur, the fuel truck driver, who all needed a ride back to the store. Sol let Justin get in to drive and as Sol was getting in he heard someone from behind him clearing their throat. He turned to look and there was a strikingly beautiful young woman with light olive colored skin who looked well tanned with almost coal black eyes grinning at him wearing a blue jumpsuit with pilots wings holding a medium size flight bag that held several changes of clothes in it.

"Where do I sit sir?"

He looked at her and said "where did you come from?"

"I was you're pilot, I the Princess from Jordan, my father is the King of Jordan, didn't they tell you your packages would be valuable?"

"Well yes of course ma'am but no one said anything about a female coming along that I remember let alone a princess!"

While they were talking she urged them to get going; "Please, we must get away from the airplane, she will be leaving quickly and you don't want to be back here when she fires up those engines, our two engineers loaded two JATO bottles onto the sides of the airplane as well." JATO stood for Jet Assisted Take Off. It helps planes take off quickly from smaller airfields or from the water like sea planes.

The two in the back seat suddenly said together; "she can sit on my lap Sol."

Sol helped her into the back seat and onto Richards lap and the van pulled slowly away from the airplane just as the female pilot fired up the engines and the hot exhaust caught the grass on fire behind them.

"Wave her on Justin, wave her on quickly;" Sol was hollering from the back seat. The fire was spreading with a little help from a light breeze. The plane seemed to stand still, not moving at all as the fire crept close to the wing then the pilot noticed the smoke blowing past her window from behind and knew exactly what she had to do, she gunned the engines, taxied down the field where she would have to turn the plane around and take off into the wind right through the fire. She did just that. As pretty as a picture the plane lifted off with the help of the two JATO bottles she fired up as they took off right through the burning grass. The plane seemed to leap into the air from the burning runway and into the sky then soon disappeared from sight.

The Driver of the fuel truck Arthur then spoke up, "Sol you had better get this thing moving and fast, when the fire reaches that tanker she's going to blow even though there isn't much fuel in her she's full of fumes and she will blow sky high. Lord only knows where the wreckage may land."

"You heard the man Justin get this thing moving and fast son!" They had all been marveling at the way the plane had taken off and weren't watching where the fire was headed.

"Yes sir Mr. Devine I'm on it but I got to go around this fence before we can get to the gate." The fire was now racing in their direction and Justin cleared the end of the fence and turned back to the right hard and headed for the demolished double gates and just as they passed over the flattened gates the fuel truck blew up and the concussion from the explosion almost tipped the van over and now the entire airport was now on fire.

"Use back streets son, do you know your way back to the store from here?"

"Yes sir, I was born near here, its no problem. I know you want to avoid the police and fire trucks, I'll get us all back in one piece." Just as he finished that sentence the wrecked cab of the fuel truck crashed down nearly on top of them landing ultimately right in front of them.

Instinctively all of them covered the faces with their hands in case they crashed into the burning pieces of debris that had been the cab of the truck. Justin whipped the wheel hard one way and then back the other but was careful no to upset the two crates in the back enough to damage the lost books which they had packed newspapers tightly around to act as a cushion. They went past the almost unrecognizable burning cab like it was walk in the park. "No sweat sir, this baby handles like a race car." They drove the rest of the way in silence, each person alone with their own thoughts. Sol was now thinking; what have I gotten myself into, a Princess and a King looking over my shoulder? When they were driving past some of the streets that led to the old Airport Fire Trucks were driving past a block away led by Police Cars in the opposite direction.

"Whew;" Sol said as he exhaled some extra air, "that was a close call!"

"You Americans know nothing of close calls;" piped up the Princess. "You and your people though are to be commended for what you have done these past few days though. I don't know when I have ever seen a more complicated operation go any smoother."

"Thank you Princess. Listen are you supposed to be staying with me, I mean us, are you in some kind of exile or something and where did those two men come from, I didn't see them on the plane?"

"No, father just wanted me out of the country because there is trouble brewing in the area among the Israelis, Syria, Jordan, Afghans and there are others, many others involved not excluding the Untied States and Russia's involvement to answer your first question and secondly the guards as you called them were in a room behind the cockpit, they are both trained navigators, flight engineers and mechanics and are well qualified as my personal body guards. They had orders to kill you both in case of treachery and we would return back to Turkey without you, anymore questions?"

"No ma'am!" He gave a hard look at Richard who just shrugged his shoulders. He was also amazed at the events now unfolding.

"As you saw when we left Afghanistan we were fired upon by rebels," said the Princess.

"Yes, so I saw from the airplane windows, the fight looks as though its already started."

"That is correct. If it will make you feel better Sol, I am a Colonel in the Air Force of Jordan, I can fly nearly anything with wings on it and I am fluent in several languages. I hold a Doctorate from a University here in America in Political Science and a Masters in Engineering also from the States. My father saw to it that his children all got a good education; we are not the backward country some think us to be."

"Even I can see that Miss; what do I call you anyway, I can't go around calling you Princess this and that very well now can I? We'll blow your cover."

"We know about your Store and your great accomplishments in the preservation of books and Documents, that's why father chose you to do this operation for us."

"Richard I have a feeling you're holding something back from me."

"Honestly Sol, I knew nothing about this, all I did was arrange for us to pick up the two crates through another party, I had no idea of this complication, nothing was mentioned about a woman and or a Princess Pilot to boot."

"He speaks the truth;" the Princess offered, "father heard about this and decided it was time for me to go underground as you people say. Why not put me to work in your store and you can call me Susan Prentiss and say I am from somewhere in Ohio. I promise to be a good girl."

"But your dark skin color, won't people know that you're from out of the Country?"

"Not if you keep them straight. My parents could have had some Middle East Ancestry in their background and you could say and that I was born here right in the U.S. in Ohio."

"Okay I know when I'm whipped, I can set you up with an identity and an apartment in our building, I have a couple vacancies."

"Yes, we knew all that before you got onto my airplane."

"Your airplane, but I thought!"

"Do not think, you are out classed when it comes to National Politics of this magnitude. The airplane you were in is my personal plane, just like you Americans own several cars we own several airplanes of different sizes and descriptions."

"Okay I know when I'm licked, I'll turn you over to Greta and she'll show you the ropes, take us home Justin."

"Yes Sir Mister Devine, right away."

"Oh and Justin, you and your friend didn't see or hear any of this conversation."

"But sir, what conversation, I've been busy driving and my friend Mike is giving me directions, right Mike?"

"Uh yeah, right, what were we talking about anyway?"

"We were talking about how nice the weather has been."

"Right; gotcha Justin!" The two of them shared a rollicking laugh. What they did not realize was that their lives depended on their keeping quiet about what had just taken place. The two boys were completely unaware about what was going on overall. One slip up by either one of them would seal there fate permanently and their bodies would never be discovered. They still haven't found Jimmy Hoffa and a lot of people were looking at Sol. After many side streets and detours they finally arrived back at the store. Sol had the boys unload everything and put the crates in the basement with Fred.

"Arthur, I thought you said on the phone you were bringing five thousand gallons of fuel, how come you only brought thirty five hundred gallons?"

"I took what I could get my hands on Sol with such short notice, be happy that I got here at all, its not easy stealing a big fuel truck rig you know even when its only partially full."

"I got it now Arthur, thank you. I know that size of truck it would hold at least ten thousand gallons of fuel."

Arthur would receive a letter in the mail in a couple of days giving him an account number with five thousand dollars in it with Sol's thanks and the King of Jordan would pay for it because without his help the airplane and the rest of them could have been caught by the authorities. Sol sent Justin to give a ride home to his friend Mike and Arthur, the driver of the fuel truck.

When the operation was over Richard and Sol cleared almost exactly one million five hundred thousand dollars apiece for their services. Richard couldn't have been happier, he had never seen so much danger and action in all his life. Sol and Richard would take their girlfriends on an around the world cruise to celebrate their latest caper. Fred stayed behind this time but he knew his time would come whenever he decided it was his turn to take some time off. Someone had to mind the store was what Fred always said when Sol would take off. Fred was only too happy to stay where he was the happiest and that was with his work. When all was said and done Sol and Richard had been gone for seventy three and a half hours, it was the quickest whirlwind trip they would ever make together.

CHAPTER - 91

At FBI Headquarters everyone was still busy with their own files and Agent Jefferies had a question. "Jane, have you got a minute?"

"Sure Dick, what do you have in mind?"

"One thing I want our people to check more closely; I've been thinking about those rubbers our killer wore over his shoes, I want everything re-checked for any shoe prints or the prints left by the rubbers. I'm thinking this guy went to a lot of trouble to throw us off track with different shoe prints even the depth of the prints in mud or soft dirt where he had to be wearing some type of weights around his middle to appear heavier than he really is just like the difference in his height and hair descriptions that we have received from different witnesses, none of them match. Somewhere along the line he is going to run out of disguises and will have to reuse them and we'll be there with the different descriptions to catch him. I want our people to go through them over and over until we have a mental picture of this guy. Then I'll need a forensic artist who can draw a description of each disguise and they will need to be in color to see the different hair colors. What I'm getting at is that he probably doesn't have a huge assortment of wigs, hair pieces or skull caps, this guy could be completely bald anyway and we'll need a rendering of that.

Now judging from the length of time this guy has been out there killing people I'm also guessing that he's between fifty five and sixty five years old. I want this guy on ice before he retires otherwise we may never catch him. Now one thing more because I want to get this all out to every single branch of the

F.B.I. as soon as possible I want a rush put on this! Are you going to be able to help me or are you tied down with another file?"

"No, I can drop what I'm doing, I've been working on the wall map with another Agent checking and rechecking reports that we may have missed and trust me, these departments around the country have dropped the ball and really messed up some crime scenes in an attempt to quickly close a case. Instead of digging deeper they took the obvious route which is what our perp. wants them to do. Let me make a call to personnel and see about an artist for us. I'm sure there has to be a good one in the building somewhere but I don't know of any personally and I think we're on the right track with this. You never cease to amaze me Dick, this is the best idea yet, we've been stuck going through files and haven't had time to think things through."

Jane picked up her phone. In just under an hour she had the names of three outstanding artists who could do this kind of work. She quickly narrowed it down to the one closest to FBI Headquarters and it was a woman in Virginia a little over a hundred miles away. While she had been on the phone Dick had gone out to talk with some of the other Agents about what they had found that may be new. Jane found him near their huge wall map. "Dick, I've got a possible in Virginia and the closest to Headquarters, do you want to give her a call?"

"Who does she work for now?"

"She's an independent contractor Forensic Artist who goes around the Country assisting other departments with the similar problems, I read her file on our computer and she sounds like the best bet for what we need. She works with color as well as black and white like traditional artists use for the authorities who employ her."

"Alright Jane, why don't you give her a call and stress that we need her as soon as she can get here and tell her to use the underground parking garage then call Donny and tell him when she will be arriving and give him a description so he will know she belongs here."

"You're skipping channels Dick, we could get hot water over this, she should go through the front door and get her temporary visitor I D like everyone else."

"I know, we'll take her up front ourselves and get her a temporary I D once we have a chance to talk to her, if she doesn't work out we'll just send her home, okay?"

"Sure thing Dick, I know the pressure you're under, don't forget we're partners in this."

"I know Jane; I'm still upset about all those innocent people in New Mexico."

"I understand Dick, but you can't let it get to you, you'll lose your effectiveness as a Detective if you do."

"I can't help it, I'm only human like you and don't you tell me that it doesn't get to you as well."

"I got it Dick, trust me I got it! Let me call this woman and see if she is still unattached and can get here soon." Jane left Dick staring at the map and went back to their office.

Twenty minutes later she had her answer. She went to find Dick again. He was with the lab people going over some photos of shoe prints they had been able to get pictures of from some of the crime scenes. "Agent Jefferies, I have your answer, she can be here tomorrow afternoon about 3:00 if that's alright with you."

"That's fine Agent Marlowe we'll try and be ready for her by then and see what she can do for us. What about lodging for her?"

"We'll cross that bridge if she says yes, if she can do what we're asking of her. We have a couple empty suites for Federal witnesses at the Hotel just up the street, we can put up her in there until we can arrange for another room for her if need be."

"Okay, I like that suggestion, did you call Donny yet?"

"No, I think its better that you call him about mid morning tomorrow and I'll tell you what kind of car she is driving and I have a photo on the computer that I can have copy off and give to him so he can be on the look out for her and in the meantime I'll call her back and give her directions to get here and who to ask for."

"Okay Agent Marlowe, thank you for everything."

"Something else is troubling you isn't it Agent Jefferies, may I ask what it is?"

"Yes Agent Marlowe, I still feel like we're missing that one piece of the puzzle and I can't put my finger on it. I'm going to spend the day out here among the lab techs and our Agents in hopes I can figure it out by listening to them and hear the latest information they have uncovered instead of waiting for their reports."

"Okay Agent Jefferies, I'll be in our office if you need me.

"I need you more than you could know;" he said very quietly under his breath.

"What was that, I didn't quite get it, something about needing something?" asked Agent Marlowe.

He leaned over closer to her ear and whispered, "I need you Agent Marlowe." He straightened up when he saw the look on her face. She had the look of surprise and shock and she wondered herself if she had heard him right. She turned around and headed back to their office to call the female artist back and tell her to come in as soon as she could. After she got off the phone for the last time she began to mull over in her mind what Dick had whispered in her ear and tried to figure out what he meant by it; he had never tried to made a pass so she was confused by what he had said and just how he had meant it. Finally she let it go and went back to re-checking files for tidbits of information someone may have overlooked.

The next day at 3:15 in the afternoon Donny called their Office to say he was letting in the woman they were waiting for, her name was Lisa Browne. Jane took the call and went to find Dick who wasn't far away.

"Agent Jefferies our Artist is here, come along and we'll go meet her."

"You go ahead she's probably some old prune faced woman in her sixties."

"Oh alright, you're an old stick in the mud when it comes to meeting new people, I'll go on without you." She took off for the back door and met the woman as she came in through the door that Donny opened for her. She was a remarkably gorgeous woman and her file said she was thirty six years old, divorced, had fifteen years experience as a forensic artist and could draw faces for bodies that were just a pile of bones and make them out of modeling clay to a very close likeness of the deceased person if and when an I D was made and someone came up with a picture. In the world of forensic science in her field she was number two in the Nation and the FBI had used her before in kidnap cases where the victim had been killed and she helped bring the murderer to justice. She looked to be about five feet eight inches tall just like her file said, she had shoulder length auburn hair, brown eyes that sparkled in the light and a perfect figure that most men would rate a ten any day of the week, a real head turner. Jane knew right away there may be trouble because there were several unmarried men in the lab and among the other

Agents who she would be working with so it may be hard to get them to keep their minds on their work and she hoped that it didn't affect Dick too much because he was single as well. Secretly Jane had a crush on Dick but she kept it to herself, now she felt threatened by this new youthful body and face. Jane walked straight up to her and extended her hand. "Good afternoon Miss Browne, I'm Special Agent Marlowe, we spoke on the phone yesterday, I'm so happy to see you, we really do need your help and insights into a problem we have."

Miss Browne took the offered hand and said; "it's good to finally meet you. I'm glad the FBI has seen fit to hire women in a traditionally male area of Law Enforcement."

Uh oh Jane immediately thought, we're going to have a problem with her male chauvinistic ideas. "Won't you follow me please, I'll introduce you around then we'll have to find a place for you to work."

"This whole place has the sterile look of a laboratory."

"That's because it is and this is where you'll find our problem and its in theory only and that's the easy part." She took her to every station and introduced her to the lab folks and then found the other six Agents who were hovering near the wall map, then she went to find Dick who had disappeared now altogether, she found him back in their office.

"Miss Browne this Special Agent Jefferies, he and I are partners working on this case by order of the Director, between us we'll explain what the problem is. Dick Miss Browne, Miss Browne, Special Agent Jefferies."

Dick stuck his hand out to shake her hand as if she were a man and his mouth was agape as he looked up and if his jaw dropped another inch they'd have to help him up off the floor. He regained his composure and stuttered just to say hello. Finally he blurted out; "pleased to make your acquaintance Miss Browne."

They had both over looked the fact that they had no place for her to work, something would have to be worked out but where was the question, every square inch of the lab and surrounding areas had been taken up with the extra Agents assigned to help Dick and Jane.

"Jane would you like to explain to Miss Browne what it is we are looking for and what the problem is, in the meantime if she works out we'll need to create a space for her to work in."

"If you think I'm working down here in this male infested environment you call a lab you're sadly mistaken Agent Jefferies!"

Uh oh, she's done it now Jane was thinking; Dick will certainly throw her out on her ear. She doesn't realize who she is talking to, he could be the new Director at any given moment. Dick's face grew beet red and Jane thought for sure he would throw her out right now. Dick sat back down in his chair and composed himself. He folded his hands and put them on the top of the desk and said; "Obviously Miss Browne we have made a mistake, we thought you were a professional like the rest of us here who don't give a rat's ass whether their partners are male or female. We all work together and fraternization is strictly forbidden and if you don't like what you see then perhaps it is best for all around that you leave right now. This person over here is Special Agent Jane Marlowe, around here she's called just plain Marlowe or Agent Marlowe, we don't concern ourselves whether one is male or female, we are professionals of the highest caliber and if you don't like it then I suggest you leave right now. And one more thing for the record I am Special Agent Jefferies and everyone down here calls me that, not Richard, not Dick, do you understand the meaning of professionalism at all Miss Browne?"

"Of course I do, just who do you think I am?" She stood there with her hands on her hips with a better than you attitude which Dick didn't cotton to either.

"Well obviously you have never worked with the FBI before or you would know how to address people and converse with them with respect."

"Uh Miss Browne before you answer him I should tell you that Agent Jefferies is the Boss down here and I do mean the 'Boss' end of quotes and if you would care to take your prejudices up with the Director of the FBI he himself will have you thrown out of here on your ear instead of kicking your butt down the street."

"Perhaps the two of you misunderstood me, all I meant was is this is a male place of employment, I see no women around here anywhere."

"Well that's probably because to work down here is the highest of achievements anyone can rise to. Only the finest minds in our business are down here and extremely happy to be working here together as well. Now you have two choices, work with us as we are and don't disrupt our work but instead help us catch the perp. we're after. When you're done down here you may leave at any time. In fact as of this minute we have no place for you to even sit down.

Agent Jefferies pulled some really big strings to get you here and all you have done is to bitch and complain so far. Am I clear on what I am saying and as far as the chain of command in this entire building you're looking at number two and number three in the entire FBI Organization in the world?" She gestured towards Dick when she said number two and pointed to herself as number three. "What did you expect a fully furnished office bigger than anyone else's here? This office we are in both Agent Jefferies and myself share. This is the phone that I called you from, there are six other Agents out there who don't even have an office and they all work together, is any of this getting through to you?" asked Jane.

"Yes of course it is, what you're saying is that you're underfunded, underpaid and frustrated as hell."

"Get her out of here Agent Marlowe, I'm afraid we wasted out time on this one, she probably couldn't draw a picture of a rabbit let alone a human face from the descriptions of witnesses."

"Now you wait just a minute there Dickey!" said Miss Browne.

"That's it Agent Marlowe get her out of here and now! I've had it with trying to work around her, she isn't fit to be among the lowest of the low around here, she's not fit to sweep the floor. Get her out of here and now damn it!" He was standing up and pointing to the door of their office, his face flushed tomato red, the veins on his forehead were turning blue as well.

"Well you've done it now Miss, you'll probably never work for any law enforcement agency anywhere ever again, you've really made him mad. I've never once seen him loose his temper, you'd best leave the way you came in."

"Can he really keep me from ever getting hired anywhere again?"

"Yes, I just told you he's number two here, you can't get much higher up than that. He's next in line to be Director and if something happened to him then I would be next in line, am I not clear on that? All he has to do is to put a note in your file on the computer that you were dismissed before being hired on grounds of chauvinism and insubordination, those two words will haunt you forever. You're one stupid woman, I've never met anyone quite like you."

"I'm sorry, what can I do to make it up to the both of you?"

"Nothing, I wouldn't blame Agent Jefferies if he blackballed you across the board, one word is all it takes to ruin your career and all I know is that you're one hell of an artist and we desperately need your help and Agent Jefferies, like I mentioned, went way out on a limb to get you here because frankly we're desperate for help from a person like you. People are dying out there because of your stupidity over men, just who the hell do you think you are? On second thought come with me right now and that's an order, you don't belong here or anywhere else but there is someone I want you to meet right now!"

CHAPTER - 92

Jane went outside with Miss Browne who was on the verge of tears after being chewed out by her. She went looking for Donny. "Donny, could you come over here please, this lady needs to know a few things about Agent Jefferies, she's confused and thinks he's a jerk."

"When you are done Miss Browne there are two choices and now I'm sticking my neck out! You can come back in and apologize to everyone including Special Agent Jefferies or you can get in your car and crawl back into whatever hole you came out of, understood?"

"Yes, but I don't know what any of this can change. I blew it and I know it but I've had some bad experiences around men."

"Did you ever stop to think that maybe you're the problem and not the men, how dumb are you? I could understand maybe if you were a blond but you aren't and your references were great, why blow it?"

"Oh I don't know; I just can't stand men in power I guess."

"Did you ever think that maybe people like Jefferies deserve to be where they are?"

"Never gave it a thought, all men are pigs."

Jane didn't say a word, by now she was fuming and her face flushed just as red as Jefferies had done. She turned around abruptly on her heel and went back inside to her work and colleagues. She left the woman in Donny's hands.

Donny didn't say a word just yet, he asked her to follow him. They went to a small building which served as Donny's office in the parking lot. He sat her down and asked her to just listen. He went all the way thorough his story of how he and Dick used to be partners and what he had done for him and his family when the FBI was about to kick him out because of his disability due to the loss of his leg. When he finished he said to her; "I guess you can leave now, I know Jane wanted me to tell you my story. Agent Jefferies nearly lost his job by going to bat for me and my family, so think what you will but that man in there is a saint and everyone knows it. I don't know what your problem is Miss Browne, but you've made the biggest mistake of your life, that man went out on a limb for you and you threw it away because you don't like men! All the Agents in that building owe something to Agent Jefferies for their being there at all. Without him some of them wouldn't even have a job, he goes above and beyond anything that's expected of him. Right now he's working on a case that is driving them all bonkers and I can't help them. All I can do it is to be here for them when they need someone to talk to.

I do know that two weeks ago this serial killer we're looking for took the lives of eleven people, died at the killer's hands for no reason whatsoever, two couples and a family of five and two more men in a truck who never did any harm to anyone. Then a few days later the Fire Marshall died, he too was murdered and if it hadn't been for Dick no one would have known, just so the killer could cover his tracks he killed them and you just threw a pile of shit in their faces before they could tell you why it was so important to them for you to be here. Lord only knows how many more will die now because you don't like men!"

She finally lost it completely, through her tears she asked; "why didn't someone tell me?"

"Did you give anyone a chance to tell you or did you have diarrhea of the mouth because you had a bad time with a man?"

"I never gave them a chance." She broke down completely now and cried uncontrollably. "What will I to do now?"

"Agent Marlowe told you that you had one chance and one chance only. I don't know exactly what was said in there but you must have been a first class bitch to piss off Agent Marlowe the way you did."

"I made an ass out of myself, I can see that now, I was a dumb blond with auburn hair at the time, but I'll do anything, say anything to set things right."

"That won't do Miss, I can tell you that because even I know its not coming from the heart, just think about all those people who have already died, you didn't give them a chance either and then there are those yet to die because of your petty bullshit about men."

Donny walked away from his small office in disgust and left her there crying her eyes out. About twenty minutes later he looked back and she was gone. Her car was still there but she wasn't. What he didn't know was that she went around to the front of the building and came in the right way saying she had an appointment with Agents Jefferies and Marlowe and that she was expected. The woman at the counter called downstairs and verified the appointment and said alright I'll send her right down with her temporary I D badge. Then Agents Marlowe and Jefferies waited to see what would happen next. Miss Bowne had gone through the proper channels that Jefferies had skipped then went down to the basement to where the laboratory was. She walked boldly thorough the double doors and asked the first person she saw to direct her to one of them. Jane was the first one she ran into.

"I understand ma'am you are looking for a qualified forensic artist, is that correct?"

"Yes Miss that's what we're looking for!" Jane's voice was stern and hard and she stood with her arms crossed defiantly.

"Well I would like to apply for the position, here are my credentials," she handed Jane a file of her information which she had not taken in with her before with several of her artist renderings inside.

"Uh huh, yes I see, very good, Miss Browne was it?"

"Yes ma'am Miss Browne will be fine."

"Alright, come with me please." She led the way back to their office where Dick was sitting going over another one of their files.

"Agent Jefferies, a Miss Browne is here to see us, do you have moment?"

"Yes of course Agent Marlowe, please come in," he barely looked up.

They started over, she took the Professional path instead of the bossy aggressive one she had taken when she arrived.

"Uh huh, you must have talked to Donny, right Miss Browne?" asked Dick.

"Yes, he straightened some things out for me and I have decided to give you, or rather us a second chance."

"You do realize there will be no third chance and what I say is final?"

"Yes of course, I understand that you're in charge and I will have to answer to you both."

"Correct Miss Browne. I have gone over the file that we have on you in your absence on our computer and I saw nothing to show why you went into a tirade a little while ago, but it will not be tolerated again, am I clear on that?" asked Jefferies.

"Yes, it is very clear where I stand.'"

"You stand, Miss Browne, amongst the finest professionals in the business, no one here is treated any differently, we are all equal down here and we have one cause and that is to catch a mass murderer and nothing will stand in our way of catching him. Enough people have died already, we need it to stop here and now! That's why Agent Marlowe contacted you and no one else. Now if you wish you may start over and we'll see what we can do to meet your immediate needs but don't expect to have your own office, we're all cramped down here out of necessity because this is where the brain trust is. We have been tasked by the Director to do this and we'll do it come hell or high water, let the chips fall where they may. Anybody fails, they get reassigned no questions asked, nothing goes in their file and we work around the clock some days and go weeks without time off but we survive because we know this guy will kill again and again until we stop him and that's where you come in. We need to know what he looks like. We have several good descriptions of him and if you'll go out there in the lab and asked anyone for Tim he'll show you what we're up against and now if you'll tell me what you need I'll see what I can do to get some of it for you."

"Well hopefully there are things in the building that you can pilfer for me. First I'll need a drafting table that tilts and a light attached, any clamp on light will do, then I need a high stool or chair to sit on and the rest I have with me, so those things will do and I'm in business and you can put me anywhere, in a corner if you like facing the wall because I've been a bad girl." Dick and Jane both got a kick out of her pun and laughed half heartedly but laughed just the same, it helped to relieve the tension in the air.

"Leave those things to me; you and Agent Marlowe can look around for a suitable corner while I make some inquires around the building for what you need. I may have to go to a office supply store but I know exactly the things you're talking about, I took some drafting in College before I changed my major and went to the University."

"You actually went to school Agent Jefferies?"

"Yes Miss Browne, I have two degrees with a major in Criminology and theory."

"I didn't know they had criminology in schools as a major, I thought it was always OJT, On the Job Training."

The two girls laughed and went on their way to find room for Miss Browne, it was now apparent that she would fit in with her new attitude.

A couple of hours went by and a small but adequate space was found but the problem with it was it was behind a door and anyone opening the door would bump into the desk that Miss Browne would be using. Dick studied the problem for a few minutes while the two girls made trips to Miss Browne's car to bring in all of her accessories that she needed to work with.

Dick finally called maintenance and asked them to temporarily remove the door from its hinges as soon as it was determined that it wouldn't violate any fire or evacuation codes.

Miss Browne didn't waste any time getting her things set up then she went across the room to locate the tech. called Tim. She found him and got the information she needed and began to draw faces and bodies together from the descriptions from eye witnesses. She saw little of Dick or Jane catching only a glimpse of them as they talked to different agents around the room among the lab techs: It soon became clear to Miss Browne that every person in the huge room was entirely to busy to stop and talk amongst themselves let alone with her. Little did she know that Dick and Jane had called a meeting in Miss Browne's absence to tell them the importance of her work and not make small talk with her or bother her until she was done or they were asked a question by her for help in clarifying something with a description that she didn't agree with or worse didn't understand.

A week went and on a Tuesday morning Miss Browne went looking for Agent Jefferies and Marlowe. She found them in their office discussing propane tanks, explosives and the ratios needed to make them work together to cause a huge explosion and also the timeline to get away from the blast area so the killer was nowhere around when it blew up.

"Excuse me Agents Jefferies and Marlowe, I'm through with my preliminary sketches and would like to go over them with you."

"Yes of course Miss Browne, come in or would you rather we came to you?"

"No right here is fine," she laid six penciled sketches before them.

"You know it's a good thing I had a minor in engineering or I never could have gotten these sketches this close." They went over each and every one of them very carefully.

"Umm, these are awfully good Miss Browne."

"Thank you Agent Jefferies, I took every single description into account including your guess as to age and so forth. The biggest trouble I had was with the shoes for his feet. I have never seen a pair of elevated shoes and I sure could use a pair to go by, any ideas on that?"

"We ran into the same problem Miss Browne, I checked out all of the Manufactures of elevated shoes across the States and everyone of them said they only make one elevated shoe for people who have one leg that is shorter than the other, They seldom if ever make a complete pair except for the movie actors and those are a closely guarded secret to save embarrassment for the actors who are what they call height challenged. I couldn't even get them to lend me a pair. They claimed it would ruin their reputation if it ever got out and besides they make the actor's pants or pant suits as it were for the ladies, longer than usual to cover the elevated shoes. I even went so far as to ask them to make me several pairs and they said no, it was a trade secret so unless our guy is an actor he wouldn't have access to the shoes anywhere in the U.S."

"Mind if I take a shot at it Agent Jefferies?" asked Miss Browne.

"Why no, we welcome all the help we can get, what are you thinking?"

"Somewhere other than the Untied States perhaps the United Kingdom or somewhere else in Europe. You know even the Germans make excellent products like shoes, maybe I'll give them a look as well."

"What did you have in mind, calling Interpol?"

"That and I have a friend of a friend who is height challenged you might say, he plays a lot of sports except for basketball, they would probably call him down for cheating."

"Uh huh, I see your point, if we start snooping around Interpol it could get back to our guy and you're absolutely right to use other resources, we don't want to tip our hand just yet to the bad guy. Go ahead and use this phone if you like and close the door, I'd rather not know your sources in case we have to arrest one of them some day."

He laughed lightly and he and Agent Marlowe left their office and closed the door behind them so she could use their phone.

Two days later Dick got a strange call for Miss Browne, they asked to speak to Lisa only so they figured it had to be one of her contacts. They hated to count on a civilian in this way but they had little choice, if they rattled too many chains it was bound to get back to the bad guy.

CHAPTER - 93

The around the world cruise the men had taken with their girlfriends was about to be over and their ship was to dock in Los Angeles California after a tour of Alaska. They had departed from Ft Lauderdale Florida six weeks earlier and it had been a simply superb trip for them all. They hadn't really run into any bad weather, no Hurricanes or Typhoons, just really mild weather all round. They had some rain in Hawaii and some other tropical spots but it was of short duration and didn't dampen their spirits. Soon the ship docked, they disembarked and headed to the Los Angeles International airport, LAX for short, for their flight back to New York and then home. They hadn't deviated from their schedule one bit, really lucky in that respect for such a long cruise. Everyone knew they would be at the mercy of the weather and finicky tides when they reached some of the smaller Island chains. Every layover in ports were great and they had lots of time for shopping and taking in local cuisine. Sol never once went into a book store, this was a vacation and he meant to keep it that way.

They arrived in New York and BJ picked them up as planned, he was out of school for Spring Break for a week and decided to work instead of play, he knew he'd have plenty of time to play in the future. He picked them up at the baggage level of the airport, loaded their suitcases into the van and greeted the women by their first names then Richard and last Sol, just like a perfect gentleman would have done. Sol was so proud of him he thought he would burst.

BJ could hardly get a word in edge wise as the four of them rattled on and on about their fantastic around the world cruise. By the time BJ got them back to the store and unloaded the van he was beat. The four of them decided to spend the night in Sol's apartment then tomorrow Sol and Richard would take the ladies home to Buffalo.

Sol had to see Fred for a moment to let him know that he was back and say hello to his old friend and partner. He got a rather cool reception from Fred who appeared a little agitated. Sol shrugged it off and went upstairs to his apartment.

BJ went back to the store. He also had an apartment that Fred and Sol had set up for him to use anytime he was there.

The next morning Sol and Richard, with BJ's help, loaded the ladies luggage into the van and they left for Buffalo and home. He had a feeling that the trip for them was not quite over and he was right, Sol and Richard were gone two more days.

Finally on the fourth day Sol and Richard were back. They parked the van and brought in their overnight bags and settled back into a routine. Two days later Richard asked Sol if BJ could take him back to the airport that he really should check in at home. Sol agreed and BJ made another trip into New York City to the Airport.

The next day Sol was finally ready to get back to work. He went down to the basement to see his old friend and colleague Fred. "Fred my boy how have you been?" Sol asked in a jovial mood.

"Just fine Sol, but 'we' have a problem!" Fred said in a very serious tone of voice.

"Oh, what is it?"

"This stuff you brought back from Turkey or where ever you went is a lot of hooey."

"What are you saying, is it all fake?"

"On the contrary, one third of it is pure History and relates to the Bible but the rest is a reconstruction by others made from conversations and third party stories from still others and then it was put down in print and has been apparently re-copied over the years, even the paper is of a poor quality and the inks are atrocious. This is very amateurish work that we'll have to redo and re-work completely. I hope your man is ready to get a huge bill from us but once he gets it back in his hands he can write his own ticket, is he ready for that do you know? I mean he asked us to do this restoration and preservation work after all and someone has to pay for it!"

"No I don't know, I was led to believe that it was all in perfect order and condition but now we know that was a lie, he probably couldn't tell the difference but a second year student of religious archeology artifacts could tell they were mostly poor reproductions."

"That's pretty much it in a nut shell," said Fred. "I'm thinking your man only got to see a small portion of the real works and was never shown the poor quality junk and I doubt he would know the difference like you and I so I guess we can give him the benefit of doubt but I'd really like to know where he got his hands on this much work outside of a museum, none have reported such a find or a loss so I doubt that its been stolen. I think he truly believes he has found the missing pieces from the original Bible and is ready to die to protect it with his life. What I'd really like to know is if there is anymore of this that may have been overlooked by others."

"Me too Fred, I guess I'd better contact Richard and see what's up with him. Oh and before I forget, how is our Princess coming along in the store?"

"Oh Sol she is a real find, she has a gift of sharing with the customers some of her background and she's selling more books than you could ever imagine. People come in for a certain book and they leave with several books totally unrelated to what they came in for. They come in for mystery books for instance and leave with geography or history books. We're going to have to re-stock a lot of our books through legal channels just to keep up with her."

"Well I think that's great as long as she doesn't tip her hand and someone finds out who she really is; we could be in really big trouble! Now back to what we're going to do about the phony junk we brought back. Can any of it be salvaged by redoing the impossible and recreating the stuff on new paper using our ink and paper technology?"

"Yes of course it can but I wish we had the originals to work from, that's what I thought you brought back."

"I know, so did Richard and I. We had no idea that any other junk was mixed in with the originals, but when and if we redo it I don't think even the experts will be able to tell the difference if we take our time and do it right."

"First we need someone who knows Hebrew to help us out and that's what I worry about right now, the least little mistake we make in our translation could be our undoing and ruin us."

"Suppose we ask BJ and see if he knows anyone at school who might be in financial trouble that we could bail out who knows Hebrew or is studying Hebrew."

"Yeah Sol. but this is the Ancient Text we're talking about you know, not modern."

"Well it's worth a shot, let me see if I can find him, maybe he'll have an idea to bail us out of this mess."

"Okay, go ahead it can't hurt and we might just get lucky and he'll earn another gold star on his report card with us."

Sol left Fred in the basement and went up to his apartment to look for BJ and check with his schedule to see when he'd have to be back at school. He found BJ and he told Sol that he should leave tomorrow morning so he would be ready for school the next day after that. Then Sol told him what they needed and why. He confided in him to a point and made him swear not to tell anyone back at school, he passed it off as just needing help translating the Hebrew Language for a book. BJ said he'd give it a try and see what he could come up with. Sol went back to talk it over with Fred.

"Well Fred it will be a few more days before we have an answer, BJ is leaving in the morning for school so he'll have a little rest before school starts up again on Tuesday. He doesn't know of anyone right off hand but says he has a friend who might be able to help him out who is taking Theology at the University."

"At least it's a start Sol, all we can do is to hope he finds us someone who knows the old text language who can read and understand it."

"Exactly Fred, I'm going upstairs to check on the Princess then I'll call Richard and get on his case about the junk we brought back, but the thing is it still may be gold mine if we do it right and in the meantime he can check with his contact and see about the money end of this." Sol went back upstairs to the Store and found Susan, their Princess.

"Good morning Susan, how are you today?"

"I am fine Mr. Devine and how have you been, I heard you were on an around the World Cruise with Richard and your girlfriends?"

"I'm fine and the trip, well lets just say that it was a once in a lifetime experience for us all, we had a fantastic time. Listen, I've heard nothing but rave reviews about your work here at the store but you know you don't have to lift a finger around here, we'll take good care of you."

"I know but it would be so boring I couldn't stand it. I miss flying and getting out and having fun but I do enjoy helping your customers find books of interest."

"I understand that but we have to protect your real identity, if someone were to find out they would stop at nothing to find you and bring harm to you. By the way, how is your father?"

"He is in exile as of last Thursday in another Country, he wasn't able to tell me where but he is safe and waiting for the Civil War to be over so he can go back and reclaim his throne. Until then I am to remain here and be safe myself, there is always a chance the rebels could find me and kidnap me to use me as leverage to get to father and kill him. The rebel leader will stop at nothing to overthrow our way of government and then I'm afraid the Russians would have a foot hold in our Country and the entire country could go Communist and that would be disastrous for us all. Your Country, I understand, is helping my people resist but they can only do so much or we'll have World War III on our heads."

"Yes you're correct in that assumption Princess. We're all afraid of that happening, it wouldn't take much to set it off and we've come close before. If you need anything just let Greta or I know and you can always trust Fred in the basement and please call me Sol, everyone does."

"Alright Sol, thank you for all you have done, my father will show his appreciation when the time comes."

"Okay, well I need call my old friend Richard and see how he is as well. Oh and one more thing, how are your Hebrew language skills?"

"Slim to none Sol, sorry is it important?"

"No, think nothing of it." Sol knew she had limited knowledge about the lost books.

Sol left Susan and went back upstairs to his apartment to call Richard. He put the call through and soon had him on the line. "Richard my friend how are you?"

"I'm overjoyed Sol, I can't thank you enough for the cruise we had, I intended to pay my way and my girlfriend's as well, you really didn't have to absorb all the expense."

"Nonsense Richard, it will be on my tax return as payment for services rendered in some way, I have a great tax accountant, he's as crooked as a plate of over done spaghetti." Sol could hear Richard laughing in the background. "Seriously Richard, I do have a small problem that perhaps you can help me with." He went into great detail about the works they had brought back and the problems they were having with it.

"Sol, all I can do is to call my contact and explain what you have discovered, he will probably bounce from floor to ceiling because he swore to me that it was one hundred percent legitimate, he's probably going to be very mad at someone and I wouldn't want to be that person when he hears about it. I'll give him a call right away; can he wire money to the same account?"

"Yes, tell him any amount would help kick start us, we're looking at perhaps a year to a year and a half more work to pull this off an do it right."

"Okay Sol, I'll relay the message and see what happens."

Three more days went by without word from Richard. Then on the fourth day Sol's phone rang late one evening around 10:00 pm. when he was just about to go to bed with a new Unsolved Mystery Anthology. "Yes, hello?" he said in a gruff voice. "Oh Richard, it's you, I'd almost given up hearing back from you." Sol listened intently as Richard relayed message after message to him. "You don't say, really?" Richard went on to tell him all the details he had learned over the past several days. Sol finally hung up the phone after saying goodbye. He turned to his book once again, opened it up and began reading and before he knew it he was sound asleep with the lights on.

CHAPTER - 94

The next morning after breakfast Sol got dressed and went to the basement to see Fred. "Morning Fred, how are you this fine day?"

"Just fine Sol, finally hear from our friend did we?"

"Yes as a matter of fact he called late last night and relayed several messages."

"Anything of any interest to us?"

"Yes actually, there is money on its way by way of wire service from bank to bank and our man, or Richards contact, is in Jordan as of today, He's been to Syria, Turkey and Israel but someone always had a tail on him, they want what we have. Somehow word leaked out that he had the original missing Books and other works himself. He's afraid of being captured by the head of the insurgent's party that's trying to over throw his Government and he's gone into hiding or exile again with some others."

"Any chance we could be found out, if so we could be in danger as well!"

"None that I know of Fred but there's always going to be that chance until we rid ourselves of the problem. I think maybe it would be a good idea to move the entire collection into our new safe down here by you. No one knows that we have this one and when you look at it, it looks like a brick wall that's part of the old basement. Let me know when you're ready to tackle the thing and I'll work with you and maybe with the two of us we can get it done it six or eight month's rather than you working it alone and with our other dealings it could take you up to eighteen months or more to finish it. I'd like to get it done and out of here as soon as possible. Oh and one more thing. I think it is best to take the crates they were shipped in and put them upstairs on the second floor in the storage area and prematurely age them there so that they don't look like they were built yesterday."

"I concur with you on that, also I think we will have to start back at square one and just work our way though this whole thing, its an awful lot of writing by hand and if you miss one small detail an expert will pick it up and we could be found out."

"Yes, that's why I told Richard that we would be requesting more money as we go. By the way, Richard said his man knew nothing of the altered works, he was only shown a small amount and probably the good work so he has no idea what we're up against but Richard reassured him that when we're done it will look as real and original as can be and will have the aged appearance it should have, so our man will be happy with whatever we do."

"Have you told Susan about her father yet?"

"No, she'll probably know as much as we do when she hears what's going on with the World News on TV."

"Do you know where her father is from yet, I mean which Country for sure?"

"No, she says that the less we know the better it will be for us, that's what she told me a few days ago anyway. I'll check with her anyhow. Let me know when you need me and I'll be right here. She did let something slip about his being the King of Jordan once but it could be a ruse to keep us guessing." Sol left and headed for the store to check with Susan.

"Good morning Susan, is everything alright with you and your father?"

"Yes for now it is, father is on the move in and out of different Countries in disguise which he is constantly changing to throw off his pursuers. He'll lose them in heavy traffic in one Country or another; he has many, many friends everywhere. You did not meet him during your travels to pick up the early works of the Bible?"

"No, Susan at least I don't think so, we weren't allowed off the plane as you know and there was lots of shooting when we joined up with you and you flew us out of trouble."

"That was nothing; I have been shot at many times in a plane and on the ground. There is danger everywhere in the region where we live."

"I do have one nagging question still and that is, who is the rightful owner of what we brought back with you, I mean which Country?"

"That is a very good question; the cave where the works were discovered is on the border of three Countries."

"Yes we know all of that but who is laying claim to it now?"

"That I am not allowed to tell you for your own safety, it is enough that you have helped us to rescue the works from the enemies of Christianity."

"Are you a Christian my dear?"

"But of course, if I were not I would have ordered it all burned to a crisp which is what the militants want to do and I'll not tell you who they are either. You could be in for some real trouble if you were found out. I would die in silence before I divulged the location of this prize because it belongs to the Christian World and no one else. There are religions out there that would stop at nothing to discredit we infidels if you know what I mean."

"Yes I know exactly what you are saying and I have to agree with you on that point. We could all be in real danger but I can assure you that Fred and I have covered one contingency and that is that the works are safe now deep underground as people like to say. If we were attacked in this building I would not hesitate to join the works in the same place as they are right now, we'd be safe from any bombs or missiles they may hurl at us."

"Are you telling me that you have a bomb shelter in this building?"

"You could call it that, we'll all be able to fit in there and we'd be safe for days, months if we put provisions in there with us."

"Oh Sol, I do feel better now, let the bastards come, we will hide with you."

"What do you mean we?"

"Why the works of course, I wouldn't let them out of my sight."

"Okay, for a minute there I thought you had someone else in mind. I'm going back to my apartment, if you hear or see something call my apartment or head to the basement and Fred will take care of you."

"Yes Sol and thank you for what you are doing, you have put yourself perhaps in great peril and as I said before father will reward you generously for your help with all this."

"Yes I know Susan, thank you for your concern as well." Sol left and went back to upstairs to his apartment.

Later that day BJ called Sol about someone to help with Hebrew Translations he and Fred needed. BJ was about to graduate and he told Sol about a friend who had a friend who was in a little bit of trouble financially and grade wise and that he may not graduate if he couldn't pass his final exams and he asked if Sol could help him and his major was Theology and its roots. Sol asked him about Hebrew and BJ told him that Hebrew was his native language and he had to learn English as a secondary language and it was the English he had trouble with understanding and that's why his grade point average was down. Sol had suggested a tutor for the young man and that they would pay for it to help him graduate and would also see to it that his grade point average came up and that all of his bills would be taken care of but in return he had to work for Fred and Sol for up to eighteen months with all of his expenses paid for including rent and food, electric and phone and a suitable wage. Sol told him to pass it on then get back to him as soon as possible. This was extremely important but he couldn't say why over the phone.

Several days went by and finally the call Sol had been waiting for came through from BJ.

He told Sol how much the young man needed in finances and he told him that the tutor idea was greatly appreciated and welcomed and he had agreed to everything else once he had met BJ and talked to him in private. He told Sol that he had to tell the young man that it involved working in a book store that also dealt with the restoration of the great works of the best of intelligent minds of the Ancients, Philosophers, Theologians and great Authors of Literature. Sol told him that it was okay to tell him that much and that he hadn't said anything specific enough to sink their ship. Then Sol asked the big question, how soon could the two of them come to the store and start work on the super secret project. BJ told him if they passed their exams and if the University stayed on schedule they would graduate in as little as six weeks but the young man needed help like yesterday. Sol asked him about his finding a tutor for him. BJ said that if Sol could send him a thousand dollars cash that he could probably get things moving in the right direction. Sol also asked for the Professor's name that was teaching the young man and was failing him due to his lack of English skills. BJ gave him the name and address of the Professor and the conversation was over.

The next day Sol met with BJ and gave him an envelope with two thousand dollars in it.

"Sol this is too much, I think I can get it started for less."

"That may be BJ but we're in a bit of a hurry at the store, I can't tell you why right now, suffice to say we have a huge job ahead of us and speed is King on this one. We don't want to hang onto what we have much longer. While I'm here could you point the way to the Professor's house for me, I'd like to have word with him so I can understand more about this young man's struggle to graduate."

"Sure Sol, he lives here on campus, you go down this street, turn left for two blocks, when you come to the stop sign turn right and he's the third house on the left."

"Do you have his address with you?"

"Yes I have it and I can find it easily now with your directions, thank you and don't worry about the money if you need some go ahead and take it, call it a finder's fee for locating this young man for us, anything else you want or need right now?"

"No I'm all set for graduation, you'll be here won't you?"

"Yes of course I will, Fred will be here as well, we wouldn't miss it for the world."

They said their goodbyes and Sol left for the Professor's house. All Sol had was the young man's last name. After Sol's talk with the Professor the young man would graduate with a passing grade, low but respectful enough that he could hold his head high for the rest of his life and the University would receive a special donation and the next building erected there would be called Solomon Hall. Sol got back in the Van and headed back to Poughkeepsie and the store.

CHAPTER - 95

Back in Washington Agents Jefferies and Marlowe had been getting a general picture of what their man might look like with six completely different descriptions of what eye witnesses thought they remembered seeing. Lisa Browne was trying to figure out the real height of the man so she took the lowest one in stature and started with that then she took the thinnest one in stature and brought it to the shortest one in stature. The height and weight were the easiest to come to a conclusion on, the hair, the face and the rest would be educated guess work but she was good at it and they, the Agents, all knew it by now. It was amazing to them how she drew and reworked her sketches. Soon a figure took place, the man was about five feet six inches tall and weighed about one hundred and thirty five pounds give or take five pounds. She presented her final sketch to Agent Jefferies one afternoon in the lab. "Well here you are Agent Jefferies, your killer is this man but the hair color and whether or not he is bald remains a question because a man that good with a disguise can use a skull cap to appear bald. After taking in all considerations of time I can estimate his age at between sixty two and sixty six give or take as much as two years either way. So you are not dealing with someone who is quick and agile. I believe he is slow and methodical and he takes his time to set up his targets so he can be far away from the actual scene so he can't be tied any of the murders. This man is clever alright and could have some stage or circus background or none at all. It may be that he just picked it up and through trial and error as he got better at it. Now as to the shoes, between Agent Marlowe and myself we located a shoe manufacturer in Germany who has a client in New York City or at least that's where he ships the shoes to and I'm betting that it's a Post Office rental place where people have things drop shipped to them and they only check in there occasionally to pick up mail or packages. At least that's the way I'm leaning. A Physiotherapist might be able to help you better but I doubt they would tell you any different."

"How did you arrive at the age of the man?" asked Jefferies.

"I take it that he is very smart and had to attend a College or a University then given the oldest confirmed killing he made deducted from this year I came up with an average age. I also understand that the first confirmed killing is based on conjecture as well, you could be a year or two off either way."

"Yes that's correct Miss Browne and I think that you are right on target with what Agent Marlowe and I already have guessed him to be age wise so we have more conformation now. Now on the manufacturer of the elevated shoes, how many different sizes of elevations has he shipped to this supposed address for the man over the years?"

"Well I asked him to go all the way back as far as he could and because of World War II and the destruction of so many buildings and their records he could only go back to 1946 and confirmed that at least that long he has ordered several different kinds of shoes to keep up with the trends of fashion as well as the different elevations."

"So our man is also fashion conscious so he won't stick out in a crowd."

"I would definitely say that you are right on the money there as well."

"Did your man say if he had another order to be sent out soon?"

"No, he said he hadn't had any for a year or more but then not much has changed in men's foot wear for the past two years."

"Are you done now with all of this or can you look at some more eye witness accounts?"

"You have more for me?" Miss Browne asked as if she were shocked by the news.

"Yes! Every now and then someone goes to the police and gives them new information which they forward on to us. I have a half a dozen or more on my desk right now!"

"Are you asking me to go through them for you?"

"Yes Miss Browne," his voice softened once more, "I'd like for you to do that and see if something new jumps out for you."

"Okay Agent Jefferies, but I do have to leave by this Friday; I have to go to LA to work on a case for them."

"That's fine Miss Browne the whole FBI applauds your service with us, this is a huge case and after you leave here I'd like for you to take my card and Agent Marlowe's card with our phone number on it so if you think of something give one of us a call."

"I'll do that and may I say thank you for your putting up with me. I came in with the wrong attitude and I'll never let that happen again. Everyone in this building has been most kind and courteous to me every single day. I'm sorry we got off on the wrong foot but now that I know all of you I am grateful for the opportunity you gave me to work with you all."

"The feeling is mutual and don't forget to say good bye to Donny before you leave, he really likes you and respects you as well."

"I'll do that, I still have a couple of days, today's only Wednesday but I do have plane tickets for 1:00 pm on Saturday and I have to go home and take care of mail etc before I leave for LA."

The two of them shook hands in front of everyone in the Lab and it was so quiet you could have heard a pin drop to the floor. Everyone was watching them to see if Dick would make some kind of a move on her. She followed Dick into his office and retrieved the eye witness accounts he had mentioned and went back to her drafting table to study them. She had been there almost three weeks now poring over file after file after file for the FBI and she had a great feeling of accomplishment under her belt by now. She also felt some warmth from Dick Jefferies but she never said anything to him about it because she saw something that the others apparently didn't see and that was when he and Jane were together they seemed to feed off from one another's energies and she felt that there was something more between them and she wasn't about to interfere with that. She sensed some electricity between them which they both tended to ignore but she felt that one day it would surface and they would have to deal with it then. Secretly she wished both of them luck but if they had a falling out she would like to be there to pick up the pieces for Dick and be there to comfort him.

Another day went by and on the following morning Miss Browne had a much better picture of the man's face. She went looking for Dick or Jane.

She found Jefferies first. "Agent Jefferies take a look at this sketch now, someone finally described the man's face as having average features, no protruding nose, no big ears, no weird looking eye brows that meet in the middle. Now I can put a face on this man and there it is as best as I can guess and I put in a few wrinkles that he must have due to his age." She didn't know it at the time but it was very close to Sol's real face right down to his bald head.

Dick looked at it long and hard. "Are you sure of this Miss Browne?"

"As sure as I'll ever be, that's the approximate look of your man, I'd bet my life on it."

"But how do you know, he wore a wig and different makeup every time."

"That's right, but take it all away and your man looks just like this."

"Okay Miss Browne, but this could be anyone in the U.S. is what bothers me, he has no tattoos or big ears, nothing to make him stand out from the crowd. He's just an average man. Wait just a minute, that's it! He's just an average sixty something year old man of average build and everything else. By George you've done it Miss Browne you've hit the old nail in the head. He's our man alright no wonder no one noticed him, he doesn't stand out from the crowd at all, he blends in no matter the disguise at the time. Oh Miss Browne I could kiss you for this."

"Don't you dare! Mind your manners Agent Jefferies! And its hit the nail on the head not in the head." but she was smiling just a bit.

It was too late, Duck picked her up in his powerful arms and swung her around in sight of everyone in the lab. He kissed her lightly on her cheek. He was just displaying his happiness and that's the way everyone saw it including Jane who stood near by. "Oh I am sorry everyone but she's done it, just look at the sketch, it's our man for sure." Jefferies started to pass it around and everyone looked wide eyed as they saw their killer for the first time.

Jane finally got her hands on it and looked it over carefully. "Miss Browne I have to admit it girl, you've done the impossible, great job, I'd kiss you myself if we were alone." The whole Lab broke out in laughter as congratulations were passed all around the room to her. There were lots of hugs and one or two kisses on her cheek especially when it came to Tim, he had grown very fond of her.

Next Agent Jefferies had a request. "Miss Browne, I'm going to ask you for a special favor for me and Jane. Would you mind taking this out and showing it to Donny, he and I were working on this case when he was shot in an unfortunate incident unrelated to this."

"Yes I know all about Donny and you and I'd be pleased to share it with him." She took the sketch, straightened her skirt and went out to the parking garage and found him.

"Donny, have you got a minute?"

"Yes of course Miss Browne, anything for a real lady."

"Take a look at this sketch; this is the man you and Agent Jefferies were looking for."

"You're kidding, why he's just an average Joe, nothing strange about him whatsoever."

"Yes, that's exactly what your partner said."

Those words must have struck a nerve because Donny began to sob slightly; "my partner, you called him," as he suddenly became teary eyed.

"That's right; he'll always be your partner no matter what."

He wrapped his arms around her and hugged the stuffing out of her.

"Here now Donny mind your manners, you're a married man."

"Oh I couldn't help myself, I miss the old days with him as my partner, no man could ever have had a better partner than Dick. He would do the same thing as I did for anyone. I just happened to be the one there at that day and time. It's the comradely thing you see among us all, man or woman, it makes no difference when it comes down to life or death, every single one of them would lay down their life for their partner."

"Yes I know that now, I've learned so much these past few weeks and I can't begin to thank you enough for enlightening me or this would not have happened if it were not for you straightening me out like you did."

"You're welcome Miss Browne, anytime you have a problem just drop by ole Donny's Parking Garage, I'm open for business twenty four seven."

"You are too kind Donny, bless you for who you are, you're one hell of a man and I hope your wife appreciates you in that light."

"Oh she does Miss Browne, she worships the ground I walk on when I come home every night because she knows how bad things can get. She saw the shooting on TV and didn't know that I was even there. It wasn't until the Director himself showed up at our house that she knew I was in some kind of trouble; all she knew was that an Agent had died and when she saw the Director at the door she thought it had been me. She was really relieved when she found out that I was one of the wounded Agents and not the deceased Agent. We have a wonderful marriage and Dick is still my best friend."

"Yes I know that now, he's a wonderful man and if he weren't married to his job I could fall for him but he is married and it would never work and don't you dare tell him I said that!"

"No ma'am, yes ma'am, your secret is safe with me."

"Thank you Donny, now I'd better go back inside I've got a lot of people to thank and to say goodbye to but you'll be the last one I say goodbye to, so see you in a little while. I won't be leaving until tomorrow morning when I have to go to LA on another case."

"See you later Miss Browne, bye for now."

"Bye Donny." She turned and walked back inside sobbing softly a little herself now, she went straight to Dick's Office hoping he wouldn't be there, he wasn't but Jane was.

"Really hard to say goodbye huh Miss Browne?"

"Yes Agent Marlowe I feel so bad for Donny, he's such a wonderful man. He doesn't deserve his fate, why do bad things happen to good people all the time?"

"I don't know Miss Browne, but here's a tissue try to dry your eyes before Dick returns."

"Dick, but I thought?"

"Don't think Miss Browne, its Dick and Jane when we're alone, out there it's Agent Jefferies and Marlowe. If we had our way we would all be on a first name basis."

"I wondered about that because one of the Lab Tech's out there you both refer to as Tim but not the others."

"Tim is one of the few who isn't an Agent, he is a chemist and forensic pathologist but the FBI doesn't own him like the rest of us. He's plain Joe citizen when he leaves this building."

"How many other Lab techs' are like him?"

"He's the only one who isn't licensed to carry a gun."

"Oh, so you mean he was valuable enough to employ and stick in that basement?"

"Yes something like that and if it will make you feel better Dick and I will go back to our own Office's upstairs once this is case is closed. The Director and Dick both thought he should be at the heart of the matter and in case you didn't notice the lab is the heartbeat of the FBI."

"Yes well I guessed that right off, that's some Lab alright, I didn't know just how big it actually was."

"Well now you've had your baptism under fire so to speak Miss Browne and I can't tell you how badly we needed your help. Just among us two, thank you so much for answering my call if you hadn't of come we might have ended up with some geek with thick glasses."

They shared a good laugh for she was no geek, she was a looker and Jane knew it. She finally dried the last tear and was still giggling quietly when Dick walked in.

"What's so funny, did I miss something?"

"Yes and no Dick, we were just reminiscing about when Miss Browne first came here."

"Yes well that's fine but we still have work to do. I've got to get this out to all the Law Enforcement Agencies around the U.S. and the sooner the better. Right now the Director wants him as number three on our top ten list of criminals so it will also go out on the air, maybe we can scare him enough to make him jittery and force him to make a mistake. When he does it I want to be there and of course that includes you Agent Marlowe. I wouldn't tackle this guy alone he's too slippery, almost like an eel."

"Yes well we know at least who we are looking for now, now if only we had a name or a City or a location of some kind, we could actually go out and look for him."

"I'm in total agreement with you Agent Marlowe; we're so close yet so far away."

The next morning was Friday and time for Miss Browne to gather her things and get ready to leave. Both Dick and Jane helped her out to her car and stayed with her to say goodbye.

Miss Browne said, "I don't mean to be rude to the two of you but there is someone special I must see before I leave so if you'll excuse me," she turned and walked away.

"Oh Dick, maybe we should go back inside, we already said goodbye to her."

"No, just wait a second; I want to see her and Donny together."

He watched as Donny picked her up off of her feet, he hugged her then set her down.

"Come on Jane we mustn't stand around here gawking."

"Yes Dick, that's what I said a minute ago."

They turned around and went back inside to go back to work. Once inside they could talk again. "You know Jane that woman was a big help to us, the only thing I wish we had was a suspect with an outstanding feature or two, our guy is just too homogenous, I mean he could be anybody out there on the street."

"I know Dick, but it's the best we have had so far, let's run with it and see where it goes."

"What do you mean Jane?"

"Let's go back to our witnesses who described him best and show them the sketch and see what they have to say, I want to see if it jogs anyone's memory."

"You do realize that these people are spread out across the United States don't you?"

"Yes of course I do but what other choice do we have?"

"There's one other thing we could do, we could contact each Law Enforcement Agency that sent them in and let them take their copy and go back to their witnesses and check them out, it would save a lot of time."

"Oh I know you're right Dick, I'm just frustrated is all, sitting around twiddling my thumbs is not in my nature."

"So you think I'm right then?"

"Yes of course you are Dick, I'm just getting anxious about our man, and I want him behind bars like yesterday. Go ahead and do your thing and contact those with the best witnesses."

Dick did just that, it was Friday and it looked as if they would all have a full weekend off while they waited for more evidence to surface. Dick contacted a total of eight states to start with and asked if their Detective teams could go back out and re-interview their star witnesses and get back to them as soon as they had finished. The entire Lab was given the weekend off after Jane and Dick told the Director of their success with the sketch and none too soon. It had taken a lot longer than usual due to the many disguises their man was capable of wearing plus the innumerable crimes they could tie him to that spanned now some twenty five years now give or take two years either way. Dick and Jane told everyone what a good job they had done and wished them a happy weekend off. Dick even managed to get the Director to give Donny a 'well done' to go into his file because he had saved the day by getting Miss Browne to give it another shot after her falling out with Dick and Jane.

CHAPTER - 96

At the Book Store in Poughkeepsie Sol was waiting for final word from BJ about his Graduation and what time he and Fred should be there. They didn't want to miss a thing. Then there was the new young man they had yet to meet. He would be coming back with BJ as soon as they could clean out their Dorm rooms and get on the road. Sol envisioned having to rent a small enclosed trailer to haul all of their belongings back to Poughkeepsie because the van would only hold so much of their stuff plus four passengers including himself. The call came on a Friday night. BJ told Sol they had their final exams and Graduation would be a week from this Saturday and gave him directions to the location they were being held. The next week seemed to go by at a snail's pace. Both Fred and Sol were excited to get BJ and his new friend back to the Store and get him set up in his apartment.

On the following Friday Fred and Sol left for the University. They had made Motel arrangements for two days just in case they needed an extra day, they both knew how impetuous University Grads could be after graduation. They arrived at their Motel at six o'clock Friday evening and called BJ immediately to let him know they were in town and gave him their number in case he needed anything before hand.

The next day the Graduation ceremonies went very smoothly, the weather was beautiful and in the low seventies. They watched as BJ walked across the Stage to receive his Degree and shake hands with the Dean of the school. It was as little after 2:00 pm when the ceremonies were over. BJ met Sol and Fred at a predetermined area under a huge oak tree whose branches spread out like an enormous umbrella. "BJ we couldn't be more proud of you, you've done more than either of us could have imagined or asked for," Sol said. "You looked like a real man walking across that stage, in fact you looked as though you owned it, good job. Now then, where is this young man you told us all about?"

BJ gave them a startled look. "Oh, uh, he'll be here any minute, he had to say goodbye to some classmates."

While they were talking about The Book Store a figure strolled up to where they standing in a cap and gown. "Are these your friends BJ that you told me about?"

"Yes Doris, this is Sol Devine and Fred Samuel; they own the store I told you about."

"Excuse me BJ," said Sol very quietly, "I thought you said this was a young man you were talking about, she's a girl!" he said in a quiet but shocked tone of voice.

"I'm sorry Sol if you were mislead by our conversations, I didn't think you would want to hire a young lady but trust me she is very sharp when it comes to Hebrew writing and speaking and she is fluent in two other languages as well, Latin and Greek."

"You don't say, well that does shed some light on the subject but will she be able to work at the store in what Fred calls his doom and gloom room."

"Oh yes sir," the young lady broke in. "I am from Israel which is my native land and tongue. We live in a very small three room house with two windows so it can be very dark in there with the houses so close together and I've learned so much while at the University and if it weren't for the two of you and BJ I may not have graduated until next year, I may have had to take advanced English all over again."

"Oh I see, then it isn't today's English you did poorly on."

"That is correct, my parents are working class people who work for the Government in Israel and they had little money with which to send me to school. When I told them of your offer to do translations for you they were quite excited about it and told me to stay as long as I liked and to save whatever money you paid me so I can return one day soon to Israel. The Advanced English I mentioned is based on the very old English Language."

"If things work out you will be able to return home in style and if it's any comfort to you I don't understand the old English either. The project we are working on is herculean in scope but don't let it frighten you; we need you to tell us what the Text says so we can understand what we are doing and it needs to be in the ancient Hebrew language. Do the two of you have a lot of stuff for us to take back with us?"

"I only have a few things to bring back and it's the same things I brought with me originally and remember I've been living on a shoe string but I can't speak for Doris, I've never seen her room," answered BJ.

"Oh I don't have a lot either BJ, mostly clothes my books and papers. Is there a problem with transportation gentlemen?"

"No not at all, we brought the van so we have lots of room, don't we BJ?"

He nodded his head in the affirmative, but he was busy staring at Doris.

"Listen kids, it's late in the day and we have a Motel room for the night and that ought to give you both time to pack up all of your things and be ready to go in the morning, how does that sound?" asked Sol.

"Sounds fine with me how about you Doris?"

"Yes that's alright, BJ knows where my dorm building is, it's only two buildings over from his, you can pick him up first and then come and get me."

"Okay that's fine, don't you have some classmates to see before you leave?"

"Oh, I almost forgot all about graduation, come on Doris we'll say our goodbyes then we can go pack and I'll meet you in the cafeteria for one last meal before we leave."

The next morning Sol and Fred met BJ at his Dorm and loaded his things in the van then went to Doris's Dorm and loaded her things and like she had said was mostly clothes and a few books and papers. Sol asked BJ to drive and let Doris ride shotgun so they could talk. The first item on their agenda was breakfast and that's the direction BJ took. He knew exactly the right place to go after being away at school for four years. They all ate a hearty breakfast and soon they were on the road again headed for Poughkeepsie.

They rolled into town close to 5:00 pm. BJ expertly parked the van under the store, they unloaded everything and took it upstairs to their apartments. Sol had prepared one for Doris close to his apartment. Then the four of them went across the street to Louie's for supper. Doris was full of questions.

"When do we start work Mr. Divine?"

"Number one Doris you may call me Sol just as BJ does and number two you need to get yourselves settled into your apartments then we'll talk. If you need Fred or I, Greta will know where we are at any given time. She is the lady that runs our store on street level. Why don't the two of you take tomorrow off so BJ can show you around the building and show you where everything is except for what we need your help with my dear. I want to save that for Tuesday morning when you and BJ can both be there. BJ can show you the factory in the basement, the lab and everything else. The work I am alluding to is locked up for safe keeping and once you see it you'll know why secrecy is the most important thing in our case. Neither of you are to discuss any of this outside of yourselves, understood?" Sol said it in a stern voice so as to make an impression on the two of them.

"Yes Sol, I told her that whatever it was would be top secret and she had to swear to keep the secret or she could start World War III." BJ said.

"It is that valuable Sol?" Doris asked in now anxious voice.

"Yes my dear, more valuable than life itself. I can't wait to see the look on your faces when we reveal to you what we have. It will rock your boat, just don't let it overwhelm the two of you and sink our reputation."

The four of them headed back across the street to the store. Sol went to his apartment, Fred went to his lab in the basement. BJ and Doris went into the store, she was anxious to meet Greta and Susan, BJ didn't know who Susan really was, her secrecy was that great and BJ was anxious to show Doris off.

"Why are there so many elevators here BJ?"

"Don't ask too many questions right now, just try to take it all in a little at a time, once you start to use the elevators you'll notice right away that only one goes to the apartments floor, workmen and others have no business in our living quarters unless Sol says okay first. Now this is Sols Apartment, this next one is Fred's, then Greta's, then mine and yours is across the the hall there and around the corner of the hall lies more apartments for staff in the store."

"So everyone who works here has their own apartment as well?"

"Only if they want to and its rent free for employees, we have to pay our own phone and utilities but Sol will take care of all of yours. I go on the books tomorrow full time. The phone and the rest will be put into my name on the first of the month which is next week anyway. You'll learn to love it here. The Book Store is probably the biggest in the Nation right now and they sell their books internationally as well and that's what you'll be working on with Fred mostly but Sol and I will be around to help out now and then. We have an entire shipping and receiving department, this place is busting at the seams! I am so glad you were able help us out."

"Me too BJ, me too." They hugged one another and went to their own apartments to finish unpacking and get settled in. BJ had all day to show her around and show her all the best places to eat and shop.

CHAPTER - 97

Tuesday morning came almost too soon for the young ones but they were up and raring to go right after breakfast.

BJ ushered Doris downstairs to the basement to where Fred and Sol were both waiting.

"Alright you two, BJ has a small inkling of what we are up to but isn't quite sure what a chore its going to be. Before we reveal it to either of you I need your solemn promise that you will tell no one and I do mean no one what we have here. Do I have your sworn promise, both of you?"

"Yes Sol of course."

"Thank you BJ."

"Doris?"

"Can't I tell my parents what important work I'll be doing?"

"No Doris, especially not your parents and you'll soon see why, then you'll understand just how dangerous this could be for all of us if the word of this project got out."

"Alright then I swear, I'll not tell a soul outside this building."

"Okay then follow me." They walked down a hall a little ways and stopped; "Well here we are," Sol announced.

BJ looked at Doris and then back to Sol. "But Sol there isn't anything here."

"Ah ye of little faith my boy, we've added something new."

Sol pressed a button hidden in the wall and the wall swung open, exposing a huge cavity of a room. He switched on a light so they could see inside. "In here you will find what we are working on, go ahead and look, one of the boxes is open."

They had unloaded the crates and boxed every thing up in cardboard boxes for better storage. Doris was the first to peer into an open box, she took out a few loose papers. "No! this can't be, it not possible, where did you get these Sol?" asked Doris, who was totally shocked, paled and trembling with fright.

"That I cannot tell you, you'll have to trust me on this, you don't want to know."

"But these look like original Bible verses in Hebrew, what you have appears to be The Lost Books of the Bible, aren't they?"

"That's exactly right my child. They are going back to their rightful owner when we are done with our work. We are going to restore and preserve the Bible as it was originally intended to be."

"But this is beyond comprehension, are you sure these are real?" asked Doris.

"Yes, they are very real my child."

"BJ do you know what this means?" Doris asked.

"I'm not at all sure I do."

"It means that whoever possesses this can literally rule the world of religion. If this is authenticated it will unhinge the world as we know it, brother against brother, Muslim against Christian and so on. In the wrong hands World War III could easily erupt."

"Now you know why secrecy is paramount, once we are done this will go back to the rightful owner and the world will go on as usual but in the wrong hands, well you said it Doris, a new World War," Sol added.

"I've heard rumors all my life about the lost books but I never thought I'd see the day when I would actually see them and hold them in my own hands, I thought it was only rumors."

"Yes well now you both know the reason I had you swear you wouldn't tell a soul. The area this came from is in turmoil and Civil War right now. Don't try guessing where because I've already done that and have been told the general area is where three countries converge and they are fighting over territory and their boundaries all the time just like now. What's possibly worse is this could become a religious war that no one could win. Each country would claim ownership and that's why we removed them at a great cost I might add."

"Oh Sol this is too good to true, please tell me I'm dreaming," Doris asked now wild eyed and still trembling a little.

"No my child, what you see is very real, it is our job to see that the works are preserved and restored forever and correctly I might add."

"But this is too important a find not to share with the world," said Doris.

"What you don't realize my child is that there are Countries out there who would stop at nothing to prevent the world from ever knowing about this. We have been instructed to restore and do conversancy work on the papers, we will make a copy for the Museum in Egypt, one copy is to go to Israel and the originals and a copy will be returned to the benefactor who gave this to us for safe keeping. Doing it our way no one but us will know where the original really is so no matter how many Churches they bomb or burn down, no matter how many Museums they loot and burn, they will never find both of them and the originals will be returned to the cave where they were discovered and sealed in for all eternity. Its the only safe and reasonable thing to do my child."

"So you are going to entrust a copy to my Country and one to Egypt as well keeping it out of the hands of the Greek Orthodox, Catholics, Muslims, religious Zealots and everyone else then?"

"Yes, that is our goal and our benefactor's as well. What you fail to understand is that our work will even fool the experts. Our inks are made just like the ancients made theirs and the paper it was printed on has been painstakingly duplicated so that no one tell an original from a copy which we reproduce. We have several patents for our paper and inks which have made us so rich that we would never have to work again. Once this is done we intend to turn this operation over to BJ for his own, everything will be put in his name. Our goal has always been to make a difference in the World and by doing this it will cumulate our life's ambitions so we can retire in luxury and BJ will have a company that is debt free, we owe no one, no bank or anyone else has ever helped us. We built this Company on our own initiative and neither Fred or I have any heirs to leave anything to. BJ you see is our unofficial adopted son."

"Well now I do understand. If you don't do this your way there is a definite possibility of a new Religious World War and I know how painful War can be first hand so I will do as you ask and do it willingly because I believe you are correct in all of your assumptions Sol."

"Thank you my child, you can see why all the secrecy now. No one must ever know what lies here. Doris I will leave you with Fred, this is the time I told you about, time to go to work, bless you my child," he patted her on her head softly

BJ and Sol went upstairs. "Sol that was quite a speech, I knew you and Fred had something real important to do but seeing the fear in Doris's eyes made a believer out of me."

"By the way BJ what is her last name?"

"Its David with an s like in David's."

"For real?"

"Yes Sol for real, no kidding."

"Well I'll be darned, how strange is that; it gave me goose bumps that she is the one and she is here. Do me a favor, I have a funny feeling about all of this and I don't know why, will you make yourself available to Fred and Doris if they need you?"

"Yes of course Sol, I already understand the need for keeping this quiet and getting the job done as soon as possible to get this dynamite stuff out of the basement before word leaks out which it undoubtedly will, its only a matter of time and we both know it."

"Thank you BJ, I knew we could count on you and now you also know why I preferred that it was a man who was here."

"I do now, you aren't thinking about snuffing out her candle are you?"

"Only as a last resort but once she is back home she'll naturally want to tell her folks so we need a new hiding place as well for the books because we are also making a copy for ourselves. Someone I assure you will come looking for them some day and when they do you can show them the empty safe and tell them that the stuff was removed by Fred and I under cover of darkness to a place you know nothing about. Fred and I will find another place for our copy and its best that you don't know where it is but I will leave you a detailed instructions in my safe deposit box in New York City with the key should you ever need it. I will give you all the details later. Right now all that is in the box are our patents and as soon as we conclude our business here we will re-file them in your name with the Government in Washington. If need be you could live off the income of those patents for the rest of your life, they are clean and completely legal."

"Thank you for everything Sol, you and Fred have been much too kind."

"You are welcome my boy, now I have work to do and so do you, what you do from now on is your business and I mean that in every sense of the word. Fred and I will be here to assist you in every way until we decide to retire." Sol left BJ standing in the entrance to the store with his mouth agape; he now had everything a person could ever need. He had money, fame and a growing legal business; or so he thought.

A week went by and the progress was slow but gaining in momentum as Doris correlated the papers in her care and translated them for Fred and there were some important dates in there some of which were BC and some writing from the time of Moses. She saw writings with a notation, 'from the house of David' and when she saw her family name she wondered, was it possible she and her family were distantly related in some way. That thought alone sent shivers up and down her spine. How fitting she thought that she was chosen to do this work. It had to come from above she reasoned and she kept working.

Weeks turned into weeks and then there came a day when things got easier and moved faster and she enlisted BJ's help with Fred so they could keep up with her. She deciphered words relating to both the paper of the day and the way ink was created and relayed all of that to Fred which helped immensely with his preservation techniques. He found that he had all the necessary items to reproduce the different inks and paper type of each era lending even more credence to their work and Doris turned out to be indispensable in all of their work.

CHAPTER - 98

A little over a week after Miss Browne left the phone rang in Agent Jefferies Office. Jane was the closest so she picked it up. It was Miss Browne with some disturbing but important information for them. She told them that she was working on a case involving a wealthy heiress who had died in a horse riding accident in LA County in California and her cousin inherited everything rather than her nieces or nephews. Jane told her that they had been there and investigated the case because their perp. had bought the book collection from the heiress who mysteriously died a few days later but they had nothing concrete to go on. She told Jane they should hurry up and fly out there because the butler was about to crack up over feelings of guilt and if he cracked maybe others in the household would break their silence as well including the stable help who didn't like the new owner.

Jane asked her if she needed to talk to Dick and she said no that she had to run some errands but she'd see them when they got to LA. They could find her at the Sheriff's Office most any time and hung up the phone after giving Jane her Motel phone number. Well I declare, I wonder what she learned that we didn't Jane wondered and she set off to find Dick.

She found him in the lab, "Dick, we just had a call from Miss Browne, she thinks we should grab a plane and head for LA right away, she said the butler is ready to crack up and if we get there in time we might learn something new about our man who had definitely been there which we already know. She said for us to bring along one of our sketches and that she doesn't trust the Sheriff's Office for some reason and to hurry up before the guy ends up in a loony bin.

She wants us to re-interview the butler and show him our sketch because when she talked with him he kept giving her different descriptions as though he were hiding something. She said he was fidgeting a lot in his chair at the mansion when she talked to him last."

"Alright I guess we can go, I'll clear it with the boss, can you see about the plane arrangements and I'll go to the Director's office right now. Are your traveling bags still packed?"

"Yes, how about yours?"

"Same here, I'm ready to leave at a moments notice. See you in a few minutes with or without the Directors okay."

Dick took off for the elevators and Jane picked up the phone and began calling Airlines.

Dick was back in a few minutes. "How did the plane tickets go Jane?"

"In this case its going to be up to you, we can catch one at 7:15 tonight or wait until the day after tomorrow, everything else is booked for the next few days."

"How about a Hotel or Motel?"

"That's even worse; I could only find one room with two queen size beds and that was it. Apparently there's a football Game in a couple of days and the rooms are going fast so I had to take what I could get. Everything close into town is gone as well. If it's alright with you I had to guarantee the room for today. We'll have to pay for a day we won't be there."

"Yes, of course its alright with me, its you I'm concerned about. Maybe we can get Donny to take us to the airport in our car, he'd get a bang out of that."

"Sounds okay with me, do you want to set that up with him?"

"Sure Jane, I'll take care of it. We need to leave here by 5:30 to get to the airport and checked in and so forth, is that alright with you?"

"Sure Dick, no problem the only question for me is, where do you want to meet him to pick us up?"

"What about right here it's as good a place as any, the night shift will be on so there will be people around, we can get a bite to eat and come back here unless you have something you need to do at home first."

"No, I'm ready to go, everything a lady needs I have with me here in my overnight bag."

"Well okay then I'll go ask Donny if he'll take us to the airport this afternoon, I hope he doesn't have any plans."

They got into LA after midnight; they were tired but had a decent nap on the plane. Jane had Miss Browne's phone number in LA where she was staying and called her as soon as they had a chance to confirm their reservations. She told her when they would be in town and where they were staying and that they had rented a car already and they could meet at the Sheriff's Office Sub Station around 10:00A.M. if she wanted and she agreed that it was a good jumping off point for them all.

Dick and Jane had yet to talk about the Motel room with the two queen size beds, it seemed as though they were both avoiding the issue until bedtime.

Dick broke the ice and started a dialogue between them. "Jane why don't you use the bathroom first and get ready for bed at the same time, we're both adults and should be able to work this out between us."

"That's fine with me, I can change in there so I'll take you up on your offer."

"That's fine and while you're in there I'll get ready for bed out here, I did manage to throw in a robe since the last time we traveled together."

That settled they went their separate ways and she took over the bathroom while Dick changed in the room. He was all done and laying on the bed closest to the door because that's where he had thrown his luggage when they first came in. Jane obviously preferred the bed nearest the window because that's where she had tossed her bags. Dick was watching a TV program while he waited for his turn in the bathroom.

Soon she was done and came out of the bathroom. "All yours Dick, I'm done for now."

"Thank you Jane, I won't be long. Dick noticed that Jane was wearing a robe and he could see her night gown that was a little longer than her robe and that it was black. Dick closed the bathroom door brushed his teeth and would wait until morning to shave and shower. Then he thought, wait a minute, I wonder if Jane wants to shower the first thing in the morning as well. He put on his robe and opened the bathroom door a little and asked, "Did you want to shower first thing in the morning Jane?"

"Yes if its alright with you Dick?"

"Would you mind terribly if we got up a little early then because I'd like to shave and shower as well in the morning."

"No that will be fine, we can work it out in the morning; you'll take less time in there than I will so after we take care of our individual nature routines you can shave and shower and then I'll use the bathroom to shower and put my face on."

"Sounds like a plan to me." Dick turned towards the hall outside of the bathroom and slid his robe off and tossed it onto the foot of the bed and got under the covers. Jane dutifully turned her head away from Dick towards the window where she couldn't see him in his pajamas; she was already under the covers. "Well Jane that all worked out very nicely didn't it?"

"Yes Dick, thank you for respecting my privacy as well."

"Sure, are you ready to go to sleep or did you want to talk or watch TV some?"

"I'm ready for sleep, why don't you leave a wake up call for 7:30 in the morning unless that's too early for you?"

"No that's fine; I'm an early riser anyway." Dick picked up the phone and called the front desk and left a wake up call and hung up the phone.

"You know Dick we're acting like a couple of frightened children don't you?"

"I guess you could say that but I'm only trying to respect your feelings towards men, I'm not sure where you are on the subject these days."

"Hopefully I'm over it, I'll know by the time we leave here to go back to Washington, goodnight Dick."

"Goodnight Jane."

They turned off the individual lights above their beds.

Before they knew it the morning sun was just coming in their window and the phone rang with their wake up call.

"Jane you first in the bathroom, I can hold out for a few minutes if you like."

"Thank you Dick."

She got up hurriedly and went into the bathroom to take care of her nature call. Dick screwed up by not looking away fast enough and caught a glimpse of her in her nightgown. It was just sheer enough for him to catch a glimpse of her figure. My God, he thought, she's beautiful everywhere it counts. He felt guilty for stealing a glimpse then he thought, wait a minute, I'm a grown man with male feelings and she didn't bother to put on her robe so she must have thought I would take a quick look and didn't bother with the robe.

Just then Jane called out to him from the bathroom. "Dick, would you be a dear and bring me my robe, I had to go to the bathroom so bad I neglected to put it on." "Sure thing Jane, I'll get it for you." He bounded out of bed without thinking, retrieved her robe and handed it to her through the door opening.

"Oh nice jams Dick, quite the thing."

Dick's face turned red when he realized he had done the same thing. They broke out laughing at their own predicaments. It was too late for Dick to grab his robe so he winged it from there. He shaved and showered then came out of the bathroom to free it up for Jane and got dressed while she showered and put her face on as she called it. Dick turned on the TV and was surprised when he saw the mansion he and Jane had been to where the heiress died. The story was about a reinvestigation by the local Sheriff's Department when they realized discrepancies in the servant's stories. It seemed they weren't matching up and were constantly changing, it was headline news. As soon as Jane was out of the bathroom he told her about the story he'd seen.

"We'd better get a move on Dick, would you mind waiting in the bathroom while I get dressed?"

"No problem Jane, I'll sit on the john while I wait for you, give me a holler when you're decent."

Dick quickly headed for the bathroom and Jane hurriedly got dressed. She called out to Dick that she was ready and they went looking for a place to eat a good breakfast where they could talk about the case in private which let out all of the fast food restaurants in town.

They met up with Miss Browne at the Sheriff's Office and were surprised when the Sheriff was there and he welcomed them with open arms and a handshake; he was at the Sub Station after he had heard they were coming.

"Well isn't this just like a homecoming, good to see you folks again. Miss Browne here works magic with her fingers using words to come up with a picture of a killer, she told me that she just got through working with you two as well."

"Yes and its good to see you again Sheriff, she worked up a man's picture for us from head to toe quite literally, she's a wonder alright. But we're not quite sure why she asked us here, I suppose we'll find out soon enough," Dick answered.

'Good morning Miss Browne, lovely to see you again," Dick Said.

"Sheriff you remember Special Agent Marlowe don't you?"

"Yes of course, how are you Ms. Marlowe? I do forget whether it is Miss or just Ms."

"It's Miss Sheriff, I've never been married; I haven't found the right man yet."

"Sheriff is there somewhere we could sit down in private with Miss Browne for a few minutes?"

"Of course Agent Jefferies, right this way." He took them to the area used as break room by the Deputies stationed there. "I'll leave you here; I'll be right out in front," said the Sheriff.

"What's this about the staff in the household getting nervous Miss Browne?"

"Well Agent Jefferies, I wanted the two of you to talk to the butler alone, he seems shifty and he keeps changing his story, he's hiding something I'm sure of it. I'd like you both to sit down and talk to him like old friends and see if he'll open up to you. All the Sheriff manages to do is to scare the hell out of him and he's ready to crack up altogether. I think if you show him my sketch and watch his eye's he will give himself away and tell you everything he knows."

"Since when did you become a Detective Miss Browne?"

"You know I'm not but I have a feeling about this guy, every time I ask him a question about the killer he says he doesn't know anything but never looks me in the eyes, his eyes shift left and right, up and down, he's scared to death that he'll come back and off him as well."

"Where did you get this bit of off a guy from?"

"From TV Agent Jefferies, where else."

"Okay we'll talk to him and see how nervous he really is, are you going there today?"

"Yes, I'm not through yet and when we're done maybe you should show your sketch to the Sheriff and ring his memory bell. I asked him whether or not he got your sketch and he couldn't say."

"Someone is stonewalling us again Agent Jefferies."

"Yes Agent Marlowe same as before."

"I know you've dealt with these people before and they don't really like outsiders butting in but in this case either they are blind or stupid."

"I agree with you Miss Browne, lets go have a chat with the Butler and see where the chips fall when we start to cut his tree down. Let's give the Sheriff one more chance."

The three of them stood up and went back out front.

"What, have you solved the case already?," said the Sheriff sarcastically.

"Actually Sheriff we know what the killer looks like, we found out a little over a week ago but our friend Miss Browne here insists that the butler knows something and is afraid to talk to anyone. Would you like to take a ride with us while we talk to the man?"

"I'd love to, I don't see how you can find out anything more than we already have, he won't talk straight to any of my men."

"Have you talked to him yourself Sheriff?"

"Actually I haven't, I have Detectives who do that, I'm more of an Administrator rather than an Investigator, mainly I'm PR between our Department and downtown if you get my gist."

"Yes its a nice post but no longer hands on as they say."

"That's it exactly Agent Jefferies and I do miss it."

"Well now you have an opportunity to take a crack at this guy before he goes to pieces, why not ride along with us as back up or something, get your feet wet once more."

"I'll take you up on that, I'd do anything to get out of the Office for a while."

"Good then its done; Miss Browne, lead on, we'll follow you. Sheriff why don't you ride with Miss Browne to keep her company."

They got into their cars and with Miss Browne in the lead with the Sheriff, Dick and Jane followed in their rental car.

"Are you crazy Dick bringing him along?" Jane asked.

"Got an Ace up my sleeve Jane, lets see what happens when we lay our cards on the table with the Butler."

"You're liable to drive him over the edge Dick."

"I hope not, you and I will be his pals and we'll make the Sheriff the bad guy."

"Oh that's terrible thing to do setting the Sheriff up like that."

"Might be fun at that Jane," Dick was chuckling to himself.

CHAPTER - 99

They drove up to the mansion, got out of their individual cars and went up to the house. The butler opened the door and let them all in. Dick spoke up first. "I guess you know why we are back don't you?"

"Huh? I don't know you!"

"This is Special Agent Marlowe and I'm Special Agent Jefferies of the FBI."

"You people ought to leave me alone, I don't know anything and I'm not going to tell you anything you don't already know," answered a very nervous Henry.

"Here, here, come here, calm down, we just want to have a chat with you, can we go to the sitting room where it's quiet," coaxed Jefferies.

"Alright, but I'm telling you I don't know anything, I already told everything I know."

They three of them went into the sitting room where they sat down to chat as Dick called it. Dick started the conversation leaving Miss Browne and the Sheriff out in the hall.

"We think we know who killed your boss, we just want to know if maybe you saw him, like maybe the man who bought the books from your boss."

"I don't know what you're talking about, I didn't see anyone, he'll kill me for sure if I tell. Oh God I never should have agreed with him. I'm so sorry I lost my boss, she was a grand lady and her cousin who runs the place now, well he's a complete jerk, he doesn't know anything about horses and is using this place as a tax write off I'm sure, oh please leave me be I don't know anything."

"Jane would you excuse us for a moment, I'd like to talk to him alone, someone has him scared of out of his wits."

"Right you are Agent Jefferies." She left the sitting room and went out into the hall where Miss Browne and the Sheriff were waiting.

"My name is Dick, what is your name?"

"Its Henry sir."

"Henry, it's only me and you here now, you do remember me don't you? Why don't you tell me what's happened, why are you afraid of someone coming back."

"Oh sir, I never should have done it, I mean Dick, I never should have agreed. A man came here to buy my boss's books and took me into his confidence when he found out that I loved books. He told me to take whatever books I wanted too from the Library before the truck came to pick them up and so I did. Oh I know it was wrong to do it but those books, they tell all kinds of stories and when my boss was killed and she was killed mind you, it weren't no accident, she was too good of a rider and the horse was too good of a horse. She never would have fallen and he never would have reared up like the police said he did, they wanted to kill the poor horse but it wasn't the horse's fault, I just know that man done it. Come with me and I'll show you what I took. I never should have listened to him he scares the hell out of me now." Henry took Dick to his private quarters and showed him the books. Some were westerns, murder mysteries, Atlas's with maps of the world, he had a little of everything. "See, this is what I took. In one book there's a story about a wealthy woman with horses and how she was killed and made to look like and accident the same way as my boss was and the killer got away with it."

"Would you remember the man if you saw his picture again?"

"Yes of course, he was a nice man, older, he was bald, wasn't very tall, a real nice man or at least I thought he was but now I know different. He offered me money to keep quiet and to tell different stories about what happened to get the cops off his trail but when I refused and he made a remark that sent chills up and down my spine, he said and I quote," "I don't leave no witnesses behind when I do a job." "He means to get me, I just know he does."

"Alright Henry calm down, we're here now and we need your help, we're you're friends now and probably the only real friends you have left."

"Thank you Dick for understanding. Can we go back now, I think I'll be alright?"

"Sure lead the way, we'll go back to the sitting room."

Dick followed as Henry led the way though a labyrinth of rooms then downstairs until they were in the main hall again. "Henry, would you mind if I asked Agent Marlowe to join us for a minute, she wants to show you something and see if you remember anything else."

"Sure, just as long as you don't let that Sheriff man near me, they scared the hell out of me the last time they was here, threatened me with jail if I didn't cooperate."

"Fine Henry, you're doing just fine now."

"Agent Marlowe, would you come in with us and bring the envelope with you?"

He signaled for the Sheriff and Miss Browne to follow but to stay out of sight. "Jane this is Henry, he's really sorry for something he thinks he did wrong but I have assured him that its alright, we're not here to take him to jail, we just need his help. Would you hand me the envelope please Jane?"

She passed the large envelope to Dick and he said, "thank you Jane!"

"Now Henry, inside here we have what we believe is a drawing of the man who was responsible for killing your boss but we need you to look at it and tell us if it is him, take your time and just look at the sketch for us."

"Well okay if you think it will help Dick."

He slid the sketch out of the big envelope and Henry gasped immediately. "That's him, that's the man what done it, oh my God I am so sorry ma'am," he said shaking all over.

"Look Henry it's not your fault, all he did was give you the books which he stole from your boss lady, he didn't pay for them did he?"

"No sir Dick, she gave them to him for being so good in bed with her, she was awful lonely you know. He spent several days here going through all kinds of things and wooing her at the same time, then he killed her to keep her quiet and he will do the same thing to me if you don't get him soon. And one more thing, I think her cousin had something to do with the murder, I seen them arrive together and leave together in different cars, that man drove around in a Chauffer driven rented Bentley limo and her cousin was in a maroon stretch limo."

"The Bentley, do you know where a person could rent one?"

"Sure there's a couple of places that rent them or lease them but I'll give you the phone number of the one that man used, I copied it off from a pad of paper he used to write the number down on a couple of times."

"We'd love to be able to lift his finger prints from something, is there somewhere in the house that hasn't been cleaned up real good yet?"

"As a matter of fact there is a room in the basement, he was all over the place and I thought it was funny when he asked me to be sure to have it all cleaned up right down to the woodwork. I haven't done it yet, I've been to scared to even answer the door but it's my job."

"Henry you have no idea how much help you have been, would you show me the room in the basement so I can see it and if its alright I'd like the Sheriff to come along with us, his men can dust the place for fingerprints and trust me, you are in no trouble whatsoever, we'll catch the man who killed your boss, I promise you that and we'll tell the Sheriff to lay off you as well."

They all followed Henry down to the basement and he pointed out the strange reading room where the books had been kept in huge bookcases.

"Sheriff, have your people dust this entire room for prints, from what Henry here has told me there should be no more than three sets of prints on anything in there and one set has to be our man, the other sets, well, both of them are dead but I'm sure their prints are on file at the Courthouse especially when someone has died. Don't they take prints of the deceased before burial and put them in a file Sheriff?"

"Actually yes they do, I'll make a call and get my forensics team right out here now."

"Thank you Sheriff."

"Well I guess that's it Miss Browne, its the same man we have been hunting." The Sheriff had gone upstairs when Dick talked to Miss Browne once more. "Miss Browne, I'm dying to know, was it the Sheriff who contacted you to come out here and do a sketch?"

"Yes Dick, it was."

"Well at least you can justify your fee and tell him this is the same guy, you hang onto to this and handle it anyway you'd like, at least this trip we aren't yelling and screaming at one another like the last time huh Jane?"

"Yes, everything was quite cordial Dick," answered Jane.

"Henry if you'll lead the way we'll follow you and if the man calls you again tell him you'll do anything he asks then call us. Here's my card and Miss Marlowe's card as well and we can't thank you enough for your help. Please don't be afraid, you have nothing to fear any more. We'll take care of everything" They followed Henry back upstairs to the sitting room.

"Miss Browne, do you need us anymore?"

"No Agent Jefferies, thank you both for what you have done, this man has his sanity back. The two of you handled that very well, do you always play good cop bad cop?"

"Who was playing, the Sheriff was the bad cop in this case, he's the one, or rather his men were who almost pushed poor Henry over the edge?"

Jane added; "Yes Miss Browne, you should have been around the first time we met, it was as comical as it gets when it comes to stupid cops. I thought Dick was going to clean one the of the Deputy's clocks. He stood up to a room full of Deputies and told them off in no uncertain terms on how they had all botched their jobs. One of them wanted to fight real bad but once he was on the floor he had second thoughts."

"Did Dick hit him?"

"No, I tossed him across the room in front of his buddies and that quieted the place down real quick. They knew then who was in charge, there was only one man among them that took up the challenge to get to work and Dick here wrote a nice letter of a commendation for him to the Sheriff. Funny but I didn't see him today; so maybe he's out on patrol or something."

They spent some time talking with Henry and just as Dick and Jane were about to leave an unmarked patrol car and a forensics van pulled up out in front. The first one in the door was their young friend from the Sheriff's Sub Station.

"Well look who's here, how are you my boy?" Dick asked.

"I'm just fine sir and thank you for the letter you sent to the Sheriff, I've been promoted to detective now, gold badge and all and I run the forensic team as well. Its Lieutenant now, I'm no longer just a Patrolmen. I don't know what you said to the Sheriff but he said I was the only Officer who had the balls to get out and go to work rather than sit around drinking coffee and eating doughnuts all day."

"What happened to the troublemakers?"

"The Sheriff split them all up, every single one was demoted one grade and are spread throughout the County Lord only knows where, probably school cross walk duties, the Sheriff was pretty mad when he got back from his talk with you after lunch."

"I guess he must have been, it was a pretty sad day for all of you, not one person but you knew what the hell to do."

"Well I wanted to thank you in person, when I heard that the FBI was in town I hoped it would be the two of you."

He shook both their hands and followed Henry as he led the team to the basement.

"Well Jane it appears we're no longer needed here, shall we take our leave and leave?"

"Sounds good to me Dick but when did you become a poet rhyming words?"

Dick let the remark slide with a small smirk of his lips and tongue in cheek looking at Jane. "Just be glad I didn't say something like maybe we should make like a tree and leave."

"Oh Dick sometimes you're incorrigible."

Dick let the remark pass without answering her. "Miss Browne care to have lunch with a couple of Feds?" Dick asked.

"It would be an honor but I insist on buying."

"I do hope you can do better than a fast food burger joint."

"I think I can handle it alright, want to follow me?"

"That will be fine the Sheriff can find his own way back to his office, there's two vehicles at his disposal."

"Dick, wait a minute, don't you think we should ask him to come along, he's been straight with us? It was his detectives that screwed this thing up with Henry."

"If you insist Agent Marlowe." Dick turned around and went back inside to ask the Sheriff if he would like to go to lunch and he decided he would.

"I really appreciate the invite you two and of course our Miss Browne, you've done us all a great service," the Sheriff said.

"Sounds to me like the Sheriff is buying lunch," answered Dick.

"Right you are son, someone lead the way, I'll buy and it's my pleasure."

After lunch Dick and Jane went back to their Motel room and she made some calls to the airlines for a flight back to Washington. "Dick what are you thinking about?"

"I'm betting that you're wondering why we didn't get that information from the butler and the others the first time we were here."

"You're absolutely right, I guess some people need an extra shove to come clean like our friend the butler but at least this time he didn't do the crime." They both broke out laughing.

After a couple of phone calls Jane asked; "well Dick, how much do you like LA?"

"It's alright, why?"

"No flights out of here for three more days unless there's a cancellation, however I can put us on a priority list to be called if there is one."

"Let me guess, fans going home after the football game?"

"You got it, we screwed up coming here so early, if we had waited a few days we could have conceivably flown in and out the same day."

"Yeah I suppose but then the butler could have gone over the edge in that amount of time and that's called hindsight."

"I agree."

"Jane did you check the redeye flights out of here as well?"

"Yes, I covered every single one of them, there's a lot of people apparently who have to get back to work same as us."

"Well then looks like we're stuck here for a few more days, I'm open to suggestions and don't even think about driving a rental car all the way back home."

"Got it, shall we call Miss Browne and see what she has planned for the next few days and evenings?"

"I guess so; she's the only real friend either of us have here."

"Wait a minute you're forgetting the Sheriff and his wife, remember the great time we had with them one evening?"

"Sure do and I did forget, would you like for me to call him?"

"Yes, it would sound better coming from you."

Dick called the Sheriff's Office and was told he was still out so he left a call back for him to call them at the Motel. In the meantime they relaxed while they waited for the phone to ring.

About 3:00 that afternoon the phone rang and it was the Sheriff. Dick and he chatted a while then the Sheriff said he'd check things out at home with his wife and would and get back to them. He called back at 3:45 and said he'd pick them up around 6:00 if that would be alright. They didn't know that he'd already invited Miss Browne to go along with them.

They all went out to dinner and had a lot of laughs and some dancing. Dick got worn out dancing with two single women.

On their forth day in LA they got lucky and found an early flight out that morning due to a cancellation of a family of five. Flying back with them was Miss Browne, they were able to all sit together and chat on the way back to Washington for at least Agents Jefferies and Marlowe.

Miss Browne informed them that she had to fly out to Albuquerque New Mexico the following Monday morning on another mysterious case.

"Don't tell me Miss Browne, three houses burned to the ground killing nine people and a truck in the ditch that killed two men who also burned to death."

"That's right but how did you know?"

"We already worked that case and there are no survivors who saw the killer or at least none that came forward with information."

"Well my sources say that there was one, a neighbor across the street from the house in the center saw two men coming and going then they came back with a truck and loaded all of the books from the house and an hour later or so the house in the middle was blown off its foundation and the two on either side caught fire and also burned down. The witness saw the neighbors from the house on the left side go into the center house but the house blew up before they could get out. She claims she can identify the men if she saw their picture."

"Let me guess, someone is putting up a reward now?"

"That's right, how did you know?"

"Educated guess Miss Browne, don't waste your time, take along a few of your different sketches and if the witness identifies the right man then we have something to go on but try to sway the person one way or the other before showing her the right sketch. Oh and one more thing that just occurred to me, take along only the sketches you made for us and see if she identifies one of them because our guy may have been in disguise. I'm guessing you see that your witness is a she and that she is the block's busy body who knows everyone's business but own, am I right?"

"Right again, you've been there alright."

"One more thing, check her eyes, if she's wearing thick glasses she may have seen them but I doubt she could identify them, and remember people are our business and we checked with all the possible neighbors and no one saw anyone including the old lady across the street. Didn't you talk to her Jane?"

"Yes actually and she said she saw no one but she was pretty badly shaken by the whole ordeal and may have been too scared to talk so let's err on the side of judgment and see what Miss Browne can find out. We can always fly back out there if she's right."

"I feel like we're the dog that's chasing its tail around and around never catching it."

"I know Dick but look at the bright side, we know what this guy looks like in all of his disguises now."

"Yes I know but it's only a question of time before some dumb cop somewhere blurts out that we have all six disguises down pat and the perp. will come up with a new one. I'm hoping our friends back in LA can come up with some useable fingerprints and maybe just maybe this guy has been finger printed for a license of some kind that will tip his hand, at least that's what I'm hoping for. He has to have a license of some kind, even a driver's license; I know some States require a finger print to get some different kinds of licenses. As soon as we get one, assuming we do, we'll run it through that new Computer the Director spent so much money on and see what comes up, we tried it once and came up empty handed because the print we weren't sure of but maybe now it's our turn to get lucky."

"You know the more I get to know the two of you the more ifs and holes I see in your case, no wonder this guy has everyone confused, with his disguises he can alter each one differently if he wants too into one of any number of different looks."

"You have a point there Miss Browne and a very good one."

"Thank you Agent Jefferies, I've learned quite a lot from the two of you."

After a nap almost before they knew it they were landing in back Washington.

"Before I forget Miss Browne give us a call if you think you have something when you're in Albuquerque."

"I'll do that, may I call you Dick now if I have anything?"

"Yes you may call me Dick and you can call her Jane if you like when we're away from the Office but any other place that's full of cops, there we'd prefer Special Agents Jefferies and Marlowe. "

"Consider it done and you two can call me Lisa anytime."

CHAPTER - 100

Work was proceeding at a greater pace on the translation of the Lost Books. Doris threw herself into the work enthusiastically working side by side with Fred. She was amazed at the knowledge Fred had for recreating ancient paper and ink so it looked hundreds or even thousands of years old. She spent a lot of time studying the loose papers and putting them in the correct order because someone obviously did not know what they were doing and had apparently started to go through them but didn't know the order of the pages or where they should be relating to the Books of the known Bible. It was painstaking work just getting started but once Doris had the books in some semblance of order things picked up and Fred was able to keep up with her in recreating some of the old worn pages and some of them were extremely fragile. Sometimes they had to remake the entire page occasionally using an educated guess as to the word or words missing from the holes in the pages due to the decomposition of the old paper. Some of the pages were so deteriorated that they fell apart and turned almost instantly into dust. Doris however was enthralled with what she was seeing and was unperturbed by the challenges. Fred was also in his element, he felt as though he was recreating history right in his own hands. Doris used lady size white cotton gloves when she handled the most damaged pages of the historic documents. She could hold a page up to the light when she had to and latex gloves were just too slippery to hold onto a page securely.

BJ and Sol made themselves available for the grunt work when it came to the duplicator machine that he and Fred had engineered and built almost from scratch. Fred had paper all ready in stacks that would mimic the old paper and text but it was safe enough for anyone to handle, it only looked fragile. As Fred and Doris completed a page or pages they would put the proper paper in the special duplicator's tray for the year that they were recreating and would run it through the machine making four copies of every page. One to keep for themselves, one for the client and one for the Museum in Egypt and one for Israel. The museums would keep the copies under lock and key away from prying eyes knowing full well the ramifications if they were found in their possession. The museum could be looted and burned to the ground to keep the books from ever being released to the public.

Secrecy was still at its highest level in the basement, no one else in the building knew what they had or what they were working on. One thing Fred had come up with was to photograph a fragile page with an overhead camera he had set up so if the page did crumble into dust from being handled they still had the photo which they could blow up right there in the basement and in that way they had the text even if the page had disintegrated into nothingness. Fred was also amazed that the books had made it so far with the aircraft having to make so many quick turns, descending movements over and around mountains while flying at such low altitudes to avoid radar and some landings which were sometimes harsh on the aircraft according to Sol.

Fred made sure that all of the dirt and dust in the boxes or crates was saved and he would use it when the papers were re-crated for redelivery back to the cave where they were found. Some of the interpretations of the original text had been handed down by word of mouth and in places where the sentence made no sense Doris would have to work it out with her knowledge of the Bible as to what the author had been trying to say. She found that in many instances an individual page made no sense at all, it was as if someone illiterate was writing it down from someone else's memory. She struggled with some of it for days on end but as they got deeper into the books it became clearer to her. It was the very early languages that gave her pause.

Four months had now gone by and the pace in the basement began to pick up a little more each day. Instead of spending a day or more on one page Doris was up to several pages a day. They took the poor copies when they came to them and redid them so that no one could tell they weren't the real thing on Fred's recreated paper. The project seemed to take on a new life as they progressed. BJ did his best to stay away from Doris when she was working because he didn't want to interrupt her train of thought. They did manage once in a while to have a meal together across the street at the restaurant but mostly Fred and Doris had their meals sent in.

Things in the store were going so well that Greta had to constantly re-order books from Publishing Houses and their inventory of first edition and rare books was being depleted despite Sol's attempts to keep duplicating originals so that each buyer thought that they had the only first edition original in the country sometimes signed by the Author and they were happy to pay Sol's inflated prices for the privilege of owning such a copy. Finally Sol had made up his mind about the critical shortage of inventory and he went down to the basement to see Fred.

"Fred, how is it all progressing today?"

"Just fine Sol we're making great headway with all of your help and BJ's, we may have the project done in twelve months instead of eighteen. This girl is a real find Sol, can we keep her on indefinitely?"

"Oh I don't know about that, I think she's probably homesick for her own country and her family but perhaps we could have her come back and stay on a work visa for a while. I think you can get one for months or perhaps a few years, I'm not sure but its worth looking into. As long she was in school it was no problem. Greta and I have set up a fake school for her learning the trade for preserving and reproducing old documents and I even set Greta up as her professor. We have given her grades to send to the Federal Government so they won't bother her as long as she's in School here with us but we can't keep it up forever."

"You're a master Sol, a real master of manipulations."

"I'll take that as a compliment Fred."

"I meant it that way. Now what is it you need from me today, you came down here to make small talk for another reason I'm sure?"

"Okay then I'll get right to the point. We're running low on inventory on the second floor, our supply is terribly small and I need to get out and find some new material soon. We've been so busy in the store that I let the inventory run down and its my fault for not keeping an eye on it. I let one of Greta's young men who hustles things for her keep to keep her going bring books down without checking on our backlog of material and making note of what he had brought down for the store so I could keep track with Greta. Its time for a new road trip or I'll loose my edge and we need new inventory anyway."

"I knew it wouldn't be long before we ran low on inventory again, go ahead and plan your trip, we can handle things down here and Doris is really good with the machinery and I've taught her what inks and paper to use for the period we're working on. It has freed me up a lot; I could use BJ for a couple of days to collate some more of what we've completed but you can have him too when you need him. After you send him down here we'll show him what we want him to do and we can probably get caught up before you're ready for your next road trip.

"Thanks Fred, it may take me some time to find a target Book Store sale so I'll let you know when I've got one selected and in the meantime you have BJ to yourself."

Sol went back upstairs to tell BJ.

"BJ, feel like a road trip soon?"

"Sure Sol, anytime you're ready just let me know."

"Okay, it will be a few days before I find a store to look over and in the meantime Fred asked me to send you downstairs to help he and Doris collate some of what they have completed so they can keep going with what they're doing which is fantastic work. I've never seen Fred do better work. So give me a few days while I look around and see what I can find and I'll give you a holler as soon as I find something suitable for us to go and look at."

Sol left BJ and went upstairs to his apartment to look through his old mail which he had overlooked because of the few bills that Greta didn't pay for him out of the Store's account just as she did for Fred's personal bills, those he paid right away. Soon he came across a couple of trade flyers which he usually found book store's sales in. Everything he saw was already past the sale date so he discarded those and he kept looking. He didn't realize how far behind he had become in reading his mail. He didn't find one that remotely interested him. He spent two whole days reading mail, magazines and other literature he had received but still found nothing. Exasperated he went back down to the store to help out and wait for fresh mail to be delivered. He was feeling like a fish out of water, he missed being out there searching for the big haul of rare books. He loved the challenge of the search when he got a lead and then he had to figure out a way to get the books without actually spending any money for them and that completed his challenge and then of course he had to get away with it and that's where he got his highs. The next day he got a call from Richard advising him that the FBI had been back to the Wynn Mansion asking more questions of the help. He felt Henry may have caved into the pressure and wanted to warn his friend that he may be found out soon. Sol told him he had made a mistake by letting Henry live but now it was too late to kill him so he asked just how unstable he was and asked if anyone was watching the mansion. Richard told him that Henry was near the edge of mental collapse but after the Feds questioned him he felt better and they said they would get you and he wouldn't have to worry. Sol thanked him for the heads up and told him not to worry, he had alibis for every job he had done, no one could be in two places at once. He said nothing about a whirlwind trip to pay Henry a visit. Sol silently made arrangements to go to LA one day and return the same day using one of his aliases, he figured he needed a new one for this trip. It was Tuesday and he got a flight for Thursday morning and a return flight for that evening. He called the rental company that Richard had used for the Bentley and asked if they had any Utility Company trucks used in the area. They told him they didn't have one and asked when he wanted it and said they could make it happen in the form of a gas, telephone or electrical service truck if need be. He told them that a Gas Company truck would be fine and asked them to pick him up at the airport in a car and take him to their lot. He got the necessary information and began getting a disguise together so he would look the part of a gas company employee.

On Thursday morning BJ took him to the airport and dropped him off, he told BJ to be back there tonight to pick him up again.

"Quick trip Sol?"

"You might say BJ but its best you don't know, just pick me up here at the baggage side of the airport as usual."

"Okay then, I'll see you later tonight."

BJ left and Sol headed for the ticket counter with his ticket information he had received over the phone with his reservation number so he could go right to the plane's gate as soon as he found out where it was. He carried only an overnight bag. He traveled under an assumed name to LA and using a different name to come back with along with forged credentials for each alias.

He landed in LA and called the rental car company and in a very short time a car pulled up to the curb with a gorgeous blond woman driving, he recognized her even with the dark glasses.

"So we meet again sir, but under different circumstances?"

"You might say that Sissy."

"I understand you want a small Gas Company Utility Repair Truck, is that right?"

"Yes, that's right!"

"Very good then, we have a man out selecting the perfect vehicle for you right now, a white pickup truck with the gas company's Logo and Name on the door. It should be there at the office when we get there."

"Fine, thank you for all your help."

"My husband and I run the office and we get a lot of unusual requests from people. You do realize that the truck will be hot but you'll have a couple of hours with which to do whatever it is you have planned and no questions asked. Our fee will depend on the difficulty of procuring the truck with as little trouble as possible. Sometimes we simply pay employees of companies to walk away from the vehicle for a couple of hours and we pay them handsomely for the use of their vehicle then return it from where it was taken within a certain amount of time. That way there are no cops involved, however there is sometimes a hitch or unseen risk then we have to steal the vehicle and dispose of the person who was driving it. Sometimes we just tie them up wearing masks so they can't identify our people. Hopefully your vehicle can be procured without any violence and we'll let you know how much time you have behind the wheel until we either have to give the vehicle back or dispose of it some way."

"That is very interesting. I've done the same kind of thing but when I need to get rid of a vehicle I take it to a friend who has an automobile salvage yard with a crusher, he crushes the thing into a square cube that no one could recognize and the vehicle disappears forever along with everything in it. Most of the time its shipped as scrap to other countries."

"Oh I like that idea but we don't have any crushers near us."

"Here's a hint, you'll generally find one close to the railroad tracks where they can load the stuff into railcars or ships to be shipped to steel plants anywhere in the world."

"I like it, nice and clean as they say. Well here we are, my husband would like to meet you and no names are fine with us, a handshake is all we ever expect with our cash customers."

"That's fine, I'd like to meet him as well."

Just as they stepped out of the car a white pickup truck pulled in and the man got out wearing regular coveralls with no company name on them. The man handed Sissy the keys and she asked; "how much time do we have?"

"We have until 1:30, if it isn't back on time the guy said he'd wait fifteen minutes more then report it stolen from a Convenience Store."

"Can you run your errand in that amount of time?" Sissy asked Sol.

"Well you tell me miss, I'm going to the same Mansion and will be there only a few minutes, then I'll come back here with the truck."

"Well lets see, its twenty minutes from here to the Mansion, ten minutes there then twenty minutes back here. Lets say an hour tops, that should leave you enough time, better reset your watch its 11:00 now. Tell you what, if you make good time come back here as soon as you are done and we'll buy lunch, how does that sound?"

"Sounds fine with me, is there gas in the truck?"

"Sure mister, she's got three quarters of a tank."

"Well alright, do you mind if I use your restroom inside to change clothes, I want to surprise someone when I arrive?"

"Yes, come in and meet my husband and I'll show you where to change." They walked into the office where her husband was waiting.

"Honey this is our friend from out of town, you remember Richard's friend, this is my husband and please no names need to be used, we're all just friends."

Sol reached out his hand and shook the man's hand vigorously.

"Pleased to finally meet you," said Sissy's husband, "many of our clients never set eyes on us, it's a cash only business we run on the side. The rest of out clients are well known to us and keep us in business. Several movie stars and entertainers who want to be invisible when they are in town and we make it happen for them. If you need to change you can use this room over here, there are coat hooks behind the door so when you return you can change back into street clothes, that way you don't have to carry a lot of things with you, quick and clean is the way we like things to happen."

"Me too and thank your for your kindness and hospitality."

"Don't forget we're buying lunch when you get back. When is your return flight?"

"Not until 4:15 this afternoon, I have all the time in the world," he told Sissy.

Sol went into the small office area and changed his clothes into a white shirt, black tie and black pants like he'd been told that gas company workers wore when making house calls. In a few minutes he was in the truck on his way to the mansion.

Twenty minutes later he pulled into the drive and up to the front of the house. He hoped Henry would be the one to answer the door. He knocked on the door and rang the door bell then stood with his back to the door and looked off into the distance. Soon the door opened and it was Henry. He glanced at the truck and the man standing with his back to him.

"Listen you, no one called the gas company, what are you doing here?"

Sol turned around slowly and looked straight up at Henry. "I understand you talked to the cops as well as the Feds. I'm here to kill you, you son of a bitch!" He reached beneath his shirt and pulled out his huge long barrel shiny357 magnum revolver and shoved it right up under Henrys chin. "I'm going to splatter your brains all over the door, I told you I'd come back to kill you if you talked."

Henry was shaking from head to toe, before Sol could threaten him anymore his eyes rolled back in this head and he collapsed in the doorway passed out cold. Sol was thinking, I wish he had gone nuts before he passed out now I'll never know how he reacted, I can't kill him now, the cops will know I've been back. Sol quietly replaced his pistol under his shirt, got in the truck and drove back to the rental place to drop it off and have lunch.

After the three of them had lunch and were waiting for their check somewhere in the Restaurant there was a TV on and the news was on with this top story. "We just learned that Henry Wertz, long time butler at the Wynn Mansion, was found dead of an apparent heart attack just before noon today by a maid who found him in the open doorway of the mansion where he fell. No foul play is suspected but the Sheriff of LA County is investigating this afternoon."

"Imagine that, the butler must have died of some kind of fright honey," said Sissy.

"Yes it looks that way dear but you know the word was that he knew something about his bosses' deaths and had a hard time living with it. It probably just caught up with him all of a sudden and he felt hot so he went out for some fresh air," replied her husband.

"Yeah, talk was that he was about to crack up over all the guilt he felt," answered Sissy.

Little did they know that the morning's papers would say the very same thing that it was a tragic death of an apparent heart attack brought on by stress and the feeling of guilt in the complicity of his employer's deaths.

Sol simply smiled when the couple he was with looked at him. He shrugged his shoulders and said, "I took two friends with me to meet poor Henry, Mr. Smith and Mr. Wesson, I guess the strain of his guilt caused his heart to stop."

The other two gave a knowing smile back, they knew exactly what Sol had done, he had scared the hell out of Henry. The couple paid for the meals then they all returned to their office for coffee and some small talk. When it was time for Sol to leave he peeled off a wad of one hundred dollars bills to pay his bill for the truck rental and Sissy drove him back to the airport.

BJ picked him up at the time Sol had told had him too and they headed back to the store. "Was your trip successful Sol?"

"Yes BJ, I tied up a loose end that had been bothering me." They rode the rest of the way back to Poughkeepsie in silence, the jet lag had apparently had caught up with Sol and BJ knew not to press him for details. Sol napped most of the way back to the Store.

CHAPTER - 101

At FBI Headquarters more than four months had passed with nothing new on the horizon. Dick and Jane were once again going over details waiting for the call they were sure would come from their Miss Browne. Then one day Dick got a notice from the Sheriff's Office in LA saying that the Butler for the Wynn residence had been found dead of an apparent heart attack and that an autopsy had been done that confirmed he did die of a heart attack. End of message. Dick and Jane were in their office comparing notes when the mail came.

"I'll be a son of a bitch, that bastard got to him after all Jane."

"Who got to who Dick?"

He handed Jane the note from the Sheriff he had just received.

"Damn it Dick you're right, the bastard got to him somehow and scared the snot out of him but good."

"Yeah I'll wager that he showed up at the front door a couple of weeks ago and was ready to kill him and it scared the man so bad that his heart stopped."

"I have to agree with you on this one but how did he get in and out of town with no one noticing him?"

"I'll bet he came up with a new disguise, flew in as one passenger and out again as another passenger a day or so apart and we don't have names for the descriptions. I wonder just how many aliases he has with I Ds to match?"

"I wish we knew, this guy is getting more and more clever all the time."

"Say, remember what Henry said the last time we saw him?"

"Huh?"

"You know about the new owner of the Mansion, how he didn't trust him and that he thought he may have had something to do with his Boss's death, Ms. Lorelei Wynn.

"Yeah I remember, he said he didn't know or care anything about horses and that he needed the place to use as a tax write off but Ms. Wynn wouldn't sell him the place."

"Yes that's it, that was the conversation. I think I'll wire the Sheriff and tell him he ought to check out the cousin more closely along with his comings and goings as well. Maybe he'll spill something useful for us."

"Good idea Dick, need some help?"

"Nope, I'll handle this one." Dick went to their secretary and with her help they drafted a note back to the Sheriff and he had her send it right out. Dick went back to their office.

"Say Jane, I just had a thought, our man hasn't struck again for some time now, did you look through all the literature we've been getting from the Trade Papers?"

"Yes I did but like you I didn't see anything that would draw our man out again."

"I'll bet he will go out on the next sale that comes up, it's been several months and he probably has cabin fever by now."

"So as usual we wait for an opportunity then we pounce."

"Yeah something like that." Another three weeks went by when they both received a flyer in the mail.

"Bingo Jane, we got one!" hollered Dick.

"What's with the bingo thing all the time Dick, you've got me saying it now and then, are you a bingo player or something?"

"No, I just get excited when we get a lead, it gets us closer to catching our man."

"Okay, let me get my mail then I'll catch up with you." Jane left and went to check her mail and sure enough there was a flyer in her mail as well. It was advertising 'The Sale of the Century, the Largest Book Store sale in History.' It was going to be held in three weeks in a small town in Rhode Island called Warwick, a very old community with Historical Stores and homes as well. The Book Store was being touted as the oldest in the northeast still in the same building for more than a hundred years in the same family. The sale was predicated on the fact that there were no heirs who wanted to run the store, it was being sold out to the bare walls; everything must go according to the flyer. It went on to say that there was a second floor in the building that was the first owners Apartment and that it hadn't been touched in years by the family, they left it intact as a testament to their great grandfather, the Antiques and odd collection of books were to be sold as well. It was an all or nothing sale, it would not be broken up. The hope by the family was that someone would come forward who liked old books and would run the business as a Historic site. The building was a three story stand alone building with other buildings close to it in the downtown area. The entire third floor of the structure held four large apartments that were all rented. 'Here was the opportunity of a lifetime,' said the article.

"Wow Dick, what an odd thing to do, sounds like to me they are offering to sell out the first floor and second floor to the walls in one package and the option is there to buy the whole building. That's an awful odd thing to do, why not just sell the whole building kit and caboodle."

"Beats me Jane, the heirs must be hoping for some kind of miracle it sounds like to me."

"I agree, why not just sell the business as a business along with the building. All in one nice neat package."

"I think I know Jane, think about it a minute, it doesn't name the business other than it's a book store, maybe the family is trying to sell the name of the Business as well, something like Uncle Ed's Fine Books."

"You're grasping at straws again Dick."

"Oh I don't know Jane, think about it for a minute, Business names have been bought and sold for Centuries for big bucks. It may be the family is selling their trade name as well? They left a couple of options open for a buyer and I'm betting they will take the one contract with the highest dollar amount to benefit them all."

"Okay maybe you have a point but suppose that the name of the store is called Warwick's

Fine Book Store? They can't very well sell the name of the city it's in and make money off it."

"True Jane, well let's have a look at it anyway and we'll hang around until our guy shows up. I don't see how he can miss it, its way too tantalizing of a prize."

They had three weeks to play with, they knew their man wouldn't be there first, he would be among the last so he could out bid anyone else. Jane went ahead and made the Airline arrangements and found a Motel not too far from the airport and she also learned that the Providence Airport was actually in Warwick and not in Providence which put them even closer to the book store in question. They got hold of a city map where the Store was located and even found the Motel where they would be staying, it was only a couple of miles from town.

"Dick, is there anything to do in Rhode Island other than go to the beaches?"

"I don't know Jane, I've never been there. Guess we'll have to wait and see when we arrive and find out what's available in the way of Restaurants and Nightclubs."

"I didn't say anything about a Nightclub Dick!"

"Well you never know, some of them have the best meals in town."

"Oh I see what you're getting at; I thought maybe you were thinking about a date."

"If and when we have a date it will be more like the Twin Willows in Virginia, I already promised the Director I would take him there."

"I haven't forgotten what an ass I made out of myself over a harmless lunch with you there, I don't know if I'm ready to go back there again."

"You know what they say Jane, if you get thrown by a horse the best thing to do is to get right back on and ride him again and if you fall again get right back on again."

"Oh I know all about that crap but I wasn't thrown, I did the throwing in the way of tantrums. I still feel terrible about the whole thing."

"Don't think a thing about it Jane, its over and done with. The next time you go there whether it's with me or someone else I know you'll act every bit the lady that you are."

"Well thank you for the vote of confidence Dick, I'll surely try to be on my best behavior then." The two of them split up and went back to work.

Two weeks later they had their gear together ready for their trip, they were planning for four to five days so they would get there ahead of their man and have time to check things out and they didn't want anyone to know that the FBI was snooping around so they would play it different this time. They would be the rich playboy, playgirl tourist kind of a thing, just being rather nosey instead of serious buyers, they would act like it could be a great tax write off if they bought it. The time was getting close for them to leave for Providence; it wasn't a long flight according to their flight information. Donny took them to the airport and they were on their way.

They arrived at the airport in Providence close to 1:00 pm and the first thing on their agenda was lunch. They stopped at a place called the Greenwood Inn on the outskirts of Warwick that was said to have a great reputation for great steaks and seafood. Inside it appeared to be a very old Restaurant and the ambience was to their liking. After eating they decided that this was their kind of place, they were open for lunch and dinner only. They would have to find another restaurant for breakfast. They rented a white four door sedan that wouldn't stand out. They marveled at all of the old buildings as they drove all around town up and down side streets trying to familiarize themselves somewhat before taking a look at the Book Store which they passed by a couple times. It was just off from Main Street but was visible by the sign that hung out from the building towards the street. The building was all brick and looked to be in very good condition. The entire bottom floor consisted of the book store and they knew it was huge even before they went in. They spent the rest of the day sight seeing along what was called the Shore Road that literally followed the sea shore. There they saw many stately large homes facing the bay with stonewalls abundant everywhere.

"Dick, I've never seen so many stonewalls in all my life, where did they all come from, the stones I mean?"

"I heard somewhere that when they began farming here there were so many rocks in the fields that the farmers began piling them up to get rid of them and they made perfect property lines in the form of walls from farm to farm, some houses early on were also built of field stone."

"You read up on the History before we left didn't you?"

"Well yes and no, I was a little curious about the littlest State in the US so I read up on it a little."

"Uh huh, just a little, you sound like a National Geographic Magazine."

"Sorry about that. Listen, it's getting late, how about some supper or rather dinner?"

"Sounds great to me!"

They went back to the Greenwood Inn where they ate lunch. Supper was fantastic, the steak you could cut with a fork and they served wine, beer or mixed drinks. They both had steak and baked potatoes, Dick had green beans and Jane asked for corn that came as a side in a small bowl. For desert they both had pie a la mode, dick had apple and Jane opted for peach.

"You know Jane that was a great meal and look at this place there's no place to sit and there is a line at the front door."

"I guess we picked the right place to eat then."

"Yeah, how lucky can we get, this is close to everything and everything is close to us."

"Well you said it earlier; we're in the smallest State, everything has to be close or they would fall in the ocean."

"Oh Jane you aren't funny, just look how close we are to the ocean"

"That's my point silly!"

While they were talking they heard faint piano music coming from somewhere in the Restaurant. They strained their ears trying to listen and figured that they must have a piano bar in another room. Anyway it was beautiful music perfect for a restaurant and lounge as big as this was. They stayed put and had a couple of drinks before heading back to their Motel where they had separate rooms this time.

The next morning they were in no rush to get going, they took their time taking showers and putting on what they considered to be playboy, playgirl clothes and they wanted to look the part of tourists as well. They had spotted a family type restaurant that advertised home cooked meals and headed there in the downtown area for breakfast. It was very close to the book store as well. After they ate they figured they would pay the Store a visit like regular customers and maybe find a book or magazine to buy and try not to appear too obvious.

It worked just fine; they prowled each and every isle trying to take it all in. The windows were covered with sale posters and the books were discounted to try and sell off as much inventory as possible. Every sale was carefully monitored and they noticed someone who could have been a bookkeeper or an accountant. Dick bought a book on Rhode Island History and other interesting facts and Jane bought a women's magazine to have something to read. They spent the better part of an hour and a half in there taking their time and checking out the customers who appeared to be all locals, no one stood out and there were only two days left before the sale. Today was Thursday and they knew they were a little early but it gave them a chance to check the place out and they both found a corner where they could see every part of the store from.

CHAPTER - 102

At the Book Store in Poughkeepsie Doris and Fred had been working hard on the Lost Books of the Bible and were still making great progress. Sol received a flyer in his mail one day that intrigued him. It advertised a sale in Warwick Rhode Island which said everything must go. It went on to say that the building may also be purchased and the second floor was the owner's apartment and no one had been in there in years, The family left it as is as a testament to their grandfather. Sol read it and re-read it several times then realized the apartment had a collection of odd books and wondered what the ad meant by an odd. Could this be a misprint that was meant to say old rather than odd? The more he read it the more confused he became. He had trouble isolating the different slants on the sale. He decided that someone, whoever it was, didn't know stink about selling a business or anything else for that matter. He decided maybe he would take a look knowing now that the FBI was on the case. He knew he would have to be more careful from here on.

He went to the basement Lab to see Fred and check on the progress of what they were working on and to let him know about this latest book store sale. He didn't know if there were enough books to restock their store or not so he would have to go have a look for himself. From there he went to the store and saw Greta and asked her where he could find reference books on the States.

She told him where so he went to find a book on the History of Rhode Island, a State he had never been to before. He found what he wanted and showed it to Greta so she could make a note of where the book was. He took it upstairs and read it through and through until he was comfortable with some of the knowledge and jargon of the State. He went ahead and made his airline reservations then looked for some information for a Motel or Hotel not to far from the airport. He knew if he made a deal and he needed the van BJ could drive up from Poughkeepsie in just a few hours to meet him. He was a little uncomfortable about this sale due to the confusing sales pitch he had read. He came up with a new disguise, one he not used before so he would fit in anywhere in Rhode Island without giving himself away. He chose to go into town and buy the things he needed in Rhode Island.. He would use two different disguises this trip to confuse the issue in case there were local Cops or Fed's watching the sale and may be in the building watching for him. He knew the best place to hide was in amongst the locals. When he had been reading he learned that a lot of Rhode Island's people were fishermen and it wasn't unusual to see them in or around town. He could use the excuse that his boat was in dry dock receiving some much needed attention what with Warrick being on the water and all. Her bottom needed scraping, repairing, painting and work needed to be done on her two diesel engines. He came up with a name for his boat and he would call it the Virginia M out of Warwick and if anyone questioned him he could say that the boat was from Massachusetts originally, he bought it a few months ago and decided to move to Warwick and make this his home rather than New Bedford, it seemed plausible to him. Everyone knew where the famous New Bedford Fishing Seaport was. The other disguise was that of a Farmer. He also learned that there were plenty of small farms around the State and the authorities wouldn't be looking for a farmer or a fisherman, at least he hoped that they .wouldn't. He figured they may have some descriptions of his past characters and would be looking for them and not two completely new disguises. He wouldn't play it up too big, just wear country type clothes and a well worn baseball cap that he could age in the basement using materials there and the same went for the fisherman's outfit, it had too look well worn but not worn out.

Within a week he was ready to go but still had lots of time before leaving for Rhode Island. Then he decided just for the heck of it to ask BJ if he'd like to go along and play Sol's first mate from their fishing boat but after that he would have to lie low so as not to attract attention. He knew that if the FBI knew about him because of Richard's heads up phone call about the Fed's and the Sheriff's Department coming back and asking questions and if they'd done their proper investigating work they would know that BJ had been seen with him on at least one deal. He decided to chance it anyway, bold always worked before why not again.

The next few of days crawled by until Thursday and time for Sol to catch his plane. At the last minute he changed his mind about bringing BJ along, he didn't want to chance it and thought he would do better alone. He planned on leaving Thursday noon and returning on Monday if successful otherwise if there was a problem he would leave on the earliest flight out and if it wasn't safe he could call BJ to come and get him in the van. He had everything planned out the best he could. He would travel to Rhode Island in street clothes then change at the airport and rent a car to drive around town with. Everything so far was going like clock work.

Sol arrived at the Providence Airport, changed into his fisherman's clothes with his elevated shoes then rented a car for five days to get the lower rate they were offering. He drove causally into town and drove around checking places out. He found the store and at the time he saw nothing unusual so he looked for a place to park about a half a block away. He checked around carefully for any police presence and saw none so either the Feds weren't here or they were and didn't tell the local cops. By now it was late Thursday afternoon and he watched customers who were coming and going from the store but saw nothing out of the ordinary so he decided to get some supper and he would make himself known tomorrow afternoon when he would case the scene as he called it. He wouldn't change disguises that he had recently purchased until after he saw the store then he had his choice of street clothes like many of the locals with which he would make the deal or in the farmer's clothes if he saw anything suspicious.

Unbeknown to Sol Dick and Jane were already in the Book Store when he showed up and they would leave just minutes behind Sol's coming in and they didn't take notice of one another.

Sol then opted to go to a small family restaurant he had seen close to the store where he could ask questions about the store and people in general. He had a good meal of Shepherds' Pie which was the special of the day and he engaged the waitress in conversation asking questions he thought he could get away with without looking suspicious. He made out like he was reasonably new in town and gave her the story about his boat being laid up in dry dock and it wasn't fishing season so that wouldn't look suspicious. He played the part extremely well and wondered about asking her for a date when he saw no rings on her fingers or tan lines where she may have worn one. He found the meal to be excellent and to his liking. He paid his bill and left the waitress a generous tip. He wanted her to remember his name was Bill, at least that's what he told her. Then on the next night perchance the Feds were there to eat he would look like any other customer and he hoped she would remember his name then he went back to his Motel.

Tomorrow being Friday he planned to case the Store as the fisherman who needed something to do with his time by looking for something to read and nonchalantly he would ask about the price of the store from someone. He just wanted to sound like an interested customer and whether or not the store would still be open for a few more weeks while his boat was in dry dock.

He was up early, shaved, showered, got his disguise together, a dark brown wig that matched the hair on the sides of his own hair line so no additional makeup was needed there. He went back to the same restaurant early to eat breakfast then befriended another waitress and gave her his name as Bill. As he was paying his check with his back turned, Dick and Jane walked in not noticing the fisherman. Even with their get ups Sol smelled cops or Feds. He had left the girl a healthy tip hoping that she'd remember his name was Bill in case the Feds or someone else asked her any questions. He smiled as he left; they never saw his face from the front, just a slight side view. They just happened to sit at his table where the same waitress was clearing the table. Dick being curious of everyone asked about the man who just left, the hair was standing up on the back of his neck giving him an eerie feeling.

"Excuse me Miss; do you know the man who just left?"

"Sure his name is Bill, he's the Captain of the Virginia M that's in dry dock getting her bottom scraped and painted for the fishing season. He's from New Bedford but he moved here because he likes our town better I guess." "Thank you Miss." He let it go as nothing but something still nagged at him. He rubbed the back of his neck again and again.

Sol went about his business and headed directly for the store to give it a another quick look see. He went in and looked all around and found a book to occupy his time, Moby Dick a well known fishing novel. He inquired briefly at the counter about the sale. He was told the final sale would be Saturday at

5:00 pm. They would accept the highest and best offer to date then and if someone wanted it bad enough they could make another offer then. He was told a local Attorney would be handling the final sale on site at the store. He got the Attorney's name and planned a new strategy. He would stake out the Attorney's office and catch him alone as he returned from the sale with or without the buyer. He already knew now there was an offer from an out of town buyer and if he worked his cards right he could beat them all to the punch. Sol decided to lay low and not go back to the restaurant afraid that he may run into the Feds again. On Saturday he would change into his farmers outfit and hang around town for a while.

Saturday morning came and Sol found a new place for breakfast, he decided that the one near the store was a poor choice. He found one three blocks away on the other side of Main Street. He ate both breakfast and lunch there and left a different story with the waitress that his name was George and he was looking for some new clothes but was picky. That got the waitress to talking and she gave him several leads of places to shop for coveralls and other farm style work clothes. He gave her the sob story that his wife had died just prior to spring planting and now that the harvest season was over he was forced to do things his wife always took care of. He flashed a considerable amount of money in front of the gal to get her attention so she would remember him in case the Feds went looking for a stranger about town. It all went very smoothly. Sol thought seriously about going back to the store but he didn't want to have another chance encounter with the Feds. He hung around close by and watched from across the street where he could see inside of the store and waited. Finally the closed sign went up on the door and he watched as the Attorney left followed closely by the two Federal Agents, Jefferies and Marlowe. Now he knew for sure what they looked like but they had yet to spot him. They walked with the attorney to the corner and not seeing anyone suspicious they headed back up the street away from the store towards their car.

Sol watched the attorney and already knew where he was going. As the Attorney opened his Office door to go in Sol was right behind him and followed him in like he owned the place.

"Say what is this, who are you old man?"

"I'm not an old man and I'd like you to accept one more offer for the store."

"What, that's impossible the sale is done and over with. An out of State Buyer has bought the whole place lock, stock and barrel. He's sending movers to start loading everything up on Monday morning."

"Just what is his name may I ask?"

"No you may not ask, the sale is final I tell you, over and done with, now please leave!"

"Have the movers been called already?" Sol asked quietly and politely trying to calm the agitated attorney down some.

"They have, so you see you're about fifteen minutes too late."

"Oh I see, you're sure you won't listen to my offer, I can top the other man's easy if you'll just listen to me for a moment."

"No sir! I am sorry but I've already notified the other party they got the deal so its done, now please leave my Office."

"No sir! I don't think you understand. You didn't make any call or I would have seen you make it. I'm prepared to offer you an amount that no reasonable man would refuse plus double the fee you'll make on this deal."

"Double my fee you say?"

"That's what I said; I'll double your fee and pay it in cash as well as cash for the store."

"This is highly irregular but cash is cash, where would a farmer like you get that kind of money?"

"Number one I am not a farmer but a savvy businessman who buys and sells things like stores and I want this one no matter what the price."

"How about triple my fee, then we can talk terms?"

"No terms; cash I told you!"

"Well I don't know, that's an awful lot of money for anyone to carry around, where's your money?"

"In my Motel room in two suitcases full of $100.00 dollar bills. I have just under two million with me, how much was your deal?"

"Well I can tell you that it was nowhere near that."

"Alright, I can see you don't believe me, here's a number for you to call, its my Banker's home phone, I'll write it down and give you my name and you can check with him about my honesty and my bank account if you like."

"Well alright, we'll try it your way, let's have it?"

Sol wrote down a fictitious name and Fred's number back at the store. It worked once before giving Sol time to rig everything up and a little time was all he needed now. The attorney dialed the number and listened. "Hmm, two million dollars withdrawn in cash just two days ago and he has that kind of money in the bank still?""Yes, yes I'm listening, okay I'll tell him."

"Your Banker said he wishes you would quit doing business on weekends and said if you kept this up he'll start charging you a fee for bothering him on the weekends. Alright I guess I know when I've been trumped, the other deal was $1,235,000.00 and my fee was a flat 35,000 with no strings attached so all you need to hand over $1,340,000.00 which includes my triple fee you agreed to pay."

"Uh huh, so now you understand." Sol reached out his hand to shake the attorney's hand.

"Put her right there and we have a deal." They shook hands. "Alright now if you will call your buyer back and explain that another bid came in dated and timed ahead of his and your secretary missed you at the store and that you're sorry but they got the deal, tell him anything like that."

"Alright I'll do it because he has to stop his moving people from coming here on Monday. If you want you can go to your Motel and get the money while I make the call."

"Thanks, but I'll wait for you to be sure everything is alright, then I'll go get the money and meet you back here in a few minutes."

"Alright, but I'd prefer you didn't listen in on my calls."

"Okay I'll step outside until your done." Sol opened the door and went outside and waited for the greedy Attorney to make his call to whoever he had to make excuses but Sol could hear everything. He was a man of his word when it came to money; his out of State buyer was a little upset as he thought he had bought the whole kit and caboodle. The Attorney told the lie to him just as Sol had told him to almost word for word, he apologized and said goodbye.

"You can come back in sir, it's done," The Attorney called out.

"What about the moving company you told me about."

"He's taking care of that himself."

"May I ask you one more thing, then I'll go get the money so you can go home?"

"Sure what is it, I'm on your time now?"

"Is there a local moving company around here that can keep things quiet, I mean move things with as little disruption as possible?"

"Of course, I know someone who can keep their mouth shut and work discreetly, is that what you're getting at?"

"Exactly, and I'd like for them to start on Tuesday morning if possible, load everything up and I do mean everything, I have plans for the building myself. I'm going to do a lot of renovating and rent the entire building out as apartments and store fronts, I think I can get two stores in there at double the rent."

"What a great idea, let me see if I can get a hold of my friend, I suppose you'll want him so that he won't disrupt traffic in front of the store and you'll pay him with cash as well sir?"

"That's right and he'll need a big rig, we have a long haul to make."

"Can I tell him where he'll be going?"

"No, just tell him to fill the tanks to the brim, I'll tell him on Tuesday morning when I see him at the store what his final destination will be. Oh and if he's worried tell him that's it less than a thousand miles one way. I have to check a couple of locations on Monday during the day out of town before I decide where I want it all to go."

"How are you going to do that and get back here in time?"

"With my private plane I came in on, it's over at the far side of the airport on the civilian side, it's a new Business Jet."

"Shall I describe you to the man?"

"No, just tell him myself or my representative will be there to supervise and pay them half down when they are loaded and they'll get the other half at the final destination. As soon as everything is settled I'll go get the money and be right back, then maybe you'll allow me to buy you dinner this evening."

"Well I don't know;" he scratched his chin with his right hand, "I don't have any real plans for tonight; I'm recently divorced and in debt over my eyeballs, but other than that I'd be honored to have dinner with you this evening."

The Attorney didn't know it but he had just signed his death own warrant. That's exactly what Sol wanted to hear. The Attorney made his call, retrieved the papers from his briefcase and told Sol he would put everything in whatever name he wanted so Sol told him to put it all in the name a fictitious Store, one of his shell companies. The Attorney agreed and Sol left in his car which wasn't far away and drove around for about a half an hour. He had two bags already in the rental car like he had described to the Attorney.

Sol drove back into the Attorneys parking lot and checked all around, people were still leaving work and were so busy leaving town that they didn't notice the Attorney's Office. He got out and went inside. The Attorney was just finishing up the transfer for the deed from the previous owner. Sol watched intently knowing that the man before him was about to die.

"Would you care to check over the papers I prepared for you sir?" asked the Attorney.

"Yes if you don't mind." Sol read over everything like he was really interested but he was watching for anything beneath the paperwork that may leave an impression on any other paper. He didn't see any carbon copies and the copy machine was still off so he guessed the Attorney wanted everything under the table so his ex wife couldn't get a dime and he was right. Sol had one more problem, he needed to make the car and the Attorney disappear. He had only a vague idea what he would do with the attorney's body and his car when he remembered the fishing docks near the end of the street where the Book Store was. It wasn't far away and he could shove the car off the wharf when it was deserted and it would be months before anyone found the car or the body. His plan was fool proof except for the FBI Agents who were still in town. He was sure they knew the moving truck would be picking everything up on Monday morning and he assumed correctly they would return to Washington empty handed. Now all he had to do was kill the attorney. He was now flying by the seat of his pants, he needed to know just how hungry this Attorney was to get his hands on over thirty five thousand dollars times three equaling $105,000.00 in cash tonight. He didn't have to wait long.

"Are you ready to finish up our transaction sir?" asked the Attorney once again,

"I sure am," replied Sol, "and I want to thank you for taking such good care of me."

"Think nothing of it; you caught me at a good time is all."

"Well why don't you lock up and if it's alright with you can we take your car to go to dinner, I'm not that familiar with Warwick. We can take the money from my car and put it in yours first if you like."

"I'd like that and I will put my car in my garage when I get home, then go to the Bank Monday morning."

Sol hesitated as the man opened his trunk and waited for Sol to bring the two suitcases of money over. Sol took both bags of money over to his car and set them in the trunk, I've already counted the money but you're welcome to check it you like, one has your fee in it and the other has the cash for the store."

"The Attorney bent over to look inside the trunk and then undid the straps of one suitcase and lifted the cover. What he saw he wasn't quite sure of so he looked again and said; "Hey wait a minute mister, it's not all here."

Those were the last words the man ever spoke. Sol shot him in the back of his head with his 9mm silenced pistol. He pushed the body all the way into the trunk after retrieving his two suitcases. He put the suitcases back in his trunk again, got in the attorneys car with the Attorney's keys and drove towards the waterfront a few blocks away. Sol already had his cotton gloves on so as not to leave any prints. He was careful while in the Attorneys office not to touch anything at all and he stood around holding his hands clasped in front of him. The Attorney was so greedy he took no notice of Sol's movements or actions. Sol drove to the waterfront and parked the car in a likely spot. There were quite a few people milling around for some reason so he got out and just kind of sauntered around. Finally he slipped away to get his own rental car to come back with. He had to wait an additional hour until the docks were finally quiet enough and he placed the ignition key back in the Attorney's ignition, started the car, put it in gear and stepped out of the way letting the momentum of the weight of the car carry it over the edge of the wharf and into the deep channel meant for large fishing boats. It hit the higher edge of the channel and kind of stood on end there for a minute or two making Sol extremely nervous until the weight of the heavy car and the incoming tide carried it out into the deeper part of the channel to where it finally settled completely out of sight in the murky green water. Sol got back in his car and headed for his Motel. That was almost too easy he thought with no trace left anywhere.

On Monday morning he knew the Feds would leave by noon time when no one had showed up and on Tuesday morning his moving truck would be there to pack everything and get it ready to go to the Store back in Poughkeepsie. Now he had to figure out a way so the moving truck would also disappear and couldn't be traced back to them along with the drivers. He thought long and hard on the problem and decided he would take care of it like the last time. Kill the drivers and take the moving truck to the scrap yard to be crushed with them inside. He went back to the motel after supper at the same restaurant in his farmers disguise and no one was the wiser for it, no one recognized him. It would be months or perhaps years before the Attorney's car would be discovered he was thinking.

CHAPTER -103

Dick and Jane were frustrated in Warwick that Saturday afternoon. They didn't see a anyone who even closely resembled or even looked their man anywhere. No one in elevated shoes which they were sure they would have noticed. A complete strike out as they searched faces in small crowds frequently checking their sketches for their man in their minds. They went to the sale and stayed there while the Attorney for the family told the small crowd of seven potential buyers that the sale was final and he read aloud the Bid he had received and no one would top it so he declared the sale over and done with. They asked the Attorney to name the faceless buyer but he said he didn't have that information. They showed their badges and he said he couldn't because he didn't know. He was acting as their agent and it would be listed in the newspapers the following Monday or Tuesday a week from now. The name was that of a large Brokerage Firm in New York City and they were fronting for one of their clients so he couldn't disclose the name because again he didn't know who it was. He said they were so sure that they would get the place that they already had moving trucks ready to show up Monday morning to move everything to an undisclosed location in New York City. They thanked the Attorney and headed back for their Motel dejected.

"I don't understand Dick, you and I were so cock sure our man would be here."

"We don't know that he wasn't, maybe we got fooled like everyone else by the sealed bid of the Brokerage House in New York, maybe that was a hoax by him to do a legal transaction this time to where he didn't have to be here in person."

"There must be something awfully valuable here for someone to buy this sight unseen."

"I have a feeling we've been had Jane, something isn't right with this whole set up. Let's see if we can find a newsstand somewhere. We'll go back to Washington but in the meantime I want next week's newspaper sent to us at the Office."

"What are you worried about Dick?"

"The Attorney Jane, he was too sure of himself, he never batted an eye at the other's who wanted to buy the Store, when he asked if anyone wanted to up their price they were willing to pay he never really gave anyone a chance to speak up, he was too quick, too sure of himself and that damned envelope he held in his hand. Did you notice he held it up but never opened it to show the price that the other buyer was going to pay?"

"I see now what you're getting at, a side deal with the Attorney acting as someone's agent to buy the place at a higher undisclosed price."

"Exactly what I was thinking. I'd really like to stay around and watch the Attorney but I have no real reason too. Just because I'm skeptical doesn't mean he isn't on the up and up and the others seemed to know him and just let their offers fade into oblivion. I'm beginning to think this whole thing was a set up for the family to milk as much money out of a deal as they could. They may have already signed papers over to the new buyer ahead of time and held the sale to see if they were getting a fair price before they signed the deed."

"Okay I see where you're going now. We're getting off track here, what about our man Dick, where was he?"

"I have a feeling he was here somewhere but blended in with the locals so well that we didn't notice him and maybe the Attorney was acting on his behalf and this time it was on the up and up, all legal like."

"You know I searched every face, every height and weight against everyone I saw. I couldn't have missed him and neither could you. I'm beginning to think he didn't show at all or maybe the Attorney represented him like you said."

"Here's a Newsstand, lets check inside and see how many papers they handle and see if we can get some sent to us in Washington."

The two of them went inside the small newsstand. There were newspapers from everywhere along with magazines of every sort imaginable. The store was not very wide inside only three isles but it went deep into the back of the building so it was much larger than one would think when looking in from outside. Dick saw a young man looking at a dirty magazine.

"Careful son, looking at things like that will stunt the growth between your legs."

The young man looked up startled, saw an older man smiling down at him, dropped the magazine and ran out of the store.

"Dick that was a terrible thing to say to that young man."

"Yeah maybe but he'll remember it for a long time."

They both started laughing. They found the proprietor and engaged him in some conversation. "May I help you folks?"

"My name is Special Agent Jefferies of the FBI and this is Special Agent Marlowe. I have a question I'd like to ask of you."

The man was completely startled when he heard FBI. "Please mister I didn't do anything, I run a good clean place here."

"You're mistaken sir, I have a favor to ask of you, that's all. If I leave you our names and address, would you be able to mail copies of your local newspaper starting with Monday's copy for two weeks to us in Washington DC?"

"Whew mister, you gave me a start! For a minute there I thought maybe the IRS sent you. I'd be only to happy to help, just write down the information. I get lots of calls from people who are vacationing in Florida to send them newspapers for four or five months so I'm familiar with the rate, will it be first class or something else?"

"No first class please and I'll give you my Federal Credit Card number to use so I'll have a receipt to give my boss." Dick wrote everything down for the man and gave him his credit card to run through his card machine and he handed it back to Dick when he was done. "Now that's twelve papers and don't try to pad the bill, we weren't born yesterday you know."

"Oh no sir, I would never do that."

"Oh, then why did you think we were here on behalf of the IRS?"

"Well, you know how things get exaggerated now and then when filling out all those Income Tax forms, you know how it is I'm sure."

"Nope, can't say that we do!"

"You did just say Special Agents didn't you?"

"Why yes, is there a problem?" asked Dick.

"Well no sir I was just wondering why such high powered Agents such as yourselves could possibly want with our little ole town?"

"We're here on Official business and that's enough for you to know."

"Yes sir, uh yes ma'am, pleased to make your acquaintance."

They left the store and the short balding man behind the counter was sure glad to see them leave; they heard him sigh deeply as they left. He had the look of the type of man who didn't know any other work. He was short in stature, average weight and wore one of those shade things on his head that had a green piece of plastic in the bill to keep the bright sun out of his eyes or in his case maybe the bright lights of the store but his bald head shown through just the same. He was sweating profusely as they left.

"Why the newspapers Dick?"

"I want to see the announcement of the sale in the paper and see when the Deed is recorded which usually takes ten days to two weeks and see if there is any other news to tie in with this sale."

"Okay, just wondering again out loud to be sure we're on the same page still."

They went out to dinner at the Greenwood Inn and returned back to the Motel to prepare to leave on Sunday Morning. They had left their original reservations for the airplane stand as it was, they could have cancelled if necessary and stayed longer.

Sunday morning they were on their way back to Washington, they had called Donny the night before and asked him to pick them up again at the airport, he was only to happy to do it because he got to get behind the wheel of Dick and Jane's new Galaxie 500 and get the old feeling back from the power beneath that hood.

CHAPTER - 104

Monday morning they were back to the same old grind, trying to ferret out their man once again. Thursday a newspaper came in the mail which was actually Tuesday's paper from Warwick with bold headline news, 'Attorney absconds with funds from Book Store Sale, he's missing declared his wife and I want my share of the commission. He owes me big time.'

Dick and Jane glanced at it and didn't think too much about it. The following Tuesday they got Friday's newspaper from Warwick Rhode Island. Headline News read, 'Fisherman gets big haul from the bay, pulls up missing Attorney's car with his body in the trunk, he had been shot in the head, caliber undetermined at press time.'

"Jane, take a look at this, we got trouble in paradise."

"Huh, let me see." She took the paper and read the article. "We missed him but how, where, when?"

"I'm guessing understand but maybe our man saw us before we saw him and waited for the Attorney at his Office and ambushed him there, he could have easily forged the papers, killed the man, got rid of the car and body after dark. Alright Jane lets go back and pick up the pieces and figure this out."

"You mean go back there and talk to people about all this?"

"That's exactly what I mean, somehow we missed him but he made us."

Jane went into their office and got them the first flight out that she could to Providence once again. The first flight that she could get them both one was Wednesday afternoon but they couldn't sit together, one seat was up forward and the other one all the way back by the restroom.

Donny took them to the airport once again and they were off. They planned their return trip for the following Sunday afternoon. Jane got the same Motel this time and they rented a car at the airport and drove the few miles back into Warwick to have a look around and talk to anyone they could find who might have seen something out of the ordinary. First thing they did was to get hold of the ex wife and she was still boiling mad at her dead husband. She couldn't shed any light on his death either. They called on the Attorney's secretary who was doing her best to clear out his office of all files, books and other paperwork. They introduced themselves and asked her all kinds of questions.

"I'm sorry," said the secretary, "but he didn't confide in me about the book store sale, he said he would handle everything for the New York City buyers, some Brokerage House was what he told me."

"Surely miss, he had to make a deposit of a rather large amount of money after the sale?"

"No Ma'am, he made no deposit whatsoever, that's why everyone thought he took off with the money but there wasn't a dime found in the car and its not in the bank either, I already checked for the Warwick Police Department who has been in and out of here since he disappeared. They tore this place apart and even made me a suspect for a while but once they checked me out real good they slacked off on me. What a mess I have to clean up here and I'm not getting paid for it either. When I came in here on Monday morning after he had disappeared all I found was his open empty safe, all the papers regarding the sale of the Book Store were gone as well and they weren't in the car either. He had a huge file he had built for the sale and its gone, everything's gone."

"How about the book store Miss, is everything still there?"

"Why no, the moving truck came just as my boss had told me it would but it was a day late and they cleaned the place out and there were some people who were there watching and they asked where it was all going and the moving men said some Brokerage Firm in New York City. Now you have all the same information as everyone else."

"I'm sorry Miss, you said the movers were a day late, do you remember the name of the company your boss was using?"

"No! I am sorry but he handled everything from here by phone."

"Wait a minute Jane, phone records may give us a clue. When do you get the next phone bill for the office Miss?"

"I already settled with the Phone company, paid the bill out of petty cash, my boss's checking account and his Escrow account had a zero balance when I checked on it for the police, the escrow of $100,000 from the buyer was gone as well as other escrow deposits for other clients, all the money's gone!"

"Do you have a copy of the phone bill anywhere around here still, we really do need it?"

"I don't know ma'am the Police may have it for all I know."

"Would you mind if we looked around some, we promise not to disturb a thing."

"No ma'am, I'm really tired, I've got to go and hunt me a new job now."

Dick and Jane got busy looking for any phone bill. For an hour and a half they hunted, they went through what they swore was a ton of paper but stayed in the front near the secretary's desk because she paid all the bills for the Office. Finally Jane called out, "got one Dick, its for last month but there are several calls to New York Phone Numbers here."

"Close enough Jane, Miss would you mind if we made a copy of this?"

"No go right ahead the electric won't get cut off until 5:00 pm today."

"We're truly sorry for your loss, he must have been a good man."

"Actually he was a good boss and a good Attorney but he was a womanizer and his wife caught him out one day with a female client in a motel room, she let him have it then filed for a divorce the very next day They didn't have any children, he couldn't make babies, something about bad sperm count or something. Anyway the ladies loved him especially the married ones.

He never once hit on me but he did say one day he didn't mix business with pleasure, bull crap!"

"Thank you Miss." Jane's face was getting red.

Dick made the copy of the phone bill and they were off again. "Well Jane what do you think? I personally feel she filled in all the blanks for us better than anyone else could have done. How about we head back to our office and make some phone calls and see what develops."

"Sounds like a plan to me Dick! Wait, hold on a minute, what about the bullet in the Attorney's head, we ought talk to the local cops to see if its our old friend with the 9mm pistol."

"Good thought Jane lets give that a whirl."

They headed for the Warwick Police station which wasn't far away. They found the desk Sergeant, introduced themselves as tactfully as they could so as not to upset the applecart like they had done a couple of times in other towns. They found the man to be very helpful. He said the autopsy wasn't complete yet so they gave the Sergeant their names and address and asked him to send a copy of the report along when he could. They told him that they were looking for a killer who used a 9mm pistol in his murders and didn't say more. They shook hands and went back to their Motel.

"Well Jane this is one of the shortest visits we ever had. What do you say we get some dinner and call the airlines and see if we can get out of here tomorrow sometime."

"Sounds like a plan to me Dick."

"You say that a lot Jane, sounds like a plan to me, where did you pick that up?"

"Why from you Dick, you used to say it a lot."

"You're kidding, I don't remember saying that."

They both laughed and headed for the Greenwood Inn for one more meal.

The next day they were on their way back to Washington hoping what they had in the way of phone numbers would shed some light on their case. Donny picked them up again and took them to their individual apartments.

The next day they both got on telephones and made inquiries into the New York Phone numbers. On one of Dick's calls he got a disgruntled gentlemen who wanted to know when they were going to get back the one hundred thousand dollar earnest money deposit for the bungled sale. Dick had to tell him that the Attorney or someone else had cleaned out all of his accounts and the man died broke and in debt. It didn't set well with the well healed Stock Broker who had been acting as the representative for an Investor whom he would not name. He went on to tell Dick that they didn't get the deal and the Attorney had called him and told him that their deal had fallen through when another out of state buyer showed up with cash before the deadline and trumped their price. The man said the Attorney apologized and said he'd return their deposit the first thing Monday morning but they never got it. Dick listened intently as he put two and two together.

Jane was getting almost the same response from the men and women she talked to. They were all mad that the money had disappeared and wanted it back. By that afternoon they were done chasing phone calls. Sometimes they had to wait on hold for a long time while someone was found to talk to them who had the authority to discuss the deal.

"Well Jane it appears that our man was there somewhere but I swear I never saw him and neither did you which means he made us before we made him. I guess we take off the gloves now and take everyone we can next time. We'll put them in place ahead of time so no one will notice them."

"I agree with you Dick we've tried it with the soft touch and either one of us could have taken him down but either he's really smart or really lucky or maybe both."

"Good point Jane, what do you say we have a meeting with our people and lay things out for them so we can keep them well informed. Not that we haven't but this is such an unusual case covering an awful lot of years."

They called a meeting for 9:00 the following morning and held it in one of the conference rooms that would hold eight to twelve people comfortably. Dick and Jane shared the chairing of the session. They went over every aspect of the case from day one when they knew about it to the last one in Warwick when they never even saw their man. They laid out the two instances when an Attorney figured into the scenario and both times the Attorney ended up dead as well as the owner of the store in question. Their man, they explained, was so well disguised and fit in so well with the crowds of people that it was hard to pick him out and that's why they were enlisting the help in the field from all of them for the next go round, they wanted to leave nothing to chance ever again. They went on to explain that up to until now they didn't even know where the killer's base of operations was and that it could be anywhere.

"Now one more thing before we wrap this up," said Dick. "Even with the sketches that we had with us in Rhode Island we still didn't pick this guy out of the crowd, we suspect he made us and avoided us completely as well as at the actual sale and he waited for the Attorney to come back to his office and ambushed him there. We're not sure how he did it but somehow he got all of the paperwork changed over into his name or the name of one of his shell companies of which we suspect he has many and he cleaned out the Attorney's safe then forged a check for over a hundred thousand dollars cleaning out the Attorney's Escrow account and his business account as well. The Attorney died dead broke and in debt. This guy is either a great forger or has his victims sign checks before he kills them. We've got to stop him and stop him now! We're pulling out all of the stops on the next Book Store Sale that comes along that might bring our man out, it may be weeks, months maybe a year but we're going to get this guy because we know so much about him now and how he mixes in well with small crowds. Nothing makes him stand out. Each one of you will be in some kind of work clothes and we'll let you pick out the kind of worker you want to portray. You can be telephone repairmen or installers, TV Cable Installers to private homes, a banker in suit and tie or anything else you can think of, even a garbage man if that's what you're comfortable with but when the time comes and we know the city or town where we're going that will be the time to get into our own disguises and you'll all be wired so we can keep in touch with one another. I'd love to have someone up a telephone pole keeping an eye on everyone for us but he's got to be convincing and we need to be in place so that we fit in and be there a week or so ahead of time so we can spot our guy when he shows and he will show and when he does we'll grab him at the right time so he can't slip away which he's done twice to us already that we know of. Questions anyone?"

Dick didn't anticipate the questions he got and he got a bunch. He and Jane fielded questions and did more brainstorming until it was almost quitting time.

CHAPTER - 105

Sol was a few hours ahead of the moving tractor trailer truck on his way back to the Book Store. The big long haul truck was bringing the contents of the book store and the contents of the man's apartment back from Warwick Rhode Island. As soon as he met with the movers Tuesday morning and had supervised the loading he was on a plane headed back to New York just a short hop away. BJ picked him up at the airport and because Sol seemed in a bit of a hurry he drove rather fast getting back to the store in Poughkeepsie. BJ didn't ask a lot of questions, he could see that Sol was busy thinking. They were nearly back to the store before he saw a smile come across Sol's face and he knew that whatever the problem was he had just solved it.

"BJ, do you know how to drive a big rig, not like the one we bought and brought back here from Buffalo but uh, what you call I think a semi-tractor trailer moving truck with a really big trailer that looks a mile long?"

"No Sol but I have a friend who can."

"Is he close by, I mean can you get him here real quick like?"

"Yeah if he isn't busy he can be here in a few minutes, he did a job for us once before and has worked part time in the Store for Greta. What do you have in mind?"

"We're going to hijack our own truck and bring it back here but the drivers will stay in New York City permanently. We won't get our hands dirty or have any connection with the truck and it won't be reported stolen until the truck doesn't show back up in Rhode Island at the moving company and I used an assumed name with a new disguise. I have a friend whom you haven't met yet who will handle everything for us. I gave the driver an address in the City that's actually a garage that's big enough to lose the trailer in and I could have met them there with you and led them back to our store but I've changed my mind now. What I want to do now is to have you and your friend come to the City with me, pick up the tractor trailer and drive it back here and he can follow you. I've got to call my friend and have him detain the two men in the truck and when you show up you grab the truck and trailer and bring it back here and they'll take care of the drivers of the moving truck and we're clean. It's perfect, I thought of the details on the way back here. I'll ride with you so I can make the final arrangements with my friend in the City but first I'll call him and give him a heads up about my plan. The driver of the tractor trailer won't have any trouble locating the garage, there's a sign on the street that shows exactly where the Garage is however there are two entrances, one every-one uses and then the one that I use on a side street. It's like two garages in one; one side does legal work on cars and trucks for folks in the City who are working and the other side, well that's where everything else happens. In fact on my last visit there I showed it to Richard and he freaked out with the whole set up and then my friend saw our van asked me if he could use it while Richard and I were doing up the town and he liked it so much he wanted to order one for himself right away so I put him in touch with my guy who built ours and got them together. So now he owes me another favor. We don't usually pay each other for anything we do, usually we work out a trade and he likes that even better because he knows we are on top of everything that's going on and he knows about our innovations and everything else we have done to our build-ing. He seems to think that Fred and I are some kind of geniuses or something. So get hold of your guy, give me time to clean up and change clothes and let me know as soon as you're ready to head back to New York City and we don't have a lot of time to kill. I may already be cutting it a little short so I'll call my guy and give him a heads up to detain our friends if I'm not back there in time."

The two of them split up and in a half an hour BJ and his friend were ready to go. BJ warned his friend not to ask questions, that Sol would pay him very well for driving the truck and if he did well Sol may pay him extra to help unload the truck when they returned.

When they arrived in the City Sol directed BJ where to turn and which street to take and soon they were driving towards the brick wall that he had shown to Richard. "Slow down BJ and watch the wall ahead. Now blow the horn only twice and slow down a little and above your head on the visor is a small black box with a button on it like a garage door opener, press it once and keep driving real slow."

Right before his eyes the wall started to move up and go inside on a track he guessed then it disappeared from sight all at the same time.

"Amazing Sol, I've only seen that in the movies."

"Well where do you think my friend got the idea? By the way this is a new door set up the old one slid left and right on tracks and took too much time to open and close, this one goes in and up overhead in the garage on tracks that go up the wall. I suggested this set up and now you can see how its done and how it resembles our own back at the store."

"Oh I see," BJ pulled the van into a cavernous garage with vehicles of every type parked in an orderly fashion.

"Okay, sit tight and tell your friend what he saw he didn't really see, he was never here." Sol got out and went to greet his friend.

"Did you get your new van yet John?"

"You might say I did, take a look around and see if you can pick it out."

Sol looked all around at all of the vehicles. "Sorry I don't see it."

"I got two of them, one in white and one in black for obvious reasons, funeral homes use one color or the other.."

"Understood but where are they?"

"They are the ones parked over there with magnetic signs on their sides so I can change them out whenever I need to, now what's this deal of yours?"

"Like I said on the phone I have a large load of books, furniture, shelving and antiques that I need to get back to my store without the drivers who are bringing it in. You can do as you please with them. I was thinking of a nice cold swim in the bay myself, no mess no fuss no bother."

"Okay, so you want to be rid of them?"

"That's it, have you got someone out front watching for them?"

"Actually I do with orders to get them to come inside and we'll detain them."

"Okay then, I have a driver and BJ with me in the van, they work for me. One will drive the moving truck and the other will drive me. You know it's too bad those tractor trailers cost so much to sand down to bare metal to cover the name of the firm on them, one of those would make you a nice rig."

His friends eyebrows went up and he scratched his head slightly like he had an itch.

"Well now that you mention it, I might be interested in it after all, just how old of a rig is it and what kind of shape is it in?"

"Only a couple of years I think, it has a big sleeper on it."

"What was your plan for it, just the truck, less the trailer?"

"I was going to have the whole rig put through the crusher over near me, that's what I've done with the other vehicles but they were old and worn out but this one isn't, it looked pretty nice actually, want to take a quick look at it before we leave?"

"Yes if you don't mind.

If I like it can I have it?"

"Of course you can my friend, but remember we'll have to move quickly when the moving truck gets reported stolen it will be hot. What do you have in mind?"

"Well I was just thinking mind you but I don't have a big rig in my stables here and sometimes loads come our way where we could use the big rig to haul trailers with. There are hundreds of trailers dropped off at loading docks every day and the drivers leave them there to be unloaded later then go out for another load, get my drift?"

"I got it, sounds clean and good."

The two of them went over to look at the two new vans John had. While they were checking them out a man came sprinting across the floor to the owner of the garage.

"They're here boss, out front."

"Excuse me my friend I have a customer," and he winked at Sol.

Sol went over to his van to talk to the boys. "Things may change here in a few minutes, my friend wants to check out the tractor trailer before we leave. He may want it and if so we can let his man drive it back following us and when we're done BJ can show him where to take the trailer then he can bring the rig back here and we won't have to fool with it and don't worry son, if they want it and you don't have to drive it I'll pay you for it just the same as if you drove it back to our store, okay with you two?"

"Yes sir, its okay but it sure would be fun to get behind the wheel of another big one anyway," said the young man.

"We'll see, maybe you can drive it back to Poughkeepsie and the other fellow can bring it back here and remember you saw nothing and heard nothing either or you."

"We got it Sol," answered BJ.

Soon the owner of the garage came back to where they were standing. "Well I like the rig Sol, I can send a man along with you to bring it back here if that's alright with you?"

"Of course it is old friend, do you mind if I send my driver along with yours, he really wants to drive the rig back to Poughkeepsie and it will give him a thrill then when we're done unloading BJ and your man can take the trailer to the crusher and drop it off and I can have BJ picked up there and your man can head back here."

"Sounds good to me, I'm going to owe you big time for this one."

"Not necessarily my friend, you still have to take care of the drivers out front."

"Not to worry, they are already getting cold on a blue plastic tarp in the back of the garage out in front in a work room which is out of the way and has a side entrance as well so we're ready to go when you are."

"Sol signaled to BJ's friend, time to go son you know the way back and you're going to have a passenger, when we're done the rig is coming back here and his man that is going to ride with you will bring it back here."

"Yes Sir Mr. Devine I'm on it."

"Hush my boy, only first names are used here, even then very sparingly."

He followed the owner of the garage out front and introduced himself to the other driver, they shook hands but the other man never gave his name.

"Rule number one here Bud, never give the bloke you're with your real name, got it?"

"Yes sir, I got it, this is a little new to me you know."

"You can drive a rig this big can't you?"

"Just watch the smoke and we're out of here." He started the engine and they were off lost in traffic and as soon as he could he swung the rig around they headed for Poughkeepsie.

BJ and Sol hung around for a few minutes before leaving then the three of them shook hands and Sol and BJ got back in the van and headed back for Poughkeepsie as well.

They caught up with the tractor trailer just outside of town and followed them to the store. Everyone pitched in and got the truck unloaded then BJ and his friend led the way to the crusher to drop off the trailer with the other man following. They dropped off the trailer and it soon disappeared, Sol had called his friend and told him that the trailer may be hot and to get rid of it a.s.a.p. BJ handed the man an envelope to pay for his services that Sol had handed him.

The man driving the tractor part of the rig would make the trip back in the dark but he knew where he was going and he knew that the rig he was driving would get reported stolen soon and would be hot so he didn't waste any time.

After dark back in the City the garage owner had a couple of his men load the bodies in one of his unmarked van's and take them to the waterfront and drop the bodies overboard so to speak loaded down with concrete blocks tied to the bodies one inside each small tarp and then the tarps were tied up as well so they looked like big blue bags and all of it would sink to the murky bottom never to be seen again. It was all done very cleanly so no one really got dirty over the disposal of the men who'd been shot in the head once with a silenced pistol. All of the gore and blood was on the tarps now on the bottom of the bay for the crabs and fish to feed on.

Late that evening or early morning, the man driving the big rig arrived back at the garage and pulled the truck inside the garage and work would start on it in the morning sanding the entire rig down to bare metal and it would be repainted another color. Sol would take care of a new forged registration for his friend and license plates.

In Poughkeepsie everyone there was tired, they unloaded in a hurry and left a lot of it on the loading dock overnight. Sol asked BJ's friend if he would like to work tomorrow and help put everything inside the store. Sol and his friend John worked it out between them that when the cops came around they hadn't seen the truck and they would tell the cops they knew nothing about a moving truck, they hadn't seen one and maybe they had got hijacked when they stopped for fuel or food.. The cops would figure that the address was real but phony for the driver of the truck and that they were hijacked en-route. They wouldn't figure it was a set up from the get go so they would spend the next several weeks looking for a tuck and trailer that no longer existed nor did the drivers.

They spent the next several days in the store moving the books to the second floor and the furniture they took upstairs and stored in several of vacant apartments. Then Sol went downstairs to the basement to see Fred. "Well Fred how goes it today, find anything more interesting?"

"Actually Sol this is all very interesting, the more I read the more intriguing it becomes like I've seen the words before almost verbatim in the Bible. It sends shivers up and down my spine sometimes."

"Good, how is the whole copying thing coming along, do you know about how much longer this will take?"

"Not much longer, this girl that's helping is such a whiz it's like she was born to do this. Oh before I forget Sol, how was your trip now that everything's been put away?"

"Just fine, there were a couple of Feds at the sale but I made them before they made me. They always stick out with their neatly trimmed haircuts and its getting so I can spot them a mile away. By the way in Apartments twelve, thirteen and fourteen I put all of the old man's antique furniture in there, take a look and see if there is anything in there you would like to have for yourself, if you see something you want you have first dibs on it then Greta then BJ."

"Thank you Sol that's very kind of you. Is there anything special about the furniture?"

"Actually yes, I believe there are some very rare antique tables and chairs there that could be Queen Anne Style or older and a couple of end tables also in that style, a huge wardrobe, a complete dining room set that's also huge. He must have entertained a lot and you've got to see his collection of rare books, they're in there with the furniture as well temporally. I'll have them brought down here to you once the lost books are out of here. All of the store's merchandise is on the second floor including the book cases and other items we hauled away. You ought to see the Antique cash register we found in the back of the store covered with a sheet, its one of those huge brass cash registers with the crank on the side of it, might be worth quite a lot to a collector, check it out as well, its in the apartment too. Walking into that man's apartment was like walking into a time capsule, it was actually quite well done with the old wall paper still intact and everything that wasn't covered by sheets has a lot of dust on it as well. I don't think the family had a clue as to the value of it all. It was obvious that no one had been in there in years and years, it was like a shrine. Hard to believe I was able to make off with all of it and none of the family members even came around but I guess by now they are upset that the money they thought they were going to get isall gone. I even cleaned out the Attorney's safe and his bank accounts, all three of them.

"Wow, then you did make a big haul."

"Yes Fred one our best, we've got close to two hundred thousand dollars all in cash. But we must still be careful, the Feds are around and will one day come here again. We need to unload anything that can connect us to any of our special deals as soon as we can but the lost books take precedence I'm afraid. I don't like having them here, the sooner they are gone the better, we'll keep the one copy in our safe that's well hidden but that's all that I want to hang onto for now. I'm afraid someone will trace it back to us one day and some idiot from the mid east may come looking for it, the lost books of the Bible that is and we can show them we never had them by showing them around with no fear. Well Fred let me know if I can help, do you have a time in mind that we may be able to ship all of this out again?"

"Oh shoot, I nearly forgot, we got to talking about furniture and all, give me maybe ten more days or so and we should be done."

"Oh that is good news although I'm going to hate to lose the two girls. I think probably the Princess may want to accompany the lost books home and take the originals we made along with her." Sol left and went back upstairs to the store to check on the rest of his employees.

CHAPTER - 106

Dick and Jane were at FBI Headquarters planning for their next field trip into the jaws of the unknown. They were still reeling over the killings of eleven people at two crime scenes where a Fire Marshal died two days later making it twelve dead in New Mexico and the fact that they were there but not in the right place at the right time. Obviously they weren't going to let it happen again. Now they were armed to the teeth with six different sketches of the man in disguise so they knew what to look for and who to look for and felt they alone could pick him out but they had been proven wrong again in Warwick Rhode Island. Not only was he there but out witted them and they did not notice him. They didn't realize he had two new disguises and they weren't looking for those. He got clean away by waiting at the Attorney's own office then took it from there adlib. Dick and Jane were still upset with themselves for not covering all avenues but this was a first that he pulled right under their noses and that's why they needed help. Dick was standing by their wall map when Jane approached.

"Agent Jefferies, we need to talk in private, can we use our Office please?"

"Sure Agent Marlowe, lead on."

Once in their office Dick closed the door and asked, "now then, what's up Jane, your

tone of voice made it sound serious!"

"It is; have you noticed any grousing among the troops around the building Dick?"

"Just the usual, too many hours, not enough pay other than that I haven't heard anything."

"Well I have and only because I was in the ladies room at the right time. I overheard a couple of the female Agents complaining that they would like to be brought in on the case and soon. They heard about our failed exploits and they think we need more people on the case and all they want is a chance to help. They may be right, a few women could be an asset?"

"Uh, I don't know Jane, bringing in fresh blood may be all that gets spilled. We would have to spend weeks or more briefing new people when we already have six men ready to go plus ourselves. Let me think about it because it does make sense. I need time to mull it over and see if we have the luxury of time on our side to make that kind of adjustment. Then we'll get our heads together once more. Give me a couple of hours and I'll let you know my thoughts on it."

After lunch Jane approached Dick and didn't have to say a word. She saw the sly smile on his face and instinctively knew he had an idea and a good one. "I recognize that look Agent Jefferies you have the look of a fox caught in the hen house when someone turned the lights on."

"Damn it Agent Marlowe, are you reading my mind?"

"Precisely, I'll bet you dinner at Twin Willows that I know exactly you're thinking."

"Alright Miss Marlowe, shoot!"

"You are about to ask me about some women in the building who may be free right now who have worked undercover before and can pass themselves off as almost anyone."

"Close but no dinner."

"What do you mean that's exactly the look I saw on your face."

"Not quite, you left out that I wanted you to be the one to send out an inner office memo to all undercover women who are not on a case right now."

"Oh come on Dick we both had the same idea. You owe me dinner at Twin Willows and no waffling."

"If you insist but did you think about you're being the one to send out the memo?"

"No, I have to admit it, I thought that you would be the one to send it out."

"Okay then, Dutch Treat at Twin Willows when this is done."

"Okay you win, how soon do you want me to do this.?"

"Right now and I'll help if you like?"

"I'd like. What about the Director Dick, shouldn't we tell him or ask him first?"

"Already did that, that's why I didn't go to lunch."

"Oh fine, so now you're skipping meals again, not good Dick. I'll go ahead and word the memo in my own words and then you can check it and make any changes you like."

"Thanks Jane. We also need a place for interviews if we get any takers."

"How about the conference room we use for meetings with our own people?"

"That will do just fine, tell them if interested to report there at 9:00 A.M. tomorrow morning. One caveat, this could be extremely dangerous, we prefer single women, no families."

"Good thinking Dick, really good idea. We don't want any pussy willows showing up either, we want only the best."

"You might add that their proficiencies with firearms and self defense be up to date."

"Wow another great idea!" Jane got busy typing on a word processor and when she was done she asked Dick to read it over.

"That looks fine Jane that will give us the cream of the crop I think, go ahead and send it out and we'll see what happens. The last thing we need is someone who's been behind a desk too long and is bound to make mistakes and it happens all too often what with budget constraints."

"Yes we need people who are not only sharp but quick and agile on their feet. And we are going to need vehicles like, cars, utility trucks, utility vans with ladders on a rack so it looks real is what I'd like to have. I think we better check it out inter agency and see who has anything available we can use. A lot of the satellite Offices have some really weird vehicles at their disposal, even those would be helpful."

While Jane was finishing up the memo Dick got on the phone to put out an inter agency memo for vehicles using their secretary. He included Donny in his calls to see what they had available right there in DC. It wasn't long before the teletype began to sing in their office showing lists of available vehicles in all areas of the States.

"Well, would you look at this Jane, someone's awake out there in no man's land. We got oodles and oodles of vehicles available, all kinds and makes. I like the looks of this already. Hang the rental cars we'll take what we can get from the local constabulary if we're close enough, if not we can have them driven in to our location for us, with enough notice of course."

"Right Dick, but now the cats going to be out of the bag, we may have a lot of unnecessary people in the way that we don't know, someone else could get hurt."

"I'll take care of that Jane, I'll have a memo sent out that this is a high profile very dangerous case being handled directly by the main Office and no questions asked, we can't afford a possible leak by some Junior Agent mouthing off over coffee some morning in a Restaurant."

"Oh that is good Dick, you're really hot today!"

"Well you don't have to be sarcastic about it; I was only trying to make a point."

"Point well taken, I was just trying to get a rise out of you."

"Well you did and it hit a nerve, I was serious about this. More than one Junior Agent has died in his or her first year of service because they were not paying close enough attention then got in the way of a bullet that could have been avoided, even the best of Agents die sometimes for no good reason."

"Okay, Dick I get it, I'm one of the veterans you know."

"Yes I know that Jane but sometimes we need a wake up call."

"You're still hurting inside because of what happened to Donny aren't you?"

"Am I, I didn't know it showed?"

"Well it does, it's not something one can forget overnight you know."

"Listen to who's talking, its taken you a long time to get past your own trauma as well."

"I know that Dick but I'm way past that now and trust me, it is in the past, I have moved on. I realize that every time you see Donny you are reminded about how and when he was shot."

"Yes but don't forget that another Agent was also killed who shouldn't have died because we were way out classed. The bad guys had heavier fire-power than we did and were wearing body armor and we weren't, they caught us flat footed and no pun intended there."

"None taken, now can we get back to the job at hand, we should be ready with questions tomorrow morning in case we have more than two or three applicants."

"Okay, I give up; you're right as usual, that's why I like you."

"Are you trying to pay me a compliment or something Dick?"

"I just did, can we move on please?"

Jane noticed that Dicks face appeared to have flushed red all of a sudden.

"How about if we compose a list of questions to ask anyone who shows up tomorrow?"

"Good idea Jane, I was just about to suggest that."

They sat down one on either side of the desks in their Office and began writing out questions that needed to be asked.

When they were done they went through them one at a time and decided they would both ask a question alternating one for him and one for her because Jane had some tough questions for a female Agent that Dick wasn't comfortable in asking. They worked right through lunch without noticing people were coming and going to lunch.

At 1:30 Dick said; "I like what we have Jane, its well thought out and I think they are really tough soul searching questions for a female Agent. I would have never thought to ask some of them on how they would feel if they got injured by a bullet and could never have children. It's not something men think about in that sense."

"Wait a minute, suppose you or another man took a bullet to the groin and it finished off his baby making capabilities."

"Men don't really dwell on it but it is a chance, that's why you will notice some men have a protector that hangs down there below the belt that is optional body armor wear for men."

"Do you ever wear one Dick?"

"I have a couple of times but it inhibits my being able to break and run after a criminal so I don't wear one anymore."

"Well how about some lunch Dick?"

"I'm ready what time is it?"

"Its half past lunch time is what it is."

"Okay let's go eat somewhere and I'll buy, we've earned a good lunch out today."

The two of them left to get their car and go to lunch, anywhere away from the Office.

At 3:30 they were back at their desks.

"Well Dick anything you'd like to add to before I have the questionnaires typed for us?"

"No Jane, I think we've covered everything, go ahead and have someone type it up."

Jane left Dick alone in their small sparse office while she went out to the lab and find a secretary who wasn't too busy to do some extra typing.

CHAPTER - 107

At 9:00am the next morning they were astonished to see eleven women of all descriptions waiting for them outside the conference room in the hall.

"Good morning everyone!"

They answered Dick collectively, "Good morning Agent Jefferies."

"For those of you who don't know Agent Marlowe yet, this is Special Agent Marlowe."

"Good morning ladies!" said Jane.

"Alright whoever is first please come into the conference room, we have some questions to ask each one of you to see if we can use you in the up coming difficult and possibly dangerous investigation?" Dick opened the door and was followed in by Jane and the first woman applicant. It took them all morning and into the afternoon to go through all of them but in the end they had picked out four that seemed tough enough and wise enough to carry off their performances in disguise. These were well rounded professional Agents who knew their job and wouldn't flinch at dropping the hammer on a bad guy. They were so tired they told the ladies they would make their decision by tomorrow noon and would let them know who was chosen. They didn't have to do a lot of thinking but they would discuss their individual choices tomorrow morning. Special Agents Jefferies and Marlowe had pretty well made up their minds on the same four but wanted to sleep on it over overnight.

The following morning they made their final decision on the same four without reservation. These were the cream of the crop of veteran Agents who had worked undercover before. Their assignments would be relatively easy on the surface, all they had to do was to observe and report to either Dick or Jane on what they observed so they could make the final decision on when to move in if and when they had their man.

They brought the four of them in that afternoon and started working with them right away. They were introduced to the other six male Agents who would be working with them. The briefings started and would be endless but necessary, each one of them had to memorize the six known disguises and also had to look for a possible new disguise like the one that fooled Marlowe and Jefferies in Rhode Island when they didn't recognize the subject in two new disguises and they missed him by inches twice but they didn't know how close they had really come to identifying him. They broke down each disguise and explained the elevated shoes the man wore which were almost indistinguishable from normal shoes. They talked about the fact that he had a fat suit so he could look overweight or thin, tall or short and they had guessed his real height at five feet six inches tall.

Days grew into weeks and the four new Agents worked right along side the others until they were all comfortable with one another. Like the men, Agents Jefferies and Marlowe let the women pick a disguise and hairdo especially so they wouldn't look like Feds and be so easy to pick out. They knew their disguises had to fit the region they would be headed to such as New England, Colorado, California or Florida. Each region had their own identity from beachwear to western wear with cowboy hats and jeans. Dick and Jane also told them to have a bag packed at the Office so it was on hand at all times in case they had to leave at a moments notice. All they could do now was to practice with their radios and wires for all of them. Two of the Agents were sent out to experience climbing telephone poles like a lineman, cable TV repairman or telephone repairman. They had to look the part and not stand out. In each case they would be able to use portable hand held radios to communicate and wouldn't look out of place. The weeks of practice were paying off for everyone, they practiced different scenarios with each other in and out of the building and went to stores to practice talking with one another in public but remaining anonymous in the eyes of others.

Two more months went by and everyone stayed sharp because they knew the day would come sooner or later and the longer they waited the more proficient they became and the shorter the time they had to wait for the next book store sale.

Then the day came, a flyer arrived in the mail advertising a huge book store sale. This time it was only the books and the owner's private collection that was for sale. None of the shelving or anything else would be sold. The flyer stated clearly, INVENTORY ONLY BOOK SALE, owner of store suddenly passed away and left only a niece for an heir who is a Doctor and has no interest in the store or the owner's private collection of rare literature. It further stated that prospective buyers could purchase one or the other or all together. Viewings for the entire inventory could be seen at the store and the owner's home and the addresses were listed and would be held on Friday the18th of August1973 with the sale on the following Saturday morning at 9:00am. Value of complete Inventory has been priced by a Rare Book Auctioneer who valued the combined Inventory of both locations at $875,000.00 and the successful bidder must have a certified check or letter of credit in at least that amount to bid. This was the first time they had seen the word Auction used in an ad. The city and State were listed as Burlington Vermont.

"Dick have you seen the new flyer that just came in?"

"No Jane I haven't checked my mail yet today, what do you have?"

She showed him the ad and he had a questioning look on his face.

"I don't know anything about the area Jane, do you?"

"I sure don't, we'll have to check an Atlas to see where it is."

They searched the offices high and low and finally found an up to date Atlas that wasn't all torn apart by others who were working cases and just needed a page or two.

"Here it is Jane, looks like its right on Lake Champlain, how long does it say that it's been in business?"

"Ninety three years in the same building according to the ad, third generation was running it until he died suddenly."

"I don't know Jane if it's valuable enough for our guy to go for and there doesn't seem to be anyone in danger other than the Auctioneer. Let's give the representative a call and see what all is involved, how big the store is and how extensive the old man's collection is?"

"Okay Dick good thought, would you like for me to make the calls or did you want to make the calls?"

"How about you doing it, check the store and the old man's collection for numbers and also the Auctioneer, give him a call as well and see what his take is on the sale, I know what the brochure says but its what it doesn't say that we need to know."

Got it Dick, I'm on it!"

"Jane, wait up a second, I have another idea, while you're on the phone see if they have a Chamber of Commerce and give them a call and get a map of the town or City and see if you can find out when it was incorporated and how long it has been there and if it is like a Sea Port seeing as though its on the Chain of Lakes."

"Whew, is that all you can think of Dick, maybe you should come help me, that way we can work two phones at a time?"

"Good idea, I'll be right there."

Eventually the two of them manned the two new phones in their Office and made several calls. The Chamber of Commerce was one they began making notes about as to transportation, airports and directions. Jane asked to have a couple of maps mailed to them from the Chamber of Commerce regarding the city layout and the location of stores. The reason Dick wanted to see the age of the City was to try and date the age of the Book Store and how long it may have been in business, the flyer did say ninety three years in the same location. What they wanted to know was, did it start out in another location and was it bought by someone else then moved to the present location or not. They also needed to get a lay of the land to see where other stores were, roof tops for surveillance and a place for a possible sniper in case of trouble with an arrest. Dick was covering all the bases this time and he knew that the older the Store the more interested their perp. would be in buying it all along with the old man's own private collection. He wanted a history on the age of the building and the business. Lots of answers were needed before they shipped this many people to arrest one man possibly two. He wanted every avenue covered to leave no chance for their guy to disappear into thin air again.

"How are you coming Jane?"

"I'm doing all right, I got hold of the Chamber of commerce and they are sending us a history of the town along with a map of the downtown area."

"How about the adjacent stores in the same block?"

"I asked them for an aerial view of stores in a two block square area surrounding the book store identifying what kind of store they were and number of stories."

"Okay that sounds good!"

"How about you Dick, how is your progress?"

"Just fine so far, I asked the City for Demographics of their City and they were only too glad to help. They too are sending early maps of the downtown area showing the locations of points of interest to us. I asked them for specifics and didn't explain why.

"Good, I did the same thing when I talked with the Chamber, they know we called but I told them the same basic thing you told the City Commissioners. I told them not to divulge to anyone that they had a call from us. They did ask one good question though; they wanted to know if an advance team was coming to their City because the President may come there for some reason. I told them I didn't have any such information just that we were looking for an individual who may or may not come there, we were just covering our bases in case we got word he was headed in their direction."

"Very good Jane, we don't need interference from the local cops, they'll just get in our way. We can sort things out later if we have a shootout but I doubt it will come to that I think we can take our guy down with overwhelming surprise and numbers. If we make our net large enough there is no way he can slip through it."

"Sounds good in theory Dick but we both know now how slippery this guy is, we need everybody on high alert twenty four seven while we're there if we even go."

"Jane, I was just thinking, if we called the Chamber of Commerce, maybe our guy will too, maybe that's why he's been so well prepared for all these heists and murders."

While they were chatting someone knocked on the door of their Office and it was Tim.

"Hi Tim, come in."

"Hello Agent Jefferies, Agent Marlowe, I just got a heads up from the Rhode Island State Police, they are looking for a very large tractor trailer moving truck that disappeared from somewhere in or near New York City. We have the last known address for it but it never arrived there and the location is a downtown automobile repair garage. The Police think that the address was bogus to begin with and that the truck with the drivers were hijacked close to New York maybe when they stopped for fuel or to get something to eat. The load on the truck is estimated to be over one million two hundred and fifty thousand dollars and was insured for that amount and it involves us now especially since the Attorney who was tied to this was found murdered and because money crossed State lines, over two hundred thousand dollars in cash from the Attorney's safe and his Accounts are missing, they were Federally Insured Bank Accounts."

"Thanks Tim, we were there when this went down but we couldn't find the guy but we weren't sure he got the deal, we were told otherwise, looks like our man alright, thanks Tim."

He handed the update to Dick and left. "Well Jane this confirms our suspicions, if we could only find the truck and the drivers' maybe we could pinpoint where the truck went from the hijack point. That's the one piece of this puzzle that escapes us."

"I agree Dick, this guy's a real pro and is more slippery than a well greased eel."

"Don't you mean a greased pig Jane?"

"No, he's no pig; he's like an eel that slips from your fingers every time you think you have him and if you get to close he hits you with an electrical shock."

"Okay I get the analogy now."

They worked the phones on and off right up through quitting time.

"Well Jane, I think we've earned our pay this week and especially today, my ear hurts from bending peoples wills to our way of thinking, why can't they make a soft sponge type of ear piece for telephones so it doesn't hurt your ears so much when you're on the phone all day?"

"Beats me Dick, I feel the same way, my ear hurts as well."

Another week went by and little by little they began to get what they wanted from Burlington Vermont and it surprised both of them as to what they learned.

"Hey Jane listen to this, Burlington is the biggest smallest city in the U.S. and the City was incorporated in 1865 so conceivably this store could have been in use close to the last one hundred years."

"Sounds good for our guy who likes old original stores and I've got some old maps here showing the digging of the Erie Canal in 1825 and the Lake Champlain canal done in 1823 and it says that this was a huge Lumbering and Manufacturing area due to the Canals connecting with the railroads and steamships that used to ply these waters like you thought ships might use."

"That could be a problem; our guy will have several avenues of escape open to him by water, air, train or bus, even a taxi according what I'm reading here."

"Boy, am I glad we made those calls."

"Me too Jane, we need all the information that he will be using as well. I think that the week of the sale I'd like to check in with the Chamber of Commerce in person and see if they got a late call from our guy asking for the same type of information and the same with the City. Your average buyer wouldn't give a damn about those things; only someone planning something devious would need that information."

"True Dick but sometimes this guy may just do a real up front deal and spend the money to get what he wants rather than steal it."

"No Jane, you are over looking one important fact and that is he likes the idea of the hunt and kill then getting away Scott Free with the goods and sometimes a lot of cash as well just like in Rhode Island where he cleaned the Attorney's office completely out including all of his cash and the other buyer's deposit of one hundred thousand dollars in earnest money he put down in the Attorney's Escrow Account. All of that was in the Newspaper accounts of the crime along now with a tractor trailer and two employee's of the Moving Company. Take my word for it those men are dead somewhere and if I had to guess I'd say they were dumped in the sea for the crabs and fishes to eat."

"That's quite an imagination you have there Dick."

"Well put yourself in the criminal's place, where would you dump two bodies in the New York area?"

"Why I'd put one in a dumpster and the other in another dumpster far away from the first one and they would both end up in a landfill somewhere"

"That's not bad Jane but its been done before. I'm betting our guy doesn't ever want the bodies recovered, that's why I think someone put concrete overshoes on them and dropped them off from a dock on the waterfront."

"But why do you think it was done in the City where literally thousands of people who could see you, why not kill them shortly after stealing the truck and dump the bodies somewhere other than in town."

"I don't know Jane; it's just that I feel they're in New York Harbor somewhere. I'm getting all new vibes about our guy. I'm betting he has a network somewhere close by. This isn't the first time we've traced things to New York City. Our man could be in there somewhere in the heart of the City for all we know. That's where a lot of mail and phone calls have been traced to including the guy's elevator shoes, someone has to be picking those packages up from somewhere and taking them to our perp. He wouldn't pick them up himself, he would use somebody else I believe for a courier. He wouldn't take the chance of being identified. I'm really hoping that the shoe company in Germany calls us back when they get a new order from him. I'd love to put a tail on the person that picks them up and see where they lead us. Another thing, look at all of his M/Os concerning the killings, no two are alike."

"I know Dick, we can only hope he loses a pair of shoes, damages a pair or just wants a new pair for esthetic or fashion reasons, it sure would reduce the amount of manpower we have to extend this time to catch him. I don't want to give up on this shoe thing though, sooner or later he'll order new shoes, maybe even hiking boots."

CHAPTER - 108

Sol was happy things were going so well at their Store. One day he called the Princess in to talk and called her by her name Susan instead of addressing her as Princess therefore causing a problem. "Susan, have you been in touch with your father lately?"

"Yes I have the night before last. He said things have quieted down some in our Country but it sill wasn't safe for me to come back yet. He said he would call me in a few more days."

"Good, I'm glad things are better than when Richard and I were there. There were a few moments when I didn't know if we'd get the plane off the ground or not and I certainly didn't know you would be flying us back here. What we have been working on has gone better than expected and as soon as they are done I would like to make arrangements to fly the boxes back to your father with the corrected books inside a separate case within the one box, kind of a two for one sort of thing. We'll pack them separately so there's no chance of mixing up the different books. Now what Fred is working on is a way to tie the pages together using a twine material similar to the kind used back then to bind pages together, it was crude then but effective, we found remnants of string within the pages of some books. Everything will be clearly marked for your father so they can return the originals to their cave again and he can hide what we did somewhere else that's very safe."

"I don't know how father can ever thank you Sol, you and Fred who is a real dear like you have been wonderful with a complete stranger in your midst."

"Why thank you my dear, I wish you could stay longer and that we weren't so busy, we could show you around this beautiful Country of ours."

"I wish for that as well but alas my Country needs me, we have some rebuilding of our own to do. Would it be alright with you if I told father what a wonderful building you have here. I absolutely love what you have done with this old Manufacturing Mill.

"Why thank you for your compliment Susan and yes you may tell your father all about it and if you would like there are some aspects of the building I'm sure your father may be interested in and I'd be pleased to give you another grand tour tomorrow if you like?"

"I'd like that Sol. Wait, you mean there's more for to see than what I've already seen?"

"Oh yes, there are things here your father would love to have for his own use and safety. You have seen very little, only what we have chosen to show you for your own safety in case we were attacked by terrorists."

"Okay, so then until tomorrow, if you are done I'll go back to the store."

"That's just fine Susan, tomorrow you'll get the whole picture."

The next morning at 9:30 true to his word Sol went to the store and asked Greta if it would be alright to borrow the little lady for a while.

"Susan, come with me and we will start upstairs with my suite then we'll work our way down to the garage level."

She started for the elevator and Sol slowed her down just in time.

"No my dear the other one."

"I don't see another one Sol."

Sol reached out and touched a place on a corner molding and the wall slid open.

"Oh my goodness, I didn't know this was here."

"This is my private elevator to my apartment alone, Fred has his own in the basement to his apartment as well, we installed them a while back, this one goes to the garage as well so either one of us can come and go without being seen by anyone we don't want to be seen by, here we are." He let the door open and they stepped out into Sol's private apartment.

"Wow Sol, this is really very nice."

"My dear you haven't seen anything yet, we came up the back way, its my emergency entrance and exit, follow me." He showed her his rooms, two bedrooms and two baths for company like Richard or Francis he explained. They went through a door and were in the front of his apartment, a small space really, bedroom, bathroom, living area and eat in kitchen. Very plain compared to the other side.

"I don't understand Sol, where are we now?"

"We're in my apartment, watch?" He closed the door behind him by pressing an unseen button and the door which was part of the wall closed behind them and when it was shut it looked like a plain ordinary wall.

"Now Princess, if someone wanted to harm me, this is all they would find. The wall between here and my real apartment is bullet proof two inch thick steel with wall board over it so it looks like a real wall and it sounds like one if you pound on it with a fist."

"Is Fred's anything like this?"

"A little bit but he has his own tastes just as I have mine, we both use the front kitchen occasionally to keep cooking odors in here so it looks and smells lived in.. Now you already know about the main private elevator that comes upstairs to everyone else's apartments, we fixed it so no one could come up here except tenants who we wanted to come here."

"This is just too clever Sol, how did the two of you ever figure this all out?"

"Reading literature my dear from the ages when Kings and Queens needed private and safe places to call their own."

"Oh I see what you mean, yes of course, why not, oh this is just too wonderful!"

"You haven't seen anything yet, my private elevator awaits you." He held out his hand again towards the wall and it opened again as if by magic, she didn't see him press any button this time but a door opened in the wall and they stepped into the elevator. "Down please," said Sol. The elevator door closed and the elevator started down and didn't stop until the basement. "Voice actuated as well in case my arms are full of groceries or books."

"So we're in the level where Fred is?"

"Yes more of less, I'll show you the underground garage and how I come in and out without being seen. Here we are, there's our van, this underground garage is completely lit and I can come in through the wall behind the van, it opens from both sides on a hidden track and the wall is concrete and steel ten inches thick." He pressed a button and the wall separated in the middle and slid noiselessly open and they stepped out onto the loading dock area of the building and enclosed warehouse. "This is the rear of the building where we get all of our deliveries. On the loading dock there's a freight elevator that only goes to the first and second floors. But from the garage we can go anywhere we want in the building. If someone were to try and break into our place they wouldn't get far. Now then lets go see Fred and I'll show you around his little world as we call it.

"Well he showed me around all the machinery and explained it to me."

"Yes my dear but there is more. If you're father should be interested I can send him plans for anything we have in the building. In fact we have already installed elevators in the center of the building in anticipation of more tenants and stores who may wish to become part of our little home here. We are training BJ in all of the aspects of running the whole show in hopes that Fred and I can retire to wherever we want and BJ will be the new owner of the building and all that is in it, that is our gift to him for his helping us. We can live off our inventions and patents for years and years to come and when we're gone they too will be willed to BJ because Fred and I have no one other than our girlfriends." Sol escorted her over to where Fred was working.

"Hello Fred, I've been showing Susan here around the building and all of its little intricacies. Would you like to continue showing her around your world down here?"

"Thank you for the offer Sol but I really need to finish what I'm working on, I'm nearly done with this project, we could be done by tomorrow noon as a matter of fact."

"Okay Fred, great work, I'll show her around then." He walked her by some of the machinery she had already seen then showed her the safety margins they had built in for themselves. "Susan this is our fire suppression system, it's a dry powder compound so it can put out any kind of fire with minimal damage to equipment, it cleans up with a Shop Style Vacuum Cleaner. Here is Fred's private elevator I told you about."

"Looks like a brick wall to me."

"Sol let her watch as he pressed a button that wasn't a button at all or at least it didn't look like anything important, it just looked as though it was an imperfection in the brick when it was made. A door slid open revealing Fred's private elevator. "This goes to any floor just like mine but only to Fred's apartment on the top floor. Did you happen to see anything in the line of machinery that may be of interest to your father?"

"No Sol but I will tell him about all of the wonderful things you have here. One thing though I should mention, I believe the best way to get the Lost Books of the Bible back to our country would be to pick them up the same way we brought them in, no one will be looking for another airplane to land here."

"Well alright, may I think about it a little. I know of another airport where you could possibly land and take off from a lot safer and its only a few miles from here, its like on a mountain top, the only thing is I'm not sure of the length of the runway. I've got to check that out, that airport is mine and Fred's escape route should we need to leave the area quickly."

"That's okay I just need to pass on the information to father so he can have a plane come for me and the books."

"Alright then, I'll check it out later this afternoon and let you know what the runway length is, I've never seen a jet land or take off from there but knowing your plane's capabilities I believe it could be done."

"Can't be any worse than when we arrived here, that was a very short runway."

"Well this is owned by the same airport people. When housing boomed close by the airport the public started complaining about the comings and goings of low flying aircraft and then there was an accident in which a pilot overshot or undershot the runway and struck a house and the people in the house and on the plane were all killed."

"Oh my that is too bad, I hate to see innocent people get injured or killed."

"Me too but it happens around airports all too often I'm afraid. Now one more thing we added recently was the room over here we are keeping the lost books of the Bible is in this room over this way." He led her to a brick wall that looked square and looked like it supported the upper floors of the building. He reached out and touched the wall in a place unseen by her. The wall kind of opened outward towards her in a four foot wide section which was actually a very big thick steel door like a vault would have. "This is what Fred and I call our safe room. Its large enough you see to accommodate everyone in the store and there's still room left over to store food and water etc. It has its own generator in case of power failure and we could be safe in here from any attack by a foreign country or terrorists. We built this after you arrived with the lost books and it turned out better than expected. The walls are impenetrable to any kind of weapons save an atomic bomb. I'll bet you didn't even know there was construction going on right under your feet when you were up in the store did you?"

"No Sol, I had no idea improvements were being made to your building at any time."

"That's because we insulated every floor and the walls as well as the interior of building are almost completely sound proof everywhere. Come I'll take you back to the Store by way of my other elevator and surprise Greta, I drive her crazy sometimes when I seem to walk through walls and it could freak out a customer as well."

Sol and Fred had purposefully kept Doris from running into the Princess. They may have seen one another in passing but were never introduced to one another by the men. As far as the two of them were concerned they were just another employee fluttering about the premises. The two of them headed back to the store.

That afternoon Sol called his friend at the airport to talk with him about the length of the runway to see if their plane could land and take off again safely. The manager had some tough questions for Sol. Number one he was suspicious when Sol mentioned a private airplane that was actually a customized military style aircraft and he asked straight out if Sol had anything to do with the one that landed in town and took off again setting the fields around the airport on fire that everyone had heard about. The talk he had heard was that it had been smugglers bringing in contraband from another Country. Number two he wanted to know if it were an illegal flight and Sol told him no on that count but didn't really answer his first question so the man figured Sol had something to do with it and Sol told him that had he heard that it was an emergency flight and left it at that. Then the manager asked Sol if this was the same kind of flight and Sol had to tell him yes or he wouldn't get the information he needed. The man told Sol that if he allowed it he could lose his license to operate an airport and Sol told him to relax that he would handle it for him if it came to that. Then he told Sol, it would cost him twenty five thousand dollars in cash and Sol told him alright, that seemed fair for the aircraft to land and refuel if needed and the fuel would be extra. Sol told him no problem and asked him if he could get fuel for a turbo prop aircraft without any trouble. He told Sol, he would get it the same way Sol did, hijack a fuel truck en route to an airport and asked, give me twenty four hours notice and the exact time the plane would land. Sol said okay then asked about the runway length. He was told that the runway had just been lengthened to be able to land the new Business Jet class aircraft but then the man turned around and told Sol that the aircraft he wanted to land and take off again would need more runway than they had to take off from. Sol told him, no problem, this was a new STOL aircraft and the runway length would be sufficient and Sol had spilled the beans by a simple mistake.

Finally the airport manager gave him the go ahead but the money had to be there before the plane was to land and Sol agreed, he had that much on hand plus plenty more from the last job he pulled. Now had to get the final plan into gear so the Princess could call her father and make the final arrangements and he would simply pass on the amount of money that was extra for the plane to land etc. to her father and would get reimbursed by him. This whole operation had made Sol verynervous since it began and he would be glad to finally be rid of the lost books.

CHAPTER - 109

Sol was anxious to get the Lost Books out of Poughkeepsie and their store. He went to find the Princess then he would talk to Fred. Sol found her in the Store talking with Greta. "Susan may I have a word with you please?"

"Sure Sol, what's up?"

"A small change of plans, I want us to use the other airport for safety concerns, it's not far from here and they have lengthened the runway to facilitate the landing and take offs of the new Business size Jets . The manager is an old friend of mine and tells me the new runway is one thousand yards long and it's about five hundred yards longer than the runway your plane took off from here in town. You may not need any assistance in taking off with your aircraft. I do have one question and he asked the same thing, can you quiet down the noise of your engines on take off and landing so as not to disturb anyone like we did here in town, we made quite a racket as you know with the use of the JATO bottles?"

"I think we can do that because we have more runway to play with, remember this aircraft is built for short runways for takeoffs and landings so we can get in and out of tight places where modern aircraft have more of a problem. That's why so many countries with limited Airports are wanting an aircraft like ours and we can't tell them that it was once a U.S. Military airplane that we acquired through shaky channels shall we say. We removed all of the I-D Tags from the plane so it would be hard to identify if someone got too close. It looks like a stubby passenger airplane and that effect is fine with us. Originally it had four standard prop engines and they were powerful but didn't have the capabilities of our four bigger turbo prop engines like the ones we put on which are made by Rolls Royce. Once again we had some difficulty getting the engines but we got them much the same was as we did the airplane. We spent a total of five years improving the airplane aerodynamically but now it flies like a dream, it's the kind of aircraft real pilots like to fly because it what they call a pilots airplane, you fly it and don't have to rely solely on gauges other than fuel and air speed etc. therefore the few test pilots who have flown it like myself fall in love with it."

"I see; I didn't realize your country had spent so much time on building it to your specs."

"Yes, we spent several million on it and now countries like Israel are really interested on getting their hands on some just like ours, we've offered them our engineering drawings if they want them but we hadn't heard back from them as of the time I left. They will probably buy them from America so that could be the delay. So Sol, I suppose you'd like to set a time for us to pack up our freight and leave."

"That's what I came to talk to you about. We need to set a date and time so it all comes together quickly and your aircraft isn't on the ground any longer than it needs to be and I have made arrangements for the right fuel to be delivered to the airport for your aircraft. Is there anything special you need in the fuel?"

"As long as you tell them its for turbo prop engines its alright. We use a different variant in our fuel in the desert environment than you do here in the States for your prop jet engines but the basics still have to be there."

"Wonderful, we need to talk to Fred and see how he's coming along then we'll make a tentative decision and you can call your father later and we'll firm up our timeline because we have lots to do to make this work smoothly. My friend at the airport is asking for twenty five thousand dollars to let you land and refuel and the fuel is extra. He is really sticking his neck out. If we are caught he could lose his License to operate the airport and it could put him out of business."

"Well then, we can't let that happen very well can we. We may need him again some day, who knows, father may want to come here and meet you some day and see your operation first hand."

"I'd like that, he sounds like a fine man, let's go check in with Fred."

The two of them went down to the basement. "Morning Fred, how are you today?"

"Hi Sol, hi Susan. I'm good, we should be able to start crating this up by 1:00 this afternoon. In fact I'll be done in a few minutes with this page I did over, I didn't like the looks of it, it didn't feel right for the paper it is was on but I like the new one now."

Sol picked up the page and held it up to the light. "Great job Fred this looks like it's a couple of thousand years old stored in a dry climate. What we need Fred is a time for packing all of this off to the new Poughkeepsie Airport."

"You mean you are going to fly in and out of that new mountain top place?"

"That's the idea."

"I sure hope the pilot of that big plane you described to me is really a good one or they could end up crispy critters in the surrounding forest."

"No problem there. I talked with Charlie a while ago and he said that they recently lengthened the main runway another five hundred yards and that's plenty big enough for them."

"If you say so, how about you Susan?"

"No problem at all Fred, in fact it will make the pilot very happy when I tell her or him, that its longer than the one we came in on and that was no problem other than we lit the airport on fire."

"So tell me Fred in hours, how long do you need?"

"If BJ can stay around to help me and Doris along BJ's other friend maybe I can have it all safely packed and crated by 5:00 this afternoon."

"Do you have all the crating and packing materials you need?"

"I won't know until we start packing, we're sending four times as much as what they brought in but then neither crate was full. I had Greta save all the newspapers for the past several months; we've got them stacked up over there to help with the crating and so forth."

"Wow, I didn't notice that pile before, that's going to add some weight to it all.

"Princess, is that going to be a problem weight wise for your aircraft?"

"I don't think so Sol but I'll ask father to add in a few extra gallons of fuel anyway and we'll top off with your fuel at the airport and if there is enough we'll top of the auxiliary tanks as well. How big of a tanker are you expecting to refuel us?"

"At least a five thousand gallon tanker."

"Trust me Sol; bigger would be better so we don't have to make too many stops on the way home and we'll be carrying extra weight as you know. When I heard back from the other pilot she said she had to stop at a friendly country and top off to get home so bigger is better.

One thing we can do with this aircraft is feather the props some and stretch the fuel consumption. It will add a little time in getting these back home but we could save a lot of fuel in the process by flying higher over the oceans we have to cross,, there is less drag at higher elevations..This aircraft, as I explained earlier is a go anywhere, do anything type of aircraft."

"Okay, then I'll make the call after we have a firm timeline of getting things to the airport in time to meet your plane."

"I can safely say we could do it by noon tomorrow at the airport", Fred said.

"That's what I needed to hear. Susan you can wait here with Fred or go back to the store or start packing your things, I'll leave it up to you and of course you'll have to call your father and make firm arrangements for the airplane to land around noon tomorrow eastern standard time."

"Then I'd best call father first Sol, he's been getting antsy with me here in the States for such a long time. Every day that I'm here I get closer to the danger of someone finding me." She followed Sol up to the store and Sol went on up to his apartment while Susan talked with Greta to give her a heads up as well. After talking with her father he asked her if it would be possible to pack the copies going to Israel and Egypt in separate crates with zero I-Ds on them other than the Country's name that is to receive them, it would save a lot of time separating them when they got to his Country and home. She went right back to see Sol so they could talk it over with Fred.

"Fred, we have a small hiccup in our plans, Susan's father would like us to split up the load of what is going back so that one crate will be going to Israel and another crate will go to Egypt, we'll have four crates instead of two bigger ones, can you manage that or is it too late?"

"I can send BJ to one of the local Lumber Yards and give him the approximate dimensions of the crates we'll have to build and the yard can sell him the necessary materials to build them with and we can start on those as soon as he get's back here, you might want to delay the trip for twenty four hours though to give us time to build the crates and separate everything for him. I'll ask our Shipping Department to build the crates to my specs. and they can bring them to me as soon as they are finished."

"As long as its okay with you Fred because it means extra work for you."

"Not a problem Sol, what I've already crated is separated with a white bed sheet that I've folded to fit the crate and they are marked clearly between layers. We'll just have to repack them in a new crate for each Country but it shouldn't be too hard at this stage of the game."

"I should have known you'd have a handle on it, thanks Fred. Susan can tell her father to delay another twenty four hours."

The next day they were busy with the new crates and on the second day they began packing everything in the van and had everything ready to go in record time, the extra day was all they needed.

Susan's father said he could make the timeline alright; they had the aircraft ready to go for the past two weeks waiting in a friendly Country to save time when he had received the last update from the Princess. Sol asked Fred if he'd like to ride along with them and he said why not he'd like to see the big bird that could land and take off on shorter runways than the big jets.

Soon they were all crammed into the van with the Princess and her luggage which was only one large suitcase and an overnight bag and another with some odds and ends she had picked up as gifts for her family. BJ drove with Sol in the right seat and Fred and the Princess in the back seat along with BJ's friend whom they would use to help unload the van and put everything on the aircraft as quickly as possible. Speed was of the essence just in case the plane got picked up on radar coming in over Canada.

At one minute of 12:00 the airplane touched down easily and ever so quietly and taxied to a place reserved for them. From there things went like clockwork, they unloaded everything and loaded it on the aircraft but the tanker truck hadn't arrived yet. A man came running towards Sol whom he recognized as his friend Charlie, the airport's manager.

He ran up to Sol all out of breath. "Sol, the truck is late but should be here any minute, there was a problem getting the right fuel truck. Is this the airplane you told me about?"

"Yes it is Charlie but you never saw it understatd."

"Just what the hell kind of airplane is it Sol, it looks fat and stubby both."

"Trust me Charlie, you don't want to know, what you saw was never here, got it?"

"If you say so Sol, but you know I still have my pilot's license; I'd sure like to see inside her while we wait."

"I'll ask the boss." He climbed on board and went forward to the flight deck to tell Susan that the truck was on its way but running a little late and told her what Charlie had asked.

"Well Sol if he's the man taking all the chances for us and is a pilot it's alright but he has to keep his mouth shut."

"I'll pass the word."

Sol went back to the open door and motioned for Charlie to climb on board but to hurry. Charlie followed Sol to the flight deck to meet the Princess.

"Susan this is Charlie, he's the owner and manager of the airport and has arranged everything for your return trip home."

"Pleased to meet you Charlie, how do you like my custom aircraft?"

"From what I know about airplanes this is a standard C130 with Rolls Royce turbo prop engines with huge paddle props, but how, why?"

"All in good time Charlie, this is my personal toy. Father bought it for me and I designed it to look more like a passenger plane rather than a cargo plane."

The girl who flew it in was now sitting in the co pilot's seat. "Excuse me from interrupting Princess Saheed but the fuel truck is approaching."

"Princess, the hell you say!" said a surprised Charlie with a shock of disbelief on his face.

"Yes I am afraid it is true, your friend Sol was kind enough to put up with me for nearly a year now but now I must go home, father needs me."

"Is he King or something?"

"Yes he is the King of our Country but it is safer that you don't know and you never saw me here. There are people in the world who are power hungry and would stop at nothing to capture me and use me for leverage against father. I would like to thank you for the use of your airport and I will see to it that you are properly rewarded."

"Wow, oh wow, I've never met a Princess before, a real live Princess, oh wow!"

"You are to tell no one under penalty of death I am afraid. If I get word that you talked you will die, friend or no friend, our security is that important. Even Sol knows the penalty for talking and it doesn't bother him because he is a man of honor. You must also give me your word and keep it. Like I said you will be handsomely rewarded for your help."

"On my honor I will tell no one, hell I'm in hot water just for stealing a fuel truck to get you out of here, I still have to get rid of the fuel truck plus I had to suspend all the flights in and out of here from 11:00 until 3:00 this afternoon to get you in and out of here quickly and quietly, everyone thinks we're doing maintenance on the runways"

"Thank you for that and take my word on this, talk to Sol; he can make it happen for you nice and clean, the truck will disappear, your hands will not be soiled."

"Got it, and thank you Princess it was a thrill to meet you and to see your aircraft."

"The pleasure was all mine I assure you and thank you for being Sol's friend he may one day tell you what part you have played in this odyssey of what we carry."

"I'm afraid to look."

"Then trust me you don't want to know what we carry, I will leave it up to Sol to tell you if he wishes but trust me on this, you put yourself in mortal danger the longer we are delayed."

"Yes ma'am, thank you for the heads up, have a nice trip home ladies."

Charlie ran the length of the entire loading deck to get off the airplane.

He approached Sol, "Sol, I need a favor, this fuel truck is going to be hot, real hot and the female pilot said you may be able to help me to get rid of it."

"Certainly Charlie, may I use your phone for a minute?"

"Yes take me back to the terminal and you can use my office phone."

Everyone piled into the van and BJ pulled away from the airplane and then stopped for a minute where they could all watch it take off.

The fuel truck arrived, a large tractor trailer of gleaming aluminum and immediately began refueling the airplane under Susan's directions from the cockpit window. As soon as the tanks were filled with what was on the truck and it took every drop, the truck pulled away a safe distance and Susan fired up the engines and taxied towards the runway to get ready for takeoff.

Receiving clearance from the small Tower she gunned the engines, headed down the runway and the engines were barely heard.

"Ah, tis a thing of beauty Sol, look at that bird fly, whisper quiet as well." commented Charlie. "Those large paddle props gives her extra lift and speed huh?"

They took off with runway to spare and they all watched it as it rose quickly into the air and was gone. The powerful engines did not even smoke as they sped north towards Canada.

"BJ, take us to the terminal building we have another chore to do before we're done."

He drove up to where Charlie was pointing, Sol went inside and was gone for a few minutes then came back again. "BJ, would your friend be willing to drive this truck to the same scrap yard as before, we need to dump it like the moving tractor trailer truck only this time it all goes to the crusher?"

BJ looked over his shoulder and the look he got back from his friend was one of, what are you waiting for lets get the show on the road, he loved this part of living dangerously. They took him over to the fuel truck and the young man climbed in after the other driver got out to stay with Charlie, he had his own ride coming to pick him up. Norman, the young man who worked on and off at the store, fired it up and they were off to the crusher once again. By 3:30 that afternoon they were all back at the Store.

Sol asked BJ and Norman to follow him inside the store and he gave both or them a handsome bonus of one thousand dollars cash in hundred dollar bills.

"Not bad for a few hours work and you also realize that the money says you saw nothing and heard nothing today."

"Yes sir Sol we both get it, my friend has enjoyed working for you now and then and would like to know if maybe you could find something for him to do around the store or warehouse full time so he can quit his other boring job which he hates. By the way Sol his name is Norman, he's done several jobs for us now and dangerous ones as well."

"Yes BJ I recognized him, I just didn't use his name in case there was trouble. I think maybe we can find something for him to do permanently. Take him to see Greta and tell her I said he's okay, he's earned a shot at working here full time now just like you earned yours."

"Thank you Sol.

Fred was smiling from ear to ear staring dreamily out into space inside the store.

"What's up Fred, why the big smile?"

"The Princess, she kissed me on the lips and told me what a wonderful a man I was for the work we did, oh my, she is wonderful, if I were twenty years younger I could fall for her."

"I think you already did just as the rest of us have."

Sol had not looked at the last several days of mail. He'd been preoccupied about getting the Lost Books of the Bible out of town and on their way back to where they came from. He called Richard to let him know they were done and that the Princess was on her way back home safely. BJ would take Doris to the airport in New York City two days layer for her return trip to Israel and she said she would like to come back soon and work close to BJ.

That evening instead of relaxing Sol decided to catch up on his mail. He started going through it then it dawned on him; it had been several weeks since he even looked at his mail. Greta always went through it for him and took out the bills that needed to be paid and she took care of all that so all Sol had was a lot of advertisements, booklets mail order catalogs and a mixture of a few flyers. One flyer in particular caught his eye; it was a Book Store sale of inventory only and the owner's private collection of old books that was in Burlington Vermont, a place he'd never been to. He read and re-read the flyer on and off during the evening trying to decide whether not to go to the sale. It was unusual for him to go to an Auction because he had competition whom he didn't know and he would rather deal one on one but he thought he may make an exception in this case. In the end he decided to sleep on it.

The next day he made a call to request information regarding the age of the store and whatever history he could come by. It was a very brief call and he requested a map of the downtown area from the Chamber of Commerce. He would call again when and if he decided to go.

A few days later he got the map and checked it out, it showed Hotels and the airport where he could fly in and out of. If he decided to buy the Inventory he could use the same type of moving company he had been using. The problem with it was that it was a very public sale and there might be a lot of interest because it was an auction and people were always trying to buy things for next to nothing. That part was holding him back. He decided to sleep on it for a while before finally deciding, he had about a week and a half until the sale.

The next day he got up, went downstairs to talk with Fred about it. He had the flyer with him. "Fred, good morning, everything okay around here now that our worries have taken wing?"

"Yes Sol now its back to a more normal routine, what have you got with you?"

"I have a flyer about a Book Store being sold due to the owner's untimely death and none of the heirs want it. The trouble I'm having with it is that it is a Public Auction and you know how much I dislike Auctions."

"I don't care for them either Sol. What's the age of the Store? How long has it been in business?"

"I don't have the specifics just yet, I'm not sure that I want to mix with a large crowd of hawkers and on lookers and such but especially the shills who try to drive up the prices from within the crowd."

CHAPTER - 110

About the same time the FBI Agents were getting close to the auction date and had made their Airline Reservations for everyone to arrive en masse with disguises in their luggage. Motel rooms had been arranged with four different Motels and Hotels spreading everyone out just in case they spotted their man at one of the few Motels in Town. At the time there were only five Hotel Motel choices available close in to the City. Dick and Jane would stay at one of the more modest Motels hoping that their man was thinking the same way so as not to stand out by using a more expensive Motel or the least expensive one. They hoped to have made their choices wisely. They now had the six Agents from the lab, four new female Agents and themselves bringing their total of manpower to twelve. They broke people up so there would be two to a room, two men, two women with the exception of Dick and Jane who would have separate but connecting rooms for communication purposes. They gave themselves almost a week to set up and practice. They arrived on Monday afternoon before the Saturday Auction. They knew from experience their man would be there late, probably arriving on Friday to scope out the territory then show up an hour or less before the sale hammer fell.

Tuesday morning the teams began practice for Friday and Saturday wanting to be in place and in disguise before Friday noon just in case he came in on an earlier flight. Things were a bit rocky getting started, the vehicles from around New England they requested didn't start showing up until very late Tuesday right through late Wednesday afternoon. They still had adequate time to get the vehicles requested ready to be put into use but fell short on some important details like getting the names and logos just right with magnetic signs. They ended up with a Telephone Repair van, a TV Cable Repair van and a Plumbing Repair truck that were almost identical to the real ones that were in town. The men worked mostly one man to a truck so they could have an agent in the Store and a sniper on a roof across the street from the store for insurance purposes in case things went sour and they had orders to shoot to kill. Each van and the trucks had sets of different ladders on them and were fully equipped with items necessary to fool anyone. They set the vehicles up around the same blocks in a perimeter as the store but not so close as to draw attention to them.

On Thursday morning a local cop stopped by one of the vehicles and said they had to move it, if they didn't it would be towed, if they caused trouble they would be arrested because the truck had been in the location way too long to make repairs and it seemed very suspicious to the Officer. Dick was called on the radio to come over to where the cop was so he could talk to him.

"I'm afraid we're not moving the vehicle Officer" Dick said We're conducting a surveillance of this area for a wanted criminal and you and your people will stay out of our way!"

"Bull crap mister, just who the hell do you think you are telling me what to do you bum?"

"I was hoping you would leave us alone, if you don't I'll have you locked up in your own jail to keep that big mouth of yours shut and if you don't like it you can go to hell." Dick opened his protective folder containing his badge showing it to the uniformed cop.

"That don't cut no ice around here mister, you're in the State of Vermont and in the City of Burlington and around here we take care of our own problems."

"Have it your way, get your boss on the phone or be arrested for disrupting a Federal Investigation, where's your car?"

"I don't have one; I walk the same beat every day."

"Fine, take me to your boss and no guff or I'll have you in cuffs before you know it."

"Are you threatening me Jack, because if you are I can take you out in a heartbeat."

"Oh no," he sighed, "Agent Marlowe, you're up," he said quietly on his wire, "I'm afraid he won't listen."

Agent Marlowe was standing close enough to overhear the conversation anyway. She stepped up and took the cop by the elbow and walked him away from Dick a few feet. She reached into her suit jacket pocket, pulled out her badge and showed it to the cop. "Now then Officer, just so you understand we don't give a hoot about your little ole town here. We're hoping to avoid a gun battle if we find our man. If we do have to shoot we don't want any locals getting in the way of the gunfire, we have twelve men and women on the streets right now watching for our man to show. Rest assured if you open that mouth of yours once more you will be singing soprano for the rest of your natural born days, do I make myself clear. You see that man you were just talking with, he's the very same officer you've seen on TV when a FBI Agent was shot and killed. His partner was also shot and nearly died. That man shot and killed one bad guy taking four bullets himself. Now he's a real mean man and I'm his new partner and I'm a hell of a lot meaner than he is so he gives me his light weight chores to take care of and he takes care of the heavy weight guys. Now we don't have all day to explain the situation to you and I doubt you have read one bulletin that we sent you, so run along and be a good boy. Bring your boss back here and we'll talk. But I warn you, do not interfere with us again. If we had to tell you what we are doing it would take us months to get you up to speed and by then just like the last time we'd lose our man because some dumb local cop wouldn't listen and didn't read the bulletins we sent out because if you had we wouldn't be standing here right now. Now then, with that said, I suggest you hightail it out of here or risk going to jail for interfering with us and while you're cooling your heels in your own jail you can catch up on your reading by reading all of the bulletins we put out to keep wise guys and loud mouths like you from butting in and the last thing we need is a uniformed cop running around here looking stupid and scaring our man away. Now make a decision and make it the right one I don't fell in the mood to hurt you and carry you off to your own jail, how would your boss react to that?"

"You're not threatening me too are you Miss?"

"The name is Special Agent Marlowe, FBI, not Miss so and so and that man you were talking with is in charge here not you, not your boss, his name is Special Agent Jefferies.

"Say, I've heard that name before, is that really him for sure?"

"Yes you shit head, you saw his I D."

"Well now I'd like to shake his hand and introduce him to our squad."

"Listen to me closely once more, we are conducting a Federal Investigation here right now, we'll be here through late Saturday and we'll leave here sometime Sunday with or without our man. He doesn't have time to talk small talk with you, now get going and don't go spreading the word that we're in town or you'll blow our cover and if that happens I guarantee you we'll take out Federal Charges against you and your entire department, now is that clear enough?"

"Do you mean I can't even tell my boss?"

"That's right, tell him what you want but no one is to be in this area for the next few days, no uniformed cops, no detectives or anyone else. If there is a shootout we don't want to be responsible for any of you getting injured or killed. Now if that isn't clear enough go ahead and get your boss but he had better be in street clothes, we don't want to see another uniformed cop around here before Sunday and that means you too. Now get the hell out of here!"

"Uh yes sir, I mean yes ma'am, I'm going." The cop started walking away briskly and Jane figured he was headed for the station house. An hour and a half later two men were seen walking down the sidewalk dressed in suits and ties trying to look the part of widow shoppers, something a woman would do but not two men.

"Oh my word Jane would you look at what's coming?"

"Yes Dick, I saw them."

The two men walked up to Dick and the one who seemed to be in charge said, "Are you sure this bum is the man Corporal?"

"Yes sir, this is FBI Special Agent Jefferies."

"If you say so."

"I'm Deputy Chief Ramsey of the Burlington Police Department. My Corporal here told me what you were up to so I went back though a bunch of directives and reports that you people sent us. Our Chief thought no one in the world would want to come here to do a crime but by the communiqués I just read I stand corrected, this is exactly the place your man would show up to do a crime, Now then, what can we do to help?"

"You can start by keeping your people away from here, you men stick out like Cops frozen in another time zone on another planet.. Our man would make you both as cops without a second look. Tell me Chief Ramsey, I have a total of twelve people here in this block alone, how many FBI Agents do you see?"

"Well I don't know, maybe two or three."

"Point out just one of them if you please."

"Well there's one, uh my mistake, well there's one over, uh oh, my mistake again. I don't see any actually."

"Do you see the lady with the baby carriage with the child in it?"

"Sure, she's a new mother."

"Federal Agent, how about the TV Cable repairman up that pole?"

"No he's a repairman alright. No, now wait a minute we don't have cable TV here yet."

"That's right but our man doesn't know it, he's a Federal Agent. Have I made my case Chief?"

"Well I guess so but I hate being out of the loop."

"Sorry, but we did tell you we were coming and asked to be left alone didn't we?"

"Well yes I saw that, but we didn't think it was possible until just now."

"Damn it all Chief, don't you people ever pay attention to requests that are sent to you?"

"Well of course we do but this time our Chief thought that you would never come up here to this sleepy little town."

"Trust me when I tell you that this man is a serial killer as well as a mass murderer. The job before the last one he killed twelve people, burned down three homes with the owners in them, then wrecked a truck and burned it with two men inside it and God knows what other things he did while he was there. If and when he shows up here I want to prevent him from ever hurting another person and I'll do just that if I have to kill him myself with my bare hands and we're all committed to that end. Each man and woman are hand picked by myself and Special Agent Marlowe standing next to you."

"Who? What? Where?"

"Right next to you!"

"You mean to tell me that this little lady isn't a tourist?"

"Special Agent Marlowe FBI, pleased to meet you Deputy Chief Ramsey." She stuck her hand out to shake his.

"Well I am impressed by all this, are you sure we can't help you all in some small way?"

"I'm sure Chief, the best thing you can do for us is to stay way away from this area of downtown. If and when we catch our perp. I'll mention in my report to the Director that it was you who assisted us along with your Department and that's the best I have to offer you."

"I thank you for that much and I'll make sure to let the Chief know as soon as he's back from vacation next week."

"Where did he go?"

"Somewhere in Florida, Miami Beach I think."

"I'll be sure he gets a personal letter from me when he gets back thanking him for staying away from our investigation and out of the way as well, it will be terse and to the point. You may very well be the next Chief when this is over, I won't let this slide!"

"Oh I hope not. I can retire with thirty years on the force next year and that would upset my wife something awful if I got the job. I promised her a real vacation when I retire and I'm not going back on my promise, have a nice day Agent Jefferies, you too ma'am."

"Its Special Agent Marlowe to you Chief!" she hollered back at him almost standing on her tip toes as she hollered back at him.

He gave a little wave over his shoulder as they quickly walked away at fast pace.

"I hope that's the last of them Jane."

"Me too Dick, where do they find these people, who takes care of them, they should be institutionalized, at least some of them anyway."

"I agree Jane and they probably feel the same way about us for the way we look. Now lets get back to work, that should be the last of the interruptions." They went back to what they were doing which was really little or nothing. Jane was supposed to be a tourist about town and really looked the part and Dick was a vagrant pan handler who had seen better days. Every town has some. He was simply standing around looking totally disinterested in life and killing time between his next free meal from someone who felt sorry for him. He had an empty wine bottle in a small paper sack that was well worn and wrinkled. One man walked by him and mentioned;

"Why don't you get a real job you bum?"

That was validation enough for him. He even tossed his soft worn out wide brimmed hat to the ground near his feet and someone passing by dropped a quarter in it and he just left it in there for effect. He was leaning against a telephone pole wearing an old raggedy worn out suit with no tie and his shirt unbuttoned for the first two button holes with the buttons missing. Jane walked down one side of the street and back on the other side covering two to three blocks at a time window shopping.

And so it went with people constantly changing sides of the street and telephone poles so as not to stand out too much.

On Friday morning Dick and Jane met in his room before going out to their posts. Dick called the Chamber of Commerce to see if anyone had called looking for a lot of details about the City that was maybe interested in the sale of the Book Store's Inventory. He identified himself and wasn't surprised when they said that two people had called a man, then a woman asking about details just like what he and Jane had asked for. Dick thanked them and they went back to their posts and when Dick caught someone's eye he would given them a thumbs up meaning their guy had made contact. No one wanted to over use their radios and at night they all plugged them into chargers to keep the battery power up.

Now all that was left to do was to wait and see if he showed today or tomorrow when the sale was too be held. It was now Friday at 11:45 am.

CHAPTER - 111

Sol decided to waste no more time. He went ahead and made his airline reservations the following day. That gave him almost a week before he would have to leave. He told Fred, Greta and BJ he would be going after all and asked BJ for a ride to the plane Thursday morning. That gave him the rest of the week to get packed and get this disguises ready to go as well. He chose three to start with then decided he had better throw in a fourth one just in case the Feds were there. Safety first he had always had told Fred and BJ. Now he was taking his own advice.

He called the City of Burlington for a more complete description of the City and asked to have some other information ready for him to pick up at the Chamber of Commerce Office tomorrow which was Friday, the day before the sale. He asked for demographics of the town and History of the block where the Book Store was. He was ready to move even if he had to do it legally. This time he would own the books he so desperately wanted rather than needed.

BJ drove him to New York to catch a plane for Burlington. He could have driven there but changed his mind taking the plane rather than a long road trip that would take several hours to make even with BJ driving, something inside told him to fly rather than involve BJ. He couldn't put his finger on it but he had a foreboding about this job. He almost didn't get on the plane. His two bags were checked through and before he knew it the plane was backing away from the terminal and began to roll towards the runway. His intuitions had always been right but this time the signals he was getting were all jumbled up somehow in his mind. Was it the Auction part of the job he didn't like or was it that they, the FBI, who may be waiting for him? He brushed that thought aside. They wouldn't catch him. They were too easy to spot just like any other undercover cops of the day. The clean haircuts clean shaves and being well dressed always gave them away even when they were undercover. Little by little he lost his wariness and his confidence began to show through. He would spot a cop before they saw him. He was too good to ever get caught. His confidence grew and grew as the plane began to descend into the Burlington Airport and the Captain told everyone they would be at their gate within fifteen minutes. He tightened his seat belt like everyone else and suddenly without warning the plane hit the runway kind of hard, the engines were thrown into reverse immediately and the plane shuddered then slowed as it reached the small maze of taxiways as Sol watched them roll by the plane's window. He knew he had one more chance to run, go back he thought, get on the next plane out of here, danger waits. He shrugged it off, got off the plane with everyone else but his head was now on a swivel, every muscle taut, every nerve tingling, he couldn't wait to get his rental car, go to the Chamber of Commerce and pick up the things he had asked for then check into his Hotel. In disguise he looked like any other middle aged businessman on a trip going somewhere, anywhere. He had on a sandy color wig of neatly trimmed hair, his elevated shoes so he looked to be about five feet nine inches tall, an average height. He was well dressed and looked very distinguished and successful with his wide brimmed brown soft hat and he saw some women as he passed them by as he was walking and they were smiling at him while they definitely checking him out. He thought to himself, I must look really good getting all of those stares and the women looking weren't bad looking either.

He went to the Rental Car desk and was handed his keys and shown which exit to take that would lead him to his car, a white four door Ford full size sedan. Sol if nothing else was a meticulous man for details. Everything he could think of he was prepared for. Any eventuality, at least that's what he thought. He had yet to meet Agents Jefferies or Marlowe in person, so he wasn't positively sure what they looked like when he Saw them in Rhode Island but he would be on the look out for those two again. If he spotted someone who resembled them he would go to the airport and take the first flight out.

He drove straight to the Chamber of Commerce and picked up the package of information he had requested. He wasn't prepared for the thick package he was handed. He drove to his Hotel, checked in and spent the evening going over every morsel of what he called intelligence he could memorize. He fell asleep lying across the bed. He had forgotten for the first time he could remember to call the desk and leave a wakeup call. When he awoke it was 8:30am Friday and he was hungry. He didn't remember eating supper after getting to the Hotel. He thought to himself, you're getting old Sol, this would not have happened ten years ago or even five years ago. He shaved, took a shower and put his business suit back on so he looked the same as when he had arrived. It had worked so far and he saw no one that remotely looked like a cop. He got his car and drove around looking for a restaurant that the Hotel's Concierge had told him about that served great food all day long and they didn't close until 9:00 pm. He found it and had a big breakfast. The man had been right the food was out of this world, done exactly to his taste. He relaxed there for a little while and read the local paper from end to end, he missed nothing. He knew sometimes undercover operations leaked out unintentionally, it had happened before and he'd caught it and by passed those places where there were just too many cops around to his liking even though they weren't looking for him necessarily but he didn't want to have so much as a chance meeting with anyone from law enforcement.

It was close to noon now Friday morning and he felt pretty good so he decided to take a quick look at the book store. It took him a little time to find it but he soon did. He found a parking space behind a telephone repair truck although it had a traffic cone behind it so no one would park too close for the man to get in and out of the back of the vehicle. He was tempted to get out and move the cone to the sidewalk when a man walked up to his car window and said; "just a minute Mack, I'll be moving and you can have this spot."

"Thank you, you're much too kind," Sol said.

The repairman didn't give him a second look so he felt safe but he'd been made; the repairman was an FBI Agent. He put his ladder atop his repair van and threw some tools in the back along with the traffic cone and pulled away from the curb.

"Johnson to crew, behind my truck, white Ford four door sedan, check out the driver real careful like, he could be our man, he looks awfully familiar."

Every undercover Agent heard the news. There was no response, none was needed, all eyes were on the space where the telephone repair van had been. Their eyes were locked onto the man as he got out of the car that had pulled forward into the vacant spot the repair van left and he strolled across the street towards the book store. He walked right in and started looking around until he heard a voice say; "May I help you sir, is there a particular subject you are interested in?"

"Yes actually, I'm an attorney from out of town and I like to read mystery novels from time to time."

"This way sir, that section is right over here."

The man was an Agent and the female behind the counter was also an Agent. The two regular personnel were busy stocking shelves by staying out of the way and had Sol been more aware he would have realized that the books they put on the shelves went back into the box and back onto the shelves again then they would move up the isle a little more and do the same thing. It was all a set up with the employees close by in case an Agent couldn't answer a question but they were out of harms way as much as possible.

Dick and Jane had worked a miracle this time. Everyone had time to practice and rehearse any responses.

Sol stood among the books as he perused them and found one he hadn't read yet so he took it up to the counter to check out and found the middle aged lady there especially attractive. He felt like asking her for a date, she was that beautiful and around his own age he thought.

"That will be $14.31 cents sir including tax that is. Sorry about the tax but the Governor, well he has rather expensive tastes; we'll elect a new one soon and toss this one out on his ear."

They both chuckled at her remark. It was just the down home kind of folksy remark that put Sol at ease. Then he popped the big question. "This sale, uh rather the Auction, like the sign in the window says, will it be held right here in the store?"

"Why yes sir, I guess so, we haven't been told very much but I do know the owner of the store also has a really large collection of books at his home, here's a flyer with directions if you are here during the sale tomorrow."

"Well I may stay over another day, our conference is over today at five, I'm just killing time until my plane leaves later this evening." He made no commitment and she didn't push him. Under the counter she held a 9mm pistol pointed at Sol's belt buckle just in case.

"What's your name dear?"

"Why its Shelia sir, Shelia Brown."

"Thank you my dear, you have been a big help."

Sol turned to his left slightly carefully watching his surroundings but saw no threatening movements from any angle so he left and returned to his car with the brochure and book in hand.

"Agent Jefferies, Sheila at the store, he's our man I'd bet my life on it, he has the coldest eyes of any man I've ever seen."

"Thank you Shelia, everyone copy?"

Everyone that heard them hit their squelch key twice in response for yes or if wired said affirmative over theirradios.

Later that evening Dick and Jane met with everyone after supper.

"Listen up folks we have three definite sightings for today but don't look for the same man tomorrow, however keep an eye out for that sedan. I doubt he'll switch cars, he believes his disguises will get him through this with no one being the wiser. Where's Jerry?" Jerry was driving the plumbing repair truck.

"Over here Agent Jefferies."

"Jerry, you had the residence, did he show up there?"

"Yes he did boss, he went through the man's library with a fine tooth comb and I heard him sigh several times and say under his breath, well, well, isn't this nice and oh my, would you look at this. I don't think he saw our bugs and if he did he was awfully cool about it."

"Alright, I need a volunteer to check him out and soon. I want to know which airline he came in on and from where, the airport isn't all that busy and I need them to check the rental car companies to see who rents that particular sedan and get the name he used to rent it. Some of us wont' get a lot of sleep tonight but we'll all make up for it after we cuff this guy, this is the absolute closest we've gotten yet guys, don't lets blow it now!" Dick said it tongue in cheek mixing up the words to relieve tension he knew everyone had to be feeling.

They broke up and spread out, one man alone headed for the airport and the rest broke up into teams of twos to go to the middle priced Restaurants to try and catch another glimpse of their man.

Before Sol went to super he called the store and asked for BJ. He caught him just before he left to go out to eat. "BJ, can you run up here to Vermont and stand by in case I need you?"

"I guess so; I don't have any plans that can't be changed, where are you, Burlington?"

"Yes that's it, I'll give you directions. Can you find your way to Interstate 91 alright?"

"Sure Sol, I know just how to get to it, I've been up there snow skiing before."

"Good, then pick up Intestate 89 off of 91 and it will bring you into Burlington, look for signs for the Best Western Hotel and that's where I'm staying. I need you for a safety valve I think. I have a bad feeling tonight, can't put my finger on it but some of the hairs on the back of my neck keep standing up. When you get to the Hotel come upstairs to room 313, that's my room. Knock on the door and I'll let you in. Drive all night if you have to but I need you son, tonight if not early in the morning. I'll see to it you get some food and some sleep."

"Okay Sol, you know I'd do anything for you."

"This may be it for you to get a gold star rather than a silver star on your report card

"I understand Sol, a.s.a.p. and don't spare the horses."

"Exactly my boy, now it's quite a drive but my money is on you to make it. I won't leave the room until you arrive. Oh and one more thing, throw in a few of those magnetic signs I had made up for things like the Telephone Company, Cable TV Repairs, Plumbing and things like that whatever you think we might need to throw people off our trail just in case."

"Okay Sol, I'll grab a bite to eat, throw in some gear and be there as soon as I can."

"Thank you BJ, bless you my son."

Wow BJ thought, he called me son again. He must really be worried. Rest assured my friend I won't waste any time coming for you. Then he thought to himself. It was roughly a six hour drive observing the speed limits and all but with the turbo charged diesel engine in the van and the extra fuel tank BJ knew he could make it in less time than that.

CHAPTER - 113

At 1:30 that morning Sol heard a knock at his door called out, "BJ that you?"

"Yes Sol it's me, I'm alone."

Sol opened the door and hugged BJ like he'd never been hugged before. "Thank God, you made really good time son, did you stop to eat?"

"Yes sir but I brought an extra sandwich just in case I got hungry; I made it in five and a half hours, not bad for over a three hundred mile trip from the store."

"Let's both get some sleep son then I'll fill you in come morning."

All BJ brought with him was an overnight bag with a change of under ware and socks in it along with a comb, toothbrush and toothpaste.

Both Sol and BJ were awake by 8:00am, BJ being younger was able to bounce back real quick and was in the bathroom first, he shaved, showered and was out in time for Sol, who was just getting out of bed. They barely spoke; Sol seemed possessed by some primordial urge to move on like the famous quote, 'damn the torpedoes, full speed ahead.' Sol acted as though he was going to a slaughter of sorts but wouldn't change his mind. BJ was happy that Sol had called him just in case they needed to make a quick getaway. The van was specifically designed by Sol partly for that purpose. He called it his 'just in case truck,' he didn't much like the use of the word van, it sounded too much like a work vehicle which this was but it was also a sanctuary type of vehicle if needed. There was plenty of room in the back for one or two people to lie down and sleep. The two captain chairs in the front reclined fully so someone could take a nap and the third seat that the sometimes carried made into a bed when laid down similar to the captain's chairs. Sol had really thought it through and planned the customization of the van thoroughly, he felt invincible in his well armored rolling tank as he sometimes referred to it.

They ate breakfast and talked a little about the sale of the Book Store. Sol seemed really preoccupied to BJ so he spoke up first. "Sol, if you are having misgivings about this deal why not skip this one and wait for another sale to come along, it might be safer to do that?"

"Yes of course it would but I've already checked the place out and saw nothing out of order and I really want the collection of old books that the owner has. When we get started I want you to stay away from me and keep an eye out for trouble such as FBI Agents or Cops. Stay about a block away with the van, do you have any other clothes with you or did you leave in such a hurry you forgot to throw extra's in?"

"This is all I have; I figured that it may be a short trip so I only threw in a change of under ware and socks."

"Well the first thing then is to find a thrift store and find you some other older kinds of duds, right now you'll stick out too much and I want you to look like the locals around here. We'll find a phone booth and look in the yellow pages for a thrift store near by. I'll pay the tab for breakfast, after that we get you changed into something other than what you are wearing. Then I'll run by the store with you in the rental car so you can see where it is and you can also take a curious walk through a little later, just don't appear too obvious. I'm going to go by the rules if I buy the books and pay with a good check. No funny business here and we're both going to be disguised as someone other than who we are. If worse comes to worse keep the van near by at all times, put one of the magnetic sets of signs on it."

They went about their chores, found a thrift store and got BJ a couple of tee shirts, a pair of well worn blue jeans and a well worn baseball cap that said Boston Red Socks on it. They took Sol's rental car and Sol drove him past the Book Store pointing it out to him and gave him specific instructions. They went back to the Hotel so BJ could change clothes then he headed back to the book store with the van alone. Sol had told him to walk around warily and watch the employees for anything that looked out of place and buy any book that interested him. Sol went upstairs to his room to rest and wait for BJ to return.

BJ got in the van and went to the Book Store and parked a block away like Sol had suggested. He surveyed the area looking for any sign of trouble. He didn't see anyone that remotely resembled a FBI Agent. He saw a telephone man up a pole and a cable TV guy up another pole, someone was washing windows, he saw a lady with a baby carriage but it was a small one like they make for new born babies and she was just strolling like she was going to the store but he didn't see her go in any of them. Good he thought to himself, lets give it a whirl, he got out of the van and walked across the street and up one block to the book store.

He walked into the store and began to walk the isles as if he were looking for something. A few minutes went by and a man approached and asked if he could help him find anything.

"Yes as a matter of fact, I'm going to restore an old motorcycle and was looking for any books on older motorcycles, I doubt you'd have manuals on how to restore one but I'd like to find a description of the one I intend to fix up."

"What kind of a bike is it?"

"It's an old Harley, a 1946 model street bike, it says on the gas tank, Cruiser."

"I'm familiar with that model; it was a great bike in its day meant for highway cruising cross country for World War II Veterans who yearned for the open road. I may not have exactly what you want but over here in the magazine isle you'll find all kinds of Motorcycle Magazines dealing with everything from buying and selling to repair and restoring. Come with me, I'm sure we can fix you up with something that would do for you."

"Thank you, that would be a big help."

"Is this your first bike young man, you don't look like a seasoned veteran of the road."

"Yes it is, in fact I've never ridden one but my Uncle left me this one in his will when he passed away and I'd like to get it in running order and try it out. I just graduated from the University of Connecticut and I'm in between jobs if you know what I mean. I'm up here with my folks to see the mountains of Vermont; they tell me it's beautiful up here."

"Oh it is marvelous; you should come here closer to fall though when the leaves are turning, its really beautiful then." They walked a little further then stopped. "Well here we are young man, this is the section I was telling you about. If you need any more help my name is Jack and I'll be around the store, we're getting ready for the big sale this afternoon."

"Big sale huh, should I wait for the sale to start, will these be any cheaper, you know like marked down maybe?"

"No, I'm afraid that once the sale is over this store will be closed for good. The owner passed away and they aren't any heirs left who wanted the business so they are selling all of the inventory. Myself and one of the ladies are here from our Publishing House to over see the daily sales and make sure the final sale is proper when it is done. We have to protect our interests as well you know." The man walked away and left BJ alone to check out the magazines.

He hadn't had the chance to go up and down every isle like Sol had asked him to but at least now he knew that two of the people here were from one of the Publishing Houses and the other two, a man and a woman, must actually work for the previous owner and are on their last day on the job. He spent a long time looking as if he couldn't make up his mind so he picked up a magazine finally that showed a Harley on the cover and went to the front counter to check out.

There was an attractive older woman in her forties he guessed working the cash register. "Will that be all young man?" she asked.

"Yes that's it for now thank you."

"Alright then, that will be $3.07 please."

"Here you are" and he handed her a five dollar bill and she handed him back his change as she counted it out. She put the magazine in a small beige plastic bag with the stores name on it in black and he left and headed back for the van which was down the street.

On the radio Dick heard, "contact with secondary person Agent Jefferies, a young man in his early twenties was just in the store asking about motorcycle books and he fits the description of the same young man that we were told about and he said he had recently graduated from the University of Connecticut, I think we have the pair of them this time."

"Great, watch and see what kind of vehicle he gets into and check the plates somebody and hurry before he gets out of sight but don't stop him just observe. Get that tag number and

State and run it through that States DMV and get the registered owners name and address and put a rush on it and I do mean rush, 10/4?"

The radio fell quiet which meant that they were all working to get the information before he got out of sight. An hour went by and Dick heard his radio again. "Agent Jefferies, the plate is registered to a Steven Shultz at a Funeral Home in New York City and the address is a P.O. Box as it turns out. The van the young man was driving had on it Plumbing Supplies New York, New York, also no address or phone number."

"That's them then, it has to be. Now we need to know where their base of operations is and I think that the P.O. Box is real but bogus for where they live and is probably used only as a drop shipment address. I doubt they live anywhere close to New York City. In fact it would not surprise me if they were from out of State given the circumstances but still I feel that they are within a couple of hundred miles in any direction. That young man had to arrive from their home base overnight."

Jane was the next one to speak. "Agent Jefferies, do you feel as though they made us?"

"No, I think that he is being overly cautious though because he made us once but I think this time we will beat him at his own game." The radio fell silent once more.

After a good fifteen minutes Dick spoke on the radio again. "Listen up everyone, we may need a chopper and or a light plane in case they make a run for it The van is the one we follow, not the rental car. I'm betting the van is the clue to finding out where they are located. Somebody take a few minutes and contact the State Police to see if the have an airplane available for surveillance of the van and Agent Marlowe if you're not to busy maybe you could contact the Director and get us a chopper or small plane in the air, unmarked of course."

The radio fell silent again as people scrambled to get Dick what he wanted but also made sure that every base was still covered.

BJ went back to the Hotel to meet with Sol and tell him what he saw and didn't see. He laid it all out for him, the conversation with the male clerk and the pretty woman behind the cash register and about the motorcycles of which BJ knew very little but the man was very helpful and probed very gently into BJs background but not overly friendly. He told Sol he saw nothing that could be the cops or any surveillance of any kind.

"You know BJ, it's sometimes what you don't see that you have to question. Did you see anyone stocking shelves or anything like that?"

"Can't say that I did. There were a total of four people in the store, two employees and two from a Publishing House or so they said."

"Ah but did they say which Publishing House they represented or steer you towards any of their books so you'd purchase what they wanted you to buy?"

"Well no come to think of it I was steered away from books to magazines."

"Do you get the feeling that they wanted you to hurry and make your purchase and get out of the store?"

"Yes, well sort of, well no, I mean yeah now that you put it that way, I was steered away from the book section of the store."

"Did you see any cameras hidden any where or feel like you were being watched?"

"No not at all but like I said the man had me cold, I don't know squat about motorcycles but that was all that came to mind when he approached me."

"Its okay son, it's your first time out like this where they may be danger ahead. Let's get some lunch and sometime this afternoon I'll decide whether or not to proceed with the sale. For some reason I don't feel threatened anymore it's more like they are waiting for me to make a move but I've yet to see a Cop or an FBI Agent anywhere."

They went to lunch then back to the Hotel. Sol still had some questions to answer in his mind as to if they were here why didn't they grab him right away unless they don't have a case yet and are holding back waiting for him to make a mistake of robbing someone and killing them at the same time like he had done before. Sol lay down and BJ grabbed a short nap as well just in case they had to make a run for it they would be rested.

Little by little the FBI Agents went to lunch as well but made sure someone was covering every aspect just in case they made an early move on the store or the house. Two Agents were at the house as well and had radios with them just in case Sol went for the collection of books and tried to kill someone along the way. There were a total of five people in the house, three were there to show the collection to prospective buyers and the other two were FBI Agents. The afternoon went by slowly for everyone on the stakeouts. Waiting and watching were the most difficult parts of their jobs. Each Agent involved was watching the other Agents to be sure everyone got to eat and the stakeout was not compromised in any way. Literally months and months of planning and coordinating had gone into this and they had incurred a huge expense in man hours and many other things that had to be accounted for once the case was closed. They knew to a man or woman that the Director would be mad if one of them slipped up after all of this planning. They felt their own jobs may be in jeopardy if one of them screwed this up

CHAPTER - 112

It was 4:30 in the afternoon half an hour before the Auction was to begin, people were gathering from around town as curious onlookers flocked together along with five serious bidders for the sale. Each bidder was required to sign a piece of paper with their name, address, phone number and show a letter of credit for the minimum value of the sale which to start with included everything and the bidders also had to state what they were interested in, Item #1. 'The Store's Inventory alone, Item #2. the private collection or Item #3.the inventory together with the private collection. All the parties opted for item #3 so the Inventories would not be bid on separately making the job of the Auctioneer much easier. One final bid would take it all.

It was ten minutes to five and Sol hadn't showed himself yet but there was ten minutes left for anyone to sign up for a bidder's number. Minute by minute ticked by then Sol showed up in a different disguise altogether. He was now a toddling little old man walking with a cane and was hunched over with spectacles that could have come from the late 1800s to early 20th century, they were gold wire rimmed glasses and very effective. Dick and Jane both did a double take before realizing this had to be their man. Hunched over as he was he looked shorter than any of their sketches and they had no sketch of a little old man such as this but Dick saw through this disguise. He whispered to Jane; "it's him Agent Marlowe he's coming through the crowd right now to the Auctioneer table to sign in."

"Are you sure about this man Agent Jefferies?"

"Damn sure, that's the reason we didn't spot him at the last sale, a couple of new disguises, damn he's good."

"Agent Richardson, check the name he signed in under and give it to me, I'm curious about this alias."

"10/4 Agent Jefferies, give me a moment." He played the part of nosey on looker and went to the table where everyone had signed in to check the name and then slid back away out of ear shot of anyone in the small crowd of people. "Agent Jefferies," he whispered.

"Yes, what is it?"

"He signed in as a Professor Stevens and listed an address in Utica New York."

"I'll wager there is no Professor Stevens in Utica, anyone want to take me up on it?"

There was silence from everyone. They could hear him through their ear pieces and resembled a hearing aid but it was very small as was the wire, it was also very hard to detect. All ears were listening for the Auctioneer to start the Auction.

At five minutes past five the Auctioneer declared the sale was about to commence and cautioned the crowd to be quiet and to keep their hands down. He said only the bidders were allowed to raise their hands and they had to show the number on their individual card to be recognized and they were in the forefront of the small crowd. He started the sale at one hundred thousand dollars and no one stirred, then he explained the rules once more that the minimum bid was one hundred thousand dollars and tried again. This time Sol feebly raised his bidder's card and held it just high enough for the Auctioneer to see it and the Auctioneer said; "I have a bid of one hundred thousand dollars," and before he started his spiel he added, "now listen here folks; the store's Inventory alone is worth more than two hundred thousand dollars, lets get on the ball and start your bidding," he went directly into his spiel. He was about out of breath when someone said, "one hundred and twenty five thousand dollars." He looked for the bidder then saw a small woman in her forties he guessed then the bidding got a little better but when they got to one hundred and sixty five thousand dollars it stalled so he upped the bid by one thousand dollars and she quit and the bid went to Sol. He got the whole shooting match for less than the Store's inventory alone at one hundred and sixty six thousand dollars and got the rare collection of books literately free.

Sol ambled up to where the Auctioneer was motioning him and signed some papers and wrote the man out a check. After he examined the check and his line of credit which was in the millions he shook his hand and asked him how he was going to box all of this up and move it by Tuesday which was the deadline for the store to be cleared out.

Sol looked up at him and said; "I guess I'll need a moving company, has anyone come forward to offer their services for the job?" he asked in a very raspy voice.

"Why yes, there's a local company who has asked the right of first refusal to do the job and the man is standing here next to me."

Sol stepped over and shook the man's hand and asked him what the charge would be. He was out of State and told him it was in the vicinity of New York City.

The driver said he wanted a flat rate in State and a little more per mile if were out of State. . Sol said no problem and the driver asked how soon Sol wanted he and his men to start boxing the merchandise up?

Sol told him to go ahead and start right now, do the store first then go to the house and box that up and load it and cautioned him to put the oldest books on top of the newer ones from the store and don't make the stacks more than three boxes high. He told him he would be around to give additional instructions and would give the man the address as soon as they were loaded.

Meanwhile the FBI Agents waited for a sign from Dick to take the man down but he resisted, he wanted the whole operation shut down not just the kingpin. He finally spoke into his radio; "everyone relax, we'll follow the white van, stay on your toes it could be a while and watch for his accomplice, he can't be far away. He bought everything and it looks completely legal. Some of you watch the movers and some of you go ahead and deploy around the house, that will be their next stop and be sure the house is de-bugged, we heard him say he would give the truck driver directions as to where the load is going and mentioned New York City but I doubt that. Everyone fade away and those with vehicles get them filled with fuel and be ready to leave. Split in half, make your own decisions, just keep in touch, nothing else is going down until the moving truck is ready to leave the owner's residence then everyone be prepared to leave at a moments notice. One more thing, having this many people here in downtown is one thing but at the residence we can't all bunch up so spread out around a couple of blocks and try to be as invisible as possible, I don't want this guy to rabbit without warning which he is apparently ready to do."

The teams were capable of going their own way, they all knew what had to be covered. They had to eat and be ready to go at any time and they also knew their man wasn't going anywhere until the moving truck was loaded and that could take hours. What they didn't know was how resourceful their man was. That he could go all night and the next day if he had to with or without food, with or without sleep. In that respect Sol had the upper hand but Dick was prepared to do the same. He would put his teams into their vehicles in pairs and let one drive and one nap and they would switch when one got tired. It was well thought out from their stand point. They also had magnetic signs for their vans and trucks that they could switch out and whoever they were following wouldn't necessarily know this. With the best preparations in mind behind them the FBI Agents went about their business and were getting themselves ready for a long haul if necessary. Dick had set up a way for them to travel where they would leap frog one another at irregular intervals even passing the Moving Truck or van occasionally then getting off at a rest stop if they were on an Interstate Highway to change out their magnetic signs and change drivers then get back onto the highway. Other agents were in four door model cars of different makes and colors so as not to draw attention. Dick Jefferies had effectively put a net around the vehicles once they were on the highway and changing drivers would help as well because it was believed and correctly so that the criminals would be concentrating on the drivers of vehicles and not the passengers who would appear asleep as they passed them. Of course all of this was hypothetical when and if the van followed the moving truck, if not they would split up into two groups. One group following the moving truck and one following the criminal's white van. Dick had prepared everyone as best he could so as not to lose them as they tailed them back to their home base of operations.

They gathered around the residence of the Store's owner and watched from nearby as they loaded the balance of the books. The white van with its 'Plumbing Supply's' magnetic signs was there with Sol and BJ. They watched the young man in the van as he sat there at the ready with Sol in the house supervising the boxing of those precious books, he wanted no mishaps. It was close to dark when the loading was complete.

Sol handed the driver of the moving truck a piece of paper obviously with their destination written on it and Dick had theorized they would take different routes to get back to their home base. Sol climbed into the van along side of BJ and they pulled away leaving the moving truck which was just about ready to leave. The movers had an army of sorts ready to pack up the store and the house and it didn't take them long to accomplish their task. One group was already at the house preparing to pack when the moving truck driver called them and said go ahead and pack we have the job and told them per Sol's instructions to be extra careful at the house, pack those books with extreme care.

Dick called on the radio and told everyone to take up their respective positions that the van and the moving truck had apparently split up. The van took to some secondary highways and the moving truck headed straight for the interstate. Dick and Jane were in the group following the van. They were guessing that the group may lay over for the night depending on how far they had to travel.

The moving truck took Interstate Highway 89 south to State Highway 7 south to State Highway 22A west then picked up State highway 74 over to Interstate Highway 87 south and followed it to Albany New York where it looked as though the group would spend the night. The two truckers checked into a Motel then went to get something to eat.

The second group following Sol and BJ in their van arrived about forty five minutes later after taking mainly secondary roads most of the way before switching over to the Interstate Highway 87 south, they went to a different Motel about a mile from the moving truck. As soon as they stopped the respective Agents checked into different Motels but close enough so they could keep an eye on the van and the Moving Truck.

Everyone bedded down for the night; well almost everyone, one person stayed awake in both groups who could watch the van and the moving truck in case they took off again in the middle of the night.

At 6:00am Sol and BJ got up as did the Moving truck's drivers. It was all very well coordinated. As soon as the two people who were standing watch saw the lights come on in the two respective rooms the Agents radios took off on a life of their own with, "They're on the move people, up and at em."

CHAPTER - 114

Everyone was up early and ready for breakfast in record time when the alert was given including Dick and Jane. Someone was detailed to watch the moving truck and the van while others ate then they switched so the watchers could grab a bite to eat.

By 8:00 they were on the move again. The moving truck took I 87 south again and stayed on it. The white van however with Sol and BJ driving took another route, they took a couple of streets east and before long they pulled onto State Highway 9 south and stayed on it.

"Where do you think they are headed Dick?"

"Jane I don't think but the next sizable city is Poughkeepsie according to my memory, they may be headed there. I remember a couple of our agents already checked out a really big store there a while back and said it was clean. That could be where they are going or they could head for Pennsylvania or Ohio, who knows," he shrugged his shoulders for effect.

The moving truck stayed on course until it intersected State Highway 56, then they turned east until they hit route 44 that took them right into Poughkeepsie. A small group of cars, pickup trucks and vans followed well behind but close enough to see where they would turn next.

Dick and Jane did the same thing following Sol and BJ in their van, it stayed on route 9 which took them right into Poughkeepsie.

Soon the radio chattered and it was from the group following the moving truck. "Agent Jefferies we're entering Poughkeepsie," came a call from the group behind the moving truck.

"So is the van," answered Jefferies, "we're not too far behind, careful not to blow your cover now, this could be it or it could be another way to change routes or stop for lunch or maybe its home to our man." It wasn't long before the van pulled ahead of the Moving Truck and the Moving Truck followed. "Here we go folks, lets hope this ends soon, I 'm tired of the run around. This guy is pretty clever alright, string it out, keep the vehicle in front of you in sight." Vehicles began to leap frog one another and string out the line of automobiles and vans.

"Dick called out, "everyone watch for them to pull off somewhere, don't stop until you find a place where we can all gather together preferably in two groups so we aren't all bunched up and easily seen."

"Wow that's tall order said one of the Agents."

"Pipe down and cut the chatter," asked Jefferies. "we'll move in when we have time to check the place out." They found a small shopping strip mall, half of them went in there and parked away from one another and the others found a old dilapidated boarded up restaurant around the corner from there and parked behind it away from the street.

"Did anyone see where the moving truck went and the white van?" asked Dick.

"Yes Agent Jefferies, we were in the lead behind the moving truck and it went behind that huge warehouse or factory across the street from our location right behind the white van," answered Agent Johnson.

"Okay then, I want two men to go behind the warehouse and check it out and report back, don't let anyone see you."

"Got it boss, we're the closet so we'll go."

"Was that you Richardson?"

"Yes sir."

"Good man, go ahead, check it out and hurry but don't let anyone see you."

Two men in street clothes walked causally across the street and walked away from the building until they couldn't be seen then doubled back to the end of the Warehouse. Dick and Jane couldn't see them because they were around the corner of the small shopping mall where the first group had stopped and set up. Several minutes passed and soon Richardson was back on the radio. "Agent Jefferies, Richardson here, the moving truck is backed into the warehouse portion loading dock and it looks like they are going to off load the books soon."

"How about the van?"

"Its parked several yards away in its own garage and there is what looks to be a big overhead door that matches the wall of the warehouse, wait a minute, damn, they just closed the door but this end of the building is still open, great camouflage I'd say."

"Alright hang tight there for a minute; I need to have a look for myself."

Dick took off at a run around the corner to where the others were. He pulled up short and was about to ask one of the men where the others were when he felt a close presence that smelled lightly of perfume. He turned slightly and standing right behind him was Agent Marlowe. "Jane what do you think you're doing?" he whispered.

"I'm covering your butt, we're partners Dick, I'm doing what any partner would do!"

"Alright hush for a minute."

"Anyone see where Richardson went?"

"Agent Jefferies, he's across the street at this end of the warehouse, if you look real hard you can see the two of them in the shade of the building at this end near the street."

"Okay, I see them. Alright listen up everyone, Agent Marlowe and I are going to cross the street like we're a couple of locals and meet them over there to check the place out and see if we can see more than one way in. I noticed the Book Store in the front so that's one way in. I'd like to hit the back at the same time, stand by we're going to cross the street now." Dick and Jane walked boldly out from amongst the vehicles and walked diagonally across the street away from the Book Store so they wouldn't attract attention in case someone was watching. The last thing they wanted was to be seen now. They joined Richardson and he showed them the layout he saw.

"My, my, how cozy is this?" Jefferies remarked.

"It's a perfect set up Agent Jefferies."

"Yes, I can see that, Agent Marlowe, let's study the situation so we can come up with a plan, Richardson that includes you as well."

"Yes sir, I wish I could see inside though, that's an awfully big building for us to cover. I make it to be at least three floors, maybe four with a basement.

That place could be a fortress of anything and everything imaginable complete with booby traps and if I were the man I'd have the back covered and leave the front open, anyway that's the way I see it Jefferies."

"Yes, and well thought out. I doubt this is a gang. I believe it's a one or two man operation and maybe they are grooming the young man to take over for them one day."

"Sounds plausible to me," said Richardson.

"So we leave four men in the back of the building with two separate vehicles, the fastest cars so in case they make a run for it, make those four men our best shots, how about that Richardson?"

"I like it just fine Agent Jefferies, it would be a bad move to rush the back of the building and if they run we'll park the heaviest vehicles to block the way of the van, something tells me there's something special about that rig the kid and old man were driving. I can't put my finger on it, call it a hunch, but I'd bet money on it that the van is very fast and may be armored."

"Instruct the four men they are to shoot to kill, we are not going to pussy foot around with these people, they've killed dozens of people that we know of and maybe two to three times that many over the years."

"Yes sir, do you want me to pick the four men sir?"

"Yes go ahead, you know them as well as we do Richardson."

"Would you mind if I included two of the women as well instead of just the four men?"

"That's fine with me, mix them up; they won't expect to see a couple of women armed to the teeth. Okay then let's get set up and ready to go, watch out for the drivers of the moving truck, make sure they don't get hit or taken hostage."

"I agree, maybe we should delay a little bit and let them get clear of here?"

"That's a good idea, we'll do it that way, then anybody that gets shot is a bad guy. Let's get back across the street and talk this over with everyone; I'll need about four more in front to cover it in case someone gets past us and tries for the front door."

They went back across the street like they weren't together except for Dick and Jane, they held hands and appeared to be chatting as they walked. Agent Jefferies decided to move everyone out of sight around back of the closed restaurant where he could draw a diagram on piece of paper.

"Alright everyone gather round, we won't make entry through the back of the building due to fears that this guy may have some kind of nasty ambush or booby traps set up back there. We'll be precipitous. I want six people to cover the back, Agent Richardson has an idea for that, your ball Richardson."

"I want two more men and two women, our best shooters should be there and if someone tries to run shoot to kill, give no quarter because he's killed indiscriminately many innocent people already. You four know who you are because I already picked you. Agent Jefferies you have the ball now."

"Now then to the front of the building. I want four more out front to cover the ones who are going inside and cover anyone who might make a run for it out the front door. Agent Marlowe and I will go in the front posing as husband and wife looking for books. I'm guessing mind you but if I were the man in there I'd have security all over the place, maybe a panic button at the front cash register so Marlowe and I will approach the counter with a couple of books like we're going to buy them and we'll incapacitate the man or woman behind the counter so they can't send an alarm throughout the building. All of this is conjecture, there could be alarms everywhere so any employees we come across we'll handcuff out of harms way as we encounter them because they may very well be innocent of any crime and just employees. Keep your eyes out for our man and the young man whom most of you saw. He may be or may not be an innocent employee but I want him arrested and let the Court figure it out, questions anyone?"

"Yes Agent Jefferies, who else is going in with you and Agent Marlowe?"

"I want Agents Johnson and Tyler to come in separately later and the other two cover the front like I asked. I have no real basis for all the precautions but I don't want to lose another Agent, stay on your toes and watch for a gun. If you see one shoot to kill, anymore questions?"

"Agent Jefferies, may I make a suggestion?"

"Yes Agent Marlowe, what is it?"

"When we go in and hand cuff people why not tell them we are the IRS and assure them they are not in any trouble, all we want to do is to go over the books with the owner and see if we can get an employee to summon him to the store from wherever he may be."

"Good idea, that might put them all at ease. If we have to show our badges we'll flash them quickly if we have to and hope they take the bait, it could save us time and keep anyone from getting hurt. Alright, now before we go in we need to get the vehicles around the corner deployed to our advantage to anywhere but where they are. Take four vehicles out back of the warehouse like we suggested for blocking purposes the others can be strewn around the building where we can get to them quickly if we have to in case someone tries to run. Agent Marlowe and I will take our sedan and park it right in front, take two more vehicles and park them randomly around ours those of you who are covering the front. If we need help inside we will have two other people in there to back us up, one man and one woman. The two out in front will need to be flexible. Like I said I don't think anyone will run from the front of the building so if you hear gunfire from out back get around there to help your fellow Agents and watch for the white van in case he's able to get through our blocking efforts. One more thing, all of you with rifles make sure you have the new armor piercing rounds in your magazines, I want these people stopped for good at all cost.

CHAPTER - 114

Dick and Jane drove across the street and parked their car in front of the book store in the first available parking place closest the entrance. They causally walked towards the front double glass doors chatting and holding hands. Everyone else were in their assigned positions or on their way. The moving truck left and was clear of the scene. They had extra help to load the truck back in Burlington and here they had enough help to quickly unload with the help of the three men in the moving truck as well and BJ and Norman.

Dick opened the right hand glass door to the store gentlemanly like for Jane and it was now 11:30am. as they strolled inside the Store. As planned they made complimentary comments about the store as they walked around. They spoke quietly as if in a Library.

"Dick, this is a wonderful Store, just look at all of the books and sections and how they are arranged."

"I agree, it's a wonderful store lets see if we can find something of interest to read."

That was the clue for them to split up. Eventually they would arrive at the front counter with some books to ostensibly purchase. A young woman of college age approached Dick.

"Can I help you find something sir?"

"Maybe, I'm looking for an adventure type of book, you know like, oh I don't know, some adventure on the high seas with pirates or something or maybe something more modern like a mystery of some kind, I'm a little tired of reading westerns right now."

"Well sir if you'll follow me I'll show you both sections and as you can see we have a wide variety of books for sale and more arrive every week. In fact we just got in a new shipment this morning, its being unloaded now."

"Maybe I'll stick around and see if something new comes in."

"I wouldn't wait sir, it may take us two or three days to catalogue all of it before putting any of it on the shelves and it's a big shipment so it could take longer."

"Does that mean you haven't seen the shipment yet?"

"Yes that's right, we won't see it here until it's all been sorted through. I understand that there are some rare and valuable books in the load and they will undoubtedly be offered to the many collectors that we have waiting for new selections as we get them in."

"Does that mean that the most valuable books don't always make it in here to the store?"

"That's right, we have a second floor that's storage for all our books. Once catalogued they go up there in their sections then we get the cards for them and as we run low on certain copies we check the cards then go upstairs and get more books to restock the shelves with, it's a great inventory system."

"I agree, it sounds very efficient."

"Well here's the Mystery section and just down from here on the same side is the Adventure section."

"Yes I see it now, thank your for your assistance, I'll look around and see what catches my eye, I want something exciting."

The young lady disappeared towards the front of the store. Dick picked up a book every now and then and set it down as he listened for Jane's voice in his ear piece. About ten minutes went by when he got the go word from both the team out front and the team out back. Their backups were in the store with them now careful to keep their distance from one another so it didn't appear they were together. Then Jane whispered in Dick's ear piece, "ready when you are Agent Jefferies."

They strolled towards the front counter, Dick with two books and Jane with three books in her arms. Greta was behind the cash register at the counter to wait on customers.

"Did you folks find everything you wanted?" Greta asked cheerfully.

"Yes ma'am, we have everything. This is a wonderful store. You see ma'am we're new in town and don't know our way around yet." Jane had a small piece of paper about the size of a three by five recipe card with handwriting on it and she carelessly slid it past the books to where it fell off the counter onto the floor behind the sales counter.

"I'm sorry ma'am, I'll get that," Agent Marlowe said as she stooped towards it.

"Not necessary Miss, its right here, I'll get it, customers aren't allowed on this side of the counter."

Greta reached down to pick up the piece of paper and as she did Jane grabbed her right arm twisting it behind Greta and hauled her away from the counter and cuffed her hands behind her back before she could protest. "I'm sorry ma'am but we're with the IRS and we're doing an on the spot audit." She flashed her badge to where Greta could glance at it and Dick did as well.

Greta was speechless. "Please, you don't need the handcuffs, they hurt my wrists."

"Sorry about the cuffs, they won't be on too long, its policy you see. I'll remove them as soon as we think you aren't a threat to us, we're not very popular as you probably know."

"Yes I'm aware of that but trust me our books are in perfect order."

"Yes ma'am that may be and that may be why we were sent here to investigate. Someone may have though they were a little too perfect."

"Oh I see, well I'll cooperate, we have nothing to hide, we're just employees here, we're not the owners," replied Greta.

"Where are the owners' ma'am?"

"Well Mr. Devine is upstairs in his apartment and Fred Samuel, his partner, is in the laboratory in the basement."

"Can you summon one of them without them knowing we're here?"

"I suppose so; I can call them by telephone one at a time."

"Agent Marlowe, hold onto her for a moment while I check behind the counter?"

"Yes of course Agent Jefferies."

Dick walked gingerly around the back of the counter and found two buzzers to summon help probably, one was on the floor within easy reach of Greta's feet and the other was under the counter below the cash register where anyone could reach it. Dick spoke into his radio quietly.

"In the store, pick up anyone who isn't a customer, cuff them and bring them to the front and hurry up about it."

"Ma'am, care to tell me what the buzzers are for behind the counter?" asked Jefferies.

"Sure, its no secret, its part of the Security system Mr. Devine had installed a few years back in case of a robbery. If you look hard enough there's another one for the City Police."

"What about the others who do they notify?"

"Why Mr. Devine, the gentleman who owns the Store."

"Uh huh, so you can declare an emergency in many ways then, do all of the employees know about these?"

"Of course they do and they are instructed not to try and stop anyone, just give the robbers or thieves what they want."

"This Mr. Devine, if he came downstairs in an emergency would he be armed?"

"Of course he would, he wants to protect our people in here, he's no fool you know!" Greta said in a confident way.

"You said our people, are you one of the owners as well?"

"No sir but they have been setting aside a fund for my old age when I retire one day, they have both been very kind to me over the years. I'm their store manager," Greta replied proudly.

Just as she finished the sentence their backups appeared at the counter, one had two young women, the other one had two young men of college age one who just was nineteen the other one was twenty.

"What do you want to do with these four employees Agent Jefferies?"

"Take them outside and turn them over to the other team for safe keeping. If I'm right we'll turn them loose soon, this one I'm not quite sure of yet. Oh and pick up a couple more pairs of cuffs for Agent Marlowe and I please."

"Just how many of you are there, Agent Jefferies is it?" asked Greta.

"More than enough to handle everyone in here, we know there's another young man hereabouts, where is he?"

"You must mean BJ; he's busy unloading the truck with another employee."

"Uh huh, are either of them armed or dangerous?"

"Of course not they're both very nice young men, BJ just graduated from the University this past summer."

"Let me guess, it was the University of Connecticut"

"That's what people think but I know better. Mr. Devine and Fred paid for him to go to school and he went to Boston, I seen the check stubs."

"Thank you ma'am for being so candid with us, what was your name again?"

"I didn't give you my name but its Greta, Greta Snodgrass and don't you dare laugh at me because of my name," she stiffened and straightened up in Jane's grasp.

"I wouldn't do such a thing Greta, I am a professional after all."

"Well thank you sir for not picking on me because of my name," and she relaxed a little.

"How can we get the two young men to come in here without any trouble Greta, we don't want anyone to get hurt you know?"

"I would have to go and call them in here by telephone."

"Is there no other way around that, you don't have a hidden buzzer here somewhere?"

"Actually there is another one; we use it when there is a phone call for someone on the loading dock."

"Can you show me where it is?"

"Sure if you'll loosen up my cuffs then I want to see an I D again before I say another word." Now Greta was getting suspicious of the whole proceeding.

"Alright, but promise me you won't scream because if you do I'll have to get a little rough and shut you up, I'll punch your lights out if I have to."

"Now you are scaring me, I don't believe you're with the IRS at all!"

"Dick took out his badge and held it up close where she could see it real good."

"My God, you're FBI Agents?" her face drained white as a sheet at the revelation.

"Yes ma'am and if you don't want to do jail time you'll cooperate with us."

"Yes of course, you are a lot more dangerous than the IRS; you kill people over nothing."

"Show me how you call them in now please, I'm starting to lose my patience here."

"Yes sir, but I'll have to point it out to you."

"Jane loosen up a little so she can point it out to you but hold her firm, she may still try to rabbit on us."

Jane loosened her grip just a little so Greta could go behind the counter but not close enough to hit a buzzer and she pointed to a blue and white button that was round and looked like an old door bell.

"Got it Agent Jefferies, around here, she says to press it once for BJ, that's the code."

Dick went around and pressed it once and they waited and watched. Greta pointed out a door where he would be coming through. BJs friend Norman was the first one through the door with BJ close behind.

Just then Greta screamed at the top of her lungs; "FBI BJ, run for it!!!"

BJ pushed Norman through the door and he fell forward to the floor. BJ slammed the door and took off running.

Dick drew his arm back as if he was going to punch Greta's lights out but before he could strike her she fainted dead away after seeing his fist and collapsed silently to the floor. Dick was on his radio, "watch the back, a young man called BJ is making a run for it, somebody get the cuffs on a young man called Norman in here."

All Dick heard was, "we're on it."

The store was suddenly silent. Jane signaled the others out in front for help to come in and get Greta, "and don't use kid gloves, she's a bitch," she added on her radio.

Soon Greta was outside and the other two inside Agents came back in and they returned to where Dick and Jane were waiting for them after hand cuffing a surprised Norman who had stayed on the floor when he saw what was happening, now there were four of them again.

"Alright listen up we know there's man in the basement who may not have heard Greta, she gave the alarm and a young man called BJ that we saw at the Book Store Sale ran out the back we think. The man downstairs name is Fred something; he is in what Greta called the lab. Go down there and get him under arrest and let me know when you have cuffs on him. The kid that ran wasn't armed; I'm not sure about the guy in the basement."

Two men went down to the basement to see about Fred. They found him immersed in his work as usual. They walked up to him and casually asked, "are you Fred?"

"Yes I'm Fred, what are you doing down here, what the hell what do you want?"

"We want you for now, put your hands behind your back and come along quietly and there won't be any trouble."

"Say, who are you to order me around in my own building?"

"FBI sir, you're under arrest."

"Are you crazy, I've done nothing wrong, I'm a chemist and a respected member of this community, you have no call to —" and he stopped mid sentence as the cuffs tightened around his wrists. "Say, you guys aren't fooling are you?"

"No sir, we're dead serious, we'll let the Courts decide who's guilty and who isn't."

They walked him back up the same stairs they came down. They walked over to where Dick and Jane were standing and talking.

"Here he is Agent Jefferies, this is Fred somebody."

"It's Fred Samuel and I'm somebody alright, you'll see, you're making a terrible mistake."

"I know, I know, you're innocent, you never killed nobody right?"

"That's right, so let me go."

"Can't do it Fred, we still haven't found your friend Mr. Devine or is it Shultz."

"Oh I can tell you, you won't take him alive either! He's got more tricks and disappearing acts than you'll ever see!"

"Well thanks for the heads up there Fred, take him and the other young man outside and put him with the others."

"Lets have a look around Jane he must be upstairs, I noticed curtains on some of the windows, I'm betting there are some apartments up there." They found an elevator and took it but it only went to the second floor.

"Jane, there must be more than one elevator in here, lets go back and have another look." Back on the ground floor they started looking for another elevator. Then they heard one faintly in the wall but didn't see any elevator doors anywhere. It's got to be around here somewhere, let's have a look in the basement."

They found the stairs and walked down one flight to the basement and started to look for an elevator. They didn't see one right away but heard the electric motor faintly whirring through the walls as the elevator moved up or down, they weren't sure which.

"Jane lets get Greta and have her show us where the elevator is, obviously it's hidden somewhere." They went back upstairs to get Greta who was still recovering after fainting out in front of the store along with the others. Once outside they confronted her. "Ma'am in case you don't know it you're under arrest for suspicion of murder, now you can help us out or not, its your choice. If you decide to help us we'll take it up with the Judge when its time, if not it may be the electric chair for you as an accomplice to murder."

"But I've harmed no one."

"Ah, but you work for the man who did and in the eyes of the law you're an accomplice pure and simple by withholding evidence from us and giving aid to the murderer by warning him. We want you to show us how to get upstairs where he lives."

"I'll do no such thing!"

"Alright, you all heard her it's on her head now if anyone dies. She'll be charged with another murder. Let's go Agent Marlowe, we're done here."

They were almost to the front door and Greta suddenly hollered; "wait, I'll show you."

One man and a woman Agent escorted her into the store and she walked over to a back portion of the wall.

"The button, there on the wall, press it."

"Sorry but I don't see one," said Dick.

"Oh for heavens sakes un-cuff me and I'll show you."

Jane un-cuffed one hand but left the cuff attached to one wrist so she could yank her around if she had to. Greta reached out and pressed something on the wall that neither one of them could see. The five of them got on the elevator after a hidden door opened as she pressed a button marked Apts.

"This is the top floor," she whispered, "where we all live. Sol's, Mr. Devine's that is, is number one right here." She pointed to his door then began to ease backwards towards the elevator and Dick saw what she was doing. He motioned to Jane and the others to move back quietly as well. Dick reached out with his arm and knocked on the door three times very loudly. A voice on the other side barked out with a gruff booming voice, "who is it?"

"FBI Mr. Devine, we'd like to talk to you!"

Almost before he finished speaking bullets tore through the door from at least two guns shredding the door from off its hinges. Smoke, dust, bullets and wood splinters were flying everywhere surprising the two Agents at the ferocity. Dick shielded Jane with his body to protect her and they were covered with dust and debris from the sudden and violent outburst of gunfire. They let the dust and smoke clear a little bit and Dick gingerly peered around the corner of the battered doorway to where he could see into the apartment. There was no one there but he heard the faintest gentle whirr of an elevator again. "Downstairs everyone and hurry!"

"What is it Agent Jefferies?" asked Jane as she dragged Greta along by her handcuffs.

"He's headed for the basement is my guess, I think he's going to try and run for it." They got back to the ground floor and dropped Greta off with another female Agent. Dick, Jane and two other male Agents continued on down the stairs to the basement on the elevator. They heard a vehicle's diesel engine start and Dick hurriedly spoke into his radio, "out back people, they're coming out in the van, stop them anyway you can."

The van sped out from the now open garage door from deep within the bowels of the store its engine screaming in high revolutions as it turned to the left and vaulted forward at high speed shocking the Agents standing there behind their blocking vehicles with their guns at the ready. Would they be able to stop the speeding van, would their vehicles slow it down or would they be knocked aside like so many bowling pins from the smoking smelly hulk of the turbo charged diesel piece of machinery bearing down on them with darkened windows which made it almost impossible to see inside?

Dick and Jane ran towards where the van had been parked and suddenly heard a fusillade of guns going off, shot guns, rifles and pistols. By the time they got outside the van had stopped just short of reaching the street, the windshield completely obliterated and the front tires shot out. Dick and Jane ran up to the van and found that the two inside were nearly dead. BJ was moaning for his mother and Sol was dying slowly as he bled out, no one was going to attempt to help him after what he had done. Their bodies were riddled with bullets and the inside of the van was splattered everywhere with their blood and brain matter.

"He didn't give us any choice Agent Jefferies," said one of the Agents, "we told them to stop but he gunned it and we had to shoot. They knocked our blocking vehicles out of the way as if they were toys. That van sure has some kind of power under the hood. The older man was firing at us as the van came at us with the young man driving" At least four armor piercing rounds went through the engine block and the engine sized up stopping the van, the remaining engine oil and anti freeze dripping out from several holes in the oversized radiator and engine block.

"That's alright men at least we got him now."

Shortly after that they heard lots of sirens. The local police were called by people in Louie's restaurant who thought the Store was being robbed when they saw the van being shot up by what appeared to be strangers as it stopped just short of the street, its tires and radiator shot out. Sol and BJ died before the local cops got there and they were upset because no one had called them earlier for help.

Just as they thought it was all over the remaining Agent who had been with Dick and Jane along with another female Agent had gotten turned around and ran down a darkened hall and he was nearly cut in half by booby traps of shotguns embedded in the walls killing him instantly. They all heard multiple gunshots that sounded like automatic weapons. Two Agents went running back into the back of the building to see what had happened. They didn't venture further when they saw the body of their fallen comrade. They came back out to see Dick and tell him who it was, their faces ashen.

"Who is it, what happened?" asked Jefferies.

"It's Johnson Agent Jefferies, he never saw it coming, booby traps with automatic shot guns embedded within the walls just like Richardson and you warned us there might be, he's dead, nearly cut in two, he must have gotten turned around in there with all the excitement."

"These deaths go on that woman's head, Greta somebody or other. Put in your report that she failed to tell us or warn us about any of this. It all could have all been avoided if she hadn't warned the young man in the van. Three people died here that didn't have to because of her big mouth, for two cents I'd shoot her myself."

"Agent Marlowe, lets let our people handle the local cops, I need to sit down. I lost another fine Agent today who didn't have to die and I feel absolutely powerless because I couldn't stop this from happening and before you say anything I know all about hind sight being twenty-twenty but I'm not talking about that, it's the wasting of so many human lives, the misery that man caused for so many, that's what just hit me."

"Come on Agent Jefferies you need a rest." Jane put her arm around him in moral support as they walked back out front to their car.

Meanwhile there were city cops running around everywhere threatening the FBI Agents with their own guns drawn. When the FBI Agents showed their badges the cops were still pissed off because they were not informed about 'the take down' as they called it. One of the Agents finally got them calmed down explaining that it had just happened when they tried to arrest a man. No one figured on a shoot out of this magnitude. Six Agents had emptied their weapons, rifles, shotguns and pistols into the van, every weapon they had on them was empty. The armored van didn't stand a chance because the FBI Agents were using new armor piercing rounds on the van and the bullet proof windshield did no good at all against those rounds.

People who had been in the restaurant diagonally across the street called Louie's filed out two and three at a time to see what happened and were aghast when they learned that their friends of many years were either dead or under arrest. One Agent put a closed sign in the window of the store and on it he wrote, 'Permanently.' Agent Richardson made an assessment of the scene and his fellow Agents. There were no other injuries other than Johnson who never knew what hit him in the back hall of the building leading from the Store along side of the loading dock which was dark and unlit at the time. Agent Jefferies and Marlowe and the other female Agent had gone through the lab to the far end and then out through the door where the van had been parked. No one knew how Johnson got separated and turned around in the back of the building apparently disoriented.

Agent Jefferies was beside himself sick with guilt as he sat in the front seat of his car. He held his head in his hands and mumbled to Jane; "why did this have to happen, we planned everything down to every possible situation. Its all on my head, I'll have to explain it to the Director why I lost another Agent today."

"Dick, this wasn't your fault,' said Jane, "it was that bitch's fault for warning the young man who then ran and told the older man upstairs we were there. Upstairs we both could have been killed as well if not for your vigilance, you saved all our lives. What happened to Johnson was unavoidable, it could have been easily any one of us as well. You couldn't have known for sure about booby traps. Its all on that woman's head for this, not yours!"

"I know that Jane, what you have to understand is that I am the Agent in charge, it was my job to keep everyone safe. I'm the one who has to tell the Director what's happened here."

When the Agents searched the van and both men they recovered the two pistols that Sol had used during his rein of crime, his 357 magnum and his 9 mm semi automatic pistol. Ballistics would show that both guns had been used in twenty eight crimes of murder over the past twenty six years.

Now it was time for the paperwork. Reports had to be written, interviews of each person handcuffed had to be done. They asked the local Police Department to take care of the ones' in handcuffs to be held temporally for the FBI while they finished their investigation of everyone and the building itself had to be gone through, checked out and cleaned out for records and anything else that may be important when the survivors came up for trial.

CHAPTER - 115

Later back in Washington Dick and Jane made out their final reports to the last detail as did all of the other Agents involved. The Director wasn't happy about losing another Agent in a gun battle but as everyone said in their reports there was no way to foresee the accident that claimed Agent Johnson's life, he made a mistake and had paid the ultimate price. Both Dick and Jane along with the rest received commendations for the years and months of work they had put in on the case. The Director wrote in his report that every precaution that could have been taken was taken by his Agents.

Six weeks later the Director summoned Dick and Jane to his Office. They were back in their own Offices now on the third floor where Dick and the others had been previously before this case got so out of hand and he moved to the basement to be closer to the actual action as did the others. The lab was once again only a lab only but the mural map stayed on the wall.

They walked into the secretary's outer office and she ushered them directly into the Director's Office.

"Sit down you two."

"Feeling any better Agent Jefferies?"

"I guess so sir but its hard to get Johnson out of my mind, he was a good man."

"How about you Miss Marlowe, everything alright with you?"

"Yes sir but like Dick says, we wish it hadn't happened this way but it did."

"Well for your information all of the reports were turned into the DA, he is seeking the death penalty for both Greta Snodgrass and Fred Samuel. There is no doubt in his mind that what happened could have been avoided if that woman hadn't warned the young man. Their deaths are on her head as well as for being a party to the end of this thing. She could have played along and maybe she would have gotten a few years in jail but now she is up on charges for three deaths. She has no one to blame but herself, at the very least she will get life in prison without the possibility of parole. Tell me Agent Jefferies what all did you find when you searched the man's apartment who was killed?"

"Unbelievable sir, he had an apartment within an apartment and a private elevator where he could come and go completely unseen. We found it by destroying a few walls looking for his disguises, elevated shoes and we found six pairs of them, six pairs of rubbers, the old fashioned kind you don't see anymore and eight disguises and several hair pieces and or wigs. He had a complete makeup kit in the bathroom and he obviously had a woman on the side. We found her name along with some others and they are being questioned by the local authorities and I guarantee you this time they won't be so sloppy with their investigations. Oh one more thing, his apartment was full of books on unsolved murders, he had circled some of them in red and I'm betting that if someone goes back far enough some unsolved murders can be linked to our man"

"What's this I read about in your report about an excavation going on in the basement of the factory where his headquarters was Dick?"

"That's even worse sir, both Agent Marlowe and I smelled something like the odor of dead bodies permeating the concrete floor. I got a guy with an air compressor and jack hammer to break up part of the floor that looked recently poured and while he was digging he let out a scream and took off up the stairs. He had uncovered a corpse. They are still digging and the last I heard from the coroner there was that they had a dozen bodies exhumed and I've ordered all of the parts of the floor that looks recent to be dug up. Its easy to see the old original floor next to the newer sections. I'm guessing you understand, but we have dozens of homeless people missing from around the area. I think we've found the workers who built the place for the dead man named Devine. I'm thinking he hired skilled men and women who were out of work and down on their luck and when their part was done he killed them then buried them in the unfinished part of the basement then poured concrete over the bodies and then had other homeless folks dig a large grave for more. Its what you could call cheap labor. Each section of concrete is about eight feet wide and twenty feet long and as soon as the concrete cured he put more machinery down there to cover it up. Also we learned that several mailboxes for the apartments have lots of mail for folks who don't exist, they may be part of what's under the floor as well."

"That's a pretty big chore to get away with all that without help isn't it Jefferies?"

"Of course sir but he had help to dig and help to build and he just kept on going. Nobody missed the homeless people until I put out a bulletin asking local agencies about missing persons and we got back over a of hundred missing people. I'm betting there are twenty five to thirty bodies or more down there. I hope that I'm wrong, but sir you'd have to see the enormity of the thing, its monstrous, the whole layout was well thought out way ahead of time. This investigation is not over sir, we've only scratched the surface. They have been in that building for the past twenty six years. Ballistics have shown that the two pistols we recovered from the van, a 357 magnum and a 9mm semi automatic pistol have been traced to more than twenty murders now."

"Thank you for everything you both have done. Now then we have one more small piece of unfinished business to discuss Dick. You owe me dinner at Twin Willows. I'd like to go tomorrow night with my wife. Its Friday and you two have the weekend off and more if you like, take a week if you want to, you've both earned it."

"Well sir tomorrow night is alright with me sir but I'll have to find a date to go with."

Jane was busy suddenly clearing her throat.

"Did you say something Agent Marlowe?"

"No, just had a frog in my throat, but well, oh shoot Dick, can't I go with you all as a chaperone an escort or something?"

"You know its against rules for Agents to fraternize don't you?" Dick replied.

"Of course I do, I'm not one to skirt around the rules, the Director will vouch for that."

"Yes I can and no you won't be going on a date. If you go with us it will be a working dinner, we'll find something to talk about business wise and that will shake up my wife, she hates it when I discuss business during a meal. So now that's all settled what time tomorrow night would you like us to be ready?"

"Make it convenient for you and your wife and I think we should take two cars and while in the Restaurant there's a rule against discussing any sort of business so it better be said out in the parking lot if you have something to say about the case sir."

"Okay Agent Jefferies but why two cars?"

"Because Director, something's always happening to me when I'm with Jane and I don't want her or me to have to walk home."

They started laughing hysterically but Dick winked at Jane so she knew he wasn't serious.

The next evening true to his word Dick and Jane followed the Director home so he could pick up his wife and they could follow them to the Twin Willows across the Virginia State line. Everything went fine right up to when Sam, who was also the owner, met them at the front door.

"Table for four tonight!" Dick said.

"Yes sir Mr. Jefferies, I take it this is the Director you told me about?"

"That's right Sam and his lovely wife Sylvia but we all call him Director he'd rather be called that than his real name and of course you've met this lady, Miss Marlowe."

"Yes sir, I understand perfectly," he said rather coolly while eyeing Jane up and down, "follow me please," giving one more guarded sideways glance at Jane.

The four of them followed him as he walked them though the maze of cubbies and dark corners with candles only for light."

"Will this be alright with you Mr. Jefferies?"

Dick didn't say anything, he watched the Director as he looked around. Finally the Director was speechless and gasped, "oh my word Dick, how did you pull this off?"

"It was easy sir, I own a considerable amount of this restaurant."

"But this means we have our own table from now on to eat here whenever we want to?"

"Yes sir, that s right."

"Would you look at that dear, my name on a brass plate on the wall, we're members now. Oh my gosh Dick, how can I; or better yet, how can we ever thank you?"

"You can thank me by picking up the tab if you like."

"My pleasure my boy, my pleasure."

They pulled the chairs out for Silva and Jane and they sat down.

The four inch by eight inch brass plate above their table read in bold letters in two lines.

'DRECTOR OF THE FBI
AND SYLVIA'

"Sorry I couldn't think of something more eloquent sir but I wanted to surprise you and you can have it changed anytime you like, make it more personal for you and Sylvia," said Dick.

"Oh I am surprised my boy am I ever. I have dreamed about just eating a meal here but to become a member all at the same time, well its overwhelming my boy."

"You're welcome sir, you too Sylvia."

"Yes thank you Dick, this is beyond our wildest dreams; you know you have to be somebody special to belong here, I know of several Presidents who weren't even allowed in here." the Director added.

"Yes dear, now remember no shop talk over dinner," replied Sylvia.

"Yes Sylvia, we all understand dear," answered the Director.

They ordered different meals; no one ate the same thing tonight, Dick had champagne brought to the table with a note, 'Compliments of the house for its newest members.' After desert they were all stuffed and well satisfied.

"My but that was the best meal I've ever had out with my wife, it was worth every penny and the ambience superb, absolutely perfect. Now Dick how do I go about calling here for reservations?"

"You don't need them but a courtesy call would be nice to let the house know that you'll be in on a certain day. That way if you have a favorite food or drink they will be sure to have it on hand, some items are seasonal though just like anywhere else."

"I noticed them on the menu, venison, rabbit, duck, pheasant under glass, buffalo, mid western black angus beef, sea food, moose etc. the list went on forever."

"Before you leave here sir they will hand you a card, keep it close to you, don't let anyone know or you'll be pestered by folks to bring them here as your guests."

"I understand Dick, I've pestered you for years, mum's the word alright."

"You'd better remember that dear on your poker nights or you'll be camping out here," added Sylvia.

"Yes dear, you're right dear."

After a couple more drinks they decided it was time to leave. The Director paid the bill and was handed a brochure to fill out about his favorite food and drinks for he and his wife and he left a generous tip as they headed out to their respective cars.

"Going to follow us home Dick?"

"No sir, I have a couple of things to do here in town first, old friends you know."

"Yes Dick I understand."

"Well Jane see you both at the office on Monday then."

"Yes sir, Monday it is."

"What do you have up your sleeve Dick Jefferies?" asked Agent Marlowe curiously.

"For starters, I reserved two Motel rooms for the night, I've had too much to drink to drive all the way back to DC tonight, I hope you don't mind Jane."

"Let me guess, are they adjoining rooms?"

"Well actually I believe they are, will that be a problem?"

"Well actually it is, you're wasting good money on me."

"Why do you say that Jane?"

"If you think for a minute I'm spending the night in a room all alone you're crazy, you should have gotten a room with two queen-size beds instead of two separate rooms."

Dick's heart suddenly sank, he thought for sure she would come around and sleep with him in the same bed tonight of all nights.

"Oh and by the way Dick, you don't need the second bed unless you plan to cover it with luggage and I didn't see you put any in the car."

"That's right but I did put in our two overnight bags, just in case you understand."

They both laughed all the way to the Motel which was only a couple of minutes away. Dick had finally found the love of his life and he would tell her tonight that it was her and Jane was feeling the same way about him.

IS IT THE END OF THE BEGINNING
OR IS IT
THE BEGINNING OF THE END?
"Winston Churchill"

ONLY TIME WILL TELL!

THE END